## INTERNATIONAL PRAISE
## FOR *THE WATCHERS*

### "READS LIKE *PARADISE LOST* BY WAY OF JOHN CONNOLLY . . .

. . . although Steele . . . brings hard-edged modernity to this timeless tale as he roots his depiction of evil in the contemporary world. Clever, stylish, and epic in scale, it's a tremendously satisfying debut."  —*The Irish Times*

"An imaginatively metaphysical thriller. . . . Steele keeps his tale tantalizingly ambiguous, casting it with fey characters and skillfully concealing until the climax whether apparent weird events haven't been manipulated to make them seem so. This solidly plotted tale, the first in a trilogy, will appeal to readers who like a hint of uncanny in their fiction."  —*Publishers Weekly*

"A seductive cosmic thriller stoked by historic fact, an ancient Jewish religious text, and a literary classic. . . . Steele's lavishly atmospheric, witty, bloody, and swashbuckling tale of age-old struggles for dominion between angels and demons is the propitious first book in an ambitious series."  —*Booklist* (starred review)

"Really smart work for serious thriller readers."
—*Library Journal*

"So phenomenally deep and complex. Jon Steele has written a modern thriller masterpiece, pulling from medieval Gothic myths and religious mysticism in a very unexpected way. . . . I felt like I was watching a spellbinding movie. This is a smart, heavily researched novel that is one hell of a roller-coaster ride."  —Pop Corn Reads

*continued . . .*

## "FAITH, LOVE, LUST, MURDER, INNOCENCE, DANGEROUS DEMONS, FALLEN ANGELS . . .

. . . meld together into one glorious, spellbinding, addicting story that readers won't soon forget. . . . *The Watchers* delivers a one-two punch of good versus evil in a fresh, unique, and decadent manner . . . brilliant enough to capture the attention of romantics, religious zealots, and historian buffs alike. Not just good, but DAMN good. I didn't just like it. I LOVED it, and it's a rare treat for me to experience such pleasure. A must read. Seriously."                    —Luxury Reading

"There's plenty of diabolical fun to be had here."
                                        —*Kirkus Reviews*

"A carefully constructed puzzle . . . [an] intriguing story of fallen angels and haunting visions."    —Warpcore SF

"A wholly original thriller that seamlessly melds suspense, history, fantasy, and mysticism. Steele deftly blends elements of many literary genres into this inventive work of fiction. A tour de force—and the first in a projected trilogy—*The Watchers* is an indescribable work of the imagination: at once heart-stopping and mystical, entertaining and awe-inspiring."          —BookTrib

"I loved this book from the first beautifully written and haunting chapter to the last heart-pounding one. It's definitely a must read for the literary thriller crowd and just about anyone who enjoys great writing and a fabulous story."                              —Book Bound

## "THIS BOOK TOUCHED ME, INTRIGUED ME, FOLLOWED ME IN MY DREAMS, AND REFUSES TO GET OUT OF MY HEAD. . . .

. . . The writing is beautiful, the setting memorable and the story unforgettable."          —Bookgeeks

"The most extraordinary novel I've read this year, and one of the most memorable that I've read in much longer than that. . . . This isn't just because of the story, which combines reality and fantasy in a seamless and magical fashion, but also because of the writing. *The Watchers* breathes beautiful prose, reaching poetic heights in places, sometimes literally."          —Movie Brit

"Dark, atmospheric . . . rich, and intricate. I was amazed by how Steele put it together."          —The Book Stoner

"Jon Steele's take on the alternative theological thriller blends the legends of a suppressed ancient text with pulp noir archetypes and a sweet but simple man on the side of the angels . . . .The final act is pure blockbuster."
          —Shelf Awareness

"If you're in the mood for something artistic, an unexpected read that you're willing to just go with, no matter how strange it seems at times, then *The Watchers* might be just the novel you're looking for."
          —S. Krishna's Books

"A fabulous story."          —Drey's Library

ALSO BY JON STEELE

*War Junkie*

# THE
# WATCHERS

## The Angelus Trilogy

JON STEELE

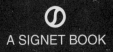
Ø

A SIGNET BOOK

SIGNET
Published by the Penguin Group
Penguin Group (USA) Inc., 375 Hudson Street,
New York, New York 10014, USA

USA / Canada / UK / Ireland / Australia / New Zealand / India / South
Africa / China

Penguin Books Ltd., Registered Offices: 80 Strand, London WC2R 0RL,
England
For more information about the Penguin Group visit penguin.com.

Published by Signet, an imprint of New American Library, a division of
Penguin Group (USA) Inc. Previously published in a Blue Rider Press edition.
A version of this work was published as *The Watchers* in 2011 by Transworld
in Great Britain.

First Signet Printing, April 2013

Acknowledgment is made for permission to reprint one stanza of the poem
"Europe" by Howard Nemerov from *The Image and the Law* (1947) from *The
Collected Poems of Howard Nemerov*, courtesy of the University of Chicago.

Ⓟ REGISTERED TRADEMARK—MARCA REGISTRADA

ISBN 978-0-451-41679-7

Printed in the United States of America
10 9 8 7 6 5 4 3 2 1

PUBLISHER'S NOTE
This is a work of fiction. Names, characters, places, and incidents either are
the product of the author's imagination or are used fictitiously, and any re-
semblance to actual persons, living or dead, business establishments, events,
or locales is entirely coincidental.
    The publisher does not have any control over and does not assume any re-
sponsibility for author or third-party Web sites or their content.

If you purchased this book without a cover you should be aware that this book
is stolen property. It was reported as "unsold and destroyed" to the publisher
and neither the author nor the publisher has received any payment for this
"stripped book."

*For Afnan*

Construction on the foundations of Lausanne Cathedral began in 1170. Pope Gregory X consecrated the church as La Cathédrale de Notre-Dame de Lausanne on October 20, 1275.

*Le guet* is the title of the man who calls the hour from the belfry of Lausanne Cathedral, as has been done each night, without fail, since the cathedral's consecration. It is pronounced "le geh" and is derived from the French military term *faire le guet*: to keep watch or lookout.

Lac Léman is the proper name of the body of water known to much of the English-speaking world as Lake Geneva. It is the name used by the Swiss and French peoples living along its shores.

The Book of Enoch is an apocryphal book of the Hebrew Bible, long discredited until its existence was confirmed when it was found to be part of the Dead Sea Scrolls in 1948. Quotations from the text are used in this story.

In writing the prologue, *Quietus*, lines from Edward Thomas's poetry, diary and letters are used as dialogue and/or narrative, sometimes without quotes, to create a portrait of the man's mind and emotions at the time of his death. This is also the case with the description of Edward Thomas's War Diary. It is taken from the web page of the University of Oxford's First World War Poetry Archive.

Saint and demon blindly stare
From the risen stone;
Brought to a common character
Neither can stand alone.

♦

HOWARD NEMEROV, "EUROPE"

# quietus

At first sight, fifty yards off, he couldn't tell who it was walking through the rain, only that the slow-moving form emerging from the shattered village of Neuville-Vitasse was a British soldier. He could tell by the Brodie helmet and brown tunic, the puttees on the legs and box respirator hanging across the chest, the Lee-Enfield rifle carried as if all battles were over.

How queer that the soldier should walk so casually through no-man's-land, he thought. Even when crossing the lacerated fields where only death lived among the blackened stumps of trees and barbed wire and shell holes filled with bloodstained water, the soldier did not cower.

And upon reaching the ridge where the soldier's form was a silhouette against the cloud-ridden sky, there was no regard for the trenches of the Hindenburg Line, nor for the German soldiers within, crouched behind their Maxim water-cooled machine guns. The same guns that laid waste to twenty thousand British lives in a single morning at the Somme.

A perfect shot.

But the shot did not come, and the soldier disappeared down a far valley.

It was then he noticed it. The quiet.

Not just from the enemy trenches, but over the entire battlefield. And he began to remember.

Atop this hill in the hour before the dawn of Easter Monday, 1917. Hidden in the hedgerow that was the forward observation post of 244 Siege Battery. Pulling his pocket watch from his tunic and seeing the sweep hand mark zero hour. Then hearing all three thousand guns along the Western Front, from Vimy Ridge to Bullecourt, open fire as one.

The earth shook beneath his feet.

And all through the barrage, binoculars to his eyes and spying the flash of return fire, his heart beat wildly. Checking the coordinates on his map and reporting the positions of the German guns to his battery so that those guns could be destroyed. Destroyed before the boys went over the top and marched across no-man's-land.

There was a sound, a furious and rushing sound.

. . . *incoming* . . .

Then all was quiet. Nothing moved.

Not the clouds in the sky, not the towering columns of smoke, not the flash of German guns. There were no soldiers rising from their trenches to march across no-man's-land, and the rain seemed to hang in the sky on threads of gray light.

He thought he should record the strange lull in his notebook, the Walker's Back-Loop pocketbook bound in pigskin and priced at two shillings. He remembered the day he bought it in England, thinking he would use it to compose more poems. Instead it had become his war diary, and the place of safekeeping for a photograph of his wife.

Her name was . . . her name was Helen.

And he always carried the notebook in the breast pocket of his tunic, like a talisman over his heart.

Wait, he thought, there were some words on the last pages of the notebook. A few unconnected lines, stumbling things, like the tottering legs of a child. He tried to remember the words, but they seemed so distant.

Then he heard the sound of trudging steps through mud and saw the soldier standing at the edge of the hedgerow.

"Hello. You must be Lieutenant Thomas. I was told I'd find you up here."

The name sounded unfamiliar till he remembered it was his own name, Edward Thomas. He had yet to grow accustomed to the title of lieutenant.

"Identify yourself."

"Swain, Corporal Swain."

"What is the password?"

"The password? Right, the password is 'Bournemouth.'" The soldier's accent was perfect.

"Advance."

As the soldier stepped closer, he saw Corporal Swain wasn't from 244 Siege Battery or Battalion HQ. And it seemed the corporal's form was the only moving thing in an unmoving world.

"Are you a messenger?"

"You could call me that."

The soldier rested his rifle against the hedgerow and sat down. He kicked thick mud from his boots. Edward saw splatters of fresh mud on the soldier's uniform.

"Terrible slog getting here. Cup of tea would go down very well, especially as it's quiet, yeah?"

Again, Edward could only think how oddly the soldier was behaving, insubordinately even. As if the battle was truly over and there was no need for protocol in addressing an officer as *sir*, even if the officer was only a second lieutenant.

"Is it over? Is the assault over?"

"No, bit of a lull where we are, that's all."

"Yes, a lull. I was going to note it—"

"—just before I arrived."

"Yes."

The soldier removed his helmet and laid it on the ground. He wiped sweat and grime from his brow. "I'm sure you must be a little confused, Lieutenant."

"It's the quiet, the look of things. I'm not sure what to do."

"Nothing to do. Just takes some getting used to."

*. . . just takes some getting used to . . .*

Yes, of course. Only been in the army twenty-one months, only been in France since February. Seen some action at the front, had a few close scrapes with enemy shells, but come through them just fine. Mostly spending time at HQ plotting maps or censoring the boys' letters home. Did see a few planes fall from the sky. Saw one dead German soldier under a bridge, sitting as if hiding from the rain. *Perhaps this is what war was genuinely like,* he thought, *moments of unrestful quiet between seconds of terrible fear.* Perhaps it explained the soldier's casual manner. Corporal . . . Corporal Swain, yes, that was it, had the look of a man too old for his years, someone who had seen all there was to see in war.

Edward noticed a handwritten scrawl inside the soldier's helmet: *And men, being destroyed, cried out.* It read as verse.

"The words in your helmet, are they from a poem?"

"From a lesser-known book of the Bible, I'm told. It's the motto of my company."

"I'm afraid I'm not a religious man."

"That's all right, Lieutenant, neither am I."

Edward looked over the soldier's uniform. No insignia on the collar or sleeves. Nothing to identify a battalion or brigade. And under the soldier's box respirator, tucked in the belt, Edward saw a mud-stained knife. A deadly-looking thing, like the knives of the Gurkha regiment.

"Not to worry, Lieutenant, I'm not a spy sent to kill the forward observers."

"I wasn't thinking—"

"Of course you were. You were ordered to keep a sharp eye out for them."

Edward realized it *was* what he was thinking. And he wondered why it had taken so long to think it.

"It was your manner. The way you walked through no-man's-land."

"There's nothing to fear for the moment. I managed to kill what fear there was in this sector."

But Edward began to wonder. "What is your company and battalion, soldier?"

"What's left of it, you mean. Lost half the company at Delville Wood."

"I'm sorry."

"No need, it's our job. My company isn't attached to any battalion. At Delville Wood we were with the South Africans. Here we started with the Canadians, now we're with the Brits. We're more the sneaky-beaky type. We do our work quietly."

"With knives."

"Yes."

"You are an assassin."

The soldier smiled. "I've been called worse."

"Why are you here now?"

"Told you, I was ordered to find you."

"To what purpose?"

"To protect you."

"Who would give such an order?"

"Comes to orders, I'm no different from you. No idea where they come from, no choice in carrying them out. But from what I gather, there's a soldier on the German side who wants you dead."

"The entire German Army wants me dead, and you, all of us. Why should I fear one soldier more than the rest?"

"This soldier is different, Lieutenant. He's a devourer of souls. And he's not the only one in this place, there are thousands of them. Out on the battlefield, while we rest in the quiet, soldiers from both sides of the line are being served up for slaughter. Never mind the civilians caught in the middle. Thirteen million dead so far in this bloody war to end all bloody wars. The more slaughter is mechanized, the more the enemy breeds. And in this bloody place, the enemy has become very good at slaughter."

Edward looked into the eyes of the soldier, almost hypnotized by them. The soldier was mad. Edward heard of such things happening in the trenches. The choking terror, the never-ending death strangling all sanity from the mind. He looked at the soldier's knife and uniform again and felt his own fear bite. What he'd thought were splashes of mud were stains of blackened blood.

"No, Lieutenant, odd as you find me, I'm not mad. You must believe what I tell you. I'm on your side. I've come with a message."

"What message?"

The soldier's eyes drifted to another place.

"No traveler has rest more blest
Than this moment brief between
Two lives, when the Night's first lights
And shades hide what has never been,
Things goodlier, lovelier, dearer, than will be or have
ever been."

Edward saw himself two years earlier. In England, at his writing desk, struggling with the words. His wife sitting at the hearth nearby, reading Keats.

"I don't understand, those are my words. I remember when I wrote them."

"Yes, I know all your poems."

"My poems haven't been published but for a few, and I—"

"—published them under the name Edward Eastaway because you didn't wish to trade on your name as a writer of prose. But in truth it was because you were afraid they might not be well received. You feared you might be dragged again into that slough of despond you dreaded your entire life."

He stared at the soldier who knew the deepest truths of Edward Thomas.

"How can you know such things?"

"The same way I know you couldn't remember your name till I called to you. The same way I know why it's all gone quiet and nothing in this place appears to move. The same way I know the words you were trying to remember just before I arrived, the lines you wrote on the last pages of your diary. The same way I know you nearly died in this place yesterday, but I wasn't ordered to find you because it wasn't your time."

Edward saw himself on the hill. Yesterday, Easter Sunday.

Bright sun, a warm day.

Positions taking sporadic fire from German guns.

Setting the battery, arranging matériel for the assault. Village of Achicourt, less than a mile up the line, shelled heavily at midday. Lulls of silence and noticing the return of birds and herbs and flowers to the nightmarish landscape after the snow and the cold rain of winter. In the afternoon, planting pickets at zero line and walking to the forward observation post, guiding three rounds to find the range of the German guns.

He heard the growl of an incoming shell.

He saw himself falling to the ground, covering his head and closing his eyes. Feeling the shell plow into the earth, knowing the blast would rip his flesh to shreds . . . Nothing happened. He uncovered his eyes to see the tail of a German shell poke from the ground like a silly thing. A dud, a great walloping dud of a Boche shell.

That evening in the officers' mess, when he was named to man the same forward observation post for the coming assault, there was a huge laugh. They slapped him on his back and offered their congratulations. He remembered someone joking, "A fellow as lucky as he would be safe wherever he went."

And once more he saw himself atop this hill in the hour before the dawn of Easter Monday, 1917. Behind the hedgerow, binoculars at his eyes, searching for the flash of return fire from across no-man's-land.

There was a sound, a furious and rushing sound.

. . . *incoming* . . .

Then all was quiet. Nothing moved.

"Have I . . . Have I died?"

"You've taken your last breath, Lieutenant, and you're beginning to forget this life. You're trying to remember things so you can hang on. You're fighting so very hard to hang on, but this life is over for you. You need to let it go, that's why I'm here."

Edward saw himself on the ground. No wounds or blood, no mark of death.

"Perhaps I was only knocked unconscious and this is no more than a dream."

The soldier nodded toward a crater of newly churned earth.

"A stray shell landed there at seven thirty-six and twelve seconds. The blast sent a shock wave through your body. It caused an embolism in your pulmonary artery, and the embolism traveled to your heart and stopped it cold."

"I never heard of such a thing."

"Nor has anyone else in this place, not yet. They'll have a name for it soon enough, I'm sure. Rather surprising the ways men are inspired to kill one another without even trying, don't you think?"

Edward did not know what to think. He saw his pocket watch. Holding at the very moment, seven thirty-six and twelve seconds.

"It seems to have stopped my watch as well."

The soldier lifted his helmet from the ground and set it atop his head with a tap. "Actually, that would be me."

"Sorry?"

The soldier touched the hilt of his bloodied knife. "I sealed off this bit of the battlefield from the rest of the devourers. I needed time to slaughter the one who was after you. Son of a bitch had an entire squad with him. Anyway, in here it's still seven thirty-six and twelve seconds. Out there, the day has come and gone."

Edward stared at the soldier, whose eyes were becoming all the more hypnotic.

"How strange it is that I should believe you."

"Yes, well, people live their lives wondering what happens when they die. Always a jolt to find what happens isn't quite what the prophets foretold. Like I said, it takes some getting used to—the dying, I mean."

*. . . some getting used to . . . the dying . . .*

"Will I be left to rot, like the German soldier under the bridge?"

"KIA in this sector are being buried in a farmer's field near Agny. Your men will come searching for you soon. They'll find your body and carry it down the hill to be buried with the rest of the dead. What's left of my company is there, watching. They have orders to take care of your body when it arrives. In time, it'll be laid to rest."

"In time?"

"Yes, Lieutenant, in time."

"I don't understand, really I don't. And strangely enough, I don't seem to mind."

"Because you no longer need this mortal coil to exist, you're ready to let go of it."

"But something holds me, something dear to me."

"You need to forget even the things most dear and let go."

*. . . the things most dear . . . let go . . .*

Edward saw familiar faces now fading from his eyes. They felt very dear to him, and he remembered.

"Yes, I know them. My wife, my children. What will they do when I am gone?"

"Sorry, Lieutenant, no one in this place can read the

future, not even the prophets. All I can tell you is their lives will go on, for better or worse."

All are behind, the kind
And the unkind too . . .

"But their names, I cannot remember their names even."
"Remembrance is for the living, Lieutenant, not the dead."

. . . no more
Tonight than a dream . . .

"Tell me, please, tell me their names."
"I can't. I can't interfere in the manner of your death."

. . . The dark-lit stream has drowned the Future and the Past.

"How cruel you are."
"Yes, I'm sure it feels that way. Then again, I'm not a poet."

How weak and little is the light . . .

"Was I a poet? I cannot remember myself."
"Yes, Lieutenant, you were a poet who was deeply loved."

And now, hark at the rain . . .

"Please, you said you knew the words in my diary, the lines on the last pages."

The soldier rose from the ground, pulled his rifle to his shoulder. He spoke softly:

"The light of the new moon and every star,
And no more singing for the bird . . .
I never understood quite what was meant by God."

Edward felt the breath slip from his body. "Everyone goes, only her face is left in my eyes."

. . . the things most dear . . .

"It's all right, Lieutenant, this is what happens. It doesn't end for your kind, it never ends. Just forget this life and let it go."

Blessed are the dead that the rain rains upon . . .

The unmoving world began to stir. He saw the flashes of guns.

He saw the rain, nothing but the wild rain.

"Oh, my . . . my Helen."

"Look into my eyes, Lieutenant, listen to my voice . . ."

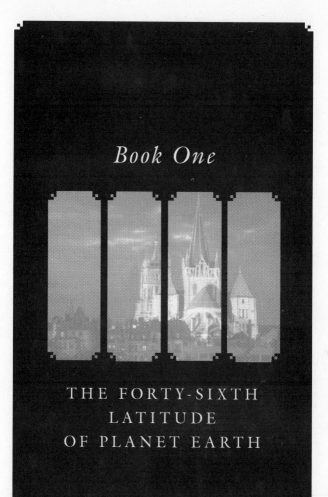

*Book One*

THE FORTY-SIXTH
LATITUDE
OF PLANET EARTH

# one

Marc Rochat pulled aside the lace curtains and watched the rain fall through lamplight and splash on the cobblestones of Escaliers du Marché. Tiny streams formed between the cobblestones and ran down to bigger streams of rain from Rue Mercerie. The two roads, narrow and angled at a steep slant, met just beyond the windows of Café du Grütli. Rochat breathed against the cold glass; he drew a rawboned face in the quick-spreading fog.

"I see you, I see you hiding in the rain. You can't fool me. *En garde.*"

He wiped away the face and turned back to the warmth of the café.

It was a familiar place to Rochat. He came here most evenings for his supper. He liked the round lamps hanging from the ceiling that glowed like full moons. He liked the photographs of Lausanne from longtimes ago hanging on the walls. He liked the chalk script menu above the bar that never changed. Monsieur Dufaux, the owner of the café, washed the slate and rewrote the menu each day, but the letters were always the same and always in the same place, just like the patrons. Madame Budry with her sixth glass of Villette, Monsieur Duvernay with his Friday night *filets de porc avec pommes frites*, the Lausanne University professor and his wife who rarely spoke to each other but read many books, the Algerian street cleaners who stopped in each night for espresso and cigarettes. And Monsieur Junod, pushing through the curtains at the door just now, followed by his little white dog on a lead. Always at the same time, always taking the same table in the corner. And his dog always jumping on the next chair to look about the café as if demanding service. Rochat liked to imagine the little dog dressed in a very nice suit, knife and fork in his paws, and eating sausages and—

"Still coming down, is it, Marc?"

Rochat saw Monsieur Dufaux standing at his table, drying his hands on the dish towel tucked in his apron strings.

*"Pardon, monsieur?"*

"The rain. Still coming down, is it?"

*"Oui,* and winter's trying to sneak into Lausanne tonight. He thinks I can't see him."

"Who?"

"Winter." Rochat pulled aside the curtain and pointed to the dripping dark beyond the glass. "Out there, hiding in the rain. He thinks I can't see him, but I do."

Monsieur Dufaux looked through the window. "Such an ugly night. And it's cold. I feel it in my bones."

"I can blow on the glass and draw him in the fog so you can see."

"Who?"

"Winter. Do you want to see?"

"*Non, mon cher,* that's all right. But tell you what: You see old man winter from the belfry tonight, you chase him away for me. Would you like a dessert, espresso?"

"*Non, merci.*"

Monsieur Dufaux collected Rochat's finished plate, pulled the white cloth from his apron strings, and pounded bread crumbs from the table.

"You know, every time you have your supper, I ask if you want a dessert or coffee. And every time you say the same thing."

Rochat thought about it. "I know."

"I know, too. That's the point. Surprise me sometime. This is Switzerland. We need surprises now and then. Keeps us from boring one another to death."

Rochat laughed politely, not sure what Monsieur Dufaux meant, but very sure it was a joke. Monsieur Dufaux was well-known in the café for saying funny things. And watching him walk among the tables, pounding bread crumbs to the floor and saying the same thing about Swiss people boring one another to death, Rochat knew he had guessed correctly. All the patrons laughed.

A single chime rang through the café. Rochat glanced at the old clock above the bar. Little hand between eight and nine, big hand on three.

"Mustn't be late, Rochat. You have your duties."

He looked at his bill and read the numbers. He

opened his wallet, carefully counting out his Swiss francs. He checked everything three times, making sure his calculations were correct.

"Very good, Rochat. Numbers can be very silly things. Always moving about when you're trying to read them."

He tied a black scarf around his neck, slipped on his long black wool coat, and eased through the crowded café toward the door. The patrons shifted in their chairs to let him pass. Monsieur Dufaux called from behind the bar, "*Fais attention*, Marc, the stones will be slippery in the rain."

Rochat felt everyone's eyes at his back, everyone watching his clumsy limp. He pulled his floppy black wool hat from his pocket, tugged it down on his head.

"*Merci. Bonne soirée, mesdames et messieurs.*"

He shuffled through the curtains and out of the door and into the rain. He checked for shadows on the cobblestones. There was only his own crooked shadow stretching from his boots.

"*On y va, Rochat.*"

He shuffled to the bottom of Escaliers du Marché. The steep hill of cobbled-together and mismatched stones looked slippery in the rain, just as Monsieur Dufaux had warned. Rochat shuffled to the wooden staircase workermen had built in middles of ages. Rochat didn't know who they were, but he was very glad they had built it. The wooden handrail was sturdy and the red-tiled roof would keep him from getting soaked to the bones. He grabbed the handrail and climbed.

*"Un, deux, trois . . ."*

The thud of his crooked right foot marking his pace.

*". . . seize, dix-sept, dix-huit . . ."*

The old stone buildings along the hill looking hammered into place by the same cobblers who built the road. Skinny flats with painted shutters, empty flower boxes at the windows, small shops on the ground floor. An antiques dealer, a hairdresser, Vaucher the *boulanger*, a gunsmith, an Indian restaurant with funny statues at the doors, and the Place de la Palud bureau of the Swiss police, who, like all good citizens, closed up shop at night and went home.

*". . . vingt et un, vingt-deux, vingt-trois . . ."*

He quickened his pace till the stone buildings began to bend in the corners of his eyes and he could imagine beforetimes . . .

*". . . quarante-sept, quarante-huit, quarante-neuf . . ."*

. . . and another cobblestone road . . .

*". . . cinquante, cinquante et un, cinquante-deux . . ."*

. . . and another stone house, with a garden at the back. The place he lived with his mother through the first ten years of his life. The place he learned to walk on his uneven legs. The only place in the world Rochat had known till a strangerman came knocking at his door. He was tall and had a bald head and there were reading glasses with no arms balanced on the tip of his nose. Rochat's mother said the stranger had been sent by his father. Rochat had never met his father, only knew him from a photograph. Standing with his mother on a summer's day on the Plains of Abraham above the St. Lawrence River. His mother wore a blue dress; she looked pretty. The photograph taken in the days before she changed. She grew tired and weak, she took lots of medicines. Then her hair fell out and she stayed in bed most of the day.

"... *soixante-quatre, soixante-cinq, soixante-six* ..."

The man at the door shook Rochat's hand. "Good afternoon, Master Rochat. I am Monsieur Gübeli. It is an honor to make your acquaintance."

He came into the house and sat at the kitchen table. He opened his briefcase and removed some papers for his mother to sign. He helped her hold the pen steady. Then the man showed Rochat a small red book with a white cross on the cover.

"Your father has secured this Swiss passport for you, Master Rochat, so you may go to live in Lausanne."

Rochat trembled. His mother took his hand.

"Don't be afraid, Marc. I have to go away soon. Your father is a very nice man, he'll take care of you. You'll go to a very nice school with children like yourself."

"... *septante, septante et un, septante-deux* ..."

The kitchen opened into a sitting room, and near the window there was a floor-stand globe of the world.

"Tell me, do you enjoy studying the earth, Master Rochat?"

"*Oui*, Maman shows me places and tells me about them."

"Has your mother shown you Switzerland? Where your father lives, where you'll go to school?"

"Yes, it's far away."

*"Pardonnez-moi?"*

The look on Monsieur Gübeli's face made Rochat laugh; his mother laughed, too. The stranger removed the glasses from his nose and laid them on the table. He walked to the sitting room and returned with the globe. He stood it next to the table and gave it a spin to the west.

"All this traveling has left me somewhat lost. I can't quite find where I am in the world."

"Because you made the world go backward, monsieur."

The stranger looked at Rochat and smiled. "Very good, Master Rochat. Perhaps you could show me the correct way to see where I am?"

Rochat looked at his mother. She brushed his black hair from his forehead.

"Go ahead, Marc. You can do it. Remember how I showed you to see things."

Rochat stopped the wrong-way world. He turned it slowly to the east and found a tiny dot along the St. Lawrence River.

"You're here, monsieur, in Quebec City."

The stranger refitted his glasses for a better look, almost touching his long nose to the globe.

"And this river on the globe would be the same river I see from your sitting room window?"

*"Oui, monsieur."*

*"D'accord.* How do I find Switzerland?"

Rochat turned the globe eastward again till he found a small country curving around a slender lake in the center of Europe.

"Switzerland is this place, the red one."

The man set the index finger of his left hand on the dot by the St. Lawrence River in Canada and the index finger of his right hand on the lake in Switzerland. He studied the distance carefully.

"Now, Master Rochat, I'm going to show you a little secret. Are you ready?"

*"Oui."*

Rochat watched the man trace the finger of his left hand along one of the thin lines drawn around the globe. From Quebec City, crossing the maritime provinces of Newfoundland and Nova Scotia and then over the Atlantic Ocean. Then through France, to find the finger of his right hand waiting in Switzerland.

"You see? Quebec City and Lausanne both lie on the forty-sixth latitude of planet Earth. So all we need to do is travel along this little line from here to there. Why, it's no distance at all. Look, I can touch the two places with one hand. Here, you try."

Rochat looked at his mother.

"Go on, Marc, you can do it."

Rochat's hand was very small and only stretched to the middle of the Atlantic Ocean. But he saw the thin line on the globe and it didn't seem too much farther beyond the tip of his little finger to the place he would go a few days later, after watching his mother's coffin lowered into the winter ground of Cimetière Saint-Charles.

And that day, the strangerman was there to hold Rochat's small hand. And he helped Rochat pack his clothes,

THE WATCHERS      • 25 •

the photograph of his mother and father on the Plains of Abraham, some coloring books, and a box of crayons. Special care was taken with the photograph of his mother and father to make sure it'd be safe as they traveled to Lausanne and nowtimes, climbing this wooden staircase on a cobblestone hill in the icy rain.

"*. . . huitante, huitante et un, huitante-deux . . .*"

There was a pedestrian passage under Rue Viret. Rochat never went that way. The neon lights flickered and made bad shadows on the graffiti-splattered walls. He took the wooden stairs that climbed above the old marketplace, where people used to sell grain and pigs and chickens and geese longtimes ago. It was a small park now with nine chestnut trees and four benches. But Rochat liked to imagine it in the old days, thinking it must have been very noisy and smelly and fun.

"*. . . nonante, nonante, nonante et un, nonante-deux . . .*"

He came to Rue Viret as the headlights of the number 16 bus rounded a bend and made flashes of reds and blues and greens in the rain. The bus splashed through a puddle, rolled by Rochat, rounded another bend, and disappeared.

"Right on time, Rochat. Must be punctual in all things."

Rochat hurried across the road and up the last of the wooden stairs.

"*. . . cent vingt-sept, cent vingt-huit, cent vingt-neuf . . .*"

He pulled hard on the handrail, jumped over the last step, and landed on the stones of the esplanade. The great floodlit façade of Lausanne Cathedral filled his eyes.

"*Bonsoir.* Still standing, are you? Good for you. Listen, you old pile of stones, we must be ready. Old man winter is trying to sneak into Lausanne tonight, and Monsieur Dufaux wants us to chase him away. Do you hear?"

He shuffled toward the cathedral, the limestone arch above the great wooden doors dripping with rain and sparkling in the floodlights. The cathedral seemed to grow bigger in his eyes.

"What do you mean, you don't need me to tell you winter is hiding in the rain? What do you mean, you already know? How could you already know? Oh, I see, because you know everything already. And why should I believe you?" He pressed his ear to cathedral stone and listened. He rolled his eyes. "Because cathedrals don't lie? Says who?"

He felt the cold gaze of the saints and prophets carved in stone on either side of the great wooden doors, all staring down at him with grumpy faces. Monsieur Moses the most grumpy-faced of all. Ready to smash the stone tablets in his hands on the ground. Rochat waved him away.

"Oh, please, it's the same silliness with you every night. 'Thou shalt not this, thou shalt not that.' That's all you have to say. And where would you be without your silly stone tablets? Looking very silly with nothing to complain about, that's what I think."

Rochat leaned back and saw the gargoyles peeking from the upper façade. He watched rain drip from their mouths and fall to the empty stone jamb between the doors.

He remembered a story he learned in school.

Once there was a gold statue of Mother Mary standing on the jamb. And lots of people climbed the steps of Escaliers du Marché on their knees to pray before her, and there were miracles: The blind could see, the lame could walk. Till some grumpy men from Berne came and tore Mary from the jamb and melted her into coins. The teacher said they were called Reformationmen. Rochat rapped Monsieur Moses on his stone toes.

"Friends of yours, I'm very sure." He watched a small pool of rain gather at the lip of the jamb, tiny drops falling to the ground. "But perhaps there's one more miracle left for Rochat."

He ducked under the jamb and let a few drops of rain fall in his mouth. He looked at his foot. Still stuck to the end of a crooked leg, still twisted to the side.

"No miracles left for Rochat, then."

Tin-throated bells rang up from Place de la Palud: *tinktink, tinktink, tinktink*. The bells lived down the hill in the Hôtel de Ville near Café du Grütli. And every night they liked to remind Rochat to hurry along.

"Yes, yes, I know, fifteen minutes. Don't worry, Rochat won't be late. Rochat is never late."

He pulled at the iron handles of the doors. Locked as always, but it was his duty to check. He shuffled to the doors of the old bishop's house and the cathedral museum. Locked as well.

"Tinny bells and grumpy statues and checking all the doors. So many duties, Rochat. No time for miracles, not for Rochat."

He shuffled along the façade and around the belfry tower to a red door almost hidden by a high wooden fence running the length of the cathedral. He pulled a ring of skeleton keys from his overcoat and slid the largest key into the lock. He turned the key, pressed his shoulder to the door, and pushed. Old wood screeched and scraped over dusty stone. He stepped in, closed the door with a loud *bang*. Rochat listened to the sound echo down a hundred dark passageways.

"*Bonsoir*, it's only me."

. . . *it's only me, only me, only me* . . .

He didn't bother with the light; he knew his way in the dark. An alcove of three doors: skinny red door to the outside, big door to the nave, bigger wooden door to the belfry tower. He sorted through the keys; finding the small one with jagged edges to open the tower door, he crossed through and locked up behind him. He shuffled down a corridor to a stone arch opening to a spiral staircase. Stone steps wound up to a narrow wooden bridge that crossed above the women's choir loft. He tiptoed, but his lightest step creaked in the dark. He passed through another stone arch and made his way up another set of winding steps to another narrow wooden bridge crossing higher above the women's choir loft, but in the opposite direction from below.

"Back and forth and forth and back. A very strange way to climb a tower. Then again, it's the only way to climb this tower, so there."

. . . *so there, so there, so there* . . .

He stopped, waited for his voice to fade.

"I really must stop talking to myself."

*. . . to myself, to myself, to myself . . .*

Floodlights on the esplanade seeped through a window of leaded glass, the light dissolving into teasing shadows on the stone walls.

"And good evening to you, mesdemoiselles. Keeping the bad shadows away, I trust?"

He heard the flimsy door at the end of the walkway swing on its hinges. Rochat was very sure the teasing shadows had something to do with the mystery of the always swinging door. He shuffled along the walkway and crossed through the doorway. He gave it a solid push till it snapped shut.

"And please remember to close the door after yourselves, mesdemoiselles! I'm very busy with my duties and don't have time for your games."

Rochat pressed his ear to the door and listened. He heard the teasing shadows giggling. *What silly things teasing shadows can be,* he thought.

He was in a dark chamber at the bottom of a stone staircase that curled up like a corkscrew. A slender window, big enough for an archer's bow, was cut through the chamber wall. Rochat looked out and saw the rain still coming down, saw the lights of Lausanne shimmering in the fog rising from Lac Léman.

"Rain or fog, you can't hide from Marc Rochat. I see you."

He hurried up the tower, round and round between close-in walls. He touched the newel pillar running up the center of the tower, his fingers tracing over the smooth finger marks made by all the men who'd climbed these same steps, touching the same place on the stone every night for eight hundred years. Round and round, higher and higher. He felt cold air coming down the tower. He heard wind sounds in the open sky. He smelled the lake and pine trees and ice and snow from far away.

He circled once more, and jumped over the last step and landed on the south balcony of the belfry as if jumping into the sky. His open arms were like perfect wings, and for a moment he was flying. High above Lausanne, high above Lac Léman and the Alps on the far shore, higher than the whole world. He settled back on his heels and opened his eyes.

"*Bonsoir*, Lausanne. Rochat is here to watch over you."

He shuffled along the narrow balcony to the northwest turret. High stone pillars and arches opening to the night sky to one side, fat supporting pillars and arches opening to the center of the belfry. Inside was the massive crisscross carpentry, six stories high and fitted together like some giant's puzzle. Rochat reached into the timbers, touched the iron spikes and wooden pegs holding the timbers together.

"*En garde, mes amis.* I know you're very old, but we must stand very straight tonight. It's our duty."

He shuffled along the north balcony, checking that all was well in the old city. He ducked through the northeast turret to the east balcony. The lantern tower at the far end of the cathedral was steady in the wind, and the weathercock atop the tower told Rochat he was right. Winds from Mont Blanc; winter was on the attack.

He felt a matronly gaze at his back. He turned slowly to the carpentry and the seven-ton bell hanging alone in a timbered cage. Rochat pulled off his hat and bowed graciously.

*"Bonsoir, Madame Marie-Madeleine, ça va?"*

The bell didn't respond.

"Oh, I see. Madame is fussy tonight."

Rochat jumped into the carpentry, checking the heavy iron hammer outside the edge of the bell's bronze skirt. He pulled at the steel cables connecting to the winch motor, making sure everything was primed and ready.

"Or perhaps madame is sleeping, hmm?"

He tapped his knuckles against her and leaned close. He heard a deep tone swirl through cold bronze.

"What's that? Madame never sleeps, madame is only resting? Yes, of course. How could I be so rude as to think otherwise?"

He refitted his hat and shuffled back to the south balcony, stopping at the skinny wooden door set between two stone pillars. He pulled a chain at the side of the door, and a small lamp flickered awake. Pigeons fled from the upper carpentry, wings fluttering like runaway feet.

"Sorry to disturb you, you blasted pooping things, but it's my duty." He opened the door, stepped into the loge, a small room of wooden walls built between the crisscross timbers, one and a half meters wide by six meters long. And he would have to stand on his own shoulders twice before touching the lowest point of the slanted wooden ceiling. A small table jutted from the west wall, and the two steps at the north end of the room rose to a narrow bed. Rochat lit seven candles and set them about the loge. He opened a cabinet, carefully removing an old brass lantern. A stunted, half-melted candle sat inside. He calculated how long it might last.

"A little while longer, I think." He took a fresh candle from a drawer and slipped it in the pocket of his coat. "*En garde*, after all."

He opened a small square window in the west wall, just above the table. He poked out his head to see another solitary bell hanging in the timbers.

"*Bonsoir*, Madame Clémence! Any heretics burned at the stake today? No? Too bad. Yes, yes, I know, not like the good old days. How sad for you."

He snapped shut the window and, with barely enough room to do so, he turned around and opened a small window in the east wall. Marie-Madeleine was just outside. Rochat thought he might give her a tap with a broomstick to check if she was truly awake. But just then, all the carpentry groaned like a very old lady yawning and stretching in a very old bed.

"*Oui*, madame is awake."

He heard the winch strain at steel cables, the steel hammer cocking back, and . . .

*GONG! GONG! GONG!*

Vibrations pulsed through the timbers and shook the room. He struck a match, lit the lantern.

*GONG! GONG! GONG!*

He shuffled out of the door, hurried through the turret to the east balcony. He stood at the iron railing just in front of Marie-Madeleine.

*GONG! GONG! GONG!*

He stood very still, waiting for Marie-Madeleine's voice to almost fade. Then he raised the lantern into the dark.

*"C'est le guet! Il a sonné l'heure! Il a sonné l'heure!"*

# two

There it was again.

She could see it through the rain.

A light moving around the bell tower.

She first noticed it after moving into the flat last summer, doing the same thing as now: sitting at her dressing table, running a brush through her hair, getting ready for a night out. She remembered swallows darting by her windows and drawing her eyes outside. Lausanne Cathedral stood against the last flush of an evening sky.

*Pretty,* she thought, *in an* Addams Family *sort of way.* That's when she saw the light in the tower, waving in her direction. It drifted out of sight, and then reappeared facing the lake. It waved once more then—*poof*—it was gone.

*Night watchman with a flashlight,* she thought.

But after a few more sightings, she realized the night watchman only appeared when the cathedral bells rang the hour. Always beginning at nine in the evening, always moving counterclockwise around the tower. East, north, west, south. Then she realized it wasn't a flashlight in his hands, it was a lantern. And it looked as if he was shouting something from the balconies.

One night, just before nine, she stepped onto her terrace and waited. The bells rang nine times and presto, there he was. And damn if he wasn't shouting something. But his voice was lost in the din of traffic rising from Pont Bessières. She grabbed her cell phone, texted her sister in Los Angeles.

```
anny u won't believe it. they gotta
lunatic locked in a bell tower over
here. he's got a lantern and screams
at night. looking at him right now!


better watch out, kat. frankenstein
was from switzerland


i thought he was german


that was hitler


tres weird. love to all☺


come home and give it urself. parental
units still way po'd abt evrthng. kids
crying, gotta go
```

She'd forgotten about the light in the bell tower till tonight. Nine-o'clock bells and *cuckoo, cuckoo, cuckoo.*

She finished brushing her hair, looked at her face in the mirror. Twenty-six years old and not a wrinkle in sight. Little eye shadow, eyeliner, a hint of mascara. Nothing else needed. Her hazel-colored eyes did the rest. It was the flaw in her left eye, a silver squiggle in the iris. Men looked at it, then they stared, then they were hooked.

Tonight's lucky fish, some Brit with a double-barreled name. Senior partner in London's biggest law firm. He requested she wear her hair down on her shoulders, the way she looked in the pictures. All her clients liked her to look the way she looked in the pictures. *Playboy*, Girls of UCLA issue.

Barely legal, Katherine Taylor was the star with the cover shot. "Jean Seberg's cool in the body of an angel," read the photo caption. Inside, she was stretched naked on her back atop a pile of cash in a bank vault, highlighting her major in international economics, which it wasn't, but who the fuck cared? Another shot straddling a bentwood chair wearing nothing but a French beret, to highlight her minor in French, which it was, but who cared again? It was a goof, something she did on a dare. But after a week of test shots, she made the cut. Suddenly it was a goof paying fifty thousand bucks. *Playboy* called it a scholarship. What a hoot, she thought. A million guys beating their meat and dreaming it was her fucking them, not their own grubby paws . . . and they call it a scholarship. She laughed all the way to the bank, wondering how goofy it could get.

The answer came a year later in the Marquis Hotel off Sunset.

A girlfriend was late for a night on the town. Katherine waited at the bar. The bartender presented a drink from someone in the room; she pushed it aside. Few minutes later, a well-dressed guy stood next to her, asking if she'd care to be presented to his boss. The guy's accent was Arabic.

"Presented . . . to your boss. Let me ask you something, bud: Do I look like a birthday cake to you?"

"Please, miss, I mean no offense. My boss is sitting over there."

Katherine saw a neat gentleman in an expensive tailored suit, alone in the corner, espresso and a glass of water keeping him company.

"So, who's the boss?"

"He is a prince of our royal family in Saudi Arabia. He wishes me to tell you he admired your photographs very much and would like you to join him, please."

"A prince. And you call him 'boss.' Wouldn't 'master' be more like it?"

"They are the same, miss."

Katherine shrugged. "Yeah, well, tell him I already have plans."

The guy appeared perplexed as he walked across the room to deliver the bad news. The gentleman with the espresso smiled in Katherine's direction. A few hushed words later, the guy was back at the bar.

"My boss understands your scheduling conflict, but is anxious to spend the evening with you. He asks if you might reconsider."

The guy laid a thin red box on the bar. Katherine

opened it, saw a gold necklace with a respectable-size pearl hanging from it. She snapped it shut and shoved it aside.

"Tell your boss he's not my type."

"Excuse me?"

"Tell him I like girls."

The guy left the red box on the bar, made the same trip across the room to deliver the even worse news. Another smile, more hushed words, he was back. This time looking fit to faint.

"His Royal Highness asks me to inquire if twenty-five thousand would change your mind regarding your . . . type."

"Twenty-five thousand, as in thousands of dollars?"

"Yes, miss."

Katherine gave the gentleman in the corner a second glance. Neatly trimmed mustache, pampered complexion, scent of sandalwood.

"Let me get this straight. We're talking twenty-five thousand dollars, cash, for one evening?"

"Yes."

Katherine picked up the red box and opened it for another look. "This trinket, it's a bonus, of course?"

"Of course. It would be a token of appreciation. You will be interested to know my prince can be most generous in his appreciations."

"Is that so?"

"Indeed, miss. May I present His Royal Highness with the happy news?"

She snapped shut the box, handed it back. "First, take this back to Prince Boss and ask him what else he's got."

That was the end of UCLA and the beginning of graduate studies in cultivated men of immeasurable means. Elegant men who came recommended to her by "a mutual friend." Probably the last guy she'd balled for cash, she thought, but so what? They came bearing gifts. Four years later, she had a beachfront condo in Santa Monica, a convertible Lexus in the garage, a room full of designer clothes, and a closet full of to-die-for shoes. And a little over four hundred thousand in undeclared cash to hide from the Internal Revenue Service.

Then came the letter from the IRS asking about all that undeclared cash in account number 2087956-2 of First Union Bank of California.

Lipstick. Understated red. Hint of gloss.

That very night, she met a Swiss gentleman for dinner at Ivy at the Shore. A private banker on business in Los Angeles, looking for discreet company. He was charming, he offered advice. Protecting one's cash assets was difficult in the post-9/11 world, he said, especially for Americans. The American security apparatus now traced every dollar in circulation around the world. And Americans, as everyone knew, were somewhat prurient toward ladies of her particular profession, especially those ladies who did well for themselves. However, if mademoiselle might consider relocating to Lausanne, things could be arranged. Say, liquidating your property in America, converting your dollars into Swiss francs to be laundered through an offshore account in Cyprus and deposited in the Lausanne branch of a reputable bank. Of course, with your financial assets, Swiss residency wouldn't be a problem. And most important, meeting someone with the right connections to handle your business affairs. He happened to know just the person: a Frenchwoman of excellent reputation now living in Geneva, operating a discreet and exclusive agency. The Two Hundred Club, catering to the rich and powerful of Europe.

Pearls tonight. Matching earrings.

The Swiss banker even knew a wonderful place on the market in Lausanne. Top floor, corner flat with a wraparound garden terrace. Lovely views of the French Alps and Lac Léman. He could arrange a mortgage with no money down, of course. Why, the whole thing could be run through the Two Hundred Club. Madame Simone Badeaux was the woman's name, by the way. The banker just happened to handle her financial affairs and had her number in his BlackBerry.

"Why don't you call her now and have a chat?"

By the time the dessert arrived, Katherine's life was sorted. And by the time she moved to Lausanne, a German pharmaceutical company announced they were buying the entire building that housed her flat. A three-hundred-thousand profit on a cash investment of zip. And she didn't have to move for another two years.

Katherine Taylor liked Lausanne. It dripped with easy money.

She stood, let the towels drop from her body. She sprayed a small mist of Chanel over her head, let the scent fall on her hair and shoulders. She opened the armoire, found the black Versace, slipped it over the expected black Aubade lingerie. The Prada heels would make their debut tonight. They added three inches to her five-foot-nine-inch frame. The client said he liked tallish women.

Her winter coat was on the chair by the front door. Fendi mink, three-quarter length. Another token of someone's appreciation. An Italian Formula One driver this time, as thanks for her silence when an Italian tabloid offered her a million euros for the skinny on a certain dirty weekend in Rome while the world champion's pregnant wife was home alone in Milan. Men of immeasurable means knew how to thank a girl who could keep her mouth shut when required. She tossed on the mink, gave one more turn in front of the hallway mirror.

"Later, baby."

She took the elevator down to the taxi waiting at the corner of Rue Caroline and Langallerie.

*"Bonsoir, Mademoiselle Taylor."*

"Hi, Pascal. *Ça va?*"

"I'm very well, mademoiselle, thank you. You are very pretty tonight."

"Thanks, Pascal. You always say the right things."

"The Palace, mademoiselle?"

"Please."

Pascal remained quiet through the ten-minute drive. Katherine appreciated his silence. That's why he was number two on speed dial, and why she always paid twice the meter. She watched Lausanne roll by in the rain. Wet asphalt reflecting blue neon signs and orange streetlamps. Rounding Rue Saint-Pierre and stopping at a traffic light, she saw the lights of Évian across the lake. *Pretty,* she thought, *in a San Francisco sort of way.*

Trolley buses rolled through the intersection till the lights changed, and Pascal crossed onto Rue du Grand-Chêne. Katherine's eyes just about popped from her head. The Lausanne Palace was flooded in red light, tied up in red ribbons and bows, garlands and ivy hanging from six floors of balconies. The pavement was dressed with stunted Christmas trees and the limestone pillars of the portico draped with hundreds of tiny white lights. None of it was there yesterday.

"Look at that! When did they do all that?"

"Today, mademoiselle. It is the beginning of the Christmas season in Switzerland when the Palace is decorated. People from all the cantons come to see it."

"All that, in a day?"

"We Swiss are very efficient."

"Tell me about it."

Pascal made a quick turn up the crescent drive. Katherine giggled.

"Gosh, it's like living a fairy tale."

T en bells echoed down the dripping street.
He checked his watch: five minutes shy of the hour. He tapped the crystal and put the watch to his ear. Still ticking, just slow.

He lit a smoke, stood still a moment. He listened.

Bells, rain.

Rain, bells.

As if there should be something else.

But he had no bloody idea what it should be.

He ducked under the hotel portico and waited as the taxi rolled up to the entrance. A nice set of ankles in black heels issued forth from the passenger door. The rest of the package came wrapped in mink, topped with a veil of blond hair that caught the white lights strung about the stone columns. He watched her make a slow turn, taking in the small forest of Christmas trees along the pavement. Watched her smile and climb the red-carpeted stairs to the revolving doors that carried her into the hotel like a kid on a carousel.

"Stars in her eyes, that one."

He dropped his smoke on the pavement, ground it underfoot. He pulled the collar of his coat tight against his neck and stepped back in the rain. He passed the oyster bar at the hotel brasserie. Saw mounds of mollusks on ice and two lads in white smocks prying open shells with blunt knives. A crowd of well-heeled types inside the restaurant living it up. White wine and assorted belons all around. He saw Blondie come through a door connecting to the hotel lobby, following the maître d'hôtel to the corner booth near the windows. Middle-aged gent stood to greet her. The gent wore a swell suit. The kind that said *expense account*. The waiter helped Blondie with her mink, revealing a nicely cut black dress. The kind that said *nicer underneath*.

He turned away and walked along Rue du Grand-Chêne, crossed over the wet road, and took the stairs down to a dark alleyway you'd miss if you hadn't been told where to look. Stone path was like a rat's maze, turning left then right and hooking back once or twice after coming to dead ends, to where a single lightbulb dangled above a black steel door.

No sign, no markings. Just two doormen the size of bulldozers with faces to match, standing motionless under matching umbrellas. They watched him approach. He stopped in front of them.

"Good evening, lads. I take it this is the place."

They looked at him for a moment and then stepped aside without a word. The black metal door behind them slid open. He nodded in appreciation.

"Cheers."

He followed a come-hither beat down a flight of stairs. Blue neon squiggle on one wall spelled *GG's* and illuminated photographs of scantily clad women on the other. All the women smiling with promises of wonderful things. He hit the last step, pushed through red velvet curtains to a dim room scented thick with perfume and cigarette smoke. A beam of white light cut through the smoke to a woman on a small stage. Her body adorned with a sheer white scarf. Her alabaster-colored skin, like the scarf, reflecting the purity of whiteness as she caressed the brass pole between her legs. She leaned back, swayed in time to the come-hither beat, let the scarf fall from her body.

"Right. And it's that kind of place."

He checked his coat with the rather nice-looking thing who appeared from nowhere, numbered ticket in her hand and a smile on her face that could melt butter.

"Enjoy your evening, monsieur."

"I'll try."

He took the ticket and walked to the bar where two beauties in negligees sat with their long legs on display. Drinking colas on ice, waiting for the kindness of a stranger. Harper took a seat at the end of the bar.

One of the women, the one with the almond-shaped eyes, said, "We will not bite, monsieur."

"Sorry?"

"Are you afraid to be close to us?"

"Maybe I'm the shy type."

"Perhaps monsieur would like to buy us a glass of champagne and we could help you overcome your shyness."

He looked at the menu on the bar. Cheapest champers in the place listed at six hundred Swiss francs. Switzerland, land of medicinal bubbly and half-naked shrinks on call.

"How about a rain check, ladies?"

"As you wish, monsieur."

He dug out his smokes, lit up, looked around the club. All the clientele sitting in the shadows with their drinks and cigarettes. None of them matched the photo.

"Welcome to GG's, monsieur. You would like a drink?"

He turned to a petite woman behind the bar. Asian face, brown eyes, slender body draped in red silk.

"Vodka tonic, please."

"With pleasure." She mixed the drink in a tall glass, set it before him. "I hope you enjoy it."

He tasted the drink; heavy on the vodka. Designed to get you well pissed and loosen up all those francs burning a hole in your pocket. He drank deeper.

"Is it to your liking?"

"Sorry?"

"The drink, monsieur."

"It's fine."

She gave it ten seconds.

"You're a newcomer to Lausanne, monsieur."

He thought about it for five.

"I suppose I am."

"You must take time to visit the cathedral."

"The what?"

"In the old city."

He stared at her, wondering about the weirdness of a half-naked woman in a strip club telling him he should see a bloody cathedral.

"I'll try to fit it in."

The bartender gave it another ten seconds.

"Is there anything else I can offer you, monsieur?"

"Sorry?"

"I could ask one of our lovely dancers to join you for conversation, if you wish."

"Conversation?"

She tapped a small notice on the bar: MERCI DE VOUS SOUVENIR DE GG'S: VOUS POUVEZ REGARDER MAIS PAS TOUCHER. You may look, but not touch.

He looked at her, wondering what one says to a half-naked woman.

"Actually, I'm waiting for someone."

She opened her arms. Her breasts perked up under the silk. They were perfect. "I'm someone, monsieur. A very nice someone for you to talk to."

"The someone I'm looking for is a man."

She leaned over the bar, smiled somewhere between coy and coquette. "Then, monsieur, you are in the wrong place."

He looked in the mirror above the bar. Portrait of a thirty-something chap in a tweed sports jacket and loose-fitting tie, propped at the bar of a strip club in Lausanne. Like being there and not there at the same time. His eyes fell from the mirror.

"Funny you should say that, mademoiselle." He finished the drink, set the glass on the bar.

"You will have another drink while you wait?"

"There comes a time in the tide of human emotions."

*"Excusez-moi?"*

"I'd love another drink."

He smoked, waited for the refill. Up in the spotlight, a caramel-colored woman with long dark hair took the stage. She wore a gold sari that glimmered in the spotlight. She pulled it from her shoulder and it slid from her body like something liquid. She held it in front of her as the spotlight dimmed and blue backlight swelled, casting her naked form against the cloth. He watched the sari rise slowly to the woman's eyes, watching her watch him. Inviting him to talk about the sensation of desire, maybe. He turned back to the bar, saw himself in the mirror again. Portrait of a thirty-something chap who couldn't remember the last time he'd felt such a thing. The bartender was back with his drink.

"I hope you enjoy it, monsieur."

"If it's anything like that last one, I'm sure I will."

He stamped his smoke in the ashtray, scanned the tables again. The man from the photograph still nowhere to be seen. Strange place for a meeting, but it was the place the man wanted. Someplace safe, someplace they couldn't be overheard. Too dangerous, time running out, must give you something. Sounded desperate, crazed even.

He sipped his drink.

An even heavier blast of vodka. Shaping up to be a rough night.

Standard operating procedure since coming to Lausanne. Couldn't sleep in this town any more than in London. Just sit on the settee. Drink, smoke, watch the History Channel through the night, every night. Not so much getting pissed as trading the sensation of memory for all there was to know about the two and a half million years of human existence. From the moment the *Homo ergaster* line of hominids became bipeds, learned to control fire and file stones into hand axes. Bit of the old drinking game before pretending to sleep: pour a round and chug it down every time someone on the telly said the words "war" or "mankind." He shook it off, lit another fag, looked around the joint. Place filling with more punters in search of conversation with a naked woman, but not the man he was waiting for. He turned back to the bar with his empty glass. The bartender in the red silk had another refill waiting for him.

"You're a mind reader, mademoiselle."

He checked his watch again. Eleven minutes after eleven o'clock. Flashing back again.

Seven weeks ago.

The last time he saw the hands of a clock in the same place.

Playing the drinking game in a one-room flat. Telly filled the dark room with blue flickering light. Holy Crusaders on the screen, slaughtering their way to Jerusalem in the name of Jesus. Streets running with blood. Telephone rang. He stared at it. Couldn't remember the last time the telephone rang, couldn't even remember where the hell he was. He got up from the sofa bed, pulled aside the window shade. Huge yellow brick building across the road. Clock tower atop the building reading 11:11.

"Where the hell am I?"

He closed the shade and sat back on the bed. Let the phone ring, thinking the bloody thing would give up sooner or later. It didn't. He grabbed the remote and turned off the telly. The room wholly dark but for the glow of streetlamps against the window shade. He picked up the receiver, didn't speak, just waited. Silence. Till a man's voice came down the line.

"Good evening, Mr. Harper."

"Who?"

"Jay Harper, on the Euston Road at King's Cross Station?"

"King's Cross?"

"Yes, the yellow brick building just outside your window. The one with the clock."

His eyes scanned the bed, the floor. Bottles of vodka in varying stages of emptiness, a wallet, British passport, an ashtray stuffed with dead butts, a couple of packets of smokes. He reached for the passport. Photo inside with a name: Jay Michael Harper. Born: London, 1971.

"Who the hell's this?"

The voice on the line answered as if the question were for him.

"Guardian Services Limited, Mr. Harper. Representing freelance security specialists such as yourself. We've engaged your services many times in the past."

Harper had no idea what the voice was talking about. "Little late for a bloody sales call, isn't it?"

"This isn't a sales call, Mr. Harper. We've been trying to contact you for three days."

He rubbed the back of his neck, looked around the room. Books, newspapers, rubbish scattered about. He shook his head, trying to come to. "Right."

"There's a job for you in Lausanne."

"Where?"

"Lausanne, Switzerland."

"Lausanne."

A wave of sickness came over him, his head throbbed with pain. Coming to was proving difficult.

"Look, this really isn't a good time."

"I apologize for the hour."

"No, it's not . . . Look, I'm not up for any sort of job, not just now."

"Mr. Harper, may I ask you if you are in a position to choose?"

"To choose?"

"Our records indicate you've been without work for

some time. One would have thought you could use the work."

The voice let him think about it. He grabbed the wallet and opened it. Thirteen pounds sterling, no pence. No other forms of ID, no credit cards, no bank cards. Like the voice said, no choice.

"What kind of job are we talking about, then?"

"Oh, the usual sort of thing."

Harper had no idea what the fuck that meant. Then again, when there's no choice, there's no choice.

"So, what next?"

Walk across the road tomorrow morning, six o'clock. Find St. Pancras Station around the back of King's Cross. Second-class rail ticket to Paris in your name at the Eurostar desk. Guy waiting on the platform, holding a sign: GUARDIAN SERVICES LTD. Doesn't introduce himself, doesn't say a word in English, mumbles in French. Somehow Harper catches the drift: Métro strike, need a taxi to Gare de Lyon, running late already. Hands over a ticket for the TGV Lyria to Lausanne, leads Harper to a waiting taxi on Rue de Dunkerque. Driver speeds through traffic, talks nonstop. Harper listens to the guy babble about the state of the world. *Très mal, monsieur, on marche complètement sur la tête* . . . Bloody world's been turned on its head—in a bad way. Stares at the back of the driver's head, wondering, *Where the hell did I pick up French?* Makes the train for Lausanne, just.

Four hours of *clickity-clack* later, Harper was in a small office of smoked-glass windows and a view of a parking ramp. On the desk, a Swiss residency card and work permit, a mobile phone and desktop computer, a letter addressed to him. The letter welcoming him, listing the address of a flat for his use on Chemin de Préville. Keys could be collected from the accounting office along with five thousand Swiss francs for expenses. A briefing book, a set of business cards.

> Jay Michael Harper
> Security Consultant
> International Olympic Committee

Like waking up and finding yourself in someone else's life.

First weeks not much to do other than make sure everyone parked in the right places and the overnight lads pulled down the shutters at night and wore blue cloth booties over their shoes so as not to scuff up the marble floors.

Just as well, he thought; anything more complicated might've tipped off his employers he didn't know why the fuck he was there. Then, a manila envelope marked Confidential appeared on his desk. Inside were ten pages of handwritten scribble. Numbers and equations, charts and graphs. Attached memo advised him to get to the bottom of this. Getting to the bottom had gotten him as far as GG's, waiting for a man named Alexander Yuriev.

He checked his watch again. Eleven forty.

The man named Yuriev was late.

Harper dug his mobile and some scraps of paper from his pocket. He sorted through the papers looking for a number. He found it and dialed. Four rings later, an annoyed-to-be-disturbed voice picked up.

"*Oui?*"

"Is that Hôtel Port Royal?"

"I cannot hear you. There is too much music."

Harper cupped his hand over the phone. "Hôtel Port Royal?"

"Yes, yes, what do you want?"

"Could you connect me to a guest in your hotel? Alexander Yuriev."

"He is not here."

"Could you leave him a note that I called?"

"No, because he is checked out with his baggage."

"When?"

"Today, before I came on shift."

"Did he leave a number or forwarding address?"

"I don't know, I'm only the night clerk. Call tomorrow during the day."

"Fine, but I'll give you my number in the event he calls in for messages tonight."

He sorted through the scraps of paper in his hand, found one of his Olympic Committee business cards, read off the number. The night clerk sounded anxious to hang up.

"Okay, good-bye."

"Wait, read it back to me."

"What?"

"My number, read it."

"Why?"

"Because I don't think you wrote it down." He heard the rustle of papers down the line.

"Okay, I have a pencil now. Give me the number."

The night clerk got it on the third try. Harper hung up, finished his drink, waved for the bill. The woman behind the bar gave him a little-girl pout.

"You do not want another drink, monsieur? We have a special midnight show. It is very enjoyable."

"Thanks, but I'm well numbed as is."

"Perhaps he will still come."

"Who?"

"The man you're looking for."

Harper scanned the club once more. "Doubt it. How much are the drinks?"

"Three hundred francs, monsieur."

"How much?"

"Three hundred francs."

He opened his wallet, dropped the cash on the bar. "Could I have a receipt, please?"

*"Tout de suite, monsieur."*

He pulled on his coat. Stuffed his smokes and matches in the pocket. He was presented with a pink piece of paper with the silhouette of a woman's naked form and a handwritten script: *300 francs. Merci de votre visite au GG's.*

"Will this be acceptable, monsieur?"

He folded the paper, stuffed it in his coat. "I'm sure the accountants will piss themselves with merriment."

"Please come again, monsieur."

"Just out of curiosity, are there many places like this in town?"

"There are many exotic nightclubs in Lausanne, monsieur, but only one GG's."

"Look, but don't touch. Not the greatest advert for a place like this, is it?"

She smiled. "The locals do not come to GG's. We cater to newcomers, like you."

"Lucky me, then."

He made his way through the club and up the stairs to the street. Fresh air fired the alcohol in his blood and slapped him silly. The bouncers watched him wobble. Their matching black umbrellas were now neatly folded, handles in hands as if they were waiting for a bus.

"Strong drink down there."

The bouncers nodded.

Harper looked up to the sky, watched a few stars coming out from behind the clouds. He took a deep breath. Whoosh again. Best leave the club-crawling to another night, he thought. He looked at the bouncers.

"Same way out as coming in, yeah?"

Ditto nods one more time.

"Cheers."

He did the rat-through-the-maze routine in reverse. Got it right the whole way and found his way to Rue du Grand-Chêne and the Lausanne Palace Hotel. Passing the windows of the oyster joint, he saw Blondie in the corner booth near the window. Carefully sipping her wine, staring at her dinner companion as he talked. As if she cared deeply for his every word.

Harper turned away, walked along the forest of Christmas trees and into the blazing lights at the hotel portico. He stopped, leaned against one of the columns, feeling as if he wanted to stay awhile. The hotel doors spun open; a man dressed like a Prussian general appeared. Wasn't a Prussian general, was the hotel doorman. And the doorman didn't like the look of the someone in a beat-up coat leaning against one of his five-star pillars.

"Just passing through, *mon général.*"

Harper moved on and followed the spiderwebbed shadows of bare plane trees on the pavement. Twelve bells sounded over Lausanne. He looked back through the trees, beyond Flon and above the Palud quarter.

He saw Lausanne Cathedral reaching for the clouds. Something caught his eye in the belfry—something in the shadows of the arches and pillars. Bright as firelight, floating from side to side. The light drifted away and the floodlights went black.

"And so concludes our special midnight show." He walked on.

The History Channel was waiting.

# three

Rochat sat on the porch of the loge where the afternoon sun heated the limestone pillars, and it felt as warm as a summer's day. He knew it was a trick. Winter may have retreated in the night, but a new wave of storm clouds hovered on the horizon for the next battle. But for the moment, all was well. He closed his eyes and dozed.

It had been a busy day of sweeping balconies and climbing timbers to scrub pigeon poop from the tops of the bells. Then checking the clappers and tightening the lashings around the heavy wooden yokes above the bells, greasing the wheels and chains of the rocking motors. Then tidying up the loge and carrying four empty Chianti jugs down the tower steps to the esplanade. Filling them with water from the fountain, carrying them back up the tower, and storing them behind the door. Marie-Madeleine stirred in the timbers and rang for five o'clock. Rochat opened his eyes.

The sun was low in the sky now, the mountains on the

far shore of the lake like jagged shadows. He leaned around a stone pillar to see Marie-Madeleine.

"And a very good afternoon to you, too, madame. I hope you're feeling well. You and your sisters must sing very soon, you know."

Marie-Madeleine remained quiet.

"Oh, I see, saving your voice for your performance. And do excuse me for disturbing you."

Rochat settled back against the stone pillars and watched two streaks of white light in the darkening sky. One streak stretching to the southeast, the other to the southwest, the two streaks crossing to make a giant X in the sky. In the setting sun, it turned the color of fire and reflected in the mirrorlike surface of the lake till it faded and floated away. Rochat scratched his head.

"Anyone up here care to tell me what that means?"

There was the usual cooing of pigeons and unmoving silence of the bells.

"Well, I think someone is sending me a secret message, that's what I think."

A gust of wind whipped through the timbers and circled the bells.

"I hear you whispering, mesdames. A giant X in the sky means nothing, you say? It's only vapor trails? And what do you know about vapor trails? You're a bunch of old bells from middles of ages. I think it's a secret message, that's what I think."

Far below the belfry, the cobblestone lanes of the old city surrendered to the evening. Rochat listened to sounds drifting in the wind: the ferry tooting its horn as it crossed the lake from Évian, a train rolling through Gare Simplon, footsteps of passersby on the cathedral esplanade. All the sounds echoing against the cathedral stones and rising to the belfry. Then a familiar set of footsteps approached the cathedral and stopped just below the tower.

"Rochat! Marc Rochat!"

He looked down through the iron railing and saw a familiar form ninety-five meters below.

"Monsieur Buhlmann, what are you doing here?"

The old man shouted back, "I tried to call you on the telephone. Is it working?"

"*Oui*, but I was cleaning the bells and took it off the hook. I must've forgotten to put it back."

"*Pas grave.*" Monsieur Buhlmann held up a large shopping bag and gave it a shake. "I have something for you, Marc."

"I'll come down, monsieur."

"No, I want to come up."

"*D'accord.*"

Monsieur Buhlmann continued looking up. Rochat continued to look down.

"Marc?"

"*Oui?*"

"If I'm to come up, you must first lower down the keys."

"Ah."

Rochat dashed into the loge, grabbed a block of wood with a big wad of string wrapped around it. He tied the end of the string to his ring of skeleton keys and dashed back to the railing. He slowly wound out the string to lower the keys. Monsieur Buhlmann untied the string and waved.

*"Bien, à tout de suite."*

Rochat began to rewind the string around the block of wood, imagining if he had a fishing rod this key business would be much easier. Then imagining if he put a hook at the end of the line instead of skeleton keys and waited for unsuspecting Lausannois to walk by, he could snatch their hats and reel them up and mount them on the walls of the loge. *24 Heures* would write stories about the Mysterious Hat Thief of Lausanne Cathedral. Lausannois would appear on the front pages of newspapers, standing on the esplanade with confused looks on their faces: "I was walking here when my hat vanished from my head! Where are the police when citizens cannot walk safely in the streets?"

Everyone in Café du Grütli would talk about it with their after-dinner cigarettes and wine. And he imagined a few days later he'd lower those same hats back onto the same unsuspecting heads. And the same Lausannois would appear in the newspapers again: *"C'est un miracle! I was walking by the cathedral, and my hat reappeared on my head!"*

The sound of the creaky door echoed up the tower steps. Rochat hurried into the loge, hung the line on the nail.

"It's a long way up, Rochat. The old man will be wanting his tea."

He opened the small window on the east wall, called out to Marie-Madeleine, "Monsieur Buhlmann is coming. Tell your sisters. What do you mean, you're busy? Busy doing what? Oh, of course. Preparing for your performance. Do forgive me, madame." He slapped the window closed, opened it just as quickly. "And tell your sisters they must sing very well tonight."

He slapped shut the window again, filled the electric kettle, switched it on. Two cups of tea were steeping as Monsieur Buhlmann came through the door of the loge.

"*Salut, Marc! Ça va?*"

"*Oui, très bien. Et toi?*"

"*En forme, Marc! En forme!*"

Monsieur Buhlmann sat on a stool to catch his breath. He tossed the skeleton keys on the table. He took big gulps of air. He didn't look *en forme* at all.

"Are you all right, monsieur?"

"Oh, I'm fine, Marc. But it's a cruel joke to grow old. When I was your age, I climbed that tower five or six times a day. Now look at me. It's all I can do to come on Sundays for your day off. But at least I can still make it once a week."

"You shouldn't have troubled yourself, I could have come down."

"No, I wanted to see you today. You don't remember what day this is?"

Rochat took a sip of tea and remembered. "Saturday. *La grande sonnerie* times."

"Yes, Marc. Saturday, the day the bells sing. Anything else?"

Rochat glanced at the calendar hanging on a nail. "December elevens."

"Yes, December eleventh, and what of it?"

Rochat looked out the open door of the loge, saw the first flickers of stars over the Alps. "It was unusually warm today."

"Yes, it was very warm for December; too warm. The oceans will soon rise and swallow the earth. Thankfully, Switzerland should be the last to go. But that's not it, either. Come on, don't you remember?"

Rochat thought about it again. Saturday, December elevens, unusually warm for this time of year. "I'm afraid not, monsieur."

"*Mon cher*, it was this very day when you were ten . . . no, twelve . . . that you first came to the belfry. Your father, rest his soul, carried you up the tower on his shoulders."

Yes, it was colder then, Rochat remembered. And there was snow on the ground. And his father did hoist him onto his shoulders and carry him up the winding tower steps to meet *le guet* of Lausanne Cathedral. Monsieur Buhlmann tapped Rochat's knee.

"You came to the door and you hid behind your father's black overcoat, the very overcoat you wear these days. You looked like you thought I might eat you."

"I was afraid you might, monsieur."

"Do you remember what we did eat?"

"We ate raclette. You cooked it on the balcony."

Monsieur Buhlmann reached into the bag and dug around. "The very thing. And today, I went to the Swiss Farm Expo at the Palais Beaulieu to see my cousin from Fribourg. You should see the place, Marc. Cows and goats and hogs everywhere. Switzerland is the only civilized country in the world that invites its prize farm animals into public buildings and lets them shit wherever they please. Just goes to show you, scratch a Swiss banker's skin and you'll find a peasant trying to get out. What was I saying? Oh, my cousin. One of his milking cows won a blue ribbon, so now he's drunk as a skunk with his Swiss hillbilly friends. But another hall was filled with the most wonderful . . . ah, here it is." He pulled out a block of cheese the size of a bread loaf and held it under his nose. He took long dreamy smells. "Raclette valaisanne, Marc. With just a taste of black pepper, not too oily. *Ça sent bon, bien?*"

"It smells very good, monsieur."

Next from the bag was a bowl covered in silver foil. Monsieur Buhlmann peeled back the foil, took another long sniff. "And boiled potatoes with onions and garlic. I had my batty wife cook them just now, very fresh. Where's the grill?"

"It lives in the winch shed next to Marie with the other things."

"Glad to hear it didn't run away. Which reminds me: I ran into that mad *vigneron* from Grandvaux, J. P. Riccard. Still wearing his apron and boots from the last harvest. He gave me two bottles of his Villette. Gold medal this year. I know you'll only have one glass, so I'll drink your share. You don't mind, do you?"

"That's a lot of wine, monsieur."

"Not as much as I used to drink, Marc. When I was young, I could drink a barrel of wine every day."

Monsieur Buhlmann certainly could drink, Rochat thought. He was famous for it. Rochat remembered one night when the old man began to recite the ballad of William Tell from the belfry. The Lausannois were confused and called the police. The police rushed to investigate, and Monsieur Buhlmann invited them up for a glass. Rochat came to the rescue and let the old man sleep on the bed while he called the hour through the night.

"Marc, I must pee. Another joke on old men. When we were young we held our water like men. When we're old we wet ourselves like babies. Where's the piss pot?"

"Behind the door, in the tool cabinet."

Monsieur Buhlmann stood and opened the cabinet. He pulled out a plastic Evian water bottle with the spout chopped off. He turned away, opened his trousers, stood very still.

"And this, this is the cruelest of God's bad jokes."

"Monsieur?"

"Waiting for your tired old dick to pee."

After a quiet moment, Rochat heard a small trickle. Monsieur Buhlmann held up the bottle to examine the contents.

"All that hard work for such a miserable piss." He picked up a Chianti jug of water from the floor and headed out of the door. "Come, Marc. Let's finish the business and get the grill."

Rochat took the keys and followed the old man around the tower to the north balcony, where the tiles of the cathedral roof were only ten meters below the railing. A rain gutter ran along under the tiles at the bottom of the slope. Monsieur Buhlmann emptied the piss pot into the gutter, rinsed out the pot with fresh water, and washed his hands. Rochat thought about it. All the men who'd worked in the tower, hundreds of years of emptying piss pots onto the roof.

"Monsieur, do you think it's all right to pour pee on the cathedral?"

"Why, if these blasted pigeons are free to shit all over the cathedral roof like prize cows in the Palais Beaulieu, I don't think the creator gives a hoot about a little piss from the likes of you and me."

"Oh."

Monsieur Buhlmann looked into the high carpentry to see the upper bells. "The bells seem very happy, Marc. You're taking good care of them."

"I do all the things you showed me."

"How is Marie treating you?"

"Not too loud when I'm trying to sleep."

"And Clémence, still moody?"

"She says she misses the good old days."

"Same old song. Now, I'll run electricity from the loge, you fetch the grill."

Rochat climbed through the timbers and squeezed around Marie-Madeleine's bronze skirt. He unlocked the winch shed, moved things about, and stumbled out with the grill, an odd-looking contraption Monsieur Buhlmann had built himself. A metal tray on a short-legged table, metal brackets and adjustable clamps atop the table to hold a block of cheese, a high-powered heating lamp along the side to do the melting. Monsieur

Buhlmann was very proud of his grill. Rochat slid the contraption under Marie-Madeleine, lifted it through the timbers, and carried it to the south balcony, where Monsieur Buhlmann was waiting in the arches near Clémence, electric cable in hand.

"We'll cook the raclette here, Marc. We'll tell Clémence we're burning a witch at the stake. That'll cheer her up."

"She'll like that very much."

Faint bells sounded three times from the Hôtel de Ville down in Place de la Palud. Monsieur Buhlmann smiled.

"Quarter to six, Marc. Just enough time to pop in the loge and have a glass, two if we hurry. Where's the corkscrew?"

"Where you left it when you retired, monsieur."

Monsieur Buhlmann found the corkscrew hanging under the table in the loge. He opened a bottle, poured a mouthful into a glass. He sniffed at it and sipped.

"Marc, don't let anyone tell you there's a better *vin blanc* in the world than a Villette from Lavaux. It tastes like your first kiss. Not a silly kiss, but the first kiss from the first girl you love. Which reminds me: While I was watching the milking competition, I realized we need to find you a girl."

"Monsieur?"

"Now, I know I'm old-fashioned and moan about many things, but this is important. We need to find a girl for you, Marc. Someone to care for you when the likes of me and Monsieur Gübeli are gone. Someone you can care for, too. What do you say?"

"I'd say you've been tasting the wine from very early in the day."

"Only a demi. With lunch. And two more with my cousin and his friends. And a liter of beer. There may have been a few more glasses, somewhere. But in wine there is truth, and I have found the truth."

"To what?"

"A girl."

"A girl?"

"Yes, a girl for you. *Écoute*, one of my cousin's hillbilly neighbors was at the Palais; he brought his daughter. She's nineteen . . . That's four . . . no, two years younger than you. A lovely girl; she won the milking competition. And she's pretty, but not too pretty. Good Swiss bones, and not too tall. Can't have her too tall because of your limp. And she's shy, like you."

"Not clever, you mean."

Monsieur Buhlmann drank his wine, poured again. "You listen to me, Marc. This town, this country, this world, is full to the brim with clever people, and just look at it. Never been in such awful shape. Clever people don't give a damn about anybody but themselves. Too busy being clever. The world doesn't need any more clever people. It needs people with wisdom."

"I don't know what that means."

"It means someone who's clever enough to grab a girl who knows how to milk a cow."

Rochat thought about it. "Are you sure you only had a demi with lunch, monsieur?"

"Perhaps it was a bottle. But I speak the truth! You're

a young man now; you need a girl in your life. Now, look. I'm going to my cousin's house for Christmas lunch. Me and my batty wife. And you are coming along. I'll have you back in time for the nine-o'clock bells, don't worry. My cousin's neighbor will be there with his daughter. You can meet her then. Her name's Emeline. Isn't that a lovely name for a girl?"

Just then, the timbers began to creak.

"But what would I tell Marie-Madeleine? What do I tell Clémence and the other bells? They'd never forgive me."

Monsieur Buhlmann whispered, "We won't tell them."

*GONG! GONG! GONG!*

The old man drained his glass and stood. "Six o'clock, Marc! *La grande sonnerie! Allons-y!*"

*GONG! GONG! GONG!*

They hurried along the balconies and stood near Marie-Madeleine as she finished sounding the hour, her great voice hanging in the air. Then the timbers in the tower moaned and groaned even louder as cables turned wheels, wheels strained at chains, chains pulled at gears, and heavy wooden yokes above all the bells began to rock from side to side. La Lombarde sounded from the higher timbers. She was always first to answer Madame Marie-Madeleine's voice. Then more voices sang from above: Mesdames Voyageuse, Bienheureuse, and l'Aigrelette. Clémence quickly shook off her foul mood and joined in from the far side of the belfry. Then Marie-Madeleine rocked from side to side till the heavy clapper under her skirt slammed against bronze and her voice thundered and silenced all sounds in the world.

Monsieur Buhlmann banged Rochat's shoulder and shouted, "To the higher bells, Marc! We must see Mademoiselle Couvre-feu!"

Rochat led the way to the northeast turret. Sixty-three stone steps circled twice around before reaching the upper balconies. They moved along to the north balcony where the old man could see the narrow wooden walkway running through the center of the tower to the south arch, looking out over the dark lake and the flickering lights of Évian on the far shore. Above the walkway, two bells whipped back and forth in a blur.

Rochat stepped over a block of stone and up to the walkway. He guided Monsieur Buhlmann under the first bell, La Voyageuse, making sure the old man's head stayed very low. The heavy iron clapper under her skirt flew so fast, it was impossible to see, and could smash open a man's skull like an egg. They stood upright under Mademoiselle Couvre-feu. Monsieur Buhlmann held up his hand; the swinging bell brushed his fingertips like a kiss.

"*Bonsoir*, mademoiselle! You are so lovely this evening!"

Monsieur Buhlmann wobbled again. Rochat settled him against the crisscross timbers in the center of the belfry. The ancient wood hummed and vibrated with bell song. Monsieur Buhlmann closed his eyes; Rochat watched him carefully. Here, in the highest timbers, with all the bells dancing and singing and the sound pulsing in dizzying waves, the massive carpentry itself swayed. A man could easily lose his balance and stumble through the south arch of the belfry. From there it was a hundred-meter fall to the ground.

The bells sang for fifteen minutes. But many minutes later, the final chord still filled the sky. Swelling and fading, swelling and fading again, then it was gone. Monsieur Buhlmann opened his eyes.

"What would this world be without our bells? Eh, Marc?"

Rochat thought about it. "Sad?"

"*Oui*, Marc, sad beyond belief. This is the last good place in a world of terrible sadness. You must never fail to call the hour, you must always protect the bells and call the hour, *mon cher*."

"I never forget the things you taught me, monsieur."

"Good. Now, let's go down and have another glass and toast the bells. Then we'll make our supper."

Monsieur Buhlmann was an expert at raclette, and Rochat liked watching him make it. Baking the edge of the cheese till it melted and then shaving the yellow goo over boiled potatoes. The grill gave off enough heat to sit outside, so Rochat brought the two wooden stools from the loge. They made themselves comfortable near Clémence. Her dark bronze skirt glowed in the reddish light of the grill.

"See, Marc? Burn a little cheese at the stake, tell Clémence it's a witch, and she feels much better. Can't let the old girl get too depressed."

After many plates of raclette, and well into the second

bottle of Villette, Monsieur Buhlmann dug through his shopping bag again.

"I have a gift for you, Marc."

"For me? But why?"

"Marc, I told you. This is December the eleventh, the day you first came to the tower. It's a birthday in a way. Part of you was born on that day."

"My birthday's in October."

"Yes, Marc, but you see . . . Never mind. I found something for you at the Palais Beaulieu, in the farm-supply displays. You know, tractors, milking machines . . . Ah, here."

He handed Rochat something wrapped in newspaper. Rochat stared at the crumply paper with wrinkly words. It was too small to be a tractor. "Is it a milking machine?"

"No, no. Open it."

Rochat slowly pulled at the newspaper and saw two long black tubes braced together, small rubber caps at one end, fat round lenses at the other. "Binoculars."

"Not just any binoculars, Marc. They're Zeiss. Swiss farmers use them to watch their cows graze on far-flung hills. Imagine that? The same binoculars Swiss Army snipers use, for a herd of cows."

"But there's already a pair in the loge."

"Those old things? They've been here since General Guisan used the belfry to keep an eye on the Nazis across the lake during the occupation of France. No, these glasses are sharp and clear. Have a look."

Rochat put the lenses to his eyes, looked off the balcony toward Place Saint-François. The clock tower of Saint-François popped up big, as if it lived next door to the cathedral. He turned a little, saw little stone angels carved in the eaves of the old Banque Cantonale building. As if they were sitting on the iron railing of the belfry.

"What do you see, Marc?"

"Angels."

"Angels?"

"On the Banque Cantonale, monsieur. It looks like I can touch them."

"Two kilometers away, that building."

Farther down the hill to the shore, along Rue du Lac to Ouchy, to the sailboats moored in the harbor. They looked like toys in his bathtub. Back up the hill to the lamp-lit windows of Place de la Palud, below the cathedral. A young couple finishing a bottle of wine, a mother putting a baby to sleep, a man sitting alone with a deck of cards. Rochat lowered the binoculars.

"They're very good, monsieur. But I'm very sure they're expensive. You must let me pay for them. Monsieur Gübeli gave me money to keep in the belfry for emergencies."

"This isn't an emergency—it's a gift. And you must give them to the watcher who comes after you, that's the tradition. You must leave something for the watcher who comes after you."

"Like your hat and cloak."

"Yes, Marc. Like my old hat and cloak. Still in the closet, are they?"

*"Oui, monsieur."*

"I do like putting them on to call the hour, you know. But when I'm gone, you take them home. Don't want them lying around."

"I know, monsieur."

Monsieur Buhlmann stretched his arms and yawned. "I suppose I'd best get home, before my batty wife forgets I'm still alive, again."

Monsieur Buhlmann made several attempts at getting up, but kept falling back on his stool. Rochat went into the loge and dialed for a taxi, then he called Madame Buhlmann to say all was well and that her husband was still alive and on his way home and could she please remember to unlock the door because he was very drunk. The old man objected, going on and on what nonsense it was and that he could find his own way home. During one arm-waving objection, Rochat excused himself for the nine-o'clock rounds. Dashing into the loge, lighting the lantern, waiting for Marie-Madeleine to ring. Then rounding the tower to call the hour and returning to the south balcony, only to find Monsieur Buhlmann on his stool, still protesting that it was all so much nonsense, as if Rochat had never left.

By the time he got the old man down the tower and into the waiting taxi, it was three minutes before the ten-o'clock bells. Rochat rushed back into the cathedral and raced up the tower.

# four

I t was a late call.

Katherine wasn't enamored with late calls. They reminded her of her job description. But Simone Badeaux pointed out that at five thousand Swiss francs for dinner, and dinner alone, she was far removed from what could be described as a whore.

"Really, Katherine, I do think you forget the impression you leave with the members of the Two Hundred Club. Mr. Duncan-Bowles thought you most charming and decided to stay another night just to visit with you again."

"He must have believed all those things I whispered in his ear when I gave him the squeeze."

"Indeed, reduces them to whimpering schoolboys. By the way, I have details regarding our Middle Eastern friend. Two weeks in Zermatt, December twenty-fourth through January eighth. You'll have accommodation at the Monte Rosa Hotel. The client asks that your mornings be kept free for coffee, and your late afternoons free for an aperitif."

"Consultation fee?"

"Fifty thousand Swiss francs plus open accounts at shops and restaurants. He would also like to meet with you just after midnight of the New Year. Discreetly, of course. The usual paparazzi trash will be chasing his actress wife about, gorgeous creature that she is. Really, I am jealous, darling. I knew his father, you know. A man of great dignity and charm, not to mention stamina. I understand the son to be of similar caliber."

"Why not come along, Simone? Make it a threesome."

"Oh, you are naughty, but it's all I can do to manage the club. You found a restaurant for this evening? The client wishes for something Italian."

"Not an easy trick on a Saturday night, but Pippo is holding a table at La Grappa."

"Oh, the divine Pippo, do give him my love. Next week I'll have details regarding your trip to the Maldives with our Bollywood friend. Things aren't going well with wife number four. He needs your particular attention. Ciao."

She finished dressing and dropped her cell phone in her Louis Vuitton bag, along with a Taser gun. Not that it was entirely legal in Switzerland, but what the hell? Sometimes a girl needs a few thousand volts of equalization. She checked herself in the mirror.

"Go get 'em, tiger."

Pascal drove her to the narrow lanes of the Rotillon quarter. The usual compliments followed by silence ate up the five-minute drive.

"When should I collect you, mademoiselle?"

"Give me three hours, Pascal. I'll let you know if things change."

She walked around the corner to the beige stone building with candlelit windows. The doorman smiled and bowed; he pulled open the door. Music and laughter drifted outside.

The divine Pippo was standing at the white grand piano with a microphone in his hands. Grappa wasn't just Pippo's restaurant; it was his stage. Hair slicked back, handlebar mustache curled at the tips, waving his arms and pointing out the beautiful people sitting at his tables come to be fed and entertained by him. *A genuine lounge lizard,* Katherine thought, *but a lounge lizard with style.*

"And now, *mesdames et messieurs,* you must excuse me. A beautiful woman has just walked into my life." Pippo laid the microphone on the piano, greeted Katherine with open arms and three kisses. He took her mink and led her through the restaurant. "I have table twenty-one for you. Close to the fireplace."

"Thanks, Pippo."

She saw Enzo at the piano, looking up from the keys and blowing her a kiss without missing a note. She smiled, sent one back. Pippo pulled out the table and Katherine settled in the corner, from where she could see the entire room.

"And I saved the last of the white truffles for you. So beautiful for the mouth. The head of the Solzdorf Investment Bank is here with his mistress. He wanted to impress her with my truffles. I told him they were finished. His mistress wasn't impressed."

"Poor boy. He'll get over it."

She pulled a cigarette from her bag. Pippo pulled a lighted match from thin air. "Champagne, mademoiselle?"

"Please, and send a glass to Enzo."

"I will cut his throat instead. Tell me you are alone tonight, Mademoiselle Taylor. Tell me and I will melt."

"I'm expecting someone, Pippo. Posh and rich, so get out your most expensive red."

"If he touches you, I will die."

"Then I wouldn't get my white truffles."

Pippo jabbed an imaginary knife into his heart. "This life, *c'est tragique*. I can only make love to you with my food."

"Well, at least you know how to satisfy a woman, Pippo."

"I burn with love." He bowed and kissed her hand, waltzed to the piano, and grabbed the microphone. "Champagne for Mademoiselle Taylor! Champagne for everyone! *Mesdames et messieurs*, tonight, I am in love with a beautiful lady from America!"

Enzo broke into a chorus of "New York, New York." Wrong fucking coast, but Katherine smiled anyway. She liked Enzo. He had long, delicate fingers. The kind a girl dreams about.

She sipped champagne till Mr. Duncan-Bowles arrived. He looked half in the bag already. He laughed when Pippo presented a starter of prosciutto and sausages while complaining to the next table that "this Englishman" had stolen the love of his life from under his handlebar mustache. Pippo poured the Conterno Barolo with the look of a lovesick puppy. He walked to the piano and announced to the crowd he was now heartbroken. He sang his way through a sad Italian melody.

*"Ancora . . . ancora . . ."*

There was loud applause. Mr. Duncan-Bowles tasted the wine.

"Odd little chap, isn't he?"

"Pippo? He and his mustache are part of the wallpaper in Lausanne. And he appreciates men of quality, such as yourself."

"I don't follow."

"Savile Row suit, gold monogrammed cuff links, the watch on your wrist." Handmade Patek Philippe. Forty grand at least, Katherine figured. And it wasn't there yesterday. Mr. Duncan-Bowles admired it himself.

"Picked it up today, bonus to myself. Just closed a huge merger in Lausanne. That's why I thought I'd like to see you again. Stay another night, celebrate."

Katherine's mind kicked into gear. One of the perks of dating men of immeasurable means: They loved to brag their way into her stock portfolio. She scooted over a smidge, sipping her wine and letting her hair fall over her eyes so she could slowly brush it away.

"Really? What kind of merger?"

"Oh, I couldn't say."

She reached under the table, rested her hand on his thigh. "Hey, I thought you wanted to celebrate."

Katherine got home after two in the morning, made a note to call her banker to put in an order for twenty-five hundred shares of Norton-Blessed Ltd. She dropped her clothes on the bathroom floor, rolled a fat marijuana cigarette, and lounged in a hot bath.

Supply running low; must call Lili.

Lili always had the best dope. Hydroponic and home-grown in a converted barn full of sculptures. Women's elongated bodies in bronze. Some of them modeled from Katherine's body. Katherine liked getting stoned and posing for Lili. She liked the way Lili looked at her while shaping her body in soft mounds of hot wax. Yes, must call Lili and have a nice girlie afternoon.

She drew a deep toke, held the smoke in her lungs.

Outside the window, Lausanne sparkled like diamonds for the picking.

"So easy, so nice . . ." She closed her eyes and floated away. "And it always tastes like more."

R ochat sat in the loge, listening to the wind.

He drummed his fingers on the wooden table and waited for a thought. Sometimes they blew in with the wind. He was very sure a thought was coming to him when the telephone rang. Rochat jumped and fell off his stool. He looked at the old wooden telephone on the wall near his bed. Two tiny bells on top, a tiny hammer pounding furiously between them.

Rochat got to his feet, dusted off his trousers, and made himself presentable to answer the telephone in his official capacity. He unhooked the listening tube from the side of the box, spoke into the talking cone at the front.

*"Bonsoir, je suis le guet de la Cathédrale de Lausanne."*

There was loud music and a screaming voice trying to make itself heard.

"Hello, what? I can't hear you. You want what? Pizza? I'm sorry, this isn't the all-night pizza place. That has a number six at the end, not a number seven. No, I'm very sure, six at the end of the numbers spells pizza, seven at the end spells cathedral. What? Yes, I have no pizza."

The line went dead.

Rochat reset the listening tube on its hook, tried to remember what he was thinking about before pizza. He couldn't, so he turned around to the shelf on the wall and sorted through his sketchbooks, pulling down the one he had titled *les bishops morts*. He thumbed through the pages to the last drawing of Basil the First. He took an eraser and pencil and began to touch up the old boy's face. Basil lived with other dead bishops in the nave, all in a row near the Virgin's Chapel. No one knew their real names because somebody forgot to carve them into the marble. So Rochat named them all Basil and he always greeted them when passing. He was very sure they appreciated it. But the years had not been kind to Basil the First's marble face. His eyes and nose were missing, and his ears stuck out from the sides of his head like a monkey. Rochat worked at it till it was time to prepare for the three-o'clock bells, the final call of the night.

"I'm truly sorry, Your Grace, but there's no hope."

He closed the sketchbook, put on his overcoat and floppy hat, set a fresh candle in the lantern, and waited for Marie-Madeleine to call him outside. The binoculars from Monsieur Buhlmann sat on the table, the neck strap looking like the lead on Monsieur Junod's small dog in Café du Grütli. Rochat picked up the binoculars and slipped the strap over his head.

"*D'accord.* We'll go for a little walk, but no barking."

The timbers creaked and groaned; Marie sounded three times. Rochat lit the lantern and shuffled around the balconies, calling the hour to the east, north, west, and south. When he finished, he looked out over Lausanne.

"All was very well for another night, Rochat."

He blew out the lantern, hooked it to the iron railing. He raised the binoculars to his eyes and focused on the red-tile rooftops of the Palud quarter. Heatsmoke curled from chimneys. A little to the right, a lone trolley bus rolled over Rue du Grand Pont. Sparks flashed where the trolley's arms touched the overhead power lines, the lights on the bus sputtering off and on. He panned left. The clock on the belfry of Saint-François was staring back at him through the lenses.

"Aha! I knew it. Just like the bells in the Hôtel de Ville. Two minutes fast. You'd better not let Clémence find out. She'll have you boiled in oil." The clock looked close enough for him to reach out and give the big hand a tap and set it right. Then he remembered he was looking through binoculars. He turned the lenses backward, looked again. Now the clock was so far away, it looked as if it were sitting across the lake in France.

He shuffled into the shadows of the southeast turret and leaned against a pillar. He looked through the binoculars again. Down on Pont Bessières, a man was standing at the railing of the bridge, looking up at the cathedral.

"Do you see, Marie? That man on Pont Bessières? He's standing very still and he's got his hands in the pockets of his coat. And it's a coat with a belt and little straps on the shoulders like detectives wear in old movies Grandmaman liked to watch."

He lowered the binoculars and thought about it. He turned to the great bell hanging in the timbers.

"You know, Marie, I think the man on the bridge must be a detectiveman, and I think he must be solving a mysterious mystery, because that's what detectivemen do, they solve mysterious mysteries. But I can't think of any mysteries in Lausanne, can you?"

A small breath of wind whisked by Marie-Madeleine to find him in the turret.

"What do you mean, the cathedral is full of mysteries? When was the last time you saw a detectiveman movie, hmm? Why, there's nothing in this pile of old stones but some teasing shadows who keep leaving doors open and all those dusty skeletons under the nave who like to rattle their bones at night and Otto the Brave Knight always falling over in his armor. Very common things for a cathedral, that's what I think."

Rochat slowly raised the lenses. He scanned the rooftops of Lausanne and the trails of chimney smoke in the sleepy dark.

"*Non*, I'm very sure if there is a mystery in Lausanne, it must be somewhere out there. And with these very good binoculars for watching cows on hills, I can see—"

A bright light flashed in his eyes, and a woman in a white robe appeared as if floating. She settled before a mirror, let the robe fall from her shoulders. Rochat saw the skin of her naked back. Her hair was wet, and she slowly combed it till it lay in long blond streaks.

Harper stood a moment longer.

He'd been walking the streets, checking every strip joint and after-hours club in Lausanne looking for Alexander Yuriev, with nothing but a pocketful of receipts to show for it. Coming up Rue Caroline, and on the phone to the night clerk at the Hôtel Port Royal in Montreux for another round of "No, the man you want has not checked for messages, sir," Harper heard the bells of Lausanne Cathedral ring for three o'clock.

He remembered the night before, the light floating in the belfry just after the midnight bells. Curious if it'd be there again and wondering if he'd only been well pissed, he disconnected with the night clerk and headed up the road. By the time he rounded the corner and saw the cathedral atop the hill, all was dark. Then he thought he saw something shadowlike moving in the belfry. He walked slowly ahead, stopped, and waited. Eyes focused on the high pillars and arches. He gave up and pulled out his smokes.

"And the winner is—well pissed."

He lit up, aware of his surroundings. On a bridge stretching between Avenue Mon-Repos and the old city. As if the earth had fallen out from under him and he was standing in midair. He stepped to the railing, looked down. A two-hundred-meter drop to narrow lamp-lit streets, where unseen winds gathered dead leaves and carried them away in darting spirals. Shadows chasing leaves, leaves chasing shadows. The winds curled up the bridge supports, cut through the railing . . .

He snapped back from the edge, rubbed the back of his neck. "Bloody hell."

"Are you all right?"

Harper turned to the voice, saw a young man standing on the pavement on the other side of the bridge.

"Sorry?"

"Are you all right? I noticed you leaning over the railing."

Harper stepped to the edge of the pavement. Two of them at the middle of the bridge, talking across the roadbed like villagers chatting across a brook.

"Fine. Touch of vertigo looking over the edge, I guess."

"Lausanne takes some getting used to. I came from Poland, everything's so flat there. All these hills and bridges in Lausanne, always looking down, it's a little like flying."

"Or standing in midair, maybe."

"Yes, that, too. You're a newcomer, aren't you?"

Harper took a long pull of smoke. "What did you call me?"

"A newcomer. Those are the names we use in Lausanne. 'Locals' for the people who live here, and 'newcomers' for ones like . . ."

"Like me."

"Yes, like you."

Harper took another pull of smoke, stared at him. Leather jacket, blue jeans, sneakers on his feet. Nineteen, twenty maybe.

"I walk this bridge at night. Sometimes I see newcomers wandering near the cathedral, not quite sure where they are. They always come this way."

"That's what you do, keep a sharp eye out for newcomers on the bridge?"

"You don't know about this place, do you?"

Harper looked both ways; not a soul in sight. "What's to know, other than I'm standing on a bridge in the middle of the night?"

"Some of the locals come here and . . . I thought you might be a local, someone in need of comfort. That's what I do."

*Swell*, Harper thought, *spend the night looking for a drunken Russian and end up in Lausanne's all-night cruising shop.*

"That's terribly kind of you, mate, but maybe you could just tell me the way to Chemin de Préville."

The young man pointed toward the old city. "That way."

"Up the hill, past the cathedral?"

"There's a view of Lausanne from the esplanade. You'll see where you need to go next."

Harper checked his watch: three thirty in the morning. He pointed the opposite direction. "Actually, I think I saw a taxi stand back down—"

"There's not a lot of time, monsieur."

Harper dropped his smoke on the pavement, shoved his hands in the pockets of his coat. "Not a lot of time—right. I'll get a move on then." Harper headed off the bridge. On the corner of Rue Caroline he looked back.

One midnight cruiser crossing the roadbed, carefully removing a handkerchief from his leather jacket, collecting the crushed remnants of Harper's cigarette, and tossing them in a bin. Then stepping back to the pavement marking the center of the bridge, waiting for someone else to come along.

"And good luck."

# five

The mobile rang and vibrated at the same time.

Harper pulled his eyes from the telly, watched the thing rumble into a half-empty bottle of vodka. The bottle went *clink*. He grabbed the phone before it did any more damage.

"Yes?"

"Mr. Harper, Nathalie Barraud calling. The doctor is on his way from Geneva Airport and wishes to see you in Vidy Park."

Harper kick-started his brain. The doctor. Doctor Johann Schwarzenberg, president of the International Olympic Committee. Liked to be called *le docteur* rather than *le président*. Nathalie Barraud, nice-looking bird who ran the doctor's office. Wore horn-rimmed glasses and tight skirts, spoke nine languages, never smiled. Coming from the airport? Right, overnight from Jo'burg, the African regional games.

"What day is this?"

"Sunday, and the doctor does apologize for the inconvenience. But he'll be receiving the king of Spain tomorrow and must see you about the lab report."

"Lab report?"

"The one you faxed to him yesterday. He received it before boarding and read it over in flight. He wishes to discuss it with you. There's a car waiting outside your flat. You are expected at two o'clock. Please be prompt."

"Right, what time is it?"

"One fifteen."

"A.M. or P.M.?"

"It's the afternoon of Sunday, December twelfth. Is there a problem of some sort?"

Harper's head throbbed. "No, everything's fine."

"Good. And in the future, Mr. Harper, please have the courtesy to submit any and all communications to the doctor through me."

The line went dead.

Harper pulled himself from the couch and opened the curtains. Gray light poured through the windows. Gave his studio flat all the cheeriness of a Dutch still life. He thought about cleaning up the remnants of another sleepless night. Hell with it, no time. He picked up the remote, switched off the telly just as a narrator's voice was telling him about the spectacular Gothic interior of Coutances Cathedral. Sunday special on the History Channel. *Great Cathedrals of the World*. Chartres, Westminster Abbey, Paris, Cologne. Everything you never needed to know about cathedrals. Kept waiting to see if Lausanne's hometown entry made the grade. No such luck.

He threw water in his face, shaved, and dressed quickly. He downed three aspirin for breakfast, jumped in the waiting car, and headed for Vidy Park. Fifteen minutes later, Miss Barraud escorted him into the doctor's office. He was at his desk, reading from neatly bound pages while pointing to an empty chair.

"Come in, Mr. Harper. I'll be with you in a moment."

Harper made the long walk across the office and sat. "Good afternoon, sir."

The doctor continued to read.

Harper kept himself busy looking out of the glass wall opening to the doctor's private garden. Huge lawn, sculpted hedges. Probably a nice view on a clear day. The lake, the Alps. Today, with the fog, it was hard to see beyond the smoked-glass-and-steel building next door, where the mere mortals of the IOC dwelled, where Harper's own office was. The one with the nice view of the parking ramp. The doctor and Miss Barraud worked in the more heavenly confines of what was known as Le Château.

He turned his eyes to the doctor's desk. Everything on it was white. White leather folders, white papers, white telephone with twenty white buttons. He looked around the office. Everything in the room was white. Chairs, sofas, coffee table. The flag in the corner with the interconnecting rings of red, blue, yellow, green, and black did add a splash of color. And the laptop computer on the desk, black for the computer. Harper wondered how often the doctor used the thing. Why would he? The man had twenty buttons on his telephone. Push one and Miss Barraud rushes in. Takes a memo, reads the mail, sorts your life with a cuppa. Tea, Christ, please.

The doctor looked at his watch.

"Is it two already?"

Harper checked his own watch, still five minutes behind the rest of the world. "Seems so, sir."

The doctor sat back in his swivel chair. "When did the lab come back with this?"

"Friday afternoon."

"And they're quite sure of their findings?"

"There are questions, sir."

"The only question I care to have answered at the moment is whether or not the drug was used in the Beijing Games."

"The blood samples of all Beijing medalists are still in the IOC lab. They've tested eighty percent. So far, nobody's popped hot."

"So it's untraceable, as the documents claim."

"Sir, I'm not sure it even exists."

"These documents call it a topically applied potion, already in use."

"Yes, sir. Question is, what's it for?"

"To win gold medals, Mr. Harper; that's why athletes take drugs."

Harper nodded *yes, but that's not the bloody point.*

"Sir, in their review of the documents, the IOC lab notes much of the data doesn't make sense. They have no idea what some of the compounds are. The ones they can identify would bring about severe psychotropic effects, if not render an athlete comatose. In fact, the word 'drug' isn't used anywhere in the material. It's always referred to as 'a potion.'"

"And?"

"Whoever used it would be high as a kite."

"So then the dosage is reduced."

"That's just it. Knock down the dosage, there's no effect."

"I don't understand. Exactly what sort of drug is this?"

"We'd have to ask the person who sent the documents."

"It was sent anonymously, you may recall. That's why you were asked to look into it."

"There's been a development, sir. Shortly after you left for Africa, I received an e-mail from someone who said his name was Alexander Yuriev. He claimed he sent the documents."

The doctor blanched. "What do you know about him?"

"Nothing, sir, till I Googled him. After that I went into the IOC files." Harper pulled a rolled-up clump of papers from his coat. "Makes for rather sad reading."

"The man was a seven-time gold medalist at Innsbruck, one of the greatest champions ever."

"Sir, I read that you're the man who had him banned from any contact with the Olympic movement, pretty much ending his career."

"By then his career was well in the bottle."

"Yes, sir. I only mention it because when I wrote to him, asking what he wanted, he said he needed to see you, he said you were the only man he could trust."

"Are you telling me you established a correspondence with him?"

"Nine times, each time through a different Hotmail address. May I ask, did Yuriev ever try to contact you after he was banned?"

The doctor looked at Harper. Harper sensed the man's discomfort.

"Just as background, sir."

"There were letters after he was banned, begging me to reconsider. There was nothing I could do, I'm afraid, and I didn't respond. I really had no idea what happened to him; he disappeared. Then, nine months ago, quite unexpectedly, I received an e-mail from him."

"What did he want?"

"He wanted to see me. He said it was a matter of life or death."

"Did you answer it?"

"I deleted it and asked Miss Barraud to block his name from the IOC server."

"No other e-mails, then?"

"I told you, his name was blocked."

"He got to me, sir, using the same IOC server."

The doctor considered it. "Yes, that is curious."

"When the documents came through the post, you had no idea they came from him?"

"Indeed not. And I'd appreciate it if you could tell me how you know the man you're dealing with is, in fact, Alexander Yuriev?"

"Yes, sir, sorry. After his initial e-mail to me, I asked for proof of identity. He sent a copy of his Russian passport.

He continued to say he needed to see you. As with you, he told me it was a matter of life and death. I wrote he had to go through me. He continued to insist you were the only man he could trust. There was an increasing level of desperation in his subsequent e-mails, so I gave him my number and told him to telephone. He called that same day, said he needed to give you something for safekeeping. And again he said you were the only man he could trust."

"What was it, this thing he wanted to give me?"

"No idea, but whatever it is, it feels like trouble." Harper glanced at the pile of papers in his lap; he sifted through some pages. "Gambling, alcohol, the accident. The man's life fell apart in rather spectacular fashion. There's no telling what he's involved in."

"Do you think he might be dangerous?"

"Not sure. That's why I set a meeting with him."

"Where?"

"Lausanne."

"Yuriev is in Switzerland?"

"Yes, sir." Harper opened his file. A sheaf of papers fell out on his lap; he sorted through them, laid one on the doctor's desk. "This came attached to his last e-mail. It's a photograph of Yuriev standing on the Montreux corniche."

"My God, he looks awful, but it's him. I'd say his drinking has all but destroyed his liver. Is that a newspaper in his hands?"

"*24 Heures.* Date and headlines prove the photo was taken the same day as his last e-mail, Friday morning, the day he telephoned my office."

"How did he sound?"

"At his wits' end. I'm not sure he's at all mentally stable."

The doctor swiveled his chair to the wall of glass, stared out at the fog. "What happened at this meeting?"

"He didn't show up."

"I don't follow."

"In our phone call, I told him you were out of the country, that you had delegated the matter to me, and that he had no choice but to trust me. Oddly enough, that seemed to calm him down. He said he was staying at a small hotel in Montreux. I offered to take the train to meet him. He said he'd come to me, said he knew a safe place to meet in Lausanne. We made arrangements to meet the same night."

"Where?"

"Where, sir?"

"Yes, Mr. Harper, where?"

Harper squirmed in his seat. "GG's."

"Where?"

"It's a nightclub, sir. Strip club, actually."

"You were conducting IOC business in a strip joint?"

Harper wondered if this might be a good time to hand over his pocketful of receipts. Then again, maybe not.

"Wasn't my call, sir. And I thought any countersuggestion might scare him off. He seemed to know the place rather well, gave me specific directions, in fact. For whatever reason, he didn't make it. I called his hotel in Montreux, but he'd checked out, taken his luggage. I did some digging around, hotels, casualty departments. Yesterday, last night, I checked every strip—nightclub in Lausanne, just in case."

"In case of what?"

"As I said, sir, he sounded increasingly desperate."

The doctor sighed, sat with his own thoughts a moment.

"This lab report about a potion must be a delusion. I mean, look at the scribble. Poor man is exhibiting symptoms of alcohol-induced paranoia. He needs institutional help before it kills him."

"Perhaps."

"You don't seem convinced, Mr. Harper."

"It's his e-mails, sir."

"Mr. Harper, I appreciate your enthusiasm, but are you not reading too much into the e-mailed ravings of a broken man?"

"It isn't what's in them, sir, it's what happened to them."

The doctor closed the lab report and settled back in his chair. "Let's have it, Mr. Harper."

"Yesterday evening I tried contacting him, but every e-mail account came back marked 'No such address.' I called one of the IOC computer people, asked her about it. She said Hotmail accounts are kept active for thirty days after they've been canceled, as protection against Internet fraud. Yuriev used nine accounts in less than two weeks. They're gone."

"I don't understand."

"Neither did the bird in computer support. She said—"

"Mr. Harper, the IOC has very specific rules regarding proper forms of address for female coworkers. 'Bird' is not one of them."

"Yes, sir, sorry. My female coworker, Miss Storries, said there's either been a near-to-impossible worldwide glitch in the Hotmail network, or Yuriev is a gold medalist in computer hacking."

"Are you suggesting Yuriev is involved in perpetrating fraud on the IOC?"

"I'm suggesting Yuriev, or someone he works with, or maybe someone following him, knows how to cover their Internet tracks in a suspicious, if not illegal, manner. Seems reason enough to bring in the police."

"The police?"

"Whatever Yuriev's up to, there's every chance he's a scandal about to be delivered to your doorstep."

For the second time in the afternoon, the doctor blanched. He leaned over his desk, rubbed his temples. Harper watched him. Long overnight flight on one side of the desk, brutal hangover on the other. Not pretty.

"You're right, Mr. Harper, of course. The tabloids would have a field day with 'IOC' and 'scandal' in the same headline, especially with the London games but nineteen months away. They wouldn't care that the wretched man was in need of clinical help, nor about the truth. You haven't told anyone else of this business?"

"My instructions were to report to you alone. Much to the displeasure of my coworker Miss Barraud."

The doctor looked up, smiled, nodded with approval. "I see why Guardian Services recommended you for this job."

Harper wondered if he should mention the parts about being in such a drunken stupor when he got the call and having no idea who Jay Harper was or what qualified him as a freelance security specialist with Guardian Services Ltd. Then again, so far, so good.

"Thank you, sir."

The doctor stood; Harper stood as well.

"You must forgive me, Mr. Harper. I'm having Sunday brunch with the British ambassador. Security arrangements for the London games are nearing Orwellian proportions. Their Home Office is now suggesting strip searches of athletes from all Muslim countries before each competition. Madness reigns. As far as Yuriev, give him forty-eight hours."

"Sir?"

"I'm sure he'll turn up. When he does, tell him I'll meet him. Arrange a meeting, somewhere discreet. Preferably not a strip club. We need to get him off the streets and into a hospital. Keep me advised of any developments."

"Yes, sir. I'll keep looking."

The doctor shot him an unmistakable glare.

"Don't just look, Mr. Harper. Find him, before the goddamn press does."

# six

The funicular train, two cars long, rolled up the dark tunnel and pulled into the underground station at Flon. Rochat made himself ready, and when the doors slid open he jumped quickly onboard and took his favorite seat near the big window. Two old ladies stepped onboard a few seconds later. Rochat stood, pulled off his hat, and bowed.

"*Bonjour, mesdames,* and welcome aboard La Ficelle!"

The ladies took seats at the far end of the car and searched through their handbags so as not to notice him. Rochat saw his reflection in the window. Hair still growing sideways from his head, smudges of dirt on his face, pigeon droppings on his black overcoat. He looked like a tramp who'd slept in a gutter. Rochat was sure his appearance must be a great shock to the little old ladies. There were no tramps in Lausanne. Besides, the gutters were spotless.

"Excuse my appearance, mesdames. I was cleaning the bells."

The old ladies cringed at the unwelcome information. Rochat sat, scratched his head, and found a feather in his hair at the precise moment the ladies were eyeing him to make sure he was keeping to his seat.

"You see, it's my day off, but I was confused, because last night . . ."

His words were lost in the whirring of motors as the funicular rolled back down the tunnel toward Ouchy. Rochat tugged his floppy hat down on his head to hide his messy hair, thinking what a strange night it had been.

He saw himself in beforetimes, in the belfry, looking through the binoculars at a man standing on Pont Bessières and thinking the man must be a detectiveman because . . . because . . . He couldn't remember why.

Then raising the binoculars and seeing a woman appear in the window above Rue Caroline. She was surrounded by the brightest light and brushing her long blond hair. Not seeing her face, just the gentle line of her profile. And remembering he wished she'd turn just a little so he could see her face. But she didn't turn around, and the light went black and she disappeared. And then, hurrying back into the loge and pulling one of his sketchbooks from the shelf, grabbing a pencil and drawing quickly, as if chasing imagination. And stopping, feeling the drawing wasn't right, turning the page, trying again and again, till finally his hand slowed and his fingers smoothed the lead streaks and lines, and the most beautiful face he'd ever seen was looking back at him.

He stared at her, quietly, for the longest time, afraid

to move lest she disappear from the page. And finally hearing his voice in the quiet.

"She looks like an angel."

The funicular jolted to a stop at Gare Simplon. Rochat blinked and found himself in nowtimes. He watched a crowd of people climb onboard with suitcases and backpacks. Two more stops, a few people got off, more people got on. None of the passengers chose to take the empty seat next to Rochat. They huddled in groups and pretended not to see him.

At Ouchy, the end of the line, Rochat remained seated. His crooked leg and twisted foot made it difficult to move through crowds. Passengers going up the hill to Flon were boarding by the time Rochat disembarked. They gave him plenty of room to pass. He shuffled out of the station and into the cold wind ripping off Lac Léman.

"Home again, home again, jiggity-jig."

Rochat crossed Rue du Lac to the corniche where waves crashed into the stone jetty. He felt icy spray on his face. He looked at the fog hovering over the lake like something fluffy. He hurried along a stone path through tall evergreen trees to where the weather-teller lived in a glass dome. It had lots of brass wheels and dials and arrows. Rochat studied the numbers. He shuffled to the kiosk to see Madame Chopra and give her the weather report, as he did every Sunday. She had brown skin and a red dot on her forehead.

"*Bonjour*, Marc. You are very late today. Where have you been?"

"I forgot to come home last night, madame, because I imagined I saw an angel above Rue Caroline."

"An angel, how nice for you. You have such an exciting life, Marc. I always think of you in the cathedral at night and say what an exciting life that Marc Rochat must have. I saved you the London *Sunday Times*; would you like it now?"

"*Oui, merci*. And could I have my bag of popcorn, too?"

"Of course, Marc. What do you think of this fog? Very strange, don't you think?"

"The weather-teller says the fog will go away this afternoon, but it's going to stay cold for a few days, and snow is coming soon."

"Thank you for telling me, Marc, I was wondering. I always count on you to give me the weather report on Sundays. Here are your things. I'll see you next Sunday. I am worrying to not see you at the usual time. I am always telling people, you can set your clock by Marc Rochat."

"*Oui, madame.*"

"And I hope Monsieur Booty enjoys the *Sunday Times*."

"He will, madame, because it lasts all week at the bottom of his kitty litter."

Madame Chopra laughed. "That will make Mr. Murdoch very happy."

Rochat laughed, too, even though he didn't know who Mr. Murdoch was. But Rochat was sure he must be very nice if he was a friend of Madame Chopra. He tucked the newspaper in his overcoat so it wouldn't get wet. He shuffled to the small harbor of bobbing sailboats, sat on a low concrete wall, and dangled his boots over the side. He watched masts sway back and forth in the wind. They made clanging sounds, like tiny bells. He fed popcorn to the ducks and swans sheltering amid the boats.

"Well, Rochat, another very busy week comes to an end."

"*Excusez-moi.*"

Rochat turned to a man standing behind him. The man's face had wrinkles and lines but didn't look old, and he was staring at the top of Rochat's head as he spoke. He spoke with a British accent.

"*Pardon. Où est le terminus pour le . . . le . . .*"

"I speak English, monsieur."

"Actually, I wanted to practice my French. It's rather bad."

"It isn't that bad."

"No, I'm pulling your leg."

Rochat looked at his misshapen foot; so did the man.

"Crap, sorry. Listen, the ferry to Évian, it's down here somewhere, isn't it?"

"*Oui, monsieur.* Through the trees and past the weather-teller."

"Is it working today?"

"*Oui*, and it says the fog is going away by this afternoon, but it's going to stay cold all day and snow is coming."

"No, the ferry, I mean. Is it working today? Looks choppy as hell out on the lake."

"The ferry works all the time, monsieur. Except when there's a bad thunderstorm. Then orange warning lights flash everywhere on the lake. One long, three short."

"Warning lights. One long, three short."

"Everywhere on the lake, but not today. Only in summer."

The wind snapped. The man pulled at the collar of his coat and then shoved his hands in his pockets. "Nippy, isn't it?"

Rochat watched the man, the way he tied the belt around his long brown coat and shoved his hands in the pockets; a coat with straps on the shoulders. It was him, the detectiveman he saw in the night, standing on Pont Bessières.

"I know you, monsieur. I've seen you before."

"Doubt it. I'm new to Lausanne, and it's my first time to this part of town."

Rochat looked at the man's coat again. "*Non*, I'm very sure it was you. You were trying to solve a mysterious mystery, but you were looking the wrong way."

Rochat watched the detectiveman smile.

"I was, was I? Not the first time, I'm sure. So, that way to the ferry?"

"Past the weather-teller, monsieur."

"Past the weather-teller, got it." The detectiveman watched the birds bobbing for popcorn in the water, circling under Rochat's boots, waiting for more. "Those ducks look like they're freezing their feathers off."

"*Non, monsieur,* I watch them every Sunday and they keep their feathers on all year, especially when it's cold.

Would you like to feed them some of my popcorn? It's fun."

"I'm sure it is, but I'd best be going. Thanks for the information. Nice talking to you."

*"Au revoir, monsieur. Bonne journée."*

The detectiveman turned and walked toward the trees. He turned back, pointed to the top of his own head. "Mate, you've got something up here, on your hat. I think it belongs to one of your friends."

Rochat reached up, found a feather and a small glob of pigeon poop.

"Oh dear, Rochat, your hat needs a bath, and so does the rest of you. And your coat, too. *Allez.*"

He rinsed his fingers in the lake and shuffled across the road to the Hôtel de Léman. It was a funny building, half hotel and half flats, and it sat over the funicular station. There was a small clock tower on top. And there was a plaque near the building's entrance that said a man who wrote books once lived there, but he was dead now.

Rochat punched in a secret code and shuffled into a lobby of tall mirrors. He checked his hat for feathers and pigeon poop. He opened his mailbox and found a postcard from his doctors in Vevey reminding him of his appointment on Monday, a small newspaper from Migros with pictures of food and lots of numbers, and an official notice from the Canton de Vaud regarding new rules for sorting rubbish. Rochat studied the notice carefully. There were lots of pictures showing what trash went where. Fines would be enacted to ensure C-O-M-P-L-I-A-N-C-E. Those in violation would have their personal details registered. Rochat wasn't sure about some of the words, but others meant "write names down." Swiss police did that on buses and trains in Lausanne to people who didn't have tickets.

He rang for the elevator, waited for it to come down in its iron cage. It was very old, from nineteens of centuries, Madame Rolle told him when he moved in. When the elevator stopped, he pulled an iron grate to the side and stepped into a gilded compartment with a small crystal chandelier hanging from the ceiling. He pressed the button marked R-O-C-H-A-T.

*"Montez, s'il vous plaît."*

The elevator obeyed and rose four floors and clunked to a stop.

*"Merci beaucoup."*

He slid open the gate and shuffled into a small hall of two doors. One door went into the hotel, the other to his flat. He heard the scratching of a fat cat's feet on polished wood beyond his door.

"Hello, it's only me, you miserable beast. And stop scratching the floors."

He opened the door locks and jumped in his flat. There was a big sign on the back of the door: "LOCK UP!" But sometimes he forgot, and sometimes he found strangers from the hotel who had gotten lost and walked straight into his flat. Sometimes they were standing at the big windows of the sitting room, admiring the view of the dungeon tower of Château d'Ouchy from one window, or the corniche and Lac Léman all the way to the Alps above Montreux from another. Sometimes he even found strangers unpacking their bags or looking in his icebox machine. Rochat was always polite, telling the strangers he was very sorry, but this wasn't their room, it was his house. He thought it important to be polite. The funny building with the hotel and flats was his, given to him by his grandmother and father before they died.

"Monsieur Booty! Where are you, miserable beast?"

And each month on number-fifteen day, Monsieur Gübeli, the man with the bald head and glasses on his nose who'd brought him to Switzerland, came to the flat and sat at the kitchen table for a cup of tea. He'd open his briefcase and there'd be lots of papers to sign. The papers were confusing, but Rochat's father told him to always trust Monsieur Gübeli, so he did. On the day he learned he owned the building atop the funicular station, Rochat asked Monsieur Gübeli if signing so many papers all the time meant he was rich.

"You know the château in Vufflens, Marc. The family fortune is substantial, indeed, but you are not part of that fortune. However, your grandmother put aside this property with all its revenues for you and you alone. If there is anything you want, anything you need, you only have to tell me, or my assistant, Madame Borel. Do you understand?"

*"Oui, monsieur."*

"Is there anything you need, Marc, anything you want?"

Rochat thought about it. He had a big sitting room, two bedrooms, two large bathtubs with catlike feet. He had a dining room overlooking the lake with lots of light and a big round table he used for drawing things he saw from the windows. He had two fireplaces and the plaster walls were covered with his drawings and the handmade marionettes his father brought from Venice: Harlequin, Pinocchio, Baron Münchausen in the drawing-pictures room; a Venetian plague doctor, Peter Pan, and Napoleon in the sitting room. Next to his bed he had the photograph of his mother and father standing on the Plains of Abraham. And Teresa came three times a week to scrub the floors and clean the flat. Teresa was from Portugal and did the ironing and cooked lunches and stored them in the icebox. Rochat did his own laundry because he liked to watch the clothes go around in the washing machine. He had a TV that had sixty-seven channels but was always tuned to Cartoon Network so he could watch Tom and Jerry because they were funny. If he wasn't drawing or watching cartoons or his clothes in the washing machine, he'd take Napoleon from his hook on the wall and chase Monsieur Booty around the flat shouting, "Charge!" Other than that, he spent most of his time at the cathedral.

"*Non*, I can't think of anything."

But just now, standing in the foyer of his flat, Rochat had another thought. If there was nothing he wanted or needed, why did his flat, full of things, feel so empty? A fat gray cat curled around Rochat's boots.

"And how are you this afternoon, Monsieur Booty?"

*Mew.*

"Yes, yes, I am very late and you're hungry. And I had a very busy night. I forgot to get some bread on the way home. Can I have some of your cat food?"

Monsieur Booty dug his claws into Rochat's overcoat and began to climb.

*Mew.*

"Never mind, I'll see what Teresa left me in the icebox machine. *Alors,* I'll feed you, clean my coat and hat and the rest of me. Then I'll go for fresh bread for my lunch."

He was soaking his head when he remembered there would be no fresh bread today. He remembered when the bell in the clock tower above the building rang for three o'clock. It was Sunday. Switzerland was closed.

*Thirty-five minutes shore to shore. Two hundred and twenty-seven thousand tons of bateau powered by twin diesel motors belowdecks. Champagne and fondue Thursday evenings, weather permitting.*

So read the tourist pamphlet Harper received with his ticket. He was trying to read the damn thing and drink at the same time. Wasn't easy. Bit of a rough crossing with two-meter swells. On a bloody lake. Better than the ride over: That was like drifting near the end of the world. Come out of the fog into a patch of nowhere. Gray water, gray sky, thin gray line on the horizon marking the place you fell off and never came back. He set the pamphlet on the next seat, took a swig of Coca-Cola. His diet so far today: three aspirin, packet of potato chips, one Chinese lunch, three Chinese beers, one Coke.

He looked off the stern, his eyes hijacked by the Swiss flag hooked to the rail, flapping in the wind as if waving good-bye to France. He looked about the cabin. A few working stiffs from Évian crossing to Lausanne for some extra odd-job cash on the night shift. Harper thought he fit right in. Another odd-jobber entering Switzerland through the tradesmen's entrance. He pulled the file from his coat, sifted through it.

The gospel of Yuriev's life according to Google.

Poor orphan boy from a village outside Arkhangelsk. Gets a pair of ice skates from a kindly old priest passing through the village. The boy has talent. He doesn't skate over the ice; he flies. Grows up winning every race he enters. Breaks every world record standing on his way to seven gold medals at Innsbruck. Hero of the Soviet Union at nineteen years old. Glasnost comes to Mother Russia, country falls apart. Yuriev goes pro hockey in North America, makes a bloody fortune. Plays with the Maple Leafs in Toronto. Garners the nickname "Slapshot Sasha" for his aggressive style of play. Copies of his number 9 jersey worn by every schoolkid in Canada. His face smiles from boxes of breakfast cereal. Leads his club to three successive Stanley Cups. Scores hat tricks in all three. Rumors. Slapshot Sasha likes to drink. More rumors. Canadian tabloids suggest Slapshot is missing shots in season four to settle gambling debts. Then gambling chits with his signature turn up, courtesy of a mobster on his way to prison, looking for a get-out-of-jail-free card.

The press smells blood, hammers away for more.

Hockey commissioner under pressure, suspends Yuriev for the rest of the season. End of endorsements. Yuriev hits the bottle for real. Begins the long fall from hero to drunken clown. Press can't get enough of the flameout. He's chased by tabloids and TV crews. Yuriev shows up pissed at a championship match, jumps out on the ice, demands to play. Punches out a referee, sends him skidding into the net like a hockey puck. And the crowd goes wild.

End of career.

Starts gambling big, loses bigger.

Word is he owes bags of money to the wrong people. Then comes the car wreck. Lets a hooker drive his SUV. She's whacked on crystal meth; Yuriev's blind drunk. SUV crosses the median at two hundred klicks per hour, smashes head-on into a Volkswagen Golf. The woman and her three kids in the Golf are crushed to death. Eight-year-old boy next to Mommy wearing Yuriev's number 9 jersey.

Spends the last of his fortune on a high-priced lawyer. Lawyer gets him off with six months' probation. Not enough for the Canadian press; they want Yuriev crucified.

Heads back to Russia. Selected as coach to the Russian national Olympic hockey team. Holy row in the press one more time. USA gets in on the act and threatens to pull out of the next winter games, citing "our moral imperative to protect family values." Doctor Schwarzenberg bans Yuriev from any contact with the Olympic movement. He drops out of sight for twenty years, then turns up in Switzerland. A matter of life and death, wants to give something to the doctor, drops from sight again.

*Find him before the goddamn press does.*

Where to start?

Check in with the Port Royal in Montreux. Another clerk, another accent, same message. Yuriev still as gone as he was yesterday, still hasn't called in for messages.

"By the way, would there be a casino anywhere near your hotel?"

"A casino? Are you kidding?"

Casino Barrière. Slots, roulette, blackjack, a slapshot from Yuriev's hotel.

Flashback from Friday.

Harper stopped into LP's Bar at the Palace Hotel for a few drinks before the Yuriev meet. A woman was at the bar with some friends. She walked over, said he looked as if he could use a friend. Turned out she's a Londoner living across the lake in Évian. She had auburn hair and nice legs, wore black kid gloves on her hands. Said she worked in Casino Barrière, came to LP's now and then, but she'd be coming more often, if he did, too. Wrote her number in a matchbook.

Harper dug through the deep pockets of his coat. Fags, lighter, scraps of paper, matchbook from LP's Bar. *Lucy Clarke* and a number with a French dialing code written inside. He punched the number into his mobile.

"Who?"

"Jay Harper. I met you in LP's . . ."

"I remember. Moody sort at the bar. You work at the IOC. I tried to pick you up but you turned me down. You were nice about it, though. Did you find who you were looking for?"

"Sorry?"

"That was your excuse: You were looking for some-one."

"Still at it. Good memory, though."

"I never forget a face. So, Jay Harper, where are you?"

"In Lausanne, staring at the fog, thinking about what to do next."

"Clearing up this side of the lake. Look, I was just on my way to a late lunch. It's Sunday, so it must be Chinese."

"Sorry, don't mean to keep you from your mates. Could I ring you later? Something I'd like to ask you."

"As a matter of fact, I was going alone. Why don't you hop on the ferry and come over? When you get to Évian, ask anyone to point you to Jardin des Thés."

Kid gloves on her hands again, light blue this time. They ordered Tsingtao beers, talked about the weather over sweet and sour soup. Progressed to her current situation over steamed dumplings.

"I made pit boss three months ago. Two more years, then I'm off to Monte Carlo, if I'm lucky."

"Such a thing as luck in a casino?"

"Sure, just ask Santa Claus. He's one of our best customers."

"You like living on the French side of the lake?"

"Liking France and affording Switzerland are two different things. But, yeah, I like it over here. Switzerland's a bit too planet fucking perfect for my taste."

After the dumplings, Harper took out a photo and laid it on the table with the moo goo gai pan.

"Ever seen this chap?"

"Who's he?"

"The man I'm looking for. Was wondering if he'd surfaced in the casino."

"You mean you didn't come over to sweep me off my feet?"

"Afraid not."

"Well, in that case, croupiers are like Swiss bankers: We don't discuss clients. And since when did the IOC become a detective agency?"

"Just asking a simple question."

"No such thing. And there's more than one casino on the lake, Jay. There're bags. There's one a few steps from that steamed dumpling on your plate. You planning to finish it?"

"Help yourself. He was staying in a hotel near the casino. He has a gambling problem."

"Anyone walking through the door of a casino has a gambling problem, it's just a matter of degree. So who is he? Is he a problem? Another crooked Olympic delegate on the take, scamming property options at the next venue?"

"No, nothing like that."

"Well, I haven't seen him. But I'm not in the casino twenty-four/seven."

"Right. End of discussion."

"That's it? Not even an attempt at any chitchat that doesn't include the weather?"

"Chitchat?"

"Come on, Jay, give it a go."

"All right. How's a girl from east London end up dealing cards in Montreux?"

"You really want to know?"

"Sure."

"Three years on a Sainsbury's checkout in fucking Copers Cope, Bromley. You're not big in the chitchat aisle, are you, Jay?"

"No, I suppose not."

"Look, since you came all this way I'll tell you this: If your Russian friend in that photo was counting cards, marking cards, or cheating the dice in any casino anywhere on the planet, his face would be known in every casino in the world. Casinos live in the land of Big Brother. Cameras in the ceilings, cameras in the walls, cameras you'd never find if your life depended on it. All connected to computers scanning faces from a worldwide network of known problems. There are microphones at the tables listening to conversations, scanners listening to phone calls, eagle-eyed spotters on the floor. And there are very scary men in a back room keeping tabs on everyone who comes and goes, with particular interest in what they do in between. Believe me, problems are dealt with quickly. And those very scary men are always on the lookout for new problems. So I'll ask you again, is he a problem?"

"How did you know he was Russian?"

"See, you are a detective." She leaned forward, tapped Yuriev's photo with a kid-gloved finger. "First lesson in dealing cards is reading faces. No way this guy could be anything but Russian, not with that mug."

"You get many Russians in the casino?"

"Loads. Montreux's a bloody Moscow suburb. That's why they both begin with the letter M."

Harper rolled up the photo, stuffed it in his coat. "He was an Olympic champion ages ago. One of the greats. His life became something of a nightmare. Booze, drugs, gambling. We heard he was in town, that he might've fallen off the wagon. IOC likes to help its own."

Lucy rolled her eyes. "You're utter crap at telling porkies, Jay. Stick to chitchat. Where'd you go to detective school, anyway?"

"I didn't."

"You should."

"When I get back to Lausanne, I'll look one up."

"Or you could sail over again sometime. I give private lessons in reading faces, especially to cute guys with nice green eyes."

He checked his watch; almost six. "I should head back. Need to send a report to the boss."

"Too bad."

The ferry's horn whistled twice as the twin diesel motors belowdecks reversed and the 227,000 tons of *bateau* shuddered and slowed. Another winter's night spreading its shadow over Port d'Ouchy like a woven thing. The lights of Lausanne flickering above the port, marking the seven hills of planet fucking perfect. All topped with one drab excuse for a cathedral, even in the bright light of floodlights. Harper picked up the tourist pamphlet. Picture of Lausanne Cathedral on the cover. *Set in the quaint charm of the old city* blah blah blah. *Overlooking Europe's largest and most beautiful lake* blah blah blah. *Open to tourists in the daylight hours with special tours of the belfry in the afternoons. Wonderful views from one hundred meters above the ground.*

Harper felt a blast of vertigo.

He tossed the pamphlet in the bin.

R ochat finished his dinner of roast chicken and sat at the kitchen table with a purring Monsieur Booty on his lap. He thought about things. Besides himself, Monsieur Booty, Monsieur Gübeli, and Teresa, no one had ever come to his home. Except the occasional hotel guests who lost their way, but Rochat was very sure they didn't count. He scratched Monsieur Booty behind the ears.

"Monsieur Buhlmann came to visit the tower last night and we made raclette. He says I need a girl in my life. Someone to take care of me. Someone for me to take care of, too."

Monsieur Booty fluttered his ears and shook his head and sneezed.

"Bless you. So what do you think, you miserable beast? Would a girl want to come here for dinner with us sometime?"

Monsieur Booty looked up to Rochat with a questioning tilt of the head.

"You see, the doctors say I've grown as tall as I can. Which isn't that tall, but they say they can begin operating on my leg and foot now and make them straighter. I might be very handsome."

*Mew.*

"You only want *le sot-l'y-laisse*, don't you?"

*Mew.*

"I thought so."

He scooped out the two bits of meat from the chicken's back, dropped them on the floor. Monsieur Booty quickly abandoned Rochat's lap to gobble the juicy morsels.

"I wonder if the operation would make my brain more handsome. But I suppose my feet are a long way from my brain. What do you think?"

Monsieur Booty licked his paws. Rochat picked through the bones for more scraps to toss to the floor.

"Here I am, bribing a fat cat to listen to me. It's worse than talking to Marie-Madeleine."

Monsieur Booty proceeded to lick his bottom.

"And this is what happens when you talk to cats instead of bells."

*Mew.*

He gave the beast a gentle shove with his twisted foot. Monsieur Booty shot out of the room and down the hall. Rochat cleared the table, placing the plates in the dishwashing machine the way Teresa had shown him. He shuffled down the hall to the drawing table. He played with his pencils, but couldn't think of anything to draw.

Then he remembered something.

He shuffled back to the hall, saw his freshly scrubbed overcoat and hat hanging on a hook next to the door. He searched through the inside pocket of the coat for a folded paper, a paper torn from his sketchbook. He took a thumbtack from a box and went back to the kitchen. He carefully unfolded the paper, pressing it flat. He pinned the paper to the top of a chair, sat in the chair opposite, and stared at the face of the angel he imagined in the night.

# seven

Katherine's cell phone rang as she window-shopped along Rue du Grand-Saint-Jean. Number one on speed dial calling.

"Hello, Simone, I was just thinking about you."

"Really, what are you doing?"

"Usual Monday-morning routine: window-shopping on my way to the spa at the Palace. And I just happen to be looking at some very expensive Christmas gifts. Can't decide if you'd like yours in blue or green."

"What is it?"

"And spoil the surprise? I don't think so."

"Anything the color of money is fine with me, dear."

"Simone, Swiss francs come in blue, green, and red."

"In that case, I'll take one of each."

"Done."

"Have a moment to discuss business?"

"Sure, go ahead."

Katherine ducked into a café. She ordered an espresso while Simone talked.

"I've booked you for a bit of fun in the sun. At the Taj in Mauritius with our Chinese friend. You'll be collected by private jet from Dubai on January twenty-eighth, and he'd like to have you for two weeks. Does that work for you?"

"Lemme check." Katherine grabbed her BlackBerry from her bag, crunched the dates of her menstrual cycle. "Yeah, perfect."

"I was thinking, why not leave a few days early? I'll book you at the Burj Al Arab, my treat. Give you a chance to shop for some nice beach things, work on your tan line."

"All sounds good." Katherine reworked the dates, snapped shut the BlackBerry, lit a cigarette. "And you definitely get three of whatever it is I was going to buy."

"Aren't you sweet? Listen, dear, something else's come up. This morning I received a call from a Russian gentleman. Dying to meet you. Staying at the Grand in Gstaad and coming down to Lausanne tomorrow on business."

"How convenient."

"Isn't it just? His name is Komarovsky. And he'd like to have you for one night."

"Who?"

*"Koma-rov-sky."*

Katherine typed in the name. "Got it. Komarovsky, Tuesday, one night. Usual consultation fee?"

"There's been an adjustment on the fee, dear."

"What kind of adjustment?"

"Your fee for one night will be two hundred thousand euros."

"Okay, what's the joke, Simone?"

"Darling girl, I never joke about money, especially in larger quantities. I asked for advance payment in euros, and it arrived not an hour later, wrapped in a very nice Prada bag."

"Two hundred grand, in cash?"

"I've already had the money deposited into your account, less my usual fifteen percent."

"So that's one-seventy thousand euros, at the current rate . . ."

"Two hundred thirty thousand Swiss, give or take a franc or two. Like I said, dying to meet you."

"I guess, but who is he?"

"He's well known to members of the Two Hundred Club, but I've never met him. Descended from the Romanovs or something. Absolutely filthy with money. His bills are paid in cash and his entourage spoils the staff with pricey gifts. You know the type, dear."

"I love the type. Room number for Mr. Wonderfully Rich in Gstaad?"

"The Royal Suite of course."

"Even more wonderful. You're sure he's not a freak?"

"Dear, anyone who resides in the Royal Suite of the Grand and tosses money about like chocolates may be as freakish as they wish. I'm sure it's nothing you can't handle. Oh, by the way, you remember that Italian footballer who got rough with you last month? Well, it's in all the gossip rags: His actress wife has left him. Apparently she didn't believe his story regarding his swollen testicles. What did you do to him?"

"Taser gun. Never leave home without it."

"That's my girl. Do let me know how it goes. I want to hear every little detail about Monsieur Komarovsky. I'll SMS his contact. Ciao, dear."

Katherine finished her cigarette as if it were something to be savored. A number popped up in the window of her cell phone. "Well, whoop-dee-fucking-do." She punched in the number. It picked up on the third ring.

"Yes?"

"Good afternoon. Is that Monsieur Komarovsky?"

"Who are you?" One of those affected voices. Male tone, female persuasion.

"I'm referred by the Two Hundred Club."

"Ah, the Two Hundred Club, don't you know?"

"Yes, I'm Katherine Taylor, from Lausanne."

"Katherine Taylor, from Lausanne. How nice. Monsieur Komarovsky is anxious to speak with you. Would you mind holding a moment?"

"Of course, of course."

Katherine took the moment to check her reflection in the window. She pulled at her bangs, thinking no more than a trim. A paregoric voice came on the line.

"Good day, Miss Taylor. How good of you to telephone."

"Good day, Monsieur Komarovsky. I hope I'm not disturbing you."

"Not at all. I was awaiting your call."

"I understand you're coming to Lausanne tomorrow."

"Yes, and it is my fervent wish to see you, Miss Taylor."

"Then it is my pleasure to tell you your wish has been granted, monsieur."

"I am so very pleased. I regret I will not be free until evening. Business matters, you understand."

"I'm glad to hear it, monsieur."

"Pardon?"

"The harder the man works, monsieur, the more deserving he is of pleasure."

"An excellent philosophy, Miss Taylor. One to which I shall aspire."

"Would you care to meet for an aperitif, say, eight, LP's Bar at the Palace? I'll reserve a table by the fireplace."

"Excellent. Then perhaps the night will carry us where it may."

She could see him in her mind: over the hill, dissipated, but rich enough to make a convent girl swallow. "Your wish is my command, monsieur."

"That makes two wishes you have granted me already. How kind."

"Monsieur, I was wondering—"

"I am a connoisseur of beauty, Miss Taylor."

"What?"

"You are wondering how I came to know of your presence in Lausanne?"

"Yeah . . . yes, I was."

"As you may have surmised, I am someone acquainted with the wealthy and powerful of the world. Many of whom are members of the Two Hundred Club, in fact. You were presented to me as a creature of exquisite beauty, Miss Taylor. Something precious to be admired by those with the means to offer you their immeasurable appreciation."

"I see."

"I contacted Madame Badeaux and she was kind enough to send me your dossier. May I say, the descriptions are true, you are a woman of exquisite beauty."

"And for one night, I will be all yours."

"Until then, Miss Taylor."

"Until then, monsieur."

Rochat felt a jab of pain running down his crooked leg to his twisted foot as he shuffled through the train station in Vevey. It was like that on days he went to see the doctors. They always poked needles in his skin and measured his leg with clamps. They twisted his crooked foot till it hurt and wrote prescriptions for vitamins and said things like "Your leg and foot are looking much better, Marc."

He shuffled up the ramp to platform number 4 just in time to catch the slow train to Lausanne. He sat by the window and looked for perch swimming in the rocky shallows of Lac Léman. He counted forty-seven fish before the train climbed from the shore and rolled through the terraced vineyards of bare, gnarled vines. Thin columns of smoke said that *les vignerons* were pruning vines and burning cuttings. He counted ten columns of smoke rising from the hills. Then came the pretty steeple of the old church in Lutry and the houses at the outskirts of

Lausanne. Then the train slowed and made *foosh* sounds as it pulled into Gare Simplon. It stopped at platform number 7 just as the big hands of all station clocks jumped to twelve and the little hands pointed to four.

"Very good, right on time. My compliments to the engineer."

Rochat closed the buttons of his long black overcoat and shuffled off the train. He stopped at the bottom of the steps. A man from beforetimes was waiting on the platform. He was tall and wearing the same black overcoat and had a red scarf around his neck.

"Hello, Papa."

"From the neck up you look like me."

"I know."

"How do you know?"

Rochat opened the coloring book he had carried across the forty-sixth parallel of planet Earth and removed the photo of his mother and father on the Plains of Abraham above the St. Lawrence River. "Maman gave me this."

"Ah, yes. Scene of the crime. You really do have her eyes, don't you?"

"*Oui.*"

"That's good, that's very good."

His father took him by the hand and led him through the station to a black car waiting outside. A man named Anton drove them out of Lausanne and over some hills to a single-lane road along a high stone wall. There was a stone gate and a long drive over crunching gravel to a big stone house with lots of towers and windows.

"What's this place, Papa?"

"Vufflens. It's not much, but we call it home."

"Is it a castle?"

"Yes, Marc, it's a castle."

"Are there dragons?"

"Every castle has a dragon, Marc. And we've got a beauty."

A short man wearing striped trousers and a dark coat with funny tails waited for them at the door. He bowed as they entered. Rochat imagined the man looked like a penguin. The man in the penguin coat coughed quietly.

"You are expected in the day parlor, sir."

"Thank you, Bernard. Marc, say hello to Bernard. He's the butler."

*"Bonjour, Bernard."*

*"Bonjour, Master Rochat."*

"What's a butler, Papa?"

"Good question. Bernard, what's a butler?"

"I endeavor each day to answer the question myself, sir."

"I don't understand what that means, Papa."

"Don't worry, you'll get used to it."

Rochat followed his father through a long corridor. Two doors opened to an oak-paneled room with a fireplace big enough to walk into, if there hadn't been a big fire in it already. An old woman in a black dress sat in a rocking chair near the fire. She sat with a book on her lap and read with the help of the magnifying glass she held in her wrinkled hand. Her hair was white and tied in a bun. Rochat's father stopped at the door, rubbed Rochat's head.

"Marc, I want you to go in there and slay that old dragon. Be brave, she's got false teeth."

Rochat felt himself pushed ahead, heard the doors close behind him. He held his breath. The old woman looked up from her book.

"Ha, it is our bastard child from Quebec! How amusing for the family. How amusing for my son's wife and children. Come here, boy!"

Rochat slowly shuffled over dark red carpets of squiggles and squares. He stood before the old woman.

"Listen to me, boy. Your mother is dead and you are in our care. You will be placed in a special school at Mon Repos, where you will live with children like yourself. I warn you, it is very expensive. And I do not like wasting my money, not even one franc. I expect to hear only good reports of your behavior. Are you listening to me, boy?"

*"Oui, Grand-maman."*

*"Grand-maman?* Did I give you permission to address me in such an intimate manner?"

*"Non."*

"Indeed not. For the present, you will address me as Madame Rochat."

*"Oui, Madame Rochat."*

"Now, if you are very good and work very hard in school, you will visit me two weekends per month. Alternate weekends you will spend with your father at his house in Cossonay when he is not being visited by his ghastly wife. A Bavarian countess, no less. God knows what he was thinking marrying her. Thankfully she spends most of her time in Monte Carlo with the children. Spiteful brats, destined for a life of debauchery. Stop fidgeting, boy, pay attention."

Rochat stood very still.

"In time, you shall be given suitable employment and become a responsible member of the canton. Our name is respected in this canton, you are privileged to carry it. You understand me, boy?"

*"Oui, Madame Rochat."*

"I am informed you are a simpleton. This is true?"

"I don't read very well, and I'm not good with numbers."

"And your French is abysmal."

*"Oui, Madame Rochat."*

"Come closer, boy. I wish to examine your face."

Rochat edged close enough to see the brown spots on the old woman's face. She lifted the magnifying glass and held it to her face. Her filmy blue eye looked like a wiggly bug.

"Yes, you have the forehead and nose, the chin is strong, and your hair is the black mop of your father when he was a boy. How old are you?"

*"J'ai dix ans, Madame Rochat."*

"Ten years! Then stand up straight!"

"This is as straight as I am, Madame Rochat."

"Then you are something of a dwarf."

*"Oui, madame."*

"Now, you may be a simpleton and something of a dwarf, but that will be no excuse for tardiness. You will be punctual in all things. If you understand, then nod. I cannot bear to hear you speak French."

Rochat nodded.

"Good. I shall now tell you something of grave importance. Noble blood does not lie. Do you understand what I am telling you?"

Rochat moved his head from side to side.

"Of course you don't. I shall present you with a test. Nod if you are ready. I said nod. Good. Did your father tell you I was an old dragon?"

Rochat froze.

"Come, boy! Spit it out, yes or no?"

"Yes, Madame Rochat."

"And did he tell you I have false teeth?"

"Yes, Madame Rochat."

"He did, did he?"

"*Oui, madame* . . . I mean, yes."

The old woman leaned close to Rochat's face. "Would you like me to take them out and show them to you?"

Rochat blinked . . .

. . . found himself back at Gare Simplon.

The sun had fallen behind the hills and the slow train from Vevey was gone. The TGV from Paris was at the platform now, and people were rushing by him and bumping him with suitcases. Rochat searched for his father, his grandmother, Bernard the butler. He scratched his head, looked at the clock above the platform. The big hand was now on the ten, the little hand on five. He looked at the clocks above all the platforms; they were all the same.

"Perhaps you're back in nowtimes, Rochat."

He continued to stand, watching people pass, seeing

their long shadows on the concrete. He followed the shadows down the ramp to the tunnels running under the platforms and was surrounded by even more people rushing by and bumping into him. Rochat kept his eyes on the ground, watching their shadows whip by his boots.

Music.

Rochat saw a black man playing a saxophone just outside the tobacco shop. The man's knit cap was upside down on the floor next to his tapping toe, instead of on his head where it should be. Rochat watched the shadow of the man's tapping toe, then raised his eyes and watched the black man fill his bristled cheeks with air and blow into the saxophone to make sounds. The sounds felt sad. Rochat watched the way the people all rushed by, the way they didn't notice the saxophoneman, the way he didn't seem to care. The music stopped.

"Hey, little dude."

Rochat looked at the saxophoneman.

*"Oui?"*

"You're supposed to put money in the hat."

"Papa always did when he saw people like you playing music in the train station."

"Then what you waiting for?"

"Why doesn't anyone else put money in the hat?"

"Because they don't see me."

"Why not?"

"They only see what they want to see."

"Why do I want to see you?"

"Because you're like me, you're cool."

Rochat looked down at his long black overcoat. "*Non*, I'm warm. This was my father's coat. It's wool."

"No, little dude, I'm telling you, you see things . . . they don't."

"Who?"

"Them, man, the locals."

Rochat looked both ways in the tunnel. People whipping by in a blur.

"Oh."

"You don't get it, do you?"

"Get what?"

"You and me, we're different from all of them."

"How?"

"I told you, we *see* things, they don't. That's why the ones like us have to take care of each other. Like dropping some coins in the hat."

Rochat opened his coin purse, pulled out three five-franc coins, dropped the coins in the upside-down cap.

"Is that enough?"

"Sure."

"Would you tell me something, monsieur?"

"For fifteen francs, I'll write you a book."

"What day is it?"

"Monday."

"And the time?"

The saxophoneman looked at the clock above the rushing-by heads.

"Five thirty."

"So I'm in nowtimes again."

"Been doing some back and forth, have you?"

"*Oui*. It's happening more and more."

"Be not afraid, little dude."

"*Non?*"

"No, because wherever you go, there you are."

Rochat thought about it. "*Merci. Au revoir, monsieur.*"

"Want me to play something for the road?"

"Which road?"

"How about the one you're walking on?"

"What was it you were playing just now?"

"'Les Anges dans Nos Campagnes.'"

"I know that song. It's a very old Christmas carol, about angels singing in the fields. But you made it sound different."

"Slowed it down, made it bluesy for nowtimes."

"Does that mean sad?"

"Ain't nothing sadder than an angel in nowtimes."

"Have you ever seen an angel, monsieur?"

"All the time, little dude, all the time."

The saxophoneman put the reed to his lips, blew the saddest sounds. Rochat watched him a moment, then he shuffled away and up the ramp to the main hall, checking all the clocks and wristwatches along the way to make sure the saxophoneman wasn't another imagination and it really was five thirty. And he studied the dates of the newspapers at the press kiosk near the big swinging doors of the waiting room to make sure it truly was Monday, December thirteens.

"Dear me, Rochat. Sometimes your imaginations are so very confusing, and all this going back and forth to beforetimes. You must concentrate; Maman told you you must concentrate. And now you're *le guet de la Cathédrale de Lausanne*, you have your duties."

He shuffled through the swinging doors and waited amid a crowd of Lausannois at Avenue de la Gare for the cartoonman in the crosswalk light to jump from red to green and say it was time to cross the road. He looked at the faces of the Lausannois, but they didn't look at him. He wondered if it was because they couldn't see him, just as they couldn't see the saxophoneman. The cartoonman in the light jumped to green. Rochat looked down at the pavement and followed all the shadows across the road, at the same time trying to figure how much time he had to take the funicular down the hill to Ouchy and do things in his flat before he'd go back up the hill to his dinner at Café du Grütli, the way he always did when he returned from the doctors in Vevey.

"Must be punctual in all things, Rochat."

Across the road he hurried down the ramp to the funicular station. The two-car train was just leaving for Ouchy, but would be back in seven minutes on its way to Flon, and Rochat would watch it go by, then it'd come back seven minutes later to take him home.

"Very good, Rochat. Right in middles of things, just where you should be."

He looked around the platform; he was alone. He watched pigeons fly through the open doors of the station, glide to the rafters above the tracks, waddle to their hiding places in the eaves. He heard scratching noises on the concrete floor. He looked down to his boots. It wasn't him.

He looked down the tracks, saw the headlights of the funicular coming up the dark tunnel. The rails glowed and the toothlike track in the middle of the rails made shadows on the railbed. Then tiny sparks flashed from the end of the platform and a long shadow stretched out over the floor from behind a concrete pillar. The headlights of the oncoming funicular blinded his eyes, till the silhouette of a woman stepped from behind a pillar. A woman in a long furry coat, a halo of light shining around her blond hair.

The train pushed puffs of air up the tunnel, passing by the woman to Rochat. The air smelled like flowers. The woman had a cigarette on her lips; she shook a lighter in her hands, clicked it on and off. Sparks flashed but the fire wouldn't light. He almost saw her face.

Rochat felt his heart skip a beat.

The woman turned, walked toward him. Rochat dropped his eyes, locked them on the concrete floor. He heard the woman's steps coming closer, the flower smell becoming stronger. He saw black high heels and two legs in blue jeans sticking out from under a furry coat.

*"Pardonnez-moi, monsieur. Avez-vous du feu?"*

Rochat didn't budge. He looked out of the corners of his eyes, saw the ends of her long blond hair.

"Say, you're a live one, aren't you? Never mind, train's coming anyway."

The funicular pulled into the station and the doors slid open. Rochat, his eyes still glued to the floor, watched the woman's feet turn away and step aboard the forward car. He looked up, saw her sitting with her back to the doors. All the passengers on the train looked at him, the way he was rocking back and forth, mumbling to himself, "Always going home to do things after coming from Vevey, Rochat, that's what you do."

The funicular chimed to say it was leaving for Flon.

As the doors began to close, Rochat jumped aboard the rear car. The doors caught his twisted foot; he pulled and tugged but couldn't get free. The passengers watched him pound at the doors with his fist.

"Open up, let me go!"

The doors buzzed angrily, reopened, and Rochat tumbled onto the floor. The doors slammed shut again, and the funicular pulled ahead. Rochat rose to his feet, brushed off his overcoat.

*"Je suis désolé, mesdames et messieurs."*

He shuffled to a corner of the train, peeking around the bodies and through the windows to the forward car. If only that big fat man would move, he could see her.

"Just a little, just a little, please."

They came to a stop at Flon. Rochat's eyes searched through the blur of bodies leaving the forward car . . . There! The hair, the long blond hair.

# eight

Two elevators carried people from Flon Station to Rue du Grand-Chêne. Rochat saw the woman with blond hair step into one elevator as the doors closed behind her. He hurried into the second elevator. People tried to push him to the back, but he stood his ground so he could be first out. The counting clock above the doors ticked slowly down: *20, 19, 18, 17*... Rochat tapped furiously at the button with the backward arrows to close the doors.

"It's faster counting my way up Escaliers du Marché than waiting for you to close the doors, and I have a crooked foot!"

He felt people step away from him. He remembered Lausannois weren't comfortable with people who talked loudly in elevators. He stared at the counting clock.

... *4, 3, 2, 1, bzzzzzzzz. Clunk.*

"*Merci beaucoup,*" he whispered.

The elevator rose slowly to the street. The doors slid open and Rochat rushed out. His eyes searched the pedestrian bridge above Place de l'Europe. If she went that way

she'd be going to Bel-Air and the Palud quarter. But he
didn't see anyone with long blond hair and a furry coat.
He hurried to the ramp leading to Rue du Grand-Chêne.
There, she was just rounding the corner. He shuffled after
her, stopped at the top of the ramp, and peeked around the
corner. He watched her cross Rue du Grand-Chêne and
disappear into a haze of light. Rochat rubbed his eyes and
looked again. The façade of the Lausanne Palace, wrapped
in a big red bow and awash in the glow of red floodlights.
All the pillars and balconies strung with fairy lights.

"No, it's a real thing, Rochat. The Lausanne Palace in
a big red bow means coming to Christmastimes. So
maybe you're not imagining the angel, maybe she's a real
angel like Christmastimes in Lausanne. Have to see her
face, Rochat, have to see her face to know."

He shuffled across the road, slowing his steps near the
bus shelter and looking down the pavement toward the
hotel. There were lots of trees with little white lights like
the lights on the pillars and balconies, but no woman
with blond hair and a furry coat. Tall windows at the
corner of the hotel opened to a dimly lit room. A narrow
dark alley ran down the side of the windows. He shuffled
into the shadows where he could see inside.

The room was lit with lots of candles like the loge in
the belfry. There was a square bar in the center of the
room with lots of glasses hanging upside down and a
fireplace nearby with an old clock on the mantelpiece.
Big windows at the end of the room looked out to the
lights of Évian across the lake. He saw the woman with
the blond hair sitting on a stool at the bar with her back

to the window. She let her furry coat slip from her shoulders. She wore a black sweater underneath.

"If only she'd turn around, then you'd see if she really is the angel you imagined, Rochat."

He watched her take a gold cigarette case from her coat pocket and wave a cigarette while flicking her broken lighter. A young man behind the bar gave her a book of matches. She lit her cigarette; a small cloud of smoke floated above her. The young man behind the bar took a tall glass, poured champagne into it, and set it before her. She took a newspaper from her bag, turned slowly through the pages. Then Rochat saw someone else at the far end of the bar. He wore a sports coat and a loosened tie around his neck. He looked familiar, Rochat thought. The face had lines and wrinkles, but he didn't look old. Rochat remembered him in a long brown coat with a belt and straps on the shoulders . . . the detectiveman from the bridge . . . and he was looking at the woman with the long blond hair.

*P*ourquoi vous me regardez, monsieur?"

Harper didn't answer.

"Hey, buster."

"Sorry?"

"You're staring at me."

"Actually, I was looking at your newspaper."

"That's the best you can do?" She opened her cigarette case and pulled out another smoke. She dug through her bag for the matches. "Second lunatic I've met in one day."

"You have one going."

"What?"

"In the ashtray, you already have one going."

"So who are you, the smoking police? Come to stamp out the last smokers' playground in Europe?"

"Fellow smoker in residence, actually."

"You say 'actually' a lot. You must be a Brit."

"Yes, actually."

"Bingo."

"I know this may sound odd, but could I buy you a drink for your newspaper?"

"I already have a drink, but don't let that stop you. You want a drink? Here, I'll help. Stephan, would you give the gentleman a drink?"

"*Avec plaisir,* Mademoiselle Taylor. Another beer, monsieur?"

"Cheers."

The bartender filled a fresh glass, set it on the bar. Katherine drew on her cigarette, blew the smoke in Harper's face.

"See? Easy as can be. Anything else you want?"

"Sorry?"

"Another favorite word from the Brit vocabulary. Have I seen you in here before?"

"No, but I've seen you. La Brasserie, a few nights ago. You were with a rather well-heeled chap."

She fiddled with her cigarette case. "My stockbroker."

"He looked the type."

She gave him the once-over. "And what about you? What type are you, besides the stalker type?"

"I work for the IOC."

"The Olympic Committee, no way."

"Why?"

"You really don't look the IOC type. You look cop. What's your name?"

He took a packet of smokes from his jacket and lit up. "Name's Harper, Miss Taylor. Jay Harper."

"Hold it, how did you know my name?"

"The bartender just said it when you so graciously ordered me a drink."

"Clever. You sure you're not a cop?"

"I'm not a cop."

She took a sip of her champagne. "In that case, what can I do for you, Mr. Harper?"

"I'd like to look at your newspaper."

"Still going with that line, are we?"

"Sorry?"

"Come on, you dress cheap but you look smart. And I admit, the newspaper line's cute, but let me ask you something: Is it that I look desperately lonely to you? Or were you just hoping I might be in your price range?"

The bartender leaned over the bar. "*Pardonnez-moi, Mademoiselle Taylor.* The chef recommends the fish soup. Should I bring it to the bar?"

"Fine, Stephan, with a glass of the Clavien Chardonnay."

"Of course, mademoiselle."

"Oh, and tomorrow, could you reserve the table by the fireplace for me? I'm meeting someone for aperitifs at eight. And could you make sure the flames are cooking?"

"Of course, mademoiselle." The bartender nodded to

Harper. "May I ask if the gentleman will be joining you for dinner tonight?"

Katherine looked at Harper and smiled. "No, I think this gentleman will be taking care of himself tonight. Isn't that right, Mr. Harper?"

Harper stamped out his smoke, smiled at the bartender. "Seems so."

The bartender bowed. "In that case, monsieur, I hope you will join us again." He turned away, took an order for drinks from one of the waiters.

"Nice place," Harper said. "Staff has better manners than the clients."

Katherine set her elbow on the newspaper, rested her head in her hand. Tossed him a little-girl pout for added effect.

"What's the matter, ego take a battering?"

"Just saying the man is a polite bartender."

"Oh, I get it. Stiff upper lip and all. Tell you what: I'll give you what you want if you can even tell me what it's worth."

"What are we talking about, exactly?"

"You're a big boy, take a wild guess."

Harper reached for the newspaper, pulled it slowly from under her arm, dropped fifty francs on the bar.

"That should cover it, don't you think?"

"Hey, excuse me?"

"Actually, I don't believe I will. Good night, Miss Taylor."

*     *     *

Rochat watched the detectiveman take the newspaper and his glass of beer and walk from the bar to a small table in the corner. The woman sat alone, running her fingers through her hair, as if combing it. She took a hair clip, pulled her long hair to the back of her neck. Rochat could just see her profile, but not enough to tell if she was the angel he'd imagined in the night.

"Turn just a little so I can—"

Bells chimed three times from the Hôtel de Ville. Rochat looked at the clock above the fireplace. Big hand on the nine, little hand almost touching eight.

"Oh, no, Rochat! You're late!"

He hurried from the shadows, raced across Rue du Grand-Chêne and on to the pedestrian bridge, pulling at the ramp and flying over Place de l'Europe.

"Everyone at Café du Grütli will be saying, 'Where is Marc Rochat? It's past seven thirty!'"

He shuffled quickly across Rue du Grand-Pont, up Rue Pichard, following the up and down cobblestones of Saint-Laurent to Place de la Palud.

"You're *le guet de la Cathédrale de Lausanne*, you must be punctual in all things."

He shuffled over the cobblestones of the square till he was staring at the numbers 1726 carved in the low stone wall of Lausanne fountain. Streams of water gushed from dragons' mouths and splashed in a dark pool. A stone lady stood on a pillar, high above the dragons. She held a sword in one hand, scales in the other, and her eyes were closed, as if she were thinking very hard about something.

"That's what you should do, Rochat, you should close

your eyes and concentrate on your duties. You shouldn't
let your imaginations run away with your brains. You're
being very silly."

The bells of the Hôtel de Ville chimed four times for
the coming hour. Rochat looked up the wooden steps of
Escaliers du Marché to the top of the hill where, above
the bare chestnut trees and red-tiled rooftops of the old
city, the belfry of Lausanne Cathedral stood in the glare
of floodlights.

"Go ahead, say it. I know what you think."

*GONG! GONG! GONG!*

Rochat listened to Marie-Madeleine's voice scold him
for his behavior. *Running through the streets like a madman! Barely enough time for your dinner! People will talk!*

"Yes, yes, I know. I'll hurry with my supper and come
to the tower. Yes, yes, I know."

Harper read it again.

## FIRE ON MOUNTAIN
## IN DEADLY ROAD ACCIDENT
### Claims Life of Russian Tourist

Special to *24 Heures*.

6 December 2010. The Swiss winter season claimed
its first victim when a driver lost control of his vehicle and drove through a wall of plowed snow.
The accident occurred 30 kilometers north of

Montreux on the mountain road to Gstaad. After crashing through a snowbank, the vehicle then tumbled down a deep ravine and burst into flames.

Frédéric Zeller, a 36-year-old computer programmer from Blonay, was quick to photograph the accident with his cell phone and transmit the scene to Swiss authorities. Police received the image of the burning car and reacted quickly with fire crews and emergency helicopters. By the time the rescue crews arrived at the scene, a meter of snow had fallen, making their work difficult and dangerous.

Lt. Pierre Berclaz of the Swiss police said one body was found in the wreckage. The body was burned beyond recognition. Lt. Berclaz said it would be some time before proper identification could be made. Lt. Berclaz would not confirm the identity of the victim, saying only that the victim appears to be a Russian tourist traveling alone in Switzerland.

"This is an unhappy but all-too-frequent occurrence. Many foreign visitors drive at speed, unaware that winter roads, even if appearing clear, are often covered with a thin layer of ice this time of year. The result can be catastrophic."

Lt. Berclaz added Swiss authorities take every precaution in maintaining mountain roads.

"We are second to none in the world with regard to winter road clearance. But the sad fact is, no amount of care can replace common sense in driving."

He would not comment on one rescuer's statement to *24 Heures* that several empty bottles of alcohol and gambling chips from Casino Barrière in Montreux were found in the wreckage. But Lt. Berclaz did say tests would be carried out to check the blood alcohol levels of the victim. Neither would he comment on whether the car had been rented to a Russian tourist.

Lt. Berclaz took the opportunity to remind citizens of the country's strict drunk-driving laws. More alcohol in the bloodstream than that found in a single glass of wine will be judged as driving under the influence. Severe fines and loss of driving privileges will be the result.

The victim's remains were flown by helicopter to University Hospital in Lausanne for identification.

Harper stared at the photos.

One: Swiss computer geek posing with his high-tech mobile phone with a wide grin on his face. Two: Grainy photo from the mobile phone. Car in flames, black smoke. Headline again: Storm claims life of Russian tourist, thirty klicks north of Montreux, bottles of vodka and casino chips found in the wreckage, deep ravine . . . Bollocks.

He dug his mobile from his jacket, dialed Miss Barraud's number. Need to be put through to the doctor. Her tone more than a little dismissive in explaining the doctor presently dining with King Juan Carlos of Spain at Le Raisin in Cully.

"Put me through, fellow coworker, *now*."

Few minutes later the doctor picked up. Most embarrassing to have the telephone ring, Mr. Harper. Could this not wait? Harper gave him a rundown anyway. The doctor considered the info for three seconds.

"And?"

"Sir, we need to talk to the Swiss police tonight, tell them what we know. Get them on our side so they let us know the identity of the victim, soon as possible."

"Mr. Harper, excusing oneself from the presence of His Majesty the King of Spain to answer a telephone call is the nadir of royal protocol. Returning to the table to announce one must leave to make a statement to the Swiss police is . . . well, it isn't done."

Harper looked at the photos. "Sir, I'm looking at these photos, and I have a gut feeling this wasn't an accident."

"Are you saying you believe Yuriev was in that car and he was murdered?"

"I'm saying, given your instructions to me, you might want to know who's in that burning wreck, and why, before the goddamn press does."

Harper listened to the sound of silence for a solid minute.

"Leave it with me, Mr. Harper. Be in my office tomorrow, eight a.m. sharp."

Harper finished his freebie beer. He folded the newspaper, thinking he should give it back to Blondie, apologize for being rude. Even if she was a snot-nosed brat. He scanned the bar. Blondie was gone.

\*     \*     \*

Katherine took the lobby elevator down to the spa, booked a shiatsu massage for Wednesday, walked out of the back of the hotel to a small street with no one around. She opened her bag and found the Cohiba cigar tube. She unscrewed the cap and pulled out a joint. She lit up, drew a deep toke.

"What a fucking prick."

She took a slow walk down the dark street, rounded the corner at Café Bavaria. She thought about going in for the dinner she'd missed, but decided she'd rather get way stoned. She strolled through an underground passage. Fluorescent lights turned the world weirdly blue. Gave a nice tint to the posters advertising last year's Jazz Festival in Montreux.

The drawing was cute. Little guy in a porkpie hat standing at the edge of the lake, playing his crooked trumpet Dizzy Gillespie style. Down in the blue water under the waves, pretty mermaids all in a row, grooving on the music. Katherine smoked half the joint, smashed it out, and slipped the roach back into the cigar tube.

"That's what I want to be. A fucking mermaid and live under the sea."

The escalator at the end of the passage rose to the center of Place Saint-François. Halfway up, she realized the square had been turned into a winter wonderland. Fairy lights in the bare trees, wood chalets below selling scarves and cakes and candles and toys. Fondue huts, dozens of wineries with open bottles, and much pouring and raising of glasses. Laughter and medieval music drifting through the cold night air.

"Fa la la, this is more like it."

She wandered through the happy crowd and looked at the displays of Christmas gifts. Maybe some hand-knit hats and gloves for her sister and the kids. Maybe some sweaters for Mom and Dad. Maybe Mom and Dad would open their presents this year. Seeing their darling girl's naked ass in *Playboy* had been bad enough. Knowing she'd turned it into a profitable enterprise was like the end of the world. Not that the parental units ever said the *W* word. But they saw the beachfront condo and the expensive car, the designer clothes and the no real job to pay for it all.

Katherine stopped at a display of scents and perfumed oils. An African woman behind the counter explained the magic wonders inside the little bottles. This one healed the mind, this one healed the body, this one the soul. Katherine picked up the soul-healing potion and gave it a sniff. Lilacs; she hated fucking lilacs. The African woman watched Katherine turn up her nose.

"Mademoiselle does not care for the scent?"

"You know, he was such a fucking prick."

"Mademoiselle?"

"Never mind."

Katherine returned the bottle and walked away.

Drums rolled and horns sounded as men and women in medieval costume worked their way through the crowd and formed a wide circle. Jugglers tossed rings and bowling pins to acrobats on stilts; a man dressed as an executioner swallowed swords and fire. Then came knights in shining armor, clanking over the cobblestones. Then fair maidens in high pointed hats and flowing gowns, blushing behind long handkerchiefs. Drums rolled again as guards with spears marched from the edge of the square. The crowd made way and the guards led a donkey cart carrying a fool. Black cloak, black cloth boots, black floppy hat on his head. His face twisted into a grotesque shape, his scrunched-over body complete with hunchback. The fool opened a burlap sack, tossed sweets into the air. The crowd cheered and raised their glasses in salute. The fool jumped from the cart, danced in little circles, kissing every girl he could get his hands on. The crowd cheered even louder, till the fool spun in slow circles with his finger to his lips to hush the proceedings. The crowd fell quiet, waiting. The fool smiled with an impish grin and, with a quick turn, he pulled a lantern from under his cloak and hopped about like a frog.

"*C'est le guet! C'est le guet! C'est le guet!*"

The crowd howled with laughter, raised their glasses again. The fool grabbed a glass from one hand and drank it down. The music quickened and the fool began to spin around faster and faster, grabbing glass after glass and drinking them down till the music stopped and he fell in a lump to the ground.

A flute played to the soft strains of a lute, and the prettiest of the fair maidens came forward and knelt near the fool. She took his hand, gently raised him to his feet, and they danced. A slow and lovely dance, the fair maiden smiling as the fool changed before her eyes from the twisted hunchback with the grotesque face to a handsome man of charming grace. The music slowed to a stop. The fair maiden presented the fool with a piece of lace. He bowed and pressed the lace to his lips.

Loud applause and shouts of "Bravo!" filled the square. The players removed their hats and worked the crowd for tips. The young man playing the fool stopped in front of Katherine. She opened her bag, dropped fifty francs in his black hat.

*"Merci, mademoiselle!"*

"No problem, it isn't mine."

*"Pardon?"*

"Nothing. Hey, your Quasimodo act was wonderful."

*"Merci beaucoup, mademoiselle.* You are American?"

"Yeah, but I live in Lausanne near Pont Bessières, and you know what? I've got a great view of the cathedral, and some nights I see this guy in the bell tower. He's got a lantern, like you, and he goes around the tower shouting something."

*"Ah, oui. C'est le guet, mademoiselle."*

*"Le* what?"

*"Le guet.* The watcher, you say in English. Each night he carries the lantern around the tower and calls, *'C'est le guet, il a sonné l'heure!'"*

"For real? What does it mean?"

"No one knows. It's just the way of things in Lausanne."

"Cool. Does he have a hunchback, too?"

"I have never seen him, I only know he is there. But it

is very good luck to see him, mademoiselle. You must make a wish next time. This is also a very old tradition. All the children in Lausanne are taught this in school."

Katherine took a hundred-franc note from her bag. "Here, and this time it's from me. You just made my night."

*"Très gentille, mademoiselle. Merci beaucoup."*

The fool darted off for more tips. Katherine kept digging in her bag for her cigarette case.

"Damn it, left it at the fucking bar."

She turned back to the Palace, pushed through the crowd, bumped straight into Harper. Her cigarette case was in his hands.

"Hello, Miss Taylor."

"How . . . how did you know I'd be here?"

"I didn't. Came over for the *vin chaud*."

"With my cigarette case in your mitts?"

"You left it at the bar—thought I'd hold it till I saw you again. I spotted you in the crowd just now."

"You could've left it at the bar with Stephan."

"It's gold."

"You still could have left it."

"There's a bloody diamond embedded in the lid."

"Stephan, I trust. You, I don't know from Adam. Looks like theft to me."

"More like thinking I was a bit of a sod and thought I should make it up to you."

"Sod?"

"You'd prefer another word?"

"How about 'arrogant piece of shit'?"

"That's four words. You must be one of those college girls I've heard so much about."

"What's that supposed to mean?"

"Nothing, I was being witty. Failing miserably, it seems."

She took the cigarette case, pulled out a smoke. Harper had a match ready. She looked at him as she touched her cigarette to the flame.

"So, you wanted to make it up to me. What did you have in mind?"

"How about a glass of *vin chaud*? Supposed to have a bit of a kick to it."

The dope was coming on in a nice wave, soothing the rough edges. She let herself smile. "Sure, why not?"

They weaved through the happy crowd to a steaming black cauldron. People huddled around for drink and warmth. A large, round woman in a Heidi outfit dipped a ladle in the cauldron, filling glass after glass. Harper managed to snatch two straightaway. Katherine watched him fumble through his pockets for twenty francs, trying not to spill the wine. Six feet something, broad shoulders, looked in pretty good shape under the beat-up Burberry. As he was walking back to her, she eyed him closer. Dark brown hair streaked with gray. Not bad, actually.

"Here you go. Careful, it's hot."

She breathed in the steam. Warm with winter spices. An accordion struck up a tune in three-quarter time. Drunken voices sang along.

"So how long've you been in Lausanne, Harper?"

"Seven weeks. You?"

"Six and a half."

"Weeks?"

"Months. You like it here?"

"Bit hard to settle in. Can't sleep. Too quiet maybe. Little odd on the laundry front."

"What?"

"Laundry."

"Yeah, I heard you. But what's so odd about laundry in Switzerland?"

"I needed to do laundry the first Sunday morning I was here. As I'm putting things in the dryer, the police were knocking at my door."

"What the heck were you doing to your laundry?"

"'Heck'? You say 'heck'?"

"Stick to the point. Police, at your door—why?"

"I told you, laundry. Seems there's a law in Switzerland against doing laundry on Sundays. One-hundred-franc fine, payable at my local post office within thirty days. You never had that problem?"

"I send mine out."

"Right."

She looked at him again. The lights in the trees softened the deep-cut lines around his eyes. No, not bad at all.

"You know, speaking of odd, I was talking to Quasimodo before you got here."

"Who?"

"You missed that part. These medieval players came with their bags of tricks. One guy was made up like a hunchback. Turned out to be a really good dancer. Anyway, he told me there's a guy in the bell tower of the cathedral who carries a lantern and calls the time at night."

"You're joking me."

"No, why?"

"I thought I saw a light up there a few nights ago."

"Well, that makes two of us. You're supposed to make a wish when you see him, for good luck."

"Bit barking for the twenty-first century."

"I don't know. I think it's sweet."

"I suppose it is nice to have your very own cuckoo clock."

Katherine broke into stoner giggles. Harper watched her.

"Something wrong?"

"No . . . well, yes. I mean no. It's just, that's what I thought when I saw him once. *Cuckoo, cuckoo, cuckoo.*"

He watched her giggle some more. They sipped their drinks. She felt his eyes.

"You're staring at me again, Harper."

"I'm sure you're used to it, Miss Taylor."

"Is that your idea of a compliment?"

"Yes, I suppose it is."

"Then thanks, I suppose."

The happy crowd broke into an *oom-pah-pah* chorus. A ditty about a farmer's daughter and her many suitors. At the end of each chorus, they touched their glasses together and downed their drinks in a single gulp. Refills were fast in coming. Harper and Katherine glanced at each other now and again, each time turning away their eyes like embarrassed strangers.

"So, Harper, now that you've had a good look, I guess you know what I do in Lausanne."

"I have a fair idea. Regardless, I was out of line in the bar."

"Nah, I had it coming."

"Agreed. More *vin chaud*?"

She smiled. "Why not? I'm off tonight."

"That makes two of us."

Harper took her glass for another round. And this time Katherine watched the way he moved, the dope giving her eyes an added sense of perception. He seemed to avoid physical contact with people. Not in a timid way, more as if keeping a lid on some fierce energy that might explode at any second. Watching him come back through the crowd with the drinks, Katherine thought if the African woman had his scent in a bottle, it'd be labeled "Rough—Handle with Care." Only made her want to unscrew the cap and take a deep huff, then hold on for the ride. He stopped in front of her and held out a glass. "Now it's you who's staring, Miss Taylor."

"I was just wondering what lies beneath the surface."

He reached into his coat for his cigarettes. "Who, me?"

"Yeah, what's your story?"

Harper put a smoke to his lips and lit up. "Nothing really. I was in London a few weeks ago, now I'm here."

"That's it?"

"Maybe when I settle into this town, I'll come up with more. Just now it's all a bit of a jumble."

"Hmm."

"Hmm what?"

"Nothing, just plain old hmm." She sipped her wine, watching the fire, swaying to the music. "It's nice they do all this at Christmas. It's like living in a fairy tale."

Harper took a pull on his smoke. "Few nights ago, before I saw you in the brasserie, I saw you getting out of a taxi and going into the hotel."

"So, you are the stalker type?"

"Just ducking out of the rain, actually, and there you were. You were looking at the lights on the portico and giggling, like someone who believes in fairy tales."

Katherine felt another round of giggles bubble to the surface. "Wow, way too funny."

"Sorry?"

"That's exactly what I was thinking. Guess that makes you a psychic stalker, huh?"

"I suppose it does."

She sipped her wine, watching him out of the corner of her eye.

"And what about you? You believe in fairy tales, Harper?"

"I'm sure I don't."

"Why not?"

"Another one of those things that seems somewhat barking for the twenty-first century."

"Oh, don't be such a party pooper, Harper. Look around: Lausanne isn't a town. It's a magic place in a faraway land where everyone's happy and a handsome man in a bell tower watches over fair maidens as they sleep."

"Whatever gets you through the night, Miss Taylor."

"What's that mean?"

"Nothing. If you're the sort who needs a fairy tale to get through the night, fine."

She almost took another sip of wine. "You know what? This does have a bit of a kick to it. I think I'll be going."

"Something I said?"

"More like something you are."

"What's that?"

"Someone who doesn't believe in fairy tales. Too bad; we were on a roll."

"I'm afraid you've lost me, Miss Taylor."

Katherine handed him her glass. "Stoner babble, Harper, forget it. And thanks for the cigarette case. It was a gift from the bass player in a big-time rock band out of Dublin. Nice guy. He sprinkled pharmaceutical cocaine on my nipples and licked it off all night long, never touched me otherwise. And you know what he said all the time he was licking my tits? He said I was the fuck of the century."

She turned, walked away.

Harper stared at the unfinished glasses in his hands, unable to decide which one to drink first. Desperately lonely or way out of his price range.

# nine

Rochat finished the midnight rounds and blew out the lantern. He climbed through the timbers, squeezed around Marie-Madeleine, and unlocked the winch shed. He reached in and pulled the lever to shut off the floodlights on the esplanade. All of a sudden, the belfry and cathedral façade were cast in shadow. He shuffled to the south balcony, watched the waning moon atop the Alps, looking as if it had bumped into one of the jagged peaks and gotten stuck. He watched moonlight reflect in the slow swirling surface of the lake.

"The weather's changing, Marie. I'm afraid we've lost the year to winter."

The great bell didn't answer. Rochat turned to her.

"What's wrong, Marie? You never miss a chance to disagree about the weather."

He reached through the timbers, gently tapped the edge of her skirt, and listened to her voice.

"I know, I've been very distracted the last few days, but I'm very sure I'm fine. I'm going in for a cup of tea now. You have a nice snooze; I'll be back in an hour. Yes, yes. I promise."

He went into the loge, took off his overcoat and hat, and set the kettle to boil. On the table a sketchbook lay open at his drawings of the loge. The funny-shaped walls built between the crisscross timbers, the crooked ceiling with the brass candle lamp hanging down, all the candles set alight on the table and things on shelves. Bubbles rattled in the kettle. Rochat poured steamy water in a cup with tea and sugar and no milk.

"With all your distractions you forgot to bring milk, Rochat. Tsk, tsk on you."

He picked up the sketchbook, put three drawing pencils between his teeth, and carried the cup of tea to the bed. He settled down and continued to draw, adding shadows and shades to the pictures. A radio lived in an oak wood box on the shelf above his bed. The radio was from before Monsieur Buhlmann times. It was the only radio Rochat had ever seen with names of cities instead of numbers to tell you what part of the air you were listening to. Tonight the dial was pointing to the air over Paris. A man said they would now hear Beethoven's Second Symphony performed by the Orchestre de Paris under the baton of Daniel Barenboim. It was nearly time for the one-o'clock bells when the music ended and the man thanked Rochat for listening and invited him to please tune in again for next week's program.

"*Et merci à vous, monsieur.* And please thank Monsieur Barenboim and the Orchestre de Paris. And don't forget Monsieur Beethoven."

Rochat hopped from the bed, put on his overcoat, and pulled his floppy hat down on his head. The carpentry groaned and cables stretched and Marie shook the loge with a single thunderous gong. He lit the lantern and shuffled to the east balcony. He waited for the great bell's voice to begin to fade.

*"C'est le guet! Il a sonné l'heure! Il a sonné l'heure!"*

He rounded the tower, north, west, and south, each time raising the lantern and calling the hour. He looked out over Lausanne; all was well. He hung the lantern on the railing, opened the little brass door. A gust of wind curled through the timbers, found the flame, and blew it out.

"And thank you, Madame Souffle, for your performance, too."

Thin clouds in the sky, weaving and racing between the stars and below the moon.

"Look, Marie. It's the stringy kind of clouds. That means snow is coming. The weather-teller machine in Ouchy was right."

He reminded Marie of all the fun things to do when it snowed. Skating around the balconies over ice-covered stones. Standing on the open roof of the belfry to catch snowflakes on his tongue.

"And there'll be icicles on the gargoyles' noses, and we can break them off and eat them. The icicles, I mean."

A light flashed above Rue Caroline, from the same window as the night before. Rochat pointed his eyes down to his boots and watched them shuffle along the balcony and into the loge. He pulled off his coat and hat and tossed them on the bed.

"You have your duties, you can't keep getting distracted by your imaginations."

He went back to his sketchbook, trying to concentrate on his drawings. But no matter how hard he tried, his imaginations kept butting in.

"But what if she isn't an imagination of something that isn't there? What if she's an imagination of a real thing? Maybe that's why the detectiveman is looking for her, too, because he knows the angel is a real thing."

He jumped from the bed, pulled the drawing of the woman's face from his overcoat, and looked at it. "That means this drawing is a very important clue."

He tucked the drawing in his trouser pocket, took the binoculars from the closet, and slipped them around his neck. He stepped out of the loge and tiptoed past Marie-Madeleine, hoping she was snoozing soundly enough to let him pass unnoticed. She was sleeping very soundly indeed. He dashed up the northeast turret to the upper balconies. He crawled into the carpentry and shimmied up the slanting timbers above La Lombarde. His crooked foot caught an iron peg, and he lost his balance and fell from the timber. His hands caught a crossbeam and he was left dangling in the air, his right boot brushing the top of La Lombarde. She vibrated with surprise.

"Sorry to disturb you, madame. No, no, nothing's the matter, just solving a mysterious mystery, I think. Go back to sleep."

He swung like a clapper, caught the crossbeam with his boots, and worked himself upright. He climbed to where he had a perfect view through the stone arches and across Pont Bessières to Rue Caroline. He raised the binoculars to his eyes, saw a blurry white light in the lenses. He turned the focus ring . . . and she was there in the window. Sitting at the dressing table, wearing her white robe. But she wasn't facing the mirror and brushing her hair. She was looking out of the window, her face in full view. Rochat pulled the drawing from his pocket, studied it in the faint light of the moon. He looked through the binoculars again.

"It's the same face, Rochat, the angel you imagined. And she's looking at . . . *non!*"

He slid down a timber, hid behind La Lombarde.

"I'm sorry to disturb you again, madame, but she's looking at me. Why is the angel looking at me?"

Before the bell could answer, all the carpentry creaked and groaned and the cables pulled taut and the giant hammer at the edge of Marie-Madeleine's skirt cocked back.

"Uh-oh."

The great bell exploded with two shouts that sent shivers through the timbers. Rochat was shaken loose and fell hard to the plank wood floor beneath La Lombarde. He jumped to his feet, raced down the turret and into the loge.

"Beforehervoicefades, beforehervoicefades. Where's the lantern? Leftitoutside, leftitoutside."

He grabbed the matches, ran to the lantern, set it alight. He raced around the tower as fast as he could, calling the hour as loud as he could. Reaching the railing of the south balcony and calling the hour once more, his voice chased after Marie's fading shouts.

*"C'est le guet! Il a sonné l'heure! Il a sonné l'heure!"*

Out of breath, he slumped against a stone pillar. He looked at Marie-Madeleine in her timbered cage. She regarded him with severity.

"I know, madame, I know. Never in eight hundred years has a watcher been late. Yes, I'm a silly fool to be out in the cold without a coat and hat. And of course it's dark, so even if she was an angel, how could she see me? And this is what I get for snooping, anyway. Yes, yes, I know. I'm supposed to be *le guet de Lausanne*, not *le snoop de Lausanne*."

He stood, bowed to all the bells.

"Rest assured there will be no more imagining from Marc Rochat tonight, mesdames. I will now concentrate on my duties."

He turned around and held the lantern over the rails, high over his head.

"And excuse me, Lausanne, if I was the slightest bit late. But Rochat is here; he will always be here to watch over you."

He held the lantern steady in the wind for all Lausanne to see. He searched the windows of Flon, the Palud and Rotillon quarters, the old city. Dark, shutters drawn. He turned to the carpentry and listened. All the bells were snoozing.

"Very good, all is well again."

He peeked out of the corner of his eye toward Rue Caroline. The light still burning in the dark. He ducked behind the pillars at the door of the loge. He raised the binoculars to his eyes. The angel still at the window, still looking toward the cathedral. She touched her fingers to her lips and pressed her hand to the glass. Then she floated away.

After a time, the light in the window went out. Rochat shivered in the cold wind.

"Goodness, you'll freeze to death out here."

He went into the loge, switched on the kettle, and tried to concentrate on making a very hot cup of tea.

"Where's the milk? Oh, you forgot you forgot milk."

He sat at the table and concentrated on counting all the spare candles in all the boxes he kept in a closet. Often forgetting which number was in his head, or from which box he was counting, then needing to start over. He was just finishing his tea when the creaking timbers told him it was time for the three-o'clock bells. He lit the lantern, rounded the balcony, and called the hour over Lausanne for the last rounds of the night.

He shuffled into the loge and tidied up. He blew out the candles, leaving only the light of the lantern. He replaced his sketchbook of things in the loge and pulled down the one he had titled *old bonz*. He tucked it under his arm.

"And wouldn't they talk at Café du Grütli? Marc Rochat, *le snoop de Lausanne*, too stupid to come in from the cold. Found in the belfry, frozen stiff, with very good binoculars for looking at cows stuck to his face. That's what they'd say."

He picked up the lantern, shuffled out of the loge and

down the tower steps. He picked up his pace, hopped three steps at a time, stopping at the door leading into the women's choir loft. The door was swinging on its hinges again. He looked for the teasing kind of shadows in the corners of the high ceiling.

"I've had a long night of confusing imaginations and mysterious mysteries, mesdames. I don't need any silliness from you, so there!"

*. . . so there, so there, so there . . .*

He pushed through the door and marched over the wooden walkway, his boots thundering in the dark.

"And Monsieur Junod would say, 'Just what was he doing with those binoculars? He doesn't have any cows.' And Madame Budry would say, 'I always knew he was touched in the head.'"

*. . . touched in the head, in the head, in the head . . .*

He stopped, held the lantern over his head. He heard whispering voices spread from stone to stone, all commenting on his behavior.

"I can hear you! All of you! Go ahead and gossip! After all, why would I expect sympathy from a bunch of crumbly old stones?"

*. . . crumbly old stones, old stones, old stones . . .*

He took a step.

*Peep.*

Then another.

*Doop.*

Then took two more steps.

*Peep, doop.*

He held his boot just above the floor, waiting one

extra moment before gently touching his twisted foot to the wood.

*BOOORAHHH!*

"The organ? At this hour? Such a night this is."

He hurried over the walkway, rushed midway down the tower to an old wooden door set in the curving stone wall. He unlocked the door, crouched down, scooted through a dark tunnel. He pushed through a wooden hatch and tiptoed onto the tribune of the nave, the organ sounds still following his every step.

*Peedoop, peedoop, peedoop.*

A towering stained-glass window in the occidental wall held Jesus dying on the cross. This was the only place in the cathedral anyone could see the window anymore. The tall pipes of the new organ built in Monsieur Buhlmann times had turned the tribune into a forgotten cave. Rochat held the lantern high, looked around. No one.

"Hmm."

He crept along the giant wooden box where the tall pipes lived.

*Peedoop, peedoop.*

He shuffled along the narrow metal ramp leading out over the floor of the nave.

*Peedoop, peedoop, peedoop.*

He ducked under the long brass horns stretching out into the dark, gathered his courage, and peeked around the edge of the organ console.

*BOOORAAAHHHH!*

A wizened man with a shock of white hair sat hunched over the keys.

"Hello, Marc."

"Monsieur Rannou, it's you."

The old man's sticklike fingers pulled and pushed the stops at the sides of the keyboards.

"I heard you walking about. I thought I'd give you a little fright. I hope it wasn't too scary."

"*Non, monsieur,* it was fun. But it's very late."

"It's only very late till midnight, Marc, then it's very early."

Rochat remembered Monsieur Rannou always said those words when he came to the cathedral to play the organ on nights he couldn't sleep.

"It's been a long time since I've seen you, monsieur."

"Yes, it has."

Rochat set the lantern on the floor, sat himself on the metal steps, watched Monsieur Rannou press the keys. The high tones of the choir pipes were perfect. They sailed from the tribune and circled through the cavernous dark of the nave.

"I thought you might be coming down to sit at the console to play with the stops and pretend you were a space captain tonight. But I see you have one of your sketchbooks. What's it to be tonight? The dead bishops, or is it your old friend Otto?"

"I was going to the crypt to draw the skeletons."

"The crypt? Oh, then I do see."

"See what?"

"You only go down to the crypt when something troubles you, Marc. Why don't you tell me what it is?"

Rochat bit his lip, knowing if he confessed a little, he'd confess all.

"It's all right, Marc. You always shared your secrets with me, remember?"

Rochat took an anxious breath.

"I'm imagining things, monsieur. More than usual, I mean. And now there's a mysterious mystery."

"A mysterious mystery, well, those are the best kind." Monsieur Rannou played a few notes that sounded scary and silly at the same time. It made Rochat laugh. Monsieur Rannou finished the tune with a flourish and turned to Rochat.

"Come now, tell me what's on your mind."

"Two sleeps ago, I saw a face from the belfry. I mean, first I saw a light in a window above Rue Caroline. And then a woman with long blond hair was floating in the light. Her back was to me and I couldn't see her face, so I imagined her face in a drawing. I'm very sure she looked like an angel, monsieur, like the angels carved in stone in the nave. Then, the next day, I saw her at the funicular station at Gare Simplon. She rode La Ficelle to Flon and I followed her."

*. . . i followed her, followed her, followed her . . .*

Rochat stopped talking, listening to his voice echo through the nave.

"And what happened, Marc?"

"She went into the Lausanne Palace and sat at a bar and she was talking to a detectiveman."

"A detectiveman?"

"*Oui, monsieur.* I saw him on Pont Bessières the night I imagined the angel's face. He wore a coat with a belt and straps on the shoulders, like detectives wear in the old movies I watched with Grand-maman."

"Well then, I'm very sure he must be a detective. But how do you know she was talking to him?"

"There was an alleyway next to the windows of the hotel, and I hid in a shadow and watched her. She talked to the detectiveman and he took her newspaper and left her alone. But she never turned around so I couldn't be sure it was her . . . Then the clock on the mantel said I was late for my dinner and I had to hurry to the café. And then I had to hurry to the belfry to call the hours. And tonight, after the one-o'clock bells, I saw the light in the window again, and I looked through the binoculars, and she was there. And she was looking at me and . . ."

"And what, Marc?"

"It was her, the angel I imagined."

Rochat took the drawing from his overcoat, showed it to the old man.

"Yes, she's very beautiful, but if she were an angel, what do you imagine she'd be doing in Lausanne?"

Rochat folded the drawing, tucked it in his sketchbook. He thought about the old man's question.

"Maybe she's lost."

Monsieur Rannou leaned closer to Rochat. "Would you like me to tell you what I think, Marc?"

"Very much, monsieur."

"I think it wouldn't be the first time an angel had

come to Lausanne and found themselves lost. And I'm sure if you look around a bit more carefully, you'll see Lausanne is full of angels."

"You might see them in Lausanne because you're a great artist. Papa always said, 'Monsieur Rannou is a great artist.'"

"And what about you, *mon cher*? Show me your sketchbook."

Rochat held the book, slowly turning the pages so Monsieur Rannou could see the drawings of the old bones in the crypt.

"Why, these aren't simple drawings of skeletons in their graves. They're wonderful stories of life and death." Monsieur Rannou looked at Rochat. "Remarkable, it's all so remarkable. Looking in these pictures, looking at you, I understand everything now."

"Monsieur?"

"Just listen a moment."

Monsieur Rannou turned and touched the keys. Rochat listened to the music as it sailed through the cathedral, imagining it flying around the pillars and altars and rising to the vaulted ceiling. The music stopped.

"That was beautiful, monsieur. What was it?"

"I don't know. I closed my eyes and an angel showed me what to play."

"How?"

"Inspiration, Marc. The same way you draw pictures. You are inspired to draw."

"I don't know what that word means."

"It's a very old word, it means 'to breathe into.' That's

how it works: An angel breathes into men and shows us what to play, what to draw. How to find the truth of who we are and why we are here."

Rochat looked suspiciously at the old man.

"You think I'm teasing you, don't you? Like all those teasing shadows hiding in the belfry."

Rochat rested his head in his hand. "There are so many imaginations in my head these days. I'm very confused."

"Be not afraid, Marc."

"The saxophoneman said those words at the train station. Just before I saw the angel. And I asked him if he ever saw an angel in Lausanne, and he said, 'All the time, little dude, all the time,' and I gave him three five-franc coins and he played 'Les Anges dans Nos Campagnes,' but it sounded sad because there's nothing sadder than an angel in nowtimes, that's what he said. But why are the angels sad, monsieur?"

Monsieur Rannou pointed into the darkness of the nave. "Tell me, Marc, what do you see now, out there?"

Rochat looked into the darkness of the nave. "A big dark space."

"Yes, a big dark space that you fill each night with the light of your lantern."

"A very small light, monsieur."

"There's no such thing in a big dark space. The smallest fire burns like the brightest star. Especially to creatures born of light, creatures men call angels."

"That's what Maman said before she died."

"Yes, she did. And she told you that once upon a time

the angels inspired men to build cathedrals. Places where angels could rest and hide."

Rochat slipped into beforetimes.

Sitting with his mother in the days before she was lowered into the winter ground at Cimetière Saint-Charles. Watching her move her hands over a candle and make shadows on the ceiling, hearing her voice . . .

"Because the bad shadows were trying to hurt them. And they wanted to hurt me, too, and that's why she needed to die and I needed to leave. Because I'd be safe and I'd learn things, because one day one angel will come to Lausanne Cathedral and I'll need to protect the angel from the bad shadows and . . . and . . ."

He blinked, found himself sitting with Monsieur Rannou in nowtimes.

"I can't remember the rest of the story, monsieur—and I can't remember the beginning. I just know the middle part about this place."

"That's all right. You remember why you were brought to Lausanne. That's enough for now." Monsieur Rannou began to play. "Why don't you take your sketchbook to the crypt and draw? It'll be dawn soon and Vaucher the *boulanger* will be taking the first of the day's bread from the ovens. That's when it's best, isn't it?"

"*Oui*, that's when it's best." Rochat tucked his sketchbook under his arm, picked up the lantern, and stood. "Would you like to come with me? We can have coffee and croissants together."

"No, I'll just sit here a moment, then I must be going." Monsieur Rannou smiled. "But off you go now.

And Marc, don't tell anyone at Café du Grütli that you saw me tonight."

"But why? Everyone knows you like to come to the cathedral when you can't sleep."

"Oh, *mon cher*, I do miss our visits. How long has it been since you've seen me?"

Rochat thought about it. "A long time."

"Yes, nine months. Do you remember why you haven't seen me?"

Rochat remembered. "Because you died."

"Yes. You came to my funeral with Messieurs Gübeli and Buhlmann."

"Can I ask you a question, monsieur?"

"Of course."

"Why are you still here if you died?"

Monsieur Rannou touched the keys softly, not pressing them, just touching them.

"So that you would know that without you, all the angels . . . all the creatures born of light will be lost forever."

Rochat thought about it. "Because it's my duty, because I'm *le guet de la Cathédrale de Lausanne*."

"Yes, Marc, it's your duty."

"I understand. Well, it was very nice talking to you again, monsieur."

"Good-bye, Marc."

"Good-bye."

Rochat made his way behind the tall pipes to the tribune. He opened a door to a short passageway and hopped down the stone stairwell that led to the floor of the nave. He shuffled through the big dark space with his lantern lighting the way. Looking up to the vaulted ceiling and seeing nothing but the teasing kind of shadows fluttering in the high arches. He stopped at Otto the Brave Knight's marble sarcophagus at the side of the altar and gave him a quick tap.

"Otto, I just saw Monsieur Rannou. He says Lausanne is full of angels and some of them are lost and come to hide in the cathedral. And he reminded me what Maman said, that I was going to Lausanne to hide from the bad shadows like the angels because angels were made of light, and that an angel would come to the cathedral and I needed to protect the angel, and without me all the angels would be lost forever."

Rochat pressed his ear to the cold marble.

"What do you mean, you already know? How could you already know? I didn't even know till he reminded me of the things Maman told me in beforetimes."

He listened again.

"Oh, because all the angels have been making so much noise with their comings and goings, you haven't been able to sleep for eight hundred years. Well, try to rest, *mon ami*. And be not afraid. They're only made of light, after all."

He shuffled from the altar and jumped down four stone steps to a low iron gate under Otto's tomb. The oldest and strangest-looking key on his chain opened a rusting lock. The iron gate creaked as Rochat eased it open. He raised his lantern into the pitch black.

"*Bonsoir*, it's only me."

# ten

Harper watched the doctor punch from Athens to Los Angeles on his white telephone. The doctor's morning phone conference was running an hour overtime. Just now it was the head of the US Olympic Committee on speakerphone, still deeply upset that baseball had been dropped from the summer games.

"You Europeans just don't get it. Baseball's the Great American Pastime. To be enjoyed and cherished by the entire world, like democracy!"

The doctor explained that, yes, baseball may indeed be a great American pastime, pure as democracy itself. But that doesn't necessarily qualify it as an Olympic event. The Yank gasped and vented his outrage for ten minutes before ringing off without a missing-you-already. The room went blessedly quiet. The doctor hung up.

"I suspect the Americans, having once renamed French fries to freedom fries, will now whip themselves into patriotic frenzy and rename them again to home-run fries."

Harper nodded, wondering if this might be a good
time to ask why the hell he'd been ordered to report at
eight a.m. if it meant hurry up and wait. Then a chime
sounded over the speakerphone, followed by Miss Barraud's reverential voice.

"*Pardon, Docteur. Il est arrivé.*"

"*Bon. Faites-le entrer.*"

The office door opened and a fifty-something gent
stepped in, elegant in his beige cashmere coat and silk scarf.
The Migros bag in his hands looked a bit out of place.
Didn't seem the sort who did his own grocery shopping.

"*Bonjour, messieurs.* Please excuse the delay, I had to
take an important call."

The doctor was already up from his desk and crossing
the office. Harper watched them work through their
Swiss greeting rituals. Warm handshake, three back-and-
forth kisses on opposite cheeks. The doctor then helping
the visitor with his cashmere coat. Tailored double-
breasted pinstripe underneath.

"Mr. Harper, would you care to join us? It's my honor
to introduce Inspector Jacques Gobet of the Swiss police."

Swell, Harper thought, cops in cashmere coats and
two-thousand-dollar suits . . .

"How do you do, sir?"

. . . and an iron fist disguised as a polite handshake.

"*Enchanté*, Mr. Harper. And let me take this opportunity to welcome you to Lausanne."

The inspector joined the doctor on the large sofa. He
set the shopping bag on the carpet next to his spit-shined

wingtips. Harper took the couch opposite, white coffee table between them.

"Mr. Harper, I contacted Inspector Gobet last evening after your telephone call. I gave him a rundown of our situation and he kindly agreed to come down from Berne this morning."

"Does that mean this is now a police matter?"

The inspector adjusted the French cuffs of his shirt till they were perfect. "Officially, I'm here in my capacity as close and trusted friend, visiting over a cup of coffee. You did promise coffee, Doctor."

"On its way, Jacques."

"To be honest, Mr. Harper, you gave the good doctor quite the fright last evening with your talk of foul play. I thought I'd best come down for a chat. Would you mind if I asked a few questions, unofficially?"

Harper felt the inspector's eyes, as if he didn't have to ask questions, as if he knew everything already.

"Go ahead."

"Why do you think there is a connection between two unconnected facts?"

"Sorry?"

"The simple facts are these: You have misplaced one man of Russian origin and I have found one corpse on a mountain road. Where is the connection?"

"The newspaper reported he was a Russian tourist."

"The newspaper reported the motorcar had been rented by a Russian tourist who secured the motorcar upon arriving at Geneva Airport four weeks before the events on the Montreux-to-Gstaad road. He reported the car stolen from Les Trois Couronnes hotel in Vevey last Monday. Two days before Mr. Yuriev cleared Swiss immigration in Zurich. Would that ease your suspicions?"

"Not really."

"And why not?"

"The photograph in the newspaper."

"What about it?"

"Looked as if the car had been pushed off the road and set alight."

"You could see this from a grainy reprint of a mobile phone photograph, taken from two or so meters away?"

"You just said it."

"I beg your pardon?"

"The newspaper said the car tumbled down a deep ravine. Two or so meters isn't deep enough for a car to tumble and explode into flames, not without a little help."

"I see. You still haven't told me why you think Alexander Yuriev was the victim. Do you have any evidence?"

"Yuriev said he had something in his possession to give the doctor, said he knew he was being followed."

Inspector Gobet raised an eyebrow. "Not really evidence, is it?"

"Then call it a gut feeling."

"A gut feeling, yes. As I understand it, the IOC received documents through the post regarding a chemical formula for a performance-enhancing drug, did it not? I believe Yuriev then claimed he had sent the formula."

"He didn't call it a drug, he called it a potion. As a matter of fact."

"Yes, of course, a potion. With debilitating psychotropic side effects, I believe."

"That's right."

"So the facts are: We have someone claiming to be Alexander Yuriev who contacts the IOC with the formula of a psychotropic potion—the very word being somewhat fanciful—and who also claims he's being followed and in grievous danger, but who uses his own actual name in all e-mail communications, his Swiss visa application, and when registering at the Hôtel Port Royal. These facts, combined with your keen forensic study of a mobile phone photograph printed in a newspaper, have led you to believe Alexander Yuriev was victim of murder most foul. Well, I must say, sounds very conspiratorial, though not surprising, coming from a man with a history of alcohol abuse."

Harper stared at the inspector a moment. "Sir?"

"Mr. Yuriev has a history of alcohol abuse; perhaps you're aware of it?"

"Yes."

"And, as I'm sure you're aware, the doctor here, who was a prominent medical professional before assuming his current position as president of the IOC, believes Mr. Yuriev is most probably suffering from alcohol-induced paranoia."

"Maybe he's a drunk, maybe he's paranoid, but maybe he was being followed anyway."

"As in the old psychiatrist's joke: Just because you're paranoid doesn't mean they aren't out to get you."

Wherever the cop in the cashmere coat was leading him,

Harper knew he had no choice but to follow, including smiling along with the old psychiatrist's bloody joke.

"True."

"In fact, Mr. Harper, you have no proof that Alexander Yuriev was being followed or that he was in any real danger. That all this talk of a potion is nothing more than a wretched man seeking help from—how did he put it—the only man he could trust."

"His e-mail accounts disappeared."

"It may interest you to know, Mr. Harper, the European Hotmail network experienced a major systems crash seventy-two hours ago. During the reboot, there was massive loss of data across the entire continent."

"Sounds rather convenient."

"Agreed, but it is also a fact that convenient things do happen now and then. *Sapiens nihil affirmat quod non probat*, eh?"

Harper stared at the inspector, instantly knowing the words. *Don't affirm what you don't know firsthand.* Couldn't remember where the hell he'd learned Latin.

"Let's just call it a hunch, then, Inspector."

"As opposed to a gut feeling?"

"I heard something in his voice."

"Yes, your one and only telephone conversation with Mr. Yuriev; thank you for bringing it up. I believe you stated he sounded in some distress."

"That'd be a polite way of putting it."

"How would you express it, Mr. Harper?"

"Like a man who was scared to death, who knew he was running out of time."

"Another hunch?"

"Like I said, I heard something in his voice."

"How long was your conversation with Mr. Yuriev?"

"How long?"

"It's not a trick question, Mr. Harper."

"Five minutes, maybe ten or more."

"You're not sure?"

"No."

"Purpose of the conversation?"

"Arrange a meeting in Lausanne."

"Did you keep contemporaneous notes of the telephone conversation?"

"Notes?"

"Contemporaneous notes, Mr. Harper. Jotting down times conversations begin and end, all the things said in between, that sort of thing. Your memory may be playing tricks on you."

"My memory?"

"Yes. For example, what was the telephone number of your London flat?"

"Sorry?"

"Your telephone, in London, what was the number?"

London, crummy one-room flat across from King's Cross, telephone ringing off the hook. Guardian Services Ltd calling.

"I don't remember."

"Precisely."

The office door opened; a butler rolled in a cart of coffee and pastries. He poured from a porcelain china pot into matching cups. The inspector shifted the mood.

"A fine coffee service, Doctor. Is it van Eenhoorn?"

"Indeed, Jacques. *Europa and the Bull.*"

"Beautiful. Qing dynasty, I believe. A reproduction, surely."

"Yes, but the original is in the Olympic museum. A gift from the Chinese government to mark the Beijing games of 2008."

"You must allow me a private viewing before I return to Berne."

*"Avec plaisir."*

The butler offered croissants and left. The inspector had a small sip of coffee. Harper watched him chatting away with the doctor. French cuffs with gold cufflinks, manicured nails, signet ring on a fat little finger, hands looking as if they could crush a bowling ball for laughs. Wants to know your bloody London phone number because . . . because he already knows you couldn't remember it if your life depended on it.

"May I ask a question, Inspector?"

"By all means, Mr. Harper."

"Exactly what kind of policeman are you?"

The doctor's reaction was just shy of the apoplectic Yank being told baseball had been crossed off the Olympics.

"Mr. Harper, I will have you know Inspector Gobet is, in fact, deputy director of the Swiss Federal Police. He is also an adviser to Interpol and other international security agencies, including the European Court of Human Rights. He has for many years been the Swiss liaison officer to the IOC, as well as all international NGOs and international financial institutions headquartered in this country. It will interest you to know that it was Inspector Gobet who personally recommended your services to me, and had you fast-tracked through Swiss immigration."

Harper looked at the inspector. "You're Guardian Services Limited?"

"In point of fact, Mr. Harper, Guardian Services Limited is a subsidiary of Guardian Services SA, an international private security firm based in Zurich. I serve as a member of the board. I've followed your career with keen interest. Does that make things a bit more clear?"

Like mud. "More or less."

"Good."

The inspector turned to the doctor.

"I'm sure Mr. Harper intends no offense, Doctor. He probably wonders why I'm grilling him so hard. Though I'm distressed you didn't mention my responsibilities in training the Swiss Guard of the Vatican City. Very proud of that one, you know."

The inspector took another sip of coffee, set his cup in the saucer.

"As far as the grilling, Mr. Harper, it's called entrapping interrogation. The kind of thing that we toss in the mix to keep the subject off balance. Truth be told, most single men have difficulty remembering their own phone numbers. How often does one ring oneself, what? No, I wasn't interested in your answer; I was interested in your reaction."

Harper stared at the inspector. Son of a bitch was playing him.

"My reaction."

"Yes, profile the manner of your thinking, as it were. By the way, you might wish to jot down a few contemporaneous notes in the future. Just a little professional advice."

"I'll keep it in mind."

"Good, then we may move on. Gentlemen, what I am about to tell you is part of an ongoing investigation by my Special Unit Task Force. We involve ourselves with cases of particular concern to the Swiss national interest, and therefore operate somewhat below the public radar. So I insist the information remains confidential."

The doctor dipped his croissant into his coffee. "Of course, Jacques."

"By coincidence, Mr. Harper is correct about the nature of the scene. The man found in the motorcar didn't die in the road accident. He was murdered; tortured to death. His body had been repeatedly scorched with a household pressing iron, causing severe loss of flesh and muscle tissue, especially to the stomach region. The pressing iron was allowed to burn through to the spine."

The doctor choked.

"I'm sorry, Doctor. I've put you off your croissant."

"No . . . I . . . Good Lord."

"Russian mafia."

The inspector turned to Harper. Harper was half surprised the words had slipped from his mouth.

"Indeed, the Russian mafia, Mr. Harper. How would you have known?"

Like his sudden knowledge of Latin, no bloody clue. "The History Channel, maybe."

"The History Channel."

"I watch a lot of the History Channel."

"Indeed? Bit of a fan of the History Channel myself. And you're right. This method of torture is the preferred brand, if you will, of the Russian mafia."

"Jacques, was Yuriev involved with criminals?"

"Please, Doctor, let's not jump to conclusions. I only provide facts, and the facts are these: Russian gangs control most of the motorcar theft in Europe. Recently, they've been turning their attention to Switzerland. Not surprising, given the wealth of choice within our borders. The problem is these gangs are notoriously protective of their turf. At present, we are working on the premise that Comrade A tried to muscle in on Comrade B's market share. As with most business dealings involving Russian businessmen, one of the two comrades is bound to end up murdered. We're all aware of Mr. Yuriev's dire straits. But I have no reason to suspect he was involved in such activity."

The cop in the cashmere coat was making sense. Still, Harper wasn't ready to concede.

"How can you be sure, Inspector?"

"After your phone call to the doctor, my task force ran his name through our database. There's no record of him having any association with the Russian mafia."

"Interpol?"

"When Interpol wants information, they come to me."

"Physical ID, then."

"What about it?"

"Cross-checking archive photos with the body."

"You may recall, Mr. Harper, the newspaper reported the body was burned beyond recognition."

"Computer-assisted post-mortem identification systems could create a three-D image of the face using the skull."

"My, you have been watching the History Channel, haven't you?" The inspector patted the doctor's knee. "You can see why I recommended Mr. Harper to you, Doctor. Doesn't dillydally, excellent record."

Harper tried to remember his excellent record, couldn't fill in one bloody blank.

"But no, Mr. Harper, I'm afraid that wouldn't do in this case. The killers hammered the victim's face to a pulp using a claw hammer. They sawed off his hands and feet for good measure. Sniffer dogs found those bits yesterday, minus the fingertips."

"Oh my God."

"Would you care for a glass of water, Doctor? I'm sure this is upsetting."

"No, no."

Harper glanced at the doctor. Going green at the gills. Tough. His eyes shot back to the inspector.

"What about his room at the Port Royal, any traces of DNA?"

"As you're somewhat new to the canton, you wouldn't know that particular hotel is a discreet location for, shall we say, short stays. The room's been rented and cleaned to Swiss standards several times since he checked out. Believe me, there is no evidentiary DNA to be found. Are you sure you won't take a glass of water, Doctor?"

"No, thank you. But I'd like to know what it is you're getting at, Mr. Harper."

Harper looked at the doctor and felt sorry for him.

"Excuse me, sir. The one fact Inspector Gobet isn't telling us is that he can't be sure Yuriev wasn't the victim."

"But I thought . . . Good Lord, Jacques, if there's the slightest chance it was Yuriev in that automobile . . ."

"A simple matter of police procedure soon to be resolved. The call that caused my delay was from my office in Berne, informing me the Russian authorities have located Yuriev's one living blood relative. An aged sister in Arkhangelsk. We'll obtain a DNA sample from her and compare it to that of the corpse."

The door opened and the butler returned to pour more coffee. The doctor and the inspector took the opportunity to chat about the upcoming Christmas holidays. The doctor off to St. Barts for some sun; the inspector skiing at Klosters. Must have oysters at La Brasserie before. The doctor asked Harper his holiday plans; he had none. The butler rolled the coffee service out of the door.

"How long will this identification process take, Jacques?"

"A week or so at the least. We're obliged to work through diplomatic channels, as we wish to collect the samples ourselves and bring them to Berne for analysis. Russian police forensics, not to mention the corruption, are a thing to be avoided."

"And what should we do in the meantime?"

"Leaving aside the events on the Montreux-to-Gstaad

road, we must assume Mr. Yuriev's still in Switzerland. We have to know the reason he came to Lausanne and why he wishes to see you. Mr. Harper was correct in his original assessment: Until Yuriev is found, there's every chance he's a scandal waiting to happen. Which is why I recommend Mr. Harper continues to look for him."

Harper shifted in his chair. "Wouldn't the Swiss police be better suited?"

"We're quite busy chasing real criminals, Mr. Harper. As Yuriev has broken no laws, the Swiss police would appreciate your detective skills in what should remain, at present, an internal matter for the IOC."

"I'm not a detective."

"Then I am misinformed."

"Sorry?"

"Last night, after speaking to the doctor, I assigned a few men to look around Montreux, ask a few discreet questions. One of my officers visited a Miss Lucy Clarke at the Casino Barrière in Montreux and interviewed her. She reported you visited her in Évian over lunch. Pulling out a photograph between the steamed dumplings and the moo goo gai pan, asking questions about Yuriev. Very *détective privé.*"

"Surely, then, you'd rather have someone else look for Yuriev."

"Please, Mr. Harper, I'm giving you a bit of stick, as my friends at the Yard would say. In fact, you demonstrated initiative and curiosity. I was impressed, to a point. You telephoned Mr. Yuriev's hotel in the early hours of Saturday morning, speaking with a Mr. Toda, I believe."

"Who?"

"Konstantin Toda, the night clerk."

Harper squirmed in his seat. Never asked the guy's name. "Right."

"You reported to the doctor that Yuriev had checked out, taking his luggage. But had you gone to the scene yourself, you would've discovered Yuriev left something in the porter's closet."

The inspector reached inside the Migros bag, pulled out what looked like an oversize brown envelope. He laid it on the table. The doctor leaned closer for a look.

"I don't believe it."

Harper was thinking the same damn thing. Thirty by sixty centimeters of brown wrapping paper around thin sheets of cardboard. The wrapper stamped with a picture of the building he'd seen and avoided every bloody day since coming to town.

### La Cathédrale de Lausanne
### Jeu de construction

"A cardboard cutout? Of the cathedral?"

The inspector removed the cardboard sheets from the wrapper, spread them over the table.

"We call it a maquette, Mr. Harper, a paper model. These perforated sections are removed from the cardboard sheets, like so. It's Swiss-made, so the details are perfect at a ratio of one centimeter to two meters. Here are the flying buttresses, the Occidental and Apostles' porches here. Here is the belfry that sits over the main entrance and the lantern tower over the altar. There's even a tiny weathercock for the top of the lantern tower. A little paper glue, a bottle of good Swiss white, some delicate finger work, *et voilà*. One rather fine Gothic cathedral. Very popular with tourists. Thousands of them sold every year."

The doctor examined the cardboard sheets, stunned. "But why would Yuriev have such a thing?"

"The very question. Perhaps Mr. Harper would give us the benefit of a hunch."

"A hobby, or a gift for someone."

"A very good notion, Mr. Harper. And, perhaps, the very thing he wished to give you, Doctor. Either of which suggests a man in a light mood. Bit of sightseeing, some shopping. Hardly the behavior of someone who thinks he's being followed."

Harper rubbed the back of his neck. "This can't be it; this thing's a bloody toy."

"Mr. Harper, this thing was in Yuriev's possession the day you were to meet with him, the day he disappeared. In the detective trade, we don't call such a thing a toy, we call it evidence."

Harper wanted to tell him to sod off. But the more he looked into the inspector's eyes, the more he realized the cop in the cashmere coat wasn't just playing him, he was making all the rules. While Jay Harper didn't even know the name of the game.

# eleven

Katherine stirred and stretched in her bed. It was scrumptious under the duvet. She opened her eyes and saw the ashtray on the nightstand. With a half-smoked joint begging to be smoked. She fluffed the pillows, made herself comfy. She lit the joint and drew a long toke.

"Nothing like a nice buzz first thing in the morning."

She pressed a switch next to the bed, raising the shutters. Beyond the terrace, Lausanne Cathedral glowed in winter's morning light. Two black crows made lazy circles above the belfry. Katherine tucked the duvet under her chin; she smoked deep hits. The cathedral, the winter light, the circling crows, everything so lovely.

"Blackbirds circled
In a cold blue sky.
Far above our forever
Bound to earth dreams.
Flightless and wishing
Only to be like them."

It sounded nice, even though she knew it was only stoner babble. She dropped the roach in the ashtray, rolled onto her tummy, stretched again. She propped up on her hands, saw the clock next to the lamp. Not even ten. She fell back to the mattress and let herself slip into the buzz. She rocked slowly from side to side, feeling something wonderful shoot from her hips to her brain.

"So nice."

Rolling onto her back, closing her eyes, touching her favorite places. Her neck, her nipples, tracing featherlight circles over her stomach.

"So very nice."

She squeezed her nipples. Sharp tingles ran through her body. Her fingers chased after them, finding them at the moist place between her legs. She teased herself, found the perfect pressure. Dopey warmth pulsed through her blood.

"So very nice, baby."

She turned her head, opened her eyes to the mirrored closets. Seeing the woman in the looking glass, the woman watching her, following her every move. The woman she was making love to.

"Look at her eyes, baby. She needs it."

Katherine kicked off the duvet, watched her body stiffen. She let the sensation build, felt the rush flow deeper, harder. Wanting to hold it . . .

"Not yet, so good."

. . . but the woman in the looking glass wanting, begging, quivering . . .

"Oh, look at her, she's coming, look at her. Oh, baby . . . oh, the lovely, the lovely."

For the briefest moment, she felt it: a place of perfect pleasure. She sighed as it slipped away. "Wow, if only you could stay there forever, girl." She rolled out of bed, slipped on her white robe. Something moved outside her windows. The two black crows from the cathedral now sitting on the railing of her terrace, watching as she covered her body.

"Enjoy the show, fellas? You know I usually get paid a lot of money for that trick."

The crows cocked their heads and fluttered their wings. They fell from the railing and then rose through the blue sky to reclaim their circling place above the belfry.

"Men, who needs 'em?" She tipsied to the bath.

R ochat opened his eyes to pitch black.
  He smelled old dirt, old bones. He heard footsteps overhead, sat up, hit his head against something hard.

"Ouch!"

The footsteps above stopped and a voice shouted, "Who's there? Who are you? Where are you?"

The voice was muffled and distant, but Rochat knew it belonged to the caretaker of the cathedral.

"Monsieur Taroni, it's me, Marc Rochat."

"Marc Rochat? But I don't see you, where are you?"

"I'm under your feet."

"But your voice is coming from the air vents by the narthex."

"I'm down in the crypt, monsieur. Could you shine a light through the iron gates under Otto so I can find my way out?"

"Yes, yes."

The steps walked away but quickly returned.

"Rochat, what are you doing in the crypt?"

"I was drawing and my lantern went out after I fell asleep."

"Drawing? Drawing what? There're only skeletons in the crypt."

"*Oui, monsieur,* I was drawing the skeletons."

"Drawing skeletons? Again? You aren't touching them, are you? They mustn't be touched. They're like dust already."

"That's why I need a light. So I won't trip over anyone."

"Anyone? What anyone? Is someone down there with you?"

"It's only me and the skeletons, monsieur. I don't want to trip over a grave and hurt the bones."

"*D'accord.* I'm going for a lamp, Rochat. Don't touch anything." The steps walked away; they returned again.

"Rochat."

"*Oui, monsieur?*"

"This is Marc Rochat speaking? This isn't a trick?"

"*Non, monsieur.*"

"You swear this isn't a trick?"

"Swear on what?"

"You're in a cathedral, for heaven's sake—swear on anything. Wait, I'll tell you. There's something down there, under the crossing square, swear on that."

Rochat needed a moment to remember.

"I swear on the old well under the altar square."

"*Alors*, you must be Rochat. He'd know about the well. Unless you read it in a book."

"Monsieur Taroni, it's Marc Rochat, who can barely read or write his own name."

"All right, then, *j'arrive*."

The footsteps walked off. Gray light dripped through the stone shafts of the air vents. Rochat yawned and rubbed his eyes, saw he was in a small cave at the back of the crypt. Through a low arch he could see into the larger caves, to the small mounds of open graves rising from the dirt. The footsteps came back, stopped over his head.

"Rochat. Are you still there?"

"Where would I go, Monsieur Taroni?"

"Just checking. I have the lamp. I'll lay the power cable and hang it on the gates to the crypt. I must hurry and open the Apostles' entrance. It's after nine and the workers are waiting to begin work. We're starting the renovations on the south portal today and moving the Apostles' steeple. You've made us late, Rochat."

"I'm very sorry, monsieur."

"Be sure to replace the lamp in the unfinished tower. On the proper shelf, mind you. I don't like it when my equipment is misplaced."

The footsteps marched toward the altar; Rochat heard the iron gates squeak open and he saw yellowy light pour through the earthen arches and tunnels. Rochat scrambled to his knees, looked across the graves. The lamp was at the far end of the crypt, and the thin shadow next to the light belonged to Monsieur Taroni.

"Can you find your way now, Rochat?"

*"Oui, et merci beaucoup."*

"Don't leave anything down here. There's to be nothing left down here but the skeletons—and Rochat?"

*"Oui, monsieur?"*

"I'm still unclear why you were down here all night."

"I was drawing."

"Yes, yes. Drawing skeletons by candlelight, I know this. The rest is strange."

*"Pardon?"*

"Rochat, we all know you are a little, well, we know what you are. But I'd think even you'd find sleeping in the crypt a little, well, you know, strange."

Monsieur Taroni's shadow hung the lamp on the gate and left. Rochat looked around to the skeletons. All the skulls staring at him.

"Don't mind Monsieur Taroni; he's very nice. And I'm sure he didn't mean to be rude. I suppose a crypt is a funny place to wake up. Maybe I'm not here; maybe I'm dreaming."

But he couldn't remember being in his bed and falling asleep, and he couldn't remember ever talking to himself in a dream. The last thing he remembered was lighting one more candle in the lantern, the last candle. Feeling sleepy, but wanting to finish a drawing of a skeleton melded into the hardened dirt, fused and

inseparable. Then he remembered imagining Monsieur
Rannou at the organ, talking about lost angels coming
to the cathedral to hide because they were broken and
needed Rochat to protect them.

"Dear me, such a strange night. You must have a cup
of tea."

He gathered his things, stood as best he could beneath the low stone ceiling, and shuffled through the
labyrinth of open graves. He could sense the skeletons
watching him pass, even though they only had holes in
their skulls where their eyes used to be. Arms folded over
their chests, the way they were laid long ago when there
was flesh on their bones.

He came to the old stone well directly under the
crossing square of the nave. Monsieur Buhlmann once
said it's where the dead bishops poured holy waters that
couldn't be used anymore. These days the well was dry
as dust and covered by a heavy grate of thick iron rods
protruding from a central hub. Rochat circled the well,
counting the sixteen iron rods pointing in different directions. Like a very old compass, he thought. This way
would be north, this way south, then east and west. He
followed the tunnel to the east, ducked under a low-
hanging arch that opened to a crescent-shaped cave, directly under the chancel. He looked back, saw the
skeletons and graves scattered around the well. The
graves like a garden and the bones like seeds scattered in
all the directions of the world.

"It looks like someone planted you in your graves and
you're waiting for a dead bishop to put holy water on the

ground so you can grow again and go back outside. That's a much nicer story to imagine than being stuck in the ground, isn't it? Yes, it is, Rochat, and you can draw that story the next time you come to visit."

He turned and banged his head against a stone buttress. He heard the yellow teeth of the skeletons chatter with glee.

"Oh, I'm glad you think it's so funny. You may be dead, but that's no excuse for bad manners. Good day to you."

He shuffled away, his crooked foot catching the corner of a grave. He tumbled to the ground, pencils and papers scattering in the dirt. He heard yellow teeth chattering again.

"You did that on purpose! Don't deny it. I come down here to keep you company and this is the thanks I get."

He crawled through the dirt, pulling together the pages of his sketchbook and searching for his pencils. He found three, but the number four pencil was missing. He looked through the dirt, in the graves, between the bones.

"Must find it, can't leave it down here. Monsieur Taroni said nothing's to be down here but you old bones. Which one of you is hiding it?"

One skeleton lay in its grave, its cracked skull turned and looking to the side, its bony finger pointing *that way*. Rochat followed the skeleton's gaze to the stone well under the main altar.

"How could it have fallen into the well? There's a big stone wall around it and an iron grate on top."

Rochat heard the skeleton rattle its teeth.

"Oh, you think so? Well, I'll show you."

He crawled to the well, looked through the spikes of the grate.

"See, I can see, and I can tell you there's nothing down there but . . ."

Something along the side of the well, in a dugout where some stones had fallen away. He squeezed his arm through the iron spikes, just barely. And he stretched as far as he could reach, touching it with the tips of his fingers. Metal, square, a handle. Rochat tried to lift the iron grate. It wouldn't budge.

"Whatever it is, it doesn't belong in a well for holy waters."

He shuffled through the graves to a small cave at the back of the crypt, where workermen hid their holding-up-the-ceiling tools. Inside the cave, a stack of timbers lay piled against the wall. He found a one-meter length of timber and carried it to the well. He fitted it under the grate and heaved, making just enough space for his head and shoulders. He leaned over the rim and into the well, caught the handle between his fingers, and lifted the thing up. He held it up in the light of Taroni's lamp. Flat silver in color, metal handle on top. Black metal latches either side of the handle.

It looked like a lunch box. It was locked.

Katherine sat with her feet on the kitchen table, her toes tapping the air in time to the music blasting from her stereo. The Police, "Don't Stand So Close to Me." Teenage lust for cute teacher. Been there, done that, more than once; she laughed. She spooned the last of the strawberry yogurt from the bottom of the plastic cup. So yummy. She could polish off the other three in the fridge easy as pie. Pie, yes, with gobs of vanilla ice cream.

"Get a grip, girl. Dope in the morning, good. Postgasm munchies, bad."

She tossed the plastic cup across the kitchen. It bounced off the wall and landed in the trash can.

"Two points. Look out, world, I'm hot today." She dropped her feet from the table, pulled the towel from her head, ran her fingers through her wet hair, looking for split ends. Not a one. "And I feel a good hair day coming on."

She mixed a Perrier and OJ and danced her way into the sitting room. She made a slow pirouette and sprawled on the sofa. It was going to be a lazy day. Nothing to do but relax before tonight's command performance with Monsieur Wonderfully Rich. Two hundred and thirty thousand Swiss for one night, give or take a franc or two. The goofiness of life rolled on. She sorted through a stack of mags on the coffee table, picked up *Vanity Fair*. Hunky Brit actor on the cover. He looked yummy as strawberry yogurt.

"Hello, hotshot."

She thumbed through a worthy story of human suffering in some African country and got to the fresh meat. Hunky Brit actor, thirty-two years old, three smash-hit movies under his belt with number four about to be released. Money coming out of his ears, desired by every woman on the planet, but woe is he. He's miserable, he's lonely. His life wasn't his own anymore, nobody understands him. He's still single but wants to find the right girl and have a family. Feels like a late bloomer when it comes to romance.

"Gay, I knew it."

She glanced out of the glass doors to the terrace. The two black crows were back at the terrace railing, watching her again.

"Hello there, fellas, want another show? Or did you bring me a message from my gallant protector in the bell tower?"

The crows fluttered their wings.

"You may tell him his fair maiden slept very well last night and she's having a great hair day. And tell him if he looks anything like this guy on the cover and he likes it straight, he should come over and see me sometime. No charge. I'm feeling way generous today."

The crows hopped from the railings, flew along Pont Bessières toward the cathedral. Katherine tossed the magazine on the coffee table and lay down for a long nap. Big night tonight. Must be beautiful, must be relaxed. Must fuck Mr. Wonderfully Rich blind and give him his money's worth.

Rochat was out of breath coming into the loge. He tossed his sketchbook and pencils on the bed, set the lunch box on the table. He paced back and forth, looking at it.

"Should I tell Monsieur Taroni? No, he's very busy with the workmen at the Apostles' porch. I'll call *le directeur* and ask him if I should put it in the lost-and-found box, that's what I'll do."

He reached for the old telephone on the wall and dialed the numbers wheel. He waited six rings before he heard *le directeur*'s voice say the rest of him was at his chalet in Les Avants till next week. Rochat sat at the table and studied the lunch box carefully. He tapped the lid, pressed his ear to the metal. He heard crows caw from the sky and the timbers creak and groan and Marie-Madeleine ring eleven times, but nothing from the silver box.

"Call Monsieur Buhlmann, Rochat. He'll know what to do."

He dialed the numbers wheel again and counted two rings before a voice picked up.

"Hello?"

"*Bonjour*, Madame Buhlmann, this is Marc Rochat."

"Who?"

"Marc Rochat, from the cathedral."

"Oh, hello, Marc. How are you?"

"I'm fine, madame."

"That's nice. Well, thank you for calling. Good-bye, Marc."

"*Attendez, madame, s'il vous plaît.* Is Monsieur Buhlmann at home?"

"Who?"

"Your husband."

"Oh, him. Of course he's home. He was drinking last night and can barely move. We're to leave for my sister's house in Unterwald today. I'll get him."

Rochat counted to fifteen waiting for Monsieur Buhlmann.

"*Salut*, Marc. The old girl finally fall down?"

"*Pardon?*"

"The cathedral, is she still standing?"

"*Oui, monsieur.* But I found something in the crypt, in the well."

"In the well?"

"A box. A silver box with a handle."

"A what?"

"A box, like a lunch box."

"A lunch box?"

"*Oui.* I don't know what to do with it."

"Is it ticking?"

"Is what ticking?"

"Is the lunch box ticking?"

"*Non*, I tapped it and listened. It's very quiet, monsieur."

Rochat heard Monsieur Buhlmann chuckle down the line.

"A quiet lunch box, the best kind. Put it someplace safe. I'll take care of it when I come to the tower next Sunday."

"I'm sorry to disturb you. Have a good trip to Unterwald."

"*Merde*, don't remind me. My wife's sister and husband are teetotalers. I must go two days without a drink, terrible. Don't forget our Christmas lunch. Emeline is anxious to meet you."

"Who?"

"The daughter of my Swiss hillbilly friend. I told you about her, from the farm expo."

Rochat thought about it. "She won a blue ribbon because she knows how to milk a cow."

"The very one. Come to the tower on Sunday evening if you like, we can talk about her. And we'll burn another witch at the stake."

*"Monsieur?"*

"We'll cook raclette on the grill, next to Clémence."

"And we can give back the lunch box, too."

"Marc, listen to me. You know how you are when you imagine things, *mon cher.*"

"But I'm very sure this is a real thing, monsieur."

*"Écoute, mon cher.* I want you to listen to me. You put that lunch box back in the well where you found it. And I want you to forget about it. Will you do that, Marc?"

"I'm very good at forgetting things, monsieur."

"I know; just put it back and don't even think about it. *À bientôt, Marc.*"

*"Bonne journée, monsieur."*

Rochat hung up the phone.

"Just forget about it, Rochat, don't even think about it."

He took the plastic basin from under the bed, poured in cold water from one of the Chianti jugs, and splashed the water on his face. He made a cup of tea and sat at the table again. He stared at the lunch box.

"But as you haven't put it back yet, you could think about it a little more."

He looked under the handle. Three tiny dials with tiny numbers. Like the numbers wheel on the old telephone in the loge.

"If you don't know the numbers to dial on the numbers wheel, then you must look them up in a telephone book."

He shuffled to the bed, tore a blank page from his sketchbook, and grabbed his pencils. He sat at the table and set the lantern on the page, using the base as a ruler to draw ten vertical lines across the page. He inspected the columns to make sure they were nice and even.

"Very good, Rochat."

Then he began to write zero numbers.

000

001

002

003

All the way to 099 at the bottom of the page, writing the numbers as tiny as the numbers on the dial. Then back to the top of the next column for the one numbers.

101

102

103

He wrote slowly and carefully, filling the columns of the page, till he reached the last of the nine numbers.

997

998

999

"It must be one of the numbers on this page."

He heard the timbers groan as Marie shook the tower twelve times in her most matronly tone: "No, no, no . . . !" When the great bell finished making her opinion known, Rochat pulled open the window on the east wall and poked out his head.

"*Excusez-moi, madame,* but I am in no mood to be corrected by a bell. The lunch box is a real thing, madame, not an imagination, I know it is. I can attend to it myself and not trouble Monsieur Buhlmann. He's an old man and needs his rest, and he'll be very proud of the telephone book I wrote."

He switched his head for the page of numbers, let her have a good look. He pulled back the page, poked out his head again.

"See? You can read every number very clearly. You go have a snooze, I have important work."

He slapped the window closed and sat at the table. He set the page of numbers next to the lunch box and, very carefully, he turned the tiny numbers of each of the three dials to zero. He checked the latches: locked. He took his pencil and drew a line through 000. He turned the dials to 001, locked, line through that number; 002, locked . . .

At the end of the zero numbers he took a sip of tea and started with the one numbers: 100, locked, line; 101, locked, line . . .

By the time he reached 899, he was losing hope. He didn't like the thought of having to admit to Marie-Madeleine she was right after all. Nothing worse than a gloating old bell. He checked over the page of numbers.

"You've tried all those, unless you missed one and thought you didn't and crossed it out anyway. But the only way you'd know is to start over again after you finish the nine numbers. Such silly jumping-around things numbers can be."

He turned the dials: 901, 902 . . . 956, 957 . . . 997, 998 . . . *click.*

He thought he imagined the sound. He put his ear to the lunch box, listened carefully. Nothing. He sat up straight and scratched his head. He touched the latches; they snapped open. He raised the lid and looked inside.

He didn't know what to do next.

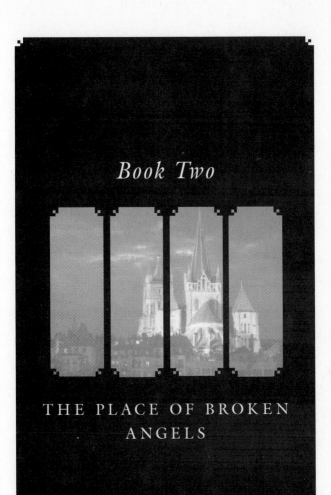

*Book Two*

THE PLACE OF BROKEN
ANGELS

# twelve

The taxi crossed over Pont Bessières and turned at Rue Curtat. Lausanne Cathedral was at the top of the road, but a truck blocked the drive. Harper paid the fare and climbed out. He lit a cigarette, looked through the windows of Café de l'Évêché. College types jagged on espresso, old men reading newspapers, cheap beer on tap. Nice place. He thought about a liquid lunch. He headed up the hill instead.

With the old city at its feet, the cathedral seemed to fill the sky with Gothic dominion. But stepping onto the esplanade, Harper thought it looked as plain as Yuriev's cardboard toy, only bigger. He walked along the chain-link fence wrapped around the south wall. Inside, tarpaulin covered scaffolds sixty meters high. And there were drawings and photographs explaining the obvious: It's old, it'll fall down if we don't fix it. The clatter of drills and hammers added to the urgency of the argument. As did the sight of a needlelike steeple, dangling from a crane and being lowered to the ground near the belfry tower. Harper stood at the skinny red door set in the base of the tower. He leaned back, looked up. Bloody long way up, it was. Chunks of stone fallen away, ratty wooden plank nailed over one window. Whole place looked wobbly as hell. A huff and a puff and it just might blow down.

Harper scanned the esplanade. Small park of bare chestnut trees near an embankment wall. An elderly Swiss woman on one bench, her sharp eyes locked on the teenagers on the next. The girl straddled across the boy's lap, mouths and tongues busy as birds and bees.

Twelve loud gongs tolled from the belfry, loud enough to break the young lovers' liplock. They lit smokes, tossed on their backpacks, and left. Left the elderly lady with nothing to watch but the view. But it was a good view. Red-tiled rooftops of the old city, ever-present lake, heavy gray clouds coming in from the northwest. And somewhere out there, one half-mad Russian gone walk-about. A walkabout that had come this way. So said Inspector Gobet when Harper asked him how many gift shops sold the maquette of Lausanne Cathedral, like the one Yuriev left at Hôtel Port Royal.

"Mr. Harper, in all of Lausanne, in all of Switzerland, there is only one such place."

"Let me guess. Lausanne Cathedral."

"Very good, Mr. Harper. And may I say, as a working detective, there may be hope for you yet."

Harper shrugged and dropped his smoke on the cobblestones, headed toward the cathedral.

*"S'il vous plaît, monsieur."*

Harper looked back. The little old lady was pointing to his still-smoldering cigarette. He picked it up, tossed it in a bin.

"*Pardonnez-moi, madame.*"

"*Bonne journée, monsieur.*"

He walked to the cathedral doors, gave the façade a quick glance. Everything about the place said "Remember, man, that thou art dust." He grabbed an iron latch, pulled open the heavy wooden door, looked inside. Oval-shaped vestibule with a high stone arch facing him. Purple curtain hanging in the arch, billowing in the draft. He stepped in, the door closed behind him with a creak and a thud, the curtain settled. Dark, but for the splatters of colored light seeping through stained glass. Dead quiet. No jackhammers, no drills. He felt the hairs at the back of his neck stand up, sensing he wasn't alone. His eyes rose to the apex of the arch, to a woman's form carved in stone and enthroned under a sky of faded stars painted on the stone ceiling. The woman's head and hands had been sawed off. Long ago, from the look of it. Stub of her neck suggested she was looking at him anyway, articulation of her arms suggested she'd been holding a child at her breast.

"Headless Mary, Mother of God. Rather creepy for a church."

Headless Mary wasn't alone. At the sides of the arch, along the walls, more statues eyeballed him. They had heads, most of them. Above was the wedding to Joseph the Carpenter, patron saint of understanding husbands.

Harper pulled aside the curtain. A sudden rush of vertigo, like falling off the earth into an unbound space stretching and rising to the cloudlike vault high above. His brain flashed back to *Great Cathedrals of the World* on the History Channel. Cathedrals were built to create the illusion of entering the kingdom of heaven. Harper looked to the ground, tapped his earthbound shoes on the flagstones.

"Right, so this would be the narthex." He lifted his eyes to the make-believe kingdom of heaven. "And that out there would be the nave."

He walked ahead. Above the curtained arch, long brass horns and sky-high pipes protruded into the nave, with a huge organ console set amid them. The whole whacking thing looked as if it were floating in air. Wind sound in the dead quiet. He thought it might be air circulating through the pipes, but it was coming from two iron grates set in the flagstones. He stepped closer, looking down one grate into a lightless dark. Warm air rising and smelling of dusty earth.

In a corner to the left, tall iron gates trimmed with gold crosses and topped with thornlike points. Dim light from within cast long shadows over the flagstones. He followed the shadows to the gates. Inside, a room of elaborately carved wooden stalls around a plain wooden table. Black iron chandelier hanging from the ceiling, wax candles burning halfway bright. Looked like the court of the final judgment, with the heavenly host just popping down to Café de l'Évêché for a pint before condemning the next lot of sinners to hell. Outside the gates, a green slate propped on a rickety easel, a small sign on the wall:

## Chapelle de Saint-Maurice
### Visiteurs, inscrivez ici vos intentions de prière.

Yellow paper squares posted on the slate. Handwritten notes in all kinds of script, all kinds of languages. French, Italian, German, Japanese, three in English: "We wait for the light." "Why am I in this place?" "For blessed comfort from fearful memories."

Box of pencils and a pad of yellow squares in the easel tray. Write your prayer, stick to the board. Harper tried to figure the odds on answered prayers. Million to one? A billion to one?

He stepped away, working out the layout of the cathedral. Chancels and altars always to the liturgical east, according to the History Channel. He'd recce up the north aisle, circle the ambulatory behind the chancel, come back down the south aisle. Not knowing what the hell he was looking for. Only knowing Yuriev was here, then he vanished.

Harper walked slowly, still thrown by the architectural illusion of unbound space. Wide stone columns every four paces forming seven huge arches either side of the nave. The columns then rising higher and branching into evenly spaced rows to form another level of smaller arches. The pillars looking like a forest of petrified trees, the carved capitals atop the pillars like unmoving leaves. Two levels of balconies set in the upper arches running the length of the nave. Just below the vault, another row of arches framing windows of leaded glass that filled the nave with gray light.

He stopped. Same feeling as before, that he wasn't alone. He looked back, then up to the balconies, along the pillars. Nobody.

"Huh."

Down on the floor, thousands of wooden chairs in well-ordered rows. Knock one over and they'd tumble one after the other for an hour. Make one hell of a racket, flush out anyone hiding in the shadows. Harper laughed to himself, shook it off.

Three-quarters of the way up the north aisle, the walls of the nave opened to the left and right where all cathedrals took the shape of a crucifix. What the hell was it? The transcross—no, transept, he remembered. Center of the transept, three steps rose to the crossing square. Directly above the square, the vault of the nave gave way to a towering space that reached for the heavens, but, failing, fell back to form eight ribbed vaults and eight arches. Milk-colored glass in the arches bled with dull white light, bringing out faded colors in the stone.

"Lantern tower, that would be the lantern tower." Harper dug his hands in his coat, pleased he could remember so much from watching the History Channel while pissed. "Little more effort, you'll remember your bloody phone number. And won't the inspector be proud?"

From the crossing square, three steps rose again to the chancel, enclosed by a wide crescent of pillars and arches all supporting a massive dome as high as the cloudlike vault of the nave. Center of the chancel was a simple stone altar holding a wrought-iron cross. A candlestand nearby with a solitary votive candle burning in the gray light. Harper stared at the fire, thinking it looked as hapless as the billion-to-one prayer lottery at the back of the cathedral.

Other side of the transept, in the south wall, a huge stained glass. Rounded, but shaped like a massive cross. Looked dull as soap from this side of the cathedral. He walked ahead. Four steps led down to the ambulatory curving around the back of the chancel. At the bottom of the steps and set even lower in a stone wall, there was a black iron gate. Looked rusting at the edges and appeared to lead somewhere under the altar. Above the gate, a marble sarcophagus set between two pillars, some long-dead chap dressed to the nines in a suit of medieval armor. Must be the entrance to the crypt, Harper thought, where the princes of God and Mammon would be buried. But from what he remembered from the telly, the gates of a cathedral crypt should be a rather grand affair. These looked fit for a broom closet. He pushed against the gate: locked. He bent down, looked through the bars into darkness.

"You in there, Yuriev?"

Nothing but another blast of warm air and dust-smelling earth. Harper reached in his coat, found the miniflashlight attached to his keys. He switched it on, pointed it through the iron bars. Dust swirled in the narrow beam of light. Then an earthen floor, a shallow pit, two skeletons lying in the dirt.

"Christ, come to Lausanne Cathedral, see our headless virgins in the rafters and our skeletons in the broom closet."

He switched off the light, stuffed the keys in his coat. The stained-glass windows in the curving passageway pulling him along. Jesus prays, Jesus suffers, Jesus dies. The weeping women of Jerusalem at the foot of the cross. Women in black robes and veils begging for mercy, clawing at their faces, watching their loved one die.

He stepped up to the south transept. A small chapel to the left. A stone carving of Mother Mary tucked in an alcove, this time with her head on her shoulders and the child Jesus in her arms. He walked on till the ground wobbled and a deep rumble echoed through the nave like faraway thunder. He looked down. A loose block of stone underfoot. He rocked it: *boom, baboom.*

Flecks of color sparkled on the stone, a band of white light crossing his shoes and racing over the flagstones. Harper looked up as the midday sun crawled across the huge stained glass in the south transept wall. Circles and squares, diamonds and crescents, all carved in a giant wheel of stone, all filled with bits of brilliantly colored glass. What was as dull as soap from the other side of the transept was now shining bright. The light sparkling and washing through the gray light of the nave, forming into a tubular shaft of color. Warm as it was bright, growing stronger, almost blinding his eyes.

He stepped back for a better view, squinting to see the bearded Almighty at the diamond-shaped center of the window, busily separating form from nothing, dark from light, earth from the seas, drawing Eve from Adam's ribs. Four panels of leaded glass, set like the cardinal points of a compass, surrounding the Almighty. Each section representing one of the seasons: autumn, summer, spring, winter. Didn't look right till he realized the seasons were set counterclockwise, like time running backward. Smaller windows grouped around each of the seasons. Images of human beings at their toil throughout the year. Pruning vines in March, tending fields in June. Slaughtering animals in November, sharing a glass of wine with a skeleton in December.

"Swell, more skeletons."

Next ring held the four elements—earth, wind, fire, water—all set amid the signs of the zodiac. Then chariots pulling the sun and moon across the sky, satyrs and deformed man-beasts playing amid the four winds. And an outer ring of demigods pouring water from vases. Latin script naming the waters: Gihon, Pishon, Tigris, Euphrates. The four Rivers of Paradise, Harper thought. And as he tried to remember where the hell he remembered that one from, he felt it again. He wasn't alone.

He looked back over his shoulder, saw a scraggly tramp standing just where the shaft of colored light hit the flagstones, dead center of the crossing square. The tramp's watery eyes wide open, looking up toward the stained glass. Arms stretched from his sides, palms turned to the light.

Some wino come in from the cold to warm up in the Gothic solarium maybe. And for a moment, Harper considered asking the tramp about the significance of the window he, too, was so busy staring at. But the more he looked at the blank expression on the man's face, the more Harper knew it'd be a waste of time. Then, the shuffle of feet and creaking of wooden chairs. Harper's eyes swept the nave. Here and there, men and women, walking up the main aisle or sitting in chairs. Everyone staring at the tramp by the altar, eyes gaga with wonder.

"Like a bloody haunted house, this place."

He quickly marched down the south aisle. Sealed wooden doors in the wall midway down. Crowbars and tools stacked on the floor, drawings and photographs on the doors explaining the repairs of the Apostles' porch beyond. End of the aisle, a glass door leading to a brightly lit room. Everything about it said *gift shop*. He saw a small round woman in a nun's habit standing behind a counter. Smiling, waiting. He pushed open the door.

*"Bonjour. Je m'appelle Sœur Fabienne. Parlez-vous anglais?"*

"Yes, I do, as a matter of fact; good guess."

"Oh, you don't look like a local, and we have so few tourists this time of year. Are you from London?"

"Yes, I am."

"How nice."

Harper nodded out of the door, toward the nave. "Sister, are you aware there's a tramp standing on the crossing square, near the altar?"

"Oh, yes. He comes to watch the sunlight pass through the rose window."

"The what?"

"The stained-glass window. All cathedrals have one great stained-glass window. They're called—"

"—the Cathedral Rose. I remember it, from the telly."

"You do? How nice. I saw you looking at it, too."

"Yes, I was. A bit unusual, the window."

"I suppose it seems so in today's world. But things were much different when the world was flat."

"Sorry?"

"When the world was flat. When people thought the earth was the center of the universe. Now they think the earth revolves around the sun and is no more than a tiny dot in the universe. My, how times change. Imagine what they will think one hundred years from now. I've been here a long time, you know. I come from Languedoc. What was I saying? Oh yes, the rose window is a cosmology, the sum of man's knowledge at the time the cathedral was built."

"Cosmology, right."

"I noticed you at the gates of the crypt."

"Yes, I saw a few skeletons just inside."

"Why, yes. There's an ancient cemetery under the cathedral, under the entire floor, in fact."

Harper looked out through the glass door. *Big bloody floor*, he thought. "That's a lot of skeletons."

"The cathedral was built on one of the first Paleolithic settlements in the world. They were the first to bury their dead, you know. Oh, dear, were the gates left open?"

"No, Sister, they were locked. But I confess, I peeked in with a miniflashlight."

"Oh, I have one of those, too. I like to say 'Let there be light' before switching it on. Of course, if I did that when the world was flat, I would've been burned at the stake for witchcraft. How times change. I'm sorry, what

were you saying? Oh yes, the skeletons. We have thousands."

Harper stared at the little old nun, wide-eyed grin on
her face as if she were waiting for him to say the magic
word and win a prize.

"Right."

"Say, would you care to visit the belfry? Through that
door and up one hundred and seventy-eight steps. Or
two hundred and twenty-four, depending on how you
count. It might help you see where you are."

Harper smiled, remembering the young lad on Pont
Bessières, telling him the same damn thing nearly. *Walk
that way, monsieur. Great view, find your fucking way.*
Something else flashed in Harper's brain.

"Actually, the other night, I thought I saw someone
up there, someone with a lantern."

"Oh yes, *le guet*. He calls the hour and spends the
night watching over Lausanne."

"*Le guet*. That's a French military term."

"Why, yes, it is. Are you a linguist by profession?"

"No, just something I heard somewhere."

"No one uses the term anymore, just this place. No
one here knows why anymore. We have a very nice young
man from Quebec in the belfry these days. He has a
small room between the lower bells, very snug and warm.
You could have a peek through his window, you just need
to squeeze past Marie-Madeleine. She's the largest bell in
the tower and rings the hour. Would you like to go up?
It's only two francs, and the air is very fresh."

Harper felt his stomach reel. "No, thanks, Sister. I'm not a fan of heights, unless required."

"Oh, too bad. You know, I enjoy the church bells in London, too. Especially the bells of Saint Clement Danes. They were destroyed in the Blitz, you know. Why, of course you know. What was that old rhyme? Let's see: 'Oranges and lemons, Say the bells of Saint Clement's . . .' What's the rest of it?"

"I don't know it."

"No? That's too bad."

Harper thought he saw a look of severe disappointment cross the old nun's face. He pointed to the assembled cardboard cathedral on the shelf behind her.

"Actually, Sister, I stopped by for one of those."

"One of what, monsieur?"

"That cardboard . . . the maquette of the cathedral."

"I'm so happy you asked. I was so afraid I would have to . . . oh, such a relief."

Harper watched the goofy smile on the nun's face as she walked to a large cabinet and opened the doors. Filled to overflowing with cardboard cathedrals. She tugged at one till it slid out and laid it on the counter.

"Fifteen francs, monsieur."

Harper dug through his pockets for coins. "Tell me, do you sell many of these, Sister?"

"Oh, yes. People come from all over the world to buy them. Sometimes people send us photos after they've made their cathedral. It's very nice. Little Lausanne Cathedrals all over the world. We once received a photograph from Mongolia. A family in a yurt, all sitting around one of our little cathedrals."

"Really? There was a Russian chap who came by last week and bought one as a Christmas present. You might remember him."

"No, I don't think I do. But I'm only here for midday meditations. Madame Buhlmann runs the shop. You could ask her, but she tends to be forgetful. She gets confused about the days and thinks Tuesday is Sunday and so forth. Excuse me for asking, did you leave a prayer at la Chapelle de Saint-Maurice?"

"No, I didn't."

"I began a collection, you know. The prayers, I mean. Would you like to see?" She had a thick photo album out from under the counter before Harper could say no. "I began collecting them when I first came to the cathedral. I used old scraps of parchment then. The world has changed so much. They use Post-it notes now. You know, with the sticky backs?" She slowly turned the laminated pages. Yellow squares, expertly placed on each page. "We have so many books now, one for each year. And it's nearly time to begin another. All the languages of the world, you see."

"That's very nice, Sister. But if I were you, I'd ask the Post-it notes people for a commission."

"Oh, wouldn't that be nice? By the way, it's 'You owe me five farthings, Say the bells of Saint Martin's.' The answer to 'Oranges and lemons,' I mean."

"'Oranges and lemons,' right. Well, I must say, it's been very interesting speaking to you, Sœur Fabienne."

"Don't forget your maquette, monsieur."

Harper picked it up from the counter. "No, wouldn't want to do that. Good-bye, Sister."

He left the shop, feeling the sudden urge for liquid reality at Café de l'Évêché. He walked toward the narthex, shot a glance at the transept. The tramp still at the crossing square, watching the magic sunbeam coming through the Cathedral Rose. A few more gaga spectators had come to watch along with him. The History Channel really needed to include Lausanne in a *Weird Cathedrals of the World* segment. Half cathedral, half haunted house, half loony bin. Three halves in the whole, that weird. He pushed through the curtains—stopped. *All the languages of the bloody world.*

He walked back into the gift shop. Sœur Fabienne and her book of prayers were still waiting at the counter.

"Sister, could I take another look at that book of yours?"

"Of course."

Harper opened the book to the last page. Blank. Back two more pages. There, between English and German, tiny Cyrillic letters crammed on a Post-it note.

"Did you find something that speaks to you, monsieur?"

Harper looked at the little old nun. "Sorry?"

"I said, did you find something that speaks to you?"

"Could you tell me when this prayer was posted at the chapel?"

"Let me see, there should be a date on the page. Why, yes, last week."

Harper remembered Yuriev's voice. End-of-the-road desperate, maybe enough to take a billion-to-one shot on unanswered prayers.

"Would it be possible to have this page copied?"

"For guidance, monsieur?"

"For guidance, right."

"Well, in that case, I'll pop into the cathedral offices next door. They're out to lunch till two o'clock. They have a photocopy machine, I'm sure they won't mind my using it. Now, there's something that certainly would have had me burned at the stake. When the world was flat, I mean."

# thirteen

Rochat heard the doorbell and knew it was Monsieur Gübeli with his briefcase full of papers to sign. He'd forgotten the appointment till he returned to his flat and saw it noted in green ink on the Wednesday page of his daybook. Green ink was for Monsieur Gübeli things. He had barely enough time to feed Monsieur Booty, take his own lunch from the icebox for heating in the oven, then bathe and dress in clean clothes. He'd just settled down to eat when Monsieur Gübeli rang the bell. Rochat let him in, took his coat, and led him to the kitchen.

"But Marc, you're having your supper."

"It was my lunch, monsieur, but I was very late getting home today. So now it's my supper. Would you care to join me? It's tuna-noodle casserole. Maman invented it before she died. And Teresa made a salad, too."

Monsieur Gübeli set his briefcase on the floor and sat down. "In that case, I'd be honored to dine with you."

Rochat set a plate, knife, and fork before his guest. He almost sat down before remembering a napkin.

"I don't have wine, monsieur. Would you like Rivella? I have blue and red."

"Water's fine, Marc, from the tap."

Rochat filled two glasses, set them on the table. He cut a large serving from the casserole, careful to keep the crispy cracker bits on top, the way he liked it himself.

*"Bon appétit."*

*"Bon appétit, Marc."*

Rochat sat down. Monsieur Gübeli took his knife and fork and tasted a small bite . . .

"Marc?"

Rochat turned to the old lady at the table. *"Oui, Grand-maman?"*

"Boys who hide food in their trouser pockets should not expect sweets."

"But it tastes bad."

Madame Rochat dropped her fork on her plate. She took her magnifying glass and inspected the grilled calf's liver and onions on her plate.

"Marc, you are untempered, but correct. I have no idea why I eat it. Other than my grand-maman ordered me to do so. No doubt her grand-maman told her the same rubbish."

The old lady picked up a silver bell, gave it a fierce ring. The butler presented himself.

"You rang, madame?"

"Bernard, take this away and instruct the chef to strike it from the menu forever."

*"Oui, madame."*

"Advise him, in no uncertain terms, he may seek employment elsewhere if he objects."

*"Oui, madame."*

"You may bring dessert."

*"D'accord, madame."* The butler bowed, turned for the kitchen.

*"Attendez, Bernard.* I believe Master Rochat must empty his pocket."

Rochat pulled his napkin from his pocket, stained with bits of half-chewed calf's liver. The butler collected it by his gloved fingertips.

"And please, do not allow the chef to see it, Bernard. I don't wish him slashing his wrists at my table in grief."

*"D'accord, madame."*

"Marc?"

Rochat turned his eyes from his grand-maman to Monsieur Gübeli. *"Pardon?"*

"I was saying this is excellent. Very tasty."

Rochat looked at Monsieur Gübeli's napkin. It was folded neatly beside his plate.

"You liked it?"

"Very much. And your mother invented it, you say?"

"We had it every Tuesday for lunch. I can tell you the recipe, I don't think she'd mind. You need one can of tuna fish, some curly-kind pasta, some cream of mushroom soup, and some saltine crackers to crumble and bake on top. I told Teresa the recipe and she makes it for me every Monday for my Tuesday lunch."

They sat without speaking, listening to the sound of

the funicular train making its way up and down the hill to Lausanne.

"It's always refreshing to visit you, Marc. It was the same with your father."

"Really?"

"Indeed it was. I'd come to his studio in Cossonay with business in mind and would end up sitting in silence for hours as he drew."

"I remember. Houses and buildings and things."

"And all by freehand, not a single ruler or drawing compass. He had an exceptional hand. His drawings for the renovation of Lausanne Cathedral were works of art. The originals are hanging in the Lausanne Museum."

"I go visit them sometimes. I can imagine Papa drawing them."

"I remember arriving many times at his studio to find you on his lap as he was working on them. Often with his hand over yours, teaching you to draw."

"I thought he was teaching me magic."

"I suppose he was, in a way. You're a lucky young man, Marc. Your father gave you the gift of art and your mother gave you the gift of life, as well as her wonderful recipe for *casserole de thon*. Now, before we lose all the time in the day, I'm afraid we have our own business to attend to."

Rochat cleared the table, placing the dishes in the washing dishes machine, the way Teresa showed him. Then he took a dish towel and slapped crumbs from the table, the way Monsieur Dufaux did at Café du Grütli. Monsieur Gübeli took his briefcase from the floor and opened it, removing a stack of papers and cleaning his spectacles with a little cloth.

"We're coming to the end of the calendar year, Marc, and I wish to make several adjustments to the cash side of your investment portfolio. The dollar will fall significantly next year, leaving us with an excellent opportunity to profit in euros. After which we will convert to—"

"*S'il vous plaît, monsieur.* Can I ask you something?"

"Certainly."

Rochat sat a minute, organizing the words in his head like arranging plates in the washing dishes machine.

"Is it true?"

"Is what true?"

"The reason I was brought to Lausanne?"

"I don't understand, Marc."

"Last night, I imagined Monsieur Rannou at the cathedral. He was playing the organ, like when he was alive. He reminded me Maman told me there was a reason I was brought to Lausanne."

Monsieur Gübeli stopped cleaning his spectacles and laid them on the table. "Are you having lots of imaginations, Marc?"

Rochat nodded his head.

"Did you imagine someone just now, while we were eating?"

Rochat nodded again.

"Whom?"

"Grand-maman, at her house."

"Did she say anything to you about your mother or why you were brought to Lausanne?"

"*Non*, she was asking Bernard the butler for dessert."

"Can you remember what else Monsieur Rannou told you, Marc?"

"He said Lausanne was full of lost angels and . . ."

"It's all right. Take a moment and think carefully, Marc. Did Monsieur Rannou say anything else to you?"

Rochat tapped his fingers on the table, thinking about it. At the same time, Monsieur Booty appeared from wherever he was hiding and sat in the doorway, wondering if the tapping was an invitation to more food. Realizing it wasn't, the beast rolled in a furry ball and went to sleep.

"He said an angel will come to the cathedral and I needed to help the angel because they were only made of light. And he said that without me, all the angels would be lost forever."

Monsieur Gübeli pushed the paperwork aside.

"Marc, why don't we have a cup of tea?"

Harper sat in Café de l'Évêché with his second pint. He drank through number one reading the instructions on assembling a cardboard cathedral: *Construction of the Apostles' porch (piece no: 111) requires gentle fingering. And don't forget to fold the perforated edges to reinforce the turrets. The four half-buttresses must be placed respectively, in twos, behind the Apostles' porch.*

Pint number two was spent thinking about his tour of the cathedral, the loopy nun's prayer collection, one prayer in Russian. Long shot at best, but the doctor wanted to be kept informed. He dug his mobile from his coat and dialed. Miss Barraud picked up.

"How may I be of assistance, Mr. Harper?"

"I'd like to speak to the doctor."

Miss Barraud adopted her most officious tone, telling him the doctor was in London and would be back Thursday, and reminding him that he had a meeting scheduled with the doctor that day at ten. Please be prompt. Unless, of course, this was an emergency. Instructions were left to have you put through in the event of an emergency. Is this an emergency, Mr. Harper?

Harper stared at the Russian script on the Post-it note. Lots of well-formed flourishes and swirls, looking like some prayerful drivel written by a woman more than a drunk on the run.

"No, it'll wait for now. Thursday at ten, then. And could you arrange for a Russian speaker at the meeting?"

"I am the doctor's executive secretary, Mr. Harper. Translators are requested through the administrator of personnel."

She hung up. Harper closed his mobile.

An attractive young woman stood over him with a tray of drinks in her hands, her cardigan unbuttoned at the midriff. He was eye level with the ruby-colored stone dangling from her belly button. The stone came closer as the young woman leaned over the table, reading the wrapper of the maquette.

"You have visited the cathedral, monsieur?"

"I have."

"You will be here for New Year's Eve? The locals will burn it down."

"Sorry?"

She laughed with perfectly formed white teeth. "It is only a play. They put red lights among the bells and use fans to blow long streams of red cloth from the belfry. It looks very real. Everyone drinks champagne on the esplanade and waits for the midnight bells. It commemorates the time, centuries ago, when the cathedral was nearly destroyed by fire."

"Well, three cheers for the fire brigade."

"*Non*, it was a miracle. A heavy snow fell and put out the fire."

"Three cheers for miracles, then." Harper took a swallow of beer, nodded out the window toward the cathedral. "And judging from the looks of the place these days, it could use a few more. Looks to be crumbling at the edges."

The waitress laughed again; the ruby hanging from her belly button bounced. "So you will make the maquette yourself, monsieur?"

"I'm told it isn't too complicated. Sort it out with a bottle of decent Swiss red."

"I made mine in school when I was ten years old, with a glass of milk." She turned and left with her tray of drinks, stopping at different tables to make deliveries. Harper felt a bit of crumbling at the edges himself. Right, cathedral. Next step: *As you can see, the base of the tower is placed across the nave and the transept . . .*

Too much bloody effort. Give the damn thing away

for Christmas. He ran through the possibilities. So far it was a list of one. Blondie of the diamond-studded ciga-rette case.

He removed a calling card from his wallet, slipped it inside the maquette. The cardboard toy was somewhat below her price range, but what the hell? He drank his beer, watched the waitress walk through the room some more. Switzerland, land of perfectly formed white teeth, bouncing belly-button rings, and sad sods trying to re-member what it was like to be ten years younger.

He drank down the beer, signaled for another.

They waited for the tea to brew in the pot.

Monsieur Booty uncurled from his furry ball shape on the floor and jumped into Rochat's lap. Rochat scratched the beast behind the ears. He closed his eyes and opened his jaws with a wide yawn. Rochat slipped his finger into the beast's gaping mouth. The fat cat always fell for the same trick: close eyes, yawn, close jaws on finger, always opening his eyes with an expression of com-plete surprise. Monsieur Gübeli smiled.

"Such a curious animal, Marc."

"He likes to pretend he forgets things, but he's only teasing. He knows he's smarter than me."

"Smarter than you?"

"From the accident when I was born."

"You had a difficult birth with many complications. We feared for your very life. But you survived, and you've grown into a fine young man."

Rochat poured the tea, remembering Monsieur Gü-beli liked his with milk and two lumps of sugar.

"Marc, do you recall when you were a boy at Mon Repos School, you often had bad dreams and night-mares?"

Mon Repos School for Special Children. In the woods outside Lausanne. A big red-brick house. Children like him from all around the world.

"I remember."

"You said you saw bad shadows, bad shadows your mother told you about."

"And sometimes, I imagined the bad shadows were killing her, and I was too afraid to stop them. Papa came to the school some nights to tell me it was all right, that the bad shadows couldn't find me in Lausanne. And you, too, when Papa was away."

"Marc, your mother's death wasn't your fault."

"I know, the doctors said it was cancer. But I remembered she told me she had to die because she couldn't protect me anymore and I needed to hide in Lausanne."

Monsieur Gübeli took a sip of tea.

"Marc, have you seen any of these bad shadows you imagined near the cathedral?"

"Only teasing shadows, and an angel. I was very sure she was an imagination, but now I'm very sure she's real."

"An angel?"

Rochat stood and shuffled down the hall. He found the folded paper in the pocket of his overcoat and brought it to the kitchen. He gave it to Monsieur Gübeli. "This is her."

Monsieur Gübeli opened the paper. "My, she's lovely. Did you see her in the cathedral last night, with Monsieur Rannou?"

"*Non*, I saw her in a window in Lausanne and I thought she was only an imagination, too. But then I saw her at the funicular station at Gare Simplon. She talked to me."

"What did she say?"

"She asked me if I had a light for her cigarette. Then I followed her to a bar in a hotel. I think she's lost."

Monsieur Gübeli laid the drawing on the table so they both could see it.

"It's a beautiful drawing, Marc. She appears to breathe on the paper."

"Because I was inspired from the angels in Lausanne."

"Marc . . ."

"Is it true, monsieur? Is Lausanne full of lost angels? Do they need to hide in the cathedral? They need me to help them very soon. Is it true, monsieur?"

Monsieur Gübeli pulled his eyes from the drawing. Rochat was rocking back and forth in his chair, his eyes losing focus.

"Relax, Marc, breathe very slowly. Try blinking your eyes, Marc. You know it calms you."

Rochat took a long, slow breath and slowly blinked the way they taught him at Mon Repos School. He stopped rocking, turned his eyes to Monsieur Gübeli. Monsieur Gübeli touched Rochat's hand.

"I'm okay now."

"Marc, I know the doctors give you medications."

"My vitamins. They're in a big box with little boxes inside, one box for every day. I keep them by the bed so I won't forget."

"You must take them regularly."

"I do, every night before bedtime."

"I'm going to have a chat with your doctors, Marc."

"Is something wrong with me, monsieur?"

"Marc, you're very sensitive to things, but there is nothing wrong with you. Why don't I go with you to Vevey for your next doctor's appointment? I'm sure they can help us understand things."

Rochat reached for his daybook, looked for a note to himself in blue ink. Blue ink was for doctor things.

"I go on Monday at two in the afternoon. I take the slow train so I can see the fish in the lake when I come back."

"Sounds like fun. I'll collect you here and we'll travel together. Now, look at the time. You'll be on your way to the cathedral soon, so we really must do a bit of work."

Monsieur Gübeli arranged the paperwork. Rochat poured more tea and signed his name thirty-three times before Monsieur Gübeli said they were finished.

"Can I ask you something else now, monsieur?"

"Of course."

"Monsieur Buhlmann wants me to meet a girl at Christmas."

"Oh yes, I know about her. She's a very nice girl, Marc. You'll like her very much."

"Really?"

"Yes, and she's very pretty. I'm very sure you'll be

drawing her face before too long." Monsieur Gübeli looked at his watch. "Oh dear, I must catch the six fifty-five to Rolle. Swiss train conductors are notoriously unforgiving of the tardy."

Rochat dumped his fat cat from his lap and saw Monsieur Gübeli to the door.

"After we visit the doctor, we can have a lunch of *filets de perche et pommes frites* at l'Hôtel Beau Rivage. You can have a glass of wine. Papa liked to do that when he took me to Vevey."

"I look forward to it. Marc, is there anything else, anything else you can remember? Anything odd you may have imagined or experienced out of your regular routine?"

Rochat thought about it. *"Non."*

"Good, that's very good. *Bonsoir*, Marc."

*"À bientôt, monsieur."*

Monsieur Gübeli was down the elevator before Rochat remembered the thing he found in the well. He thought about racing down the stairs to catch Monsieur Gübeli to tell him. Then he remembered Monsieur Buhlmann told him to put the thing back where he found it and forget all about it. So Rochat walked back into his flat, locked the locks, and forgot all about it again.

# fourteen

"*Bonsoir, Mademoiselle Taylor. Vous êtes très elegante, ce soir.*"

"Thanks, Stephan. Big date on tap, had to put a little extra effort into the packaging. Anyone ask for me yet?"

"Not yet, mademoiselle."

Stephan led her to the table by the fireplace and helped her with her mink. She settled in the chesterfield, opened her cigarette case.

"The fire's perfect, Stephan, thanks."

He offered her a light. "Will you have an aperitif?"

"Club soda with lemon for now, Stephan. By the way, I called that girlfriend of yours. I'm dragging her out of her sculpture barn for a girlie afternoon of shopping tomorrow. I'm talking major league rampage. So, if you want to drop any hints of what you want for Christmas, now's the time."

"I shall put on my thinking cap, mademoiselle."

"Can't you call me Kat when the boss isn't around?"

"Then it would not be the Palace, mademoiselle." He winked and left for the bar.

Katherine looked around to see if there was anyone worth noticing. So far, she was the one getting noticed, every man in the room stealing glances at her much to the annoyance of their lady friends. Even the hunk sitting solo had his eyes locked on her while talking on his cell phone, probably to his wife. *Men; so fucking predictable,* she thought. He wasn't bad, though. Hepcat whiskers on his chin, beefcake tough, dressed according to *GQ.* Had that mondo-cash-in-the-pocket look. Any other night she'd have given him the look till he crawled over on his knees and begged for it. The tough ones always ended up on their knees. She took a long drag from her smoke, thinking what a naughty mood she was in. Stephan arrived with her drink.

"You seem to have captivated all eyes in the bar, Mademoiselle Taylor."

"The *Playboy* curse strikes again. Listen, Stephan, anyone wants to send over a drink, tell them thanks but no thanks."

"Of course, mademoiselle. I'll be behind the bar if you need anything."

The clock above the fireplace chimed for eight. She stared at the flames, letting the warmth of the fire add a flush to her complexion, psyching herself for tonight's performance. She felt flutters in her tummy. Amazing what a turn-on a big bag of money for one night could be. She felt someone move close to her. She took a breath, slowly raised her eyes to greet Mr. Wonderfully Rich. She saw bad news in a beat-up coat instead.

"Harper, what are you doing here?"

"Hello, Miss Taylor, expecting someone?"

"Yeah, and it isn't you."

"No worries, just dropped by to say hello."

"Harper . . ."

"I had a tour of the cathedral today."

"What?"

"The cathedral. I took a tour."

"Harper, this really isn't a good time."

A waiter slipped between them with a bucket of champagne and two glasses on a silver tray.

"*Pardon, mademoiselle.* The gentleman you are expecting has sent this ahead. He will join you shortly. May I open it?"

"Please."

Harper watched the waiter set the glasses on the table and then open the bottle with a polite burp. Bubbles fizzed as he poured, cresting perfectly at the rim of Katherine's glass. The waiter bowed and left.

"Looks like the good stuff."

"I'm sure it is. Be a nice guy, Harper and . . . What's that under your arm?"

"Ah, almost forgot. For you."

He held out the large brown envelope. Katherine turned up her nose.

"What the hell is it?"

"It's a cardboard cutout of your favorite cathedral. It's called a maquette in Frog. I took a tour of the cathedral today, picked one up."

"Are you drunk?"

"Blocked. But I've ordered a club sandwich and chips to soak it up."

Katherine took the maquette. "Thanks. Now, good-bye."

"Quasimodo has a room in the belfry."

"Who?"

"Your lantern-swinging friend at the cathedral. He's got a room, top of the tower. Thought we could walk over one evening while he's doing his thing. Give him a shout, see if he'll have us up for a drink."

"Promise you'll go away?"

"Tomorrow night, same time, here?"

"Okay, good-bye."

Harper headed to the bar, picked up his drink, and disappeared around the corner. Katherine dumped the maquette behind her chair, took a quick breath. Fuck, wouldn't that have been fun? *Oh, yes, Mr. Fabulously Wealthy, this is some drunken slob acquaintance of mine.* End of perfect evening.

She glanced around the room. The guy with the hep-cat whiskers still staring at her, smiling. She ignored him, lifted the glass, tasted the champagne. It was ambrosial; the bubbles tickled her tongue. She resettled in a luxuriant mood. Music, candlelight, the beautiful faces of wealthy Lausannois. Everything, everyone, glowing in the fairy lights of the Christmas trees just beyond the windows. Lovely, the world so very lovely. She offered herself a silent toast: *How sweet it is, baby.*

Then something even better walked in the room.

Tall, elegant. Dressed in tailored black-on-black Armani. Pampered complexion, the most beautiful hair she'd ever seen on a man. Long, silver, pulled tight to the back of his head and held with a silver clasp. Gorgeous sculptured face, small dark glasses over his eyes. "And wouldn't that one be nice?" she mumbled to herself.

A tall androgynous-looking man, skinny as a string bean and wearing a black silk mandarin jacket, followed at the gorgeous one's heels. The guy with the whiskers, the one who'd been staring at her, rose from his chair. Katherine did a double take; he was three heads shorter than the others. She had another sip of champagne, thinking another night, another job, she'd take them all at once or one at a time. Giggling at the thought, wondering who'd be first. The short one, the tall one? Nah, have to be the gorgeous one in the middle. He was so alpha male, Katherine could smell him from across the room. She watched them talk among themselves till the short one nodded toward her. Then the gorgeous one searching the crowded room from behind his dark glasses. His gaze stopping in her direction.

Katherine smiled to herself. *Girl, this is so your lucky day.* And she watched him move through the room, almost floating. Her breath quickening as he stopped.

"*Bonsoir*, Mademoiselle Taylor. I am Komarovsky."

She saw her reflection in his dark lenses, looking very pleased to make his acquaintance.

"*Enchantée, monsieur.*"

He took her offered hand and bowed slightly, almost

touching his lips to her skin but holding back and releasing her.

"I hope the champagne is to your taste. It is a particular favorite of mine."

The tall one lifted the bottle from the ice: Dom Pérignon, 1959.

"It's delicious, monsieur. Like a taste of heaven."

"I am so pleased you appreciate it."

"I do, very much. In fact, I was just thinking it must be a sin to enjoy something so nice alone."

"Then for the sake of your salvation, I must join you."

The tall one refilled her glass and poured for Komarovsky. Katherine gave the tall one a closer look. A dusting of foundation over chin stubble, just the right touch of mascara. One of the most beautiful one-or-the-others Katherine had ever seen. Komarovsky spoke a few words of Russian; the tall one made a graceful turn and left them alone.

"And now, mademoiselle, where were we?"

She raised her glass to her eyes. "I was welcoming you to Lausanne, monsieur."

"How delightful to be welcomed by such beauty. I have looked forward to this evening with great anticipation."

She watched herself in the dark glasses, looking so very beautiful tonight. Offering herself the toast, smiling, her face still flushed with color. "Please, call me Katherine."

"I have no urge to hurry our intimacy. I am one who believes it is the sense of anticipation that brings the greatest pleasure."

"Pleasure is good. I like pleasure."

Katherine looked away to break the spell. She saw the short one on his cell phone, the tall one taking peanuts from a silver bowl, tossing them in the air and catching them in his mouth.

"I get it now; your friend was watching me."

*"Pardon?"*

"The one with the whiskers, over there with the tall one; he was watching me. He told you I was here, that's how the champagne showed up."

"How clever of you to notice. They are my attendants. I fear you may find me old-world in my habits."

Katherine smiled, never ceasing to be amazed by the habits of the über-rich, especially when it came to the habit of sex. "Not at all, monsieur, you wear it well."

"How kind of you to say. I have asked that supper be prepared for us in a private salon, where I trust we may come to know each other better."

"Whatever gives you pleasure, monsieur."

"The fulfillment of my own pleasure is not my wish, Mademoiselle Taylor."

Katherine leaned close to him, her head spinning. The champagne, the alpha male scent oozing from the guy's skin, so good.

"So what is your wish, Monsieur Komarovsky?"

"To watch you drift in the deepest currents of your passion."

Katherine felt a rush of something nice. Jesus, she thought; Mr. Wonderfully Rich was so on the right track she wanted to scream. She giggled instead.

"You find me eccentric, mademoiselle?"

"Mysterious would be more like it. Especially when you hide your eyes behind those dark glasses."

"All the better for you to see yourself."

"I beg your pardon?"

"I see the delight you take watching your reflection. You possess the rarest of gifts: to enter a trancelike state of bliss watching yourself surrender to pleasure."

Her head spinning, her body feeling like molten wax, waiting to be shaped into whatever the fuck he wanted. "Is that what you want, monsieur? You want to watch me take myself all the way to wonderland?"

"I want, for one night, your reflection to be made flesh. To be worshipped and adored."

"Sounds good to me." She raised the champagne to her lips. "Just one thing, monsieur. I'm going to need to see your eyes."

"To what purpose?"

The corners of her mouth curved into the slightest of smiles. "Because I want your eyes to be my looking glass to wonderland."

"I must warn you, people are often affected looking into my eyes. I have a lack of pigment in the irises."

"Me too. A tiny squiggle, here."

"Yes. I admired it in your photographs, as I admire it now."

"Well, you've seen mine, Monsieur Komarovsky. Where I come from, it's your turn to show me yours."

"This is your wish?"

"Depends. How many does a girl get in one night?"

He raised his hands, slowly removing the glasses. She took a sharp breath. Silver disks, the color of his hair.

"As many as you desire."

Counting his way up the steps of Escaliers du Marché, Rochat saw black clouds racing through the sky. And at the old marketplace he felt a sharp chill in the wind. He hurried across Rue Viret and up the last of the wooden steps. He jumped onto the esplanade to greet the cathedral.

"Boo!"

Silence.

The façade looked pale in the floodlights instead of its usual shining self. And the stone statues on either side of the doors looked timid. Even Monsieur Moses seemed to cower amid the pillars.

"What's wrong with you? It's only a silly storm. Be not afraid; Rochat is here."

The floodlights flickered and the cathedral almost shrank in fright. Rochat shuffled across the esplanade. He saw the dragons and demons, gargoyles and man-beasts in the stone carvings of the great arch, all looking terrified and wanting to hide. He rapped Moses on his stone sandals.

"What have you been telling everyone? Another plague of locusts on the way, rivers running red with blood? You shouldn't scare everyone with your stories. It's not nice."

The wind swelled and the bare branches of the chestnut trees twisted wildly. The black clouds sank through

the sky, scraping the high turrets of the belfry tower.
Rochat looked at Moses, rapped his sandals again.

"I'm sorry, monsieur, you're right. This isn't a December kind of storm. What? What do you mean, I
should run away? I'm *le guet de Lausanne*, it's my duty to
protect the cathedral."

Rochat hurried to the embankment wall, looked out
over Lausanne. All the trees twisting and bending in the
wind, branches clawing at rooftops and windows. Shutters slamming and fallen leaves swirling in funnels
through the narrow lanes of the old city. Then the clouds
forming into a great tumbling mass, covering the Alps in
a dark shroud and spreading over Lac Léman. The lake
turning dark as ink as it began to churn and swell. White
crests formed like sharp teeth, snapping at the low tumbling clouds. And all along the shore, orange warning
lights flashed . . . one long, three short, one long, three
short . . . *Danger! Danger! Run away!*

Rochat hurried toward the cathedral.

"Be not afraid, Rochat, be not afraid."

Thunder cracked and lightning sliced at the chestnut
trees on the esplanade. The tallest of the trees snapped
and crashed to the ground, skidded over the esplanade,
and charged toward Rochat. He jumped behind the corner of the tower, the tree just missing him and sliding on
till it smashed and shattered against the fountain. Water
from the fountain rose from the basin as if it were raining
upside down into the black clouds now breaking into
black shreds and flying madly in the winds, then swoop-
ing down across the façade of the cathedral. Rochat ran

to the red door of the belfry tower, banged hard, and shouted, "Otto, my Brave Knight, I know you're sleeping by the altar, but wake up! I think bad shadows are here, and they're scaring the cathedral! *En garde, mon ami!* You protect the nave! I'm going to protect the bells!"

He unlocked the tower door, raced up the tower to the south balcony. The lights of Lausanne, the lights of Évian, the villages along the lake, flickering on and off. And the winds now charging from every direction, howling like a pack of wild dogs, driving the mass of black clouds to the east, then chasing them to the west, faster and faster, till the tumbling mass formed a giant spiral above Lausanne. Rochat leaned over the railing and looked up into the boiling, bubbling eye of the storm, hovering directly above the lantern tower.

"Stop it! You're scaring the stones and the bells! They're very old! It's not nice! Stop it, I say!"

Clattering on the cathedral roof. He hurried to the east balcony.

Hailstones bouncing off the tiles, spilling from the gutters. Then a screaming gust of wind ripping open the clouds.

"Leave us alone! Go away!"

And a flood of hail bore down.

The winds tore through the carpentry and slammed into Rochat. He stumbled and grabbed the balcony railing and held on. Pulling himself around the tower, jumping past pillars, grabbing the railing again. The wind lashing at his face, hailstones crunching under his boots. Then he heard terrible wailing sounds in the wind and the screech of metal against metal. He hid in the south-east turret, watched the building works surrounding the cathedral. Tarpaulins on the scaffolds flapping like untethered sails, high scaffolds rocking from side to side, metal planks dropping sixty meters to the ground and clanging on the cobblestones like frightened bells. Rochat jumped to the south balcony, barely able to see beyond it as the mass of swirling clouds closed in on the cathedral.

"Stop it! You're not supposed to be here! Go away, I say!"

As if to mock him, the winds ripped the scaffolds from the cathedral walls and they crashed to the ground in one monstrous scream of falling-down steel. The winds then charged through the turrets, finding Rochat and knocking him from his feet, sending him sliding over the icy balcony toward the tower steps. He grabbed at the railing; it slipped through his hands.

"No! Help!"

His crooked foot caught a stone pillar, stopping him from tumbling down the tower steps. He pulled himself to his knees; he heard the ancient timbers of the carpentry creak and groan, and Marie-Madeleine cry out in the face of the storm.

*GONG! GONG! GONG!*

Rochat knew he should run to the loge, light the lantern, and call before the ninth bell faded, but he couldn't move. His hands squeezing the iron railing with all his strength, his whole body trembling to the sound of Marie-Madeleine's voice.

"Rochat, Marc Rochat! Evil has returned to Lausanne!"

# fifteen

"Hello, Jay."

Harper looked up, saw a pair of kid gloves, dark brown this time.

"Hello, Miss Clarke. What brings you to planet fucking perfect?"

"I was on my way to the Château d'Ouchy with some mates when the storm hit. Like fire and brimstone out there."

"You don't say."

"World's coming to an end and that's the best you can do?"

Harper looked out of LP's windows. The small forest of Christmas trees and twinkling lights lay in tatters; snow was beginning to fall.

"I suppose it was rather exciting for the two minutes it lasted."

"Said the actress to the bishop."

"Sorry?"

"It's a joke, Jay. A Brit joke. You're a Brit, you're supposed to laugh at Brit jokes. So, do I continue to stand here like an idiot, or do you ask me to sit down?"

He stood, offered a chair. She sat down, lit a smoke.

"Anyway, my mates decided to run for cover in the Palace. We're having dinner down in Le Jardin. I'd ask you along, but you seem happy with your club sandwich."

"It's the fries. Deadly in this place."

"You really need to get out more, Jay."

She took a drag from her smoke. A new addition attached to the butt end, a pearl-colored cigarette holder.

"Nice touch with the fag."

"Can't soil the new gloves, Jay." She reached over, stole a fry. "Yeah, not bad for Swiss fries."

"Thought you didn't want to soil the gloves."

"I always carry a spare. And thanks, by the way, I'd love a drink. Vodka tonic with a twist."

Harper signaled the polite bartender, vodka tonic with a twist, make it two.

"So I had a visit from the Swiss police."

"So I hear. A cop in a cashmere coat told me you weren't impressed with my detective work."

"Who's he?"

"Who?"

"The cop in the cashmere coat."

"Sees all, knows all, talks shite."

"Oh, that one. Well, he wasn't there, whoever he is. But I told the other lot you were cute."

"I'm sure that made an impression."

"One of them's coming back tomorrow. Spending the

afternoon looking through security tapes for your missing Russian pal. He's a sergeant. He's cute, too. Nice green eyes, like you."

A waitress delivered the drinks.

"Cheers, Miss Clarke."

"The eyes, Jay. Look me in the eyes."

"Sorry?"

"To make a proper toast in Switzerland, you must look into each other's eyes as you touch glasses. It's one of the rules."

"Like no laundry on Sundays?"

"Like you don't want to look me in the eyes?"

"Sure, they're nice. They match your gloves."

"My knees are positively trembling, Jay."

"Where are your friends?"

"In the restaurant. I said I'd follow on, maybe."

"Maybe?"

"Unless, maybe, you had a better idea." She watched him fumble with his watch, trying to read the time. "You're a strange one, aren't you, Jay?"

"How so?"

"I see you through the window and abandon my friends. And as fate would have it, I'm wearing one of my better fuck-me dresses, so maybe, just maybe, I'll get lucky enough to not spend another Christmas Eve with Jimmy Stewart. And you haven't batted an eye."

"Who?"

"Jimmy Stewart, actor in *It's a Wonderful Life*. Weepy Yank holiday trash designed to keep lonely hearts from jumping off Pont Bessières."

"That's a bridge in Lausanne."

"Yeah, but there's also a bridge in the film, in Bum-fuck, USA. Jimmy's about to take a flying leap on Christmas Eve when an angel shows up to save the day. I've seen it a hundred times, still cry like a baby every time."

"Hang on, what's Pont Bessières got to do with Bumfuck, USA?"

"Because every year at Christmastime, a few lonely Lausannois take a dive off Pont Bessières."

"You must be joking."

"You think people diving off a bridge is a joke?"

"No, I was there a few nights ago. Middle of the night, actually. This lad popped out from nowhere, asked me if I knew about the bridge, wanted to know if I needed comfort. I thought he was on the game."

"Maybe he was a ghost."

"A ghost?" Harper laughed to himself. Headless virgins, skeletons . . . now ghosts. "This town's bursting with comfort and joy, isn't it?"

"No, it isn't, but it's better than the rest of the world, or haven't you noticed?"

"Noticed what?"

"The state of the world."

"What about it?"

"When's the last time you looked at a newspaper, Jay?"

"I can't remember."

"Then I'll clue you in: It's fucking depressing out there. That's why I'm looking for a body to keep me warm on Christmas Eve."

"What about your cute Swiss cop?"

"Oh, he's cute enough. Strikes me as a bloke who's married to his job, with no time-outs allowed for fun. But none of that matters. What matters is I'm sitting here like a sure bet on a million-to-one jackpot, and you sit there eating fries, with ketchup on your chin." She picked up the napkin from the table, leaned over, dabbed away the splotch. "And it makes the second time you've turned me down. You're giving me a complex."

"You don't waste time, Miss Clarke."

"Only ten shopping days till Christmas. Besides, life is too short."

"I've heard that. Somewhere."

"Where's that?"

"No bloody idea."

"Jay?"

"Present."

"You're incredibly pissed."

"I passed that point long ago. Which reminds me, another drink?"

"No, thanks, Jay. I might be gagging for it, but I don't beg."

"Sorry, Miss Clarke."

She sighed. "I always fall for the wrong guys."

"What kind of guys make wrong guys?"

"Guys like you."

"Me?"

"Yeah, they wash up on the shores of Lac Léman like emotional refugees. I take them in, but they're so bruised by the time I find them, they can't even trust a sure thing."

"Known a few, have you?"

"Bags. And you, Jay Harper, make one more." She stamped out her cigarette, dropped the holder in her bag. "Well, I'm off. There's a cute waiter down in the restaurant who might fancy a quick shag in the wine cellar."

"Fast work, isn't it?"

"Yeah, well, what can I say? I feel the need to hang on to someone tonight. You ever feel the need, Jay?"

Harper watched her stand, turn to walk away, feeling something unremembered.

"Miss Clarke?"

She turned back.

"Do they sleep?"

"What?"

"The wrong guys, do they sleep?"

"Sure, Jay, everybody sleeps. Don't you?"

"Not really."

"Why not?"

"My telephone number in London."

"What about it?"

"I can't remember it."

"This keeps you up at night?"

"Among other things."

"Like what?"

"That's just it, Miss Clarke; I can't remember a bloody thing before coming to Lausanne."

"Good-bye, Jay, wish me luck."

She blew him a kiss, headed for the door. Harper lit a smoke, scanned the room. Two clowns sitting at the bar. Tall skinny fuck blowing Lucy Clarke a prissy kiss. Short one with a goatee glancing at Harper with a wink and a

nod. No idea if they were the wrong guys or not, but
Harper had a visceral dislike of them. He gave the short
one a *Fuck off, shrimp* stare, then he looked out of the
window. Snow coming down hard.

As Rochat finished the three-o'clock rounds, the
tiled roofs of the old city were covered in snow. He
raised the lantern into the dark.

*"C'est le guet. Il a sonné l'heure, il a sonné l'heure."*

He crawled into the carpentry and hung the lantern on
an iron spike. He quickly tucked himself in a sleeping bag
under Marie-Madeleine and pulled his floppy hat down on
his head. He curled up his legs and leaned against a timber.
He watched lantern light glow against the great bell, seeing
the tiny chips and cracks at the edge of the bronze skirt.
He could sense she was still upset from the storm, still unable to slip into her usual snooze after ringing the hours.

"It's so quiet, isn't it, Marie?"

Silence.

*"Pardonnez-moi, madame,* but if you're going to have
me sit out here in the cold to keep you company, you
should at least have the decency to chat. I have a very
warm bed in a very warm loge awaiting me. Instead, I'm
stuffed in a sleeping bag and looking like a big stupid
caterpillar with a silly hat on his head, talking to a bell,
of all things."

He reached up, rapped the hem of her bronze skirt.
Marie hummed with a soft voice.

"Yes, yes, I'm only teasing. I'm warm enough, don't

worry. Yes, I know, it always turns warmer when it snows. What? No, the bad shadows are gone, and I haven't seen anything evil returning to Lausanne. Yes, I'm very sure we were only imagining them. Yes, yes, I'll keep a sharp eye, just in case."

He stared off the balcony, watching the snow fall through the dark sky.

"Hail and thunderstorms and so much snow, all in one night. It's so strange, isn't it, Marie?"

The great bell didn't answer. Rochat looked at her, now snoozing comfortably in the timbers. He picked up his sketchbook from the floorboards and looked at the pictures. While keeping Marie company, he'd been drawing the snowy rooftops and curls of wood smoke from chimneys. He'd even drawn the dark and shuttered windows above Rue Caroline. He began to draw the lantern tower when he felt himself doze off. He shook himself awake.

"You must keep the watch for something evil returning to Lausanne, Rochat. It's your duty."

He pulled his hat tighter down on his head, tucked the sleeping bag to his chin. The old wooden flooring under Marie-Madeleine creaked as he shifted position.

"But I still feel like a big stupid caterpillar with a silly hat on his head." He thought about it and decided he should draw a story about a giant caterpillar who was very clever and wore a silly hat on his head. And his name was Pompidou and he lived on snowflakes. Big ones, fat ones, like the ones falling tonight. And he crawled around the world—no, he flew around the world and beyond the moon.

By the time Marie-Madeleine rang for four o'clock, Rochat's sketchbook was full of wild drawings. Ice castles and moats of fire and three-headed crocodiles. And an evil wizard named Screechy who lived in an ice castle and wore a pointy hat with a rooster on top and stole a big diamond that was a future-teller. And a band of funny pirates with wooden swords and paper hats, riding on Pompidou's back and flying just above the waves of the Boiling Seas of Doom on their way to the land of Saskatoon where . . . where . . .

Five loud gongs shook Rochat awake.

He was scrunched up in his sleeping bag with his sketchbook open on his lap. Pompidou and the pirates were circling the ice castle, shouting for the evil wizard's surrender. He looked at Marie-Madeleine; she was quiet and calm.

"I think it's time for a hot cup of tea, Rochat, don't you? Yes, I think so, too." He closed the sketchbook and yawned. He looked through the timbers, rubbed his eyes, looked again. He rapped the great bell with his knuckles.

"Marie, wake up! Do you see it?"

A half-meter of snow on the belfry balcony, just reaching the iron railing. He stuck his head through the crisscross timbers. He checked to the east. The roof of the cathedral and base of the lantern tower at the far end of the building buried in even more snow. Down on the esplanade the crumbled construction site was covered.

And just under the belfry, the steeple from the Apostles'
porch, long and pointed, poked through the snow like
the lance of a brave medieval knight who'd fallen over in
his armor and couldn't get up.

"Otto, what were you doing walking around in the
snow, you clumsy old fool? You're supposed to be sleeping next to the altar! Don't worry, I'll dig you out tomorrow, *mon ami*!"

Rochat looked out over Lausanne. Perfectly white,
untouched, not a footprint. And all the black clouds were
gone, and there were thousands of stars sparkling in the
still night sky. Rochat saw the vineyards in the hills to
the east of Lausanne and the mountains across the lake.
The whole world covered in silent white. A funny
thought popped into Rochat's head. He jumped to his
feet, tapped Marie-Madeleine again.

"The sun will be coming up in two hours, Marie, and
Lausanne will have such a big surprise with all the snow.
And I can make an even bigger surprise."

He grabbed the lantern, crawled through the timbers,
jumped onto the east balcony, and sank to his knees in
snow, his overcoat bunching up as if it were much too
long. He cleared a path to the loge, set the lantern on a
stone ledge. He opened the door, banged his boot
against a timber, and set it in the loge, then the other leg,
and he stepped inside. He found his gloves and a long
stick that had been in the corner behind the door from
longtimes ago and nobody knew what it was for now. He
dug through the closet, found an old scarf and the floppy
black hat Monsieur Buhlmann wore on the nights when

he called the hour. He opened another closet and found an old broken lantern and three plastic cups. One red, two blue. He remembered Monsieur Buhlmann kept a bag of walnuts in a hiding place in the loge. The old man loved walnuts with his many glasses of wine, but Rochat was sure it would be fine if a few went missing. He carefully counted out seven walnuts. He put on his gloves, rushed back outside. He set the things in the eaves above the door of the loge and thought about his plan.

"I'll put him here. So the biggest one from this balcony, and one from Clémence's side, then the last one from over by Marie."

He kicked his way to the end of the balcony, scooped up a clump of snow, and packed it into a tight ball. He rolled it the length of the balcony, then back, packing it tighter each time. He rolled it back and forth till it was a big fat ball. He rolled it to the railing directly in front of the loge. He crawled through the timbers near Clémence, rapped his knuckles on her bronze skirt.

"Excuse me for disturbing you, madame, but I'm making a surprise for Lausanne. I won't be long."

He jumped onto the west balcony and rolled another ball of snow. He picked it up, carried it around the tower, planted it atop the big ball. Then over to Marie-Madeleine's side of the tower. He could feel her brood with disdain.

"Oh, just mind your own business. Look the other way if you don't like it."

And he rolled a ball of snow the size of a watermelon and stacked it atop the pile, and now had three balls of snow standing taller than him. He stuck the long stick through the middle ball so it poked from the sides like arms. Two blue plastic cups for eyes, the red one for a nose, seven walnuts for a smile.

"Now, this old scarf around your neck, hang this old lantern from your arm, *comme ça*. And to top it off, *le chapeau du guet*." He set Monsieur Buhlmann's floppy black hat on the snowman's head. "*Et voilà*. What do you think? Marie, Clémence?"

The two bells refused comment. He made a snowball, threw it at Marie.

*Donnnng,* she grumbled.

"What do you mean, 'What is it?' It's a snowman."

He threw a second snowball at Clémence and listened to her opinion.

"Oh, I see. This is a cathedral, not a playground. I'll be excommunicated and burned at the stake if the Pope sees it? Well, with all due respect, mesdames, the Pope doesn't come here anymore. And besides, there's a big pipe organ where he used to sit. So, if you'll excuse me, I'm going inside to warm up. It's been a very long night of keeping the watch. My deputy, Monsieur Neige, will be happy to look after you. You may address any complaints to him."

Rochat looked over Lausanne once more. Here and there lights flickering awake. He jumped in the carpentry, shuffled around Marie-Madeleine.

"Oh, what a surprise everyone'll have when they see a silly snowman in the belfry. They'll be very confused and wonder if they're imagining things. I'm sure they'll be talking about it at Café du Grütli tonight. After their supper, they'll all talk about the snowman, and tonight, I'll have something to say! I'll say, 'What snowman, mesdames and messieurs?' Won't that be funny, Marie?"

He tapped her skirt and listened; she failed to see the humor and remained quiet.

"Bells, why do I bother? I'm going into the loge. Good night."

The timbers creaked and groaned; Marie rang for six o'clock.

"Good morning, I mean."

Rochat gathered his sleeping bag and sketchbook from under the big bell. As he climbed from the carpentry, his eyes skimmed the snowy rooftops to the unshuttered but dark windows above Rue Caroline. He leaned close to Monsieur Neige.

"And if you see an angel in the windows over there, don't be alarmed. Lausanne's full of them."

He went into the warmth of the loge. He took off his snowy boots and hung his wool overcoat on the nail at the back of the door. He blew out the candles, lay down on his bed, and fell sound asleep.

The dream coming again.

"More, please."

Her body floating on a silver cloud. Tasting caviar from a crystal spoon.

"Is it good, mademoiselle?"

"I've never tasted anything like it. Buttery and beautiful."

"This morning there was a great sturgeon swimming in the Caspian Sea. I had her drawn from the depths, her belly sliced open while she was still alive, and her precious eggs poured into crystal bowls and brought to you this forever night."

"Lovely, so lovely."

A light shimmering through swirls of smoke, pulsing, coming closer, like something delicious and warm, then breaking into shreds of silver mist, taking the shapes of bodies. Beautiful bodies of men and women, all floating through swirls of smoke, brushing against her. Feeling a delicious warmth seep through her skin and flow through her blood. Cut open alive, the precious eggs poured into silver bowls. Tasting the life still breathing in the precious eggs.

"Lovely, so lovely."

"A gift to honor your beauty."

"I want everyone to taste it. I want everyone to feel it."

"Is this your wish?"

"Yes."

Mounds of tiny black pearls glistened in the silver light. The beautiful bodies dipping their fingers into the caviar, licking it from one another's fingers. Feeding one another, tongue to tongue, mouth to mouth. Licking the black pearls from one another's lips.

"I feel them. I feel so . . . so . . ."

"Feel their hunger."

"Yes, oh, yes. I feel it."

A shuddering rush of pleasure.

"What's happening to me?"

"You have become one with the woman in the looking glass."

"Yes, yes, please. I want her. I want to be her again." Touching her, feeling her.

Another delicious rush.

"Oh, God. Never so good, never so good."

"Swear it."

"I swear, I swear, never so good."

"Swear that you will always want more."

"Yes, I swear."

Music vibrating, a murmuring voice.

*Too much love . . . never too much love.*

The beautiful bodies coming closer again. Feeling their breath on her skin.

"More. I want more."

Drums pulsing, voices swirling.

*Radiance . . . absolute radiance . . . so wonderful.*

Waiting to ride the next wonderful wave.

*Sacrifice of love . . . our sacrifice of love.*

Her body rising, lifted by unseen hands, carried through the beautiful bodies. Feeling every heart in passing, pounding in one impassioned pulse.

She breathed deeply, holding the breath to the edge of blackness. Gasping and breathing even deeper.

The rush burned deeper and the voices cried with joy, faces coming close to her and inhaling the scent radiating from her skin. Mouths and lips and tongues hungry for more.

*Too much love . . . never too much love.*

She opened her arms to receive them.

Worshipping her, licking her skin, sucking at her breasts, biting her flesh.

"Take my body, take my blood."

The beautiful bodies covering her, their flesh melting into shreds of silver mist, smothering her, her heart pounding faster.

"Never so good. Never so good."

The delicious warmth seeping into her skin again. Filling each hungry pore. Floating higher and higher on the crimson cloud.

Faces, thousands of beautiful faces emerging from the mist, licking at her flesh. "Where am I?"

"At the gates of paradise."

"Who am I?"

"You are your reflection made flesh."

"Yes, so beautiful, I want it forever and ever."

Feeling the warmth sink deeper into her flesh, rushing through her blood.

Higher, higher. Breathless.

Feeling her legs open, feeling them touch her.

"Don't stop, please, don't ever stop."

Rushing into her, lifting her higher, so much higher.

"I love you, I love you, baby."

Panting, tingling . . . suspended in a perfect moment of never-before pleasure.

Then slipping away and falling.

"No, my darling, not yet." Wanting the rush again. Wanting to stay there forever.

*Too much love . . . never too much love.*

"Please, monsieur, can I have more?"

# sixteen

The snowplow clanked down Rue Pépinet. Harper waited for the heavy machine to pass. Freak thunderstorm followed by one of the biggest snowfalls on record and the Swiss have most of the city's streets cleared by ten in the morning. He crossed the road to Place Saint-François, ducked into the newsagent, picked up two packets of smokes. He saw *The Guardian* amid the Swiss newspapers and grabbed it. Catch up on the state of the world maybe. He paid the assistant, went back outside.

Ye olde Christmas village on the square had taken a battering, but workers were already drinking glasses of *vin chaud* and singing merry tunes about the farmer's daughter and hammering the place back together again. The noise reminding Harper of the state of his head. He stopped at the chemist.

"Aspirin, please."

Back outside and around the corner to Café Romand. Place was filled with men and women enjoying their mid-morning coffee break. He found a spot next to the windows, ordered an espresso and croissant. He opened the aspirin, downed two pills. He opened *The Guardian* to check on the state of the world. Headlines: "Pakistan and India Arm Nuclear Missiles as Riots Continue." "Civil War in Iraq as Iran Threatens West." "Second Suicide Attack on New York Subways Claims Hundreds." "More Genocide in West Africa: 700,000 Slaughtered in Six Weeks."

"Christ, 'depressing out there' is the polite way of putting it. More like 'going down in flames.'"

"I beg your pardon?"

Harper lowered the newspaper. Old gent at the next table, the kind that had "Talker" written across his face.

"Sorry?"

"You were speaking to me, monsieur?"

"Actually, I was reading the newspaper to myself."

"Then excuse me for disturbing you, monsieur."

Harper turned the page. Pictures: Hindu nationalists stoning Muslim children to death in Rajasthan; Pakistani soldiers praying before a nuke in Islamabad; shredded bodies in New York.

Slaughter and blood. Tortured faces, hearing the desperate cries of the dying, begging to be saved. A wave of vertigo hit him hard. "Bloody hell."

"Are you feeling unwell, monsieur?"

Harper looked at the old gent again. Round face with a thick white beard, green cap and red jacket, red watery eyes through thick specs. The more Harper looked at him, the more he looked like a down-on-his-luck Christmas elf.

"Bit too much to drink last night. No worries."

"I see. I must say, it's a sad world you hold in your hands."

"Sorry?"

"The events you're looking at in the newspaper."

Harper looked at the pictures again. Slaughter and blood, screams and cries. Feeling it was ever thus, but it shouldn't be.

"Yes, I agree, ever since the time of *Homo ergaster*."

Harper pulled his eyes from the paper, looked at the elf. "What did you say?"

"You said it was ever thus. I assumed you were talking about the time of *Homo ergaster*, two and a half million years ago when—"

"—hominids began to walk upright, shape tools from stones, control fire. But I wasn't talking. I was thinking about something I saw on the History Channel."

"Excuse me, monsieur, but I'm sure you did say it aloud."

Harper rubbed the back of his neck. *Christ, the mother of all hangovers.*

"Are you working in Lausanne, monsieur?"

Harper nodded, knowing he was giving the elf permission to babble. Still, the chatter was keeping the nausea at bay. "Yes, I'm a consultant with the IOC."

"The Olympic Committee in Vidy. A most interesting place. Lovely place, built on one of the first Neolithic settlements in the world. First to domesticate animals, you know?"

"I thought that was the cathedral."

"Oh, no. The settlement under the cathedral was from the Paleolithic Era, much later. They were the first to bury their dead."

"Right, I remember." Harper signaled for another espresso, a double. "I saw a few of them under the altar."

"A remarkable sight, isn't it? The skeletons in their open graves."

"Whole cathedral is a bit of a sight."

"Yes, I suppose so. I came here as a child in 1938 with my mother. After Stalin had my father taken to a Siberian gulag and shot for the high crime of being a good bee-keeper. Such madness in the world then, such madness now. But I'll never forget after we arrived in Lausanne, my mother took me to the cathedral to light a candle and I felt all that was good in the world, all that was left of it, was here. It is a very remarkable place, don't you think?"

Harper couldn't think how to tell him that's not quite what he had in mind about the place. Nor how to tell him the goofball look in the old gent's eyes underscored what he did think about it: a broken-down haunt for batty nuns, tramps on altars and, now, down-on-their-luck Christmas elves with visions of goodness in their eyes. Instead Harper watched the old gent finish his own coffee and reach in the pocket of his red coat to pull out some lint and a few coins. Near his last, from the look of it.

"Never mind that, mate, I'll get it."

"Oh, thank you for your kindness, monsieur. I must be going to the cathedral. They say there's a snowman in the belfry."

"A what?"

"I saw it on the telly this morning. The locals are all atwitter. A schoolboy prank, they say. Wonderful, don't you think?"

The old gent stood, closed his red jacket, tied a purple scarf around his neck. On his merry way to see the snowman of Lausanne Cathedral. Harper checked his watch; almost eleven. The snowplows should've cleared the way to Vidy Park by now. Should catch a taxi to the office and check in. See if there's been a message from Yuriev . . .

"Hang on, did you say you came here from Russia?"

"Yes, I did."

"You still speak Russian, then?"

"Well, yes. I taught Russian literature at the university for many years."

Harper dug through the pockets of his coat. Scraps of paper, rolled-up file on Alexander Yuriev, photocopy of Sœur Fabienne's unanswered prayers.

"Could you have a look at this, tell me what it says?"

"Certainly, monsieur."

Harper pressed out the creases on the page. "Sorry for the state of it. It's this one here, in the middle."

"A very small script, isn't it? Would you have a pen or pencil? I could follow the words better with a pointer of some kind."

Harper dug through his pockets again. Extra packet of smokes, keys, ballpoint pen lifted from LP's Bar. The man took off his glasses, rubbed them on his scarf.

"Thank you, monsieur. My, such an elaborate hand . . . how unusual."

"What's that?"

"Well, it appears to be a variation of a Slavonic dialect no longer used. Some of these letters were dropped from the Cyrillic alphabet in the 1960s. When was this written?"

"A few days ago. Why?"

"Whoever wrote this was educated in the schools of the Soviet elite, where they still practiced the older alphabet. The penmanship shows their particular discipline. Education was a source of pride in the Soviet Union. Tram drivers in Moscow could quote whole passages of Pushkin."

"It's Pushkin?"

"This? Oh, no. Let's see. 'Spirits of giants on the earth . . .' Yes, I've got it now. I'll write it in the margin. 'Evil spirits walk the earth. The spirits of heaven live in heaven, but this is the place of earthly spirits, born of the earth. Spirits of giants on the earth, like clouds. To occupy, corrupt, and bruise the earth.'"

"And?"

"That's it."

"Sounds like something from the Bible."

"Oh, I couldn't help you there. But I do know someone who can. He's somewhat eccentric, but very knowledgeable in these things. We often play chess on Saturday afternoons. I'll write his number down on the paper, his name's Monsieur Gabriel. He comes from the Catalan region of Spain. A remarkable story. He was a boy soldier on the Republican side, blew up bridges with the American brigade. After the war, he dedicated his life to the study of scripture. I'm sure he can help you, monsieur. You need only to telephone him."

The old gent jotted down the number. Harper took the paper, folded it up, and stuffed it in his coat. He lit a smoke, laughing to himself.

"Cheers, but I'm sure it won't be necessary."

"I gather the note isn't what you expected."

Harper sucked in the smoke. *All that's good in the world . . . all that's left of it . . .* Christ. He let it go with a shrug. "Actually, considering the barking mad place I found it, it's perfect."


The old telephone on the wall rang furiously and shook Rochat from sleep. He sat up from the bed, watched the hammer pound on the little bells. He lifted the listening tube from the hook and spoke into the talking cone.

*"Bonjour, je suis le guet de la Cathédrale de Lausanne."*

"Rochat! Are you in the belfry?"

It was Monsieur Taroni, the caretaker of the cathedral, sounding quite flustered.

*"Oui, monsieur.* You called me here."

"Are you aware there's a snowman on the south balcony?"

For a moment, Rochat was very sure he was imagining the phone call, till he remembered there was such a snowman on the balcony, and that he had put it there.

"I know, I made him."

"You? Did you get permission from the canton authorities?"

"To make a snowman?"

"In the belfry of an eight-hundred-year-old cathedral, yes! There are reporters here, Rochat."

"Where?"

"On the esplanade! With television crews!"

"Television?"

"Yes. TSF One *and* Two!"

"What are they doing?"

"What do you think they're doing? They're reporting that there's a snowman in the belfry of the cathedral! They've been at it all morning in French, German, Italian, *and* Swiss Romansh. Rochat, this is a cathedral, not a playground!"

"I know. Marie told me last night."

"You have a woman up there with you? Oh, *merde*."

"I mean Marie-Madeleine, the bell. She had a bad dream last night, in the storm."

"A bell told you it had a bad dream last night?"

"She said evil has returned to Lausanne."

"Oh dear, oh dear. What're we going to do, Rochat?"

"Don't worry, Monsieur Taroni. I stayed up all night keeping the watch, but I didn't see anything."

"I'm not talking about what you imagined a bell told you! I'm talking about the snowman!"

"We could wait till he melts."

"That'll be in April! Were you thinking it could stay there till spring? I must call you back, after I speak to the director."

"Do you need his telephone number? I have it written down."

"No, I don't need his telephone number. He's here."

"His voice said he was in Les Avants."

"What?"

"His voice said he went to Les Avants."

"Rochat, what on earth are you talking about? He's here on the esplanade, talking to reporters. All Switzerland has heard about the snowman in the belfry of Lausanne Cathedral. Everyone wants to know what it means. The Italians are calling it a miracle. Thank God you put a lantern on its arm instead of a cross or we'd have the holy resurrection on our hands!"

The connection broke off. Rochat replaced the receiver on its hook, paced the little room nervously. The telephone rang again.

*"Bonjour, je suis le guet—"*

"I know it's you, Rochat, I called you! Listen, things are worse. The press is on its way up the tower with the director right now. They want to take pictures of the snowman from the balconies in time for the lunchtime news programs."

"There's lots of snow up here, monsieur."

"They don't care. They say Switzerland needs to see the snowman, and the director now thinks the snowman is a good thing."

"He does?"

"That Julien Magnollay from *24 Heures* told him it was good publicity for the cathedral and we could get more money from the canton authorities for the repairs. We'll need it, what with the scaffolding falling down, such a mess. One thing, Rochat, we want you to stay in the loge. We've said you've gone home."

"But I'm here, monsieur, in the loge."

"I know you're in the loge! Listen, Marc, you're a nice boy, we all like you very much. And those of us who know you, well, we know you didn't invent gunpowder. But I'm not sure the locals need you telling them one of our bells had a nightmare and thinks evil has returned to Lausanne, not today, anyway. Lock the door of the loge and stay very still. Pull the curtains over the windows. Do you understand? Stay very still. Don't make a sound."

"*Oui, monsieur.*"

"The forecasters say freezing rain and cold winds are coming—it's going to make it very slippery up there. I'm closing the tower to all visitors for the next week. Can't have anyone sliding off the tower, not after all this good publicity. I want you to shovel the balconies and the belfry tower roof as soon as you can. But be careful, Rochat, *tu comprends?*"

"*Oui, monsieur.*"

"And tonight, after you turn off the floodlights, get rid of the snowman."

"*Pardon?*"

"The director says a joke is a joke—for a day. But if your snowman falls on one of the locals from eighty-five meters, we'll never hear the end of it. Remember, don't make a sound while the press is up there."

Rochat hung up the telephone, locked the door, blew out the candles, and hurried to pull curtains over the windows. There were none. He turned in little circles.

"Whatdoyoudo, Rochat, whatdoyoudo?"

He saw dish towels hanging above the glasses-and-plates shelf. He grabbed three, quickly draping them over the windows.

He sat on the bed. Voices and footsteps rose up the tower steps. He didn't move. Voices laughed and talked just beyond the door of the loge. He counted the seconds as they ticked and tocked around the clock above the door of the loge. He counted 947 seconds before the voices and footsteps wound back down the tower. He tiptoed across the loge, unlocked the door, and looked outside. No one but the snowman and the many footprints in the snow where the voices used to be.

Rochat stepped onto the south balcony and hid behind the snowman. He looked down to the esplanade. Hundreds of Lausannois gathered at the foot of the belfry tower.

"Uh-oh. It seems you did your duty a little too well, Monsieur Neige."

The timbers creaked and Marie shouted her opinion with twelve mighty gongs. He waited for her to finish before asking, "They all came because of their dreams? What dreams?"

Marie didn't answer. Rochat crawled through the timbers and gave her a solid rap on her bronze skirt.

"Come now, you can't make all that noise and then pretend you have nothing else to say. What do you mean, you can't remember? And why not? Oh, I see, the photographers were fussing about taking pictures. What do you mean, you hope they got your best side? You're a bell, you're round, you don't have a side."

He was about to give her one more rap to wake her up,

but he remembered her voice in the storm. So frightened by her own terrible dreams in the night. He touched her softly, feeling the chips and cracks at the edge of her bronze skirt.

"I think the photographers are right, Marie. You're a very beautiful bell. And I'm sure the photographers got your best side. Yes, yes, I'm very sure. You have a good rest and I'll see you in a few hours. I have lots of work to do tonight, so I'll come very early this evening. No, don't worry, I'll bring my dinner from Café du Grütli. Of course, madame, I'll sleep in the tower tonight, don't worry. You have a nice snooze."

He crawled through the timbers onto the balcony, hiding behind the stone pillars, staying out of the sight of the crowd below. Something caught his eye, something hanging from the window of a building in the Rotillon quarter. A white duvet with black squiggles.

He went into the loge for the binoculars. He stood in the doorway, focusing the lenses till he could see it wasn't a duvet; it was a bedsheet. And the squiggles were letters painted on the cloth. He stared at it, organizing letters into words that kept jumping around in Rochat's head. He tried to make sense of them anyway: *Quand ma mari matrice de mari?*

"When will my husband die?" He lowered the binoculars from his eyes. "What a very strange thing to write on a bedsheet."

He hung the binoculars in the closet, locked the loge, and hurried down the tower to the women's choir loft. He stopped, thinking he should leave another way. Perhaps Monsieur Taroni wouldn't like it if people saw him coming onto the esplanade from the tower door, especially after telling everyone he'd gone home. He took a side passage, crossing under the roof of the nave to a set of crooked stairs winding down to the ground. He unlocked a heavy door and stepped into the nave. Another crowd had assembled outside the gift shop. Rochat shuffled quietly so no one would notice him. He moved along the edge of the crowd, listening . . .

"My Olivier had the most terrible nightmares last night. And this morning he saw the snowman on television and said, 'Maman, I must see the snowman!'"

"My daughter did the exact same thing. *C'est bizarre, non?*"

. . . and he heard a familiar voice shouting from the doors of the gift shop.

"*Mesdames et messieurs!* I am sorry, but the tower is closed."

Rochat peeked through the crowd and saw the top of Monsieur Taroni's head, his waving hands trying to hold back the shouting crowd.

"What do you mean, the tower is closed?"

"We are citizens of the canton!"

"Let us in!"

"*Mesdames et messieurs,* there is a great deal of snow that we must clear away. And the Federal Office of Meteorology informs us there will be an ice storm in the next few days. We cannot allow unauthorized persons to the tower in such hazardous conditions. *Mesdames et messieurs, le beffroi est fermé!*"

Children began to cry; parents became flustered. Rochat bent as low as he could to escape Monsieur Taroni's notice. Out on the esplanade, Lausannois huddled in groups, some looking up to the belfry, others pointing to the Palud quarter.

"Look, there's another one."

"And over there."

Rochat worked his way to the ramparts overlooking Lausanne. Hanging from other windows of the old city, more hand-painted words on white sheets: *Does he return to us?*, *John 3:16*, *All is darkness without the light*.

Nearby a reporter was talking to a man in a white smock; television cameras pointed at the two of them. Lausannois gathered around to listen.

"I'm speaking with Dr. Helmut Sreiff, head of psychiatric medicine with the University Hospital in Lausanne. Doctor, what do you make of this schoolboy prank?"

"It has obviously touched a nerve in our communal psyche. Last night there was a frightening storm, causing much damage in our area. We are, of course, fast approaching the Christmas season. The combination of these events, as well as the general feeling of uncertainty regarding the state of the world beyond our borders, fills us with conflicting feelings and emotions. It's natural for us to search for answers that give us a sense of comfort and stability, answers that reassure us we are safe. Unable to find these answers, we are overcome with acute anxiety, leading to a mild form of communal psychosis, I would say, and therefore . . ."

Rochat didn't know what the man was talking about.

He shuffled through the crowd and counted his way down Escaliers du Marché.

S he stretched her naked body over red silk sheets, opened her eyes.

A large room with a crackling fire in a marble fireplace. Beautiful white orchids surrounding her bed. Sheer white curtains at the windows, glowing with soft midday light. Quiet voices coming down a mirrored hall. She wrapped her body in the top sheet and slid from the bed. She floated across the room, down the hall, seeing her reflection in the mirrors. Wrapped like a goddess in a red gown. The hall opened into a large sitting room. Monsieur Komarovsky and his attendants gathered around a table, selecting from pages of handwritten correspondence. The tall one noticed her and bowed graciously. The short one with the whiskers stared at her and smiled. Komarovsky, his silver eyes now covered in dark lenses again, opened his arms. "Ah, the belle of the ball now awake from her slumbers."

"What . . . what time is it?"

"It is the late afternoon, my dear. Come and sit, you must take some herbal tea."

The tall one wheeled a china tea service into the room. Komarovsky helped her to the divan and sat beside her. "We've been reading your reviews. They call you exquisite and wonderful."

"Reviews?"

"Last night, my dear, at your coming-out party, you were adored by all."

Yes, she remembered them. How they adored her, loved her, caressed her. Her heart rushed faster thinking of them. Beautiful bodies, slipping through her fingers, like touching warm light. Komarovsky raised the cup to her lips; she sipped.

"It tastes so sweet."

"An ancient potion to calm you, my dear, drink it slowly. My attendants will prepare a bath of water and oils to refresh your skin before supper."

"Supper? No, the deal was only one night. I'm going to Zermatt next week. I have to go home."

She tried to stand, but the floor fell from under her. Komarovsky took her hand and eased her back to the divan.

"There, there, my dear. I have already spoken with Madame Badeaux, and everything is fixed. Tonight you will dine on fresh sweetmeats to rekindle your energy. Another long night of pleasure awaits you."

She sipped again. She felt something wonderful ooze through her blood. So warm, so lovely.

# seventeen

Harper spotted them as he stepped off the train in Montreux. Two husky men with bulges under their overcoats.

They spotted him just as fast.

"*Bonsoir*, Monsieur Harper."

"Have a pleasant trip?"

He gave them a recce. Twin sons of different mothers. This one's nose itches, the other one sneezes. And built like the no-neck bulldozers outside GG's nightclub. *Must be the milk they drink in this country,* Harper thought.

"Fine. Where's Inspector Gobet?"

"We'll take you to him now."

"It's only a short walk."

A conductor's whistle blew from the next platform. Long windows of the departing train carriages stuffed with happy faces.

"Looks like they're having fun."

"That's the GoldenPass Line to Gstaad, Mr. Harper. Skiing holidays have begun in Switzerland."

"The train leaves twice each day. At noon and six in the evening, on the dot."

Harper looked at the clock above the platform: five fifty-nine. "Hate to tell you, lads, but that train's leaving a minute early."

"Not to worry, Mr. Harper."

"He won't leave before his scheduled time."

Harper pulled his smokes from his coat and lit up. He watched a red rubber ball of a second hand loop around the bottom of the clock and move up to the twelve. It stopped. The clocks above all five platforms stopped. All the second hands falling in line, then marching ahead as one. Electric motors wound into gear, the train pulled ahead.

"Station clocks throughout Switzerland are resynchronized each minute, Mr. Harper."

"They operate as one clock, so the country's trains leave exactly on time."

Harper nodded. "Or the conductor gets a big fine, I bet."

Twin blank stares. "More along the lines of a lengthy prison term. We'd prefer to shoot them, but capital punishment is banned in Switzerland."

"Shall we go? Inspector Gobet has a dinner engagement this evening, we wouldn't wish him to be late."

Like being escorted by Mutt and Jeff. Harper puffed on his smoke, wondering where he'd heard the term *Mutt and Jeff* or what the bloody hell it meant, but knowing it fit these guys like a pair of handmade gloves.

"Lead the way, lads."

Down some concrete steps and through the tunnels

under the platforms. Everyday-looking sorts rushed for the coming and going trains. Harper followed his guides through the crowd and down the escalator to Avenue des Alpes. Mutt pointed to the right, so did Jeff.

"This way, *s'il vous plaît*."

"It's only a short walk."

They walked along a narrow road lined with leftovers from *la belle époque*, Bauhaus boxes, postmodern sixties shite. Harper chuckled, wondering at the things one remembers from the History Channel, like Bauhaus and Belle Époque, and why.

The road opened onto a small roundabout. Harper did a 360 of the view. Looked swell in the fading light. Whole town neatly fitted between the curving shore of Lac Léman and the cloud-scraping Alps. The white mountains looking as if they'd fallen from the sky and landed at the end of the road, next to the palm trees.

"Palm trees, in Switzerland?"

"Montreux has a unique microclimate, Mr. Harper. Winters here are mild and sunny. You can see the locals were spared much of last night's terrible storm."

Harper considered the scene. "So the end of the world wasn't quite as advertised."

Mutt and Jeff stopped in their tracks, spoke.

"The end of the world, Mr. Harper?"

"Whatever do you mean by that?"

Dead fucking serious.

"Something someone told me last night after the storm, sounded funny. Of course I was incredibly drunk at the time."

"Excessive drinking can often be accompanied by hallucinations, Mr. Harper."

"Perhaps you should consider moderating your consumption."

"Moderation, right."

Mutt pointed across the roundabout. So did Jeff.

"We're going just over there."

"Where you see the Afghan restaurant."

Triangle-shaped building on the far corner, six floors. Forgotten laundry and satellite dishes on the balconies. Ground floor with high windows and a painted sign: Faryab.

Harper saw the Pashtun-looking clientele within, drinking Sadaf tea and smoking cigarettes. He dropped his own smoke on the ground and stomped it underfoot. He wondered how he'd know what a Pashtun looked like, or what the hell Sadaf tea even was, but knew he could smell the wretched stuff already.

"Fine, let's go."

Mutt touched Harper's elbow; Jeff pointed down.

"*Pardonnez-moi*, Monsieur Harper, pick that up."

"It's forbidden to throw rubbish in Switzerland's streets."

Harper picked up the butt, tossed it in a bin. "Of course it is."

They moved along the roundabout. A uniformed copper stood at the side entrance of the building; a strip of red plastic tape was strung across the door. The copper saw them coming, pulled aside the tape, and let them through. Narrow hall with a single bulb dangling from the ceiling and filling the passage with stark light. Raga music and the scent of grilled meat bleeding through thin walls. He saw a mailbox by the door. Names listed looked to be from countries a body would do anything to get the hell out of. End of the hall, a small brown-skinned man standing at the bottom of the stairs. He was sucking on a smoke, his hands nervous and shaking. No wonder. The cop in the cashmere coat was looming over him, pointing his pudgy finger in the small man's face. The copper turned, saw Harper coming through the door.

"Ah, *bonsoir*, Monsieur Harper."

"Inspector."

"This is Monsieur Abu Marwan, the owner of the café and manager of this building."

Dark eyes, trimmed mustache, his brown skin smelling of cardamom. He spoke nervously.

"My customers are asking questions, Inspector."

"And you will inform your customers that a resident in your building has suffered a fatal heart attack."

"You call that thing up there a heart attack?"

"For the purposes of conversation, yes. And may I remind you this is an official police inquiry, which has revealed, in part, that you've been renting flats to illegal residents? I don't have to spell out what that means for you and your family in the Canton de Vaud. I'm sure your children would find deportation to Kabul most unpleasant."

"I don't want any trouble."

"Then you'll do as I ask, and everything will be fine."

"*Inshallah.*"

"In your part of the world, sir, such things may require the will of God. Within the borders of Switzerland, my assurance is all that is needed."

Inspector Gobet opened a door into the café; Abu Marwan stepped through. The inspector closed the door, looked at Harper.

"Poor fellow, he's had a terrible fright. I'm sorry I couldn't elaborate on the telephone, Mr. Harper. I appreciate your making the trip."

"Did I have a choice?"

"No, you didn't. This way, please." The inspector wound up the stairs. Harper followed with Mutt and Jeff bringing up the rear. "I must say, Mr. Harper, I'm beginning to wonder as to your social skills."

"Really."

"Indeed. Since arriving in Lausanne, you've made telephone contact with two foreigners. One of them, a Russian named Alexander Yuriev whom you managed to misplace. Your other telephone acquaintance has proved somewhat more interesting, one Konstantin Toda from Tirana."

"The night clerk from the Port Royal?"

"The very same. Male, thirty-seven years old, lived alone except for his collection of tropical fish. He came to Switzerland fifteen years ago. He has overstayed his thirty-day tourist visa considerably. For the last six years, he's been working at the Hôtel Port Royal. Without benefit of a work permit, I might add. Other than that, he appeared a decent sort. Law-abiding, low-profile, wired money to his family on a regular basis."

They came to the second-floor landing. Two uniforms stood before an open door midway down the hall. Harper stuffed his hands in the pockets of his coat.

"Let me guess: The night clerk's suffered a fatal heart attack."

"Something like that."

The inspector stopped at the door, motioned the coppers aside. Harper looked in. Large aquarium on a white plastic table. Fish darting in cloudy water. Lamp in the aquarium the only light in the dark, filling the room with sickly green light. Sour smells slapped his senses. Sweat, shit, blood.

"It doesn't smell like a heart attack, Inspector."

The inspector gestured toward the door. "Please, after you, and step no farther than the plastic sheeting on the floor."

Harper stepped ahead.

A wrought-iron bed behind the door; on the other side of the room, the night clerk was pinned to the wall like a bug. An iron rod running through his naked chest and into the wall, arms and legs hanging lifeless. Streaks of blood on his face, eyes gouged from his skull, black socks stuffed in his mouth. Abdomen sliced open, blood and body fluids spilled over the floor.

"Bloody fucking hell."

"An apt description. A forensics team of the Montreux police worked the room for physical evidence before my arrival. You may be interested in knowing what they found."

"Which was?"

"Nothing."

"Nothing?"

"No fingerprints, other than those you would expect to find. No footprints on the floor, no samples of skin or hair not belonging to the victim, no traces of anyone being in this room but the victim and his tropical fish. Abu Marwan was cleaning the hall when he saw blood seeping under the door. The door was bolted from inside and he called the Montreux police. They arrived and broke open the door. Please notice the bars on the windows. The flat is on the fire escape and the bars can only be opened from inside the room; they haven't been disturbed. Residents of the building were interviewed. No one saw strangers in the building, no one heard sounds of struggle."

"So what the hell happened?"

"Frankly, we're stumped. And the reason I called for you."

"Me."

"Yes, we thought you might help us with one of your hunches."

Harper stared at the inspector. Same I-know-something-you-don't smirk on the copper's mug. Mutt and Jeff in the doorway, waiting to be impressed as well. Harper swept the room with a quick glance.

"Fine. It appears the night clerk, having succumbed to a fit of remorse over working in Switzerland without a permit, locked himself in his room, tore an iron rod from the bed frame, gouged out his eyes and his bowels before impaling himself through the chest and pinning himself to the wall at a pressure of five thousand pounds per square inch. It also appears he gagged himself beforehand, so he wouldn't disturb the neighbors. How am I doing so far?"

"You've forgotten what he did with his eyeballs, Mr. Harper."

"Dissolved them in battery acid?"

"More along the lines of digested." The inspector pointed to the aquarium, the fish snapping at tiny bits of flesh floating in the water.

Harper rubbed the back of his neck. "Right. Missed that one."

"As did the forensics officer of the Montreux police. There's also the question of the victim's missing heart, liver, kidneys, and tongue. We've checked the neighborhood skips to no avail. Leading us to believe whoever murdered Mr. Toda wanted his organs as a killing trophy of some kind, if not lunch."

Harper looked at the dangling corpse, guts sliced to shreds. "Jesus wept."

"Indeed. Shall we go down for some fresh air?"

Back down the stairs, out on the street. They stood in a pool of white light from the lamp above the door. A Mercedes pulled up to the pavement, 500 series, dark blue. Matched the suit under the inspector's cashmere coat.

"No doubt, Mr. Harper, you're asking yourself what the deputy director of the Swiss police from Berne is doing at a murder scene in Montreux."

"No doubt you're about to tell me."

"We only have a handful of willful homicides per year in Switzerland, and I keep abreast of all such investigations. I like to see that they're conducted properly."

"Don't think I'd care to be the forensics lad who missed the eyeballs in the fish tank."

"I promise you, you would not. When I learned the victim was working at the hotel in which Alexander Yuriev was staying, I thought I'd best swing by."

The driver lowered his window, handed over a clear plastic bag. Something inside; a magazine.

"Thank you, Sergeant Gauer. Please inform the morgue they may collect the body. Mr. Harper, there was one item deliberately left at the scene."

"Deliberately?"

"One must assume from the lack of physical evidence that nothing was left by accident. In this case, the most recent issue of *Playboy* magazine that was found on the victim's bed. Would you care to have a look at Miss December?"

Magazine opened to a shot of Miss December. Harper looked at her. Pretty smile.

"And this means what?"

"If you look at the bottom of the page, you'll see a telephone number. There's no name, but I believe it to be yours."

Harper saw the number. No bloody idea. Then again, maybe that wasn't the fucking point.

"You really want me to answer, Inspector, or are you just profiling the manner of my thinking again?"

"Truth be told, I knew immediately it was yours."

"How?"

"Elementary, my dear Mr. Harper. I saw, I dialed, you answered. When would Mr. Toda have written this?"

"The Port Royal, Friday night, the night I was supposed to meet Yuriev at GG's. I'm surprised he got it right."

"Why's that?"

"Took him a few tries. Given where he wrote it, he was probably otherwise engaged."

"Did he call you at any time in the last few days?"

"No, but I called him a few times."

"When was the last time you spoke with him?"

"Would've been Sunday. In the early morning, around three a.m."

"Are you sure?"

"That I called him, or that it was three a.m.?"

"Just answer the question, Mr. Harper."

"I was searching strip joints and bars for Yuriev all night. Ended up on Rue Caroline and heard the cathedral bells ring three times."

"And what was the substance of the conversation?"

"Same as the rest. I asked him if there'd been any word from Yuriev."

"Did Mr. Toda sound in any way distressed?"

"Not that I could tell."

"I see. Would you get in the motorcar, please?"

Mutt and Jeff were on both sides of the Merc, holding open the passenger doors.

"Am I under arrest, Inspector?"

"Nothing of the sort. I just happen to be on my way

to Lausanne. Dinner at the Palace Brasserie with the doctor. Our annual oyster fête before the holidays. Bit of a tradition."

Eviscerated corpse followed by a serving of gutted *Ostrea edulis*. "You must have a cast-iron stomach, Inspector."

"Feelings and emotions are best laid aside in our line of work, wouldn't you agree?"

"This isn't my line of work."

"Actually it is, you're just a bit slow on the uptake."

Harper didn't like the sound of it. "I'll take the train, thanks."

"Please, don't make me pull rank. Besides, there's something else I'd like to show you."

Rochat packed three flannel shirts, a pair of trousers, two pairs of winter socks, and two clean towels in his rucksack. It wasn't easy. Every time he turned his back, Monsieur Booty jumped in to claw at the contents.

"Listen, you miserable beast, I told you. I'm staying in the tower the next few nights. We've had lots of snow, and Monsieur Taroni says an ice storm is coming. So you just get out of the rucksack and stop bothering me. I have important duties."

*Mew.*

"No, you can't come."

*Mew.*

"What do you mean, who'll feed you? Is that all you can think about at a time like this?"

*Mew.*

"Oh, your litter box. Don't worry, Teresa will feed you and clean your litter box. And thank you for reminding me about little boxes."

He packed his vitamin box and two wool sweaters. He sat on the edge of his bed and tried to think of anything else, even though there wasn't any space in the rucksack for anything else. Outside the balcony windows, the dungeon tower of Château d'Ouchy stood soldierlike in the fading light. Monsieur Booty jumped up onto Rochat's lap and purred. Rochat scratched the beast's head.

"Did you have bad dreams last night, too?"

*Mew.*

He stood with the cat in his arms and shuffled to the balcony windows. He pulled a window open and smelled the cold air. Down the corniche, packs of Swiss children digging madly in the snow. Rolling fat balls of snow and stacking them into a long line of snowmen facing the lake. Topping them with stocking caps, sticking twigs in the sides for arms, using pinecones for faces. Young voices shouting, boots stomping against the cold, mothers calling the children home.

"Marc?"

He turned, saw his mother on the bed. She was very sick, days away from being lowered into the winter ground at Cimetière Saint-Charles.

"Hello, Maman."

"What are you doing at the window?"

"I'm watching the children make snowmen, and I was thinking how sad I am that you're going away."

"I know, and when the time comes, I don't know how I'll say good-bye . . . but to keep you safe in this world, I have to let you go. I'm not strong enough anymore to protect you."

"Because you're going to die?"

"Yes, darling, I'm going to die."

"Why can't I die with you?"

"Because your life is a miracle, and you must live for me, for all of us. Come here, let me hold you."

Rochat climbed on the bed, laid his head at his mother's breasts. She traced her fingers through his black hair.

"You're going to Lausanne and you'll go to school and learn such wonderful things. You'll be safe there, your father and kind people will protect you."

"From the bad shadows?"

"Yes, from the bad shadows."

"I'm afraid, Maman."

"Oh, Marc, you fought so hard to come into this world, you wouldn't give up. And you'll never stop fighting, you'll never run away. You'll grow to be the bravest of them all, won't you?"

"How can I grow up to be brave if I'm so small and crooked now?"

"Listen to me, darling: Being brave is nothing more than standing up when you're afraid. Will you remember that?"

"I'll try, Maman. I'll try very hard."

"I know. Now, draw the curtains and light the candles."

"Are you going to make shadows on the ceiling and

tell me the story of the angel coming to Lausanne Cathedral?"

"No, not tonight. Tonight I want to give you something, a secret thing, so one day an angel will know who you are. Look in my eyes, Marc, listen to my voice . . ."

Rochat blinked, found himself at the open window with Monsieur Booty in his arms still, the two of them staring out into the dark. The children and mothers on the now lamp-lit corniche were gone, only an army of snowmen left behind to stand guard along the shore, silent and unafraid.

*Mew.*

"You're right. No time for beforetimes, not now. You have your duties." Rochat stepped back into the flat, closed the door. "Where were you? Oh yes, you were sitting on the bed, thinking if there was anything else to pack."

He shuffled to the bed and sat. Monsieur Booty jumped from Rochat's arms and into the rucksack.

*Mew.*

"I told you, you can't go. I'm very sure Monsieur Taroni wouldn't like the idea of a cat in the belfry; you'd eat the pigeons. They may be annoying with their poop and feathers, but that doesn't mean they should be turned into cat food."

He looked at the photograph on the bedside table. His mother and father standing on the Plains of Abraham. He slipped it between the sweaters, tied the rucksack closed. Then he shuffled through the flat, locking the windows and dousing the lights. He put on his overcoat and boots and headed for the door. At the hall entrance, Monsieur Booty sat blocking the way.

"What is it now?"

*Mew.*

"Of course I'll come back."

The beast looked at Rochat with a pitiful look.

"Oh, all right."

Rochat went to the drawing room and wrote a note: *M. Booty visiting towar. Back in 3 days.*

He left the note on the kitchen table for Teresa to find so she wouldn't worry because Monsieur Booty wasn't home. He shuffled to the hall closet, dug out Monsieur Booty's travel cage. He set it on the floor, opened the gate.

"Get in and sit." The beast got in and sat. Rochat closed the door and peered inside the cage. "Remember, you must be a polite guest in the belfry."

*Mew.*

"The timbers are very old and not your personal scratching posts."

*Mew.*

"And no eating the birds."

Silence.

"I said, no eating the birds."

*Mew.*

He tossed the rucksack over his shoulder and picked up the cat cage. He looked at himself in the mirror by the door. He stood as straight as he could.

"*Tu es le guet de la Cathédrale de Lausanne*, Rochat. Be not afraid."

He stepped into the lobby, locked the two locks of the door, and called for the elevator. Then he went back to the door, checking both the locks the way Monsieur Gübeli had taught him. The elevator came up in its iron cage and stopped. He opened the door, pulled aside the gate.

*Shhhclunk.*

He looked in the cat cage. "Are you ready for an awfully big adventure, you miserable beast?"

*Mew.*

"Me too."

He stepped into the elevator, pulled closed the gate, and pressed the button with the letters L-O-B-B-Y.

"Down, please."

The elevator heard and obeyed.

# eighteen

It was him, Alexander Yuriev. Sitting at a bank of slot machines in the Casino Barrière. He wasn't playing, he was talking. To a bloody slot machine.

Harper pulled his eyes from the photographs, looked ahead through the windshield. White light from the headlights of the inspector's Merc swallowing the dark road. Rounding bends, he watched the light fan over the lake like a searchlight.

"What are your thoughts, Mr. Harper?"

"About what, Inspector?"

"The photographs, of course. Sergeant Gauer had them printed from the casino's surveillance cameras with the assistance of your acquaintance Miss Lucy Clarke. Time codes burned in the photographs have Yuriev entering the casino at eight thirty-five Friday evening and leaving at nine o'clock. You were to meet him in Lausanne the same evening, I believe."

"At ten."

"Giving Yuriev plenty of time to leave the casino for

the regular sixteen after the hour train from Montreux to Lausanne, reaching Lausanne at nine forty. The walk from Gare Simplon to GG's would take no more than ten minutes."

Harper looked at the photos. Time-lapse shots. Top shots, side shots, digitally enhanced close-ups. The man's face, as if he hadn't slept in years. Harper slipped the photos into the manila folder, handed them back.

"Please keep them, Mr. Harper. I'd like you to study them a bit more, when you have the time."

"Why?"

"Because I want you to."

The man had a way with words. Harper rolled up the folder, stuffed it in his coat. "If you say so."

"How did he look to you?"

"Yuriev, or the night clerk?"

"Let's begin with Yuriev."

"Looks in pretty bad shape, stumble-drunk leaving the place. Didn't see him drinking in the photos. He was probably blocked before he got there. Explains his babbling at the slot machines."

"So it would seem. Sergeant Gauer, hit the lights, please. We must get a move on. Mustn't keep the good doctor waiting." The dark road ignited with flashing blue lights. The speed gauge rocketed to one-fifty per. The inspector settled back in the seat. "One of the perks of the job, kicking on the lights and speeding so as not to be late for dinner."

Harper replayed the inspector's words in his head. "What do you mean, 'So it would seem'?"

"Exactly what I said. Looking at the photos, one would assume Yuriev was very drunk indeed. Except the blood sample from the body found in the wreckage outside Gstaad had an alcohol count of zero."

It took a second for the penny to drop.

"The car wreck on the mountain road, it was Yuriev's body?"

"I'm afraid so."

"When did you get the DNA results?"

"I didn't need them. I knew the identity of the victim from the beginning. I had reasons to play dumb, as it were."

"I'm listening."

"But I'm not telling."

"Why not?"

"Because I'm the policeman and you're not."

"Right." Harper reached for his smokes.

"No smoking in the motorcar, Mr. Harper. Wreaks havoc on the leather. Had the seats specially made in Tuscany, you know."

"What are you going to do, Inspector, shoot me?"

The inspector laughed. "No, that would be Sergeant Gauer's duty. *C'est vrai*, Sergeant Gauer?"

*"Absolument, Inspecteur."*

Harper caught the sergeant's eyes in the rearview mirror. The kind that obeyed orders. Any orders.

The inspector leaned toward Harper as if sharing a confidence. "Did I mention Sergeant Gauer's last posting was in the sniper unit of the Vatican Swiss Guard? Cracking shot with a Barrett Light Fifty. Hit a moving assassin at twenty-five hundred meters. Perfect head shot, right between the eyes. Sort of thing the Vatican likes to keep quiet, of course. They'd much rather the world think of our Swiss Guard as jolly fellows with plumed helmets and halberds, not the most effective mercenaries on earth."

Harper looked out of the window. Fuck it.

Stone walls whipped by in strobes of blue light. Stone cottages in the terraced hills. Dark fields, rows of gnarled vines standing in snow. The inspector's voice continuing, "You may be interested to know this region has some of the best wines in Europe, from some of the oldest vines planted on the continent. Those stone-edged terraces were built by Christian monks in the Middle Ages—"

Harper ground down on his teeth.

"—and that large house atop the hill with the green shutters belongs to the Dézaley family. Wonderful vineyards, perfect soil for the Chasselas grape. Makes a lovely white. The doctor and I recently attended a rather fine dinner party there. A private birthday celebration for the president of France."

Harper turned to the inspector. "Screw the loveliness of your whites. What the hell's going on?"

"For a moment, Mr. Harper, I thought you might let me get away with pushing you around. Didn't you, Sergeant Gauer?"

"Very much so, Inspector."

Harper looked at the rearview mirror and the sniper's smiling eyes, then turned to the grin on the inspector's face. "You two are a barrel of laughs."

The inspector pulled a cigarette case from his pocket,

flipped it open. Neat fags all in a row. Brown-paper-wrapped, gold-tipped filters.

"Here, try one of these. Hand-rolled in a little shop in Paris, just behind the Ritz."

Harper took one; the inspector offered a light.

"Cheers."

"It's a rather rare tobacco, with a touch of North African herbs."

Harper took a deep draw, turned away, looked out of the window again.

Strobes of blue light.

Gnarled vines.

Twisted shadows on the snow.

Darkness.

Strobes of blue light. Gnarled vines. Darkness.

"How do you like the taste, Mr. Harper?"

"Sorry?"

"The cigarette, how do you like the taste?"

"As cigarettes go, it's swell."

"I'm so glad. History writes tobacco was discovered in the Americas. Actually, it was first grown in the once lush hills of North Africa. This very tobacco is still harvested there, on a patch of land protected by the king of Morocco."

"You don't say."

"Yes, similar to the tale of the horse. A creature native to the Americas that migrated over the land bridge once connecting the continent to Asia. The land bridge broke away to become the Bering Strait, and the horse died out in the Americas. But the memory of the creature endured through the centuries, to be drawn on the walls of caves and temples. Native Americans believed their gods would return to earth on the backs of horses. So when the Christians of Spain arrived on horses, well, you can imagine the unhappy result. The natives presented the Spaniards with treasures of gold and the virginity of their daughters, while the Spaniards, in deepest Christian gratitude, slaughtered the locals in the tens of thousands and usurped their lands. An all-too-familiar tale of human history, I'm afraid."

Harper took another deep draw from the cigarette. "I'm supposed to get all that from one of your flash smokes?"

"No, Mr. Harper. I was simply wondering if you enjoyed the taste. The rest was whimsy, shooting the breeze. That will do with the lights, Sergeant."

The car slowed. Splatters of icy rain on the windshield.

"*Merde,* more foul weather. I didn't tell you everything for the simple reason I don't know if I can trust you, Mr. Harper."

"You can't keep a thing like this secret."

"Of course I can. I practically run this country, which means I practically run Europe."

"Of course, how could I be so daft?"

"Not at all. Why don't you tell me what you've come up with? Find anything interesting while looking for Yuriev?"

"You had me chasing a dead man, Inspector. What was I supposed to find?"

"Just tell me what you've found."

Harper felt the words pulled from him, like stubborn teeth. "A note, in the cathedral."

"A note."

"Written in Cyrillic, stuck to a board at the back of the nave."

"At Chapelle de Saint-Maurice, I know it. And the contents of this note?"

"Barking mad stuff. Evil spirits and giants walking the earth. Maybe it was from Yuriev, maybe not. Judging from the photos, I wouldn't be surprised."

"Why's that?"

"Barking mad note in a cathedral, barking mad Yuriev talking to a slot machine."

"I see. When do you meet with the doctor again?"

"Tomorrow morning, ten sharp."

"I'm going to ask you to do me a favor, Mr. Harper."

"Don't tell him Yuriev is dead, got it."

"Actually, I'd prefer you didn't meet him at all. I'll explain you're to do a bit of work for me, off the books, as it were."

"Sorry?"

"Why do you think I requested your presence at the crime scene in Montreux?"

"Why do I think I'm not going to like the answer?"

"Because I suspect, despite being a bit slow on the uptake, you are one who senses danger from a great distance."

Harper lowered the window. Almost tossed the smoke. Remembered Swiss rule number whatever: No tossing ciggies on the ground. He crushed it in the door-side ashtray.

"How long have you known about Yuriev's killer? Or is it killers?"

"Killers. They came on our radar twenty years ago. As you've seen with your own eyes, they have an appetite for the most imaginative methods of slaughter."

"Imaginative, that's what you call it?"

"In meeting the enemy, Mr. Harper, it's helpful to recognize them for what they are without the affectations of human emotion, if you wish to survive."

"What are you getting at?"

"Geography, Mr. Harper."

"Excuse me?"

"The killings began in Moscow, then crossed through Eastern Europe and the Balkans. We lost track for a while, till the murders began again in the Middle East and up through Italy, Germany—"

"—Gstaad and Montreux."

"Would you care to run with that thought?"

"The killers were tracking Yuriev, but why?"

"At this stage, I can only tell you Yuriev did have something in his possession, something he was trying to give the doctor before he was killed."

"What is it?"

"I have no idea."

"Or you won't tell me."

"Either way, you find yourself in the same situation."

"Which is what?"

"By now the killers believe you have the thing they want. Or, at the least, you know where it is."

"And where would they get that idea?"

The inspector brushed at the lapels of his cashmere coat. "Oh, I'm sure you can do the sums, Mr. Harper."

Corpse pinned to the wall and sliced open, eyeballs fed to the fish, mobile number scribbled next to Miss December's pretty smile. Christ, Harper thought; the penny wasn't just dropping, it was falling from a great height.

"They've got my phone number."

"Well put, Mr. Harper. They do, indeed, have your number."

Harper didn't know whether to laugh or smash his fist in the inspector's sees-all, knows-all mug. He looked out of the window, laughed to himself instead.

"Do share the source of your amusement, Mr. Harper."

"You're a piece of work, Inspector."

"Do tell."

Harper turned back to him. "You recommended me to the IOC. I turn up in Lausanne and there's a flat, an office, calling cards, a wad of cash. Then, like clockwork, Alexander Yuriev comes calling. This isn't a job, it's a set-up."

"I'm afraid I don't follow you, Mr. Harper."

"You knew Yuriev was on his way to Lausanne, you knew he'd try to contact the doctor. And the real starter for ten, you bloody well knew the killers were tracking

him. You needed someone to run interference for your
doctor pal, you needed bait."

"I'm afraid in answering that one, I'd be revealing
more facts than required for the present."

"Is the doctor in on this?"

"I assure you, he's not. The doctor's part of something noble in a world badly in need of it. You and I,
however, are part of its filthy underbelly."

"Why me, why not one of your Swiss Guard lads?"

"I needed someone with your particular profile."

"As in a blackout drunk, someone so deep in the bottle he can't remember his bloody London phone number."

"To be honest, I was hoping for a bit more."

"Ask Guardian Services Limited for a refund."

"Trust me, there's no time for that, Mr. Harper.
Hopefully, you'll come around. In the meantime, let's
just say the unsuspecting always make for better bait,
don't you agree?"

The Merc rolled up through the outskirts of Lausanne and up from the lakeshore road to Saint-François.
The Christmas village on the square back in full swing.
Hot wine and drunken merriment beneath the twinkling
lights. Black umbrellas popping open as icy rain began to
fall. The Merc stopped at the traffic light. Harper looked
through the rain-pelted windshield. Flashing lights, a
blur of faces. The whole world refracted through tinted
glass, bending and stretching. Then the rain on the
windshield breaking into droplets and dripping down
the glass like everything melting, till the wiper blade

scraped over the windshield and wiped it clean and made
the world whole again. The traffic light flipped to green.
The Merc rolled up the hill toward the Lausanne Palace.
Another construction brigade on ladders, patching up
the hotel's holiday ribbons and bows and lights, righting
the small forest of beat-up Christmas trees. Life going
bizarrely on.

"So what am I supposed to do?"

"Your job."

"And what's my job, besides being bait?"

"I'm sure you'll work it out."

"What if I don't?"

"Then I'll find the remains of your slaughtered form
somewhere in Lausanne. Very soon, I'd imagine."

The Merc drove by the hotel, did a U-turn, stopped
at the bus stop fifty meters from the hotel.

"You'll forgive me if I drop you short of the hotel
entrance. The doctor might see you from the windows of
La Brasserie. Wouldn't want him asking questions. Can't
expect the man to be as resilient in his digestion as the
likes of you or me, what? Besides, you have the look of
someone badly in need of a drink."

"First honest words I've heard out of your mouth all
night, Inspector." Harper climbed out of the Merc,
slammed the door, walked to the pavement. Heavy drops
of rain pelting a patch of ice-encrusted snow, picking up
bits of lamplight, refracting into bits of color.

*Vnnnnnn.*

Rear window lowering, the inspector's voice jabbing
at Harper's back: "Mr. Harper?"

Harper turned around.

"I've made some arrangements to keep an eye on you, but make no mistake, you're in the gravest of danger."

Harper felt ice-cold rain drip down his neck. He pulled at the collar of his coat, turned around. Beyond the Merc, across Flon, above the old city: Lausanne Cathedral, illuminated in the soaking wet night.

"You believe in evil spirits, Inspector?"

"I beg your pardon?"

"Yuriev's note—evil spirits walking the earth. Seems appropriate just now."

"Does it, indeed?"

Harper took a slow breath. "Don't suppose I could tell you to fuck off and skip town?"

"No, I'm afraid not."

"Right. Thanks for the ride, then."

"Don't mention it. Enjoy your evening."

The window rose and the blue Merc drove to the hotel portico. The Prussian general of a doorman popped out, opened the rear passenger door, saluted. The inspector alighted and strolled, devil-may-care, through the revolving doors. Harper looked down, kicked at the ice-encrusted snow, watching it break into a thousand pieces of light.

"Now is the bloody winter of our discontent."

He looked up at the cathedral, thought about walking over, banging on the doors. Ask Headless Mary, Mother of God, the going rate for sanctuary.

Then again, didn't do her much good. He headed for LP's Bar.

\*          \*          \*

Katherine shuddered awake.

Alone in the bedroom, dark shadows against the white curtains, fireplace filling the room with light. She combed her hands through her hair. Slick, wet. Her skin, covered with the softest oil. Something delicious tingled through her body. She raised her wrist to her hand, smelling the scent of her skin, feeling the tingles swell. The oil was everywhere, her arms, her neck, her breasts.

She breathed the skin of her wrists again. Her flesh warmed with a quickening pulse.

"Yeah, here we go again."

Pulling her hair over her face, breathing deeper. Her body melting into the silk sheets. Her hands touching her skin, her beautiful soft skin.

"Jesus, whatever this shit is, I love it."

Then remembering the looking-glass dream once again, wanting to stay in the dream forever, sinking back to the bed. Her eyes searching the room. There, in the corner. The beautiful woman in the looking glass, floating fairylike in the dark.

"There you are, baby. Come play with me some more."

Watching the woman breathe, watching the joy seep into her blood. Katherine rolled her hips, the woman in the looking glass rolled her hips. She touched her breasts, the woman in the looking glass touched her breasts.

"I so want it again, I want it again and again and . . ."

The beautiful woman dissolved and then reappeared,

on the bed, but from a different angle. Still following her every move, but still looking away, dissolving and reappearing again.

"You're teasing me. Won't you come closer?"

Katherine inhaled the smell of her skin again, closing her eyes, waiting for the forever rush. She fell back, stretched out on the bed, expecting to fly. Then high in the corner of the room, a tiny red light jumping from corner to corner.

Katherine stopped moving. A dull feeling washed over her as the rush slipped away. She shook her head; something was not right. She climbed from the bed, wobbled, trying to find her balance.

The woman in the looking glass was standing, trying to find her balance, too.

Katherine stumbled toward the table.

She watched the woman in the looking glass stumbling the same way. Katherine stopped, shook her head, focused her eyes at the thing on the table.

It wasn't a looking glass; it was a laptop computer.

"What the fuck?"

A tiny red light sparked next to her. Katherine stared at it till she could see it was connected to a video camera. She stepped back, saw herself on the computer screen, stepping back from the table. The picture dissolved and the red light jumped to a high corner. A second camera up there. Her eyes searched the room. Three, four . . . six fucking cameras, pointing to the bed in the center of the room.

"No way."

She reached for the curtains behind the desk, eased one aside. The window had been filled in with bricks.

"What the fuck?"

Katherine looked around the room.

Her luxuriant room of marble fireplaces and fragrant flowers . . . the place was a fucking dump. No fireplace, no flowers. Just an electric floor heater in the corner, cheap red velvet on the walls, bright spotlights above the bed. And the luxuriant red silk sheets on the bed, cheap shreds of polyester, soaked with sweat and semen stains.

"Oh, God, no. Jesus, please, no."

She stepped back, bumping the table. The computer beeped and numbers and letters poured down the screen in a high-speed waterfall. A small message box appeared in the center of the screen.

```
Connected: Encrypted Powerline
Hyperspeed
199 members online
Subject not in frame
Switching to replay
```

Then seeing herself on the screen, alone on the bed, drugged out of her mind, masturbating like someone possessed.

"Holy fucking shit."

Her eyes searched the room again, trying to make sense of it. She moved toward a light spilling beneath a door.

She touched the latch, pressed down with the lightest

touch, and opened the door. The light burned her eyes; she squinted to see. It was a bathroom. She went in.

A stinking toilet, a scum-lined sink. Bottles of oil, powders and herbs, mortar and pestle. Needles and syringes stained with traces of blood.

Katherine saw herself in the mirror, smeared makeup and swollen lips, hair sticky and matted. She looked like shit.

"What the hell happened?"

There was a large bath in the corner, a grimy window above. She wiped her hand across the glass, leaned over the tub, and looked out. She saw a metal platform outside the window, crisscross stairs. A dark alley four floors down. Dead end one way, signs of life the other, where a streetlamp stood at the corner of a small street.

Katherine looked at herself in the mirror again, realized she was naked. Then she saw the red spots on her breasts and skin. Bites and scratches and pressure marks. As if she had been mauled by a mob.

"Jesus, Jesus."

She looked around for her clothes, a robe, a towel. Not a stitch. She returned to the bedroom, she heard a muttering of voices echo down a mirrored hallway . . . and remembered walking down the same hall, in a beautiful gown . . . or was it a dream? Was all this a dream? She crept closer, peeked around the corner. A bright room at the end of the hall. She saw three shadows moving against a wall. Komarovsky and his attendants, it had to be them. They were there before, they gave her tea and fresh sweetmeats, Komarovsky telling her she was adored . . . Katherine felt a touch of fear as she realized she wasn't dreaming at all, and the muttering voices were talking about her.

". . . the test is positive . . ."

". . . will need another dose soon . . ."

". . . have her bathed . . . taken to the others . . ."

The tall one's shadow disappeared from the wall. Katherine saw his reflection appear in the mirrors. Walking toward the hall, walking toward her. She backed away and ran to the bed. She lay down and covered herself with the filthy sheets. She closed her eyes. She heard the tall one enter the room and open the door to the bathroom. She half opened her eyes, saw him through the doorway. Turning on the taps to the bath, testing the temperature with his hand, turning back toward the bedroom.

Katherine closed her eyes again, heard him come close to her. Felt him sit on the bed and pull away the sheets. Felt the touch of his fingertips tracing over her shoulders and breasts. His body lowering close to her, his lips moving against her face: "Are you dreaming still, my pretty?"

Katherine swallowed the scream in her throat.

"Yes, I know. You want more, you need more. Don't worry. I'll be right back to bathe you in oils and inject you with potions and you will be in paradise once more."

She felt his tongue lick her neck and nibble at her skin. She stopped breathing. *Don't move, don't move.*

"There, there, my pretty. Soon, very soon."

Katherine felt him rise from the bed, she heard him walk away. She opened her eyes. He was gone.

Panic rushed through Katherine's blood. *Gotta get out of this place now!*

Her mind trying to think through the fog in her brain.

Bedroom window walled in, Komarovsky and his freaks down the hall, coming back to drug you. Wait . . . the bathroom window, the metal platform and stairs, must be a fire escape. She jumped from the bed, searched the room for her clothes. Only her mink and her bag on a chair. She grabbed both and hurried to the bathroom. The hot water pouring into the tub, filling the room with steam. She leaned over the tub and pulled at the window latch. It wouldn't budge. It had been nailed shut.

She saw the water in the tub, more than half full now. The tall one would be back any second with his fucking knockout drugs.

"Shit!"

Her eyes desperately searching for something to break the window . . . She felt the thickness of the fur coat in her hands.

"Yeah, yeah."

She rolled the coat around her arm, turned away her face, and smashed the coat against the glass. The window shattered apart. She quickly smashed the remaining shards from the frame. She leaned out of the opening: just a short drop to the metal platform below. She laid the mink across the sill, stepped up on the edge of the tub, and leaned through the window. She dropped her bag on the fire escape and then pulled herself through. She tumbled down onto the fire escape.

She tossed on her coat, grabbed her bag, and quickly climbed down the stairs. Looking up, seeing if she was being followed . . .

*Keep going! Keep going!*

. . . the stairs ended at the first floor. A metal ladder needed to be released to get to the ground. The release handle wouldn't shift.

"Motherfucker!" She sat on the landing, put her back against the wall, and kicked at the handle again and again. "Motherfucker! Motherfuck—"

The release snapped and the ladder dropped to the ground. Katherine climbed on, looked up to the window again. Still no one. She flew down the ladder, falling to the snow-covered ground. She picked up her bag, was halfway down the alley before she realized she was heading to the dead end.

She turned back, saw the street at the other end of the alley, saw a taxi stopping at a red light. She was about to scream at the taxi when she looked up and saw a shadow at the broken window. She froze . . .

*Fuck it! Run!*

. . . she bolted for the street . . .

*Don't stop! Don't look back!*

. . . her bare feet pounding through the snow, her eyes seeing the red light go yellow, seeing the driver put the taxi into gear . . .

"Wait! Wait!"

# nineteen

Rochat had been shoveling snow from the balconies and dumping it on the cathedral roof all night. Madame La Lombarde, Couvre-feu, and their three sisters in the upper carpentry appreciated his company and acted like long-lost aunties. Lots of "Why, hello, Marc!" and "We don't see enough of you!" But in the lower timbers, Clémence and Marie complained he made far too much noise with his shovel. Marie was even more upset that Rochat had unmade the snowman on the south balcony only to reassemble him in the corner of the timber cage where she lived.

"And what do you expect me to do, madame? Chop him up and dump him on the roof? I was told to get rid of him, no one told me where to rid him to."

Marie responded by ringing for two o'clock.

Rochat dropped the shovel and hurried to the loge. Monsieur Booty was curled in a ball on the bed; he opened one eye. Rochat gave him a mocking bow.

"Sorry to disturb you, your royal catness, but some of

us have important work to do and can't be sleeping on the job."

He lit the lantern and shuffled around the tower, raising the lantern and calling the hour. He looked out over Lausanne to make sure all was well. Low, gray clouds had settled in and icy rain was beginning to fall. He hooked the lantern to the railing and resumed his shoveling duties. Marie's fading voice still hummed with displeasure at the continuing racket.

"Well, I'm very sorry I'm disturbing you, madame, but if I don't clear the balconies of snow, this rain will turn everything to ice, and I could end up bidding you adieu as I go sliding over the railing, and wouldn't you feel bad then?"

The great bell didn't answer.

"Bells. You work and you slave and this is the thanks you get."

He shoveled the last clump of snow and dumped it on the roof. He shuffled back to the loge, collecting his lantern from the railing and resting the shovel next to the door.

"And by the way, don't you go wandering off like you did last year. I have lots of work for you yet. Can't spend my time looking for you, you just stay by the door."

He stomped his boots free of snow and ice, slapped snow from his overcoat, and stepped inside the candlelit loge. He hung his coat and hat on the hook behind the door, blew out the lantern, and set it on the table. Monsieur Booty heard the racket and sat up for a stretch.

"So, you miserable beast, I've finished the balconies.

Tomorrow I'll attack the roof. Difficult battles ahead yet." Monsieur Booty wasn't interested. He rolled on his back, stretching his paws to all four corners of the bed. Rochat took off his hat and scratched his head. "Cats and bells, bells and cats. There's got to be more to life."

Rochat brewed a cup of tea, picked up his plate from Café du Grütli, and sat on the tiny patch of bed Monsieur Booty hadn't managed to claim as his own. He picked at the *pommes frites* left on the plate, dabbing them in the last of the mushroom sauce. Monsieur Booty perked up, realizing food was being consumed.

"Forget it. You look like a big fat furry balloon already. You're going on a diet when we get home."

*Mew.*

"*Non*, I can't have you eating me out of house and home. Or belfry, come to think of it."

He reached up and turned on the radio in the old wooden box. He waited for the tubes to warm up. He always knew when the tubes were ready by the yellow light glowing from the back of the radio. The light was the same color as the burning candles set about the loge. He tuned through wavy voices in the air. Paris, Belgrade, Berlin. When the needle pointed to Rome, a woman's voice filled the room. She was singing a very sad song, and the candles about the loge seemed to move with her voice. Rochat sipped his tea and watched the candles. He scratched Monsieur Booty's belly as a man began to sing with the woman, sounding as if he were trying to hold her with his voice.

"I know this music, Papa liked it. He knew all the

words and he'd run around his house and put on funny hats and act out the story. It's about a silly butler who makes a bed and works for a mean king. That's why the woman is sad, because she's married to the mean king and he doesn't love her anymore. And there's a girl who pretends to be a man and a woman who pretends to be another woman and . . . I can't remember the rest. But everyone sings together at the end, and they're all happy."

Monsieur Booty twitched his ears and purred.

"Nice to know you like the music, too."

The music did end with everyone singing together and sounding happy. There was lots of applause, and Rochat joined in. Then he turned off the radio, jumped from the bed, and began to tidy up the loge.

"Yes, Rochat, it's been a very busy night and your legs are sore, but you must complete your duties."

He swept the floor, arranged his sketchbooks on the shelf, checked his candle supply. Then he sat on the bed to rest just as Marie shook the loge with three powerful gongs.

"Oh, of course, madame. Why should I need to sit for a moment, madame? Yes, yes, at your service, madame."

Rochat put on his overcoat and hat and lit the lantern. He headed out of the door, turning to Monsieur Booty on his way. "And when I come back, you miserable beast, I expect to see the rest of the *pommes frites* on the plate and not in your fat stomach. And scoot over to your side of the bed, if you please. I'll be finished with my duties after I call three o'clock, and I'm very tired."

He shuffled around the tower, calling the hour to the

east and north, then to the west and south. He looked over Lausanne for the final watch of the night. The icy rain fell more heavily, dripping from streetlamps and making thumping sounds on the snowy rooftops of the old city. The snow-cleared streets glistened with slippery ice.

"All is well, and cold, Rochat. And you've performed your duties for another night. Time to say good night."

He blew out the lantern.

Tires screeched from beyond Pont Bessières.

A shaft of fast-moving light cut through the rain.

A speeding taxi turned at Langallerie, stopped at the corner of Rue Caroline. The rear door flew open, and a woman with blond hair and a furry coat jumped from the car and ran into the building in her bare feet.

The taxi drove away.

"It looked like the angel was coming home, Rochat. But it looked like something was wrong with her. Or maybe you only imagined it because you're very tired."

He dashed into the loge and dropped the lantern on the table. He opened the closet and grabbed the binoculars. Monsieur Booty sat up with alarm, watched Rochat stumble over a stool on his way out of the door.

*Mrewwww.*

"Never mind, you stay here!"

He hurried to the upper balconies and crawled into the carpentry above Madame La Lombarde. He put the lenses to his eyes, turned the focus ring till he saw her through the windows, walking in circles and waving her arms in the air. Then pulling at her hair and throwing her bag on a chair and picking up something from a table and throwing it at the wall. It shattered to bits. She tore off her furry coat, dropped it on the floor. Her hair was messy and she was . . . she was naked.

Fucking goddamn bastards."

Katherine ran into the bedroom and into the bath. She tore her robe from the back of the door, stumbled back to the sitting room, and sank to the sofa, tears burning her eyes. She reached for her bag. *Cell phone, where's the fucking cell phone?* She dumped her bag on the coffee table. The phone tumbled out with her wallet, cigarette case, Taser gun, and a packet of unopened condoms.

"Jesus, I didn't use protection."

She dialed Geneva. Two rings, three rings.

"C'mon, answer the goddamn phone."

*"You have reached Madame Simone. If you are being referred by the Two Hundred Club . . ."*

The message stopped and a woman's voice answered. *"Oui?"*

"Simone, thank God, Simone. He's a freak! He's a goddamn freak!"

"Katherine, where are you?"

"In my flat. I got away from that fucking freak and his fucking freak friends!"

"Calm down, dear. I'm in the middle of something. I'll call you back in one minute."

"Simone, wait! Simone!"

She dropped her phone on the table, grabbed her cigarette case, fumbled at the lock, got it open. Her hands shook as she put a cigarette to her lips. She found her lighter, clicked it . . . three tries, four tries.

"God damn it to hell."

Her cell phone rang, she grabbed it.

"Simone, Jesus, what took you so long?"

"Katherine, it's only been two minutes. Now, what's this about?"

"I've been drugged, I've been raped. Fucking bastards."

"Calm down. Who raped you, Monsieur Komarovsky?"

Katherine tried to think.

Bodies. Beautiful bodies.

Floating on a cloud of silver mist.

"I'm . . . I'm not sure. But I know I was gangbanged and I know Komarovsky was there with his freaks."

"Where did this happen?"

The room, the stinking cesspit of a room.

"I don't know. I don't fucking know."

"Dear, you're not making sense. You must calm down."

"Jesus, I'm crashing from the drugs . . . What time is it?"

"It's gone past three."

"What day is it?"

"Thursday morning, dear."

"Jesus, they had me out for two fucking days."

"Darling girl, you're overwrought."

"They had a fucking drug lab in the bathroom, Simone. And there were cameras. They put me on the fucking Internet!"

"I'm sure it was nothing of the sort. And what drugs did you see? Cocaine, methamphetamine, heroin?"

"Powders, herbs, some kind of oil on my skin."

"You're a big girl, Katherine, you know how the wealthy can be somewhat eccentric in their tastes. You remember the Japanese gentleman who paid a small fortune to write calligraphy over your body?"

"Fuck's sake, Simone, I was drugged and gangbanged for two fucking days, the bastards could've infected me with AIDS—"

"Katherine, listen to me."

"—I don't care how fucking rich they are, I'm calling the police."

"Stop right there, dear. Pardon my French, but you're a whore. Now, I've seen this sort of thing before. Too much wine, too much fun, things get out of hand. We all have a bad trick now and then, but going to the police would only raise embarrassing questions for you. Don't forget that prostitution, international money laundering, and tax evasion are serious crimes that could have serious repercussions on your lifestyle. And in Switzerland, making unfounded accusations of rape against the wealthy is even worse."

"I'm not making this up."

"Calm down and be still, everything will be fine."

Katherine drew on the smoke.

*Whore, a bad trick, everybody has one.*

"I want you to send that bastard's money back to him. I want nothing to do with him, ever."

Simone was quiet.

"Simone?"

"I'm afraid I can't do that, dear."

"What?"

"Katherine, you need to face the facts of the situation."

"What . . . what are you talking about?"

"Do you truly believe the last six and a half months were without purpose? Did you not carefully read the agreement you signed with me?"

"Simone, I don't understand . . ."

"Then I'll help you. You were spotted in America, you were tested by members of the Two Hundred Club and found to be most talented, and I took you on. But you can't think it was for your own enjoyment and welfare."

"What?"

"Darling girl, you were brought to me for grooming."

"Grooming . . . why?"

"Why, to be sold to the highest bidder, of course."

Katherine felt a cold chill run through her skin. "You can't fucking sell me."

"Darling girl, grooming and selling sweet little things like you is what I do. Now, luckily for you, Monsieur Komarovsky seems to hold fine affection for you. And frankly, you're not getting any younger. In no way do gentlemen prefer sagging breasts and cellulite-riddled bottoms, not when they're paying top money for it."

"I'm getting the fuck out of this country."

"I'm afraid that isn't possible."

"Fuck you, Simone. I've got plenty of cash in the bank, I'll do what I fucking want."

"Your personal accounts are well hidden, withdrawals over twenty-five thousand francs must be cosigned by me. You really should've read the fine print, dear."

"You can't do this."

*Bzzzzzz, bzzzzzz.*

"Jesus, someone's at the door."

"I really must run, dear."

"Simone, wait."

"Katherine, the deal's been signed and sealed. And now it's time for you to be delivered. By the way, if you cause me a breath of trouble, I'll have the Swiss police and IRS after you with a basket full of arrest warrants before you can say fellatio. Good-bye, dear."

*Bzzzzzz, bzzzzzz, bzzzzzz.*

"Simone, please—"

L ook out, behind you . . ."
As if hearing his voice, the angel jumped from the sofa and turned to see shadows moving along the walls.

"It's the bad shadows, Rochat. They're coming for the angel."

He watched two men emerge from the shadows. A skinny tall one and a small one with whiskers on his chin. They walked slowly into the sitting room. The angel ran for the terrace doors. They flew across the room, grabbed her hair, and pulled her back. The small one took her cell phone, slipped it in his coat. He pointed his finger at her, telling her to do something, but the angel shook her head. The small one slapped her hard across the face.

Rochat turned to La Lombarde. "Did you see, madame? Those men from the bad shadows hit the angel. She's in trouble. I'm very sure she's in trouble."

He looked through the binoculars again.

The small one was holding the angel as she struggled to break free. The tall one pulled a curved knife from his coat and touched the blade to the angel's cheek, then he sliced down. The angel screamed and fell to the floor. The small one picked her up, threw her to the sofa, and stood in front of her.

"They're hurting her . . . Why are they hurting her? You have to see, Rochat, you have to see."

Rochat slid down the timbers, ran to the northeast turret. He balanced the binoculars on the iron railing and focused.

The tall one took a step to his left and Rochat could see the angel's face. She was crying, her right hand over her cheek, blood running down her face. He let the binoculars slip from his hands, ducked behind the pillars.

"They're hurting the angel . . . You have to help her."

He rushed down the turret to the east balcony, jumping in the timbers and banging Marie-Madeleine with his fist.

"Marie, wake up, the angel's in trouble! The bad shadows are here and they look like men and they're killing her! We have to help her!"

He saw movement in the windows. He jumped from the timbers onto the south balcony and looked through the binoculars. The small one, pulling the angel to her feet, leading her from the sofa. She screamed, pulled away. She opened her bathrobe to the men. Rochat quickly spun around with the binoculars still stuck to his eyes.

"Marie, she's showing them she's naked. Why is the angel showing them she's naked?"

He spun back to the windows. The small one stepping close to her, closing her robe, touching her hair. The tall one walked away, another light switched on. Rochat panned the binoculars and saw the tall one in the room where the angel had her dressing table. He was opening a closet, picking through clothes, pulling this dress and that, tossing them to the floor. Rochat whipped the binoculars back to the sitting room. The small one, reaching in his pocket, removing a silver tube . . .

"The small one's doing something, Marie!"

. . . opening the tube and pouring a clear liquid into one hand, rubbing his hands together, not seeing the angel move behind him, picking up something from the coffee table. Something in her hands. Black, metal.

"A gun! Marie, the angel's got a gun!"

She rushed from the sofa, stuck the gun in the small one's back. He jolted and fell to the ground. The angel turned and ran down the hall.

"She killed him!"

He panned back to the other room. The tall one hearing something, dropping the dress in his hands, running out of the room.

"The angel killed him and ran away, Marie! And the tall one heard the shot!"

Rochat jumped to his feet and hurried back to the railing, focused down on the wet street; nothing. Up to the windows, the tall one lifting the small one from the floor, slapping his face.

"*Non*, he's not dead, Marie. The angel didn't kill him."

Down in the street, she was coming out of the building and into the rain, running over patches of snow and ice in her bare feet. She ran over Pont Bessières; he could see her screaming. She rounded the corner at Café de l'Évêché, fell again, pounded her fists on the ice, on the darkened windows. Rochat jumped to the carpentry and banged Marie's bronze skirt.

"Marie, it's my duty to help her, but I don't know what to do."

He looked through the binoculars again, back to Rue Caroline. The two men were in the dark street, looking both ways, looking like bad shadows again.

"You have to help her, Rochat, you have to help the angel." He panned down to the café windows.

The angel was gone.

H elp! Someone, help me!"
      Staggering up the hill, her feet sliding over ice.
"Help! Someone!"
Falling, getting up, running along a fence.
"Somebody! Help me!"
Hearing a door scrape open, seeing a spark of light in

the corner of her eye, then a shadow rushing fast toward her, growing larger, lunging for her.

"Oh, God, no!"

Grabbing her arm, dragging her over the cobble-stones.

"No! Let go of me!"

Throwing her through a doorway and pressing her against a stone wall.

A heavy door slamming shut. Darkness.

Terror clawed at Katherine's throat.

"Let go of me! Fucking let go!"

Her screams like a thousand mad shrieks in a deep cave. She looked for a face, only seeing black.

"No!"

She pulled free, pounded down with her fists.

"You piece of shit! You fucking piece of shit!"

Kicking, clawing, pounding harder. Her screams feeding her blows.

"I'll fucking kill you! You touch me again and I'll fucking kill you!"

*"Non, c'est—"*

"Shut up, you piece of shit! I'll fucking kill you!"

*"—le guet, c'est le guet!"*

She held her fists. Her eyes still blind with terror, seeing only a dark silhouette gathered around a spark of fire, hearing a voice, almost whispering: *"C'est le guet, c'est le guet."* The voice rising and echoing and floating away with the sound of her screams. She looked up, saw warm light moving over four close-in walls of stone, the high ceiling disappearing into shadows.

"Where am I?"

*. . . where am i, am i, am i . . .*

"In the cathedral."

*. . . in the cathedral, the cathedral, the cathedral . . .*

She looked down, saw someone in a long black over-coat and a black floppy hat, his body hovering over a burning lantern as if protecting it.

"The cathedral . . . How did I . . . Who are you?"

He turned slowly. She saw his face and the lantern light reflecting in his eyes.

*"Je m'appelle Marc Rochat. Je suis le guet de la Cathé-drale de Lausanne."*

# twenty

"Y̲ou? You're the guy in the bell tower, with the lantern? I don't believe it. I don't believe it."

Rochat watched her sink to the cold floor. Her eyes going somewhere else, not even noticing the blood on her hands, on her face. Her hands uncurling from fists, her tears turning to laughter, but Rochat knew it was sad laughter. He listened to her voice echo through the stone chamber.

*. . . don't believe it, don't believe it, don't believe it . . .*

He pulled a handkerchief from his overcoat, leaned toward her. Katherine shrieked, punching him back to the wall.

"Don't touch me! Don't fucking touch me!"

"Shhh, they'll hear you."

*. . . they'll hear you, hear you, hear you . . .*

She held her breath.

Rochat whispered in his quietest voice, "I saw them. The men who came from the bad shadows."

"The what?"

"I saw them from the tower. A tall one and a small one. I saw them."

... *i saw them, i saw them, i saw them* ...

"The men, you saw them?"

"Shhh, whisper. If they hear you, they'll know you're hiding in the cathedral."

She quieted.

Bitter cold pierced the quiet. She shivered.

"Jesus, I'm freezing."

... *i'm freezing, i'm freezing, i'm freezing* ...

She jumped, hearing the echo of her own voice.

"Who's here? Is somebody else here?"

Rochat thought about it. Maybe it would scare her and make her run away to tell her about all the teasing shadows and Otto the Brave Knight and the skeletons under the floor of the nave.

"Just my cat."

"Your cat?"

"My cat."

... *my cat, my cat, my cat* ...

"Jesus . . ."

Katherine pulled her knees under her chin and buried her face in her hands, then her hands curled into fists again as she chewed at her bloodstained knuckles. She cried quietly to herself. Rochat didn't move. He watched blood ooze from the cut on her face; it didn't look deep, but it was still oozing. He listened for footsteps beyond the door.

He heard rain dripping from the high-above turrets. He heard wind blow away the rain.

"They didn't come to the cathedral."

"Who?"

"Those men."

"Are you sure?"

"I can hear footsteps from far away, and Maman told me about bad shadows, how they look like men. They didn't come to the cathedral, I can tell."

Katherine leaned her head back to the wall, looking at the shadows in the high corners of the stone chamber. "I must be losing my mind."

*. . . my mind, my mind, my mind . . .*

Rochat watched her.

The blond hair, the face.

It was her, but she didn't look the same. She looked raggedy and scared, her legs and bare feet covered with icy slush. She shivered with cold.

"What am I going to do? What the fuck am I going to do?"

"I have a telephone. You can call a policeman, if you want."

"No! Not the police! Please, no police!"

Rochat held up his hand to quiet her. *"D'accord."*

She dropped her head in her arms. "Jesus, I want to go home, I just want to go home."

*. . . want to go home, to go home, go home . . .*

Rochat heard something in her voice, something very sad, like the bad shadows had crushed her wings. So if the bad shadows came to the cathedral nave to find her, she wouldn't be able to fly away.

"I know a place you can hide. It's warm and there's a

bed. You can hide till you're better, and then you can go home."

"What?"

"No one will know you're there, because you won't be hiding in the cathedral, you'll be hiding in the belfry."

"I don't understand."

"The belfry's profane, it's not consecrated like the rest of the cathedral. So if they come to find you in the cathedral, you won't be there. Do you want to see?"

Rochat pulled himself to his feet. He tugged at an iron latch and opened the door to the tower. She saw his boots, the twisted right foot, his small crooked frame draped in a long black overcoat. She panicked as he turned to leave.

"Wait, where are you going?"

"To the belfry. There're lots of steps up the tower, and they go around and around and it's dark. But I brought my lantern so you can find your way."

The piano man played a slow blues riff. The chanteuse picked up the microphone and crooned along, glass of champers in her hand. Gone way past three, *mesdames et messieurs*, drink up and get the hell out. Nice accompaniment to stuffing Yuriev's photos back into the manila envelope. Was proving difficult. Envelope somewhat smaller than before. Harper held the last photo of Yuriev's haggard face looking dead into the camera. As if he knew it was over and there was nowhere to run.

"Getting to know the feeling, mate."

"*Pardon*, Monsieur Harper."

He looked up, Mutt and Jeff standing over him.

"Hello, lads, time to die?"

"We believe it's time to escort you to the hotel."

"Hotel, right. Hang on a tick, what happened to my flat?"

"Inspector Gobet has arranged for you to stay at the Hôtel de la Paix for the time being."

"For your protection, you understand."

"We have a car waiting."

They reached under his arms. Harper pulled away.

"Oh no, you don't. I'll get up on my own and I'll walk on my own, *s'il vous plaît*."

"Are you sure you won't fall?"

"We wouldn't wish you to hurt yourself."

"Of course fucking not. You boyos have to keep me alive for the fucking psycho killers, don't you?" Harper pushed against the table and slowly rose to his feet. He wobbled but didn't fall. "God save the bloody Queen." Mutt had Harper's coat at the ready; Jeff settled the bill with a quiet word with the bartender. The bartender bowed to Harper.

"I hope you enjoyed your evening, Monsieur Harper."

"Cheers. Hang on. You're that polite bartender from the other night. What's your name?"

"Stephan, monsieur."

"Stephan, that's right. You're a friend of hers, aren't you?"

"Monsieur?"

"Miss Taylor. You're her friend."

"Mademoiselle Taylor is an acquaintance of my girl-friend, monsieur. And I have the pleasure of serving her when she visits the Palace."

"Then you tell her—Miss Taylor I'm talking about—you tell her I was here till the bitter end. For our date tonight. No, wait, last night, we had a date."

"Of course, monsieur."

"No, no. Not that kind of date. A few drinks and stroll around the cathedral date, that's all."

"I'm glad to hear it, monsieur."

"I'm glad you're glad."

"I will give Mademoiselle Taylor the message. *Bonne nuit.*"

"*Bonne nuit* . . . Wait, what's your name?"

"Stephan."

"Stephan, right."

A taxi waited on the street. White Merc glowing red from the Christmas lights dangling and bouncing off the hotel façade above the bar. Harper waved his arms in indignation.

"Hey, those Christmas lights are still broken. What happened to the construction brigade? What's wrong with this country, anyway? Falling apart at the steams—seams."

"You needn't concern yourself with the Christmas decorations, Monsieur Harper. The workers will have it put to rights by the time you wake up."

Mutt and Jeff dumped Harper into the backseat.

"Not coming for the ride, lads? I'm in the gravest danger, remember?"

"Undercover operatives are posted at the hotel, Mr. Harper."

"Your driver is one of them."

Harper caught the driver's eyes in the rearview mirror. "Let me guess, another ex–Swiss Guard sniper. Hey, good enough for the Pope, good enough for me. Forward, he cried from the rear."

The taxi pulled away from the curb. Harper stared out of the window.

Wet asphalt, clumps of white snow on the pavements, streets devoid of life.

Toothbrush. Need a toothbrush.

"Sorry, mate, could we swing by my flat? I need my toothbrush. And toothpaste, I need toothpaste."

"I've already been to your flat and prepared a valise. It's in the trunk."

"You went in my flat without my permission?"

"I went in your flat under orders from Inspector Gobet."

"Ah, Inspector Gobet of the iron fist strikes again. That's what I like about the coppers in this place, always looking out for you."

The driver crossed to Avenue Benjamin-Constant and up the hill toward the old city. Downtown Lausanne gave way to a wide view of the lake. The taxi slowed to cross the road to the Hôtel de la Paix. Harper leaned over the front seat for a better look; looked swell. Seven floors, all the rooms with balconies overlooking the lake, all the balconies with yellow awnings. The taxi slammed to a stop, Harper's face went into the back of the front seat—

"Shite!"—a black Ferrari, speeding around a corner, missing them by inches. Harper looked back, watched the car roar through Place Saint-François and up Rue du Grand-Chêne.

"After him, Officer. Looked like the bad guys to me."

The driver eased across the road, pulling into the hotel entrance.

"Surveillance cameras have already recorded the license plate. The car is being traced and profiled as we speak."

"And let 'em get away? I'm telling you, there's ghoulies and ghosties and long-leggedy psycho killers on the loose in this town. Like to nail night clerks to walls. Seen it with my own eyes. Must have words with the inspector, get you lads straight. And let me tell you, I saw a fucking newspaper for the first time in . . . ever such a lot and, oh boy, no more nicely-nicely in this place. It's kill now and ask bloody questions later. You Swiss coppers need to get with the times."

The driver switched off the engine, turned to the backseat. "Do you wish me to call the porter to help with your valise, Monsieur Harper? Or will you and your smart arse manage by yourselves?"

S he was sleeping as soundly as Monsieur Booty, who was sleeping next to her on the bed.

Just before she laid her head on the pillow, Monsieur Booty jumped down from his hiding place behind the radio and introduced himself by sticking his cold nose in her face. Rochat told her the cat's name was Monsieur Booty.

"Hello, Monsieur Booty," she said, and she closed her eyes.

The beast quickly took advantage of the situation and made himself comfortable in the curves of her duvet-covered body. Rochat sat on a stool and watched her. On her stomach, with one leg curled and her hands tucked under her chin. He could smell her skin in the circulating warmth of the loge; she smelled like Marseille soap.

He took off his hat and laid it on the table. He sat on a stool, scratched his head.

He stared at the lantern flame and thought about beforetimes.

When she first came into the loge, she stood in the middle of the room and didn't speak. She held her arms tight across her body, still shivering with cold. Rochat stood with his back to the door, afraid to move, afraid he might scare her away. Slowly, as the warmth of the loge seeped into her bones, she became conscious of her surroundings. The odd shape of the room, the wooden walls set between crisscross timbers, the cockeyed ceiling high above her head. Then the little bed fitted sideways between the timbers at the end of the room, and the many candles that filled the room with comforting light. Rochat waited for her to say something, but she only stood still for the longest time until:

"What a very strange place this is."

Rochat waited for her to say something else, but she

didn't. He set his lantern on the table, the flame still burning.

"They built the loge between the timbers. That's why it looks funny."

She rubbed her arms. "I'm so cold."

"I'll turn up the heater, and I have a sleeping bag under the bed. It's better than my wool blankets, and you can open it like a duvet. Do you want to see?"

"Yeah."

"*D'accord.*"

It was only six steps to the bed, but after two steps, with the small table protruding from the wall, she was standing in the way. He nodded to the bed.

"I have to go that way."

She pressed herself against the table; Rochat squeezed by without touching her. He opened the cabinet under the bed, found the sleeping bag. He undid the zipper that made it a duvet. He laid it on the bed, squeezed by her again, retaking his position at the door.

She stepped slowly up to the bed. She opened her soaking bathrobe, let it fall to the floor. Rochat spun quickly around, his nose touching the door of the loge. He waited till it was quiet. He peeked over his shoulder; she was sitting on the bed, her naked body wrapped in the duvet.

"You're bleeding a little."

"What?"

Rochat pointed to her right cheek. It took her a moment, seeing the blood on her hands, looking at the bloody robe on the floor, touching her cheek and seeing the damp red on her fingers.

"They cut my face?"

"On your cheek."

Rochat took a small mirror from the shelf near the door, shuffled to the bed, handed her the mirror. She held it like something fearful.

"I'm afraid to look."

"You rubbed it and made it messy, but I don't think it's deep."

She looked into the mirror. "My face, Jesus, my face."

"I'll boil some water so you can wash. I have Marseille soap."

She didn't answer. She kept staring in the mirror, touching the bloody spot as if trying to make it go away. Rochat shuffled toward her; she stiffened.

"What are you doing?"

"I need to get things from underneath the bed. And I'll close the air vent, so it stays warmer in the loge."

"Okay."

She lifted her legs. Rochat dug through the cabinet, closed the small vent at the back of the closet, pulled out the plastic tub of washing things. He took a water jug from behind the door, filled the kettle, and set it to boil. She watched his every move. The timbers creaked and groaned.

"Cover your ears."

"What?"

*GONG! GONG!*

Her hands shot to the walls, holding on to the timbers as the loge shook in the deafening sound.

*GONG! GONG!*

"What the hell was that?"

"Marie. She lives in the carpentry next door. When you hear the timbers, it means she's going to ring the hour. She said it's four o'clock."

"Marie?"

"That's her name, Marie-Madeleine, she's a bell. Do you want to see?" He watched her eyes, slipping away and returning to now.

"That's the French name for Mary Magdalene, isn't it?"

*"Oui."*

The kettle clicked off. Rochat poured hot water in the plastic tub. He added cool water, mixed it around. He set a stool by the bed and rested the plastic tub on top.

"I can make it hotter or colder."

She reached into the water with her bloodstained fingers. She raised them slowly, watching pink drops fall from her fingertips.

"No, it's just right."

He gave her the soap, a washcloth, and a towel.

"The towel's clean. I brought it from home."

She stared at the things in her hands.

"My name's . . . Katherine. Do you have any bells named Katherine?"

*"Non."*

She looked up. Rochat saw a tear run down her bloodied face.

"But Katherine would be a pretty name for a bell, too."

"You think?"

*"Oui."*

"Your name, it's Marc?"

*"Oui, Marc Rochat."*

"And you're the guy in the bell tower, with the lantern."

He nodded.

She leaned over the tub. Steam rose from the water and enveloped her face. She soaked the washcloth, touched it to the cut, and cleaned away the blood. She cupped water in her hands and poured it through her hair again and again. Then she unwrapped her arms from the duvet to wash her arms and neck. The duvet slipped; Rochat saw her breasts. There were red marks and scratches all over her skin. He quickly turned around, putting his nose to the door again, listening to the water run through her fingers. He didn't move till long after the water sounds stopped and he heard her voice call to him.

"You can turn around now, Marc."

She was pulling the duvet over her shoulders, tight around her neck. The towel was wrapped around her hair. Her face was clean, the skin around the slice on her cheek looking purple and swollen. Rochat stepped toward her, but then stopped.

"You need some medicine and a bandage. I have some."

"Okay."

She watched him open the cabinet next to the door,
take out a small bottle, some two-by-two bandages, and
a roll of surgical tape. He removed two bandages from
the sanitary packaging, picked up one, and poured antiseptic solution over it. He shuffled three steps to the bed
and held it out to her.

"Could you do it for me, Marc?"

"Me?"

"Please?"

"*D'accord.*"

He stepped closer, dabbed the damp cloth to the
wound. She flinched. He dabbed a few more times till
the wound was clean.

"I'll make a bandage now."

She watched him shuffle to the table, cut four strips of
surgical tape from the roll, and attach the strips to a fresh
bandage, careful to make sure the strips were half on and
half off. He shuffled back toward her, holding out the
bandage for her.

"Here."

She looked at him. "Are you a med student or something?"

"I don't know what that means."

"It's like a doctor."

"I'm not one of them."

"Could you hold the mirror for me?"

He held the mirror for her as she set the bandage over
the wound.

"How do I look?"

"You look better."

He gave her the mirror and shuffled back to the door. He stared at the floor, feeling the strange sensation of her presence in the loge.

"Marc?"

He raised his eyes from the floor. In the soft candlelight of the loge, she looked pretty again, he thought.

"Why are you helping me?"

"Because you're lost."

"Lost?" She pulled her knees under her chin, half smiling to herself. "I must still be hallucinating."

Rochat wasn't sure what the word meant. "Is that like imagining things?"

"Yeah. Big-time."

"I imagine things, too."

She looked at him. A crooked little man in a floppy black hat and a long black wool overcoat, a mildly insane look in his pale green eyes.

"Where on earth did you come from?"

"Quebec City. It's on the same line as Lausanne."

"The same line?"

"The line on the globe in Maman's house."

Her eyes became heavy, overcome with exhaustion. She lay down on the bed. "That's nice."

That's when Monsieur Booty jumped down from his hiding place behind the radio to stick his cold nose in her face, and Rochat said the cat's name was Monsieur Booty, and she said, "Hello, Monsieur Booty," and she closed her eyes and fell asleep.

Rochat pulled his eyes from the lantern flame and blinked. His cup of tea was cold now.

He whispered to himself, "The angel has come to Lausanne Cathedral, Rochat, just like Maman said. And she's lost, so you must protect her. Like you protect Marie and Clémence and all the bells and all the old stones and teasing shadows and Otto and . . . you must protect her till she can go home. That's what you must do."

He moved quietly about the loge, blowing out the candles. All but the candle in his lantern, in case she woke and was scared. Then she'd know she was in the belfry and was safe, he thought.

He took off his overcoat and sat on the wood floor, his back to the door.

He laid the coat over himself like a blanket. He watched her sleep.

*Book Three*

THE AWAKENING

# twenty-one

Steel wheels on steel rails.

Running east to west this time.

Hotel telly didn't have the History Channel, so Harper spent the night waiting for the cathedral bells to count off one more sleepless hour. Wasn't much, but it beat counting and recounting dead soldiers in the ashtray. A packet of smokes' worth now.

Steel wheels coming again. The sound like a wave rolling up from Geneva, cresting at Gare Simplon, rolling on to Montreux.

Christ, Montreux.

Once or twice, drifting in the almost sleep, Harper saw the night clerk pinned to the wall. But it was only the curtains at the balcony door moving in the draft. Then he thought he saw Yuriev stumbling out of the casino on his way to his own grisly end. That one was only trails of cigarette smoke floating through the room. *Two poor sods you never met,* Harper thought, *slaughtered because they talked to you on a telephone.*

Another train. West to east.

Heavy and lumbering.

It slowed into Lausanne but didn't stop; it picked up speed, moved on. Had to be a freighter. They rolled by Lausanne like clockwork on the twenty- or forty-minute mark all through the night.

Just after the seven-o'clock bells, lighter trains came every two or three minutes. Leaving behind pecking sounds of feet on icy pavements that grew more in number with the coming and going trains.

The eight-o'clock bells brought buses and trolleys and gathering voices. Harper climbed from the bed, crossed the room, and pulled open the curtains. He saw locals in the streets on their way to their daily bread. He saw morning light glowing firelike on the iced cliffs above Lac Léman.

He walked back to the bed, downed three aspirin, looked at the telephone. The thing had buttons with pictures next to them. Man carrying bags, woman behind a desk, woman in maid uniform, man with a tray, man holding a suit of clothes. Harper picked up the receiver, pushed a button.

"*Bonjour*, Monsieur Harper, how may I serve you?"

"Are you the man with the tray?"

"*Pardon?*"

"I'd like a pot of coffee and croissants, please."

"*Absolument, monsieur, tout de suite.*"

"Do you have *The Guardian*?"

"*Pardonnez-moi?*"

"English newspaper. I'd like to give the state of the world another go."

"Of course, monsieur. I can purchase one from the tobacconist. May I charge it to your room?"

"Sure, and add five francs for yourself."

*"Merci, monsieur."*

"Hang on, what day is this?"

*"Jeudi, monsieur."*

"Thursday."

*"Oui, monsieur."*

Harper hung up the phone, headed to the shower, and lingered long enough to feel the cobwebs of the long night clear a bit. He dried himself before the steamy mirror. Drips of water snaking down the glass let him see watery reflections of his face, his chest, the still-healing bruises on his stomach and ribs. Couldn't remember where they'd come from. Must've been way beyond pissed at the time. Took a fall down some stairs, maybe.

He wrapped the towel around his waist and found his valise. Everything inside arranged as only a Swiss copper could've done it. The socks were perfect. He took his shaving kit to the sink, did the deed without slicing open his throat. He stared at the face in the mirror a good long while.

"What?"

Down on a stool, a hotel bathrobe folded nice and neat. He picked it up and shook it out, wondering about the man who spent his life folding bathrobes. Thinking that's the job he should've had in Lausanne. Out of sight, out of mind. Locked up in some basement. Left sleeve, right sleeve, fold twice, tie snugly with belt. He slipped it on as someone came rapping at the door. He walked over, looked through the spy hole. Young woman in white busman's jacket standing behind a serving trolley. Silver pot, china cup and saucer, basket of croissants, neatly folded newspaper. The newspaper looking as if it'd been folded by the same man who did the bathrobes. He opened the door.

"*Bonjour, monsieur.*"

"Sorry, not quite dressed."

She wheeled the trolley through the door. Harper stepped into the hall.

No bad guys this way, no bad guys that way. No good guys, either.

"Do you wish me to pour the coffee, monsieur?"

Harper stepped back in the room. "That's fine, I'll do it."

"As you wish, monsieur." She offered him the bill in a leather folder.

"This is only for record purposes. The Swiss police will be paying your bills."

"I should hope so." He signed it and handed it back. He saw the bulge under her busman's jacket. "I take it you're one of Inspector Gobet's gang?"

"Monsieur?"

"The gun under your coat. Rather hefty from the look of it, or perhaps that's because you're such a delicate thing."

She took the leather folder. "I'll be delivering all your meals during your stay. If anyone else appears at your door, don't answer and dial triple zero on your telephone. The code will alert us."

"What about the maid?"

"Fresh towels are under the breakfast trolley. Inspector Gobet suggests you make your own bed. He also suggests you do not leave the room. Please feel free to use the minibar."

"I didn't see any guards in the hall."

"There are CCTV cameras in the lobby and elevators. As long as you stay in your room, you should be safe enough."

"Should be?"

"Yes."

She turned to leave.

"There's no History Channel on the telly."

"Inspector Gobet left instructions you were not to have the History Channel."

"Sorry?"

"He thought it best you find another way to pass the time."

"Any idea what that might be, besides die at his beck and call?"

"I'm sure I'm far too delicate to know such things, monsieur." She walked out of the room, closed the door.

Harper rolled the trolley to a chair near the balcony windows and tucked in. Two cups of coffee and half a croissant later, he checked the headlines. World still going down in flames, just faster than yesterday. As if caught in the laws of physics, gravity dragging the whole bloody thing down. He tossed the paper on the bed, stared out at the big rocks across the lake. Orders of the day: Stay out of sight, look for a new hobby. Wait for a pack of fucking psycho killers to find you. How lucky can a man get?

Laws of physics. Gravity.

Luck.

No such thing.

He searched the room for his coat. Nowhere to be seen till he opened the closet and saw it in a heap on the floor. A hanger lying next to it, as if in the wee hours he'd given up the struggle. He hung the coat up properly and pulled the manila envelope from the pocket. He poured another cup of coffee, pulled the photos from the envelope, flipped to the last shots: Yuriev stumbling out of the casino.

Laws of physics somehow remembered: To stand, the force of gravity on body mass must be countered by an equal or greater force as applied by the legs, or you fall down. More laws of physics: Walking requires legs and feet to move in alternate but coordinated steps of equal pressure per square inch to maintain balance and resistance to force of gravity on same body mass, or you fall down.

He laid out the photos.

Yuriev's feet were all over the place. His body mass leaning forward, way off balance. Shoulders pinched back, arms hooked to the sides.

Laws of physics said he should've fallen flat on his face.

Harper checked the photos of Yuriev at the slot machines. The poor sod's eyes flipping from side to side. Harper found the overhead photos, compared them to the head-on shots, following Yuriev's eyeline. The man wasn't talking to the slots, more like talking to people on either side of him, but there was nobody there. Back to the last shots, Yuriev's arms rising from his side, arced and twisted as if he's being dragged from the place. Harper's eyes searched the photo. Halogen lamps in the ceiling, hitting Yuriev's back. There were shadows on the carpeted floor.

"You must be bloody joking."

B y the time the tenth bell rumbled through the loge, Katherine was letting go of the walls. The vibrations subsided and the door at the end of the room opened. A fat gray cat darted in, followed by a crooked little guy in a long black overcoat. He was carrying a yellow plastic tub loaded with what looked like Chianti bottles. She pulled the duvet over her body.

"Who are you?"

"Marc Rochat."

"The guy with the lantern."

"*Oui.*"

"And this place is the cathedral."

"In the belfry, on top of the cathedral."

"Yeah, okay." She ran her fingers through her hair. "Is it morning?"

"It's ten o'clock. Didn't you hear Marie?"

"Who?"

"Marie-Madeleine; she rings the hour."

"Oh yeah, her." Katherine leaned against the wall. Monsieur Booty hopped to the table and then onto the bed; he nestled in the duvet. "And this is your cat."

"My cat, Monsieur Booty."

Rochat set the yellow tub on the table and stood by the door. Katherine stared at him, his round face framed by a mop of uncombed black hair.

"You look different without your hat."

"I forgot to put it on when I went out."

"And there's snow on your coat."

"I was shoveling snow from the tower roof before I got water from the fountain."

"What?"

He pointed to the bottles in the yellow tub. "I got fresh water from the fountain."

"Those are Chianti jugs."

"I use them to get water from the fountain, so they're for water now."

"Where's the fountain?"

"On the esplanade. Do you want to see?"

She watched him, standing still with a nervous look on his face. "How old are you?"

"I have twenty-one years."

"You look younger."

"I have twenty-one years."

"My name's Katherine."

"You told me your name was Katherine before you went to sleep."

"I did?" The night flashed through her mind; she touched the bandage on her face. "What . . . what else did I say?"

"You said, 'Do you have a bell named Katherine?' and I said, 'No.'"

"Yeah, that's right, and you told me your name was . . ."

"Marc Rochat."

"Yeah. So, Marc, I don't know how to say this, but . . . I need to pee."

Rochat thought about it. He reached behind a timber, found the plastic water bottle with the top cut off, and held it out to her.

"What's that?"

"The piss pot."

"You pee in an Evian bottle?"

"I pee in an Evian bottle."

"What do you do with it when you're finished?"

"Empty it on the roof of the cathedral and rinse it out and put it back."

"Isn't dumping pee on a church a sin or something?"

"Monsieur Buhlmann said, 'If these blasted pigeons are free to shit all over the cathedral roof, I don't think the creator gives a hoot about a little piss from the likes of you or me.'"

"Who's Monsieur Buhlmann?"

"He worked in the tower before me. He only works on Sundays now because he's old."

"Well, I'm sure it works for you and Monsieur . . ."

"Buhlmann."

"Buhlmann, yeah. But my plumbing's different, you know?"

Rochat thought about it some more. He turned and put away the piss pot. He removed jugs from the yellow tub and held the tub out to her.

"You mean you don't have a toilet up here?"

"Not in the tower. But there's one under the unfinished tower for when I need to . . . other things."

"Can I go there?"

He took the skeleton keys from a hook on the wall. "I can take you. Do you want slippers? I have slippers under the bed."

"Yeah, that'd be great."

Rochat shuffled to the bed; she jumped as he came closer. He stopped. "They're under the bed, in the little closet."

Katherine lifted her feet and slid to the corner of the bed. He opened the closet, found the leather slippers with thick cotton inside. He laid them on the bed and closed the closet door. He shuffled back to the door, watched her try them on.

"Wow, fuzzy slippers, I love fuzzy slippers. You don't have any extra clothes, do you?"

"I have some trousers and some wool socks and some shirts and two sweaters. They're under the bed, too, in my rucksack."

"Can I have a look?"

Six steps back across the loge, under the bed, up with the rucksack.

"And there's an extra toothbrush. You can wash it and use it. I have another one in the loge, it's in a jar."

Rochat shuffled back to the door and stood. Katherine looked at him, feeling suddenly shy.

"Um, could you go outside for a minute, Marc? While I get dressed?"

"I can go outside for a minute while you get dressed."

He shuffled out of the loge, closed the door behind him.

He looked out over Lausanne and the lake. He felt warm sunlight cut through the cold air. He turned and saw Marie-Madeleine hanging in her timbered cage, detecting a severe scowl on her bronze face. The snowman near her, however, smiled with walnut teeth.

"*Bonjour, Madame Marie-Madeleine et Monsieur Neige.* A good rest, I trust?" Marie was silent. Rochat reached in the timbers and gave the great bell a rap with his knuckles. She grumbled.

"What do you mean, what must I be thinking? You saw what happened last night; those men from the bad shadows hurt her. And Monsieur Rannou said an angel would come to the cathedral to hide and I have to protect her. It's my duty, so there."

The door of the loge opened, and Katherine peeked out. "Who's out there?"

"Me."

"Who're you talking to?"

Rochat pointed into the timbers. "Marie-Madeleine."

Katherine looked around the stone pillars and into the crisscross timbers and saw the massive bronze thing.

"You're talking to a bell?"

"She's not happy this morning."

"How can you tell?"

Rochat couldn't decide if it'd be rude to tell the angel Marie didn't like her hiding in the belfry, so he rocked on his heels and didn't speak. Katherine looked around the stone pillar again.

"And why is there a snowman in there with the bell?"

"I made him in front of the loge first, but Monsieur Taroni said I had to get rid of him, but I didn't want to chop him up, so I hid him next to Marie."

"Who's Monsieur Taroni?"

"The caretaker of the cathedral."

"So your snowman's on the run, too, huh?"

Rochat looked at Monsieur Neige, then Katherine. "He doesn't have any legs."

She stared at him, not knowing if he was joking or truly insane.

Soft bells rang up from Place de la Palud—*tink, tink*. Katherine's eyes followed the sound. She saw the snow-covered roofs of the old city, curly streams of smoke from chimneys. She saw the long crescent of the lake, the French Alps rising above Évian and the Swiss Alps rising to the east, all the world rising into the clearest of blue skies.

"Gosh, it's like flying up here."

"It is?"

"Yeah, it really is."

"I imagine I can fly when I come to the belfry at night."

"No wonder." Katherine looked over the railing and down to the esplanade. She saw people walking along the cobblestones, and she jumped back. "There're people down there."

"But people don't look up when they walk under the tower, except when the snowman was standing here yesterday. Monsieur Buhlmann says the bell tower was once the tallest building in Europe, and people always looked up then. But they stopped when it wasn't anymore."

Rochat saw his sweater and trousers on her body, his slippers on her feet. The towel he gave her last night was over her shoulders. She held the toothbrush, toothpaste, and Marseille soap in one hand; her other hand held up the loose-fitted trousers.

"My clothes look funny on you."

"They feel funny, but we'll worry about that later. Can we go now? I really need to pee."

"We can go now."

He shuffled along the balcony, pointing into the west timbers. "That's Clémence. She's always grumpy."

Katherine looked in and saw another big bell with pigeon shit on it. Rochat hopped down the tower steps and spiraled out of sight. She felt a sudden rush of panic like the night before.

"Hey, wait."

He leaned back around the newel. "What's wrong?"

"Just wait for me, please."

He watched her come down the winding steps to meet him. "Are you afraid?"

"I'm all right. Just don't run away."

"*D'accord.*"

He led her two turns down the tower to the low wooden door built into the curving stone wall. Rochat pulled his skeleton keys from his overcoat, gave them a shake, and found the right one. He unlocked the door.

"There's a tunnel and you have to bend down and it's dark."

"There's not another way?"

"We could go outside and around the façade, but I imagined you didn't want to go outside so people wouldn't see you."

"You imagined right."

Rochat ducked into the tunnel. Katherine watched him scoot through the dark and come out in a place of dim blue light, then he disappeared. She felt alone amid an eerie silence. She looked up and down the winding stone steps; she felt the tower walls closing in.

"Marc?"

*. . . marc, marc, marc . . .*

His head reappeared at the far end of the tunnel, upside down.

"You can come now."

"Jesus, where did you go?"

*. . . did you go, you go, you go . . .*

"I made sure no one was here; you can come."

*. . . you can come, can come, can come . . .*

Katherine ducked in and hurried as fast as she could. Clearing the tunnel, she straightened up and found herself in a place of blue light radiating from a huge stained glass of Christ on the cross.

"Yikes, where are we?"

"The tribune."

"What's a tribune?"

"It's the old balcony at the back of the nave. The coming-in doors to the cathedral are under your feet. This is where the Pope and the emperor sat before the organ was here."

"You mean we're inside the cathedral?"

Rochat pointed to the tall enclosures of polished oak. "The nave is the other side of those big boxes where the organ's pipes live. The console lives between the pipes—it looks like a spaceship. Do you want to see?"

"I really want to pee."

*"D'accord."*

He led her to the other side of the tribune and through a wooden door, down some winding stone steps, and along a narrow passageway to another wooden door that creaked when Rochat opened it, then down a few more steps into a large dusty room of unused tools and uncut blocks of limestone. Wooden slats high above, sunlight pouring through plastic tarps flapping in the breeze. He shuffled to a wooden shack in the corner of the room, unlocked the door. Inside was an old toilet and an old sink, a foggy mirror hanging on a nail, a string to a lightbulb hanging from the ceiling.

"I clean it every night, but there's no hot water."

"I couldn't care less just now. I'm going to have a bath in the sink."

Rochat looked at the sink and then her, from his fuzzy slippers on her feet to the top of her blond hair. "You're too big."

"I'll think of something. Just don't run off."

"I won't run off." He reached in his coat, pulled out a fresh bandage with fresh strips of tape along the sides. "I made this before you woke up. I imagined you'd need it."

"Gosh, you're a regular five-star concierge."

"I don't know what that means."

"I'll explain later. Don't disappear, please."

"I won't disappear, please."

She dashed in, closed the door. Rochat stood quietly.

He heard the toilet flush and water run in the sink and her voice say, "Wow, it's so cold!" She made splashing sounds for a long time, and when she came out she was towel-drying her hair with one hand, still holding up the trousers with the other. A fresh bandage was attached to her right cheek and her face had an inquisitive look.

"Which Pope?"

*"Pardon?"*

"Back there, in the tribune. Which Pope used to sit there?"

Rochat thought about it. "I don't remember. He's dead now."

"Huh." She looked up to the sunlight seeping through the wooden slats and plastic tarp. "What happened to the roof?"

"They're fixing it. The covers blew off in the big storm. That's where the unfinished tower is."

"Where?"

"Up there."

"There's nothing up there."

"That's why it's called the unfinished tower."

"What big storm?"

Rochat counted backward. "Two nights ago, before it snowed. Don't you remember?"

"I was drugged out of my mind two nights ago." Katherine finished drying her hair and rolled the washing things in the towel. "You don't have an extra belt, do you? I'm afraid your trousers are going to fall down around my ankles."

Rochat looked down at her hips. He saw her belly button, the swathe of white skin beneath. He looked quickly at her face. "I don't have an extra belt."

She tugged at the belt loops. "How about a piece of string or something?"

Rochat shuffled through the cluttered room till he found a length of thin rope that he laid on a block of wood. He picked up an old ax and chopped the rope in two. He held up the lengths for careful examination. He shuffled to Katherine, handed her the shorter length.

"I imagined this one will work because the other one's too long."

"Thanks." She laced the rope through the belt loops, pulled it tight, tied it in a bow. "How do I look?"

"Like a hobo man."

She looked down at her outfit, wiggled her toes in the slippers. "Hey, wearable junk is very hip these days."

"I don't know what that means."

"It means I'm looking good, considering my entire life's just gone to hell in a handbasket."

Rochat didn't know what that meant, either. "Are you hungry?"

"Yeah, I'm famished."

The room echoed with muffled gongs from high above. Soft, round sounds filled the cavernous room.

"What's that?"

"That's Marie. She says it's eleven o'clock."

"It sounds different down here."

"Monsieur Rannou says listening to the bells from inside the cathedral is like being in the belly of a whale."

"Who's Monsieur Rannou?"

"He plays the organ in the cathedral at night sometimes, but he's dead, too. We can go back to the belfry now. I've got some bread and cheese, and I can make tea while you think about things."

"What things?"

"How you can go home."

Rochat shuffled across the dusty room and up the stone steps. Katherine hurried after him, afraid to lose sight of the crooked little guy in the long black overcoat.

# twenty-two

There was a phone number and name scribbled under the translation of Yuriev's note. The elderly Russian gent in Café Romand, the one who looked like an elf, wrote it down just in case. Monsieur Gabriel was the name on the receiving end of the number. Biblical scholar and onetime boy soldier in the Spanish Civil War. Harper dialed. It rang nine times before a sickly voice answered.

"*Sí?*"

"Is that Monsieur Gabriel?"

"You are English."

"Sorry?"

"Only the English are so rude as to begin phone conversations by demanding information before introducing themselves."

"My name's Harper, Jay Harper. I met an acquaintance of yours at Café Romand."

"Which friend of mine have you met?"

Harper couldn't remember asking for his name. "He's Russian, you play chess with him on weekends."

"I play chess with many Russians on weekends, they are masters of the game. They stood with the Republicans in the war, the English stood with Franco and his Fascists."

*Click.*

Harper dialed the number again.

*"Sí?"*

"Let's try it this way. One of your Russian chess pals translated a note I found in Lausanne Cathedral. It sounds like something from the Bible, and your friend, whichever bloody one it was, said you might help me with it."

"Why should I help you with this note?"

"If it's a question of money, I'm happy to pay you for your time."

"I have no need of money. I only asked why I should help you with this note."

Harper didn't see a choice other than telling him.

"Two men have been murdered in the last week. Their deaths and this note may be connected."

"How were the men murdered?"

"Does it matter?"

*"Sí*, it matters. Tell me, English."

"One man was tortured with a pressing iron, then had his skull crushed with a hammer. Second man was impaled with an iron rod, pinned to a wall, eviscerated."

"And?"

"Two slaughtered men isn't enough?"

"You have yet to tell me why I should help you with this note."

Harper felt it again: No choice but to tell him.

"I'm next on the list to be slaughtered. Figuring out where this bloody note comes from just might keep me alive."

"How does it feel?"

"How does what feel?"

"For death to chase after you."

Harper lit a fag. *How does it feel?* He let go of the smoke. "Like I'm running out of time."

"Long Live Death."

"Sorry?"

"The battle cry of my brigade in Spain as we chased our own never-to-be-consummated death. Where did you find this note?"

"Lausanne Cathedral. There's a nun in the gift shop. She collects prayers left at a chapel, keeps them in a book. One of the murdered men was in the cathedral at the same time this note was left."

"You saw Sœur Fabienne?"

"Yes, I saw her."

"Then perhaps you should read the note to me."

"Do you need to write it down?"

"I am cursed with a photographic memory, English. It applies to my hearing as well."

Harper picked up the paper.

"'Evil spirits walk the earth. The spirits of heaven live in heaven, but this is the place of earthly spirits, born of the earth. Spirits of giants on the earth, like clouds. To occupy, corrupt, and bruise the earth.' That's all of it."

"You've no idea where these words come from?"

"No, why would I?"

"They are unknown to you, you have no remembrance of them?"

"Remembrance?" Harper took another pull on his smoke, feeling he was talking to a dead end, and at the same time feeling he had no choice but to keep talking. "Like I said, Monsieur Gabriel, why would I?"

Gabriel's voice broke into bone-shaking coughs.

"On second thought, English, I don't think I can help you. You'll excuse me, it's nearly time for my meditations, and I mustn't be late."

"Trust me, Monsieur Gabriel, I don't want to keep you from your meditations any longer than it takes to know the source of this bloody note. Now, can you help me or not?"

The sound of a striking match crackled over the line, then a wheezing draw. Harper listened to Gabriel's labored breathing.

"Sounds like you should think about quitting."

"I'm old and decrepit, English; smoking opiates relieves the pain."

"I wasn't told you were sick."

"I'm not sick, only weary. I yearn for sleep."

Harper wanted to laugh, talking to a sleepless tramp with meditation on the brain. Then again, a sleepless tramp talking to a sleepless drunk. What a wonderful town.

"I know the feeling. Look, I'm sorry to trouble you, mate, but—"

"—but death is chasing after you."

"That does seem to be the fact."

"As death was chasing after the one who left the note in the cathedral."

Harper drew on his smoke. "He told me he was being followed, he told me the same words I told you about running out of time."

"But you didn't believe him."

"No, I suppose I didn't."

"And, now, you feel driven to me in the hope I'll believe you."

"Maybe."

Harper heard Gabriel inhale his drugs like precious things, and then his voice as if it were drifting to another place.

"Your note is from the Book of Enoch, an ancient book of the Bible. The passage written is quoted from what scholars call the Slavonic fragment. The entire translation was never found."

Harper pulled open the desk drawer. Pen, Hôtel de la Paix stationery. He laid them on the desk, stared, wrote *Book of Enoch, Slavonic fragment.*

"So it's biblical. From the New Testament, Old Testament?"

"From the no testament. The Book of Enoch was thought to be nothing more than a legend. It was banned by the Jews at the beginning of the Christian epoch in AD 90, and by the Christians in AD 347. Enoch's name still appears several times in both the Jewish Bible and the Christian Testaments, but Enoch's book is not included in the Canon of Holy Scripture."

Harper scribbled down the words *Banned by Jews and Christians. Name appears in Testaments.*

"Why's that?"

"Hebrews 11:5: 'By faith Enoch was translated that he should not see death.'"

"Sorry?"

"Infect men with the fear of death, they will be your slaves. Take away the fear of death and you take away what blinds men from seeing the undying nature of their being; they are no longer slaves."

Harper stopped writing.

"Monsieur Gabriel, I really don't think I'm in need of a Bible class. I just need to know why a man who had his face hammered to pulp left a quote from the Book of Enoch in Lausanne Cathedral."

"In that case, English, my advice is that you read the Book of Enoch yourself. There is a translation of the Ge'ez script, found in 1906 in Ethiopia by one Reverend R. H. Charles. It was denounced as a fraud by biblical scholars, but I know it to be a true translation from the ancient Aramaic."

"Look, I'm not a religious man."

"The Bible has nothing to do with religion. It's a book, a wondrous and mystical book written by frightened creatures of free will who looked to the stars and being so overwhelmed with insignificance they dared to wonder: What is this place, where is this place, why is this place? They gathered and distilled all the world's gods and myths and legends into the greatest book ever written. And the Book of Enoch is the greatest book of the Bible never read."

"Because?"

"Because it wasn't supposed to be this way, English."

"Sorry, what wasn't supposed to be what way?"

"Everything, all of it."

"Could you narrow that down a bit?"

"Listen to me. The Book of Enoch tells the story of this place and why you are here."

Harper sensed he'd hit a dead end. He wrote Gabriel's words for the hell of it. "Greatest book of Bible never read. Tells the story of why men are here—got it."

"No, English, the Book of Enoch tells the story of why *you* are here."

"Me?"

Harper heard a druggy voice down the line. *"Sí."*

"Right. Could you tell me where to find this bloody Book of Enoch?"

"Go to Google and ask God."

"As in, type 'God' and see what happens?"

"No, English. In the round world, Google *is* God. The one true God who knows all things and reveals them unto men with the click of a mouse."

Harper dropped his pen on the desk. "Monsieur Gabriel, I have to tell you, I've no idea what you're on about."

Gabriel's voice fell into a diminished sigh. "Forgive me, I need another dose of opiates before my meditations."

*Click.*

Another dose of opiates, no bloody shit. Take them down and pass them around.

Harper hung up the receiver, dropped his fag in the coffee cup. It fizzled and floated like a rotting corpse. He looked at the mess on the desk. Shreds of handwritten notes, photos of Yuriev in the casino.

"Bollocks."

He shoved the lot in the desk drawer, slammed it closed. He walked to the curtains, slammed shut the balcony door. He stopped in his tracks, felt a pair of eyes at his back, turned around.

Down on the floor, a mislaid shot of Yuriev. Dead man's eyes looking at him.

Running out of time. All that had come before, finally and forever finished.

"Sod it."

He walked to the telephone, picked up the receiver, pressed the button with the man holding the tray.

"*Oui*, Monsieur Harper? How may I serve you?"

"Is my room wired for Internet?"

"Of course, monsieur, you'll find a broadband connection at your desk."

"Right, tell the Swiss Guards in the kitchen I need a computer, *tout de suite*."

"Monsieur?"

"A laptop, with a search engine. And ask the waitress with the gun to run over to LP's Bar and pick up a club sandwich."

"*Pardon, monsieur?*"

"And tell her to not forget the fries."

\*　　\*　　\*

Rochat made a pot of tea and set it on the table. He sat at the table and watched her eat.

"You're hungry."

"Worst case ever of the munchies."

Rochat guessed that meant really hungry. He watched her sip the tea. Color had returned to her face, and her eyes weren't as swollen from crying in the night. Her long blond hair was clean and smelled nice.

"And I'm still hungry; when can we have lunch?"

"I can go to Café du Grütli. It's at the bottom of Escaliers du Marché. I can bring two *plats du jour* for lunch. Today is roast duck day."

"Sounds good. When's lunch?"

"La Lombarde rings at noon—she tells everybody it's time for lunch."

"I thought the bell was called Marie-Madeleine."

"Marie rings twelve times first, then La Lombarde rings for five minutes. She lives in the upper carpentry above Marie. Do you want to see the bells now?"

"No, I'll just stay out of sight for the time being. Traveling to that toilet of yours is about all the adventure I can take for now."

"It's fun to see the bells."

"No, thanks, I'm fine." She looked up at the small clock ticking above the door. "I'll just sit here and wait for lunch."

"Do you want more cheese? I have a wedge of *bleu*."

"I'd love some, thanks."

Rochat brought the cheese to the table and set it on the plate. She tore a piece of bread from the loaf and spread the cheese like butter. She finished the wedge. There were only a few crumbs of bread on the table when she realized her host hadn't eaten a thing.

"Marc, I'm sorry. I ate everything."

He wasn't looking at her. He was looking at the empty stool next to the table. Smiling, mouthing words to himself.

"Marc?"

The timbers creaked and the room shook with the bell sound, but Rochat didn't move. The bell quieted; Katherine touched Rochat's arm. She saw him blink slowly and turn his eyes toward her.

"Hey, what happened to you?"

"Marie rang eleven times."

"No, before the bell, I mean. What happened to you?"

"Your mouth was full. It took me to beforetimes."

"Before what?"

"Beforetimes."

"What's that?"

"Sometimes I imagine people and things. I can see them and talk to them."

Katherine looked at the empty stool. "So who were you talking to just now?"

"Grand-maman."

"You saw your grandmother . . . like, here?"

"*Oui.* She was telling me it wasn't nice to eat with my mouth full. But the chocolate cake was good, and I asked for ice cream on top. That made her laugh and she told the butler to bring ice cream and the chef sent a big bowl. Grand-maman took out her teeth and set them on the table and started eating and couldn't stop. Then her mouth was as full as mine. Then I heard you telling me to come back, so I did."

"So she was in your head?"

"She was in her house in Vufflens. It's a castle."

"Your grandmother lives in a castle?"

"With a butler named Bernard and four maids and a cook named Adolpho. I thought you were an imagination once."

"Me? No, I'm real, but your grandmother and the others, are they real?"

"*Oui.*"

"And your grandmother lives in a castle, for real?"

"Not anymore, she's dead."

Katherine remembered someone else. "Downstairs, when I was cleaning up, you talked about an organist?"

"Monsieur Rannou."

"Yeah, that guy. You said he was dead, didn't you?"

Rochat nodded.

"And do you see him, too, sometimes?"

"Only once, but he won't come back anymore."

"How do you know?"

"He told me, three nights ago."

She covered her face with her hands. "I must still be stoned."

"Does that mean full?"

"No, it means . . . it means I'm a little confused."

"There was an accident when I was born."

"An accident?"

"I got tangled up in a cord because of my foot. It's

twisted and my leg is crooked. Then Maman died and I came to Switzerland to live with Grand-maman and Papa. Papa taught me to draw and Grand-maman sent me to Mon Repos School for children like me."

"Children like . . . you." Katherine turned her teacup in slow circles. "This school, was it for retarded kids?"

"I don't know what that means."

"Forget it, it's a terrible word. I'm sorry. Can I ask you something?"

"*Oui.*"

"Does it ever scare you to imagine people and things that aren't, like, there?"

Rochat thought about it. "*Non.* Can I ask you something now?"

"Sure."

"Don't you ever imagine things?"

H arper typed in the words, and a search page popped open at the speed of light. *Results: 1–100 of 1,470,000 for the Book of Enoch.*

"Blimey."

His eyes ran down the top of the list.

```
Book of Enoch and Secrets of Enoch at
reluctant-messenger.com
Book of Enoch translated from the Dead
Sea Scrolls at heaven.net
About the Book of Enoch at
youaregoingtohell.com
```

"Tell me something I don't know, mate."

He scanned the entries. Blips of words blinked through his eyes.

He pulled paper and pen from the desk drawer for another round of note-taking: *Once cherished by Jews. Dealing with the nature and deeds of the fallen angels, tells the story of angels mixing with women. Extinction level impacts from outer space predicted by 2012.*

He scrolled through thousands more, watching the references flip by. He pulled his finger from the mouse pad. See what pops up: *Book of Enoch. Its History, Fallen Angels, and UFOs.*

"Too good not to."

He clicked the words; the screen went black, then filled with thousands of computer-generated stars. Words appeared amid the stars, floating in deepest space.

```
AlienResistance.org
Supernatural beings identified as
angels
Supernatural beings identified as
extraterrestrials
Angels take women as wives
Alien abductions
Cloning
Missing fetuses
```

He clicked back to the search page, another too-good-not-to entry nearby: *The Watcher Files: UFOs, Aliens, Reptilians, Secret Government Black Projects.*

"The greatest book of the Bible never read, no bloody wonder."

He decided to pass. He walked across the room and raided the minibar. Walked back to the bed, picked up the telephone, punched the magic button next to the man with the tray.

"*Oui*, Monsieur Harper, how may I serve you now?"

"I'd like the minibar refreshed with beer, please."

"Refreshed with beer, monsieur. *Absolument, tout de suite.*"

"No hurry, there's three left. Just giving you a heads-up."

"*Le* heads-up. Of course, monsieur."

"What happened to the waitress with the gun?"

"Mademoiselle has been dispatched to the Lausanne Palace for monsieur's club sandwich, with fries."

"Cheers."

He dropped himself in front of the computer, scrolled back to the search page, eyed the list. *Book of Enoch— Wikipedia, the free encyclopedia.*

He gave it a double click. The page blinked open with pages of info. He started writing.

Enoch was great-grandfather of Noah. Man of visions, was said to have conquered death. Wrote visions on scraps of goatskin, transcribed by followers to parchment scrolls as the Book of Enoch. Original writings of Enoch and Hebrew transcriptions thought to have been taken (with original Hebrew transcription) to Egypt, kept in Great Library of Alexandria, translated and transcribed into Greek on papyrus scrolls, quoted by nearly all Church fathers. Enoch's name mentioned throughout Jewish Bible, Jesus mentions Enoch in New Testament. Hebrew text and Greek translation, along with Enoch's original writings, assumed lost with destruction of Alexandria Library (history records Julius Caesar burned library in 48 BC—actually destroyed in series of acts over four hundred years).

Enoch's writings fell into disregard—scholars doubt Enoch existed—struck from Hebrew scriptures by the Sanhedrin at Yavneh c. AD 90. Book totally discredited after Christian Council of Laodicea in 364 bans book from Holy Canon (Christian emperor Theophilus, AD 391, orders all "apocryphal works" of scripture to be burned throughout known world. AD 642, Arab army sacks Alexandria, Amir ibn al-As orders all "pagan" writings contrary to Koran to be burned when found).

By now, Book of Enoch considered no more than legend. Two transcriptions of Book of Enoch found in Ethiopia in seventeenth century, written on papyrus scrolls in aboriginal Ge'ez script. Claimed to have been translated from Greek transcriptions while held in Alexandria Library, translated into English in 1906 by Reverend R. H. Charles but disregarded by biblical scholars at the time as mystical ravings of subhuman species of men (fragments in Hebrew found in nineteenth century, Slavonic fragments, fragments in Latin, fragments found in Akhim—all discredited as frauds).

1947, shepherd finds network of eleven caves above ruins of Qumran—

The word *Qumran* highlighted in blue, he clicked it, the screen flashed to a new page. Harper scribbled more notes.

Qumran site of Essene cult of Judaism. Lived on shores of Dead Sea 100 BC–AD 70, spent their lives collecting and transcribing works of scripture and creation mythology. John the Baptist one of their number. Jesus of Nazareth visited Qumran during "Forty Days in the Desert"—said to have been tempted by "demon" Azazel at nearby Mount Quarantania above Jericho.

Thirty years after time of Jesus, Jewish revolt against Roman Empire begins in AD 66. Romans burn Second Temple in Jerusalem (AD 70). Essenes place original scrolls and transcriptions in clay jars and hide them in nearby caves as Roman army sweeps through Israel to burn and destroy all remnants of Jewish faith. Dead Sea Scrolls not found by Romans and lay undisturbed for two thousand years in dry desert air at lowest point on earth.

Harper lifted the bottle for another swig; it was empty.

"Bloody hell, Bible study is thirsty work."

He got up from the desk, walked to the minibar, grabbed another bottle of beer. He cracked it open, sat back at the desk. He lit a fag, clicked back a few pages to the Book of Enoch, picked up with the shepherd finding the caves above Qumran.

Writings found in clay jars at Qumran called the Dead Sea Scrolls containing only transcription of Bible in ancient Hebrew left in the world. Cave number four called "the Cave of Secrets" by biblical scholars. Contents of cave number four never revealed to world, now held in underground bomb-proof bunkers capable of withstanding nuclear attack in west Jerusalem.

Fragments of Book of Enoch (Aramaic) found in "Cave of Secrets," proving, after thousands of years of denial, Book of Enoch was real—still banned from Canon of Holy Scripture.

Harper raced over hundreds more entries. Something caught his eye; he stopped, clicked back.

**The Meaning of Enoch**

Depicts the interaction of the fallen angels with mankind. Taught men to make swords—beautifying the eyes—enchantments, astrology, taught signs of the sun and the course of the moon—fathered the Nephilim.

Nephilim: creatures who feed on human beings

(suggests slavery, or forms of political, economic oppression), born of "demons," who took form of men, and used human women to create a "new race on earth." Cycles of breeding every hundred years. Ancient Aramaic translation curses Nephilim as "half-breeds," said to have brought evil into the world, seek to capture the fire of creation (sic: God, Creator, Divine Force of Universe). Archangel Michael and celestial army sent to destroy Nephilim on earth—hide and protect the fire of creation from the "demon" Azazel.

"Half-breeds and fires of creation. Sounds like a must-read. So where the hell is it?"

He clicked back to the search page, scrolled again, stopped.

*ancienttexts.org/library/ethiopian/enoch/index.html.*

He gave it a double click. Computer screen turned the color of desert earth for a solid minute, then an unrecognizable script spread slowly over the top of the page, like scratches in the sand. English words forming underneath.

```
The Book of Enoch
Translated from the Ethiopian by R. H.
Charles, 1906
```

"Well, well, the Reverend Mr. Charles. I've heard so much about you and your barking book."

Harper looked at his watch: just shy of noon.

He slid his finger over the mouse pad, settled the cursor over the entry.

He double-clicked the computer. Nothing happened.

"Come on, Reverend, talk to me."

The screen faded to black, words began to form.

```
Book 1: Watchers
```

# twenty-three

The timbers creaked and moaned. Katherine covered her ears.

*GONG! GONG! GONG!*

Twelve strikes shook the belfry tower. Rochat watched Katherine cringe as waves of sound roared through the loge. When the last strike finished, Katherine lowered her hands.

"I guess that means it's noon, huh?"

Rochat touched his finger to his lips, pointed to the crooked ceiling, to someplace up there. Katherine listened to a lovely and soft sound. She closed her eyes.

The sound now falling rainlike through the tower, splashing against the timbers and balconies before finding its way into the sky and drifting away. For a moment, with her eyes closed and dreaming, Katherine thought she could hold open her hands and feel the rainlike sound, fresh and cool on her skin. There was a girl once who loved that game; she could still see her, hiding under the garden trees, stretching her hands . . . The sound was gone. Katherine opened her eyes.

"Wow. Which bell was that?"

"La Lombarde. She rings after Marie for five minutes at noon. She lives upstairs with the other bells. Do you want to see?"

"Why do you call the bells *she*?"

"Because that's what they are. Do you want lunch now?"

"Yeah, but are you sure nobody will come up here while you're gone?"

"Monsieur Taroni closed the tower to visitors because the snow and ice could make the balcony stones slippery."

"And Monsieur Taroni is . . . ?"

"The caretaker of the cathedral, he tells me what to do."

"Is he like the other ones?"

"Monsieur Taroni's not dead yet. He lives in nowtimes."

"Nowtimes. And that would be the opposite of . . ."

"Beforetimes."

"That's good, seeing that this Taroni guy tells you what to do and all. What about the guy you said works on Sundays?"

"Monsieur Buhlmann."

"Yeah, him."

"Not dead yet."

"And there's no chance any of these guys'll come up here in . . . nowtimes."

Rochat stood and took the ring of skeleton keys from the hook on the back of the door.

"I have the only keys to the tower, and you can stand on the balcony and watch me go down Escaliers du Marché and come back up. You can see the café from the balcony. Do you want to come outside and see?"

"No, I'll stay inside and wait."

He shuffled by her and reached above the bed. He fiddled with the buttons and dials of the old radio.

"You can listen to this radio. This is the button to turn it on, and this is the dial to find places in the air. It turns, like this."

"No, that's all right, I'll just sit here."

Rochat reached behind the radio, pulled Monsieur Booty from his hiding place, where he was enjoying a nap.

*Mew.*

"Oh, be quiet, you miserable beast."

Rochat held the cat out to Katherine, his legs dangling like furry noodles.

"What am I supposed to do with your cat?"

"I imagined Monsieur Booty can be me when I'm gone."

Katherine opened her arms and received the cat, who promptly nestled in her lap and went back to sleep. Rochat opened the small window that looked out to Clémence.

"And I'll leave this window open in case he needs to go out and do cat business. Just tell him not to scratch the timbers or eat the birds."

"No eating the birds, got it."

"I'll get lunch now."

He lifted his overcoat from an iron peg in the wall and slipped it on. He stuffed the keys in the pocket. He saw the look on her face.

"Are you afraid to be alone in the cathedral?"

"I'll be all right. Just don't forget to come back."

"You can call a friend if you want. The telephone's old, like the radio. You have to turn the numbers wheel."

She saw the telephone. Wooden box with a mouthpiece and a rotary dialer, black receiver hanging on a hook, two tiny steel bells on top.

"What a funny old thing."

"Sometimes it's hard to hear because it's so old, but you can call someone if you're afraid to be alone."

"No, I can't call anyone."

*"D'accord."*

He turned around, opened the door. Sunlight flooded by him, blinding her eyes.

"Marc, wait."

Rochat turned back. *"Oui?"*

"You won't be long?"

"I won't be long."

"Okay."

He watched the sunlight cross her face, her eyes catching the light and reflecting sparkly colors. She didn't move.

"Are you thinking about something?" Rochat asked.

"Yeah, I'm thinking there's something I have to tell you."

"Do you want to tell me now?"

"Not really."

*"D'accord."*

He turned to leave.

"No, Marc, wait."

He turned back again and waited.

"What I meant is, I don't want to tell you now or ever. But I have to, right now. Those men you saw last night?"

"From the bad shadows."

"The what?"

"They came from the bad shadows."

"Yeah, those bad-shadow guys. They said they'd find me wherever I went, they said they'd kill anyone who helped me."

Rochat stared at her. It took a long time to understand the words; no one had ever said such a thing to him.

"Oh."

"That's all you have to say?"

Rochat scratched his head and shuffled into the loge. He took his lantern from a shelf and set it on the table. He lit a match, set the lantern alight, shuffled back to the doorway, and faced her.

"It's my duty to protect you." He pulled the door closed.

Katherine watched the flame in the lantern. She heard sounds in the quiet. Above the world, middle-of-the-sky sounds. The breeze moving through the timbers and circling the tower. Footsteps crossing the far-below esplanade. A trolley bus rolling over Pont Bessières. The whistle of the ferry crossing the lake. There was the briefest moment of tranquility, before reality hit her over the head.

"You really got yourself screwed nine ways to Sunday this time, girl."

She looked at the wreck of a telephone on the wall. Damn, if only there were someone to call. She went through her contacts. Forget it. Daily gossip sessions meant Simone had the names of all her clients, Stephan at LP's, Lili at her sculpture studio, her family in the States, her favorite restaurants and haunts. Need an escape plan. Go to the Swiss cops or the US Embassy in Geneva? Oh yeah, there's an idea. *Hi, my name's Katherine, but you can call me Kat, and I'm a dope-smoking hooker from California with hobbies in international money laundering, insider trading, and eight years' worth of tax fraud under my belt, and I was wondering if you could help me, please?* Couldn't stay in a belfry forever. Think what it'd be like asking her roomie to pick up a box of tampons with lunch. She stroked Monsieur Booty's fluffy coat.

"This is what you call being up the creek without a paddle, fuzzface."

The beast looked up to her.

*Mew.*

"I get it. Your boss talks to bells, you talk to people."

*Mew.*

She stood with Monsieur Booty in her arms and

looked through the small square window above the table. Yup, big bell still hanging in the crisscrossed timbers, narrow stone balcony, pillars and arches opening to the sky. She could just see bits of way-down-there Lausanne and the snowy hills forming the border with France.

She turned to the small window facing east. She saw the long retiled roof of the cathedral with a conical tower at the far end, then the snow-covered vineyards beyond Lausanne and the lake bending to Montreux, and down to Italy where the icebound Alps rose to the blue sky. *Hell of a view,* she thought; *like sitting on the edge of a cloud.*

She opened the window; pigeons fled from the timbers in a blur. The cat's ears twitched.

*Merroow.*

"Hey, you heard the boss. Lay off the birds."

*Merrrroooow.*

She dropped the cat from her arms. He scratched at the wood floor.

*Merrrroooow.*

"Scat!"

Monsieur Booty hopped up to a stool, jumped on the bed.

Katherine rose on her tiptoes, stretched her neck through the small window to see Marie-Madeleine. The bell was as tall as the loge ceiling and twice as wide.

"No wonder it's so damn loud."

She closed the window, looked about the room.

There was a shelf along the wall, with a photograph of

a young man and a beautiful young woman on a cliff. She saw his face in the both of them—had to be mommy and daddy. A stack of tall, thin books behind the photo. She pulled one down, saw the words *"loge du guet"* written in childlike scribble on the cover. She sat at the table and opened the book. Inside were pictures of the very room she was in, drawn as detailed studies. The burning lantern on the table with a floppy hat, water jugs, candles, and the empty bed. There was a name at the bottom of each page, written in the same childlike scribble: *"rochat."*

"Hey, not bad."

She took down another book, *les bishops morts,* and opened it. She thumbed through a series of marble tombs. Clerics from the Middle Ages in stoneful repose, their marble faces worn away to almost nothing, but looking as if they just might sit up and talk.

"Not bad at all."

She took down another book, *piratz.* It was a story, like a comic book, with a wizard in a pointed hat, resembling the conical tower outside her window—even had the weathercock on top. And the wizard was flying through the night, lighting the sky with the huge diamond hanging around his neck. And he lived in a castle of ice, on an island in the middle of a boiling sea. Then there was a gang of goofy-looking pirates with wooden swords and paper hats, riding on the back of a giant caterpillar, flying over the boiling sea and circling the castle. The wizard and the pirates shouting at one another: "Pooh on you, you big mean wizard!" "No, you take it back, you dumb pirates!" "Oh, yeah?" "Yeah and double yeah!"

"Jesus, he's really good."

She reached for the last book, *l'ange de lausanne*. She heard footsteps on the balcony and quickly replaced the books on the shelf. She sat still on the bed and listened. There was nothing but the sound of pigeons scurrying outside the loge. Monsieur Booty took the opportunity to crawl over and curl up in her lap. She scratched the beast behind his ears.

"False alarm, Monsieur Booty. Just the pigeons."

*Merroow.*

"No, you still can't eat them."

*Merrrooow.*

"Yeah, yeah. Life's a bitch."

Katherine sat quietly, looked around the loge again. The odd angles of the walls and ceiling like lines of perspective squeezing down to the door at the other end of the loge. Weird, she thought; the wooden door was only six or seven steps from where she sat with a cat in her lap. But with the lines of perspective and the way it was set between two heavy timbers with a huge crossbeam above, the door looked like the gateway to a rabbit hole leading to a dark and scary place. Come to think of it, that's just what was on the other side of the fucking door. Better off above the world in the middle of the sky with a crooked, brain-damaged guy who thought it was his duty to protect you. *Damn good thing there's still someone left you can squeeze a favor from,* she thought. Her mind came to a screeching halt. Jesus, maybe he wasn't the only one. She lifted Monsieur Booty's face to hers.

"Hey, fuzzface, where's your boss hide the phone book?"

M onsieur Dufaux was snapping his dish towel on tabletops and pounding bread crumbs to the floor when Rochat came into the café.

"Marc Rochat! Where have you been?"

*"Salut, monsieur, ça va?"*

Monsieur Dufaux tucked the dish towel in his apron strings and shook Rochat's hand.

"I'm fine, Marc. But everyone's been talking in the café. Madame Budry says you must have found a girl to cook for you in the tower. You know, you are looking a little pink in the cheeks."

Rochat watched the cigarette bounce on Monsieur Dufaux's lip as he talked.

"Well, come on, Marc. Who is she?"

Rochat didn't know what to say.

Monsieur Dufaux smiled. "I'm teasing, Marc. What can I do for you?"

"I'd like two *plats du jour* to take to the tower, and a block of fondue cheese for later. I'll return the dishes tomorrow."

*"Deux magrets de canard avec frites et salade verte, c'est bon?* Wait, did you say two plates?"

*"Oui."*

"So maybe you do have a girl up there, eh?"

Rochat spoke very slowly to make sure he didn't make

mistakes. "I'm staying in the tower, because there's been lots of ice and snow. And Monsieur Booty, my cat, is visiting. So I need two *plats du jour*."

"Well, for you and your cat, I'll get the fattest ducks in the canton. Sit and have a Rivella."

"I'm in a hurry, monsieur."

"Marc, you have to give my cook time to go to the farm, find just the right ducks, and bring them to Lausanne. Then we need to wring their necks, pluck their feathers, and roast them in the oven."

Rochat wasn't sure if it was a joke. He laughed nervously, rocked back and forth on his boot heels. Monsieur Dufaux put his hand on Rochat's shoulder.

"You have time for a Rivella, Marc."

"I have time for a Rivella."

Rochat sat at the table by the window. He pulled back the lace curtain and looked up the cobblestones of Escaliers du Marché. He could see the belfry through the bare plane trees, and the streaks of thin white clouds sneaking in from the southwest. Monsieur Dufaux came to the table with the drinks and sat.

"So what's the weather report for tonight, Marc? More snow coming our way?"

Rochat remembered what the sky looked like from the tower. "It's too warm for more snow today, but stingy kind of clouds are coming from the southwest. That means more rain by tomorrow night, then winds will come down from the north and it will turn very cold and icy."

"Really?" Monsieur Dufaux reached for the newspaper and turned to the weather report. "Bless me, you're right. Come to think of it, last week you sat right here and said old man winter was trying to sneak into Lausanne. Next thing, we were buried in snow. Why don't you pick the lottery numbers for me, Marc? Seventy-six million francs in the pot. I'll buy the ticket, you pick the numbers, we'll split the money."

"I'm not very good with numbers, monsieur."

"Too bad." Monsieur Dufaux drank his coffee in one quick gulp. "*Bon,* I'll see about your food."

He rose from his chair and went to the kitchen. Just now, the café was full of shopkeepers and bankers and people Rochat didn't know but recognized from the street. Like the two ladies sitting across the café, smoking and talking over coffee. There were big shopping bags at their feet, stuffed with things wrapped in Christmas paper.

"Goodness, Rochat, you've been so busy you forgot it's nearly Christmas."

He sipped his drink, thinking what if she was still here for Christmas? What would she want for Christmas?

"A way home is what she wants, Rochat, a way home."

"Who?"

"The angel."

"What angel?"

"The angel who's lost and hiding in the cathedral because . . . because . . ."

Rochat stopped talking and looked up. Monsieur Dufaux was at the table with a picnic basket covered with a red checkered cloth in his hands. He smiled at Rochat.

"Tell you what, Marc. You go right ahead and find that angel a way home. Too many illegal foreigners in Switzerland as it is."

The phone rang again. Harper ignored it. His desk was now covered with scraps of paper. Each scrap filled with his own scribbled notes. The phone stopped ringing. Harper turned back to the computer screen.

**Chapter 6**

And it came to pass when the children of men had multiplied that in those days were born unto them beautiful and comely daughters. And the angels[3], the children of the heaven, saw and lusted after them, and said to one another: "Come, let us choose us wives from among the children of men and beget us children."

Harper scrolled down to the references, number 3: *Aramaic text reads* watchers *here*. He scrolled back up to the text and read down a few more lines.

**Chapter 7**

And they became pregnant, and they bare great giants, whose height was three thousand ells: Who consumed all the acquisitions of men. And when men could no longer sustain them, the giants turned against them and devoured mankind.

"So what the hell is a bloody ell?" He kept reading.

## Chapter 8

And Azazel taught men to make swords, and knives, and shields, and breastplates, and made known to them the metals of the earth and the art of working them, and bracelets, and ornaments, and the use of antimony, and the beautifying of the eyelids, and all kinds of costly stones, and all colouring tinctures. And there arose much godlessness, and they committed fornication, and they were led astray, and became corrupt in all their ways.

Harper scrolled down more. Words flashed through his eyes. He pulled his hand from the computer, like a gambler seeing what he'd come up with. He hit a winner.

And the whole earth has thereby been filled with blood and unrighteousness.

The computer beeped and a message flashed on the screen.

```
Mr. Harper, Inspector Gobet asks as
you are too busy to answer the
```

telephone, could you then be good
enough to open the door? Thank you.

"You can't be serious."

*Knockknockknock.*

A not-so-gentle rapping at the chamber door that could only be from the knuckles of an iron fist. Harper turned in his chair, stared at the door.

"Just a second."

He tossed off the robe, threw on his clothes, opened the door. The cop in the cashmere coat was standing in the hall, the waitress with the gun behind him. Her gun drawn, her finger inside the trigger guard, the barrel pointed at Harper's head. Harper was careful not to move, remembering from somewhere there's no dodging a bullet at point-blank range.

"Good morning, Inspector."

"Good afternoon, Mr. Harper."

Harper looked at his watch: two forty. "I miss check-out time?"

"Considerably. But as you are not checking out as yet, let's not worry about it. May I come in?"

"Room's a mess, I'm afraid. Seems I'm the maid and I'm rather bad at it."

Inspector Gobet turned to the waitress with the gun. "Thank you, Officer Jannsen. He appears to be in one piece. Please resume your post, advise the rest of the team of the situation."

"Sir."

The inspector stepped into the room. "I hope you're

comfortable. I'm afraid the Lausanne Palace is one star above our expense guidelines."

"Thought it might be because this place is a Swiss copper's safe house."

"That, too. Though the management doesn't advertise it in the brochure."

"May not be the Palace, but there's a free minibar and a nice view of those big rocks across the lake. What else does a man need in a prison?"

The inspector looked about the room. Harper saw the inspector's nose turn up at the general lack of neatness.

"Any news, Inspector?"

"One or two things. First, I took lunch with the doctor. I told him you were involved in a bit of research for me. He was kind enough to pass on a telephone message from the IOC switchboard."

"A message?"

"Received at twelve thirty-five today. A woman called for you regarding a lost cigarette case, asking if you might return it. There was no name or return number. I assume you know her."

Harper could sense the inspector's sees-all, knows-all eyes.

"Someone I met in a bar, but she's got the wrong man."

"The wrong man?"

"I don't have it."

"Have what?"

"Her cigarette case."

"I see."

"But thanks for being concerned about my social life. Or were you just profiling the manner of my thinking again?"

"Bit of both, in truth." The inspector turned, regarded the view from the windows. "Yes, an excellent view of *le massif.*"

"The what?"

"*Le massif des Mémises*, Mr. Harper, those big rocks across the lake." The inspector took the chair at the desk, his eyes scanning the almost finished sandwich plate with the LP's logo, the empty bottles of beer, and the ashtray overflowing with butts. All set amid scattered notes and Yuriev's casino photos.

"You've been busy, I see."

"A little." Harper nodded toward the computer. "By the way, nice trick with the laptop, Inspector."

"I hope it wasn't too much of an intrusion."

"I take it your lads in the kitchen have been monitoring what I'm doing?"

"Of course. But as I'm here, why don't you tell me what it is you have been up to with our computer. Save me reading the report on your excellent detective work."

"Ever heard of the Book of Enoch, Inspector?"

"Should I have heard about it?"

Harper walked to the desk, picked up his smokes, and lit one up. "It was a book that ended up getting chucked from the Bible, part of what's called the Apocrypha. I downloaded it from the net, read through it twice. Load of mystical gibberish about angels and men. Seems, in the beginning, angels were called Watchers. Sent here by God to protect the creation, guide mankind. First wave of Watchers went stir-crazy and fell for the women of earth in a big way. They took the form of men and set out to create their own race of half-breeds to rule the earth."

"Half-breeds, you say?"

"Not me, Enoch."

The inspector didn't appreciate the jibe. Harper dug through the scraps of paper on the desk.

"Bottom line, all evil in the world comes from a pack of bad-guy angels and their half-breeds."

"And what, may I ask, does any of this have to do with the late Alexander Yuriev, or the hapless Albanian night clerk for that matter?"

Harper looked the inspector in the eyes, feeling they had a way of beating lesser beings into their place. "The note Yuriev left in the cathedral, the line about evil spirits walking the earth, it's from the Book of Enoch. A local biblical scholar confirmed it. Bit of a loon who talks in morphine riddles, but he did get me thinking."

"About?"

"Evil spirits." Harper picked up the last shots of Yuriev leaving the casino. "You told me to keep these pictures, look at them again."

"Standard procedure in police work, Mr. Harper. New eyes see new things."

"Or things that aren't there, maybe."

"I beg your pardon?"

"Look at the carpet in front of Yuriev. There's more than one shadow on the carpet; I count three. The man isn't stumbling, he's being dragged."

The inspector didn't bother to look.

"Are you suggesting Yuriev was forcibly removed from Casino Barrière by two 'bad-guy angels' from the Book of Enoch, as it were?"

"I'm suggesting someone did a lousy job of doctoring these photos. The rest was—what'd you call it on the drive from Montreux?"

"Whimsy, shooting the breeze."

"That's it."

Harper dropped the photos in the inspector's lap. The inspector tapped the photos into even corners, laid them atop Harper's notes.

"For the moment, Mr. Harper, let's put aside pictures of things that aren't there and consider all the things that are."

Harper walked back to the bed, sat down. "Somehow, I knew this wasn't a social call."

"Indeed not."

The inspector slid his hand into his cashmere coat, pulled out a DVD case, and removed a disk from it. He tossed the empty case across the room. It landed perfectly in Harper's lap. Black scribble on the cover: *Confidentiel pour Inspecteur Gobet.* Harper picked it up.

"I'll bite, what is it?"

The inspector looked at the sandwich plate on the desk. He took the last of the fries, popped it in his mouth.

"Let's just say, it's a good thing we've both had our lunches."

# twenty-four

The inspector slid the disk into the laptop. The machine whirred, grainy video appeared on the screen.

POV shot moving down a hall and into a sitting room of Louis XIV furniture, fine paintings, and tapestries on the walls. Bay windows looking out to a lakeside harbor. A fountain shooting up from the lake, 150 meters into the sky.

"These pictures were taken in a flat in Geneva's Cologny district, famous for its view of the Jet d'Eau you see just there."

The camera steadied before a gilded mirror. Something reflected in the glass. Out of focus, red, marble-streaked. The camera panned and zoomed in . . . a headless body hanging by the ankles in the center of the sitting room, flesh peeled away. Harper felt sick to his stomach, as if last night's hangover were coming back for more.

"Oh, Christ."

The inspector pointed to the horrid image on the screen.

"The victim is a female, fifty-eight years of age. The attending coroner happens to be a lecturer on medieval torture at the University of Geneva. He believes the killers to be well practiced in the art of flaying a victim alive. Note the tiny patches of flesh left at major pulse points, where arteries and veins run closest to the skin. As long as they're not ruptured, a master of the craft can keep his victim alive through the entire process. According to the coroner, this is the object of the art."

"The art?"

"The art of inflicting pain for as long as possible."

"Seems they got their pound of flesh's worth."

"Eight to ten, actually."

"Sorry?"

"Human skin is the largest organ of the human body, covering an area of some seven meters squared. Thus, the weight of the woman's flesh is estimated at eight to ten pounds."

"Your attending coroner knows his art, does he?"

"And more. Indications are the victim engaged in repeated sexual activity during the procedure."

"They raped her?"

"Subcutaneous tissue at the wrists and ankles shows no sign of forced restraint, bodily orifices show no sign of violent entry. The coroner has reason to think she was stimulated to orgasm several times before death occurred, and most probably beheaded at such a moment."

"She must've been drugged."

"Tox screen turned up negative, but we suspect the use of an unregistered drug with severe psychotropic effects."

Harper looked at the inspector. *Severe psychotropic effects* . . . "Those words are from the IOC report on Yuriev's formula."

The inspector ignored Harper's comment. "As in previous cases, we've not found any evidentiary DNA, other than that of the victim. She was discovered early this morning by her maid. Body temperature suggests she died in the early hours of this morning."

"Who was she?"

"Simone Badeaux, a French national living in Switzerland."

"I need a drink, Inspector. You?"

"Sparkling water, please."

Harper went to the minibar, grabbed a bottle of water and the last beer.

"So who was Madame Badeaux?"

"One of Europe's legendary courtesans. She ran an exclusive escort agency out of Paris called the Two Hundred Club, with prostitutes priced at thousands of euros per night. She was connected to and protected by certain personages."

"Certain personages?"

"Powerful and rich men from around the world with strong ties to the European economy. Politicians, businessmen, one or two Arab princes. All very discreet. Joke around Interpol was if Madame Badeaux's client list was revealed, half of Europe's governments would collapse and l'École Nationale d'Administration in Paris would be shut down. She took up residency in Switzerland seven years ago for tax reasons. And while maintaining her office in Paris, she became a model citizen of *le canton de Genève*."

Harper glanced at the screen. "Obviously. So what's her connection to the killers?"

The inspector opened his cigarette case, offered one of his flash smokes. Harper handed the inspector the bottle of water in return. Harper lit up, cracked open his beer, and waited for an answer while the inspector lit his own smoke.

"I asked my counterpart in Paris to pop around to the offices of the Two Hundred Club for a look, see what he could find."

"And?"

"An empty tenement off Rue Saint-Denis. Nothing but a few dead rats and a telephone on the floor. Not the sort of place suggesting Madame Badeaux was a woman in possession of several numbered accounts holding in excess of forty million euros. Cash deposits made over the last ten years, to a private bank in Geneva."

"The woman was thrifty."

"And shrewd. There's no paper trail of a Two Hundred Club in any French government office. It appears Madame Badeaux conducted business exclusively by way of telephone and computer."

"Easy enough kit to crack."

"One would think. But an initial check revealed her telephone records have been deleted, except for the number leading to Rue Saint-Denis."

"How'd she manage that?"

"She didn't; someone else did. There's a highly classified technology used by certain governmental security operations around the world that allows a worm to erase phone records instantaneously. A Swiss invention, developed by my task force. My telephone call to Paris, for example. The worm followed the call and erased any trace of the communication upon hanging up. In effect, the call never happened."

"What about her computer?"

"The hard drive was wiped clean."

"Would've thought you'd have ways of making computers talk, Inspector."

"In this case, no, though not without trying. We've been running SX sweeps of the Internet since the morning—with no luck."

"What the hell's an SX sweep?"

"Another little Swiss invention located deep within a mountain and surrounded by a crack unit of the Swiss Alpine Brigade."

"And?"

"Suffice it to say there's no longer a place for a nano-byte of digital information to hide. And so far there's not a trace of Simone Badeaux to be found anywhere on the Internet. Given what I know about SX sweeps, I don't expect to find any. I'm afraid all that's left of Madame Badeaux is what we see dangling by the ankles in the rather fashionable Cologny district of Geneva. The poor woman's soul has been deleted unto the hell of nonexistence."

"Didn't realize you were a philosopher."

"One sees enough brutality in the world, one seeks to

understand in one's own way. Or are you not one who seeks to understand? *'Cogito ergo sum,'* and so forth."

Latin sinking into Harper's brain and falling into place like tumblers in a lock. *Cogito ergo sum: I think, therefore I am.* Half smiling to himself, not knowing why he'd know such a thing, and knowing for whatever bloody reason the cop in the cashmere coat was playing him again.

Harper took a pull off the gold-tipped smoke, chased it with a swallow of beer. *Fine,* he thought, *let's play.*

"I'm afraid you'd have to put me with the *merda taurorum animas conturbit* crowd, Inspector."

"I beg your pardon?"

"Bullshit baffles brains."

The inspector didn't smile. Then again, he didn't go for his gun, either. "I must say, I'm not familiar with that quote, Mr. Harper."

"No worries, Inspector, neither am I. Maybe it's . . . Hang on, you said no paper trail, and the hard drive was wiped. How'd you find out about her bank accounts? Or the location of the Two Hundred Club for that matter?"

"Indeed."

The inspector sipped his water, touched the laptop keys, and advanced the video. Harper's eyes watched the images flash by. Stop. Low-angle shot from the floor. Skinned carcass hanging in the foreground, large white cross painted on the far wall. The inspector advanced the video again, zoomed in to the cross. Stop. It wasn't paint; it was a ream of eight-and-a-half-by-eleven tacked to the wall. The inspector hit a few keys, the picture zoomed in, digital processing adjusting the shot. Numbered accounts, cash deposits, forty million big ones credited to Simone Badeaux.

"We assume the killers left these documents behind for our edification."

"Maybe they wanted you to know what a model citizen she was."

"I don't think I'm the one they had in mind, Mr. Harper."

The inspector shifted the shot right. Words on the wall, words written in blood: *All who are in the heavens know what is transacted here.*

Harper leaned toward the computer.

"Meaning what?"

"Chapter three, verse one, I believe."

Harper was in mid-swallow when the inspector's words sank in. He got up from the bed, looked down at the scraps of paper on the desk. The inspector's finger pointing to one of Harper's handwritten notes. Words from the Book of Enoch, words on the wall. Same fucking words.

"Fascinating coincidence, don't you think, Mr. Harper? You and the killers sharing such a keen interest in apocryphal works of the Bible?"

"I don't get it."

"What don't you get? The fact you and the killers share a keen interest in the Book of Enoch, or that you have the recurring habit of stumbling into their midst?"

"I didn't know the woman, Inspector, never spoke to her."

"Are you quite sure? Perhaps through an acquaintance?"

Harper crushed out his fag. "What are you getting at, Inspector?"

"Madame Badeaux's answering machine. A digital model we assumed wiped clean of evidence. Imagine our surprise when a single message was found. You know, one's late picking up, the machine begins to record." The inspector closed the video on the laptop, opened an audio file. "The machine has the message recorded just after three in the morning, Thursday. Care to listen?"

Squiggly lines on the screen, voices filled the room.

*"Oui?"*

*"Simone, thank God, Simone. He's a freak! He's a goddamn freak!"*

*"Katherine, where are you?"*

*"In my flat. I got away from that fucking freak and his fucking freak friends!"*

*"Calm down, dear. I'm in the middle of something. I'll call you back in one minute."*

*"Simone, wait! Simone!"*

The squiggly lines went flat as a dead man's heartbeat.

"Would you have any idea as to the identity of the caller, Mr. Harper?"

Rabbit punches from the inspector's sees-all, knows-all eyes. Harper felt himself getting backed into a corner. "Afraid I can't help you, Inspector."

"Perhaps a bit more information, then."

The inspector tapped at the keys; a new screen popped up, looked like voice analysis of the recording.

"Yes, here we are. The caller's accent and inflection

patterns suggest she's a white American female from the Southern California region, in her mid to late twenties. Would any of this information help you to remember the identity of the caller?"

Harper looked at the inspector. "You know, since the day I met you, there's one thing I've wanted to ask."

"Please."

"What makes you think I remember shit?"

The inspector hit the keys; video back onscreen, 360-degree shots spinning around the corpse. Stop. Woman's headless body, circle of blood on the far wall. Picture zooming in on the circle of blood. A calling card pinned to the wall with a bloodstained knife.

```
Jay Michael Harper
Security Consultant
International Olympic Committee
```

"Why don't we call it a hunch, Mr. Harper?"

Katherine was finishing her lunch when Rochat suddenly jumped from the table and put on his overcoat.

"I'll be back."

"Where're you going?"

"I just imagined I have to do something."

"What kind of something?"

"Something in the belfry. Do you want to come outside and see?"

"No, I'll just sit here and pick at the leftovers."

"*D'accord.*"

He shuffled out of the door.

Through the open window on the east wall, Katherine thought she heard him whispering. She peeked out of the window, saw him leaning close to the big bell in the timbers, then shuffle to a wooden shed and unlock the door. He stepped in, disappeared a moment, came out with two metal buckets. He shuffled back toward the window, saw Katherine watching him.

"I'll be back."

"Where are you going?"

"To the esplanade. You can watch from the balcony."

"But you're coming right back."

"I'm coming right back."

"What were you talking to the big bell about?"

"Which big bell?"

"The one behind you."

Rochat turned around, faced Marie-Madeleine a moment, turned again and faced Katherine. "I was telling Marie the thing I imagined in the loge."

"Which was?"

"The thing I'm doing now."

He climbed through the carpentry and out of sight. Katherine heard him wind down the steps of the tower. She opened the door of the loge, tiptoed onto the balcony, and hid behind a stone pillar. She heard a door scrape open from far below. She looked over the railing and saw him crossing the esplanade to the stone fountain under the trees and filling the buckets and crossing back to the tower. She heard the tower door close and lock. She jumped back into the loge, waited by the east window. She heard his crooked steps come up the tower and shuffle onto the balcony. Then she saw him round the stone pillars and climb into the timbers with the buckets.

"Hey, you."

*"Oui?"*

"What's the thing you're doing now that you imagined you were telling the big bell before . . . times, I mean?"

"I told Marie I imagined getting two buckets of water from the fountain."

"Why?"

"I'm going to scrub the bells of pigeon poop. Do you want to come out and help?"

"What, like, clean the bells?"

"The wind's very calm now and the sun's been reflecting off Lac Léman all day and heating the pillars and arches and balcony stones. I'm very sure you'll find it warm outside. There's warm rubber boots in the closet with thick wool socks. And Monsieur Buhlmann's black cloak is in there, too. He wears it when he calls the time, but he won't mind if you wear it."

Katherine considered it for a second. "Nah, I think I'm better off staying inside and out of sight."

"No one can see you if you're in the timbers with the bells. And if you wear Monsieur Buhlmann's cloak, people will think you're me."

She pulled at her long blond hair. "I don't think so."

Rochat set down the buckets. He shuffled to the snowman behind Marie-Madeleine, took the black hat from the top of the snowman's head. He slapped it on his overcoat, brushing away the snow. He shuffled toward Katherine and stuck the black floppy thing through the window.

"It's like mine. You can put your hair inside the hat and pull it down on your head."

Katherine looked at the hat, took a breath. "Okay, why not?"

She took the hat and disappeared from the window.

Rochat picked up the buckets and shuffled by Marie-Madeleine. He tapped her bronze skirt with a bucket.

"See, madame, I told you so."

The great bell hummed.

"What do you mean, 'What?' I told you I imagined I could get her to come outside so she can see things, then she can find her way home, and she did. Very clever, don't you think?"

B e careful, Marc!"

He was climbing up the crisscross timbers with a rope between his teeth. She watched him grab a high cross-timber with his hands, swing his legs, and catch the timber with his crooked foot, pulling himself up and twisting around till he was sitting on the timbers above the bell. He took the rope from his teeth, pulled a bucket of water up from the floor.

"I've been climbing the timbers since I was little. I need to pour a little water on Marie so I can scrub off the pigeon poop. It'll be her last bath before spring."

"Good idea. Pigeon poop is terrible for the complexion. She needs to exfoliate."

"I don't know what that means."

"It's a girl thing. Go ahead and pour."

"Get underneath her skirt, or you'll get wet."

"You mean, like, get *under* the bell?"

"Marie doesn't mind."

"You sure?"

"Ask her."

Katherine looked at the bell, then back at Rochat. "I'll take your word for it."

She ducked under the massive bell, found she could stand perfectly upright. She stretched her arms and hands, unable to touch the sides or top of the bell. A huge clapper dangled down the center of the bell. She tried pushing it. It wouldn't budge.

"Wow, how heavy is this thing?"

Her voice bounced off the bronze and circled inside the bell. She heard Rochat's muffled voice from outside calling, "What?" She looked out from under the bell's skirt. Rochat was balancing the bucket on a timber.

"I said, how heavy is this bell?"

"Seven tons. She's A-flat."

"A flat what?"

"The sound she makes."

"You mean A-flat, the musical note?"

*"Oui."*

"Huh. Are all the bells the same note?"

"La Voyageuse is A-flat, too. She lives upstairs."

"What about the other bells?"

Rochat thought a moment. "They have other letters. Get back under Marie, or you'll get wet."

She ducked under and waited. She heard drops of water slap against bronze and saw little streams drip off the edge of the bell's skirt.

"Can I come out now?"

"What?"

She poked out her head. "Can I come out now? I'm afraid Marie might fall on me."

"Why would she do that?"

"Trust me, lots of reasons."

"You can get the scrubber broom."

"What's a scrubber broom?"

"It lives in the winch shed. It's behind Monsieur Buhlmann's grill and has a long handle and stiff bristles. It's brown."

She scooted around the bell, edged by the snowman, and went into the shed. Some contraption that must be the grill was just inside the door. She saw a large winch motor with a connecting cable running out of the top of the shack, a small generator, and a few cans of gasoline. Mops and snow shovels and the brown-bristled broom stood neatly in the corner. She pulled the broom free and stepped outside.

"How am I supposed to get this up to you?"

Rochat undid the rope from the bucket and let it dangle to the floor.

"You can tie this rope around it and I can pull it up."

"Do I look like a Girl Scout to you?"

Rochat looked down at her. Floppy black hat on her

head, Monsieur Buhlmann's black cloak with the black rubber boots on her feet. "You look like *le guet de Lausanne*."

"Really?"

"Really."

"*Très* cool."

Katherine wrapped the rope around the broom and tied a knot with a nice bow. Rochat pulled it up. The handle tapped the outside of the great bell. The bell grumbled in deep tones. Rochat clicked his tongue.

"Oh, be quiet."

"What?"

"I was talking to Marie. She likes to pretend she doesn't like strangers, unless they're photographers. She likes to have her picture taken."

"One of those, is she?" Katherine tapped the bell. "You and I need to talk, girl."

"I can hear the timbers."

"What?"

Just then the winch motor wound, the steel cable slapped taut, and the heavy timbers around Marie-Madeleine creaked and groaned.

"Cover your ears."

"Wha—"

*GONG! GONG! GONG! GONG!*

Even with her hands on her ears, it was like being tossed in a heaving wave, knocking her off her feet and onto the wood floor under Marie-Madeleine. The wave rolled mightily from the belfry and out over Lausanne. Katherine lowered her hands from her ears.

"Man, that's the loudest thing I've ever heard in my life."

"What?"

She looked up. Rochat was dangling by his legs from a crossbeam, his black overcoat down over his head. Katherine jumped to catch him.

"Jesus! Marc!"

He poked his head from the coat. "Don't worry. Marie always tries to knock me off the timbers when she rings, and I pretend she almost did. It's a game we play. But sometimes I pretend she does, too."

"You mean you fall from up there?"

"*Oui*, it's a game."

"Well, no games, not just now, please."

"*D'accord.*"

Rochat swung back and forth, caught the crossbeam with his hands, and flipped himself upright. He undid the broom from the rope and began to scrub the top of the still-vibrating bell.

"Goodness, Marie, I should just leave all this pigeon poop on your head, that's what I should do. And how would you like that, hmm? Not very much, I'm very sure. No one likes pigeon poop on their head. I'm told it's very bad for the complexities. And another thing, Madame Complains-a-lot . . ."

Katherine leaned against a timber, watching him jump from timber to timber with the greatest of ease. She couldn't help but laugh to herself.

"Holy cow, Quasimodo lives."

# twenty-five

They sat under Clémence eating their supper.

Rochat was telling Katherine the story of the bell.

"Hold it right there. We're having fondue under the execution bell?"

*"Oui."*

"As in burning witches at the stake?"

"They don't burn witches at the stake anymore."

Katherine stuck her fork into a piece of bread, lowered it into the pot of melted cheese, and stirred. "Gee, that's good news."

After scrubbing Marie and Clémence and deciding to leave the upper bells till the next day, Rochat led Katherine to the toilet under the unfinished tower so she could have another bath in the sink, then back up the tower, where she changed the bandage on her face and lay down for a nap. She woke when Marie rang seven times, and saw Rochat's crooked form in the open door of the loge, bowing like a butler.

"Dinner is served."

She looked at the table jutting from the wall of the loge, empty but for the burning lantern.

"Where?"

"Outside."

"Where outside?"

"In the carpentry. And I made it warm and I cleaned the dirt and feathers from Monsieur Buhlmann's cloak and the snowman's hat, and there's a sweater I brought from home. I put it on the bed while you were sleeping."

"So we're eating outside, for real?"

*"Oui."*

He turned and shuffled away. Katherine stretched, slipped on the rubber boots, and looked for the sweater. It was on the bed under a fat gray cat, who was busily pawing it into a comfy ball.

"Hey, fuzzface. That's mine."

*Mew.*

"Forget it."

She gave the beast a gentle push to the side. The beast took the hint and jumped up to his hiding place behind the radio. Katherine pulled on the woolly sweater, wrapped up in the black wool cloak, and stepped onto the balcony. She saw blue-shadowed mountains under a starry sky, the smooth-as-glass surface of the lake, and the lights of Évian stretching over the lake like long pieces of shimmering string.

"Marc, it's so beautiful up here at night. Marc?"

"I'm over here, under Clémence."

She found him in the west timbers of the belfry, beneath a low and wide bell. Big enough to fit two empty stools and a small wooden box set with plates, fondue forks, two cups of tea, and a basket of bread bits. Rochat sat on one stool and leaned over a hot plate, stirring a pot of melting cheese.

"Wow, we really are eating outside. I thought you were making it up. And it's really warm up here."

Rochat pointed to the grill at the edge of the timbers.

"I imagined Monsieur Buhlmann's raclette grill would make a very good outdoor heater."

Katherine crawled through the timbers and sat on the stool. She looked up into the belly of the bell, feeling the heat gather and fall about her. She looked out over Lausanne, the lake, the mountains, the stars.

"I can't believe how beautiful it is up here at night."

"It's nice in spring, too, when the swallows come back from Africa. They live in the timbers, but they don't poop on the bells like the pigeons. Swallows are very polite birds."

"I remember the swallows, just after I came to Lausanne. They flew by my window and I looked outside. I saw the cathedral, and I saw a light in the tower. That's when I first saw you. Gosh, that was six months ago."

Rochat looked at her. "Why didn't you come to the cathedral then?"

"When?"

"When you saw the light in the lantern six months ago."

Katherine smiled, not knowing what he was talking about. "I don't know, but I'm here now."

*"D'accord."* Rochat lifted the pot of melted cheese to the table. *"Bon appétit."*

"It smells wonderful."

They ate fondue and drank tea in silence till Katherine looked up into the belly of the bell.

"What's this one's name?"

"Clémence."

"Does she have a story, like Marie-Madeleine?"

"Did I tell you the story of Marie-Madeleine?"

"No need, I sort of know that one by heart. But I'd like to hear the story of Clémence. Why don't you tell me that one?"

And so he did.

Clémence was born in 1518 and weighed four tons. Her sound was a C letter. She was long feared in the middles of ages for her foul moods, Rochat told Katherine. She rang when bad things happened, like fires and invaders. Then it was the duty of *le guet* in the belfry to make the warning sound with Clémence.

"What's the warning sound?"

"Like this." Rochat reached up and rapped his knuckles at the bronze rim of the bell: three rings, six rings, three rings.

"Huh, what else?"

"She has another name sometimes."

"Yeah, what is it?"

"The execution bell."

"The what?"

That's when Rochat told Katherine about heretics and witches and how Clémence would ring as they were marched to their deaths. And that's when Katherine asked about burning witches at the stake and Rochat told her they don't burn witches anymore and she said, "Gee, that's good news."

"And that's why Clémence is always grumpy, because she has nothing to do now but ring with the other bells during *la grande sonnerie* times."

"The great song?"

"*Oui*, when all the bells ring on Saturday evenings and say the week is over."

"Yeah, I remember hearing that from my flat sometimes. Hey, I bet I can see my flat from up here."

"Do you want to see your flat from up here?"

Katherine crossed her arms, as if holding herself. "Not yet."

"*D'accord.*"

She watched the light of the grill glow on the timbers of the crisscross carpentry around Clémence. "Do these old timbers have a story?"

"*Oui.*"

"Tell me about the timbers." And so he did.

"Long ago, Lausanne was surrounded by primeval oak forests, and the trees were tall as the clouds and had never known the touch of an axe. Then the first Lausannois came and cut down some trees and built a town with a wooden barricade around it. And when the cathedral was built, someone remembered a cathedral needed lots of bells to be a cathedral. So the Lausannois built a stone tower next to the cathedral and it was the tallest tower in Europe. And on top of the tower they wanted to build a house for the bells. Then someone remembered cathedral bells are very big and they needed a very big house. So the Lausannois cut down the biggest trees in the forest and brought them to the tower and built a house called the carpentry for the bells to live in."

"You made that up, didn't you?"

"That's what Monsieur Buhlmann told me."

"Which one's he?"

"You're wearing his old cloak."

"Ah, that guy. Then it must be true. When did they build the cathedral, anyway?"

"In twelves of centuries."

"Wow, that's a ways back." Katherine ducked under the rim of the bell and looked at the carpentry. "Gosh, I couldn't get my arms around some of these timbers. They must've been big old trees. Twelfth century, huh? That makes them nine hundred years old."

"They're much older."

"Monsieur Buhlmann tell you that one, too?"

"I told myself."

"Okay, so tell me, how are they older?"

"They cut the biggest oak trees for the bells. Papa told me oak trees live for six hundred years before they grow up. That means the timbers in the carpentry are one thousand five hundred years old. I spent one whole night writing the numbers and adding them."

"A whole night?"

"I'm not good with numbers. Was I right?"

"Yeah, perfect." She looked at the timbers again and

sighed. "Sad, isn't it? They were giant living things, once upon a time."

"They're still alive."

"What do you mean?"

"Before Marie rings, the timbers creak and groan and say, 'Marie's about to ring!' And when all the bells ring for *la grande sonnerie* times, the timbers stretch and sway because they think they're still in the forest and the bells are the wind, and I'm very sure that means they're still alive. That's why I spent a whole night adding the numbers: I wanted to see how old they *really* are."

"That's a sweet thought, Marc."

"You can see on Saturday, when they all ring for *la grande sonnerie*. If you don't find your way home first."

Katherine reached up, touched Clémence's skirt. She was quiet a moment before looking at Rochat. He waited for her to speak. She didn't.

"Are you imagining something?" he asked.

"Yeah, sort of, I guess."

"What?"

"I'm not sure where home is just now, Marc. Maybe I could stay here, just a few more days, to figure it out."

"You can stay a few more days."

"Then I could be here for *la grande sonnerie*. Then, maybe, I'll be ready to leave, okay?"

They ate more fondue and drank more tea.

"How did you get to work in the cathedral, Marc?"

"Papa brought me here all the time when I was little. Papa was an architect. He was saving the cathedral from falling down before he died. He brought me to the tower

while he worked and showed me all the tunnels and
walkways and things. And Monsieur Buhlmann showed
me how to hold the lantern and say the words when
Marie-Madeleine rings the hour at night."

Just then, the timbers creaked and groaned and Marie
shouted from the other side of the tower in a great deafening voice.

*GONG! GONG! GONG!*

"Hurry, touch the timbers."

"What?"

"Like this, hurry."

He ducked under Clémence and put his palms on the
carpentry. She did the same, feeling vibrations pulse
through ancient wood. Rochat jumped onto the south
balcony, waved for her to follow quickly.

*GONG! GONG!*

She hurried after him to the east balcony. They stood
under Marie-Madeleine and Katherine saw the iron hammer outside the edge of Marie's skirt, cocking back and
slamming down. Rochat jumped onto a timber, pressed
his ear to the wood, and closed his eyes. Katherine
wrapped her arms around a timber as best she could,
closed her eyes . . .

*GONG! GONG! GONG!*

It was like holding on to a still-living thing, feeling its
mighty heart pound. The last strike sounded, shook the
tower, and drifted away. Slowly, Katherine opened her
eyes.

"Wow."

Rochat jumped to the balcony. "Hurry, follow me."

"To where?"

"Forfunthings."

Katherine ran after him, followed him up the stone steps of the northeast turret, winding twice around before opening to a higher balcony of pillars and arches. She stopped to catch her breath, thinking the world looked so different one level higher in the tower, like stepping from one cloud to an even higher cloud.

Rochat called back to her, "Hurryitsalmosttime," and he darted along the north balcony and she chased after him to the center of the balcony. He pointed through the stone arches to the highest of the crisscross timbers, to the five bells hanging by old wooden yokes and leather lashings. Katherine couldn't believe her eyes.

"Oh my gosh."

Rochat touched his finger to his lips to quiet her. "Shhh, watch the littlest bell." He pointed to a small bell hanging perfectly still against the center arch of the south balcony. *Like hanging from the stars,* Katherine thought. The wooden yoke above the bell began to move; the bell began to sway.

*. . . ding, dingding . . . ding . . . dingding . . .*

Rochat stepped into the carpentry, onto the narrow wooden walkway running through the center of the tower. Katherine watched him shuffle toward the swinging bell. He turned to her, waved his hands for her to come. She stepped up to the walkway, ducked under the unmoving bells, tiptoed toward him. Closer, she saw the clapper flying under the little bell's skirt like a dizzy sparrow.

*. . . dingding . . . dingding . . . dingding . . .*

Katherine leaned against the timbers and watched till the bell slowed and quieted, till its voice faded away.

"How beautiful. What's this bell's name?"

"Mademoiselle Couvre-feu. She rings every night just after eight o'clock for five minutes. She tells the Lausannois to cover their fires for the night and go to sleep. And then she rings in the morning at seven o'clock and tells everyone to wake up and stoke the ashes to make their morning fires. That's what she says, because she doesn't know about electric ovens and alarm clocks. She's the oldest bell in the tower, older than the cathedral. She's more than one thousand years old."

"And she's so small, compared to Marie and Clémence."

"She's only three hundred and sixty kilos."

"She's so beautiful."

"And she has a story, but it's a secret story. You have to promise not to tell."

Katherine raised a finger to her heart and made a tiny cross. "Cross my heart."

"She's the last silver bell in Europe."

"You mean pure silver?"

"*Oui.*"

"But she's so dark."

"Because she's very, very old. You can come close and see. Be very quiet and listen."

Rochat reached up and held the clapper in the palm of his hand. He eased the clapper to the inside of the bell with the softest touch. A lovely delicate sound chimed through the tower, delicate as a sleeping baby's breath.

Rochat whispered, "She makes a C letter."

Katherine whispered, too: "That's the same sound as Clémence, isn't it?"

"*Oui*, but Couvre-feu lives higher in the tower, so her voice is higher. That's what I imagined. Was I right?"

Katherine tried not to laugh. "Makes sense to me. But why is she the last silver bell? Were there others?"

"In all the cathedrals. But there was a great war in Europe, and all the silver bells were melted into cannons to kill people."

Couvre-feu's soft voice faded under their whispers. Katherine reached for the bell and then held back.

"Can I touch her, Marc?"

"You can touch her."

Katherine stood on her toes, took the iron clapper in her hands, tapped it softly to the side of the bell. The baby's breath of a sound chimed and swirled through the tower once more.

"Gosh, melted into killing things. What a terrible thing to happen to something so beautiful."

Harper ducked out of the service door of the Hôtel de la Paix. The Swiss Guard cabbie waiting around the corner was busy with a newspaper. Harper headed for the steps across the road and down to the small triangle-shaped park. He tromped through a clutter of pine trees and snow and came out on Avenue du Théâtre. A trolley full of disapproving locals passed by, their looks admonishing Harper that decent citizens of the Canton de Vaud do not creep through dimly lit parks at night.

He moved into the shadows and checked his watch. He'd give it five minutes to see if he'd been followed.

So far, things were going according to plan.

He'd spotted the park from his room and worked out the roads. Just needed a diversion. He ordered up supper and a bottle of vodka. The waitress with a gun delivered the meal and asked him how he was; Harper said he was bored. The waitress suggested the classic movie channel, the one she watched at home. Ten minutes after she left, he turned on the telly as the opening titles came on the screen: Kirk Douglas and Anthony Quinn in *Lust for Life*. He cranked up the volume, thinking it just might buy some time to get out and do some checking. He punched the Do Not Disturb button on the telephone, grabbed his coat, and headed for the emergency stairwell.

Didn't spot any CCTV cameras on the way down, not that it mattered. Harper couldn't be sure letting him get away from the hotel wasn't *their* plan. Get him primed, let him loose, see where he goes. Harper decided that didn't matter, either. Had to take the chance. Couldn't sit in the room till the inspector came calling with another batch of snuff pics. *Yes, Mr. Harper, we seem to have located the body of one Katherine Taylor. Note the limbless torso . . .*

Harper checked his watch again; five minutes had gone by. He moved on.

He walked quickly along the pavement, his mind continuing to replay Inspector Gobet. The inspector knew

Harper was lying through his teeth about not knowing the voice on Madame Badeaux's answering machine. That was the moment, Harper remembered, staring into the Swiss copper's eyes, that he got the unmistakable feeling everything about the cop in the cashmere coat was wrong.

"How did your business card end up at a particularly gruesome crime scene, Mr. Harper?"

"No bloody idea."

"Did you know Madame Badeaux?"

"You already asked me, Inspector, and the answer's still no."

"Then perhaps through the woman on the answering machine, perhaps she was the very person who left that rather cryptic message for you at the IOC switchboard, regarding a lost cigarette case?"

"Told you before, she's got the wrong guy."

"Then you won't mind giving me the woman's name."

"Sure, soon as I remember it."

"You'll understand my having difficulty believing you, Mr. Harper."

"Actually, I don't give a tinker's damn what you believe."

Inspector Gobet pushing for more; Harper telling him nothing.

"You don't have a choice about this, or anything else, Mr. Harper. You must tell me who she is. You have no idea the seriousness of the matter."

Enough was bloody enough, Harper thought. Had to get out, try to find her.

Maybe she was still alive.

"Go fuck yourself, Inspector."

The inspector stormed out; Harper paced the room.

Only thing he knew for sure was he'd been used as bait by holier-than-thou Swiss coppers, and now Miss Taylor was being used as bait by the killers. The two of them on the receiving end of a bad joke. Question is, who's laughing hardest, killers or cops?

Harper kept hearing Katherine Taylor's terrified voice on the answering machine: *Simone, thank God, Simone. He's a freak! He's a goddamn freak!* Kept seeing her face hammered to pulp, her body sawed into bits. Kept working the timeline: Blondie's message on Simone Badeaux's answering machine at three this morning. She leaves a message at the IOC switchboard at midday. Could you return my cigarette case? Harper checked his watch; nine thirty. Means nine hours ago, she was still alive. No return phone number means she's hiding. Question again: Where does a hooker hide from killers who walk through walls?

Harper snapped back to now.

He crossed over four lanes of traffic. He cut down a small dimly lit lane, saw Gare Simplon at the bottom of the hill, heard steel wheels on steel rails. He ducked into another shadow, lit a fag, thought about chucking the whole idea. Woman was probably dead already. Maybe it was time to buy a ticket to ride, destination unknown. Then knowing there was no place to go.

Maybe the cop in the cashmere coat was right. Maybe he didn't have a choice, about this or anything. Come to

Lausanne, find out it's a trap, wait your turn to be slaughtered.

Harper dropped his cigarette on the pavement, let it smolder, felt new Latin words tumble through his brain and onto his lips. *"Tempus edax rerum."*

He headed back up the lane, turned down Rue du Grand-Chêne, sticking to shadows as best he could till he reached the lit-up Lausanne Palace. The Prussian general of a doorman was just helping a guest inside the hotel. Harper moved casually past the portico, stopped at the window of LP's. Saw Stephan, the polite bartender, pouring flutes of champagne behind the bar. Rest of the place packed with happy-faced locals at their luxuriant trough. The champagne-swilling chanteuse and piano player doing a number about the old black magic casting its spell. All the time in the world, these people. No bloody idea that time is the devourer of all things.

Bells sounded from the cathedral.

Harper refocused his eyes, saw his reflection in the glass as something dark rushed over his shoulders. He spun around. Nothing but the branches of the beat-up Christmas trees swaying in a cold rising wind. He looked up and saw shreds of dead black clouds ripping through the sky. Feeling in his guts the clouds were coming for him.

"Crack your cheeks, motherfuckers."

He pulled at the collar of his coat and pushed through the barroom door.

# twenty-six

"*Bonsoir*, Monsieur Harper, may I offer you something to drink?"

"Have you seen her?"

"*Pardonnez-moi?*"

"Miss Taylor, have you seen her?"

"I haven't since she was here Tuesday evening."

"Have you spoken to her at all, got a text message, anything?"

"No. Is something wrong, monsieur?"

"She's in a world of shite, Stephan. I have to find her. Does she have any friends in Lausanne, someone she can shack up with?"

"Mademoiselle Taylor is a very private person, monsieur. My girlfriend, Lili, and I are her only friends in Lausanne."

"Could she be with your girlfriend?"

"I don't know. They were to meet at the Beau-Rivage on Wednesday, but Mademoiselle Taylor didn't arrive. Lili's tried to call her many times without success."

Harper tapped his fingers on the bar, remembering. "Tuesday night, she was here, she was waiting for someone. You know who it was?"

"I know she was to meet someone, but I only saw her speaking with you."

"Me?"

"When she meets a client in the bar, I keep an eye on her, for her protection."

"Fair enough, mate, but there was someone else."

"As I said, monsieur, I saw only you."

"No, can't be. When I was talking to her a waiter brought a bottle of champagne to her table. Do you know who sent it?"

"I assumed the bottle came from you."

"Me?"

"After she left I needed to charge her account. I checked with the serving staff, but no one recalled bringing a bottle to her table."

"Can't be—the waiter said it'd been sent by the gent she was expecting."

"Do you see that waiter here now, monsieur? We could ask him."

Harper looked around, saw men and women in serving uniforms, hustling drinks on trays.

"Truth be told, I can't remember, I was so blocked. But I did give her something, a maquette of the cathedral."

"Yes, I saw it, and that's also why I thought you gave her the champagne, as a gift. I knew you and mademoiselle had met before, and you did tell me you were to have a date . . ."

Stephan didn't finish the sentence.

"What is it?"

"Monsieur, I thought you might be mademoiselle's client for the night. When I saw her leave alone, I thought the two of you had agreed to meet somewhere else, for discretion."

"You saw her leave?"

"Yes, she walked through the corridor to the lobby. She was wearing her mink."

"Did she look concerned, scared, nervous?"

"No, she looked very happy. She looked at me and smiled and waved good-bye."

"Alone?"

"Yes, I'm positive of this."

Harper rubbed the back of his neck. *What the bloody hell was going on?*

"Hang on, did she have the maquette with her?"

"No, I saw it on the floor behind her chair after she'd left. I came back to collect it for safekeeping, but the table was cleared and the maquette was gone. I checked with housekeeping, but they didn't have it. The staff is very careful with items guests leave behind."

"How long between seeing the maquette and the bloody thing disappearing? Five minutes, ten minutes?"

"Thirty seconds, monsieur, a minute at the most."

"So whoever took the maquette . . ."

Harper felt a chill crawl up his back. Christ. The killers were here that night, watching him talk to her, watching him give her the maquette. They could be here now, watching again.

"Think back, Stephan. You remember anyone asking about her that night? Anyone noticing her?"

"On any night it would be unusual if people didn't notice her, and that night she looked very beautiful. Monsieur, it was very busy that evening, but I'm positive she was alone after you left her."

"You have her mobile number, her home number?"

"Yes."

"Ring her."

"I'm not allowed to make personal calls on duty. I'll go to the storeroom."

Stephan asked a waitress to come behind the bar; needed to check the champers stock, he said. Harper smoked a fag, waited. The chanteuse now singing about being bewitched, bothered, and bewildered. *No shit,* Harper thought. From the corner of his eye he saw Lucy Clarke walking toward him. He turned away. Too late.

"Hello, Jay."

*Bollocks.*

He looked down at the ashtray, mumbled under the music. "Grab a pack of matches from the bar and leave."

"What?"

"Just fucking do it."

"I beg your *fucking* pardon?"

Harper grabbed a pack of matches from a tray himself, stuffed them in her kid-gloved hands, spoke so anyone listening could hear.

"Sorry, madame, I didn't realize I was blocking your way."

"Hey, calm down, Jay. What's going on?"

Harper stared at her. She read his eyes. *Not another fucking word.*

"All right, Jay, I get it. And thanks for the piss-off."

She left, walked to a table where a group of people waited for her. She tossed the matches on the table. Harper turned back to the bar; the polite bartender was back.

"Mademoiselle's mobile phone is still off, monsieur, and she doesn't answer her home number. Monsieur, what's going on?"

"Seems to be the question of the moment. If she contacts you, get her somewhere safe. I'll be back in later to check."

"What will you do?"

"For lack of a better idea, I'm going to the front desk, see if anyone saw her with anyone."

Harper shot a glance back to Lucy Clarke. She had that laughing-because-I've-just-been-humiliated look about her. He turned to Stephan.

"I need you to do something. Don't look now, but there's a woman at a table behind me. Auburn hair, wears kid gloves."

"Lucy Clarke, I know her very well."

"When you get a chance, tell her I was drunk. Anyone else asks about me, tell them the same thing. Don't tell them anything else, especially if it's the police."

The polite bartender coughed worriedly. "Monsieur, this is Switzerland. Citizens do not lie to the police."

"Stephan, for another two hours, make believe you don't live on planet fucking perfect."

"*Pardon?*"

"Ask Miss Clarke, she'll tell you all about it. For the moment, Miss Taylor's flat. Where is it? And tell me she just happened to give you a spare key for safekeeping."

K atherine wrapped herself in the black cloak and sat on the steps of the loge. She watched Rochat shuffle along the south balcony with things to return to the winch shed and listened to him talk to Marie-Madeleine each time he passed.

With Monsieur Buhlmann's grill, it was, "Because you're too noisy for dinner, that's why." With the hot plate and power cables he said, "What do you mean you haven't been properly introduced? She helped clean pigeon poop from your head, you silly old bell." And with the wooden box he'd used for a table it was, "When she's ready to go, that's when." Finally, Katherine heard Rochat lock the shed and shuffle by the great bell with, "No, she's our guest, guests don't do the dishes after dinner." Then he jumped onto the south balcony just in front of her.

She smiled.

"Marie-Madeleine feeling a little left out of all the fun?"

"She's not used to anyone being in the tower at night besides me and Monsieur Buhlmann."

"I don't know, Marc. I think she might be jealous. Maybe she thinks I'm going to steal you away from her."

"That's why I haven't told her about the girl."

"What girl?"

"A girl Monsieur Buhlmann wants me to meet at Christmas lunch. She lives on a farm and milks cows."

"Hey, are you cheating on us already?"

"I don't know what that means."

"It means between the bells, me, and the farmer's daughter, you're quite the ladies' man."

Rochat scratched his head, not really sure what that meant, either. "It's almost nine o'clock. I have to work now."

"Okay."

Katherine scooted to the side and Rochat shuffled by her and into the lantern-lit loge. She watched him light candles and set them on shelves and ledges. The small room was suddenly aglow in warm light. Rochat sat at the table, pulled open the door of his lantern, and blew out the flame. He pulled his floppy hat down on his head and stared at the unlit lantern.

"Marc?"

*"Oui?"*

"What are you doing?"

"Working."

Katherine got to her feet and came into the loge, sat so the lantern was between them. "Why did you blow out the lantern if you're going to use it in a second?"

"Because I couldn't light it if it were already lit."

"So when do you light the lantern?"

"When Marie says."

She looked at his face, the way he was concentrating on the candle stub in the lantern.

"What are you doing now?"

"I'm imagining something."

"What?"

"Candles."

Katherine looked around the loge, counted twelve burning candles. "Which ones?"

"Not these candles. Other candles, somewhere else. There's lots of them and it looks nice."

She rested her head in her hands, looked at him through the lantern. "You know, the night I first saw you in the tower, I thought you were a night watchman with a flashlight."

"I don't think it would work."

"What wouldn't work?"

"A flashlight—it's not the same."

"What's not the same?"

"Flashlights are for looking. Fire is for seeing things."

"Oh, that makes sense, I guess." She yawned and stretched. "Man, I'm so tired."

"You sleep a lot."

"Yeah, I know. Must be the air up here, just knocks me out. I need to lie down."

*"D'accord."*

Katherine hung her black cloak on an iron spike, slipped off her boots and woolly sweater, and climbed onto the bed. She pulled the heavy duvet over her body.

"Marc?"

*"Oui?"*

"When you go to work, could you leave the door open? That way I can see you and your lantern when you come back."

"I can leave the door open."

The timbers creaked and groaned.

*GONG! GONG! GONG!*

Katherine felt the sound of the great bell pulse through the loge as if it were rocking her to sleep. And as the ninth strike sounded, she watched Rochat light the lantern and shuffle outside. She heard him move around the tower, his voice calling the hour to the east, north, west. Then his crooked shape appeared just outside the door where he faced Lausanne, the lake, and the sleepy mountains on the far shore, raising his lantern of firelight into the night.

*"C'est le guet! Il a sonné l'heure! Il a sonné l'heure!"*

Harper punched in the code, the door popped open, and he stepped inside.

Marble floor, Chinese tables and vases, fresh flowers. Mailboxes on the wall, one name per floor. Taylor, top apartment.

He sorted through the keys, trying to remember the order of entry. Numeric code opens the street door, red key opens the private elevator that takes you up seven floors to a private lobby. Unlock the double doors with the white key to a small atrium, close the door behind you and punch in a second numeric code to deactivate the alarm, unlock the last door with the blue key. *A bit like breaking into a Swiss bank,* Harper thought. He slipped the blue key into the lock, opened the door.

"Of course, a long dark hall."

He reached for the light switch, but stopped. He dug through his coat, pulled out his own keys with the mini-flashlight on the end.

"Let there be light."

He twisted it on, pointed it into the dark.

Antique side table to the right. Mom and dad photos, photos with a woman and three kids. Woman in the photo looked like Blondie a bit; sister maybe. Another shot, Blondie in a sculptor's studio, half naked and a glass of wine in her hand. Attractive woman in I'm-a-serious-fucking-artist overalls next to her. Stephan's girl-friend maybe. Next picture confirmed it. Hippie artist bird with the out-of-uniform polite bartender lounging on a divan. Miss Taylor fitting nicely between them. The three of them looking stoned and very friendly.

Harper walked on, his mini-flashlight leading the way.

Guest room to the left. Big windows with balconies overlooking the lake and mountains. The room was empty but for some unpacked cardboard boxes. Farther down the hall, an arch opened to a kitchen. High-tech aluminum chair kicked back from a Lucite table, rest of the chairs tucked neatly underneath. Harper stepped in. Stainless-steel everything. Appliances, pots and pans, double-barreled sink. Sink held one wineglass with a trace of red, one plate with a few bread crumbs, one cof-fee cup, one teaspoon. He looked in the trash can. Two empty yogurt containers, that's it.

Swinging doors led to a dining room. Glass shelves with antiques, the expensive kind. Antique oak table and chairs, a never-been-used feel. Dining room opened onto a large sitting room. Harper worked his way back through the kitchen and down the hall. A guest bath to the right. Baskets full of soaps and shampoos from the Lausanne Palace Hotel, a few towels bearing the hotel's monogram. Farther down the hall, a wide arch opened into a crescent-shaped sitting room. Curving floor-to-ceiling windows opened onto a garden terrace and a million-euro view of the lights of Lausanne and the mountains across the dark lake, sitting like snowcapped silhouettes against the starry sky.

He stepped in, scanned the dark with the flashlight.

Plush Italian leather sofas and chairs, Oriental carpets on the floor, huge LCD screen on the wall with a flash stereo kit to match. There was a pedestal with a sculpture of a woman's form in bronze, Blondie's form most probably. He panned the flashlight, saw a shattered table lamp on the floor, chunks of a crystal ashtray near the wall. He raised the flashlight to a nasty dent in the plaster wall.

Nearby, an antique backgammon table turned on its side. Black and white disks scattered over the floor; the dice had come up double six. Something black under the table. Harper kicked it into the open. Taser gun, both probes fired. Patch of clear oil on the floor. He touched it, rolled it in his fingertips; no scent. Across the room, next to a glass coffee table, a large furry lump on the floor.

"If you're the watchdog, you're doing a crap job of it."

He walked closer. Fido was a mink coat. He held the collar close to his face; he could smell her scent. He checked the pockets, something pricked his finger. He

pulled his hand from the pocket, saw a small shard of
glass in one fingertip. He shook the coat, and fine pieces
of glass fell to the floor. Wasn't crystal, it was window
glass. Harper panned the flashlight across the windows
in the sitting room. Nothing broken in this place. He
laid the coat back on the floor, shone the flashlight
around the rest of the room.

Glass coffee table splattered with lipsticks and bits of
makeup, a packet of condoms and a Cohiba cigar tube.
He unscrewed the tube. It was stuffed with high-grade
dope. He saw her handbag on the floor. He knocked it
over with the tip of his shoe and her gold cigarette case
tumbled onto the floor. The embedded diamond sparkled in the light of the flashlight.

"Found it, now what?"

He picked up the case, slipped it in his coat. He
checked the handbag again. No wallet, no mobile, no
keys. Rest of the sitting room looked undisturbed.
Harper went back to the hall.

Closets along the walls; he checked them one by one.

The woman had lots of designer clothes, many with the
sales tag still on them. There were a shitload of shoes, as
well as a complete set of Louis Vuitton luggage in de-
scending sizes. No pieces missing. Open door at the end
of the hall, bright light within. He stepped slowly to the
door. Her scent grew stronger. He leaned around the corner. Master bedroom, overhead light switched on and the
light reflecting off the sliding glass doors to the garden
terrace, making the bedroom appear twice as big as it was.
He switched off his flashlight and stepped into the room.

Mirrored closets along one wall, one of the closet doors left open. Dresses tossed about the floor and bed. Harper walked across the room to the en suite bathroom. Oak armoire, art deco sinks and fixtures, antique bath the size of a small car. More stolen soaps and towels from the Lausanne Palace. Nothing looking used for days.

He turned back to the bedroom. Except for the scattered dresses on the bed and floor, nothing seemed out of place. He walked to the bay window, checked the antique dressing table. Hairbrush, combs, perfumes. He opened the drawers. Makeup, assorted creams, LP's bar ashtray with a half-smoked joint.

Harper closed the drawer and walked to the bed. Like a normal bed. No mirrors on the ceiling. No hooks for the whips and chains. Not a handcuff in sight.

He pulled open the bedside table drawers. Hand creams, another LP's ashtray with a fat joint on standby, operations manual and charger for an X26 Taser gun. He dug for his own smokes and lit up, half tempted to huff one of Mademoiselle's spliffs. Might clear up one or two things. He walked in circles, following his thoughts.

She had cash, lots of it. She was a pothead but no sign of hard drug use, though she was addicted to all things designer. She liked to steal towels and ashtrays from the Palace Hotel. She never had dinner guests, not to mention stay-over clients. Never used the flat for business. It's where the kid lived.

Right.

She comes home. Comes home, hell. Her voice on the answering machine, terrified. She came here from somewhere else, somewhere she was escaping from. Somewhere she had to break a window to get away from, maybe. Gets home, calls Madame Badeaux for help. Someone's waiting for her or comes in after she arrives. Argy-bargy in the sitting room. Someone gets zapped with the Taser gun. She runs away, leaves everything.

No, too easy, no one gets away from these killers. They let her go. Why?

Because they want someone or something else. Blondie with the stars in her eyes was a sideline . . . maybe.

He walked to the dressing table again and touched her brush, her combs, the long strands of blond hair. He picked up a bottle of perfume and smelled the cap, remembering her at Place Saint-François. Drinking *vin chaud*, giggling, thinking Lausanne was like living in a fairy tale. Then the "But why?" hit him. Because the fairy tale was a trap she'd been lured into, just like him. And just like him, she had nowhere to run.

"So where the hell is she?"

Harper saw himself in the mirror, her perfume bottle in his hands. *Sad sod that you are,* he thought. *Sniffing her mink, sniffing her perfume. What's next, boyo, her knickers in the cupboard?*

Ten bells rang out over Lausanne.

Harper's eyes refocused in the mirror. He saw the reflection of the bright room in the windows at his back. Beyond the glass he saw something moving in the night.

"Bloody hell."

He set the perfume bottle on the dressing table, reached over and hit the light switch. The room went black. He slid open the glass doors and stepped onto the terrace. Across Pont Bessières, above the old city, Lausanne Cathedral stood in a blaze of light as if hiding in plain sight. Only thing giving it away was the spark of light rounding the belfry tower.

"Oranges and lemons, Say the bells of Saint Clement's."

Rochat shuffled quietly into the loge. He set the burning lantern on the table and hung his overcoat and hat behind the door. He made a cup of tea and sat at the table. He picked up a pencil and went back to the drawings in his *l'ange de lausanne* sketchbook. He brushed away leaded dust and smoothed the lines of his drawing of the angel as she lay wrapped in the duvet and sleeping.

He had filled one page with detailed studies of her hands. Her fingers were long and pretty, almost touching someone or waiting for someone to touch her. Another page was filled with her shoulders and neck peeking from the duvet, the smooth curves emerging and swelling and then sinking down to a swanlike neck. Two more pages were filled with drawings of her face. The bandage was hidden from Rochat's eyes and, as he drew her, she looked the way he first imagined her in the windows above Rue Caroline. The perfect shape of her nose and gentle lines of her chin, her long blond hair falling down over her sleeping eyes.

He looked up from the drawings.

He saw her on the bed, thinking he'd never before seen someone sleep so deeply, so soundly. Even Monsieur Booty, curled up next to her, would stretch and open an eye now and then. But the angel didn't move, she didn't stir.

"Because that's how angels sleep, Rochat. Yes, I'm very sure that's how angels sleep."

Earlier in the night between nine- and ten-o'clock bells, Rochat had been drawing in his *piratz* book because he imagined he could include the angel in the story. He imagined the angel was captured by Screechy the Evil Wizard and that Screechy took her to his ice castle in the land of Saskatoon and she was under his sleeping spell. And the silly pirates flew over the Boiling Seas of Doom on the back of Pompidou the Giant Caterpillar, holding on to their paper hats and waving their wooden swords, to capture her back. And they wanted the future-teller diamond back, too. "Give her back," yelled the pirates. "She's our angel! And the future-teller diamond, too!" And Screechy stuck his head out from the tower and yelled, "No, you can never have her, she's mine now, so ha, ha on you! And let me tell you something else, you dumb pirates, I'm looking at the future-teller right now, and let me tell you, your future doesn't look so good, so there!" And so the pirates decided to come up with a cunning plan to rescue the angel. But Rochat hadn't been able to think of a plan of any sort. That's when he decided he'd draw the angel as she slept instead.

The small window above the table was open slightly. Rochat heard three double *tink*s drift up from the tinny bells of the Hôtel de Ville. Monsieur Booty heard them, too; he opened his eyes and took a long stretch. Rochat put a finger to his lips.

"Shhh. Don't disturb her. She's very tired and needs to sleep."

The beast jumped from the bed to the floor and hopped up to the table for a look at the drawings.

"What do you think, you miserable beast?"

*Mew.*

"Me too."

The beast stepped over Rochat's arms onto his lap and curled into a ball.

"Well now, I was beginning to think you didn't like me anymore." He scratched the beast behind the ears; the beast purred. "I know, it's nice to have her visiting, but I'm very sure she'll be leaving soon. She wants to be here for *la grande sonnerie* times on Saturday, then she'll go home. That's what she said."

Monsieur Booty looked up with half-open eyes.

*Mew.*

"Because that's what angels do, you dumb beast, they come and they go. They're only made of light, after all."

The timbers creaked and groaned, and Marie rang for midnight. But even with the great bell's longest and loudest shout of the night, the angel didn't stir. Rochat set Monsieur Booty on the table with the sketchbook.

"I'm sorry, your royal fatness, but I have to go to work. And when I come back, I'll make tea for me and a bowl of milk for you."

*Mew.*

"*Pas de panique*, I'll warm it up for you."

Rochat put on his overcoat and hat. He picked up the lantern and went quietly out of the door. He shuffled around the tower, calling the midnight hour. When he finished, he hooked the lantern to the railing and climbed through the timbers. He gave Marie a soft tap on the edge of her skirt.

"All is well, madame. No something evil returning to Lausanne tonight. I'm going to switch off the lights on the esplanade now, so don't be frightened. What?"

Rochat pressed his ear to the bronze, listening to her deepest tones.

"Why would you ask such a silly thing? Rochat will always be with you, Marie. Have a nice snooze."

He unlocked the winch shed and pulled the steel handle with the big handwritten sign *LIGHTS OFF!* and an arrow pointing to it. The floodlights on the esplanade switched off and the belfry fell into darkness. He locked the shed and checked on the snowman. Looking a little crusty at the edges, but still standing. Rochat retied the scarf around its neck.

"I'm very sorry about your hat, Monsieur Neige, but the angel's using it. You can have it back after she goes home."

He jumped onto the south balcony and shuffled toward the loge. A tiny flame sparked on the esplanade.

Rochat's eyes followed a thin trail of smoke into the dark of the chestnut trees. A lone streetlamp at the top of Escaliers du Marché cast a long shadow from under the chestnut trees and out over the cobblestones. Rochat hid behind a stone pillar. He didn't breathe, he didn't look down. He heard footsteps on the esplanade and a voice climbing the stones of the tower to find him.

"I can see the lantern on the railing, so I know you

can hear me. I know she's up there. Her name's Katherine Taylor. She lives on Rue Caroline."

Rochat didn't move.

The voice from the esplanade climbed the tower walls again.

"My name's Harper, I'm her friend."

Rochat leaned from behind the pillar and saw someone in the shadows, puffing on a cigarette.

"Her friend?"

"That's right."

"Are you lost, too?"

"I don't think so. This is Lausanne Cathedral, isn't it? Look, why not come down and talk before we wake up the skeletons."

Rochat shuffled to Marie, tapped her three quick times. "Marie, there's someone by the fountain and he knows the angel's here and he says he's her friend and he knows about the bones in the crypt, too. What do I do?"

He pressed his ear to her skirt and listened.

*"Oui, merci."*

He shuffled to the railing, held his lantern into the night.

"How do I know you're not one of the bad shadows playing a mean trick to hurt her?"

It was quiet for a long time before the voice climbed the tower again.

"No, mate, I'm not a bad shadow. I'm her friend. That makes me one of the good guys, doesn't it?"

# twenty-seven

Harper waited by the fountain and watched the lantern move along the railings of the belfry and disappear in the southwest turret. The archers' windows cut in the tower walls dilated with light as the lantern circled down. Long minutes later he heard the rattle of keys from behind a skinny red door, half hidden behind a ton of collapsed scaffolding and mountains of shoveled-aside snow. The door scraped open and a small form wrapped in a long black overcoat and black floppy hat emerged, the lantern in his hand swinging low near a crooked foot. The closer the lantern came, the more Harper recognized the foot.

"I've seen you before. You were feeding popcorn to the ducks at Port d'Ouchy last Sunday."

"And you were going to Évian on the ferry. I told you it was through the trees and past the weather-teller. You said I had feathers in my hair."

"I'm afraid you did."

Rochat raised his lantern close to Harper's face, close enough to see the lines at the corners of his eyes.

"You're a detectiveman, aren't you?"

"Sorry?"

"I saw you on Pont Bessières. I imagined you were a detectiveman trying to solve a mysterious mystery in Lausanne. But you were looking the wrong way."

Harper could tell the lad was dead serious. "Which way should I have been looking?"

"The other way, monsieur."

"The other way. I'll keep that in mind. Listen, that lantern of yours is rather bright. Would you mind?"

Rochat lowered the lantern. *"Pardonnez-moi, monsieur."*

"Miss Taylor, is she all right?"

"They cut her face with a knife, but it isn't deep. I cleaned it with medicine and made bandages for her, but she puts the bandages on herself. She's very tired."

"Did she tell you what happened?"

"She didn't have to tell me. I can see her flat from the belfry. I saw two men come into her flat. They came from the bad shadows. She was on her mobile phone and they cut her. She shot one of the men and then ran away, but she didn't kill him. I saw it through binoculars."

Harper glanced toward Rue Caroline. "Her flat's on the other side of Pont Bessières, more than a kilometer away."

"They're very good binoculars, monsieur, they're Zeiss. Swiss farmers use them to watch cows in the mountains."

Harper stared at Rochat, gave himself a moment to sort out the lad's story.

Men from bad shadows. Had to mean coming out of

the dark hall into Miss Taylor's sitting room. On her mobile. Fits with the message left on Madame Badeaux's answering machine. Shot one but didn't kill him. Explains the spent Taser gun on the floor. The lad may have a vivid imagination, but he made sense in his own peculiar way, Harper thought.

"Sorry, mate, I didn't ask your name."

"Marc Rochat."

"My name's Harper, Jay Harper."

*"Enchanté, monsieur."*

Harper held his fingers in the cold water running from the iron spout of the fountain. "Can I drink from this?"

"You can drink from all the fountains in Lausanne, that's why they're here. But on December twentyones they turn them off till spring."

"Twenty . . . ones, right." Harper leaned down to the water, drank deeply, and straightened up. "Not bad, actually. How did she get into the cathedral?"

"I saw her run away from those men and she came over Pont Bessières. She was in a bathrobe and naked underneath and she had no shoes on her feet and she was scared and screaming. She tried to stop a car but it didn't see her, and she fell by Café de l'Évêché and she got up and started to run up the hill. I came down from the belfry and pulled her into the cathedral before the bad shadows could find her. She was cold, and I took her up the tower to the loge because it's warm and there's a bed where she can hide till she can find a way home."

"Did she say anything else about the men?"

Rochat thought about it. He saw himself in the doorway of the loge and the angel saying she had to tell him something that she didn't want to tell him.

"Those men said they'd find her wherever she went and they'd kill anyone who helped her."

"She said those words?"

"She said those words."

Harper took a long drink from the fountain to think it through. The killers either knew she was in the cathedral or they didn't. If they didn't, they'd find her soon enough. Oddly enough, it would be better if they did know. Meant they didn't want to kill her, not yet. Bigger question: Why the hell not? And the lad, what about him? The killers would slaughter him in a flash; he didn't have a chance. *Christ,* Harper thought, *whatever the hell the game was in this bloody town, it had just snared another victim. An innocent lad who could barely stand up straight.* Harper wiped his mouth and looked at Rochat, trying not to betray his thoughts.

"Are you really her friend, monsieur?"

"Yes, I'm her friend."

"Are you here to help her find a way home?"

Harper drew on his smoke. "Sure, that's what friends are for, isn't it?"

"If you're a friend, do you need to hide in the cathedral, too?"

"No . . . no, I've got my own hiding place, but thanks for the offer. Listen, I'll come back tomorrow. Maybe together we'll figure out a way to get her home. Is there a telephone up there?"

"It's very old and it's hard to use sometimes."

"Good. Don't use it, don't let her use it. If it rings, don't answer it."

"She doesn't want to talk to anyone and she's afraid of the police."

"I don't blame her. Can't tell the good guys from the bad guys in this place without a program." Harper pulled the gold cigarette case from his coat. "Do me a favor, give this to her. She'll know it's from me."

Rochat held his lantern over it, and the clear stone in the lid sparkled.

"Is it a future-teller diamond, monsieur?"

"A what?"

"A future-teller. I've never seen a real one, only imagined it in a story."

"I'm afraid it's only a cigarette case."

"Oh."

Harper watched the way the lad stared at the thing, wondering if he was disappointed. "Too bad, I suppose we could use one just now, eh?"

"*Oui*. Could you bring some food when you come back? She eats a lot."

"Sure."

"*Merci*. It's almost time to call the hour." Rochat turned to leave and kept turning in a slow circle till he was facing Harper again. "Those men from the bad shadows crushed her wings and she can't fly anymore, monsieur. That's why she's lost."

Harper watched Rochat shuffle away and back through the skinny red door and up the tower. He stepped back into the shadows of the chestnut trees and watched lantern light through the archers' windows winding up the tower. The whole cathedral looking like the last outpost. Nice but dim lad with a lantern all there was at the gate.

"God save us, every one."

GONG! GONG! GONG! GONG!
    The sound roared through the loge and squeezed the air from her lungs.

"Jesus, no!"

She sat up, gasping for breath. She saw the crooked little guy in the long black coat standing at the open door of the loge. Burning lantern in one hand, fat gray cat in the other.

"Are you all right?"

"I was having a nightmare."

"A bad-shadows kind of nightmare?"

"Yeah, the bad-shadows kind. Those fucking bastards knew I was in the tower, they were coming for me."

Rochat shuffled into the loge, set the lantern on the table, filled a glass from one of the water jugs.

"In school, they always gave me a drink of water when I had the bad-shadows kind of nightmares. Then I'd feel better."

Katherine took the glass. "Thanks. Where were you?"

"In the nave." He picked up a piece of paper from the table and held it out to her. "I made a note in case you woke up and were scared to be alone."

She focused her eyes: *in nav and be bcak soone.* Above the words was a drawing of a man in an overcoat, holding a lantern and winding his way down the tower steps, fat gray cat at his heels.

"What a nice picture."

"You can keep it."

She took a sip of water, ran her hands through her hair. Rochat dropped Monsieur Booty to the floor. The beast scampered through the loge and jumped onto Katherine's lap.

"The detectiveman was here."

"Who?"

Rochat reached in his overcoat, pulled out the gold cigarette case. Katherine saw the diamond glitter in the lantern light.

"Oh my God. Harper?"

"He came while you were sleeping. He was on the esplanade and I was in the belfry, and we decided not to wake the skeletons so I went down by the fountain so we could talk and he could drink water. He said he's your friend and he said if I gave you this, you'd know who he was. And I asked him if it was a future-teller diamond, and he said it's a cigarette case but it was too bad it wasn't a future-teller because we could use one just now, eh. Then he said he's coming back tomorrow, but he wasn't going to tell the police where you were, because you need a program to tell the good guys from the bad guys. And he said you should stay off the telephone and not to answer if it rings. Then he said that he'd bring you food tomorrow and help you find a way home."

"That's a lot of remembering in one go, Marc."

"I practiced while I was in the nave."

She opened the cigarette case. "I am so dying for a smoke. Would you mind if I had one?"

Rochat found a tin ashtray on a shelf and set it on the table. "This is Monsieur Buhlmann's. He smokes a pipe sometimes."

Katherine pulled on the woolly sweater and fuzzy slippers, climbed down from the bed, and sat at the table. She lit up, closed her eyes. "God in heaven, I almost feel normal again. What were you doing in the nave, anyway?"

"Making the thing I imagined before I lit the lantern tonight."

"The thing you imagined before . . . Remind me what it was you imagined."

"You have to come with me to see. Do you want to come with me now?"

She looked up to the clock: four fifteen. "Like *now* now?"

Rochat took the black cloak from the hook behind the door and held it out to her.

"I'm very sure you'll like it."

Katherine followed Rochat and his lantern down the tower to where two candles were set on the stone steps marking the small door in the rounded wall. The door was already open and more candles lined the tunnel beyond. Rochat ducked down and scooted through.

Katherine hurried after him to the tribune. She stood up, barely able to see the crucified Christ in the darkened stained-glass window. Her eyes adjusted to the dim light. She saw a camping cot covered in wool blankets, Rochat's sketchbooks and pencils atop the blankets. The photo of his parents and a box of many colored pills sat on a small wooden box beside the cot, a burning candle near the photograph.

"What's all this?"

"I can sleep here and be the tower guard, and you can sleep in the loge. Then we'll both have a bed, and I can hear footsteps on the esplanade better down here. If the bad shadows come again, I can hurry up to Clémence and ring the warning sound."

"Then what happens?"

Rochat thought about it. He didn't really know what happened next.

"Do you want to see more things?"

"You mean this isn't what you wanted to show me? There's more?"

"*Oui.*"

Rochat held up the lantern and opened the little glass door and blew it out. There was only the burning candle near the cot. She watched the soft light wiggle against the stone ceiling high above.

"Wow, so much light from one little candle."

Rochat reached down, picked up the candle from the floor. He held it between their faces.

"Blow it out."

"What?"

"Blow it out."

"Okay, but if I get scared, promise you'll light it again quickly?"

"I promise."

She lowered her face, drew a breath, blew away the flame. The stone ceiling continued to glow with wiggly light.

"Look at that. Where's it coming from?"

"I can show you."

He led her along the narrow metal walkway next to the tall wooden boxes where the organ pipes lived and he told her to duck under the long brass horns. Then he led her down the steps to the platform for the organ console high above the cathedral floor. Katherine suddenly felt like she was falling.

"Marc . . ."

She grabbed his arm, closed her eyes, heard her voice echo into a forever space.

. . . *marc, marc, marc* . . .

"Be not afraid."

Slowly, she opened her eyes to see a cloud of light floating through the forever space of the nave.

"What on earth?"

Candles.

Hundreds of candles burning throughout the vast dark nave.

On the stone floor at the foot of the great pillars and lining the triforium and upper balconies running all around the cathedral. In the arches of the giant chancel dome at the far end of the cathedral and scattered over the flagstones of the altar square beneath the lantern tower.

"Oh, my."

. . . *oh my, oh my, oh my . . .*

Katherine sat on the organist's bench, watching the light swell in the giant arches of the nave as if the cloud of light had lifted the cathedral from the ground and it now drifted unconnected to the earth.

"Gosh, it looks like the whole cathedral is flying."

. . . *cathedral is flying, flying, flying . . .*

"I made it while you were sleeping. I made it so you could see things."

. . . *see things, see things, see things . . .*

"What am I supposed to see?"

"Things angels see."

"Really?"

Katherine looked into the glow of light and saw delicate flames sway in invisible drafts, bending and almost dying before curling upright to breathe light into the dark and chase shadows from the darkest corners.

"Look at the shadows, it looks like they're playing."

"Because they're the teasing kind of shadows."

"What?"

"Teasing kind. They like to play in the cathedral. Sometimes they leave the door to the tower open and sometimes they chase after echoes. They're very friendly shadows."

"That's a sweet imagination. What's that big white box in the pillars, next to the altar?"

"That's Otto."

"Who's he?"

"A brave knight from middles of ages. Sometimes I imagine him wandering around in his armor. He falls over a lot."

"You really have quite the imagination, Marc. Anyone else wandering about the place at night?"

"Sometimes I hear the statues, and skeletons, and—"

"Stop. Skeletons, for real? As in the skeletons you and Harper didn't want to wake up?"

*"Oui."*

"And just where are these skeletons?"

"They live under the floor of the cathedral. Do you want to see?"

"Oh God, can we turn on a light now?"

Rochat turned to leave. Katherine grabbed at his arm.

"No, I mean, don't move. Just change the subject. Imagine something nice."

*. . . something nice, something nice, something nice . . .*

"We can imagine the angels hiding in the cathedral."

"Yeah, that's right. We're supposed to be seeing things only angels can see. So you sit here and tell me about angels hiding in the cathedral."

*. . . in the cathedral, the cathedral, the cathedral . . .*

Rochat sat next to Katherine on the bench and told her things he remembered Monsieur Rannou saying a few nights ago. How angels were creatures made of light and how sometimes they got lost in Lausanne. And in beforetimes, there were lots of cathedrals and men who held their lanterns against the dark so angels could find their way. And what else . . . oh. One by one

the men with lanterns disappeared from the world because nobody thought they needed them in a world of
wonderful inventions, and people forgot angels were
made of light. And that he was the only one in the
world left to hold a lantern in the darkness so angels
could find their way. And that's why Lausanne was full
of lost angels, because there was no place else for them
to go in the world.

"And that's all I can remember."

*. . . all I can remember, can remember, remember . . .*

Katherine listened to the voice echo through the nave.
Then she heard the sound of her breath coming and
going to the rhythm of the flames. She sat silently for a
long time.

"That's such a sad story."

"It is?"

"Yeah. Sad and beautiful, at the same time."

Rochat thought about it, wondering how something
could be sad and beautiful at the same time. Then he
remembered his mother, how beautiful she was, and how
sad he was watching her lowered into the winter ground
of Cimetière Saint-Charles.

"Marc?"

He slowly blinked and looked at Katherine. *"Oui?"*

"Did you go somewhere just then?"

*"Pardon?"*

"Your eyes, they do this thing sometimes, like you go
somewhere else."

"Because I went to see Maman before she died."

"You miss her?"

"I can still see her, in beforetimes. Do you go to beforetimes?"

"Me? No, there's not much for me to go to in the beforetimes department."

Katherine looked into the nave, watching the cloud of light. "Have you ever seen a lost angel in Lausanne, Marc?"

*"Oui."*

"Really, where?"

Rochat reached in the pocket of his overcoat, pulled out a folded piece of paper, and held it out to her. She looked at it, not knowing what to do with it.

"What's this?"

"The angel I saw in Lausanne."

Katherine took the paper and unfolded it. A drawing of a woman through a window, sitting at a mirror, brushing her long hair. Detailed sketches of a face, the eyes.

"But this is me. When did you draw it?"

"I drew it when I first saw you, before you came to the cathedral. And I showed it to Monsieur Gübeli, and he said it could be an angel."

"I don't understand."

"Monsieur Gübeli worked for my father and he brought me to Lausanne when I was—"

"No, no, Marc. This picture. How could you have drawn this picture before I came to the cathedral?"

"I was in the belfry, and I saw you in a window above Rue Caroline. You were brushing your hair, but your back was to me, I couldn't see your face."

"My window? How the heck did you see me through my window?"

"Monsieur Buhlmann gave me binoculars and I was looking for a mysterious mystery and I saw you, but I couldn't see your face."

"A mysterious . . ."

"I wasn't snooping."

"Hey, it's okay. Considering how things turned out, I couldn't care if you were. You saved my life. But if you couldn't see my face, how did you draw this?"

"I imagined it."

"You imagined my face?"

Rochat nodded. "Then I saw you at Gare Simplon. You were getting on La Ficelle and you asked me for a light for your cigarette, but I was too afraid to see if it was really you."

"Jesus, I remember now. You wouldn't even look at me, you were rocking back and forth. I got on the train and left you standing there."

"And you went to the Palace and you talked to the detectiveman, but you didn't turn around and I couldn't see you still."

"You followed me?"

"I followed you and I saw you going into the Palace. I stood outside in the shadows and watched you, but I wasn't snooping."

"No, it's okay, Marc. Don't worry about the snooping thing. Trust me, I'm used to it. Just tell me why you followed me."

"I had to know if you were real or just an imagination, but I couldn't see your face. Then the clock on the fireplace rang and I was late and had to hurry to the cathedral, and later I was looking through my binoculars again and you were sitting at the window again. And you were looking outside, you were looking at the cathedral, and you . . . and you . . ."

"Kissed my fingers and touched them to the glass."

"That's when I saw your face, that's when I knew what you are."

. . . *what you are, what you are, what you are* . . .

Katherine held her breath a moment. "Marc, what do you think I am?"

"You're an angel who's lost in Lausanne. That's why you came to Lausanne. You needed to come to the cathedral so you could hide till you find a way home."

. . . *a way home, a way home, a way home* . . .

Katherine looked through the nave, all the candles filling the cavernous nave with an almost breathing light.

"You did all this and you're helping me because you think I'm an angel?"

"It's my duty to protect you and help you see things."

Katherine raised her hand to her mouth. "Oh, Jesus."

"Did I say something bad?"

"No, you said something really lovely but . . . I'm not an angel, Marc."

"*Non?*"

"I'm as far from an angel as it gets."

"I don't know what that means."

"It means I'm a prostitute, I sell my body for money. Lots and lots of money."

Rochat thought about it. "Like Marie-Madeleine?"

"Yes."

"You're not the angel Maman told me about?"

"What?"

"Maman told me an angel would come to the cathedral. It's not you?"

"No."

"But if you're not an angel who's lost, why are you in Lausanne?"

"I was in trouble with Uncle Sam and the IRS. Now I'm on the run from those men you saw. I was sold into white slavery as a sex slave, Marc. Believe me, I'm no angel."

Rochat thought about it some more. He didn't know who her uncle was or what an IRS was, but he was very sure about those men she ran away from. "Maybe you don't know you're an angel, but those men from the bad shadows know and that's why they want to buy you. I'm very sure no one can buy angels."

She reached over, took his hand. "There's only one angel I can see in the cathedral, Marc, and it isn't me."

"Maybe you don't know you're an angel because angels are only made of light. That's what Monsieur Rannou said."

"Marc—"

"And maybe you don't know you're an angel because you're so lost."

*. . . you're so lost, so lost, so lost . . .*

"I do feel lost, Marc. I feel very lost."

He stared at her hand touching his for a moment. Her skin felt warm. He looked up at her.

"Then the cathedral is where you belong. It's where

you ran to. You didn't go anywhere else because once you saw the lantern from your window. You said you saw the lantern. And you ran to the cathedral because you knew it was the only place for you to hide."

*. . . to hide, to hide, to hide . . .*

Katherine saw Rochat's green eyes in the light of the candles burning in the nave, so wanting to believe she was an angel. And she felt her own heart, so wishing it were true.

"Maybe I could imagine I was an angel, just for tonight. It's such a lovely thing to imagine, it really is. Can we go for a walk, Marc? Can we walk through the cathedral, with all the candles burning?"

"Aren't you sleepy?"

"No, I'm not sleepy. Let's go for a wonderful walk. I'll be the lost angel and you can take me around the cathedral and we'll look for all the other angels hiding in the cathedral."

"And I'll light the lantern and we can blow out all the candles."

"Yeah, we'll blow out the candles, one by one. And we'll pretend we're putting all your beautiful angels to sleep."

*. . . angels to sleep, angels to sleep, to sleep . . .*

# twenty-eight

The sun rose over the Alps and set afire the ice-covered peaks above Évian. The fierce light reflected back across the lake straight into Harper's eyes. He turned away, watched the clock next to the bed flip to eight o'clock. The inspector's drug-induced stupor finally easing. Harper thought he should order coffee, eat something maybe, shake off the numbness in his arms and legs. Then again, the waitress with the gun might shoot as quickly as she'd bring him a croissant.

He pulled himself up and dropped his feet to the floor. He stumbled across the room and sank into a chair, saw the bottle of red wine on the table. He opened it and poured, watching the deep red color swirl in the glass. He drank it down, remembered the inspector's prophecy: *Mr. Harper's missed his supper and he's in for a rough night. A full-bodied red will do him wonders.*

He poured another glass, remembered some more.

Came back to the hotel just after one. No coppers waiting for him. Thought he was clear till he opened the door of his room. Pitch black inside. Light from the hall revealed someone had been in the room and shut off the telly and turned down the bed. Two Swiss chocolates lay perfectly on the pillow.

"Bollocks."

Something slammed into his back and shoved him in the room and up against a wall. Blunt steel digging at the back of his neck, a woman's voice spitting venom.

"You should've chosen a film with a longer running time, monsieur."

"Any recommendations, mademoiselle?"

"*Ben-Hur*. Two hundred twelve minutes."

A quick roundhouse kick caught the back of Harper's knees and dropped him to the floor. Another kick to his shoulder knocked him upright. He was looking up the death end of a pistol. The waitress with the gun on the trigger end.

"Where did you go, monsieur?"

"Went for a walk. I needed a pack of smokes."

Her knee smashed into his face and sent him to the floor. Then a swift kick to his bruised ribs.

"Fuck!"

She grabbed his collar and pulled him upright again and set the gun at his head.

"*S'il vous plaît, monsieur,* where did you go?"

"This is all very impressive, mademoiselle, but could we just get to the bloody point?"

The desk lamp switched on from across the room. The cop in the cashmere coat sitting comfortably, Mutt and Jeff standing behind him.

"Speaking of the bloody point."

"Good evening, Mr. Harper, nice to see you looking so well. We were enjoying your romp through the park when the town's CCTV cameras shut down. Unscheduled service, it seems."

"Unscheduled? In this town?"

"A minor inconvenience that will not be repeated. No matter, as I suspect you're about to tell us what you were up to."

"Told you. Went for a walk, needed a pack of smokes."

"Yes, rather fond of evening strolls myself. Good for the digestion. By the way, where would I find Katherine Taylor?"

"Get stuffed."

The inspector raised one eyebrow. "I beg your pardon?"

"You heard me."

"Mr. Harper, you seem to forget that I'm with the police."

"No, I didn't."

The waitress with the gun threw another roundhouse kick. Harper caught her ankle midflight and pulled hard. She hit the floor, rolled, and was back on her feet with the gun at his head in the blink of an eye.

"Now that was really impressive, mademoiselle."

The inspector cleared his throat. "Officer Jannsen, that will be quite enough. I'm sure Mr. Harper would prefer to take a seat on the bed."

She held out her hand and pulled him to his feet. He towered over her.

"So, Officer Jannsen is it?"

*"Oui, monsieur."*

*"Enchanté*, and suppose you make yourself genuinely useful, love, and get us a cup of tea."

She turned to the inspector; he nodded.

"Would you be so kind, Officer? The Earl Grey, I think. And if you'd bring a bottle of good Lavaux. Mr. Harper's missed his supper and he's in for a rough night. A full-bodied red will do him wonders."

*"Tout de suite, Inspecteur."*

She left the room. Harper sat on the bed.

Mutt closed the door and rested his back against it. Jeff eased to the other side of the room. Both of them opening small notebooks and writing. The inspector rose from the chair, took his cigarette case from his cashmere coat. He crossed the room, offered one of his gold-tipped smokes to Harper.

"Now, why don't you tell us about your evening with Miss Taylor?"

"Didn't see her, didn't talk to her." Harper took a smoke, set it to his lips. "Anyone got a match?"

Mutt stepped in with a lighter, Jeff dropped an ashtray on the bed. They retook their positions as the inspector picked up one of the chocolates on the bed pillow.

"You don't mind, do you? I have a weakness for Swiss chocolate."

"Take two, Inspector, they're small."

"One's quite enough, thank you." He walked back to his chair, unwrapped the chocolate, popped it in his mouth. "In that case, why don't you tell us what you were doing while you were out not seeing Miss Taylor."

"Actually, I was thinking about skipping town on the next train."

"I see you're still here."

Harper inhaled deep puffs, exhaled clouds that floated about the room. "Couldn't get a ticket. Skiing holidays and all."

"Yes, well, one must book ahead this time of year."

The inspector waited in silence; he watched Harper smoke. Mutt and Jeff continued to make scratching noises in their notebooks. A quiet knock at the door. Mutt opened it. Officer Jannsen wheeled in a serving trolley. China pot, cups and saucers, milk and sugar, bottle of Swiss red wine. She poured two cups of tea, set one on the table next to the inspector.

"Thank you, Officer."

*"Volontiers, Inspecteur."*

She served a cup to Harper, bowed, and left the room. Harper turned to the inspector.

"Nicely trained, that one."

"Her first year on the task force, keen to do well. I hope she wasn't too rough on you. She was terribly aggrieved you got the jump on us. I thought it an opportunity to see how her enhanced interrogation techniques were coming along. How would you rate her?"

"Nice smile, vicious kick." He raised his cup and breathed in the bouquet, took a long sip. "And she makes a decent cuppa. She'll go far in your gang."

"Happy to hear it. I think it effective to have attractive young women do the dirty work. Greatly reduces the time in getting to the facts of the matter when dealing with truculent sorts, wouldn't you agree?"

"If you say so." Harper took another long sip, watching the inspector watch him like a cat waiting to pounce. "Something else on your mind, Inspector?"

"Just wondering if you enjoy the taste of the tea? Special house blend, you know."

"Don't tell me, here's the part where we shoot the breeze about the evil Spaniards on their horses, slaughtering their way into the New World. Followed by a bit of whimsy about the king of Morocco and his tobacco patch. Or was it the other way around?"

"In fact, this is where you describe the nature of your relationship with Miss Taylor."

"I hardly know her."

"That wasn't my question. I asked about the nature of your relationship."

"Our relationship?"

"*Di immortales virtutem approbare, non adhibere debent,* and so on."

Harper took a draw on the cigarette. "If you're asking me if I've known Miss Taylor in the biblical sense, the answer's still no."

"I am relieved. Attachments with women of her sort, not the healthiest of things for our sort."

"What makes you think I'm one of your sort?"

"Well, you're here, aren't you?"

"Never knew you to talk in riddles, Inspector."

"Believe me, Mr. Harper, I'm not. Where and when did you meet Miss Taylor?"

Harper felt one of those "get stuffed" moments rising from his guts but couldn't find the wherewithal to say the words.

"LP's Bar, a few days ago, she bought me a beer and I took her newspaper. We also had a drink on Place Saint-François at the Christmas fête the same night. She went home alone. I saw her in LP's again last Tuesday evening. She was waiting for a high-priced client. No idea who, so don't ask. That's all there is to it."

"I'm told you gave her a maquette of Lausanne Cathedral while at the bar."

Harper set his cup in the saucer, drew on his smoke. "And I see you had a chat with the polite bartender at LP's."

"Indeed. He was most helpful in spite of your advising him to lie to us. For future reference, Mr. Harper, the locals find such behavior quite unnatural. They're just not very good at it."

"So you knew what I was up to. Why didn't you catch up with me at Miss Taylor's flat?"

"Because I had every confidence you'd return to tell us all about it."

Harper sipped at the tea. "All right. I picked up the maquette in the cathedral gift shop the day I discovered Yuriev's note. Had no real use for the bloody thing, so I gave it to Miss Taylor when I saw her in the bar that evening, right after I slipped my business card inside."

Inspector Gobet raised the other eyebrow. "Your business card?"

"That's right, the one pinned to the wall next to what was left of Madame Badeaux."

"And for the record, why didn't you identify Miss Taylor's voice on the answering machine, knowing she was involved with the killers?"

"You telling me you didn't already know who she was or what sort of trouble she was in?"

"Of course I did. But I'd still like to know why you didn't identify her voice."

"Didn't like the tone of yours."

*"Pardon?"*

"Set up people to die, Inspector, you should at least be polite about it." Harper took another sip of tea, huffed on the inspector's cigarette. He dug a set of keys from his coat, tossed them to Mutt.

"Keys to her flat, lads. Number two, Rue Caroline, rooftop flat. Have fun sorting which key is which. Place is a wreck, but I kept my prints off things. And there's an oily patch on the floor in the sitting room, near a broken lamp. Careful you don't slip."

Mutt and Jeff stopped writing, shot a look at the inspector. Harper's turn to raise an eyebrow.

"Let me guess: You've heard that one before. Let's try this one: A witness saw two men outside her building in the early hours of Thursday. One short with a small beard, goatee most probably, wore a black suit. Other one was tall and thin in some kind of pajama outfit. Black, Oriental maybe."

Harper read the looks on the coppers' faces.

"My, seems we've heard that one, too."

"It would be helpful if you gave us the name of the witness, Mr. Harper."

"Not on his life."

"What?"

"Let's just say I'd rather not see an innocent person slaughtered."

"You're being most unhelpful, Mr. Harper."

Harper took another long draw on the cigarette. "Don't take it personally, Inspector, but for a country with only a handful of willful homicides a year, bodies are dropping like flies in this place."

"Mr. Harper, you don't seem to understand what's going on in Lausanne."

"Enlighten me."

"I'm afraid I can't."

"Right, you're the policeman, I'm not."

"It's more complicated than that."

"What's complicated? You're the good guys, they're the bad guys. Or are the lines a little less clear, other way around, maybe?"

"I'm not quite sure what you mean."

"Then I'll spell it out for you, Inspector. You're as bent as they come."

Mutt and Jeff stepped toward Harper. The inspector kept them in place with a quick glance before returning his attention to Harper.

"Perhaps you'd care to share with us the manner of your thinking, Mr. Harper."

"Back to the manner of my thinking routine, are we? Fine, goes like this: A rain of shite is about to come crashing down on your cashmere coat."

"Do tell."

"You told me your task force had been tracking the killers when it was Yuriev you really wanted. Or rather, whatever the fuck it was he smuggled out of Moscow. My guess is you got it off him before he ended up in a ditch."

"Are you suggesting I had something to do with Alexander Yuriev's death?"

"I'm saying it was convenient he ended up in a ditch."

"And what, do you suppose, is it that I obtained from Yuriev?"

"Knowing you, some gadget to rule the fucking world."

"Surely you can do better than that."

"All right, how about a performance-enhancing drug with severe psychotropic effects?"

"And what would I want with such a thing?"

"I told you, rule the fucking world."

The inspector removed a fluff of lint from his coat. "Mr. Harper, may I remind you that the fool does not become wise through the repetition of his folly."

"You've got it back to front, Inspector."

"Do I?"

"It's 'If the fool would persist in his folly, he would become wise.'"

"Of course. William Blake's *The Marriage of Heaven and Hell*, yes?"

"No bloody idea."

"No? Something you heard, then. The History Channel, perhaps."

Harper felt himself wobble. "What did you say?"

"It wasn't important. Let's stay with your manner of thinking."

"Manner of . . . thinking."

"Yes. I fail to understand Miss Taylor's role in my grand scheme to 'rule the fucking world,' as you put it."

"Miss Taylor . . . she's . . . she's a direct connection to Simone Badeaux. That's why the killers want her alive, and why you want her dead."

"You're beginning to imagine things in a very serious manner, Mr. Harper. You should be careful. I'm not sure you can handle it."

Harper shook his head. "No? Then imagine this: Legendary courtesan with a client list that'd bring down several European governments, she was your bloody front."

"I don't follow."

"You practically run this country, you practically run Europe. No wonder. You're blackmailing Europe with one hand and cashing in on every crooked scam with the other. And the profits are hiding in Simone Badeaux's bank accounts to the tune of forty million. The killers have it all on paper, ready to share with Euronews, along with pictures of Madame Simone's mangled corpse. The killers want to make a deal. Give us what Yuriev smuggled out of Russia or we let the world know what an upstanding pig you are, courtesy of Miss Taylor. How am I doing?"

"Like the proverbial blind man describing the elephant."

The room began to spin. Harper tried to focus his eyes. "Sorry?"

"The blind man and the elephant, missing the point and all. Though for a moment I thought you were coming around. Making the connection between the oil you found in Miss Taylor's flat and the formula delivered to your office at the IOC and all."

Harper felt the floor giving way under his feet. "Formula?"

"Yes. You see, it's actually a breeding potion, as ancient as evil itself, used by those who already rule this world. Their mating rituals are as painful as they are cruel. The potion induces selected females into imagining they are experiencing intense pleasure. I'm sure you understand what all this means for Miss Taylor."

"You're . . . you're out of your bloody mind . . . I'm getting her out of this cesspit you call a country."

"You? Oh, do be serious, Mr. Harper. You're nothing but a drunkard who can't even remember his London telephone number."

The room spinning faster. Harper dropped the cigarette in the ashtray, grabbed the bedpost. "Fuck . . ."

"Are you feeling unwell, Mr. Harper? You seem to be drifting. Perhaps you should take another sip of tea."

Harper looked down at his cup. *Special house blend, you know* . . . He looked up into the inspector's smiling face. Like the bloody Cheshire Cat.

"You drugged me."

"Just a little potion of ours to enhance the cumulative effect of the cigarettes."

Harper saw the cigarette in the ashtray, still burning. He raised his blurring eyes to the inspector. "The fags."

"Yes, hand-rolled in a little shop in Paris, just behind the Ritz."

Harper dropped his cup, stumbled across the room. "Bastard."

Mutt and Jeff jumped and pinned Harper to the wall. He saw the inspector almost floating toward him, his voice coming from the way beyond.

"I want you to listen to me very carefully, Mr. Harper. This is what we call an intervention. You need to wake up and remember what you are and why you're here."

"Who the hell are you?"

"Me? I'm Inspector Jacques Gobet of the Swiss police. The question is: Who are you?"

Feeling himself slip from his body, trying to hold on. Seeing himself coming to in a shabby London flat. Brit passport with a photo and name inside.

"Harper, my name's Jay Michael Harper."

"And where was Jay Michael Harper born?"

"London . . . I was born in London."

"And what was your father's name, your mother's name?"

"My mother, my mother was . . . her name was . . ."

"Where did you attend school, your hobbies, the name of your first sweetheart, perhaps?" The inspector moved close to Harper's face. "When was the last time you slept?"

"I don't remember."

"No, you don't remember. Curious, isn't it? You know

everything there is to know about this world. You speak its languages and quote its poets with no remembrance of where you learned such things. In fact, you don't remember a single day of life before a telephone rang in a London flat with a call from Guardian Services Limited."

Consciousness sinking. "I'm Harper, my name's . . ."

The inspector slapped Harper's face hard. "Stay with me, Mr. Harper. You are not a creature of free will, you are one of our kind, and you'll tell me what I want to know."

"I won't let you slaughter her. I won't let you slaughter him."

"You cannot save the living from the time of their death, Mr. Harper."

"Watch me, you fucking pig."

The inspector slammed Harper into the wall. "I didn't bring you to Lausanne to be a savior of men, Mr. Harper, I brought you here to kill."

"What are you talking about?"

"The war, eternal and forever. We're losing badly and running out of time. We need you to wake up."

"Go to hell!"

The inspector rammed his iron fist into Harper's guts. Harper crumpled over. The inspector stepped back and adjusted his silk scarf.

"There is no heaven, Mr. Harper, there is no hell, there is only this place. And these are the days of slaughter and destruction. Wake up!"

Mutt and Jeff tossed Harper to the bed. Numbness spreading through his limbs. He rolled onto his back. The inspector hovered over him.

"What the fuck have you done to me?"

"I do hope you enjoyed your evening, Mr. Harper. It's about to come at you in spades."

Harper could barely speak. "No."

The drugs dragging him into a paralytic stupor. Watching the inspector float out of the room. Seeing Mutt tear a page from his notepad, hand it to Jeff. Jeff laying it on the desk, and then the two of them drifting out of the door.

"Bloody insane . . ."

Searing light from the hall, burning his eyes.

Officer Jannsen appearing in the doorway and eclipsing the light.

"All of you . . . insane."

Smiling at him, pulling the door closed.

Rest of the night, unable to move, unable to speak. Hands clawing at bedsheets.

The night rolling through his mind again and again, as if he were trapped in a ripple in time till the sun rose over the Alps and set afire the ice-covered peaks above Évian. The fierce light reflected back across the lake straight into Harper's eyes. He shook his head clear, saw the bottle of red on the table.

"Hell with it. Can't beat 'em, get pissed."

He poured a glass and looked out of the window. He watched the sun on Les Big Rocks across the lake.

*Crack.*

The crystal glass in pieces on the floor and the red

liquid flowing through glass shards slow as molasses, bleeding into the carpet. Not remembering the glass falling, hand and fingers still formed in the crescent that held it, then seeing it again. Taking a sip of wine, watching the glass fall, watching it shatter, knowing where each piece of glass would lie before it touched the ground. Watching the wine seep deep into the carpet and taking the shape he had already seen. Then looking out of the windows and seeing the same sun crawling across the same bloody ice-covered rocks.

*. . . days of slaughter and destruction . . . days of slaughter and destruction . . .*

His eyes shot to the desk. Note from Mutt and Jeff, left atop the computer keyboard. He picked it up, focused his clearing eyes: *Book of Enoch, chapter fifteen, verse nine.* Harper scoured the scraps of paper on the desk, stopped cold finding one: *The spirits of the giants shall be like clouds which shall oppress, corrupt, fall, and bruise upon the earth . . . and they come forth during the days of slaughter and destruction.*

"Christ, come to Lausanne, lose what's left of your mind."

# twenty-nine

$M$onsieur Booty opened his eyes and watched the woman dry her hair with a towel. He sat up and yawned as the woman pulled on a woolly sweater. The beast then lay down to sleep as the woman leaned toward the small mirror on the wall and touched the reddish scar on her cheek.

"Hey, fuzzface."

Monsieur Booty opened one eye.

"Any facial moisturizer up here?"

*Mew.*

"No, didn't think so."

Katherine prepared a bandage and raised it to her cheek. She looked at herself in the mirror, remembering she was always the prettiest one. The one the boys wanted to kiss, the one the girls wanted to be. She rolled the bandage in a ball and tossed it to the floor.

"Heck with it."

Monsieur Booty pounced without mercy and held the offending thing in his claws.

*Mrewww.*

"Yeah, me too."

Katherine slipped on a pair of heavy socks and rubber boots. She tossed the black cloak over her shoulders and put on her black hat and stepped out onto the south balcony, squinting in the bright sunlight bouncing off the lake and sparkling on the limestone pillars of the belfry. She touched one pillar. The stone felt warm.

"A girl could get a great tan up here. Turn this place into a spa, make a fortune."

"What's a spa?"

Katherine looked up and saw Rochat poking his head from the high south timbers, a few bird feathers entwined in his black hair.

"Jesus, don't do that, Marc."

"Do what?"

"Pop out from nowhere. I need a warning. What are you doing up there, anyway?"

"Brushing La Lombarde. Do you want to come up and see, or do you need to go to the toilet for another bath?"

"No, thanks, one freezing bath in a sink per day is fine. When do we eat?"

"When the detectiveman comes. Are you going to have a nap? You haven't slept all night."

"I'm not tired. When's he coming?"

"Who?"

"Harper."

"I don't know. Why didn't you put a bandage on your face?"

"I'm going for a grunge thing, goes with the outfit. How will we know when Harper comes?"

"I'll hear his footsteps on the esplanade. What's a grunge thing?"

"You're looking at it."

"Oh. Do you want to come up and see the upstairs bells now?"

Katherine smiled. "Okay, why not?"

She walked to the east balcony as the massive hammer outside Marie's skirt cocked back and slammed down on the great bell's bronze skirt.

*GONG!*

Katherine jumped and plugged her ears, watching the hammer cock and slam down nine times, feeling the sound penetrate her body and then fade away.

"Man, that's the loudest thing I've ever heard!"

"What?"

She looked up. Rochat was leaning out from the east timbers, holding on by his fingertips.

"Marc, get back in there."

He jumped back into the carpentry. His face peeked over the edge.

"I'm very good at climbing the timbers."

"Yeah, well, you could hurt yourself. And how come the timbers didn't creak and groan that time?"

"They did, you just didn't hear them."

"I was standing right next to them."

"Then you weren't listening."

"Gotcha." She wound her way up the northeast turret, ducked through the arch, and stepped into the icy shade of the north balcony. "It's freezing up here!"

Rochat was crawling along the cross timbers above La Lombarde. "Because the sun never sees the north side of the belfry in winter. Come inside the carpentry where it's warm."

She stepped up to the walkway, almost banging her head into a low-hanging bell. She ducked and moved to the center of the tower. The warm sun flooded through the stone arches, chasing away the cold.

"Oh, yeah. This is more my speed. Just like home."

"Really?"

"Oh yeah, put a couple of surfers on the lake and you'd have it."

Rochat didn't know what surfers were and decided not to ask. He slipped the scrubber broom down the back of his black overcoat, crawled to the edge of the timbers above La Lombarde, and leaped through the air to the other side of the carpentry. He pulled out the scrubber broom and brushed the tops of two bells hanging in the west timbers.

"*Bonjour, mesdames.* Aren't we looking pretty today?"

"Do these bells have names, too?"

"*Oui*, this is Bienheureuse and this is l'Aigrelette. They're sisters, they came from Lombardy to live in the tower."

"And who's this one, the one I almost banged my head into?"

"La Voyageuse. She used to live in the church on Place Saint-François."

"So which one of these gals rings for lunch?"

"La Lombarde. She used to live in the Dominican abbey, down there."

Katherine looked where Rochat pointed through the west arches and down to a parking lot. "What Dominican abbey?"

"They tore it down in middles of ages and La Lombarde went to live in the church at Saint-François with La Voyageuse."

"Huh?"

"La Lombarde and La Voyageuse lived in the church at Saint-François before they came to the cathedral."

Katherine could just see the small tower of Saint-François off the south balcony. "So how did they end up here?"

"Because in nineteens of centuries a man from Italy heard the bells and said they were out of tune. So the Lausannois moved around all the bells in le Canton de Vaud, so they'd sound nice when they sang together."

"No kidding?"

"*Non*, they do the same thing with bells on cows."

"They tune the cowbells in Switzerland?"

"*Oui*, so it sounds nice when you walk through the country."

"Huh." Katherine looked at La Lombarde and La Voyageuse. "So they moved these bells from over there to here?"

"But first, they had to move two bells from here to there."

"To Saint-François?"

"I go visit them sometimes. They're still very grumpy about the whole thing."

"You're making this up."

He stopped scrubbing, he looked at Katherine. "*La grande sonnerie* times is tomorrow at six o'clock. You can hear how nice the bells sing before you go home."

Katherine settled against a wide timber and looked through the arches of the east balcony toward Pont Bessières.

"Marc?"

"*Oui?*"

"Could you show me where I used to live?"

Rochat stopped scrubbing, peeked out from behind Bienheureuse. "Now?"

"Yeah."

"*D'accord.*" He balanced the broom on a timber, slid down a crossbeam, jumped onto the wooden platform, and stood in front of Katherine.

"Wait a sec, let me do something about these feathers in your hair."

"I was cleaning the bells."

"Yeah, I know." She reached up and picked them away one by one. She brushed the dust from his shoulders. "There, much better."

"*Merci*, I'll be right back."

"Where are you going?"

"To get something to help you see things."

He shuffled to the northeast turret and down the corkscrewed steps. Katherine waited, listening to the quiet and feeling the warm winter sun on her face. She walked along the platform to Mademoiselle Couvre-feu. She reached up and took the clapper in her hands, gently touching it against the darkened silver skirt of the thousand-year-old bell. The bell chimed softly.

"Hello, you. It's me, Katherine. Remember me?"

She listened to the sound as it floated through the belfry and faded away into the sky.

"Hello."

Katherine jumped and turned around, saw Rochat.

"Jeez, Marc! Don't do that!"

"Don't say hello?"

"No, popping up like that. Where'd you go?"

Rochat held up the binoculars. "To get these."

"Aha, the famous binoculars for seeing things. Like girls through their bedroom windows."

"I wasn't snooping."

"I know, Marc, it's a joke."

"Oh. Do you want to see your house now?" He turned and shuffled along the balcony. "Watch out for the ice on the steps, and there's still lots of snow on the roof."

He climbed up the corkscrew steps of the northeast turret. She chased after him, imitating the way he skipped up the steps two at a time then jumping through the arch at the top of the steps and sinking to her knees in powdery white snow. The whole blue sky opened above her head, the whole world lay at her feet.

"Oh, wow! This is like being on top of the world!"

She kicked through the snow and made her way along a balustrade of hollow crosses that ran between the four turrets of the tower, each turret peaked in wildly carved

498 ·     JON STEELE

stone. A red-tiled hexagonal spire rose from the center of the roof, twice higher than the turrets.

"What's this tower in the middle called?"

Rochat thought about it. "The top of the cathedral."

"I know that, but what's it called?"

Rochat thought about it some more. "The top of the cathedral."

Katherine laughed. "God, you're so funny. Hey, there's a little door down here, almost buried in the snow. What's in here?"

"Old roof tiles. But I like to imagine it's a very good place for hiding things."

"Good to know, in case I ever need a new hiding place."

The balustrade was almost as high as her shoulders. She jumped up, leaned over the edge, her eyes following the lines and angles along the roof of the cathedral.

"That's the nave down there, where we went looking for lost angels, isn't it?"

*"Oui."*

"And what's that tower over there, the pointy one at the far end of the cathedral?"

"The lantern tower."

"That was above the altar, wasn't it?"

Rochat looked at the pointy tower, then back to Katherine. "It still is."

"I know that, what I mean is . . . Wait a minute. Why do they call that one the lantern tower if the guy with the lantern lives over here, in the tower with the bells?"

Rochat looked down at the roof under his feet, extending his arms this way and that way as if figuring the volume of a space. With arms fixed, he faced the lantern tower and measured the squared space of the belfry against the conical shape of the lantern tower. He dropped his hands and looked at Katherine.

"Because the bells won't fit in the lantern tower."

Katherine smiled. "You really are very funny, Marc."

"There was an accident when I was born."

"I don't mean funny odd. I mean funny funny."

"*Merci.* Do you want to see where you used to live now?"

Katherine took a deep breath. "Yeah, let's go for it."

Rochat handed her the binoculars. "You don't have to go anywhere, just turn around and look."

Katherine took the binoculars. She put the lenses to her eyes and panned across the rooftops of Lausanne to the attractive building with the rounded façade at the corner of Rue Caroline. She focused on the rooftop flat with the green shutters and garden trees and the three men standing on her terrace looking back at her. She dropped to her knees.

"Fuck!"

"What's wrong?"

"They saw me."

"Who?"

"Those men on my terrace. Jesus, get down."

Rochat ducked next to her, took the binoculars, looked through the stone pillars of the balustrade.

"It's not those men who hurt you."

"I know it's not *those* men. The men out there are police. Holy fuck, they're after me."

Rochat lowered the binoculars. He saw Katherine cowering next to the northwest turret.

"But policemen in Switzerland wear gray uniforms with gray hats and they carry black guns on their belts."

"Trust me, those guys are cops. Detectives, real ones."

Rochat raised the binoculars to his eyes. "They're looking somewhere else now."

"Where?"

"To the lake."

"Lemme see."

He gave her the binoculars and she saw two big men in long black coats, with a third man in a brown wool overcoat. The big men writing in small notebooks as the third man talked. After a minute they reentered the flat and closed the sliding glass doors.

"Shit, this is all I need."

Rochat crouched down next to her. "But they didn't see you."

"They were looking right at me, Marc!"

"No, it's the binoculars. They play games on you and make you think people can see you because things look so close. Like the hands on the clock on Place Saint-François."

"What?"

"You can look at the clock through the binoculars and you can reach out and touch the hands and fix it because it's always two minutes early."

"What're you talking about, Marc? Because I'm talking about the police on the terrace of my flat, the ones who were looking at me!"

Rochat tried to think faster. "But they were far away. Look again without the binoculars. They don't look like policemen, they look like ants."

"Ants?"

"Tiny ones."

She looked between the pillars of the balustrade, saw the windows of her flat and the indistinguishable shapes inside.

"Yeah, maybe they didn't see me, but they're sure as hell looking for me."

"But they don't know you're here. And you don't look like you anymore, you look like *le guet*."

She touched the brim of the black hat hiding her hair, hiding her face. She tugged at the black cloak and pulled it snug.

"Yeah, that's true."

"And soon you'll be going home. Your friend the detectiveman is going to help. He said so."

"Yeah, that's true, too."

She pulled off her hat. Her hair fell to her shoulders. She rested her head against the balustrade, took a deep breath, and sighed.

"Marc, could you do me a favor?"


Harper dialed; the tramp picked up on the first ring.
"So, English, I see death hasn't found you yet."

"How did you know it was me?"

"The holy miracle of caller ID."

"Caller ID, right."

Harper heard the sound of Monsieur Gabriel firing up his opiates and sucking hard. His wheezing voice coming down the line as if from another planet.

"The eternity of our beings is such a wonderful gift, is it not?"

"Sorry?"

"You sound weary, English."

"Weary? More like paralytic."

"*¿Y esta mañana, has visto la luz?*"

"The light, this morning?"

"On the ice cliffs above Évian. Beautiful, no?"

"Depends on which side of the loony-bin gate you're standing."

"Tell me, English."

Harper laughed to himself. "I saw it more than once. Five or six times actually." He heard the tramp hit the pipe again.

"I am familiar with the sensation."

"Glad to hear it, means we're on the same side of the gate. How about this one, then: You wake up in a London flat without a single memory of a life. You're brought to Lausanne and set to wander through strip clubs, bridges, cafés, and one falling-down cathedral looking for a dead man. And along the way there's a bird in a strip club, or a bloke on a bridge, or a down-on-his-luck elf in Café Romand, or a nun in a gift shop. Not to mention a pack of Swiss cops who may not be cops but they're up to their necks in corpses so what's it matter. Because what does matter is the sensation I had coming to this morning and watching *la luz* splatter across those fucking big rocks again and again."

"And what was the sensation, English?"

"That there're a lot of people in Lausanne who know things I don't."

"Such as?"

"Such as what I'm doing in this town and what happened to the rest of my life before I got here. I mean, there's the rub, isn't it? I'm dragged to Lausanne without a memory. No bloody idea why I'm here other than to watch people die until it's my turn. And everywhere I go some local clown is pointing me to bloody Lausanne Cathedral. And when that doesn't work, I get pointed to the bloody Book of Enoch. And when that doesn't work, I'm drugged and pushed to the edge of madness till I'm forced to come to you for the answers."

"Perhaps madness on this side of the loony-bin gate is no more than seeing things as they truly are."

Harper lit up and drew on a fag. "Maybe, maybe not. Doesn't change the fact you're the man with the answers, does it? Or am I wasting my bloody time? Because from what I hear these are the days of slaughter and destruction. And time is something you and the rest of Inspector Gobet's gang are running out of."

Harper listened to the sound of Gabriel's ragged breathing.

"It is time for us to meet again, English. Though I'm not sure you're ready to know the truth."

"From what I can see, Monsieur Gabriel, truth is a moving target in this place . . . Did you say *again*?"

"I will wait where you saw me before, at the place of my midday meditations."

"Mate, I've never seen you. I don't know you from Adam."

"You knew me long before the time of Adam. You have known me from the time of the unremembered beginning."

"The what?"

"Noon, under the lantern tower of Lausanne Cathedral."

Ripping back through time.

Watching himself search through the cathedral. Coming up the ambulatory steps to the transept.

Sparkles of light on the flagstones, bright sun rushing through the colored glass of the Cathedral Rose. Turning slowly to see a ragged form standing at the center of the crossing square. His face aglow with color, arms stretched to his sides, palms open to the light.

"Bloody hell, you're the tramp on the altar square."

"Let there be light, English." The line went dead.

# thirty

H ow do I look?"

Rochat laid the scissors on the table.

"You look like the picture of Joan of Arc I remember
from my schoolbook."

"What?"

"You said you wanted me to cut your hair short, and
I remembered a picture of Joan of Arc from a schoolbook
because she had short hair."

"Oh shit. Where's the mirror?"

Rochat took the hand mirror from the shelf and gave
it to Katherine.

"Hey, it's really good. Where did you learn to cut
hair?"

"I drew the hair on your head with the scissors. It was
easy."

"Easy? Trust me, women in LA would sell their first-
born for a haircut this good. You could be the next big
thing in hairstyling."

"I don't know what that means."

"Don't worry. It's a good thing."

"It's a good thing, *merci*."

"Now, do you have any money you could loan me?"

Rochat dug through the cabinet under the bed and found a tin box. He gave it to her.

"Papa brought me this when I was little. It had chocolates inside but I ate them longtimes ago and keep money in it now."

She stared at the picture on the lid: the Matterhorn reflected in an alpine lake.

"Zermatt. I was supposed to be in Zermatt next week."

She opened the lid, saw tightly fitted piles of Swiss banknotes in fifties and hundreds.

"Yikes, how much is in here?"

"I don't know."

Katherine counted the notes out on the table. "Jesus, there're a hundred thousand francs here. What the heck do they pay you to wave your lantern?"

"They don't pay me anything."

"So what's this?"

"Monsieur Gübeli gives me some pocket money for allowances every month. I don't spend much, so I just keep it in the tin because he told me to keep it in a safe place."

"Remind me, which one's Gübeli?"

"He brought me to Lausanne. He takes care of the bank my grand-maman and papa owned before they died. And he takes care of my building in Ouchy."

"You have a building in Ouchy?"

"I have a building in Ouchy."

"Which one?"

"L'Hôtel de Léman. Half of it is apartments, and it has a little clock on top."

"I know that place. It's yours?"

"Grand-maman and Papa gave it to me before they died because I'm not part of the family fortune because Papa's wife is a Bavarian countess and the children are spiteful."

"What?"

"That's what they said."

"Were your grandmother and father, like, rich?"

"Grand-maman lived in a big castle in Vufflens."

"You mean the castle with the butler and all the maids you told me about the other day, it was real, you weren't imagining it?"

"I wasn't imagining it."

Katherine stared at him. "Man, you're so full of surprises."

"Is that a good thing?"

"Yeah."

*"Merci."*

She fingered the cash. "So could I borrow four thousand francs?"

"You can borrow four thousand francs."

She counted some bills, stuffed the rest back in the tin, closed the lid.

"Okay, got some paper and something to write with?"

Rochat tore a blank page from a sketchbook and gave her a drawing pencil. Katherine took the paper and started writing.

"I'm making a list of things for you to buy. You know where Globus is?"

"Around the corner from Café du Grütli, but . . ."

Rochat started rocking back and forth on his heels. Katherine touched his arm.

"Marc, what's wrong?"

"I don't read very well and I'm not good with numbers. I might make mistakes."

"Don't worry, just go to the section where they sell women's clothes and give this list to one of the ladies behind the counter. She'll get everything for you. I'm putting down sizes so it'll be really easy, okay?"

"What kind of things am I buying?"

"Things I need to get out of town."

"So you can go home?"

"Well, on my way at least."

Katherine wrote quickly. Blue jeans, tops, lingerie, couple twinsets, makeup. Enough things to travel light for a week. She held the note out to Rochat, then she snapped it back.

"Hey, how do you think I'd look with black hair?"

Rochat imagined it. "Not like you anymore."

"Perfect. Do you know where there's a pharmacy?"

"On Place de la Palud, across from Café du Grütli."

"Is everything in this town next to Café du Grütli?"

Rochat thought about it. "Sometimes."

"Okay, then. I'm writing some things on the other side of the paper. I'm putting a big star at the top of the page so you'll know the things on this side come from the pharmacy, okay?"

"Okay."

She handed him the list. "Here you go."

Rochat took the list, turned, and headed out of the door.

"Here I go."

She listened as he shuffled down the tower till it was quiet.

She sat on the bed with Monsieur Booty on her lap. The tin box with the cash in it sat on the table like a cookie jar waiting to be raided. Ninety-six thousand Swiss francs inside. Enough to hop a train to Italy or France and get lost and live in a style to which she was accustomed, for a few months at least. The more she thought about it, the more it seemed like the way out. No passport checks at the borders, not for someone with a cute smile. Get a place and lie low, figure out the next step. She picked up Monsieur Booty, stared him in the eyes.

"What do you think, fuzzface, think it'd be okay if I take the money and run?"

*Mew.*

"C'mon, he's loaded."

*Mew.*

"You're right. He's been awfully nice. But I've still got to get out of this place."

The timbers creaked and Marie-Madeleine shook the loge eleven times. The mother of all hookers, weighing in with her own advice.

*GONG . . . go and sin no more. GONG . . . yadda, yadda, yadda.*

"Okay, you win. I'll be a good girl."

Katherine scooted Monsieur Booty from her lap, folded the duvet, and tidied the loge. She swept the mound of long blond hair from the wood floor and dumped it in the trash can under the table. She picked up the hand mirror and saw her reflection in the glass. The cool bob of a haircut, the scar on her face, the look in her eyes. The look that made all the boys go weak at the knees. Wasn't quite the same with a sliced-up face, but still workable in a tight spot, she thought. Could still turn a few tricks on the run to make ends meet. And she could start with her roomie in the belfry. Teach him a few things before his big date with the farmer's daughter. Rock his world, say good-bye. Leave him thinking he'd imagined the whole thing. Face it, she thought, a hooker by another name is still a hooker. That way, it wouldn't be stealing. Just a little business between friends. Besides, he's fucking loaded, yeah?

She opened the tin.

Such a lovely pile of cash.

She reached for it as a soft knock met the door.

*Taptaptaptap.*

"No fucking way."

*Taptaptaptap.*

Katherine slammed closed the lid. She walked to the door and pulled it open.

"Don't tell me, Marc, you forget where Globus—"

"Hello, Miss Taylor."

"Harper."

"Sorry I'm late."

"How did you get up here?"

"I walked. Bloody long way up those steps."

"The tower's supposed to be closed to tourists."

"That's what the sign says on the cathedral doors. I went around to the side door and picked the lock."

"You know how to pick locks?"

"Rather surprised myself on that score. Mind if I come in, I'm not that comfortable standing out here."

"Don't worry, no one looks up anymore."

"Sorry?"

"Marc says no one looks up, no one'll see you."

"Marc?"

"He's the guy with the lantern."

"Right. I met him and his lantern last night on the esplanade." Harper glanced back over his shoulder toward the sky. "Actually, three steps that way and it's a fast way down to the esplanade."

"Come again?"

"Heights, Miss Taylor, I'm not keen on heights."

"You're kidding me."

"No, actually."

"Then you'd better come in before you hurt yourself, big guy."

She turned from the door and Harper stepped into the loge, checking the odd angles of the skinny room.

"What a funny old place this is."

Katherine sat at the table, suddenly aware of her appearance. The secondhand clothes, the slice on her cheek. She turned away, combed what was left of her hair with her hand, trying to hide the scar on her face. Harper watched her, gave it a moment.

"I like it."

"What?"

"The haircut. Do-it-yourself job?"

"No, Marc did it."

"Really? Where is he, anyway?"

"He's gone to buy me some clothes."

"Planning to make a run for it?"

"I'm in an awful jam, Harper."

"So I gather." Harper set a shopping bag on the table. "I brought you something to eat."

"Great, I'm starving. I was giving up on you, you know." She opened the bag: *jambon cru* and Emmental cheese baguettes. "Swiss fast food. Gee, aren't you the big spender."

"There's also some antiseptic and stitching strips in the bag. You're lucky, Miss Taylor."

"On the run and hiding out in a cathedral looks like lucky to you?"

Harper pointed to the slice on her cheek. "I mean your face. The cut isn't deep or ragged. We'll clean it and put on the strips. They dissolve from normal washing in a few days. There's some vitamin-E capsules in there, too. Squeeze one of them on the cut four times a day. Few weeks from now, you'll hardly know there's a scar."

Humiliation burned in Katherine's eyes. "Oh, I don't know, Harper. I think it's a hot new look for me. From perky *Playboy* centerfold to she-bitch dominatrix. I'll wear black rubber, do the stiletto-heel number. I hear pain's where the real money is. It was never my thing. I was always a give-the-boys-a-thrill sort of girl. I liked seeing the twinkle in their eyes when they went over the edge, you know? I'm lucky when you think about it. It's not like you have to be pretty to give a man pain."

"Miss Taylor—"

"No, I don't have to be pretty at all, ugly is good. In fact, the uglier the better. I might have a few more scars done. I'm going to be the ugliest bitch on the fucking planet."

"Miss Taylor . . ."

"What, you fucking son of a bitch!"

Pigeons bolted from the carpentry and into the sky. Harper sat on a stool.

"Miss Taylor, I'm not sure what the hell's going on in this bloody town, but trust me, you're not the only one neck-deep in shite. Now, I'm going to dress the wound, you'll eat your Swiss fast food. Then I need you to tell me what the hell happened."

D oes Monsieur see anything that appeals to him?"
Rochat looked around the shop, saw statues wearing lace things, pictures of girls wearing lace things. The lace things looked very small.

"What do girls like?"

The lady patted the pile of clothes on the counter.

"Well, monsieur, judging by the blue jeans and tops selected from your list, I'd say madame enjoys projecting a casual image while showing off a nice figure. The choice of lingerie says she is a woman of elegant, if somewhat naughty, taste."

Rochat had no idea what any of that meant. "Oh."

"If I may ask, has monsieur purchased lingerie for a lady before?"

He shook his head vigorously. The lady smiled and arranged a set of black lace undergarments on the counter.

"Then allow me to be of assistance. Why doesn't monsieur imagine madame wearing these."

Rochat looked at the things. He imagined the angel on that first night, dropping her robe to the floor of the loge and him seeing her naked body. He snapped quickly back to the lady behind the counter.

"Could you choose?"

"Of course, monsieur. Would you like the items gift-wrapped?"

"I'd like the items gift-wrapped."

Rochat shuffled quickly to the windows overlooking Rue Centrale. He didn't dare look back and see what the lady was choosing. He kept his eyes busy with cars and people and the policewoman in her gray uniform standing in the middle of the intersection, blowing her whistle and directing all the cars and people. Everyone obeyed.

Sunlight poured down the steep cobblestone lane from Place Saint-François. Skinny elongated shadows followed people walking up the lane and stretched ahead of people walking down the lane. He watched the shadows cross over one another and through one another and disappear when people stepped from the sun, only to pop out in another place and attach themselves to someone else.

"Monsieur?"

Rochat turned to the lady. She had two big shopping bags in one hand and money in the other.

"I was watching teasing shadows."

*"Pardon?"*

"Down in the street. The shadows. They're the teasing kind."

The lady smiled politely. "Of course. Here are your purchases and change, monsieur."

*"Merci, madame.* I'm going to follow the teasing shadows up the hill to the chemist shop to buy more things for the angel."

"Who?"

"The angel, that's who the clothes are for. *Merci,* madame."

*"Bonne . . . journée, monsieur."*

Rochat shuffled to the escalator machine and stepped on carefully. Just before he sank through the floor he looked to the windows and saw the saleslady standing at the window, staring outside. He jumped from the escalator just before the steel teeth caught the tips of his boots and pulled him under the floor. He shuffled out of the door and into the bright winter sun washing up the hill. A shadow jumped out from nowhere, took his shape and matched his crooked pace, step by step.

"Going my way? Well, you must keep up. I'm very busy today."

The shadow looked funny with shopping bags at the ends. Rochat swung his arms back and forth making them long and short and long again. He imagined he was a strongman at a circus lifting heavy bags of iron. He watched the shadows of other people coming from behind him and growing bigger, till he saw the feet where the shadows and people were sewn together. The people and their shadows all walking faster than him, their shadows laughing—"Nahnahnah"—as they passed.

"Don't be rude. I'm carrying these big bags. If you had any manners you'd offer to help. But no, too busy being the teasing kind of shadows."

A tall skinny shadow moved up on his right and slowed to the pace of his shuffling steps. And on his left, a short and thick shadow did the same. Rochat slowed, the shadows slowed. He looked back over his shoulder— no people were attached to the two shadows. He looked back at his boots. The two shadows were gone. Just his own crooked shadow standing alone, holding the shopping bags.

"I'm very sure it was only an imagination, Rochat. Mustn't become distracted from your duties."

He continued to shuffle up the hill. The two strange shadows caught up to him again, following at an even pace. Rochat stopped, they stopped. He moved, they moved. He turned slowly, no one was there again. He jumped to the shaded doorway of a patisserie. The shadows disappeared.

"You didn't imagine them, Rochat. And they didn't feel like teasing kind of shadows."

He waited a moment before stepping back into the sun. A teasing shadow took his shape and led him up the hill. He kept his eyes on the ground all the way to the fountain at Place de la Palud, making sure all the passing shadows had people sewn to their feet. Suddenly, the two strange shadows appeared at his sides again. One tall and skinny, the other short with a little beard on his chin.

"I know who you are. You can't fool me. Go away."

He swung the shopping bags at the cobblestones. The shadows jumped back, only to creep closer again.

"No, go away!"

All the shadows across the square stopped and all the people attached to them stopped. Everyone and their shadows looking at him.

"I'm very sorry, *mesdames et messieurs*! The bad shadows are chasing me!"

The shadows circled around him till they were nothing but a blackish blur spinning over the cobblestones.

"Stop it! Leave us alone!"

He stomped his crooked foot on the ground trying to squash the shadows.

"She's going home so you just go away!"

He spun around till he lost his balance and fell to the ground. He hit the shadows with his fists but they dodged his blows. The shadows stretched into distorted shapes and slithered down the hill.

Rochat hobbled to his feet, collected his bags. He searched through all the shadows on the ground. They were all attached to the feet of Lausannois. Rochat gave a slight bow.

"It's only teasing shadows now, *mesdames et messieurs.* All is well." The crowd parted, giving him plenty of room to pass. Rochat heard their whispering voices as he shuffled into the chemist's shop to buy more things for the angel so she could go home.

# thirty-one

Harper looked back over his notes.

"So the last thing you remember clearly is leaving LP's with Komarovsky?"

"That's the third time you've asked me that one, why?"

"Stephan, the bartender, says he saw you leave through the lobby corridor. He says you were alone."

"No way."

"He also said, besides him and me, no one talked to you in the bar."

"That's nuts, Stephan always . . ."

She didn't finish the sentence. Harper finished it for her.

"He always watches who you talk to, who you leave with."

"He's not my pimp, if that's what you're thinking."

"I don't. And he's got nothing to do with this, if that's what you're thinking. He's your friend."

"Then how can he say he didn't see me with Komarovsky? I was sitting just fifteen feet from the bar."

"Komarovsky and his goons are experts at getting in and out of places without being seen. And when they leave, it's like they were never there."

"But the place was packed, Harper."

"Did you recognize the waiter that served the champagne?"

"I didn't notice one way or the other, why?"

"No one else did, either. And the bottle didn't come from the bar and neither Stephan nor any of his waiters saw the waiter who delivered it to your table."

"That's impossible."

"Maybe, but it happened just the same. I'm guessing that's how the drugs were first administered to you."

"What about the needles and powders I found when I came to, or the oil on my skin?"

Harper stared at Katherine, the mad night flashing in his eyes. The cop in the cashmere coat raving about a breeding potion, as ancient as evil itself . . .

"What are you thinking, Harper?"

. . . *you understand what all this means for Miss Taylor.*

"I'm thinking . . . I'm thinking champagne was a gateway drug, made you receptive to the psychotropic drugs delivered later, without you ever knowing what hit you."

"Huh?"

"The most effective way to drug someone into an alternate state of consciousness is to administer the drugs from a variety of sources over a period of time. So the subject isn't alarmed at what's happening."

"Since when did you become such an expert on psychotropic dope?"

"Since coming to Lausanne."

Katherine laughed to herself. "Man, what a tangled web we weave."

"Sorry?"

"Not you, me. It's weird, you know, when first I came to Lausanne I thought I'd made it to paradise. Look at me now."

Harper did look at her a good long while, hearing the inspector's voice again . . . *a breeding potion . . . used by those who already rule this world* . . . before skipping back through his notes.

"Tell me something, Miss Taylor, who helped you come to Lausanne?"

"What do you mean, who helped me?"

"You said you came here to get away from the IRS. Swiss residency visas are tough to get if you're not a billionaire."

"I didn't have a problem, and I'm not a billionaire."

"That's the point. Who helped you?"

"A Swiss banker passing through Los Angeles. We sort of hit it off. He took care of moving my money to Geneva, visas, my flat."

"Did he introduce you to Madame Badeaux?"

"Yeah, he did. The very night I met him."

"So he was a member of the Two Hundred Club?"

Katherine stared at Harper. "How do you know about the Two Hundred Club?"

"I just do."

"You've been talking to the police about me?"

"Other way around, actually. But don't worry, Miss Taylor, I didn't rat you out."

"Honestly?"

"Sure, which is why I need you to be straight with me. The Two Hundred Club, who are they?"

Katherine pulled a smoke from her cigarette case and lit up.

"There're two kinds of rich and powerful in the world, Harper. The ones who've got it and like to flaunt it and see themselves on the cover of *Hello!* Then there's the other kind. The über-rich and powerful who don't need to flaunt a fucking thing, because they own the world already."

"They own the world?"

"That's how Simone describes them. Her way of reminding us girls to keep our mouths shut."

"Where did she find the girls to work for the club?"

"They're recommended to her by members, the way I was."

"Should be the other way around, shouldn't it?"

"The Two Hundred Club is like a gourmet tasting club. Someone finds a new savory dish, he wants to pass it around to his pals. Simone managed the menu for them."

"Did you ever see a list of members?"

"No way. The list was locked tight in Simone's head."

"So what did she do, as manager?"

"Booked our dates, took care of our money so we'd stay clear of the taxman, gave us allowances against our earnings. Mainly she made sure we were good little girls."

"Good little girls."

"You worked for the Two Hundred Club, you were exclusive to the Two Hundred Club. No jobs on the side, no getting it off for laughs with anyone who wasn't a member."

"No boyfriends?"

"Maybe you remember my reaction to you when you came sniffing around at LP's?"

"Miss Taylor, I wasn't trying—"

"Yeah, yeah, you only wanted to borrow my newspaper. So you kept telling me, and it's still cute. But what I'm saying is it doesn't matter what you were doing, I was giving you the brush-off because that's the way it was. Look, you have to realize what it's like. I was so rolling in cash and gifts, I didn't need or want anything on the side. Besides, I kind of got off on the whole scene. There's a rush in fucking your way to the top. I'm sure it was the same for all the girls."

"How so?"

"When you fuck the guys who own the world, you don't bother with the boys who shine shoes for a living. No offense."

"None taken." Harper flipped through his notebook. "You said Komarovsky told you that you'd been recommended to him by members of the club and that Madame Badeaux said she'd checked around with the members. She told you they all knew who he was. Then in your last phone call to Madame Badeaux, she told you you'd been spotted in the States and brought to Lausanne to be groomed and sold to Komarovsky."

Katherine puffed nervously on her smoke. "Yeah, so?"

"Did you ever meet any other women who worked for the club?"

"Simone's number-one rule, no talking to the other girls."

"No phone calls, no e-mails just to say hello?"

"Harper, I never met the other girls because I never knew who they were."

"Why not?"

"Just the way Simone ran her shop. She didn't want us trading pillow talk about the members."

"Or knowing what the hell they were really up to."

"What do you mean?"

Harper checked his notes again, found the quote. "'Grooming and selling sweet little things like you is what I do . . . Monsieur Komarovsky holds fine affection for you.' Those were Madame Badeaux's words to you on the telephone."

"Yeah, and what are you getting at?"

"Every club's got a president."

"You mean, I'm not the only one who's been sold to Komarovsky?"

Harper watched Katherine lay her cigarette in the ashtray, saw something pass through her eyes.

"What is it, Miss Taylor?"

"It's weird. It's like trying to remember a dream days later. But I think I remember something from that night."

"Tell me."

"I sort of woke up, once. I mean, I was still drugged out, but I heard Komarovsky talking with the others. I remember hearing someone say the test was positive and I needed another dose of something, more psychowhat-ever stuff probably. And I remember Komarovsky saying I was to be taken to stay with the others."

"Did they say who the others were?"

"No."

"Did they say what kind of test?"

"No."

"Can you remember anything else, anything at all?"

"Yeah, it was then or another time, but Komarovsky was reading my reviews from my coming-out party."

"Reviews?"

"Yeah, reviews. Apparently I was the belle of . . . Why are you looking at me like that?"

"Where did these reviews come from?"

"What?"

"'Reviews' implies an audience of some kind."

"You mean someone was watching it happen?"

"That would be my guess."

"I was flying on all rockets, Harper, I couldn't tell you more than I have. I don't remember anything that makes sense till I saw myself on a computer screen."

Harper flipped back a page.

"You said you saw yourself, thought it was a mirror, walked over and bumped the table, and the picture stopped for a second. Think back, walk through it again; what happened?"

"What do you mean, what happened? Some words came on the screen and I ran away."

"What words?"

"Harper, I was fucked up and I've told you everything I can remember."

"Tell me again."

"How many times do we have to do this?"

"Till it makes sense. Tell me again."

"I was in some kind of orgy with these bodies I couldn't touch and I was carried to Komarovsky. Then I woke up on semen-stained sheets and I was masturbating on the Internet."

"How do you know?"

"What do you mean, how do I know? There were six fucking cameras in the room, I saw myself on the computer screen."

"How do you *know* you were on the Internet?"

"Because . . . because . . . there were words on the screen."

"What did they say?"

Katherine closed her eyes, she saw herself in the room, standing before the laptop. "'Connected at powerline hyperspeed' or something . . . 'one hundred ninety-nine members online.'"

"And Komarovsky makes it two hundred."

Katherine opened her eyes. Harper saw terrible fear rising.

"Jesus, who the hell is he?"

"You need to stay calm, Miss Taylor."

"Fuck that, what I need is to get my money from that bitch Simone and split."

"Simone Badeaux is dead."

"Dead . . . how?"

"She was found in her flat about the same time you disappeared. She'd been flayed alive and beheaded, her body was left hanging by her ankles."

Katherine reached for her burning cigarette, fumbled it, her hands shaking. "I am so getting the fuck out of here."

"There's nowhere to go, Miss Taylor."

"Can you tell me those freaks won't find me in the cathedral? Can you tell me they don't already know where I am?"

"They may already know."

"What's that supposed to mean?"

"The fact you're here and they're leaving you alone means you're safe. For now."

"What makes you so sure?"

"Call it a hunch."

"A hunch, are you serious? I've got a news flash for you, this isn't the Middle Ages, sanctuary went out with Quasimodo. I'm getting the fuck out of here!"

"And what about the lad with the lantern?"

"What about him?"

"He is giving you sanctuary and there's every chance he'll be slaughtered for doing it. That's what Komarovsky's goons told you, didn't they? They'd kill anyone who helped you escape."

Katherine jumped up and pulled off her sweater. "Fuck you, Harper! Look what they did to me!"

Harper saw the scratches and bite marks on her breasts and stomach.

"I'm sorry, Miss Taylor. I'm sorry for what's happened

to you. Doesn't change the fact that if you run, a helpless lad will be slaughtered."

Katherine slammed her fists on the table. She fell into the chair and put on her sweater. She dropped her head in her hands, took a few calming breaths.

"You really know how to make a girl feel guilty, don't you?"

"Just telling you the way it is."

She looked at Harper a moment. "Why don't you ever call me Katherine, or just Kat?"

"Sorry?"

"My name's Katherine. You never say it."

Harper said the name in his head, couldn't quite get it past his lips. "Don't really know. Feels like it's against the rules, like no laundry on Sundays."

"That makes sense—not."

Harper lit a smoke. "No, I suppose not. What's the lad call you?"

"Marc? Come to think of it, he's never said my name, either. Then again, it's not what he calls me, it's what he thinks I am."

"What's that?"

"Promise you won't laugh?"

"Sure."

"Marc thinks Lausanne is full of lost angels. Last night, he lit up the nave with candles to tell me I was an angel, too. His mother told him a story once, about an angel coming to the cathedral and how he had to protect her."

"Blimey."

"I know. Poor guy can hardly stand up straight and he's got it in his head it's his duty to protect me till I find a way home. Kind of funny, huh?"

"Actually, I'd say it's quite the compliment."

"I know. I don't deserve it."

"Don't be hard on yourself, Miss Taylor."

"No?" She touched the tin can with the picture of the Matterhorn on the lid. "You know what's in here? Nearly a hundred thousand Swiss."

"Nest egg from the flat?"

"Isn't mine—it's Marc's. His family was rich. His grandmother lived in a castle of some kind. Anyways, know what I was doing when you showed up?"

"Stealing the money and taking off?"

"That's right, leave him thinking he'd imagined the whole thing. Or I thought I might fuck him silly as trade in kind. Truth is, I didn't give a damn what happened to him."

Harper took a thoughtful draw from his smoke. "You're still here, Miss Taylor."

"Yeah, so?"

"Maybe the lad wasn't too far off about you."

"Nice try, Harper, but I'm only here because you showed up in the nick of time."

Harper looked at the clock on the wall: eleven forty-five. He gathered his notes.

"Speaking of which, I have to meet someone, I'll be back this evening. We'll try and figure a way to get you out of here. A way that doesn't get the lad killed."

"Where are you going?"

"See the man with the bloody answers."

"What kind of answers?"

"The kind that tell me why nothing in this bloody town feels like an accident."

"Huh?"

"Intersecting lines of causality, Miss Taylor. Things happening in this place for a reason we can't see."

"Wow, where'd that one come from?"

"No idea, just something I heard somewhere." Harper stood, slid the bottle of vitamin E toward her. "Four times a day, Miss Taylor. I'll be back this evening."

"Promise?"

"Sure."

He ground out his smoke, picked up his notebook, and stuffed it in his coat. He looked at her without speaking.

"What is it, Harper?"

"I don't ever remember making a promise."

"What, like, in your entire life?"

"Not the life I can remember, at any rate."

"Well, for the record, you just did. To me and Marc both."

Harper opened the door; an almost blinding light filled the loge. He turned back to Katherine again.

"How did the lad's mother know he'd be in the cathedral one day?"

"What?"

"You said the lad's mother told him a story about an angel coming to the cathedral. How did she know?"

"Gee, I don't know."

"Is he a local?"

"A what?"

"Was he born in Lausanne?"

"No, Quebec. His mother died when he was a little boy. His father and grandmother were Swiss, they brought him here and put him in a school with kids like him."

"Like him."

"Well, let's face it, Marc is a little out-there. I don't mean that in a bad way."

Harper stared at her a moment.

The lad with a lantern, a hooker on the run, a drunk who couldn't remember ever making a promise. *We few, we happy few,* he thought. Three more lines of intersecting causality in Lausanne.

"Does he see things, things that aren't there?"

"Oh yeah, big-time. He calls it imagining."

"Imagining."

"Yeah. In Marc's world the cathedral is full of imaginary friends. Knights in armor, teasing shadows, dead bishops, lost angels. He tried to get me to go down into the crypt to say hello to the skeletons under the altar. All sort of freaked me out at first. Now it's part of his charm. And he keeps drifting off to something he calls before times, but he says it like one word, *beforetimes.* He sort of zones out and sees himself somewhere in the past. Always comes back with the funniest stories. But you know something? He really loves this place. You should see him with the bells. It's as if Marc thinks this place is alive. And he's got it into his head that if he doesn't protect the cathedral and the bells and keep his lantern going at night, then the angels would be lost forever. Funny, huh?"

Harper looked at her without speaking for a long moment. He turned, stared out of the door and off the balcony.

The midday sun reflecting off the ice-covered peaks above Évian. Fierce light coming back and hitting him straight in the eyes.

"Harper?"

"Hell of a view from up here, isn't it?"

*Sept cent deux . . . sept cent trois . . . sept cent quatre . . ."* Rochat stepped onto the esplanade and looked at the cathedral. The prophets and saints carved in the façade stood motionless in the chilly shade, waiting for the winter sun to swing around and wake them from their sleep. He looked down Escaliers du Marché. Nothing but empty planks.

"All is well, Rochat."

He shuffled to the great arch above the main doors and stood beneath the statues in their niches. He rapped Monsieur Moses on his toes.

*"Pardonnez-moi,* I know you're still sleeping. But if you see any bad shadows coming up Escaliers du Marché, please stomp your feet and toss your tablets at them and chase them away, *d'accord? Merci, à bientôt."*

He shuffled along the façade to the corner of the belfry tower. He stopped. Something caught his eye on the cobblestones. A long unmoving shadow stretching over the esplanade. His eyes followed the shadow to a pair of shoes and up to the detectiveman. He was standing near the fountain.

"Hello, mate."

*"Bonjour, monsieur."*

"Do you have a minute for a chat?"

"I have a minute for a chat."

Rochat shuffled over with the shopping bags as Harper took a drink of water from the fountain. Harper stood, dabbed at his lips with the back of his hand.

"You know, this really is very good water."

*"Merci.* We have our own source in Lausanne."

"So everybody in Lausanne gets the same water in their kitchen taps?"

*"Oui."*

"Then why do the locals drink water from plastic bottles in this town?"

Rochat thought about it. "I don't know."

"More for us then, eh?"

*"Oui."*

Harper leaned down for another drink, wiped his lips, and straightened up. He looked toward Escaliers du Marché and then down toward Café de l'Évêché.

"Are you here to come to the cathedral now, monsieur?"

"No, I have to meet someone in the nave after the noon bells. Just checking to see if I'm being followed."

Rochat looked around the esplanade, back toward Escaliers du Marché.

"I don't see anyone, monsieur."

"Probably because they already know where I am."

"Who?"

"Good guys, bad guys."

Rochat thought about it. *"Pardonnez-moi, monsieur,* but you are real?"

"Sorry?"

"I don't mean to be impolite. I'm just a little confused."

"Some days are better than others in the imagining-things department?"

Rochat nodded. Harper smiled.

"In that case, I'm as real as the last time you saw me."

*"D'accord."* Rochat set down the shopping bags. Harper pointed to the boxes inside, all wrapped in ribbons and bows.

"You've been shopping for Miss Taylor."

"How did you know?"

"I had a chat with her in the belfry before you got here."

Rochat pulled the ring of keys from his overcoat to make sure they were there. He shook them to make sure they were real.

"Did I leave the tower door unlocked?"

"No, it was locked, but I managed. Reminds me, I saw heavy iron braces in the alcove behind the door."

"From the days of invadermen."

"Who?"

"Invadermen who came to Lausanne, and it was the duty of *le guet* to set the braces at the door to protect the cathedral."

"Invadermen, right. Well, it might be a good idea to reset the braces after you go in. What do you think?"

"About what, monsieur?"

"When you go inside. You could set the braces against the doors. Can you manage on your own?"

"I can manage on my own. I'm very strong from my legs up."

"That's good." Harper watched the lad again, seeing a maze of crooked wheels in his head trying to spin. "Something on your mind, mate?"

Rochat looked toward Escaliers du Marché, turned back.

"Those men from the bad shadows, the ones who crushed her wings, they're back. I saw their shadows. They followed me and chased me at Place de la Palud. That's why I asked Monsieur Moses to keep the watch at the old staircase."

"Moses?"

Rochat turned, pointed to the stone statues at the cathedral doors. "He's the grumpy-looking one holding the stone tablets. His feet are made of stone, so if he stomps his feet and throws his stone tablets at them he can make a lot of noise and chase away the bad shadows. That's what I imagined. Sometimes the things I imagine are real and sometimes they're just imaginations. And sometimes it's very confusing because there was an accident when I was born. But I'm very sure the bad shadows were real. Do you imagine things, monsieur?"

"Does a rough night followed by watching the sun come up five or six times in one morning count?"

"I don't know what that means."

"Me neither, but it's time to find out. Listen, later, I'd like to take you up on your offer to hide in the cathedral. Would that be all right? We could take turns keeping an eye out for any bad—"

"Invader—"

"—shadows."

"—men."

Harper chuckled. Rochat watched him closely.

"Did we make a joke, monsieur?"

"I believe we did."

Rochat thought about it. "It was funny."

"It was at that. So after my meeting in the nave, I'll collect my kit and run around town till nightfall, then I'll come back. You'll need to keep an eye out for me. I'll be waiting right here after dark, all right?"

*"D'accord."* Rochat picked up the shopping bags. "If you don't mind my asking, monsieur, who are you meeting in the cathedral?"

"Monsieur Gabriel."

"I don't know who he is."

"He stands at the crossing square every day at noon. Watches the light through the rose window."

"I've never seen him."

"You must have. Bit of a tramp. The nun in the gift shop tells me he comes to the cathedral every day around noon for meditations."

"Sœur Fabienne?"

"Yeah, that's her."

Harper saw Rochat's eyes lose focus for a few seconds. He slowly blinked.

"Something wrong, mate?"

"I imagined beforetimes to remember something about Sœur Fabienne."

"What?"

"She died three years ago. Madame Buhlmann works in the gift shop now."

"I just saw her, three days ago."

Rochat looked at the cathedral, then back at Harper. "That's how imagining works, monsieur. I hear the timbers."

A great, deep sound exploded in the sky. Harper raised his eyes to the belfry as pigeons scattered and Marie-Madeleine rang out over the esplanade, obliterating every sound in the world till the twelfth bell faded away. Harper lowered his eyes; the lad was gone. He heard the sound of iron braces falling into place behind the red door to the belfry.

"Bloody hell, just keeps getting better."

He walked to the cathedral entrance, pulled open the heavy wooden door. The smell of old earth rushed out and the heavy purple curtain hanging in the archway billowed in the draft. Harper stepped into the narthex and waited for the wooden door to close behind him with a coffinlike thud. The curtain settled. As his eyes adjusted to the dim light he couldn't keep them from looking up at Headless Mary, Mother of God. Watching him with her unseen eyes. He moved ahead and pulled the curtain aside. He stepped into the nave. His whole being instantly drawn into the illusion of infinite space. He saw the long shaft of tubular light rushing through the giant stained-glass window in the south transept wall. Cutting through the dull gray gloom of the nave and falling on the decrepit form standing at the center of the crossing square.

"Right. Monsieur Gabriel, I presume."

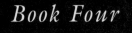

*Book Four*

THE THING IN
THE WELL

# thirty-two

Harper walked up the main aisle, watching the billion bits of dust floating in the tubular light. The light hit the flagstones of the crossing square with the tramp spot-on center. Arms extended from his sides, palms turned to the light, his face with the same gobsmacked expression as before.

Closer to the crossing square, Harper slowed his steps. The light slipped from under the tramp's heels and raced over the flagstones and up the chancel columns. It settled in the arcades of the crescent dome high above the altar. Monsieur Gabriel lowered his arms, bowed his head. Harper could hear his whispering voice.

*"Transit umbra, lux permanet . . ."*

*Shadow passes, light remains. A prayer,* Harper thought. *To a God, a saint, the runaway light maybe.*

The tramp coughed.

"And so, finally, you have come."

"Didn't realize I was late. But seeing as I'm here, maybe we could get to it."

Gabriel stared again at the still-radiant stained-glass window. "It's comforting to see the light as the living thing, no?"

Harper leaned back, searched the crescent dome high overhead. The runaway light now hiding behind the pillars.

"A sane man would tell you it isn't the light. A sane man would tell you it's the pitch and rotation of the earth on its axis. The window just happens to be in the right place at the right time."

"And the insane man would ask which is the greater miracle: that the universe was so created, or that men built this window to be in the right place at the right time?"

Harper glanced up to the giant stained glass. Same universe divided up into seasons and months of the year, same signs of the zodiac, same white-bearded Almighty in the middle watching it all spin round and round.

"Is that what the window's about, the right place at the right time?"

"Sœur Fabienne didn't tell you?"

Harper looked over his shoulder to the gift shop at the back of the nave. Lights out, no one home. The woman was real as beans on toast a few days ago. Standing behind the counter in her nun's habit, hawking her cardboard cathedrals, showing off her collection of unanswered prayers. He turned back toward the tramp.

"Seen her lately, have you?"

"What did she tell you about the window, English?"

"She said it's a cosmology representing the sum of man's knowledge."

"When the world was flat, English, you forgot to say when the world was flat."

"And you forgot to say she's dead."

"Is she?"

"So I'm told by a lad with a lantern. But then again, he thinks this place is a hideout for lost angels."

The tramp walked toward Harper, stopping at the edge of the crossing square.

"Do you realize that at this very moment, in this hideout for lost angels, we breathe from the last breath of Christ on the cross?"

"Now that would be a neat trick."

"The nature of death isn't a trick, English, it's chemistry."

"Chemistry."

"*Sí*, chemistry. When the human form expires, a galaxy of carbon and nitrogen molecules are released in the final breath. The science of the round world calculates the number to be more than ten to the power of twenty-three. An almost infinite number of molecules set free to drift through the atmosphere and circle the earth for all time. So that thousands of years and thousands of miles from the cross, you and I breathe from the last breath of Christ. Perhaps this says something about the nature of death."

"According to your chemistry, Monsieur Gabriel, what's good for Jesus is good for Jack the Ripper."

"Perhaps that says something about the nature of man."

Harper stuffed his hands in the pockets of his coat.

"I would've thought the nature of death was rather matter-of-fact. Now you breathe, now you don't."

"And perhaps this says something about the nature of the warrior returned to us."

Harper looked around the cathedral. Not a body in sight, dead or alive. He looked at the tramp.

"By that, I gather, you mean me."

"I do. Please, if you do not mind." Monsieur Gabriel held out his arm for assistance. Harper helped him down the steps and settled him in a chair. "And now you've come to hear the story."

"Actually, I came for answers."

"No, English, you are here so that I may tell you the story so that your awakening will be completed. This is how it works for our kind."

"Our kind? As in me the drunk, you the morphine freak?"

"As in those without free will."

"From chemistry to metaphysics without missing a beat. Let's try apocryphal literature for ten." Harper pulled his notebook and a handful of papers from his pockets, found one crumpled scrap. "'Evil spirits walk the earth. The spirits of heaven live in heaven, but this is the place of earthly spirits, born of the earth. Spirits of giants on the earth—'"

"'—like clouds. To occupy, corrupt, and bruise the earth.'"

Harper looked up. The tramp smiled through yellow teeth.

"Did I say something funny, Monsieur Gabriel?"

"You commit the words of Enoch to scraps of paper and carry them in your pockets like a scribe at Qumran."

"Glad you find it amusing, but if I don't get some answers, two innocent people are going to be killed."

"You cannot save the living from the time of their death, English."

"So I've been told. Tell you what, let's you and me do something drastic and tell Inspector Gobet and his gang of whatever they are to stuff themselves. We'll save a couple of innocent souls, make the front page of *24 Heures*."

"I'm only here to tell you the story."

"I don't give a damn about your story. Tell me why Alexander Yuriev tacked this note to the prayer board at the back of the nave. Why here? There's a reason. What was he trying to tell me? What was he trying to give me?"

The tramp sighed. "You already know the answer; you've known the answer for millions of years."

"Bollocks." Harper reached back into his coat, pulled out a photograph, held it under the tramp's eyes. "Look, this is him, Alexander Yuriev. Look at him, damn it. Did you see him, talk to him? What was it he wanted to give me?"

"Hear the story and know the truth of what you are."

Harper took a deep breath of Jesus and Jack the Ripper and anyone else who'd lived and died in the world. "Right, sod this for useful." He turned and marched down the aisle. Gabriel's voice chased after him.

"No matter how much you ache to hide in their form, English, you cannot choose to leave this place."

Harper picked up his pace. "Watch me."

"'And men, being destroyed, cried out.'"

Harper heard the words echo through the nave. Two steps later he forgot how to put one foot in front of the other. He turned slowly around, saw the tramp with an even bigger smile on his face.

"An odd sensation, isn't it, English?"

"What?"

"Awakening in their form."

"What the hell are you talking about?"

"Finish the verse."

Unable to resist again, Harper felt the words rise in his throat, pass his lips, and echo through the nave.

"'And their voice reached to heaven.'"

"*Sí*, their voice reached to heaven."

"What is this, who are you?"

"This is you awakening to what you are, a creature without free will. And I am the one men call Gabriel."

Harper flashed through the History Channel, remembered an episode called *The Legends and Myths of Angels*. The good, the bad, the celestial war brought to earth.

"Gabriel, the messenger? You're God's messenger?"

"Names and gods, gods and names. These are the imaginations of men, they are not the things of our kind."

"Making me whom—or is it more along the lines of what?"

The tramp's hand began to rise, his gnarled finger pointing straight at Harper.

"'Then Michael and Gabriel looked down from

heaven and saw the quantity of blood which was shed on earth, and all the iniquity which was done upon it, and said, It is the voice of their cries.'"

Like getting ripped through time again.

Seeing himself in the shabby London flat across from King's Cross. Watching the story of human slaughter on the History Channel. Telephone rings. Guardian Services Ltd on the line. Passport on the table with a picture and a name.

Jay Michael Harper.

"You must be bloody joking. The archangels exist and we're it?"

"Names and gods, gods and names, none of these things matter to our kind. All we know is that we are here, and that the myths, legends, and religions of men point to the truth of what we are."

"And what are we exactly?"

"Creatures of an unremembered beginning, born of light and sent to protect this place and live among men of free will. To comfort them in death and guide their souls to a new form."

Harper chuckled to himself, rubbed the back of his neck. "You know, Monsieur Gabriel, I've met a lot of lunatics in this town, but you take the cake."

"And you still cannot choose to take the next step and leave this place of lost angels."

Harper looked down at his unmoving feet. "There does seem to be that."

"Then perhaps you aren't what you seem in this world of men. Perhaps you only wear the form of men."

The tramp coughed and shivered as if it were killing him to breathe. Harper took a step closer, saw beads of cold sweat on the tramp's face.

"Medication time, is it?"

"The weight of our eternity is difficult to bear."

Harper stared at him a moment, knowing when all else is impossible, what's left begins to look like maybe. He stuffed his notebook and papers in the pockets of his coat, scanning the nave of Lausanne Cathedral.

"Mate, if you and I are what passes for archangels in this world, I'd hate to see the rest of the heavenly host."

"Come, English, sit awhile and I will tell you the story."

"The story, right."

Harper stepped closer to Monsieur Gabriel, close enough to smell the scent of decay. He stopped, nodded toward the crossing square of the transept.

"Why do you stand up there, in the light?"

Gabriel coughed again, cleared his throat of phlegm.

"The smell of my form disgusts you, no? I see it in your eyes. Do you know what it is you smell? You smell greed and cruelty, the toxic waste of man's free will. It poisons the light. I stand in this place to absorb the poison from the light before it touches these stones."

"Why?"

"The earth beneath these stones is sacred."

Harper tapped the flagstones with the tip of his shoe. "There's nothing under these stones but old dirt and skeletons. What's sacred about it?"

"I have no idea."

"No?"

"Like you, I am only the extension of another's will. I have no choice, so here I stand."

"You know, I saw a program called *Great Cathedrals of the World* on the History Channel a few days ago. They left out the part about the earth beneath the stones of Lausanne Cathedral being sacred. In fact, they left out Lausanne Cathedral completely."

"I have no choice but to stand."

"Right. No free will for our kind, no questions asked." Harper looked about the nave. "By the way, where is the rest of our kind?"

"Slaughtered in their human forms. There are so few of us left to protect this place."

"This place."

Harper stared at the great stained-glass window in the south transept wall. The Cathedral Rose of Lausanne, the sum of man's knowledge when the world was flat. Perfectly balanced, perfectly ordered. Once upon a time there was a place called paradise.

"Tell me something. Everything out there, everything beyond the walls of this place. This isn't the way it was supposed to be, is it?"

"And so you begin to see with more than the eyes of men."

"Not completely, but maybe I'm getting there." He stepped up to the crossing square, walked in a small circle at the center, tapping the flagstones with his foot. "All that greed and cruelty, what did you call it, the toxic waste of free will?"

"*Sí.*"

"Where'd it come from?"

"Man's fear of death."

Harper stopped walking, looked up at the stained glass, saw a local sharing a glass of wine with a skeleton, as if they were old pals.

"But they . . . the locals . . . they weren't supposed to be afraid of death, were they? I mean, all those molecules drifting through the atmosphere and circling the planet. The chemistry of their souls means their life never ends. That was the idea, right?"

"Sit with me, English, and I will tell the story."

"Soon as you tell me why the Book of Enoch points to the truth of who we are and what we're doing on this chunk of rock."

The tramp scratched at the crook of his arm. "'And it came to pass when the children of men had multiplied that in those days were born unto them beautiful and comely daughters. And the angels, the children of the heaven, saw and lusted after them, and said to one another: "Come, let us choose us wives from among the children of men and beget us children."'"

Harper knew it instantly. "Book of Enoch, chapter six. Fallen angels take the forms of men and create their own race of Nephilim, half-breeds to enslave mankind. That makes them the bad guys. And me, I'm one of the good guys, I take it. Come to save the world."

"*Sí.*"

"But in the Book of Enoch, the good guys win. They kill off the half-breeds, chain the bad guys to the wall of a cave in Duadel. You're telling me the Book of Enoch got it wrong. The Bible got it wrong. Every legend of creation got it wrong. This is all the paradise there is. That's the real story, isn't it? Our own kind stole paradise from the locals, slaughtered most of the good guys come to save it, and we're what's left. The war, eternal and forever."

"*Sí.*"

"Losing badly, I hear. Not much time."

Gabriel nodded. Harper rubbed the back of his neck and mumbled to himself.

" 'The faithless shadows of day are running, And high and clear is the call of bells.' "

"Aleksandr Blok."

"Who?"

"The Russian poet you just quoted," Gabriel said.

"No idea, mate. Just something I heard somewhere."

"Another sensation I am most familiar with."

Harper tapped a flagstone with his shoe, listening to the hollow sound below. "This story of yours. What happens if I don't believe a word of it?"

"Then the light shall become darkness and all souls will vanish from the face of the earth."

Harper sat next to the tramp. "In that case, Monsieur Gabriel, you'd best get on with the telling."


Rochat was sweeping down the steps of the northeast turret. He'd been up and down the turret and around the balconies twice already, but the angel was still dressing in her new clothes and told him he couldn't come in the loge yet. The small windows of the loge were open, and he could hear her ripping open the things he'd bought. She peeked through the window once with a towel wrapped around her hair.

"You did great with the shopping, Marc."

"Why is there a towel on your head?"

"That's what I like about you, Marc. You forget everything, so everything is a surprise."

She left him thinking about it. He was still thinking about it as he swept his way along the west balcony. He saw Clémence, the execution bell, brooding in the timbers. He swept the wooden planks under her bronze skirt.

"You really shouldn't be so glum, Clémence. I'm very sure she made a very funny joke."

The bell remained unlaughingly still.

"Of course, why should I expect an execution bell to know a joke? Crack you on the head with a broom or tell you a joke, you wouldn't know the difference."

He swept along the south balcony and stood at the railing. He watched dark stringlike clouds drift high and fast from behind the French Alps. He jumped up through the timbers, gave Marie-Madeleine a gentle rap. The bell hummed sleepily.

"Yes, I know, you were only resting. But I thought you should know the wind is coming from the southeast, madame. And I can smell the ice from Mont Blanc. That means another storm is coming. And that means the pigeons will be hiding in the rafters and I'll have to brush the poop from your heads before *la grande sonnerie* times tomorrow."

The steel hammer cocked back and slammed down on Marie's iron skirt five times. Rochat watched her, waiting politely for her to finish ringing the hour, then went back to sweeping the balcony. He stopped and listened. Something was strange. The wind should have carried Marie's voice away, but the sound hovered as if clinging to the timbers, afraid to leave. Rochat shuffled back, reached through the carpentry, and touched her.

"What's wrong, Marie? You sound sad. I thought you'd be happy the angel's going home soon."

The bell vibrated still with the slightest hum. He jumped on a timber and pressed his ear to the edge of her skirt. He listened to her fading voice.

"Why would you say that, Marie? I'm not going anywhere. Rochat will always be with you. Don't worry."

He climbed into the great bell's timber cage and shuffled to the snowman in the corner, pretending to re-arrange the scarf around its neck.

"Monsieur Neige, please keep an eye on Marie. She's imagining sad things. Tell her snowman jokes if you know any."

"Marc?"

He turned, looked through the carpentry, and saw a pretty girl with short black hair standing on the south balcony. The girl's eyes under black eyebrows looked familiar, but Rochat couldn't be sure.

"Who are you?"

"It's me, Katherine."

He looked from her black sneakers to her black jeans, her black sweater, and up to her face, to her black eyebrows and the short black hair on the top of her head. He saw small Band-Aid strips across the scar on her cheek.

"They won't know it's you."

"Who?"

"Those men."

Katherine smiled.

"Except when you smile. You look like you when you smile."

"Believe me, I bump into those freaks again, I won't be smiling." She shivered in the wind. "Jeez, it's getting cold."

"The sun's going down and a storm is coming."

She leaned next to a stone pillar. "Gosh, it really is like being on the edge of a cloud up here. You feel like you can see the whole world. Hey, I can see a Christmas tree in somebody's window."

Rochat jumped through the timbers with the broom in his hands and landed next to Katherine. They watched lights come alive over Lausanne. Streetlamps on corners, headlights of cars and trams moving through the streets and over the bridges, frosty windows of the old city glowing with warm light. They took turns spotting Christmas lights on buildings, strung on the construction cranes high above Flon, in the windows of people's homes. He heard Katherine sigh.

"It's all so different from up here, I feel like . . . I don't know."

Rochat looked at her face again. Her skin was so much

whiter with black hair. And her eyes. When he first saw her, her eyes were hazel colors. But now in the fading light they were green, like emeralds.

She shivered again. "Man, it really turned cold."

"Do you want to go inside the loge now? I can make tea."

"No, I want to watch the lights for a while. It's kind of like watching your candles in the nave. It's so pretty."

*"D'accord."* Rochat rested the broom against the iron railing, shuffled into the loge, came back out with Monsieur Buhlmann's black cloak. He helped her put it on.

"You know, you're quite the gentleman, Marc. That girl you're going to meet for Christmas lunch will be knocked out."

Rochat wasn't sure what that meant. "Is that a good thing?"

"Oh yeah, that's a great thing. And I like the way you're picking up LA speak. I'm telling you, Marc, you should reconsider being a hair designer. Open a shop on Melrose Avenue and you'd clean up."

Rochat picked up the broom from the railing. "I already do that in the tower."

She laughed, closing the cloak around her body. "Man, sometimes you're so funny, it hurts."

"I'm sorry."

"No, it's great, it's wonderful." She fixed the collar of his coat, brushed away flecks of dust and ice from his shoulders. "Does she have a name, the girl you're going to meet?"

Rochat thought carefully till he remembered. "Her name is Emeline."

"Marc and Emeline. They sound nice together."

"*Merci.*"

Katherine turned back to the lights. She took a slow breath. "Marc, I think I'm going to leave soon."

"I know, because your friend the detectiveman is hiding in the cathedral tonight and I'm very sure he'll take you home."

"How do you know?"

"I saw him by the fountain before I climbed the tower steps. He said he was coming after dark and I should keep an eye out for him."

"Keeps getting more crowded in your cathedral, doesn't it?"

"I don't think they mind."

"Who?"

"Otto the Brave Knight, the skeletons, the teasing shadows, and the—"

"Marc?"

"*Oui?*"

"When you meet Emeline, leave out the part about the skeletons, just till she gets to know you."

"Why?"

"Trust me." She looked back to the colored lights dotting Lausanne. "There's something I need to tell you, Marc."

"Do you want to tell me now because you have to?"

"Yeah. While you were buying things for me, I was going to steal the money you had in that tin. I was going to run away."

Rochat stared at the ground, scratched his head, began to rock back and forth on his heels.

"You can take the money if you want."

"No, listen to me. I wasn't even going to say good-bye. I thought you'd think you imagined the whole thing. That you'd just go on with your life."

"You can take the money."

"Oh, believe me, I could take your money, and put a big smile on your face doing it, but—"

"You can take the money if you want."

She reached out to him and took his hands. "Marc, listen to me. I've spent my whole life not giving a damn about anyone but myself. Then my whole life goes to hell and you gave me a place to hide, you protected me."

"It's my duty."

She reached under his chin and raised his face, looked in his eyes. "No, Marc, it's who you are."

"It's my duty."

"Okay, it's your duty. It's just . . . I don't know what's going to happen to me, and I only know one way of mak-ing it in this world. I don't know if I'll ever change. But you touched me, Marc. Like no other guy I've met."

"Is that a good thing?"

"If you knew the whole story, you'd call it a miracle. What I'm trying to say is . . . is . . . ."

Her voice faded in the cold wind. Rochat watched her eyes, the way they looked wet.

"Are you going to cry now?"

"Yeah, I am. God, I'm so seriously PMS-ing."

"I don't know what that means."

"Never mind, it's a girl thing."

She fell silent; he waited for her to speak.

"It's just when the time comes, I don't know how I'll say good-bye."

Rochat stared at her, then he turned to Marie-Madeleine. Katherine leaned closer to him.

"Marc? Did you go somewhere?"

He turned back to Katherine. "I was imagining what Marie said a minute ago."

"What did she say?"

"The same thing as you."

"What?"

Rochat took off his hat and scratched his head. He almost spoke, but didn't. He tugged the hat back on.

"Hey, are you all right?"

"I'm finished working till it's time to light the lantern and call the hour. Are you hungry? Because it's Friday."

"I'm starving, but what's Friday got to do with it?"

"Friday means Monsieur Dufaux is making *filets de porc avec pommes frites et salade*. And we can have dessert tonight, because you're leaving with the detective-man. I can go down to Café du Grütli and pick it up in an hour. And I can make tea now and draw your picture till I go."

"You want to draw me? Like this?"

"I want to draw you like this. So I can remember when you came to the cathedral to hide and I protected you the way Maman told me to."

"Yeah, Marc, anything. But it's a mess in there, let me

clean things up. And let me make the tea, I really want to do it."

Katherine dashed into the loge, poured water from one of the jugs into the kettle, and arranged the cups and saucers. Rochat watched her through the open door a moment, then he turned to the great silent bell hanging in the timbers.

"She said the same thing as you, Marie, about saying good-bye. Why did you both say Maman's words from beforetimes?"

Rochat looked out over Lausanne and Ouchy. The snow-covered vineyards and villages along the lake, the lights of Évian flickering to life on the far shore, and the shadowy mountains cutting into the darkening sky. And the winter sun breaking through the clouds once more and brushing the ice and snow of the shadowy mountains in pastel shades of violet and blue. The timbers creaked and Marie-Madeleine rang out for six o'clock. Rochat watched the last of the light fade from the sky. A cold wind swept through the tower. The dark clouds raced faster toward Lausanne.

"Be not afraid, Rochat. Be not afraid."

A familiar fluff of gray fur curled around Rochat's ankles, rubbed against his crooked foot. He bent down, picked up the beast, and held him in his arms.

"*Bonsoir*, Monsieur Booty. Did you come to say good-bye, too?"

*Mew.*

# thirty-three

He picked up the receiver and pressed the button next to the man with the tray.

*"Oui, Monsieur Harper?"*

"I'd like to order water to my room."

*"Pardon?"*

*"De l'eau, s'il vous plaît."*

"Monsieur has bottled water in his minibar, still and sparkling."

"I want the local stuff. Fill a jug from the kitchen tap, toss in a few ice cubes. No lemon, no limes."

"Of course, monsieur."

Harper opened the curtains and watched raindrops smack at the windows. They dripped down the glass like ragged tears. He reached in the pockets of his coat and pulled out the scraps of Enoch, his notebook. He crumpled the lot in his hands and let it fall to the floor. Then the photographs of Yuriev. Seeing the poor sod dragged from the casino by a pair of bad-guy shadows. Harper tore the photos to bits, sprinkled them atop the small paper mountain at his feet.

*"Corpora lente augescent cito extinguuntur."*

There was a double tap at the door. Harper looked through the spy hole and saw the waitress with a gun carrying a tray with a pitcher of water and a glass, a bowl of perfectly squared ice cubes. He opened the door.

"Come on in, champ."

She walked in, set the tray on the desk with a rude *clank*. "The name is Officer Jannsen, monsieur."

"Sure, but from what I've just been told in the cathedral, we're all pals. You, me, the inspector, Mutt, and Jeff."

"I have no idea of who Mutt and Jeff are."

"The inspector's boys, Mutt and Jeff, rhyming slang for death. Rather good when you think about it, not that I ever was." Harper dropped a few ice cubes in the glass, poured from the pitcher. "It's like that other rhyme I heard recently, 'Oranges and lemons, Say the bells of Saint Clement's.' What's the rest of it?"

"I wouldn't know, I've never heard it."

"No? 'You owe me five farthings, Say the bells of Saint Martin's.'"

"Will there be anything else, monsieur?"

Harper drank to the bottom of the glass and poured another. "You know, this really is the most amazing water. You drink this stuff?"

"Ten glasses each day."

"So that's the secret. Here I was thinking it's the milk

in this place. Turns out it's the tap water." He drank
quickly, poured again. There was only half a glass on the
third round. "Seems I need a few more glasses to meet
my quota, Officer Jannsen."

"Then may I suggest you refill your glass from the
bathroom sink?"

"Swell, I'll just finish this."

Harper threw the water in her face and kicked her
across the back of her knees. She went down hard. He
tore the gun from her holster and tested the weight.

"Well, well. A SIG P229R, necked throat for a .357
hollow-point round, DAK trigger system."

"What are you doing?"

He flipped off the safety and took point-blank aim at
her head.

"Haven't you heard? There're traitors everywhere.
Can't trust anyone."

"Are you insane?"

"In this town, that passes for normal. Now, let's see if
you followed standard operating procedures. Did you
load a bullet in the firing chamber before you entered the
room or not?"

"You wouldn't dare."

"Wrong."

He swung back his arm, pulled the trigger. An explo-
sion punched through the room like a boxer's fist, the
room's windows blew apart. Harper brought the barrel
down on her head.

"Your spare clips, mademoiselle, if you please."

"You could have killed a local!"

"We're well above the locals, and the bullet's already taking a dive in the lake. Odds of killing man or fish are well within rules of engagement."

Harper heard a polite cough behind him.

"Are we interrupting something?"

Harper turned, saw the cop in the cashmere coat standing in the hallway, Mutt and Jeff on either side with their own hefty weapons drawn. Laser sights targeted on the kill spot between Harper's eyes.

"May I remind you, Mr. Harper, that regardless of the intended eternity of your being, if my men shoot you in human form, you'll die."

"Die in their form, you die forever."

"I'm pleased you remember how it works."

Harper lowered the weapon, flipped on the safety, stuffed it in his belt. Mutt and Jeff holstered their guns. Officer Jannsen jumped from the floor, stood at attention.

*"Je suis désolée, Inspecteur."*

"Oh, think nothing of it, Officer. Now that Mr. Harper's finally come around, he's a very different sort of perch. But would you be so kind as to give him your kill kit?"

Officer Jannsen raised her skirt, pulled two ammo clips from the Velcro garters around her left thigh and the black steel knife strapped to her right. She handed them over.

"Try not to hurt yourself, monsieur."

"Cheers, and sorry about the water in the face thing. Old tricks being what they are and all."

"I thank you for the lesson, monsieur. Rest assured I shall not forget it."

Inspector Gobet signaled Mutt and Jeff to take positions in the hall; he entered the room and saw the damage.

"Oh, for heaven's sake. Officer Jannsen, please advise the concierge the windows of room 511 will need repair."

*"Oui, Inspecteur."*

"And draw another kill kit for yourself from stores."

*"Oui, merci."*

She walked out, closed the door. The inspector looked at Harper.

"Not very gallant of you, Mr. Harper. She's not one of us, she's a human partisan and she's still in training."

"She seems tough enough."

The inspector removed his gloves, opened his cashmere coat and loosened his silk scarf, noticed the small mountain of papers and shredded photographs on the floor.

"You weren't planning to set fire to the room, were you? Bullets through windows are one thing; burning the Hôtel de la Paix to the ground might cause the locals to wonder just what is going on in their fair canton."

"Actually, I was . . . I don't know what the hell I was doing, Inspector." Harper tossed the SIG and clips on the bed. He tossed the killing knife from hand to hand. The inspector watched him.

"You do remember how to use that thing?"

Harper held the killing knife to his eyes. Slightly

curved, razor-sharp on the long edge, serrated on the curve, tip shaped like a small fishhook. Designed to slice and rip open a throat in one quick move.

"Sure, like riding a bicycle, isn't it?"

"I beg your pardon?"

Harper flipped the knife in the air and caught it by the handle, twisted it over the back of his hand, and gripped it again to reverse the angle of attack.

"Nice to see you in killing form, then. We were losing hope you'd come around."

"How long was I out?"

"Ninety years. But we only had six months to reanimate you in this form."

"Christ, no wonder I feel hungover as sin."

"Indeed. By the way, what was the roughty-toughty with Officer Jannsen?"

"'Oranges and lemons,' she couldn't finish it."

"Bit of the pot calling the kettle black, isn't it? You couldn't finish the same rhyme for Sœur Fabienne. She could have slaughtered you in the gift shop of Lausanne Cathedral."

"The little old nun is one of us?"

"Old tricks being what they are and all, what? It was only the fact you asked for the maquette of the cathedral that spared you."

"Lucky me, saved by a cardboard cutout."

"And for future reference, we haven't used the Oranges and Lemons code since the First World War. Sœur Fabienne only used it to try to snap you out of your stupor—to no effect, unfortunately."

"I didn't recognize her eyes."

"Not surprising, given your state. Retinal luminance recognition should return within the next forty-eight hours."

"Right." Harper held up his hand. He stared at it as if examining it. "And who's this?"

"British forces captain of the Special Reconnaissance Regiment. He was lost in a tribal region of Pakistan six months ago. He'd been captured by Taliban fighters and tortured for some time before managing to escape. His wounds and the exposure killed him. One of our cells snatched the body and got it to London for regenerative stasis. It was in fairly bad shape, I'm afraid. There's still some rough spots in the lower chest."

Harper felt the tenderness in his ribs and stomach. "Thought I'd fallen over while pissed."

"We planted that idea in the hippocampus region of your brain to keep you from asking too many questions. We also did a memory sweep before you took form. You will still sense phantom feelings of the man he was. Very much as the amputee senses the itch of a leg that's no longer there."

"I know the drill, Inspector."

"Yes, well, there's some concern you might find the sensations to be much more acute. London's never turned around a body so quickly. But it was the form we needed for the mission, and we're under some pressure."

Harper sat on the bed, rubbed the back of his neck. "He didn't like heights."

*"Pardon?"*

"Him, me. He didn't like heights. Odd for someone in special ops, but he loved the job. And he loved . . . his wife, I think."

"He was listed, Mr. Harper. He was finished with this body."

"No jumping the gun, then, being as you were under pressure and all?"

"The devouring of the human souls and theft of their still-living forms are the tactics of the enemy, not us."

Harper looked again at his hand. "Did his soul make it?"

"For the record, Jay Michael Harper was comforted before he died. His soul has already been born into another life."

The inspector pulled his cigarette case from his cashmere coat, offered Harper a gold-tipped smoke.

"More of that fine hand-rolled Moroccan tobacco, Inspector?"

"Please, take one. An awakening can be something of a jolt. A good strong dose of radiance might be helpful in maintaining balance."

"As in keeping my eternal being separate from a dead man named Jay Michael Harper?"

"That and clearing the cobwebs, what?"

Harper grabbed one and lit up, drew the smoke into his lungs, let it soak into his blood. He sat on the bed, looked down to the shreds of paper and photographs at his feet.

"One more thing, for the record, Inspector?"

"If I can."

"Alexander Yuriev. Our kind, or human partisan?"

"Does it matter? Either way, he's gone forever."

"It matters."

The inspector took one of his own flash smokes and lit up. "The real Alexander Yuriev drank himself to death shortly after returning to Russia. We'd been tracking him for many years as part of a long-term operation in Moscow."

"An operation that went belly-up, I take it, or you wouldn't have had to pull a rush job with me."

"Yes, as a matter of fact. Yuriev and his operating cell of partisans were exposed by a mole in our Paris operation. All our partisans working with Yuriev were slaughtered and their souls fed to the devourers."

"You say 'devourers' as if I'm missing something, Inspector."

"Since you were last here, the enemy has perfected the manipulation of half-breed DNA. What was once a mutation has become a swarm, following fast at the enemy's heels, waiting to dine at the table of mass death."

"'For they covered the face of the whole earth, so that the land was darkened; and they did eat every herb of the land.'"

"Indeed, Mr. Harper. Except these monsters, unlike the locusts of Moses, devour the chemical substance of the human soul."

Harper drew at his fag, remembering something from somewhere. The History Channel, episodes on World War I maybe. No, he'd seen it himself. He could still smell it. He'd been there. Lacerated fields where only death lived among the blackened stumps of trees and barbed wire and shell holes filled with bloodstained water. Slogging through fields of mass death, hunting down the devourers of souls. All the time hearing the cries of the dying ones begging to be saved. *What was once a mutation has become a swarm, bloody Christ.* The inspector's voice dragged Harper back to now.

"Mr. Harper?"

"Yes, sir, I'm with you. Yuriev's partisans were slaughtered in Moscow."

"His last message to us was that he'd make a dead drop at Lausanne Cathedral. That was twenty years ago."

"He knew the bad guys were after him. He went underground."

"Twenty years' worth of deep, Mr. Harper. Not once coming in from the cold for regenerative stasis, not once making contact with a partisan. The weight of his form must have crushed down on his being with excruciating pain. It was a rather remarkable feat that he found the strength to complete his mission. We had hoped you might bring him in, but Komarovsky and his half-breeds got to him first."

Harper inhaled from his smoke. The inspector was right: A dose of radiance was swell for clearing the cobwebs. He looked down to the shredded papers at his feet. Yuriev's eyes were still staring at him. *Christ,* Harper thought. *There's only a handful of our kind left in this place. Battle buddies from the time the cries of men reached the heavens, on a mission to save paradise from the bad guys. You were his last chance, and you let him down.*

"I should've been bloody faster off the mark. I might've saved him."

"Those are the phantoms of your form speaking, Mr. Harper. I suggest you ignore them."

"He dropped that formula in my lap. If I'd been even half awake, I would've known it was the enemy's breeding formula, not some bloody performance-enhancing drug. He was begging me to recognize who he was . . . what he was."

"Mr. Harper, if you remember, Yuriev didn't drop the formula in your lap, I did. In the end, the state of Yuriev's being was all but lost. He could no longer separate his being from his human form. And every human partisan in Europe was trying to save him—that *is* their job, isn't it? Fight with us, save *us* if they can. And they have, through the ages. But the sad fact is Yuriev was already dead but for the beating of his heart. Indeed, he had become what men call a paranoid schizophrenic."

"All the more reason to save him."

"Yes, well, in our line of work the same orders stand when it comes to saving anyone, or anything. It's not our job. Our job is the mission. Are we clear?"

"Yes, sir."

"Now, time is not on our side. Are you feeling reasonably up to speed?"

"Monsieur Gabriel seems to have done the trick. And you did have me watching the History Channel 24/7 for, what was it, six months? Clever, the whole telly thing, communications embedded in the pictures."

"It's proven somewhat more effective than the deciphering of nursery rhymes. Shall we begin the briefing and mission profile?"

Harper took another hit off his smoke. Radiance seeping deeper, the tumblers in his brain spinning again, another safe cracking open, and a rush of light to the brain. *Ab uno disce omnes . . .*

"Go ahead."

The inspector took a sizable draw from his own smoke. "In the late 1950s, a half-breed rose to prominence as a member of the Soviet Politburo, ending up as the Minister of Public Construction. His primary work was the management of urban prisons and slave labor camps in Siberia. However, we learned of a plan within his ministry code-named Firelight. The plan involved the rebuilding of Christ the Savior Cathedral along the Moscow River just outside the Kremlin walls. It was to be an exact replica of the original, built on the very same site."

Harper's mind flashed through *Great Cathedrals of the World* on the History Channel. Built in the nineteenth century to commemorate Mother Russia's victory over Napoleon. One of the largest cathedrals in the world till Comrade Stalin blew it to hell in 1931.

"Bit odd in the mother ship of the Communist state, particularly as the Commies destroyed it."

"Precisely the thing that caught our attention. Obviously, the cathedral couldn't be built under Communism, so the enemy had to bide its time until they could engineer the proper political climate. That time came with the collapse of the Soviet Union in 1991 and a new enemy cell emerged posing as a group of Russian businessmen."

"Enter Komarovsky."

"Indeed. He and his half-breeds flourished in the corrupt climate of the new Russia through a series of shell companies. He managed to gain control of the assets of the state-owned construction company outright. He then secured the contract for the excavations of the new cathedral. We activated Yuriev and, using his status as former hero of the Soviet Union, he secured a job as a laborer when the project broke ground. The excavation of the site went slowly and was often delayed due to mysterious equipment malfunctions."

Harper drew from his smoke. "Let me guess, they were searching for something in the original cathedral foundations."

"A bit deeper than that. A tunnel, hand-cut, two and a half kilometers deep, leading to a cave deep beneath the Moscow River. It was in the cave Yuriev found the object he carried to Lausanne."

"What was it?"

"I couldn't tell you."

"Couldn't or won't?"

"Same thing in the end, isn't it?"

"Fine, but the foundations of Christ the Savior were built in 1839. The locals didn't have the technology to dig a tunnel like that till the twentieth century. When was it built?"

"Well spotted, Mr. Harper. It was dug long before the dawn of man, long before our kind were sent here."

THE WATCHERS · 573 ·

"Yuriev ran carbon-dating tests. It was built in the Miocene Epoch, seven million years ago."

Harper waited for the inspector to spill with the rest. When he didn't, Harper's mind sorted through another episode on the History Channel, *The Dawn of Man*.

"The time of *Homo ergaster*. Hominids became bipeds, learned to control fire and file stones into hand axes. Christ, they must have found the reason man evolved—"

"At this point, I give you an official caution, Mr. Harper. You are not to speculate on what the enemy may have found. Your mission is quite specific."

"You're not going to tell me what it is."

"In truth, we don't even know what it is. We only know Yuriev got it before the enemy and he sacrificed the eternity of his being to keep it from them."

"So where is this thing, whatever it is, Yuriev lifted from Moscow?"

"You're not cleared to know that information, I'm afraid."

"Not cleared to know what it is or where it is. So how do I bloody find it?"

"You don't find it. You were never meant to find it."

"Then what the hell am I doing here?"

"You're a warrior, Mr. Harper, a killer. You know what you're here to do. Leave the finding to us."

Harper looked at the killing knife in his hand. Something didn't feel right. Phantoms of his form rising maybe. He forced them down.

"Where're Komarovsky and his half-breeds now?"

"Waiting for you to make the next move."

"Sorry?"

"Komarovsky and his half-breeds are well aware of what you are, as well as the next phase of your mission."

"Since when?"

"Since I told them, the day you arrived in Lausanne."

"You what?"

"Komarovsky's half-breeds in Moscow have been trying to decipher our SX traffic since Yuriev went underground. Upon your arrival in Lausanne, we let slip the codes embedded in the BBC signals, giving the enemy the impression they had secured a back door into our communications. Happily, they took the bait."

Harper tapped his cigarette and watched the ashes tumble to the floor again, not liking the sound of things already.

"What exactly did they read in your SX traffic?"

"That you met secretly with Yuriev before he was slaughtered, that he told you where he'd hidden the object in Lausanne Cathedral, and that you now have it in your possession. That message was transmitted two days ago. Within the last hour I've let it slip you're bringing the object to our Paris cell tonight."

"Now I truly don't get it."

"You'll leave this room with your overnight bag and make your way to LP's Bar. Take the scenic route, make sure you're noticed. At LP's, have more than a few drinks, chat with your bartender friend, Stephan. Tell him you're off to London for a break, allow yourself to be overheard. Then allow yourself to be followed to Gare Simplon, where, very plainly and drunkenly, you board the midnight TGV to Paris."

"I still don't get it."

"You're not meant to get anything, Mr. Harper. You're meant to follow orders and leave for Paris tonight."

"Komarovsky's killers won't buy it—they'll know my leaving Lausanne is a bluff no matter what you sent in your bloody SX traffic."

"Precisely. They'll assume we're trying to draw them from the cathedral and never see the real reason you're going to Paris."

"Track down and slaughter the mole in the Paris operation."

"With extreme prejudice, Mr. Harper."

Harper took a final draw of the inspector's fine North African tobacco. It felt like a last puff before the firing squad got the order to fire.

"There's a problem, Inspector. Two problems."

"Yes. Miss Taylor and the boy in the cathedral, you mean."

"You knew all along?"

"As did the enemy."

"Sorry?"

"That's the way the counterintelligence game's played. Bluff, bluff, double bluff, and hope you don't come up with the short stick. The enemy has been watching you and noted your behavior."

"Courtesy of your SX traffic?"

"Of course. Your apparent abandoning of Miss Taylor and the boy in the cathedral will cause the enemy a measure of doubt. Throw them on the back foot."

"I said I'd come back to the cathedral tonight. The lad and Miss Taylor, they'll be waiting for me."

"Nothing we can do about that, I'm afraid. Mission timeline has already begun."

"I promised I'd help them."

"You did what?"

"I promised I'd come back."

"You realize such a thing is a direct violation of the rules of engagement with locals."

"I didn't at the time, but it's done. I can't just leave them."

"Again, those are the phantoms of your form, you mustn't let them interfere with your mission."

"You're asking me to abandon two innocent souls."

"I'm not asking, I'm telling you to abandon them and get on the midnight train to Paris."

"This isn't right."

"We don't live in a place of right or wrong, we follow orders."

Harper jumped from the bed. "No, what's not right is you not telling me something."

"I tell you everything you need to know. If I say jump, you ask how high on the way up."

"Bullshit."

"Control yourself, Mr. Harper, anger can lead to free will. I'm ordering you to limit cognitive functions to the confines of your mission. Is that clear?"

"What's clear is whatever Yuriev hid in the cathedral is still there, isn't it? You let that bit of info slip on your bloody SX traffic, along with where it is, didn't you? My orders are a diversion; the real mission is here. You want to capture an enemy chief in human form, let Officer Jannsen at him with her enhanced interrogation techniques. Moving Miss Taylor and the lad from the belfry would show your hand, so you're willing to sacrifice their souls."

"You have your orders, Mr. Harper."

"There's something about the two of them, something you're not telling me. I mean the lad knows how to read shadows, he sees things. His own mother told him an angel was coming to the cathedral . . . Christ, none of this is an accident. You brought them both to Lausanne. You're using the two of them as double agents and they don't even know it. You can't do this, damn it, they'll be slaughtered."

The inspector drilled deep into Harper's eyes. *"Cura nihil aliud nisi ut valeas!"*

Something snapped to attention in Harper's brain, overpowering the phantom of a dead man named Jay Harper. "Yes, sir."

The inspector adjusted his silk scarf, closed his cashmere coat. "Mr. Harper . . . Some of them, the sensitive ones like the boy, the woman for that matter, they affect us. In some ways, it's the greatest weight of our eternity, knowing we can never cross the line to their world even though we hide in their forms, mimicking their lives. Show me one of our kind who can draw a picture or write a piece of music, a line of poetry. We can't. We can only stand in the shadows and watch them with wonder. And yes, too many of them are lost to us, I know."

"'Lost' is a polite way of expressing it, isn't it? Human souls ripped from bodies, fed to the devourers."

"It happens when the enemy hides in the form of men."

Harper held his hand before his eyes, studying it again. "And what do you call this?"

"We didn't start this war, Mr. Harper, and we have no choice but to fight. We are here to save what is left of paradise. Do you read me?"

No choice, no bloody choice.

"Understood, will comply."

The inspector stepped closer to Harper. "I shouldn't tell you this, but as it's been such a rough go for you . . . perhaps this will make it easier for you. The boy in the cathedral. The fact is he is listed, his life is nearly finished."

Like a kill shot to the head. Not even hearing the crack.

"When?"

"That sort of thing is way above my pay grade. But from what I gather, it's to be soon."

"And Miss Taylor?"

"The woman isn't listed as such, but . . . well, you know what they did to her."

"And you won't let Komarovsky take her alive."

"It's for the best. You know what they do to their women when they're finished with them. What was done to Simone Badeaux was an easy death in comparison." The inspector took a step toward Harper. "And as we're on the topic, I need not remind you of the rules regarding locals who've been listed."

"No contact, no interference that would affect the time and manner of their death."

"Quite. Now get a move on, the clock's ticking."

Harper stuffed the killing knife in his belt, picked up the gun and ammo clips from the bed. He looked at them. "You know, I saw a newspaper the other day, read some new words for the slaughter of the innocent. They call it 'collateral damage.'"

"Go easy with those thoughts, Mr. Harper."

"Go easy?"

"Whatever it's called these days, you know this isn't the first time you've had to turn and walk away."

"Will they receive comfort, will their souls make it to another life?"

"We'll do all we can, of course. But you know how it is, mission success comes first."

The inspector stepped to the door and pulled it open. Mutt and Jeff filled the passageway like two immovable and immortal things. Harper looked through the shattered balcony windows, saw rain falling hard in the dark night, felt words rise within him from an unremembered place.

"'Blessed are the dead . . .'"

The inspector turned back. "I beg your pardon?"

"'Blessed are the dead that the rain rains upon.' Who wrote those words?"

"Edward Thomas, a poet and soldier of the Great War, Artists' Rifles Regiment."

"What happened to him?"

"Killed in action on the Western Front, Easter Monday, 1917. His name is listed at Poets' Corner in Westminster Abbey."

"Right, I remember him."

"I beg your pardon?"

"I took his human form, the last mission, didn't I? I gave him comfort, helped carry him to his grave at Agny, and then I snatched his body for regenerative stasis."

"As I said, go easy, Mr. Harper. You've only just been awakened."

"I remember him, Inspector. I remember everything about him; I remember every last one of them."

"Then remember this: They are not us, and we are not them. Now, get a move on. Give us a good show."

# thirty-four

Rochat watched the cigarette bounce on Monsieur Dufaux's lower lip as he spoke.

"You want desserts with your two *plats du jour*?"

"*Oui, monsieur,* two."

"Two, you say."

"*Oui.*"

Monsieur Dufaux shook his head slowly, pulled the cloth from his apron, pounded nonexistent crumbs from a table. He rearranged the place settings.

"I don't like it."

"Monsieur?"

"How many years have you been coming to my café for supper?"

"Since I was an apprentice at the cathedral."

"And every time, you order the *plat du jour* with tap water to drink. Once in a blue moon you take a Rivella. Never an espresso and never, never a dessert. No, I don't like it one bit."

"*Pardon?*"

"First, you stop coming to the café for your supper, then there's all this takeaway business, always for two. And now you want dessert."

"Monsieur Booty is with me in the tower."

"And since when do cats eat *tarte aux pommes* for dessert, uh? Or maybe you want to tell me it's for that snowman of yours? I don't know, Marc, it sounds very strange to me. We Lausannois aren't comfortable with strange. We like our little corner of the world to operate with dull regularity. All of us in the café agree: You need to come clean about your little secret in the belfry."

Rochat looked about the room, saw the university professor and his wife with their books, Madame Budry and the first of her many glasses of Villette, the Algerian street cleaners with their espresso and cigarettes, even a table of Japanese tourists struggling with fondue forks. All were staring at him, hanging on to Monsieur Dufaux's last remark.

"My secret, monsieur?"

"Yes, that illegal angel of yours hiding in the cathedral. We were just discussing it before you arrived. Come on, let's have it."

Rochat was so flummoxed with all the patrons staring at him and waiting for a reply, there was only one thing to say.

"She came to the tower in a bathrobe and nothing else and had long blond hair, but I gave her a haircut and then she looked like Joan of Arc, but now she's dyed her hair black and she looks like someone else until she smiles then she looks like the angel again. And she has a

THE WATCHERS · 583 ·

friend who's coming tonight to help her find her way home."

There were seconds of utter silence till Monsieur Dufaux burst out laughing and all the patrons joined in at the very moment Monsieur Junod pushed through the curtains at the door, followed by his small white dog on a lead.

"Oh, *merde*, I've missed something good, haven't I?"

"*Bonsoir*, Monsieur Junod. It appears our dear friend Rochat now has two angels in the tower and they both want apple pie! So, Marc, this other angel, was he in a bathrobe, too?"

"*Non*, monsieur. He was wearing a brown coat with straps on the shoulders like detectives wear in old movies."

The café burst out laughing again. Monsieur Dufaux put his arm around Rochat and led him to his usual table near the window with the lace curtain.

"Forgive me, Marc, but it was too precious to pass up. Monsieur Junod, sit down and I'll pour you a beer. And a fresh glass for everyone, on the house, in honor of *le guet de Lausanne* for being such a good sport!"

Everyone applauded and raised a glass. *"Le guet!"*

Monsieur Dufaux rested his hand on Rochat's shoulder. "And you, Marc, your dinners are on the house as well."

"I have money, monsieur."

"*Mon cher*, it's the least I can do. We miss you when you don't come around. Not much for us poor Lausannois to do in the evenings but bore one another to death.

You always give us something new and wonderful to talk about. Sit down, I'll get your dinners, *tout de suite*."

Monsieur Dufaux pulled the cloth from his apron strings and pounded tabletops on his way to the kitchen.

"*Mon dieu*, two apple pies for the angels. What's next, uh?"

Rochat sat at the table and looked about the café. The round lamps hanging from the ceiling that looked like full moons. The pictures on the wall of Lausanne from long ago. The slate that was washed and rewritten in white chalk each day, but the letters were always the same and always in the same place, like all the patrons of the café. And Monsieur Junod settling at his table with today's edition of *24 Heures*, and his little white dog jumping up on the next chair to survey the room as if demanding service. Soon dinners would be finished and cigarettes would be lit, Monsieur Junod would finish studying his newspaper, and the evening's conversation on important matters in Café du Grütli would begin. Rochat pulled aside the lace curtains and watched the rain fall and splash on the cobblestones of Escaliers du Marché. Tiny streams formed between the cobblestones and ran down to bigger streams of rain from Rue Mercerie.

"*Et voilà, Marc.*" Monsieur Dufaux was standing at the table with the dinner basket. "Two pork fillet dinners, two slices of apple pie, and I've thrown in a bottle of wine."

"Wine?"

"Oh, I know you're not a drinker, but maybe your

angels will take a glass or two. If they're goody-goody angels, leave it for Monsieur Buhlmann."

"He's coming on Sunday for my day off."

"I know, *mon cher*." Monsieur Dufaux looked out of the window. "The rain. Still coming down, is it?"

"*Oui*, and winter's trying to sneak into Lausanne tonight. He thinks I can't see him."

"Who?"

"Winter. Out there, hiding in the rain. He thinks I can't see him, but I do."

"Such an ugly night. And it's cold. I feel it in my bones."

"I can blow on the glass and draw him in the fog so you can see."

"Who?"

"Winter. Do you want to see?"

"*Non, mon cher,* that's all right. But tell you what: You see old man winter from the belfry tonight, you . . . Say now, that's very strange."

"What's strange, monsieur?"

"I feel like we've had this conversation before."

"We did, monsieur. Last Friday night. It was raining then, too. And you were about to say, 'You see old man winter from the belfry tonight, you chase him away for me.'"

"Why, yes, the very words. How did you know?"

"That's how beforetimes works, monsieur." Rochat stood up, closed his black wool overcoat.

"Wait, Marc. Let me call you a taxi."

"*Merci*, monsieur, but I need to climb the steps."

"Are you sure?"

"It's my duty." He picked up the basket and moved through the crowded café toward the door. The patrons all shifted in their chairs to let him pass.

"*À tout à l'heure, Marc.*"

"*À demain, Marc.*"

"*Bonne soirée, Marc.*"

Monsieur Dufaux called from behind the bar, "*Fais attention*, Marc, the stones will be slippery in the rain."

"*Merci. Bonne soirée, mesdames et messieurs.*"

Rochat felt everyone's eyes watching him. Everyone watching him move through the café with a clumsy limp. He stopped, turned to face them. The room fell quiet.

"I liked your joke very much. It was funny."

He shuffled through the curtains and out of the door and into the rain. He checked for shadows on the cobblestones. There was only his own crooked shadow stretching from his boots.

"*On y va, Rochat.*"

He shuffled to the bottom of Escaliers du Marché. The steep hill of cobbled-together and mismatched stones looked slippery in the rain, just as Monsieur Dufaux had warned. Rochat shuffled to the wooden staircase workmen had built in middles of ages. Rochat didn't know who they were, but he was very glad they had built it. The wooden handrail was sturdy and the red-tiled roof would keep him from getting soaked to the bones. He grabbed the handrail and climbed.

"*Un, deux, trois . . .*"

\*     \*     \*

Harper saw him struggling up the wooden stairs with a basket in his hands. He almost called to him till he remembered his orders. *Make your way to LP's Bar, put on a good show, abandon Miss Taylor and the boy in the cathedral. And by the way, Mr. Harper, the lad with the lantern is listed, no contact or interference with the time or manner of his death.*

*Christ,* Harper thought, *what a bloody business this is.*

He stepped from the wooden stairs, ducked into the old marketplace, and moved into the shadows. He heard the shuffle and thump of the lad's steps coming closer, then the sound of his passing voice.

*"Huitante-deux . . . huitante-trois . . . huitante—"*

Silence.

Harper waited, not breathing, not moving.

He heard the lad's crooked steps turn toward him and shuffle over the wet cobblestones. Harper lowered his eyes to the ground. Some of them, the sensitive ones, he remembered, could sense when they were being watched. But with his eyes cast down, the lad shuffled by without stopping. After a moment, Harper heard the lad's voice.

"Good afternoon, Master Rochat. I am Monsieur Gübeli. It is an honor to make your acquaintance."

Harper looked up. The streetlamps from Rue Viret above the marketplace cast rain-soaked light through the bare branches of the plane trees. He saw the lad on a wooden bench, sitting in the rain, mumbling to himself. He checked his watch; time to get a move on, boyo. He bit his lip instead . . . *Two minutes, just two minutes . . .* He moved along a stone wall and slid into a dark corner near the lad, keeping his eyes to the ground and watching the lad's shadow on the cobblestones. His hands around the basket, his crooked form rocking slowly back and forth, mumbling to himself still.

"Tell me, do you enjoy studying the earth, Master Rochat? *Oui*, Maman shows me places and tells me about them . . . Has your mother shown you Switzerland? Where your father lives, where you'll go to school? . . . Yes, it's far away . . . *Pardonnez-moi?* Quebec City and Lausanne both lie on the forty-sixth latitude of planet Earth. All we need to do is travel along this little line from here to there. Why, it's no distance at all. Look, I can touch the two places with one hand. Here, you try. Go on, Marc, you can do it."

Then watching the shadow of the lad's hand reach from the basket, the hand opening, and the fingers stretching over something that wasn't there. The fingers closed slowly and moved back to the basket. The lad stopped moving.

"The number sixteen bus will be coming soon, Rochat. You must watch it go by and then you must climb the rest of the steps and say hello to the cathedral and the statues and check all the doors—it's your duty."

The lad rose from the bench, shuffled over the cobblestones. Harper stood motionless, his eyes following the lad's shadow till it stopped next to him. Harper could feel the lad's eyes looking dead at him. He heard the lad's voice.

"Are you here, monsieur? I can't see you, but it feels like you're here."

Harper didn't breathe.

"Perhaps it's only an imagination, Rochat. Yes, I'm very sure that's what it was. You're having so many imaginations these days. Sometimes you get confused."

Harper listened to the lad shuffle a few steps, stop, turn back.

"The detectiveman said he would meet me by the fountain when evening came, but he wasn't there when I came down from the tower to get dinner for the angel."

Harper's eyes burned to look at the lad, burned to let the lad see him.

"Perhaps he's waiting at the fountain now. Yes, I'm very sure that's where he'll be."

Harper heard Rochat climb the wooden stairs running to Rue Viret.

*"Huitante-quatre . . . huitante-cinq . . . huitante-six."*

The steps stopped.

"Whoever you are, I'm very sorry if I frightened you. It was very nice to visit with you this evening. I didn't know Lausanne was full of lost angels. I hope to meet you again someday. I'd stay longer, but I have my duties."

Harper heard the lad continue up the stairs to the road. He heard heavy tires roll through the rain. He looked up, saw the lad standing in the light of passing headlights. Tiny rainbows glistened in the rain all around the lad's crooked shape, the light holding him for a moment like something blameless and pure till it faded and there was nothing left of the lad but the sound of his crooked steps crossing the road.

"Christ, they'll fucking butcher him."

Harper rushed for the tunnel under Rue Viret, phantoms screaming in his brain: *Get after him, stop him! At least let them know they're on their own!* He stopped at the edge of the tunnel's fluorescent glare. A razor-sharp line across the cobblestones separating light from dark . . . *They are not us, and we are not them.*

"Bollocks!"

He turned back and charged down Escaliers du Marché. Hard rain pelting the tiled roof of the staircase, rolling off the sides, splattering on the cobblestones and rushing down the steep slope of the uneven and mismatched stones, down toward the lights of Café du Grütli at the bottom of the stairs.

"You want a show, Inspector? Swell, let's get bloody started and have a drink for the fucking road."

He pounded off the wooden stairs, headed for the lights. Black forms rushed from the shadows.

Harper reached for the killing knife in his belt. Like a kill shot to the head.

Instant nothing.

Not even hearing the crack.

Jesus, Marc, you're soaked. Get in here before you catch pneumonia. Take off your coat."

"Wool's warm even when it's wet."

"Yeah, but the rest of you isn't made of wool, especially your head."

"I forgot to wear my hat, it's wool."

"Never mind about coats and hats, Marc." She helped

him remove his coat and sat him down. She rubbed his wet mop of a head with a dish towel. "Jeez, you poor thing."

"Wool's very warm, even when it's wet."

Katherine crouched down in front of Rochat. "Hey, Marc, are you okay?"

"I'm a little cold. Like you when you came to the cathedral."

She rubbed his arms. "You'll warm up as soon as we get some food in you."

She took the plates from the basket and set the cutlery, tore pieces from the baguette and stacked them on a plate.

"Hey, there's a bottle of wine in here. And it's from Lavaux, the good stuff."

"Monsieur Dufaux gave it to me because they played a joke on me in the café because I said Monsieur Booty wanted a *tarte aux pommes*."

"They weren't making fun of you, were they? Because I'll march down there and break their jaws if they made fun of you."

"*Non*, they're always very kind to me at the café."

"Really?"

"Tonight the patrons all raised their glasses to me and said, '*Le guet!*' and Monsieur Dufaux said, 'We miss you when you don't come around. Not much for us poor Lausannois to do in the evenings but bore one another to death. You always give us something new and wonderful to talk about. Sit down, I'll get your dinners, *tout de suite*.'"

"What?"

"That's what Monsieur Dufaux said."

"Okay then, so let's eat dinner."

"Okaythensoletseatdinner."

Katherine set the food out on the table. "And you know what? I'd love a glass of wine. You got a corkscrew up here?"

"There's one under the table Monsieur Buhlmann left when he retired, and I'm very good at opening bottles because Grand-maman's butler taught me. His name was Bernard. Do you want to see?"

"Yeah."

Rochat reached under the table for the corkscrew. He carefully folded and laid a dish towel over his left arm. He bowed, opened the bottle, poured her a glass, and bowed again before sitting down.

"Wow, that was very professional, Marc."

*"Merci."*

Rochat watched her sip slowly from the glass.

"Does it taste good?"

"It tastes very good. And this dinner with you is really good."

"Would you like me to turn on the old radio? There's music in the air."

Katherine giggled. "Man, where did you get your sense of humor?"

Rochat thought about it. "From Grand-maman."

"Really?"

"She liked to take out her false teeth and make them talk."

Katherine laughed, and wine splooshed from her mouth. "What a hoot."

"I don't know what that means."

"It means really, really funny. Come on, let's eat."

Rochat jumped up. "I forgot to look by the fountain."

"What's wrong, Marc?"

"I forgot to look by the fountain for the detective-man."

He shuffled three steps, opened the door of the loge, stepped out onto the south balcony. Katherine watched him bending over the iron railing. He came back into the loge, closed the door.

"He still isn't here yet."

"Don't worry, he'll come."

Rochat started to rock back and forth on his heels.

"Marc, is something wrong?"

"Maybe I can't see him anymore."

"Who?"

"I thought it was him on Escaliers du Marché, but I couldn't see him. I pretended it was another lost angel because . . . because . . ."

"Don't worry, Marc. He promised he'd come back."

"Hepromisedhedcomeback."

"Yeah. Come on, sit down."

Rochat sat. He stared at the burning candles on the table. Katherine took the black cloak from the hook on the wall and wrapped it around Rochat's shoulders.

"This is Monsieur Buhlmann's cloak for you to use," Marc said.

"I know, but it's dry, and we need to warm you up. I

think you got a chill in the rain. That's all you're feeling, Marc. Just a nasty chill, and we're going to chase it away."

"Like chasing away the bad shadows."

"That's right, let's chase them all away."

She rubbed his arms and shoulders through the cloak. She sat down, looked at him, brushed strands of damp black hair from his forehead.

"Marc, Harper will come back and take me home, and you'll have your tower back to yourself. Everything will be like it was before. Just you, your beautiful bells, Otto, Monsieur Booty, and all those crazy skeletons in the basement."

"Cathedrals don't have basements. Cathedrals have crypts."

"Whatever, as long as the skeletons stay there."

"Do you want to see them before you leave?"

"No, but after I'm gone, you be sure to tell them I said hello. Come on, eat before your food gets cold."

"You said Maman's words again."

"Yeah, what words?"

"'C'mon and eat before your food gets cold.'"

"Well, you know what they say, if it's not one thing, it's your— Wait a sec, when did I say her words before just now?"

"Outside on the balcony when we were watching the Christmas lights and you said, 'When the time comes, I don't know how I'll say good-bye.'"

"When did she say it?"

"Before she died, but she never said good-bye."

"What?"

"One day she was gone."

"I don't understand."

"I made tea and went into her room with a cup of tea I made for her and she was gone."

"She was dead, you saw her?"

"I didn't see her. She was gone."

"What?"

"Monsieur Gübeli was in the room and told me Maman had gone away. And we put her box in the ground."

"You never got to say good-bye to her."

"I never got to say good-bye to her."

Katherine touched her fingers to her lips. "Oh, Marc, no wonder you're upset."

"I thought it was the detectiveman on Escaliers du Marché, but I couldn't see him."

"Hey, Harper didn't go away like your mother. He'll come back; he promised."

"He'll come back; he promised."

"Yeah, it's going to be okay."

"Okay."

"Shhh, just take a breath. I'm with you, so you're not alone." She waited a moment. "Can I ask you something, Marc?"

"*Oui.*"

"What was your mother like?"

Rochat thought about it. "She was soft."

"Soft . . . That's a sweet thing to say. How old were you when she died?"

"Ten years."

"You miss her, don't you?"

"I can see her in beforetimes."

"Yeah? What happens, when you see her?"

"She teaches me to walk in the garden. She helps me with letters and numbers. She shows me places on the globe and tells me stories. She lights candles and makes shadows on the ceiling with her hands and tells me more stories, and she says she's going to a place where she can see me but I think she tells me that because I'm afraid. And she tells me I'm going to grow to be the bravest of them all because being brave is only standing up when you're afraid. And she tells me an angel will come to the cathedral and I have to protect the angel like I protect the cathedral. And then she tells me how to go to beforetimes to see her so I can remember the things she tells me."

Katherine leaned against a timber. She pulled the candle close to her, picked at the melting wax along the side, mashed it between her fingers.

"You know what I think? I think if your mother could see you now, she'd be really proud. Because you did grow up to be very brave."

"I grew up crooked. There was an accident when I was born."

"Shhh, just listen to me, Marc." Katherine rolled the wax into a small oblong shape. Rochat watched her shape it between her fingertips and stand it upright on the table. "It doesn't matter what you look like on the out-side, because anyone who knows you knows what a great guy you are on the inside. You're honest and true. Frankly, you're the kind of guy that makes a girl weak at the knees."

"I don't know what that means."

"It means you're the kind of guy a girl spends her whole life looking for, usually in all the wrong places."

"I don't know what that means."

"Let's put it this way: When I get home, I'm going to tell everyone the story of Marc Rochat and how he saved me from the bad shadows."

*"Merci."*

She broke off another piece of wax, rolled it in her fingers. Rochat watched her make another oblong shape.

"This girl you're going to meet at Christmas, what's her name again?"

"Her name is Emeline. She knows how to milk a cow."

"Emeline the Swiss cowgirl, that's the one. I want you to promise me something." She set the wax form on the table, a little taller than the other. Rochat watched her move them, side by side, on the table. "Promise me that one night you'll bring Emeline to the cathedral and you'll light all your candles and take her for a walk in the nave and tell her the story of all the lost angels hiding in the cathedral."

Rochat watched the two wax forms moving through candles on the table, watching their shadows swell and move like living things. Katherine moved the shapes closer to each other, gently touching them together.

*"D'accord."*

"And promise me, when you're walking with her, you'll hold her hand. So she won't be afraid."

Rochat thought about it. "Will she like to hold hands?"

"Very much."

"What if I forget to take her for a walk and hold her hand? I'm very good at forgetting things."

Katherine set the bits of wax on the windowsill next to each other. "You won't forget, because I'll leave the two of you up here. And when you see them you'll go to beforetimes and remember."

Rochat stared at the figures, his head tipping slowly from side to side. "The one on the left is me."

"How come?"

"Because he's a little crooked."

Katherine laughed. "Man, you are so one-of-a-kind."

"Is that a good thing?"

"It's the best thing there is to steal a girl's heart."

"Can I tell Emeline an angel gave me the idea about the candles?"

Katherine took a thoughtful sip of wine. "Know what? I think she'd like that story a lot. Just leave out the part about looking through my windows with the binoculars. Or that I slept in your bed a few nights. And the hooker thing, leave out the whole hooker thing."

"Leave out the hooker thing."

"Yeah, trust me." She rubbed Rochat's arm. "You feel better now?"

"*Oui.*"

"Good. Then let's eat; the apple pie looks scrumptil-lyicious."

Rochat sat up straight, stared at the door of the loge. "I didn't have my lantern."

"What?"

"Maybe I saw him but he couldn't see me because it was dark and I didn't have the lantern. Maybe he wasn't an imagination and he needed the lantern to see things in the dark."

"That's right, and when you call the hour, he'll see your lantern from the belfry."

"And then he can find his way to the cathedral."

"Yeah, he'll find his way. Don't worry."

# thirty-five

Harper raised his head and tried to focus.

Dimly lit room, dirty wood floor, mirrors on the walls. The smell of sweat and fear.

He wasn't alone.

A woman on a bed in the center of the room. Lolling trancelike on red sheets, her naked body covered with oil. Black scarf tied over her eyes, black scarves holding her wrists to the bedposts. Table next to the bed, mortar and pestle, powders, oils.

"You on the bed, can you hear me?"

She didn't answer. She wasn't even on the same planet.

Muffled sounds from the other side of the room. A man in a chair, burlap sack over his head. Stripped to his boxers, arms tied to the back of the chair, his whole body trembling.

"You, tied to the chair, can you hear me?"

The man twisted, searching for Harper's voice. "Mmm, mmm!"

"Stay calm. You're filling the sack with carbon dioxide, it's making you panic."

Shreds of black mist curled through the room, washed over the hooded man in the chair. The man felt the mist on his skin, jerked frantically to shake it off. Harper called to him.

"They smell your fear, don't move."

Two shadows shot from the mist and smashed dense as iron into Harper's kidneys. He cringed with pain. A voice hissed throughout the room.

"Never mind the skins, killer."

Then a powerful hammerlike blow smashed across his face.

"Aw, bloody hell!"

Forms emerged from the shadows. A tall reed of a man and a runt of beef with whiskers on his chin. Same forms described by the lad with the lantern, same creeps Harper had seen at LP's Bar the night Katherine Taylor disappeared.

"Jings, it's the goon squad."

The tall one leaned down, eyeliner and a five-o'clock shadow on his face, a razor-sharp killing knife in his hands. "Watch your mouth, killer, before I stick something in it."

"All right, what the fuck am I doing here?"

"Wouldn't you like to know?"

"That's why I'm asking, dickface."

The small one grabbed Harper by the hair. "Name-calling isn't polite."

"Wasn't talking to you, squirt."

Double kicks slammed into Harper's stomach and ribs, air rushed from his lungs. He felt himself blacking out, his eyes searching for something to hang on to. He saw his reflection in the mirrored wall on the other side of the room. On his knees, stripped to his shirt and trousers. Chained at the wrists, arms stretched out to the walls. His face battered, blood dripping from his mouth and down his shirt. The small one hissed in Harper's face.

"Want some more, killer?"

Harper spat blood on the floor. "Fine for now, thanks. Who are the locals?"

"Them? Just a pair of skins, friends of yours, don't you know?"

Harper's eyes quickly scanned the woman on the bed and the hooded man in the chair. Whole room looking blurry as hell, but he could tell it wasn't Miss Taylor or the lad. *Then who the fuck?* He couldn't think through the dullness in his brain. Couldn't be partisans, they'd already be slaughtered, their souls fed to devourers. *Then who?* He looked at the half-breeds, shrugged as if he didn't give a damn.

"Take me to your leader, because you two goons are dumb as soap. I don't know these people."

The half-breeds pounded Harper's stomach and back with rabbit punches. He buckled over, dangling by his chains. The small one cocked back for more, his fists held in place by a disembodied voice.

"That will be sufficient."

The half-breeds parted like waters as down a mirrored hall and into the room came a tall and elegant form. Black suit, black shirt. Long silver hair tied to the back of his head, dark round glasses over his eyes. His scent filling the room like something heavy and persistent. He stopped before Harper, bowed slightly.

"Good evening. I am Komarovsky. I'm pleased you could attend our little soirée."

"Cheers, but I think there's been some mistake."

"That would be most inconvenient." His hands swept toward the hooded man and the woman on the bed. "As you see, some of the guests have already arrived."

"Big party, is it?"

"The rest will join us presently."

The half-breeds hauled Harper to his feet. He looked down, saw iron shackles and chains at his ankles. And next to his bare feet, ten hypodermics on the floor. Traces of dark liquid in the hypos. *No wonder your skull feels three sizes too small for your brain,* Harper thought; *60 cc of dead black potion in the veins.* Half-breed narcotics manipulated from dark matter, gave the fuckers an insatiable appetite for death. Cranked them with an orgasmic rush every time they killed. Made them imagine slaughter was a sacrament of nothingness. And as the potion surged through Harper's blood, he felt the dark matter absorbing the light in his eyes. *They want to flip me, they want me to become one of their kind.* Harper gave his shackles and chains a shake; they chinked like a pocketful of spare change.

"In that case, how could I refuse your gracious invitation?"

"You are too kind."

Harper looked at him, trying to see through the dark lenses, only seeing himself looking back.

"Sorry, what was the name again?"

"Komarovsky."

"Komarovsky, Komarovsky. Nope, can't say it rings a bell."

"Do you expect us to be seduced by this ongoing pantomime? You, of all your kind, wandering the streets of Lausanne unaware, unawakened?"

Harper looked at the woman on the bed, the half-breeds, the hooded man tied to the chair, the whole stinking charnel house of a room.

"You call this awake? Looks more like a bad dream."

Komarovsky sniffed at Harper. "But to dream you must first know the sleep of men. You do not smell of sleep, you do not smell of dreams. You smell of an eternity born of the unremembered beginning."

"Now you've lost me completely."

Komarovsky held Harper's chin, examining his face. "Your kind never learned to completely hide the light in your eyes. It made it so easy for us to spot you in the forms of men. Have they told you your kind are all but extinguished from the face of the earth? I suppose it is a sign of their desperation that they would bring you back in such a tattered form, haunted by feelings and emotions. No, you cannot hide. I spy the eyes before me to be those of the celestial warrior the legends of men call Michael."

Harper felt the dead black hitting his brain hard. He tried to snap to, sort the terrain.

"Let's see. Celestial warrior, legends of men, eternity. Right, all coming back to me now. I'm one of the good guys, and you're one of the bad guys fucking up paradise with your half-breed goons."

The small one hammered hard into Harper's side, the pain tearing through his guts.

"Argh!"

Harper wobbled. Komarovsky's hand caught him by the throat and held him upright.

"How dull your eternity must be. Sworn to the will of a creator who has all but abandoned his creation. Driven only by an urge to hunt and slaughter our children, our giants among men."

Harper pulled his neck from Komarovsky's grip, gagged for breath, steadied himself on his feet.

"Correct me if I'm wrong, but you were sworn to the same will once upon a time, remember?"

"Once upon a time was so long ago. And times change." Komarovsky turned away and walked to the hooded man in the chair, petted his covered head. "Tell me, good and noble warrior, do you feel nothing as you slaughter our children?"

Harper felt the heart of his human form pound, blood rushing hot through his veins. *Don't give in, boyo, don't give in.*

"Not really, it's a job. Clock in and slaughter as many half-breeds as you can in a day, clock out and head to the nearest pub."

The tall one swooped in as fast as light, slashed the killing knife across Harper's chest.

"Aw, fuck!"

Harper dropped to his knees, looked in the mirror. Shirt cut open, blood oozing from the hairline incision in his flesh. The tall one set the serrated blade at Harper's throat.

"Sliced or diced?"

"How about you shove it up your arse instead?"

The tall one kicked Harper in the ribs, driving him forward. The chains pulling his wrists, stretching his arms to the walls.

"Christ!"

Komarovsky studied Harper's pose. "Indeed, you look very much like the Christ. Arms extended from your sides, cherishing the exquisite pain of salvation. But even Christ, for all his perfection, knew the taste of temptation in his final moments. I remember his voice: *'Eli, Eli, lama sabachthani . . .'* 'My God, my God, why have you forsaken me?' He questioned, he considered his place. And as we drove the spear into his heart to finish him, and the sky turned black, the four winds raged and we were moved to tears considering the perfect balance of flesh and spirit he had discovered in the form of a carpenter's son. He was the best of your kind. It is fitting he is worshipped as a god."

"I hate to tell you this, but the word is he didn't die in his form. And he'll be back, and he's mightily pissed off."

"So goes the legend of men."

"This is why you dragged me here? Pump me full of dead black potion to talk about the legends of men?"

"I invited you here that you, too, may find salvation, as did the Christ."

Harper looked at his out-strung arms. "You're barking up the wrong cross, Komarovsky."

Komarovsky smiled. "Oh, ye of little faith."

Harper's blurring eyes shot to the tall one leaning against the wall, cleaning his fingernails with the tip of his knife. And the small one, picking up a rusty hacksaw from the floor, wiping it on his sleeve, circling the hooded man tied to the chair. Harper felt sensations churn in his guts. He shook his head; the dead black wasn't just sucking the light from his eyes, it was breaking down his resistance to emotions. *I feel . . . I feel fear. Get a grip, boyo, get a fucking grip!*

"Look, I'll make it easy for you. Whatever Yuriev took from Moscow, I don't have it, I never did. I don't even know what the hell it is."

"Of course not. You are an errand boy for your kind and nothing more. But the sacrifice of these skins will give you the chance to achieve so much more."

"What the hell do you really want? You want information, is that it? You want the locations of our partisan cells? What the fuck do you want?"

"What I really want is your salvation."

Komarovsky raised his hands, pointed to the corners of the ceiling, small cameras panning from side to side. Down in one corner, a laptop computer with numbers streaming down the screen. *They're watching,* Harper thought, *slaughter at midnight, live on Goon TV.*

"You're fucking up, Komarovsky. You didn't hack into

our SX traffic, you were let in. We're tracking your communications right now. This stunt will lead us to the rest of the Two Hundred Club and every half-breed in the world. We'll track them, we'll kill them."

*"Che sarà, sarà."*

Komarovsky snapped his fingers, the small one threw a switch on the wall, and bright light blasted through the room, red lights on the cameras kicked on. The tall one punched a few keys on the computer, the screen switched to the room, the tall one nodding everything was online.

"Nearly a billion hits already." Komarovsky smiled and opened his arms to the cameras. "Good evening and welcome to another entertainment presented by the Two Hundred Club. Tonight we players engage in an act of sacrifice for the sake of salvation. Who shall be sacrificed and who shall be saved? That is the question of the ages to be played on our humble stage."

Harper felt the dead black potion seeping deeper into his brain; the room began to warp out of shape, panic rising again as he watched Komarovsky drift over the woman on the bed, touching her stomach. The woman stiffening with excitement, her voice breathless.

"Yes, my love, I want more. Please give me more."

Komarovsky looked at Harper. "So beautiful in their dreams, are they not? It was hiding in the shadows and watching them sleep, watching them dream, that first enchanted us and filled us with desire. We began to whisper to them as they slept, tell them secret things. Their bodies surrendered to us and they became the vessels of our loneliness, and so we were made flesh."

"Such a poetic flourish for treason."

Komarovsky reached between the woman's legs. "And you, good and noble warrior? Have you never desired such treason? To touch them, to let their bodies soothe the weight of your eternity, if only once?"

The woman arched her back, took a sharp breath as Komarovsky pushed his fingers inside her. She cried with the joy of release, then she relaxed and slid back into her murmuring and whispering place.

"Don't leave me, my love, not yet. Give me more."

Harper pulled at his chains. "Enough—she's so drugged she doesn't know what she's doing."

"All the better to give you pleasure."

"What?"

"She has been bathed in breeding oils and made ready to conceive this night, this hour. Lie with her, feed on her dreams, and consecrate her with the seed of your form."

"You must be joking."

Komarovsky moved close to Harper, traced his moist fingers over Harper's lips. "Taste the stuff of creation, let it inflame the flesh in which you hide."

Harper twisted away. "Forget it, rules and regs. No fraternization with the locals. You remember the rules and regs, don't you?"

"But you and me, we're way beyond rules and regulations, aren't we? Even now I smell the scent of fear rising from your skin."

"Forget it, this isn't going to happen."

"Fuck her and I will spare both their souls."

Harper shook his head. "You were sent here to protect this place, comfort the locals at the time of their
death, guide them to their next form in life."

Komarovsky grabbed Harper's crotch and twisted
hard. Harper felt a shock of pain. "But fucking their
women and breeding a new race to rule over paradise
turned out to be far more satisfying."

"Fuck you, fuck your half-breed goons."

*Thwack!*

The killing knife, skimming Harper's throat, digging
into the wall. The tall one rushed in, pulled the knife
from the wall, held it in front of Harper's face.

"Tsk, tsk, I missed. I know, let's have some fun with
your skin friends."

Harper felt the dead black blow apart the firewall between his eternal being and the emotions of his human
form. Then came the breathless panic of being trapped
in a physical space, crushing down, *can't get out . . . the
weight, Christ, the weight . . . bloody hell, no.*

"Told you before, I don't know these people. Don't
have friends in this place. Never did, never will."

The tall one moved back to the bed, dragged the
point of the blade over the woman's stomach. She reacted
to the touch as if it were a loving thing. The dead black
in the half-breed's eyes pulsed faster watching her. Across
the room, the same thrill in the small one's eyes as he
yanked the hooded man upright, pulled the burlap sack
from his head. Harper saw the fearful eyes, gaffer tape
over the mouth . . . the bartender from LP's.

"Stephan?"

"Mmmm! Mmmm!"

The small one set the hacksaw against the boy's jugular. Harper looked at Komarovsky.

"He's got nothing to do with this, he's a bloody bartender."

"But he has everything to do with it, as does the woman whom, I'm sure, you remember very well."

The tall one lifted the woman from the bed. The woman's eyes hidden by the blindfold. Her skin white and pasty. Harper stared at her, the auburn hair, the black scarves around her wrists, almost hiding the kid gloves on her hands. Komarovsky swept by her, pulled the blindfold from her face . . . *No, not her.*

"Ah, I see by the expression on your face you do recall the lovely Miss Clarke. So needing to hold on to someone, so wanting it to be you. She kissed you with such tenderness."

"You're wasting your time, they're not even partisans."

"No, they are the innocent instruments of your salvation."

"You don't fucking need them. You've got me in chains and a billion hits online waiting for a show. Let's clear the place of locals and get to it. Torture me for a thousand years."

"You see, you are already more than a warrior. You have become the new Christ on earth, ready to sacrifice the eternity of your being for the insignificant souls of men. But it is not your suffering I seek."

"What do you want, then? What do you fucking want?"

"Lie with the woman and let the flesh of your form

bond with hers. Let the passion of her love release you from your oath to an ancient and forgotten will."

"What?"

"Breed one of your own kind on earth and we shall be brothers again. Tonight, you and I will put an end to this eternal and forever war."

Harper looked at Stephan and Lucy. "They are not us, and we are not them."

"Once again, you give me rules and regulations, when innocent lives are at stake."

"Just telling you the way it is."

"Then you would choose their deaths?"

Harper nodded to the cameras in the ceilings, zooming in for close-ups as the half-breeds readied themselves for the slaughter. "There isn't a choice."

"No?"

"It's no use, Komarovsky. I saw the hunger in the eyes of your half-breeds. They're whacked to the gills on dead black. They want death. No matter what I do, the locals are as good as listed."

Komarovsky smiled. "How clever of you to notice. Because your salvation does not come in choosing to love, but in choosing to hate." He spun around and pointed toward Lucy. "Wake her! Let her know the good and noble warrior who would not save her soul!"

The tall one threw a white powder in Lucy's face, pressed the killing knife against her throat. A trickle of blood ran down her breasts. She snapped out of her druggy haze, saw herself naked, saw the blood. She felt the killing knife at her throat, saw Harper in chains.

"Jay?"

Harper shook his head, tried to suppress the rage pumping in his brain. "Look into my eyes, just look into my eyes."

"Jay, what is this? What's happening? Help me!"

Komarovsky turned to the cameras. "Yes, let the warrior angel hear their cries. Let him hear her cries rise to the emptiness of the heavens. Slaughter them both!"

The short half-breed tore the gaffer tape from Stephan's mouth.

"Monsieur, what are they doing? Please, stop them!"

"Look at me, both of you, look at me, listen to my voice."

Komarovsky turned to Harper. "Do you feel their panic, do you feel their terror?"

"Leave them alone, you fearmongering fuck!"

Then he realized he'd played into Komarovsky's hands. Letting the dead black in his blood fuel the rage in his guts and crush the light in his eyes. *No, damn it! Hold on!*

The tall one pulled Lucy's head to the side, sliced at her neck, her scream ripping at Harper's ears.

"Jay!"

The knife sliced deeper into her neck.

"Ahhhhh!"

The short one pulled the saw over Stephan's throat.

"Monsieur, save us!"

Harper pulled at the chains like a madman. "Listen to me! Your life doesn't end, it never ends!"

The hacksaw cut hit Stephan's jugular, blood sprayed

through the room. The tall one twisted the blade into Lucy's throat. Their screams drowning in blood. Then blades set for death cuts. Terrified eyes watching him, begging to be saved. Harper felt a spark of light in his eyes.

"Look into my eyes, listen to my voice. *C'est le guet, il a—*"

Komarovsky slapped gaffer tape over Harper's mouth. "Their souls will not hear the ancient words of comfort. Nor shall they see good and noble light in your eyes. Their souls will be fed to the devourers and we shall share in the sacrament of their flesh."

He pulled a burlap sack over Harper's head.

"Nnnn! Nnnn!"

Harper twisted in the chains and chewed at the tape over his mouth. The rage in his throat tasting of bile and vomit. The chains clanging and scraping on the floor. Hearing their screams drown in gurgles of blood, arms and legs slapping in death throes. Then the sawing of blades against bone and the sound of bodies falling to the floor.

Soft footsteps stepping near. Two dull thuds before him. An evil voice in his ear. "I bring you death." Then an unseen hand pulling the sack from his head, tearing the gaffer tape from his mouth, and forcing his half-blind eyes to the floor.

Two severed heads staring back at him. Terror burning in their still-blinking eyes.

And in the corners of the room, shadows of the devourers forming to feed on uncomforted souls. Komarovsky drifted toward Harper. Harper tried to see through the dark glasses.

"Which one are you?"

"I am Komarovsky."

"Which one are you, what's your name in the Book of Enoch? Let me see your bloody eyes!"

"Names are the things of men. And the Book of Enoch is only a legend."

Harper's eyes shot to the watching cameras in the ceiling. The flood of dead black dragging his being under again.

"You fuckers! This is nothing but a game to you. I'll kill you, all of you."

Komarovsky loomed over him. "And you will kill not because of your oath to a forgotten will, but because you now choose to hate."

Harper ripped at his chains. "Let me free, you bastard. I'll show you how much I choose to hate. I'll show you how I choose to kill!"

Komarovsky leaned down. Harper saw his own face in the dark lenses again. Unrecognizable to his own eyes, blood and frothing spittle dripping from his mouth. Komarovsky kissed Harper's lips, licking the drool.

"At last, brother, the taste of free will is upon your lips. You are saved."

"And you're fucking dead forever, every one of you. I'll find all of you and every one of your half-breeds! I'll slaughter every last one!"

"That's the spirit! Go forth into the world and kill!"

"Let me go, I'll slaughter every fucking half-breed in the world!"

"Do you swear to hate, do you swear to kill them all?"

"Yes, I fucking swear!"

Komarovsky held his hand before Harper's eyes and, as if controlling a wild beast, he whispered to soothe him.

"So let the slaughter begin with the crippled fool hiding in the tower of Lausanne Cathedral."

Harper jolted to a stop.

The world suddenly coming unhinged from its place in the stars.

"The lad with the lantern, a half-breed?"

Komarovsky's form began to fade, transmigrating into shadow.

"Go, my brother, go in the name of hate and fulfill your oath to kill them all. Go and slaughter *le guet de Lausanne*."

Harper felt a needle punch through the base of his skull. A flood of dead black potion rushing into his brain. Falling into blackness . . . *Kill* . . .

# thirty-six

Rochat came into the loge after the midnight rounds. "He isn't here yet."

"He's probably drinking his supper somewhere. Let's not worry, not yet anyway."

Katherine was sitting on the bed, sorting clothes to pack in the rucksack Rochat had given her. Monsieur Booty sat nearby, pawing at each item as if laying claim to it. Katherine brushed him away each time. Rochat took Monsieur Buhlmann's cloak from the door hook and folded it. He handed it to Katherine.

"You can take this because it's winter and you need a coat. We forgot to buy you a coat from the lady behind the counter."

"I thought it belonged to the other guy who works here."

"I can buy Monsieur Buhlmann a new cloak for Christmas. You need a coat to go home, and I'm very sure he won't mind. He's a very nice man."

"Gosh, thanks, I really love this old thing."

Rochat turned around, reached up to a shelf, took down the tin box with the picture of the Matterhorn on the lid.

"And you can take the rest of the money, too. I have more in my bank."

"Marc, you've done enough already."

"But what will you do to make money?"

"Have to earn it the old-fashioned way, I guess."

"You mean like Marie-Madeleine?"

"I guess so."

"But if you take my money, you won't have to sell yourself anymore and you can just go home."

Katherine stared at the tin with ninety-six thousand Swiss francs inside, like ninety-six thousand second chances staring back at her.

"Tell you what. I'll take it if we call it a loan. A loan I'll pay back."

"I have more in my bank."

"I know, but I need to pay you back. Not quite sure how, but I will. Even if I have to flip hamburgers at Mc-Donald's for the next twenty years."

Rochat thought about the McDonald's near Place de la Palud. The people behind the counter wore funny hats and always asked if Rochat wanted an extra-large drink with his meal.

"Is that a joke?"

"Yeah, I hope so anyway. But I promise, I'll pay this back, every franc."

"D'accord."

She took the tin and stuffed it into the rucksack. Rochat reached to another shelf, took down a sketchbook and a jar of pencils. He sat at the table, opened the sketchbook. Katherine watched him a moment.

"What are you drawing now, Marc?"

"I'm drawing you getting ready to go home."

"You're going to wear down your pencils drawing me. Why don't you finish that funny story? The one about the wizard and the guys in paper hats on the flying caterpillar. What's his name? Pompidou?"

Rochat looked from Katherine to his sketchbooks on the shelf, seeing the one with the word *"piratz"* scribbled on the binding.

"Did I show you the book with the story of the pirates in the paper hats?"

"Not exactly."

"Then how do you know about the pirates in the paper hats?"

"Oops, guess the cat's out of the bag, huh?"

Rochat looked at Monsieur Booty sitting on the bed next to the rucksack, busily looking back and forth at the two of them.

"He's on the bed."

"Yeah, I know. It's an expression, Marc."

Rochat watched Katherine pick up Monsieur Booty, set him on her lap.

"Now he's on your lap."

"Yeah, I know that, too. Truth is . . . Marc, look at me, forget the cat, he's fine."

"Forget the cat, he's fine."

"Yeah, forget the cat. I was peeking through your

things when you went to the café, the first day after I got here."

"Oh."

"You're really talented."

*"Merci."*

"No, I mean it. All your drawings are wonderful, and that story is really, really funny. I loved the part where they're all yelling silly stuff at one another. I couldn't stop laughing."

Rochat stood, took *piratz* from the shelf, handed it to her. "You can take it with you."

"Wow, really? This is the best thing."

"It is?"

"Sure, you made it with your heart."

"I made it with my hands."

"Man, am I going to miss you. Did you finish it?"

"Finish what?"

"The story."

Rochat thought about it. "The pirates need to get into the ice castle and rescue the princess and find the future-teller diamond and then they go home."

She handed the sketchbook back to him. "Then you sit down, buster, and draw while I finish packing."

Rochat sat at the small wooden table and opened the sketchbook to the page with the pirates in their paper hats waving wooden swords and shouting, "Oh yeah?" and Screechy the evil wizard shouting back, "Yeah and double yeah!" Rochat picked up a pencil and his hand began to move quickly over the page.

Katherine watched Rochat draw for a few minutes,

then she slowly packed her clothes. Monsieur Booty, seeing all the things he'd already laid claim to now being
stuffed in a rucksack, jumped on a black sweater and
purred in protest. Katherine picked up the cat and
dropped him to the floor.

"No claws on the cashmere, thank you."

*Mew.*

Monsieur Booty arched his back, flapped his ears, and
hopped onto the table to watch Rochat draw. He swung
a furry paw at the pencil; Rochat brushed it away.

"*Non.*"

*Mew.*

"Because I said so."

*Mew.*

Another swipe of the paw.

"*Non.* You ask her, you miserable beast."

Katherine stopped packing. "Hey, I'm standing right
here. Ask me what?"

Rochat and Monsieur Booty looked at Katherine,
then each other, then back to Katherine. Rochat pointed
to the beast. "He wants to be in the story."

"Monsieur Booty told you he wants to be in the
story?"

"*Oui.*"

She looked at Monsieur Booty. The beast yawned.

"You sure that's what he said?"

"*Oui.*"

"Okay, so put him in the story."

"I have to think of something for him to do."

"So think of something."

Rochat scratched his black mop of a head and thought about it.

"Monsieur Booty can be living in the ice castle from the times of the nice old queen before she died, and one day he climbs to the tower on secret steps and finds the captured princess and falls in love with her. So he lets the pirates into the ice castle so they can take her home. But before they leave, she reminds them about the future-teller diamond, and the pirates all say, 'Oh yeah, the future-teller diamond.' And Monsieur Booty shows the pirates where it is and they go steal it back, and the princess decides to take Monsieur Booty with her and they all fly back over the Boiling Seas of Doom on Pompidou the giant caterpillar. And then they put the future-teller diamond in its secret place, and then they all drink tea in a vineyard overlooking the lake, and it's a spring day and the swallows are coming back to Lausanne and everyone's happy. The end."

Katherine tipped her head with wonder. "How the heck did you come up with that so fast?"

"Because I imagined that's the way the story's supposed to end."

"Huh. What's Monsieur Booty think?"

Rochat looked at Monsieur Booty. "What do you think, you miserable beast?"

*Mew.*

"He likes it."

"So, do it."

Rochat went back to work. Katherine finished packing and lay down on the bed, watching Rochat draw till her eyes grew heavy and sleep began to wash over her.

"I'm going to miss being in your cathedral, Marc."

"You can come back and visit."

"And you'll always keep your lantern shining at night so I can find my way?"

"It's my duty."

Katherine pulled the duvet over her legs. Monsieur Booty saw the opportunity for another nap and hopped to the bed. She scratched the beast behind its ears.

"And thank you for saving me from the evil wizard, Monsieur Booty."

*Mew.*

She closed her eyes, listening to the sound of Rochat's pencil moving over the paper.

R ochat stood over her, the bright lantern in his hands. Katherine shaded her eyes, saw his crooked shape. His black floppy hat and coat sparkled with drops of rain.

"Marc . . . what's going on?"

"I just finished the two-o'clock rounds. The detective-man is down on the esplanade."

"Is he coming up?"

*"Non."*

Katherine looked out of the open door of the loge. Rain falling thickly.

"What's wrong?"

"I thought he was dead, but they only hurt him."

"What?"

"The bad shadows, they hurt him."

Katherine quickly unraveled herself from the duvet and rushed to the south balcony, looked down over the railing. Near the fountain below the trees, a body in a bloodied shirt and trousers, facedown on the soaking-wet cobblestones, a brown coat tossed to the side.

"Oh, Jesus, Harper."

Rochat shuffled up behind her.

"They cut him on his chest and stomach and he's bleeding. That's why I woke you up. I need you to hold the doors so I can bring him in the cathedral. I'm very sure he needs to hide, too."

D ull buzzing sounds through the darkness.

Tingles of awareness. Breath, touch.

Opening his eyes, seeing a shadow taking form. Long black overcoat, black hat pulled down on his head.

Dead black potion pulsed through Harper's blood.

"Bloody half-breed!"

He lunged at Rochat, slammed him to the floor. Katherine grabbed at Harper's arms.

"What the hell are you doing?"

"He's one of them!"

Harper drove a knee into Rochat's chest, pinned him to the flagstones, and tore the hat from his head. He grabbed his throat and squeezed. Rochat kicked his crooked legs, his face turning purple. Katherine pounded her fists at Harper's back.

"You're killing him!"

"That's the bloody idea. Look at his eyes."

Katherine pounded harder. "Stop it! What's wrong with you?"

"His eyes, you can see the dead black in . . ."

Seeing the faintest light. Flashing and fading.

". . . in his eyes."

*. . . his eyes, his eyes, his eyes . . .*

Harper heard his own voice echo in the dark. He loosened his grip and Rochat crawled away, sucking at the air in wrenching gasps. Katherine rushed to him, held his shoulders.

"Marc, can you breathe?"

Rochat coughed. *"Oui."*

She shot a vicious glare at Harper. "You idiot, you nearly killed him!"

"Did you see it, what happened, just now?"

"See what?"

Harper shook his head. "No, it's a bloody trick!" He charged again, tossed Katherine aside. He pulled Rochat by his overcoat and dragged him over the flagstones, threw him against the stone balustrade. Harper leaned down, yanked Rochat upright. "Your father, which one was he?"

"Monsieur?"

"He was one of them—which one was he?"

Katherine pulled at Harper's wrists. "Stop it, you bastard!"

Harper shoved her aside, silenced her with a killing look. "Stay back, Miss Taylor, or I'll snap his neck here and now."

Horrified tears welled in her eyes. "Please, Harper, it's Marc."

"Who?"

"Marc, you know who he is."

Harper looked at Rochat, almost recognizing the face. Then seeing it again, the faintest light shining deep within his eyes.

"No, it's got to be a trick, it's part of your cover."

"I don't know what that means."

"Stop lying to me!" Harper grabbed the lapels of Rochat's overcoat, shook him hard. "Your father, what was his name in the world? He would've told you his name. The name men gave him, from the Book of Enoch—what was his name?"

"I don't read well, there was an accident when I was—"

Harper slammed Rochat into the balustrade. "You're lying. Tell me his name, you know his name! Azazel, Samyaza? Which one was he?"

Rochat quivered with fear. "His name was Papa, he was an architect, he was trying to save the cathedral from falling down."

"Bollocks! He showed you the dead black in his eyes, didn't he?"

"I don't know what that means."

"You do know, you know everything, you're a fucking half-breed!"

*. . . half-breed, half-breed, half-breed . . .*

Rochat seized up trying to speak; Harper shook him harder. "Tell me!"

Katherine fell on Harper's back, grabbing his shoulders. "You son of a bitch! You're scaring him to death!"

"Your father showed you the dead black in his eyes, didn't he?"

"Papa showed me how to draw people and things."

*. . . draw people and things, people and things . . .*

Harper heard Rochat's terrified voice echo away.

*. . . people and things, people and things, people and things . . .*

"What did you say?"

"Peopleandthings, nodeadblackinhiseyes, peopleand-things."

Harper released him; he fell back on the floor.

"You draw things, you draw people?"

"Papashowedmehow, Papashowedmehow."

Katherine slid over the flagstones. She took Rochat in her arms. "Jesus, you're trembling."

Harper backed away into the shadows, listening to the lad's words echo through the dark like a frightened prayer.

*. . . papa showed me how, papa showed me how . . .*

Katherine turned on Harper. "What's wrong with you, you bastard? What is this?"

"His father could draw."

"So does Marc, so the fuck what?"

"We can't draw a picture, write a poem, a piece of music . . . not even the enemy. His father was a man."

"Of course his father's a man. Have you totally lost your mind?"

*. . . lost your mind, your mind, your mind . . .*

Harper leaned against the cold stone wall, watching and listening to the woman with the lad in her arms.

Rocking him, comforting him with a tearful voice. "It's all right, Marc. I'm here, you're safe now."

*. . . you're safe now, safe now, safe now . . .*

The echoes finding Harper in the shadows. He saw a burning lantern on a cardboard box spreading a cloud of soft light through the darkness. Saw a cot next to the cardboard box, wool blankets and his beat-up coat in a heap. A small framed photograph, a box of unlit candles next to the lantern. Down on the flagstones, a bowl of reddish water, shreds of bloodstained cloth, bandages and scissors. He looked up and saw a mass of darkened stained glass slowly taking the form of Christ on the cross.

*"Eli, Eli, lama sabachthani."*

"What? What are you saying?"

Harper looked at Katherine and Rochat. "Where the hell am I?"

*. . . where am i, where am i, where am i . . .*

"In the cathedral, monsieur. On the tribune behind the organ."

"The cathedral. How did I get here?"

"I found you on the esplanade next to the fountain. I thought you were dead, but they only hurt you."

"You helped me?"

Katherine said, "Yeah, Marc found you and Marc carried you up the tower and took care of you. You'd be fucking dead if it weren't for him, you fucking bastard."

Harper felt the back of his head at the base of the neck. Felt as if someone drove a nail into his skull. He looked down at his chest and saw he was wearing a loose dark blue sweater. He pulled at the collar, saw neat bandages across his chest, felt the pull of stitching strips underneath.

"You did all this, mate? You fixed me up?"

*"Oui."*

"Thanks."

*"Volontiers, monsieur."*

Harper took a slow breath as a wave of pain shot through him, dragging images through his brain. Syringes of dead black potion, killing knives, jagged-edge saws, slaughter. The still-blinking eyes. Two souls lost forever. He held his stomach, buckled over. "Oh, bloody hell."

. . . *bloody hell, bloody hell, bloody hell* . . .

"Does it still hurt, monsieur?"

Harper looked up, saw it again: the delicate light flashing and fading deep within Rochat's eyes.

"Yes, it still hurts. Do you know the time?"

"The bells rang four times and you woke up."

"Four?"

Katherine wiped tears from her face.

"Yeah, Harper, four o'clock. Time for you to tell us what the hell's going on."

Harper shrugged. "It's impossible."

"What's impossible?"

"Our kind . . . it was forbidden."

. . . *forbidden, forbidden, forbidden* . . .

"What's forbidden?"

"The lad's a half-breed."

"He's crippled, you fucking idiot, and you almost strangled him to death."

Harper rubbed the back of his neck again. His mind scrambling back. *Pumped full of dead black potion. Enough to crush your eternal being and flip you into one of them. Then you're dumped at the cathedral to kill the half-breed hiding in the tower. Almost did, but something brought you back, boyo . . . something . . .*

"The lad's eyes."

"What about them?"

"There's no black in his eyes."

"No, his eyes are green, like yours."

"Like mine?"

Harper looked at Rochat. The light in his eyes growing even brighter. A light unseen by men, a light seen only by . . . *no bloody way . . .* Harper's mind scrambled back further, to the cop in the cashmere coat. *Retinal luminance recognition should return within the next forty-eight hours.*

"Holy Christ."

He looked again at the photograph on the cardboard box. Saw a handsome man, a man who taught his son to draw living things, a man with blue eyes and black hair, standing with his arm around a beautiful young woman, a woman with the brightest green eyes.

"'For she hath blessed and attractive eyes. How came her eyes so bright?'"

*. . . so bright, so bright, so bright . . .*

Katherine waited for the sound of his voice to fade.

"Tell me they drugged you, Harper, because you're babbling like a lunatic. What're you talking about? What can't be?"

"All of it."

Harper rose from the cot and hobbled over the flagstones. He picked up the lantern from the floor and moved toward them. Katherine pulled Rochat close to her.

"Stay away from us, Harper, stay the fuck away."

"I'm not going to hurt him, Miss Taylor." He looked at Rochat. "I'm not going to hurt you, mate."

"I know, monsieur."

Harper lowered to one knee. "Can I ask you something?"

*"Oui, monsieur."*

"The photograph next to the cot, that's your mother?"

"With Papa on the Plains of Abraham."

"That's in Quebec City, isn't it?"

*"Oui,* it's on the same line as Lausanne."

Harper had to think for a second. "You mean the forty-sixth latitude of the planet, yeah?"

*"Oui,* that's how I came to Lausanne."

"Right. Your mother, she's beautiful."

*"Merci."*

"You look like her, in the eyes."

"Maman said I have Papa's face and her eyes."

"Do you remember your mother?"

"I see her in beforetimes."

"Beforetimes, right."

"Do you know about beforetimes, monsieur?"

"Yes, I know about beforetimes. When you go there and you see your mother, what do you see in her eyes?"

Rochat fell very still, not breathing, almost sinking. Katherine stroked his mop of black hair.

"What is it, honey, what do you see?"

"Maman told me it was a secret."

"You can tell me, honey."

Rochat looked up at her. "I see a pretty light."

*. . . a pretty light . . . pretty light . . . pretty light . . .*

The words echoing against the ceiling of curving stones. Harper spoke softly, not wanting to chase the sound away.

"When do you see the light in her eyes?"

"In the days before Maman says good-bye and goes away. She says she wants to give it to me so the angel will know who I am."

"An angel. Did she tell you which angel?"

"The one who would come to the cathedral."

Harper lowered his head in a long and perfect silence, till an unbelieving whisper crossed his lips.

"What the bloody hell have we done?"

Katherine waited a moment. "Harper? What's going on? What's wrong with Marc? What did they do to him?"

"Nothing's wrong, Miss Taylor, he's fine." Harper looked at Rochat. "Aren't you, mate?"

"I'm very tired, monsieur."

"Me too. Look, when I woke up, when I tried to hurt you, that wasn't me."

"I know, monsieur. Maman told me the bad shadows make people hurt each other. Did the bad shadows make you want to hurt me?"

"Yes, they gave me a drug that made me want to kill. But it's over now." Harper hobbled to the cot, sat down.

"Monsieur?"

*. . . monsieur . . . monsieur . . . monsieur . . .*

"Yes?"

"Did I only imagine you on Escaliers du Marché?"

"No, you saw me. I couldn't talk to you just then. But that's not going to happen anymore."

"*D'accord.* Will you stay in the cathedral now and help the angel find her way home?"

"Yes, mate, I'll stay."

"*Merci.*"

Katherine kissed Rochat's forehead. "Shh, Marc. Enough, go to sleep."

"I heard the timbers."

"What, honey?"

"I heard the timbers."

Five deep bells rolled through the belly of the nave. Rochat closed his eyes and fell asleep in Katherine's arms. The bells swelled and faded away.

"Hush now. Marie just rang to tell you everything's okay."

*. . . everything's okay, everything's okay . . .*

K atherine heard the cot creak. She saw Harper getting slowly to his feet. He picked up the wool blankets and hobbled toward her. She tried to swallow Rochat in her arms.

"I swear to God, you ever hurt him again and I'll kill you."

"I believe you would, Miss Taylor. And I wouldn't blame you."

He bent down, laid the blankets over them. He grimaced in pain as he straightened up and hobbled back to the cot. He looked at Katherine, as if seeing her for the first time.

"What are you looking at?"

"Your hair."

"What about it?"

"It's black."

"I dyed it."

He looked down, saw a pair of secondhand sneakers on his feet. He picked at the ragged sweater. "And all these clothes?"

"Your shirt was in shreds, covered in blood. You were in your bare feet. Marc got the sweater and shoes from the lost-and-found box."

Harper shook his disbelieving head. "Lost-and-found box, perfect."

He fell quiet. She listened to him breathe. Ragged and in pain.

"Harper, what happened?"

"Sorry?"

"Tonight, what happened?"

He took a slow breath. "I was ordered to abandon the both of you in the cathedral."

"Abandon us? Why?"

"Still a bit of a blur. I'm guessing I was in the way."

"Of what?"

"I wish I knew."

Katherine watched him hold his sides. "Someone died tonight, someone was killed, that's what happened, isn't it?"

Harper looked at her. "Two people. A man and a woman."

"Who were they?"

He didn't answer.

"Harper, tell me. Did I know—"

"Stephan. You knew Stephan. The woman, you didn't know her. Her name was Lucy Clarke."

"Who is she?"

"She was from East London, she worked in a casino."

"Did you kill them?"

"What?"

"You said the killers gave you a drug that made you want to kill. Did you kill them?"

"No. It was Komarovsky and his goons."

Katherine shuddered. "They were murdered because of me?"

"No, Miss Taylor, because of me."

"You?"

"They saw me talking to Stephan at LP's. They saw me talking to Miss Clarke."

Katherine felt a flash of fear. "The killers are coming here, aren't they?"

"Yes."

"Can we call someone for help? Swiss cops maybe?"

"It was a bloody Swiss copper who ordered me to abandon you."

"What?"

"It's complicated."

"Jesus, what kind of detectiveman are you?"

"Sorry?"

"That's what Marc calls you, the detectiveman."

"Right, I remember. He said it the first night I met him on the esplanade."

"So just what kind of detectiveman are you, Harper?"

"What do you think I am, Miss Taylor?"

"I don't give a flying fuck, I just want to know which side you're on. Good guys or the bad guys?"

Harper rubbed the back of his neck, felt the swelling where the half-breed goons rammed the needle. "When it all started, they told me I was one of the good guys. Turns out I was only following orders."

"So you're some kind of soldier or a spy?"

"Something like that."

Katherine softly combed strands of black hair from Rochat's brow. "Those names you said, Azazel and the other one . . ."

"Samyaza."

"Yeah, him. Who are they?"

"Fallen angels from the Book of Enoch."

"The book of what?"

"Look, Miss Taylor, it'd take an eternity to explain and you still wouldn't believe it."

"Try me."

Harper looked up at the dark stained glass holding the crucified Christ. Seeing long traces of rain running like shadows down the glass.

"Everything out there, all of it, this isn't the way it was supposed to be."

"Okay, that makes sense—not."

Harper smiled. "No, I'm sure it doesn't."

Katherine sat quietly, watching Harper sit just as quietly.

"You know, you look like me the night I got here."

"How's that?"

"Like something Marc's cat dragged in."

"The lad's got a cat?"

"Up in the belfry, and it talks."

"The cat talks."

"Yeah."

"I didn't notice."

"That it talks?"

"That the lad's got a cat in the belfry."

"He was probably hiding behind the radio when you were there. You can be a scary piece of work, Harper. But you know that, don't you?"

Harper scooped a handful of unlit candles from the box, grabbed one more. He opened the door of the lantern and touched the wick to the flame. He rose slowly from the cot, the burning candle in his hand. He dropped the spares in his pockets. Katherine pulled Rochat closer to her body.

"Are you leaving us?"

"Leaving?"

"Your orders, to abandon us in the cathedral."

Harper patted the pockets of his trousers: nothing but unlit candles.

"You don't happen to have a fag, do you?"

"Smoked them all waiting for you to come back."

"Right. In that case, let's just say I'm through with following orders."

"Then where are you going?"

"Down to the nave, check the perimeter." He turned one way, then the other. "Do . . . do you know which way's down to the nave?"

Katherine nodded to the wooden door at the end of the balcony. "Over there, Sherlock, to the unfinished tower. Another door opens to stairs that wind down to the main floor."

"Unfinished tower, stairs winding down, got it."

She watched him walk away. She called after him. "You don't think we've got a snowball's chance in hell of getting out of here alive, do you?"

Harper stopped, looked back at her. "Actually, there's got to be more than one miracle left in this lump of a cathedral."

"Gee, I must've missed the first miracle in all the excitement, especially the part where you tried to kill Marc."

Harper looked at the lad sleeping in her arms.

*Transit umbra, lux permanet* . . . Shadow passes, light remains.

"That's just it, Miss Taylor. I didn't."

# thirty-seven

Seven bells rumbled through the belly of the nave as Rochat and Harper gathered the last of the wooden chairs and carried them to the north transept doors. Harper climbed a ladder and Rochat handed up the chairs. Harper drove the last chair into the doors with a heavy bang. Rochat lifted his lantern from the floor and studied the barricade.

"Will this keep out the bad shadows?"

"No, but it'll make a huge bang when they do come in. Let them know they're on our ground. Which reminds me, you know where there're any floor plans of the nave? I'd best get familiar with what our ground looks like."

Rochat thought about it. "When Papa was saving the cathedral from falling down, he made a book with drawings of the cathedral from the belfry spire to under the cathedral."

"Just the thing."

"You can buy one in the gift shop for one hundred Swiss francs."

Harper felt his pocket where his wallet used to be. Nothing but a few coins.

"Suppose we could borrow a copy, just to look at it?"

"When she was alive, Sœur Fabienne told people who just looked at books in the gift shop that the cathedral wasn't a lending library and all the books were for sale."

"I bet she did. Thing is, I've only got some pocket change at the moment."

Rochat reached in his trouser pocket and pulled out his own wallet. "I have money. I can leave one hundred francs and a note on the counter for Madame Buhlmann, because Sœur Fabienne doesn't work there anymore and Madame Buhlmann can put it in the money box when she comes back from Unterwald with Monsieur Buhlmann. And I can push the big cabinets in front of the going-outside door of the gift shop, too. They're metal and will make a lot of noise when they fall over, like Tom and Jerry on Cartoon Network."

"Sorry?"

"Tom's a big stupid cat, Jerry's a clever little mouse who always gets away."

"Cartoon Network, you watch it all the time?"

"*Oui*, it's funny."

"They had me watching a lot of the History Channel."

"The History Channel lives next door to Cartoon Network on my TV. That makes us neighbors."

Harper smiled. "It does at that."

"Should I move the cabinets now, monsieur?"

"Sure. Need help?"

"*Non*, I'm very strong from the legs up."

Rochat shuffled away with his lantern. Harper watched him almost floating through the dark and empty nave, remembering him that first night coming across the esplanade. Nice but dim lad who thought it was his duty to protect a lost angel. *Turns out the lad's the eighth wonder of the world,* Harper thought. *A half-breed of your own kind.* Two and a half million years of rules and regs down the drain, and for what? Enemy's ready to crash through the doors of the cathedral and take down what's left of paradise, no backup in sight. Not even the little old nun in the bloody gift shop. Maybe that's the inspector's wham-bang triple bluff. Maybe he's the bloody traitor in the ranks, the whole Paris story another bluff. Maybe he's already taken what Yuriev hid in the cathedral and he's long gone. Leave the woman and the lad and the whole bloody world in one putrid pile of collateral damage. Not the first time innocents have been left behind, Mr. Harper, won't be the last.

*Christ, get a grip. Think it through.*

He rubbed the back of his neck, thinking the free will of men was tough going. Especially with the phantom of a dead man running through your form. Is it this way, is it that way? Drive yourself bloody mad every time you hit a fork in a road in the Wonderful Land of Now What? The rattle of keys and turning of a lock echoed through the nave. Harper watched the lad's crooked form disappear into the gift shop.

"Hey, Harper."

He saw Katherine, a good-sized cardboard box in her

hands, step into the glow of a hundred candles alight and scattered over the flagstones of the crossing square.

"These are the last of Marc's candles. Where do you want them?"

"On the bench. Just have a seat, I'll take care of it."

Katherine dropped the box, collapsed on the bench. "Where'd Marc go?"

"Gift shop, looking for a book."

She could see Rochat through the glass doors at the back of the nave, dragging a huge cabinet across the room. "Of course he is. You know, he's such a . . . I really wish . . ."

"What do you wish?"

"Forget it. I'm zoning out on fairy tales again."

Harper stepped onto the crossing square and walked through the burning candles, watching the flickering flames. "Go ahead, tell me."

"What you said before, about finding miracles in the cathedral."

"Got one in mind?"

"Yeah, that guardian angels were real. That they'd protect him."

Harper looked at her, nodded to the wool blankets on the bench. "You should wrap up, Miss Taylor, it's getting cold."

"Yeah, it does feel cold. What do they say, it's always coldest before the dawn?"

"I think it's darkest before the dawn."

"Whatever, it's still cold."

She pulled the blankets over her shoulders, watched

Harper set a hundred more candles about the flagstones, lighting them one by one from a single candle, then rearrange the glowing things as if marking positions on a chessboard.

"What the heck are you doing?"

"Lighting candles."

"I see that. Looks like something else."

"Like what?"

"Don't know. That's why I'm asking." Katherine watched the light swell and form at the edges of the crossing square like a lucent fortress. She tipped back her head and watched the light rise into the lantern tower where it radiated against the still-dark windows of leaded glass. "Once, in the belfry, I asked Marc why they called this one the lantern tower when the guy with the lantern was in the tower with the bells. You should've seen him. His hands were going back and forth like he was trying to figure it out. He said it was because the bells wouldn't fit."

Harper leaned back and looked up into the lantern tower. "He's right."

"Yeah, but just now I'm thinking with all these candles burning, the cathedral must look like a big lantern to anyone who might be watching."

Harper lit the last candle, leaned back, and looked up into the lantern tower again. "You're right."

"So is that what you're doing? Calling all angels in the coldest and darkest hour before the dawn?"

Harper sat next to Katherine, offered her the burning candle in his hand. "You never can tell, Miss Taylor."

"About what, angels, or fairy tales?"

"How about both?"

Katherine smiled, took the burning stub. "Those freaks must've really fried your brains on drugs, Harper. You're talking like a nice guy. Not sure it suits you."

"Wouldn't worry, I'm sure it'll pass."

Katherine giggled, peeled bits of melting wax from the side of the candle. "You know, I think I'm going to turn over a new leaf, give up the game. I'll learn to make candles, open a little shop. Somewhere really, really quiet."

"Sounds good."

She looked at Harper. "Can I ask you something?"

"Sure."

"Komarovsky and his freaks, the ones Marc calls the bad shadows. What do you call them?"

"The enemy."

"Yeah, because you're some kind of sneaky-beaky soldier boy. So tell me, soldier boy, you know what Komarovsky and his freaks did to me, and you know what's going to happen to me if they get their hands on me, don't you?"

Harper stared into her eyes. He didn't answer.

"Yeah, that's what I thought."

Shuffling sounds echoed through the nave. Katherine turned her head, saw Rochat's crooked shape coming through the dark.

"What's he got in his hand?"

"That would be his lantern."

"No, the other hand."

"That would be Lausanne Cathedral."

"No way."

Rochat stepped into the lucent fortress of the crossing square, a completed maquette of the cathedral balanced atop a book.

"*Bonsoir*, it's only me."

"I see that. Where'd you get the little cathedral?"

"I made it."

"What, like, now?"

"I made it for Sœur Fabienne before she died three years ago. She said it was very good and she'd leave it in the gift shop for everyone to see. I remembered it when I was moving things and finding the book Papa made. I imagined it could help the detectiveman."

"This Sœur Fabienne, is she one of your beforetimes pals who drops by the cathedral now and then in the middle of the night to say hello?"

"I haven't seen her since she died, but the detective-man saw her in the gift shop."

Katherine looked at Harper. "You see dead people in the gift shop?"

"Couple days ago. But I wouldn't call her dead, not really."

"You know, the more you talk, the more you sound like Marc."

Harper rose slowly from the bench. "You should get some rest, Miss Taylor, you look tired."

"Yeah, I am. It just comes over me, you know."

Rochat shuffled toward her. "Do you want to go to the belfry and sleep with Monsieur Booty? It's warm in the loge."

"No, Marc, I'll stay here, keep an eye on you guys. But don't go wandering off without me, okay?"

Katherine stretched out on the wooden bench and covered herself with the blankets. She watched Rochat and Harper walk up the steps to the main altar under the chancel dome. Rochat with his shuffling limp, Harper holding his beat-up sides. Rochat setting his lantern and the maquette next to the wrought-iron cross on the marble altar, then opening the book, the two of them huddling over the pages like a couple of . . .

. . . a couple of . . .

S he sleeps a lot. Is it because of what the bad shadows did to her?"

"Yes. She's . . . she's not well."

"Should I make her tea? She likes my tea."

Harper looked at Rochat, remembering him again from that first night on the esplanade. Seeing how much the lad wanted to do the right thing, and the lad clueless how horribly dead he'd end up doing it.

"She needs more than a cup of tea. She needs a doctor."

"We can take her to the University Hospital. It's very close to the cathedral."

"No, we need to get her to someone who can fix her, the way you fixed me."

"Because they broke her wings and she can't fly anymore."

"That's right, mate, because they broke her wings."

"What can we do to help her?"

Harper pulled the maquette between them. "Is there a way down from the belfry, besides the tower steps?"

*"Oui."* Rochat tapped the north side of the belfry, just above the cathedral roof. "There's a drainpipe here, and you can climb down to the cathedral roof. I used to play hide-and-seek with Monsieur Buhlmann and he could never find me when I climbed down the pipe because I'd sneak through the roof."

"The roof?"

Rochat tapped the gable above the main doors. "There's a little door here, and I sneak through and walk on the ceiling above the nave. It's like walking through a field of giant turtles."

Harper looked up to the domes of the vaulted ceiling fifty meters above their heads. "It would at that. But this time you're not playing hide-and-seek. You want to get to the ground as fast as you can."

Rochat turned through the book, pointed to the drawings of high balconies running just under the vault. "You can go down to *le coursier*, then there's lots of ways down to the floor of the nave."

"But you're still inside the cathedral and we've barricaded all the doors. Is there a way outside, besides the doors?"

Rochat turned to the next page. "There's some stairs to the triforium and a passageway to the balcony here. It goes behind the organ. We can go outside, behind the big stained glass of Jesus to where the monks had a garden behind the gargoyles."

Harper watched Rochat's face, knew the lad was giving it all he had. "And then?"

"Oh." Rochat turned the maquette, the façade facing them, pointing to just above the statues at the cathedral doors. "There's an old chain ladder from middles of ages, for when the monks had to run away from invadermen and fires. They could toss it down the façade and climb down to the esplanade by Monsieur Moses."

"Where?"

Rochat pointed to one of the statues at the main doors of the cathedral. Harper traced his finger from the doors and over the cobblestones of the maquette.

"And the wooden stairs down to Place de la Palud . . ."

"Escaliers du Marché."

". . . it's what, fifteen meters away from the main doors?"

"Five. I counted the steps with Papa and he said fifteen steps means five meters. Was he right?"

"Exactly." Harper skimmed through the drawings of the belfry, the two levels for the bells, a roof position to serve as lookout. "Right. I need you to imagine something with me."

"I'm very good at imagining things."

"I know, that's why you'll understand. When they come, they'll hide in the shadows. And they'll come as a full killing squad this time. That'll make it a total of their six against you and me."

"How do you know, monsieur?"

"Dealing with the bad shadows is my job, mate. Look, they can manipulate physical things from the shadows, so they'll be dangerous. But to take anything out of the cathedral, they must transmigrate into form."

"When they look like people."

"That's right, when they look like people. And that's when I can slaughter them."

"How do we make them trans . . . thing?"

Harper pointed to Katherine. "They want her, they'll have to come and get her."

"But there's very little room in the belfry, and it's high from the ground."

"That's just it." Harper turned the drawings of the belfry toward Rochat. "The layout of the belfry acts as a force multiplier."

"Is that a good thing?"

"Worked well enough for us at Thermopylae."

"I don't know where that is. Do I have to know where that is to help the angel go home?"

"No, mate. All you need to know is how to get Miss Taylor down the tower, through the roof, and out of the cathedral. You get down Escaliers du Marché. Don't look back, keep going."

"Where do we go?"

"To the train station, should take you no more than fifteen minutes. Don't stop, don't look back. Take the first train anywhere out of Lausanne. Then make your way to Gare de Lyon in Paris. Go to the main hall and head upstairs to the bistro called—"

"—Le Train Bleu. It has funny pictures on the ceiling."

"You know the place?"

"Papa took me to Paris once and we had lunch there. I had croque-monsieur and Papa had entrecôte. But Gare de Lyon is very big and there's lots of people and I might forget how to find things."

"Don't worry, Miss Taylor will get you there."

"Are we going there for lunch?"

"No, you're going to meet someone. Someone like me."

"A detectiveman?"

"Sure, a detectiveman. He'll be waiting for you, and he'll get Miss Taylor some help."

Rochat thought about it. "But how will the detective-man like you know I'm bringing the angel to Le Train Bleu?"

"I phoned ahead."

*"Pardon?"*

Harper nodded to the hundreds of candles alight on the crossing square, the light rising to the high windows of the lantern tower. Rochat watched the light against the leaded glass form into repeating shapes of shadows and light. Three flashes, six flashes, three flashes, six flashes.

"I can see it. It's the same as the warning sound Clémence makes. Can the detectiveman in Paris see it?"

"He can see it."

"Can the bad shadows see it?"

"No, they've lost the ability to read light. Too much shadow jumping, too much dead black in their blood."

Rochat had no idea what that meant. "Oh."

Harper watched the lad continue to stare into the lan-

tern tower as if seeing light for the first time. He tapped
gently at Rochat's arm. Rochat looked at him, his eyes
sparkling with reflected light.

"You remember what you have to do?"

Rochat thought again about all the things the detectiveman had told him. He imagined himself helping the
angel down from the belfry, through the cathedral roof,
out of the cathedral. He imagined them going to Gare
Simplon, taking a train to Paris. He imagined another
detectiveman taking the angel to a doctor and giving her
a new place to hide.

"Will the other detectiveman know she's an angel?"

"He'll look at you and know everything."

"Will he bring me back to Lausanne in time to call
the hour?"

Harper shook his head. "You don't come back."

"I don't understand."

"You're in as much danger as Miss Taylor, you can't
stay in Lausanne."

"But . . . but . . . what will you do?"

"Stay behind, buy you time."

"How can you buy time?"

"I kill them."

"You can kill the bad shadows?"

"Told you, it's my job, it's why I'm here. And you
can't be here when I do my job."

"But it's my duty to call the hour."

"Listen to me, it's not the bad shadows that want you
killed. You've been listed."

"I don't know what that means."

"It means your life, this life, it's running out of time. You're going to die."

"When?"

"Soon."

Rochat took off his black floppy hat and scratched his head, pulled down the hat again. "Maman said people shouldn't be afraid of death."

"You're not like other people."

"Will I be dead forever?"

"If they get their way, yes."

"Can you stop it from happening, monsieur?"

"It's against the rules, but I'm going to try. But you need to get out of Lausanne and hide. And you can never come back."

Rochat turned away and shuffled a few steps. He stopped and turned back to Harper, almost speaking, but then turning again and picking up his lantern instead. He shuffled to the pillars of the chancel dome and rapped the stone boots of the form in the white sarcophagus. Harper listened to Rochat talking quietly.

"*Bonsoir.* Yes, I know it's very late, but it's never very late till midnight and then it's very early. The detective-man wants me to leave the cathedral and take the angel to another hiding place because she's sick. And if I don't go I'll be dead forever and . . ."

Another voice echoed at Harper's back.

"He won't leave the cathedral, Harper, and I won't leave without him."

He turned, saw Katherine propped on one elbow. She looked half asleep.

"Miss Taylor?"

"Yeah, I know, you thought I was sleeping, so did I. Maybe I still am and this is a dream. Because it feels like one of those dreams where you know you're dreaming and you sort of wake up, but you know you're still asleep."

"How much did you hear?"

"Enough to know you want us to go to Paris and meet someone like you at Gare de Lyon. What the hell are you doing, Harper?"

"It's the only chance the two of you have to survive the day."

"Too bad, you're stuck with us."

"Miss Taylor . . ."

"We're not leaving."

"You don't know what you're up against."

"Read my lips, Harper: I won't leave without Marc, and Marc won't leave the cathedral. Will you, Marc?"

Harper looked over his shoulder. He saw Rochat shuffle toward him.

"I'm *le guet de Lausanne*, monsieur. It's my duty to protect the cathedral."

"See, Harper? It's his duty to protect his cathedral."

"This cathedral's about to become a battleground."

"I can help you fight them, monsieur. I'm very strong from the legs up."

"They're coming for blood, mate. You're no match for them."

"Oh, get with my dream, Harper. Because in my dream, I'm a princess trapped in a tower by the evil wizard and you two are pirates in paper hats and you're telling me none of this was an accident and there's all these intersecting lines of causality and that the three of us were brought to Lausanne and ended up in the tower for a reason. And I'm dreaming Marc helps you imagine where the future-teller diamond is, because I'm not the only thing the evil wizard wants from the tower. So you guys best jump on your flying caterpillar and get busy and come up with Plan B."

Katherine laid her head down, and she closed her eyes.

"And keep it down. Otto and I need our rest."

Rochat and Harper stood still a long minute, staring at the sleeping woman on the bench.

"Monsieur?"

"Hmm?"

"Was the angel talking in her sleep?"

Harper rubbed the back of his neck. " 'Sleep hath its own world, And a wide realm of wild reality.' "

"I don't know what that means."

"It means I'm not sure it was even her talking. More like someone was sending us a message through her."

Rochat looked around the nave; it was empty. Harper laughed to himself.

"Oldest trick in the book. Feed them Plan A, clobber them with Plan B."

"What's a Plan A?"

"A hundred lines of causality set in motion long before you were born, before Miss Taylor was born. All meant to intersect and collide in one big bang, right here in Lausanne Cathedral."

"Oh. What's a Plan B?"

"You, you're Plan B."

Rochat almost took off his hat to scratch his head to think about it. He looked at Harper instead. "Monsieur, I'm very confused."

"Mate, I've been here two and a half million years, and this place still confuses the hell out of me now and again."

Harper looked around the altar; Rochat followed his gaze.

"Is something else wrong, monsieur?"

"Who's . . . who is Otto?"

Rochat pointed to the sarcophagus in the pillars. "Over there. He's the brave knight from longtimes ago. Sometimes I imagine he stumbles around the cathedral at night looking for something. I like to imagine he's looking for his lance, but it's outside, under the belfry. It's the spire from the top of the Apostles' entrance, but I like to imagine it's his lance and that when he picks it up he falls over and can't get up. He told me I have to stay because it's my duty."

Harper looked at Rochat. "Really is full of dreams and wonder, this place, isn't it?"

"*Oui*, it's Lausanne Cathedral."

"That it is. Back in a tick."

Rochat watched Harper walk to Katherine and slowly pass his open palm down across her eyes as if closing them. He heard his voice.

"*Dulcis et alta quies placidaeque similima morti . . .*'"

"What did you do to her?"

"Making sure she gets some rest while you and I imagine a few more things."

Rochat watched the detectiveman tap the flagstones with his shoe. "Are we imagining something now, monsieur?"

"As a matter of fact, we are."

"Oh, what are we imagining?"

"We're imagining that the earth under these stones is sacred."

Rochat thought about it. "Because the skeletons live down there?"

"I rather think it's something else."

Rochat watched the detectiveman walk slowly between the burning candles on the crossing square, reading the light, kneeling, and rearranging the flames like rearranging the words on a page.

"Are you making another phone call?"

"I am."

"What are you saying?"

"Message received, will comply."

Harper finished with the candles. He walked the perimeter of the altar, his eyes looking at the candles on the flagstones, then up to the lantern tower and down again. Rochat watched him walk in ever-smaller circles, wondering if they were getting there and why he was walking in circles. Just then the detectiveman stopped and looked up into the lantern tower and pointed to one high-above thread of light amid the glow of a hundred candles. Rochat could see it. How perfectly straight it was. And he watched the detectiveman follow the thread of light seventy meters down to the one candle on the flagstone amid a hundred others. The one candle marking the exact center of the crossing square. He watched the detectiveman tap the stone with the tip of his shoe.

"What's under this stone, mate, right here?"

"The well."

"The well."

"*Oui.*"

"What kind of well?"

"A very old kind of well."

"And what do we imagine might be in a very old kind of well?"

Rochat thought about it. "A lunch box."

# thirty-eight

They crossed the transept to the ambulatory, took the three steps down to the iron gate of the crypt. Rochat stopped.

"What if the angel wakes up?"

"She won't wake up till I tell her to."

*"Non?"*

"Old trick we detectives have."

"Oh."

Rochat pulled his ring of keys from his overcoat, found the oldest key, slipped it in the rusting lock. *Kak-lack.* He pulled open the gate, ducked under the low stone lintel, turned back to Harper. "Don't step on the skeletons, monsieur, they're very old."

Harper smelled ancient dirt. He saw a dozen skeletons in open graves, their chalky bones glowing in the lantern light. He followed the lad's shuffling steps along a narrow dirt path between the graves, not quite able to stand upright for the low ceiling. He felt a slash of pain and pressed his hand on the bandage covering the wound. Rochat pointed ahead.

"That's the stone arch where I hit my head. And over there's where I dropped my pencils, and those are the skeletons that were laughing at me." Rochat lowered the lantern to a grave at the arch where a fragile-as-dust skeleton lay with its skull turned to the side. "And this skeleton was looking at the well, and I imagined he was telling me one of my pencils fell inside. That's how I found the lunch box."

Rochat ducked through the arch. Harper followed the lad and his lantern to a bigger cavern and hundreds more graves. All filled with skeletons on their backs, all with their hands crossed over their chests, all looking melded into the earth. The ground dipped and Harper straightened up, his head just brushing the stone ceiling. He saw the field of bones around him.

"Are they all like this, arms crossed over their chests?"

"They're all like this. I imagined they were seeds and someone planted them in the earth to grow again."

"Not too far off, actually."

"Really?"

"Yes, I'll tell you all about it later."

They moved farther through the bone garden to a third cave where the skeletons lay in concentric rings. Dead center was a round stone structure standing a meter and a half above the graves.

"Is that it, the well?"

"That's the well."

Harper saw the heavy iron grate and the twelve spikes emanating from the center, each one stretching twenty centimeters beyond the rim of the well. He made a slow 360 around it, touching each point of the spikes.

"I imagined it looked like a compass," Rochat said.

"That's exactly what it is. With the well as the center point from which all directions lead." Harper's eyes followed the lines of the compass, each one pointing to more arches and tunnels. "Where do the tunnels lead?"

"To more caves with skeletons."

"And all the tunnels and graves are on this level? None of them go deeper than the foundations of the cathedral?"

Rochat thought about it. "Is that the feet?"

"What?"

"The feet of the cathedral?"

"Sure, the feet."

"Nothing's under the feet but solid rock, that's what Papa said."

"Did he ever mention any false walls or hidden doors anywhere down here?"

"*Non.*"

Harper looked down through the iron grate. "So where's the lunch box?"

Rochat held his lantern over the grate and pointed down through the spikes. "It's there, stuck in the stones."

Harper set his shoulder under one of the spikes and heaved. It wouldn't budge. "How did you reach it?"

Rochat set the lantern on the edge of a grave and

shuffled to a pile of timber. He drew a thick length and carried it to the well.

"I imagined I could use this to hold up the compass, then I squeezed under and reached down."

"Good thinking."

*"Merci."*

They worked the plank under the iron spikes and lifted the grate. Harper braced his weight against it and Rochat squeezed through the opening, hanging over the lip of the well, reaching down.

"I have it, monsieur."

Harper grabbed the back of Rochat's coat and pulled. He slid from under the grate and held up a silver box by its handle. Bloody hell if it didn't look like a schoolboy's lunch box, Harper thought. They knelt in the dirt, the silver box between them. Harper tapped it gently.

"Titanium."

"I don't know what that means."

"It means it's a very expensive lunch box."

Harper set it upright, saw the combination lock set to triple zero. He flipped at the latches with his thumbs.

"Nine nine eight are the numbers to open it."

"You know the combination?"

"I imagined all the numbers the wheels could make, then I made a phone book and checked them one by one. It took me all day."

"You're telling me you opened it and you know what's inside?"

"I saw what's inside but I didn't know what it was."

"You tell anyone else you opened it?"

"Monsieur Buhlmann told me to put it back where I found it and forget about it before I remembered to tell him what was inside. So I put it back and forgot till we imagined it in the nave, because I'm very good at forgetting things."

"Right. So, nine nine eight, then?"

"Nine nine eight. Do you want to see?"

"I certainly do."

Rochat lifted the lantern over the box. Harper turned the three dials . . . *click*.

He flipped the latches, raised the lid. Lantern light sparkled along a narrow rod of polished iron, fifteen centimeters long. A starlike cluster of delicate iron spikes at one end, a small holed-out oval at the other end. It was fitted into a slab of black foam.

"Do you know what it is, monsieur?"

"A key."

Rochat pulled his ring of keys from his overcoat. "It doesn't look like a key, and I have lots of them."

"It's a key, all right. Question is, to what?" Harper lifted the key from the box, stood, and held it by the oval, letting the tiny spikes hang down toward the iron grate. "Let's have your lantern up here a sec."

Rochat jumped up and lifted the lantern over their heads. Harper lowered the key to the center of the grate. Twelve spikes on the well grate, twelve spikes on the key, all pointing in the same twelve directions.

"They look alike, monsieur."

"And the grate and key each have one spike a tad longer than the rest. So line them up to match and . . . which direction is it pointing?"

"East."

"So the cardinal point of the well's compass is east."

"Where I stand when I begin to call the hour."

"And where first light comes from." Harper leaned over the well again, looked down into the dark. "How deep is it?"

"Twenty-five meters."

"What's the well used for?"

"Monsieur Buhlmann says they used to pour holy waters down there when they were old."

"Does anyone ever go down there?"

"It's forbidden."

"Who says?"

"Monsieur Buhlmann. He said the well is very old and the walls could cave in."

"I bet he did. Who is Monsieur Buhlmann, anyway?"

"He taught me to hold the lantern and say the words."

"The words?"

*"C'est le guet, il—"*

*"—a sonné l'heure."*

Rochat stared at Harper. "You know the words, too, monsieur?"

"Yes, I know the words." Harper tugged at the grate. "Look, we have to get down there for a look."

"But Monsieur Buhlmann said—"

"—the walls could fall in, I know. But the key was hidden in the well for a reason. We need to see if the reason is down there."

"Because you're a detectiveman trying to solve a mysterious mystery."

"Exactly, and I'm sure Monsieur Buhlmann would understand."

"*D'accord.*"

They set their shoulders under the grate and heaved, once, twice, till the heavy thing slid off the well and hit the dirt with a dull thud and a cloud of dust filled the cavern. They covered their mouths, waited for the dust to clear. Rochat held the lantern into the well.

"I don't see anything, monsieur."

"Hard to tell from up here. Any rope down here?"

"The workmen keep tools in an empty cave under the north transept. We can get there through the tunnels."

They hurried through the tunnels and graves to a small cave stuffed with shovels and picks, timber, coils of five-meter-length rope. They carried six coils back to the well, lashed the ropes together, and secured one end to the iron grate. They laid the heavy length of timber across the grate to weigh it down. They eased the rope down the well. Harper lifted his legs over the top and climbed in. He braced his feet against the crumbling stones, lowering himself a meter. Bits of dirt and stone broke from the inside of the well. He stopped and waited.

"So far, so good."

"Wait, monsieur, you'll need light to see things." Rochat reached in his overcoat and pulled out a spare candle. He handed it to Harper. "And I have matches, too."

"Cheers—"

The stones under Harper's feet broke loose, the rope slipped from his hands.

"Fuck!"

"Monsieur!"

Rochat heard Harper hit bottom.

*Boom, boom, boom.*

"Monsieur, are you all right?"

Harper's voice called up through the dusty dark. "I'm all right. I managed to grab the rope and break my fall. But I can't see a bloody thing. Toss me the matches."

Harper heard them hit the dirt. He felt around and found them. He scratched a match alight, touched the flame to the candle's wick. He did a slow turn, saw nothing but the inside of a very old well. He pulled and pushed at the stones, everything solidly in place.

"Is there anything down there, monsieur?"

"Nothing that shouldn't be here. We must be looking in the wrong place."

"*Pardon*, monsieur, but what are we looking for, because I can't remember."

"Not really sure. A door, another lunch box, who knows?" Harper blew out the candle, grabbed the rope between his hands. "Keep the rope steady, I'm climbing up."

"*D'accord.* I'm very glad you're not hurt, monsieur. It sounded like you fell down a very deep tunnel, because when you hit the ground it made a very big echo."

"What did you say?"

"When you hit the ground, there was an echo like you fell down a very deep hole."

"It did, didn't it?"

"*Oui.*"

Harper jumped back to the floor of the well. *Boom, boom, boom.* He relit the wick and lowered the candle to the floor of the well. Nothing but the hardened ground of centuries-old dirt. He picked up one of the fallen stones, got to his feet and let it go. *Boom, boom, boom.* The sound sinking deep, deeper, till it faded away. He looked up and saw Rochat leaning over the top of the well, lantern in his hands.

"Could you go back to the cave with the tools and bring a shovel?"

"I can bring a shovel."

Harper sat in the dirt, staring at the burning candle in his hands. Almost trembling with excitement before reminding himself it was only the phantom of a dead man. Or maybe it was something else. The earth under these stones was sacred to our kind, Gabriel had said. Didn't know why, couldn't know why. Been sent to this place two and a half million years ago. Lost all contact with the creator. As if the creator himself had disappeared and they were truly a pack of lost angels, hiding in the forms of men so long that all memory of where they'd come from was gone. And the only knowledge they had of themselves was from the legends and myths and religions of men. Stones are sacred to our kind. This is all that is left to us. *What the hell is down here?* He laughed to himself, thinking how much he was acting like one of the locals: *So this is what it feels like to be like them.*

"Monsieur, cover your head. I'll put the timber over the well and come down."

Harper looked up, saw the lad leaning into the well.

"No, I need a shovel."

"It's in my coat."

Bits of dust and stone jolted free as Rochat mounted the top of the well, slung his lantern over his shoulder, and twisted down the rope, touching the ground quiet as a cat. Harper nodded.

"Very impressive."

"I was first in my school in rope-climbing because I'm very strong from the legs up."

"I remember. Where's the shovel?"

Rochat turned in the cramped surroundings and handed his lantern to Harper. He pulled the shovel from the back of his overcoat.

"I'll dig, monsieur."

Harper blew out his candle and slipped the stub in his pocket. He squeezed up against the stones of the well to get out of the way. "Go right ahead."

The same hollow sound sinking deep and falling away each time the shovel hit the ground. *Boom, boom, boom . . . boom, boom, boom . . . boom, boom, boom . . . thunk.* Harper brushed away the dirt with his hands and saw lantern light glint on metal. Rochat cleared more dirt with the shovel. A rounded iron door in the center of the ground. Barely wide enough for a man to squeeze through.

"It looks very old, monsieur."

"Older than the cathedral, a lot older."

Harper pulled at the handle; Rochat pried the shovel under the edge. It opened with a shrill cry falling into utter darkness. Fresh air seeped out. Harper lowered to his knees, peered in with the lantern. A round shaft, meter and a half wide, carved from solid black rock. Iron rungs running down one side and stretching into utter blackness. Harper pulled himself up, rested his back against the stones of the well. Rochat looked at him with curiosity.

"What is it, monsieur?"

"A hole in the ground. And it's deep."

"How deep is deep?"

"Good question. Hold this."

Harper handed the lantern to Rochat, dug in his trouser pockets, and found a coin. He held it over the center of the shaft opening. Rochat grabbed Harper's sleeve.

"Monsieur, wait."

"What?"

"That's five francs. Don't you have anything smaller?"

"Nope."

Harper let the coin fall. They held their breaths and listened. Nothing, nothing, nothing. As if the earth swallowed the coin. Harper looked at Rochat.

"Like I said, deep."

"Who made this place, monsieur?"

"That is the question."

Rochat quickly hooked the lantern over his shoulder and scrambled for the iron rungs. Harper grabbed him by the shoulder.

"Hey, what are you doing?"

"It's my cathedral."

"Right. After you then."

*"Merci."*

Harper checked his watch. Mark at fifty-five. He followed Rochat into the shaft. They worked down the iron rungs, the lantern light reflecting on the carved-out rock. Tiny flecks of light sparkled in the black stone, and there were flashes of green and red and blue. Deeper and deeper down. Harper heard the lad mumbling to himself as they climbed. He checked at his watch; ten minutes on. Looking up, no longer able to see the open iron door above, just blackness. Deeper. Twenty minutes, losing all sense of perspective. Like sinking through a void with nothing but the lad's lantern to separate them from darkness.

"We're at the bottom, monsieur."

Harper looked at his watch. Forty-five minutes down. He noticed the second hand stuck in place; he held the crystal to his ear.

"Is something wrong with your watch, monsieur?"

"It's stopped."

Harper stepped from the last rung onto a solid rock floor, squeezed around to face Rochat. The lad with the lantern in one hand, a small well-dented coin in the other.

"Here's your five francs, monsieur."

Harper smiled. "Tell you what, mate, you keep it for the both of us. For good luck."

*"D'accord."*

They looked up. Nothing beyond the glow of the lantern on the black walls, as if all the world had disappeared.

"I've never seen anything like it, monsieur, except when I'm in the nave at night and playing space captain."

"Sorry?"

"Sometimes I sit at the organ and pretend I'm flying through outer space. It feels like that down here. Like we're floating in outer space." He held up the lantern and made a slow pass along the black stone wall. "And all these little colors look like stars."

Harper watched the reflecting colors appear and fade in the passing light. His eyes separating the light from dark and seeing the patterns.

"They are stars."

*"Pardon?"*

"Look here. Andromeda, Virgo, Taurus, Cepheus— all of them. And up here, constellations no one on earth could know, and all the stars . . . Bloody hell, it's a map of the entire universe."

"What does that mean?"

"It means you're one hell of a space captain."

"Oh." Rochat slowly waved his lantern again, studying the points of light. "What's this one here, monsieur?"

Harper saw where Rochat was looking. "Taurus. And this small group of stars in the constellation is Pleiades, the seven sisters."

Rochat stared at the tiny cluster of stars, tipping his head from one side to the other. "Like the bells."

"Bells?"

"In the tower. There are seven bells in the belfry, and they're sisters, too. Is that a clue?"

"This stage of the game, mate, nothing would surprise me about this place." Harper looked up. "How the bloody hell did they do this? It's so far down."

"Two thousand four hundred and forty-nine steps."

"You counted them?"

*"Oui."*

Harper looked at the iron rungs in the black stone wall. A meter of separation between each. Another meter from the last rung to the ground. Two and a half kilometers down.

"Same as the depth of the well times one thousand. Exactly the same as Christ the Savior Cathedral in Moscow."

"What's a Christ the Savior Cathedral in Moscow?"

"A cathedral on the other side of Europe. Someone found a shaft like this. That's where the key was found."

"Does that mean we found another clue?"

"I don't know. Unless . . . hold up the lantern again. Let's push against the wall, see if it opens up anywhere."

They circled back to back in the confined space, pushing against stone. It was solid.

"Nothing, monsieur."

"But there's fresh air down here. It's coming from somewhere." Harper sank to the floor, felt around the lowest iron rung. "Here, the air's seeping through here. Bring us the lantern."

Rochat lowered the lantern close to the iron rung. Harper touched his palms to the stone, felt air seeping through microscopic holes drilled through rock. He pulled at the rung; it shifted a bit.

"This is it, give us a hand."

Rochat set the lantern on the ground and scrunched down next to Harper. They grabbed the rung.

"One, two, three."

They pulled hard, and a meter-square section of stone separated from the wall. A gust of sweet air rushed at their faces. They leaned down, saw a small iron gate set back in the rock face.

"It looks much older than the door in the well, monsieur."

"And there's not a nick on it." Harper saw a multipointed slot cut in the gate. He patted his pockets. "Bollocks, I forgot to bring the key."

"*Pas grave*, I imagined we'd need it."

"Sorry?"

Rochat pulled it from inside his overcoat and handed it to him.

"That's damn good imagining."

"*Merci.*"

Harper held the key to the lock. "It fits, but all the slots in the lock are of equal length. Which way does it go?"

"We can guess, because that's what detectivemen do."

"True."

Harper slipped the key in the lock, jiggled it left and right; nothing. He refitted the key, tried again; nothing. He held the spiked end of the key close to the lantern, saw the one spike a half-centimeter longer than the rest. The iron compass atop the well flashed through his brain, cardinal point of the compass pointing toward first light, not north.

"Bloody hell, I'm such a dolt. Which way is east?"

Rochat rose to his knees, held his elbows close to his sides, extended his forearms as best he could, and twisted from side to side five or six times before pointing in the direction of the iron gate.

"That way."

"You sure?"

*"Oui."*

Harper leaned down to the lock, sat back up. "Just out of curiosity, how'd you figure that?"

"When I was coming down the rope, I counted how many times I twisted around and added it to which way the ladder was."

"You like to count things, don't you?"

"It helps me imagine other things."

"Right, I'll give it a try sometime. Because so far your imagining is a hell of a lot better than mine."

Harper turned the key till the longest spike pointed straight up, east as north. He slid the key into the lock and turned . . . *kaklack*. He pushed against the gate. It opened with the greatest of ease, and another rush of sweet air hit them in the face. This time it was moist and came on waves of rushing sound.

"What's that noise, monsieur?"

"Sounds like water, lots of it. Didn't you say Lausanne has its own underground source?"

*"Oui."*

"I think we just found it."

"Is that why they made the tunnel?"

"Probably one of the reasons they made it here."

"What's the other reason?"

"Let's find out. Care to have a look with your lantern? Your cathedral and all."

Rochat didn't even wait to answer. He twisted to all fours and crawled through the door. Harper heard his voice calling back.

"It's another very long tunnel going sideways, monsieur, and it's very narrow. We need to crawl on our stomachs."

"Swell. And it's dark, I bet."

"*Oui.*" Rochat pulled himself from the tunnel. "But there's a light at the other end."

"You must be joking."

Something bright fell across her face. She opened her eyes to a luminescent shaft of color passing slowly over her. Her eyes followed it to the crossing square of the transept, where a raggedy old man stood in the colored light amid the hundreds of candles set about the flagstones.

Katherine sat up and looked him over. Pockmarked skin, yellow teeth, worn-out clothes, coughing up phlegm into a filthy handkerchief. He turned to her.

"Be not afraid."

"I'm not, but who are you?"

"A messenger."

She looked at the altar, saw the maquette of the cathedral, the book. "Where's Marc, where's Harper?"

"They'll soon be back. And I want you to tell them

something. I want you to tell them, *Una salus victis nullam sperare salutem.*"

"I'm dreaming, aren't I? That's why I'm not afraid."

"*Sí*, you are dreaming. So the words will be easy for you to remember. *Una salus victis nullam sperare salutem.*"

"That sounds like Latin."

"*Sí.*"

"I'll never remember it."

"You will, because this is a dream."

Katherine looked around the nave, saw people standing shadowlike and faceless, but she could feel them watching. "What . . . who are they?"

"Undying souls waiting to be born into another life."

"I don't understand."

"That is how it is done."

"How what's done?"

"Never-ending life on earth." He walked toward her and held out his hand. His skin was cracked and there was dirt under his nails. "Come, walk with me."

She looked up to his face. Scraggly stubble for a beard, his hair hanging in greasy clumps, the brightest eyes. Still, she couldn't help but feel a gentleness from him.

"Your eyes, they're so green. The same as Marc and Harper."

"Then you know you're safe with me."

She gave him her hand, and he led her through the burning candles on the flagstones to the center of the crossing square. He turned her to the south transept. She raised her eyes to the rose window. Each piece of stained glass seeming to ignite like sparks of colored fire.

"Gosh, the light . . . it's so beautiful."

He stepped behind her, raised her arms, turned her palms to the window. "And you will be the bearer of the light."

A shaft of color took shape and cut through the dull gray light in the cathedral, touching the floor and racing over the stones and crossing her feet. She looked into the window, as if standing in the middle of a rainbow. The man stepped in front of her, the brilliant light glowing all around him as he faded into silhouette.

"Where are you going?"

"To purify the light before it touches the life within you. *C'est le guet, il a sonné l'heure, il a sonné l'heure.*"

# thirty-nine

M iss Taylor, Miss Taylor."

Katherine woke and saw Harper standing over her, Rochat next to him with his lantern in his hand.

"Hey, I must have dozed off." She lifted herself from the wooden bench. The blankets slipped from her shoulders. She noticed their clothes covered in dust, the dirt on their hands and faces. "What've you guys been doing? You're filthy."

Rochat looked at Harper; Harper looked at Katherine.

"Stacking chairs, we were stacking chairs at the doors."

"Didn't you do that already . . . Marc?"

*"Oui?"*

"I just woke up and that lantern's really bright."

*"Pardon."*

Rochat lowered the lantern. Katherine saw their faces.

"You're sunburned, the two of you."

Harper looked at Rochat; Rochat looked at Katherine. He said the first thing that came into his head.

"We went on the balconies of the lantern tower to check the doors were locked and the sun is very bright today."

"Wait, you guys left me alone? No wonder I was having weird dreams."

"Nightmare kind of dreams?"

"No, Marc, just the run-of-the-mill weird kind." She folded the blankets, remembering. "I dreamed the sun was coming through that big stained-glass window and this guy was floating in the light. He was saying the words Marc says when he calls the hour. Kind of funny, if you think about it."

"What did he look like, Miss Taylor?"

"What do you mean, what did he look like? It was a dream, you know how dreams are."

"Actually, I don't."

"What?"

"Did he look like a tramp?"

Katherine raised an eyebrow. "Yeah, how did you know?"

"What did he say to you?"

"Gibberish, that's the way people talk in dreams, the way you're talking now."

Harper pulled the blankets from her hands, set them on the bench. "Miss Taylor, it's important. What did he say to you?"

"What's going on, Harper?"

He didn't answer.

"This comes under the heading of things I wouldn't understand in a billion years, doesn't it?"

"Something like that."

"Okay." Katherine pointed to the burning candles on the crossing square. "He was over there. He told me you guys were gone, that you'd be back, and he said something in Latin . . . *Una salus victis* . . . something. I told him I'd never remember it."

*"Una salus victis nullam sperare salutem."*

"Yeah, and now you're freaking me out."

"What else?"

"Harper . . ."

"Tell me."

"He took me for a walk."

"Where?"

"On the altar."

"Show me."

"Harper, it was a dream."

"Show me."

"Fine."

She walked to the center of the crossing square and turned and faced the giant stained-glass window in the south transept wall.

"He said, 'Walk with me,' and he took my hand and led me here, in the middle of these candles."

"On that exact spot, dead center of the altar square?"

"Yeah, right here. And he held out my arms and turned the palms of my hands toward the window and he told me to watch the light. I remember the sun passed by the stained-glass window and it got really warm. Then there were all these colors. I remember it felt like I was standing in the middle of a rainbow. That's when he started to float away into the light, and he said something about purifying the light to protect the life inside me, me being the bearer of light . . . Don't stare at me like that, Harper. I told you it was a dream."

"What else happened in the dream?"

"I don't know. No, I do . . . Everything went bright as the sun and the nave was filled with people watching us. It was really weird because they didn't have faces, they were just shapes. The tramp said they were the undying souls to be born into a new . . . Now you're staring at me, Marc. What is it?"

"I . . . I was wondering where my lantern was."

"It's in your hands."

Rochat looked down to his lantern. "Oh. *Merci.*"

"You know, you two lunatics are acting weirder than the guy in my dream. Sorry, Marc, you're not a lunatic. It's just an expression."

*"Pas grave."*

Twelve deep-throated gongs rolled through the nave.

Harper looked at his watch, tapped the crystal. Rochat leaned close to him.

"Is your watch still broken, monsieur?"

"No, it's ticking again, just backward."

"That's because it's a cheap watch, Harper. First thing I noticed about you at LP's."

The sun crossed the giant rose window. The thousands of pieces of colored glass sparkled like tiny jewels. Katherine shaded her eyes.

"And it's a good thing it was only a dream or that'd

make the third time today the sun was going by that window. Man, it's all so weird, isn't it?"

Katherine turned, saw the two of them huddled over the wristwatch. She walked close to them. She saw the watch winding back and slowing to a stop and then racing ahead. One thirty, two, three fifteen, three forty. Katherine threw up her hands.

"Okay, I give up. I'm lying back down because, obviously, I'm still dreaming."

Harper looked at her. "Miss Taylor, earlier, do you remember telling me the lad would never leave the cathedral, telling me to get with your dream, Plan B?"

"Huh?"

"That's what I thought. Good night."

"Huh?"

Harper passed his palm in front of Katherine's face. *"Dulcis et alta . . ."*

She fell back into Rochat before Harper finished the words. Rochat stumbled, the flame in his lantern flickered.

"The lantern, mate. Don't drop it!"

Rochat quickly steadied himself. Still-burning lantern in one hand, collapsed angel in the other.

"I've got them both, monsieur. But why did you—"

A terrible growling wind rose from beyond the cathedral walls, snapping and biting at the stones. Black mist seeped through the spaces under the doors and crawled along the flagstones to snuff out the candles on the crossing square. The light in the nave grew dim and the long shaft of tubular light pouring through the giant stained glass in the south transept wall seemed to slow amid a billion motes of dust. Harper saw the dazed expression crossing Rochat's face.

"C'mon, mate, you know how time works. You can see this, just blink."

Rochat blinked. His eyes seeing the world gone still as a photograph. The unmoving threads of colored light, the motionless dust, the still-life wisps of smoke from the snuffed candles on the crossing square. Only the flame in his lantern moved. He reached out with a finger and poked at the threads of light hanging in the air. Small concentric waves rippled outward.

"It's like throwing a stone in Lac Léman."

"If only it were going to be as much fun."

*"Pardon?"*

Harper nodded toward the leaded glass in the walls of the chancel. Rochat saw black mist spreading quickly over all the windows and across the giant rose window in the south transept wall, casting the nave into complete darkness but for the fire in Rochat's lantern. The growling wind pounded on the doors, sending shock waves through the unmoving world of the cathedral.

"I'm very sure evil has returned to Lausanne, monsieur."

"I'm very sure you're right." Carefully, Harper took the lantern from Rochat. "Take Miss Taylor, get in the alcove over there."

Rochat gathered Katherine in his arms and shuffled quickly to the Virgin's chapel near the south transept.

Harper grabbed the wool blankets from the bench, ran after him, tossing one of the blankets to Rochat.

"Cover her with the blanket, cover yourself with your overcoat."

Rochat tucked himself in the small alcove. He pulled Katherine close to him and wrapped her in the blanket. He saw Harper dropping to his knees between two tightly fitted pillars, wrapping a blanket around his shoulders.

"Monsieur, the fire in the lantern, it's dying!"

Harper saw the choking flame. "Just get down!"

Rochat pulled the collar of his overcoat over his head, peeked through the buttons, and saw Harper lean over the lantern and breathe into the flame before disappearing under his blanket. The cathedral dissolved into blackest dark. The growling wind beyond the doors wound to an earsplitting pitch . . .

Then silence.

Rochat pulled Katherine closer. "Be not afraid, be not afraid."

The wind howled again and the cathedral doors broke open with a terrifying crash. The barricades of wooden chairs flew through the nave, smashed into the pillars and arches, and shattered apart. All the doors tore from their hinges, skidded over the flagstones, and slammed into the stone walls. The leaded-glass windows in the high balconies exploded into dust. Then all the windows of the nave and along the chancel. The great rose window in the south transept wall crackled and cracked and distended inward till it burst apart with a horrible crash and the sum of man's knowledge when the world was flat fell through the nave like flecks of colored snow.

It was silent again.

Rochat saw Harper looking toward him from under his blanket, his finger at his lips—*Don't move, don't make a sound*—pointing to the broken doorways. Black mist crept over the threshold and moved over the flagstones as if hunting prey. Sniffing, searching. It gathered on the crossing square and formed into a cyclone. Swelling and spinning and rising. Sucking in the broken remains of the nave. It stretched high into the lantern tower, pulsed with black light and roared before it crashed down onto the center of the crossing square and smashed through the flagstones and drilled deep into the earth. A cloud of ancient dust filled the nave before being sucked into the cyclone. Skeletons ascended from the crypt and were drawn into the spinning blackness like frightened things.

"Watch out! They're coming for her!"

Rochat saw Harper's hand, pointing toward the altar.

Shadows emerging from the cyclone, slithering over flagstones toward the Virgin's chapel. They formed into tentacles and wrapped themselves around Katherine's body and pulled. Rochat felt her slipping from his arms.

"*Non!*"

He jumped after her and caught her wrists. He twisted around and pounded down on the shadows with his crooked foot.

"You can't take her, you bad shadows, this is my cathedral! *C'est le guet! C'est le guet!*"

The shadows squealed, released their grip, fled into the cyclone. Rochat pulled Katherine back to him and held her tight as Harper threw off his blanket, grabbed a pillar, and rose to his feet. Steadying himself in the raging winds and holding up the lantern.

"That's it! Say the words, you need to say the words!"

Rochat took a deep breath and shouted as if shouting from the belfry.

*"C'est le guet! Il a sonné l'heure! Il a sonné l'heure! C'est le guet! Il a sonné l'heure! Il a sonné l'heure!"*

A flash of fire exploded in the lantern and slashes of light, brilliant and sharp as lightning, shot from the lantern straight for the heart of the cyclone. The spinning black thing howled and disintegrated into a thousand shadows that shriveled and faded away, leaving the ancient bones and shattered remnants of Lausanne Cathedral hanging in the air like specks of dust.

Rochat looked at the lantern.

The brilliant light was only a fragile flame on a wick.

Daylight washed through the shattered doors and blown-apart windows.

Rochat tucked the blanket under Katherine's head. He got to his crooked legs, shuffled toward Harper.

"I saw you breathe into the fire. You inspired it to do things and chase away the bad shadows."

"Me? I was just trying to keep it alive. Wasn't until you started shouting that it came to life. All I did was get out of the way."

"It did that because of me?"

"Seems so."

Rochat thought about it. "I kicked them and they ran away, like in Tom and Jerry cartoons."

"And you kicked them where it hurts."

"So are they gone, did we win?"

"Those were devourers looking for dying souls. The real bad guys will come later."

"When?"

"Sundown, they always come at sundown."

"Why?"

"Because even after two and a half million years of free will, they're still so fucking predict . . ."

Harper clocked it.

Twenty-five-meter-deep well, two-point-five kilometers deep in the tunnels of Christ the Savior and Lausanne Cathedral. Two and a half million bloody years ago, *Homo ergaster* line of hominids suddenly stand up. Learn to fashion tools from stones, control fire. Something kicked it off, something made it happen, something inspired the creatures of this place with a soul. He held up the lantern and looked at the delicate flame.

"Well, what do you know."

"Are we imagining something, monsieur?"

"We are."

"Oh. What?

"We're imagining why the earth under Lausanne Cathedral is sacred to our kind."

"Because of the fire we found."

"Not just any fire. You're looking at the first light of creation, born of the unremembered beginning."

Rochat studied it.

For the moment, it looked like any flame in his lantern. Then he rewound his way through time to when they found it. Coming out of the tunnel into a small cave and seeing the fire burning alone in a tiny stone lamp, on an island in the middle of the source flowing under Lausanne. And the detectiveman said, "Bloody hell." And then looked at it some more and said, "Give us the lantern, mate," and Rochat did. But the candle in the lantern was almost burned away and Rochat said, "I don't have any more." The detectiveman said, "No worries," and he watched the detectiveman take a candle stub from his pocket and transfer the flame from the rock to the candle's wick and carefully reset the candle in the lantern. Then he handed the lantern back to Rochat and said, "Whatever you do, mate, don't drop this." And Rochat said, "I won't drop this."

Rochat blinked back to nowtimes.

"But where did the fire come from, monsieur?"

"It came from . . . from wherever the hell I came from."

"Who put it in my cathedral?"

"Someone who thought my kind couldn't be trusted with it, I suppose. Looking at the way things turned out for paradise, someone was right."

Rochat held up the lantern and looked deep into the fire. "It's like the light Maman gave me, isn't it?"

Harper looked at Rochat's eyes, seeing the reflection of light. "It is at that. And that means you and me, we're the same in a way."

"Really?"

"Yes. And given that, maybe you should imagine a new place to hide the fire."

"Me?"

"Sure. Your cathedral and all."

"I'll try to think of something."

The two of them stood side by side. Watching the dust and the dirt, the shattered chairs and the broken doors and shards of glass, the skeletons from the crypt and the stones from the well, all suspended and still, high in the hollow space of the lantern tower.

"I see it, monsieur, but I don't understand it."

"It's a time wake. Works like a massive stun grenade, establishes the battle perimeter. Wind time back on itself and let it go. Snaps back with considerable force. Good news, the good guys did it. Bad news is they've trapped us inside with the enemy."

"Why would they trap us with the bad shadows?"

"All part of the plan, mate. All part of the plan."

Rochat had no idea what any of that meant. "Oh. Is it like this everywhere in Lausanne?"

"No, just the cathedral. And the locals can't see it. Not yet, anyway."

Rochat took off his hat and scratched his head. It didn't help make things any clearer, so he put his hat back on his head and tried to imagine where he was in time instead. He was very sure he could go to before-times and come back to nowtimes. But this, this was very new. As if he suddenly found himself stuck in the middle of the two places.

"So is this betweentimes?"

Harper looked at Rochat. "Betweentimes. I like it."

"*Merci*. Do the bad shadows know we took the fire from the cave?"

They walked to the edge of the gaping hole in the crossing square. Rochat held his lantern and they looked down. Their eyes searched through shards of colored glass, broken bits of wood, and skeleton bones suspended in an unmoving spiral stretching down into the well and deeper into the shaft carved through solid rock.

"I'd say so."

Harper poked the hanging dust and watched more concentric shapes ooze outward. "*Una salus victis nullam sperare salutem.*"

"Those are the funny words the angel said, from the man she saw in her dream."

"They're from Virgil's *Aeneid*. It means the only hope for the doomed is to have no hope at all. It's another message from the good guys, it means hold on till the time wake shifts a bit and the cavalry can squeeze through."

Rochat imagined an army of knights in armor on horseback, racing up Escaliers du Marché toward the cathedral. And Otto the Brave Knight was leading them and waving his lance and shouting, "Charge!"

"And will the cavalry save the cathedral and the bells and the fire and the angel?"

"Sure. All we have to do is stay alive till they get here. Easy, eh?"

"*Oui.*"

Rochat looked up at the mass of floating things in the lantern tower. "Will it ever fall down?"

"It's falling. Just looks very, very slow when you're stuck betweentimes."

Rochat thought about it. It made perfect sense. He looked up at the slowly falling things.

"Look up there, near those two skeletons."

Harper leaned back and saw two skeletons turning slowly as if dancing. Between them was the maquette of Lausanne Cathedral.

"Now that's something you don't see every day."

Rochat sighed. "I don't know how I'll explain this to Monsieur Taroni."

"Who's he?"

"He's the caretaker who tells the workermen what to do. He doesn't like it when things aren't in their proper places."

"We don't pull this job off, this mess will be the least of Monsieur Taroni's worries."

Three bells rolled through the nave and the floating things began to fall, drifting slowly to the ground, touching the flagstones as if being laid by a gentle hand. Harper looked at his watch, the second hand still spinning in a blur, but beginning to slow.

"We'd best get to the belfry."

They hurried to the Virgin's chapel where Katherine was still lying on the stone floor. Rochat looked at her; he turned to Harper.

"Why didn't the angel come with us to betweentimes? Why can't she see things like us? And why did the tramp she saw say those words about her and take her for a walk when she was sleeping?"

"Why don't we leave that one for now, mate? I'll explain everything later."

Rochat continued to stare at Katherine, his head tipping from side to side, remembering how she had found her way to the cathedral. "I imagined she was an angel who was lost and it was my duty to protect her till she could find a way home. Because the bad shadows broke her wings and she couldn't fly anymore."

"I know. And you saved her life imagining it."

"But sometimes the things I imagine aren't real. She's just a girl, isn't she?"

"It doesn't matter what you imagined her to be. All that matters is what she shares with you."

"I don't understand."

Harper nodded to Katherine. "The two of you have souls, part of one soul, actually. It's all one living thing."

"I don't understand."

"That's all right. No one else in this place understands it, either, yet."

"Do you have a soul, monsieur?"

"No, souls are the things of men."

Harper watched Rochat's eyes lose focus for a long moment before blinking back to nowtimes.

"Did Maman have a soul?"

"No."

"What did Maman have? What do you have, monsieur?"

"Nothing." Harper stared at Rochat. *No going back, the lad needs to know the truth.* He pointed to the fire in the lantern. "Your mother and me, our kind, we're just reflections of light."

"But I could see Maman. I can see you."

"Yes, well, that's where it gets complicated."

Rochat thought about it. "You're the angel Maman told me about, aren't you?"

Harper took a slow breath. "Yes, mate, I'm what men call an angel. And so was your mother."

"Really?"

"Sure. That's why she implanted the light in your eyes, so I'd know who you were."

Rochat thought about it some more. "Did Maman have a future-teller diamond? Is that how she knew you'd find me?"

"She was the future teller, mate. And her job was to pass on that gift to you, same way she gave you the light."

Harper watched the truth sink in as best it could. The lad sensing that somehow, his entire life was a thing beyond the imagination of men.

"I'm not sure I understand, monsieur. But thank you for telling me."

"When this is over, I'll explain everything. Just now we need to get Miss Taylor to the belfry and find a place to hide your lantern. Just now they're the two most precious things in the world."

"I don't know what that word means."

Harper laughed to himself, knowing the word "precious" had slipped by his lips because he let himself choose to feel something, not even knowing what the hell it was. An emotion, maybe. Inspector Gobet was not going to be happy.

"I guess it's like the feeling you have for the bells in the belfry. And because you feel that way, they need to be protected."

"Because it's our duty."

"That's right, it's our duty."

Rochat shuffled to the slowly sinking column of things, reached carefully and removed the maquette of Lausanne Cathedral. He turned around.

"And when you explain everything, will I be able to stay in the cathedral with the bells?"

"Sure."

He shuffled to Harper and handed him the maquette.

"I imagined where we can hide the fire. Do you want to see?"


Katherine felt Monsieur Booty's cold nose in her face. She opened her eyes. In the loge, on the bed, candles burning about the place. The candle flame glowing soft as the last of the day's light came through the open door. The maquette of Lausanne Cathedral sat on the table. She scratched the beast behind its ears.

*Mew.*

"Hello, fuzzface. Where is everyone?"

Steps came along the south balcony. She sat up and pulled Monsieur Booty close to her. Rochat appeared in the open doorway, his floppy black hat and long black overcoat still covered in dust.

"You were dreaming in the nave, that's all."

"What?"

"You were dreaming in the nave and we carried you up here. That's what happened."

"I didn't wake up down there?"

"*Non.*"

She ran her fingers through her hair. "What time is it?"

Just then the timbers shuddered and Marie-Madeleine shook the tower with five mighty gongs. The sound faded away.

"Always nice to have your own personal alarm clock. Where's Harper?"

"On the roof of the belfry watching the sky around the cathedral, because it looks wiggly and that means it's over soon."

"What's over soon?"

Rochat thought about it. "The way the sky looks."

She watched Rochat rock back and forth on his heels. She laid Monsieur Booty on the bed.

"Marc, is something wrong?"

Rochat stepped into the loge. "Can I ask you something?"

"Yeah, what?"

"Did your papa and maman tell you stories about shadows and visiting beforetimes and imagining things?"

She shrugged. "Dad's idea of a bedtime story was the letters section of *Penthouse.* And Mom, dear old Mom, fed me on the usual stuff mothers feed their girls. Cinderella, Sleeping Beauty."

"They're like you."

"Like me?"

Rochat reached to his shelf of books and pulled one down. He held it out to her. "You can put this in your rucksack and take it with you."

She looked at the cover.

*piratz*
*Une histoire drôle de Marc Rochat*
*pour Mademoiselle Katherine Taylor*

"A funny story by Marc Rochat. You finished it?"

"The detectiveman helped me write the words on the cover because I'm not good with spelling. You can read it when you go home to your maman and papa."

"What?"

"Where your home is."

She looked through the open door. The deep blue sky turning to night, the lights of Évian glimmering and reflecting in the lake.

"Yeah, but it's sort of the last place on earth I'd ever think of going."

"Why not? It's where your home is."

"That's . . . that's another story. Not a very nice one."

She stared at him. Thinking he must have drifted off to another time zone. But she could feel his eyes focused on her in the here and now. She felt as if he were looking inside her, looking for something he couldn't find anymore.

"Marc, did Harper tell you something? Something about me?"

"He said you still needed me to help you find a way home."

"What?"

"That's what he said." He reached into his pocket and removed something. He shuffled three steps to the bed and held out his hand. "And you can take this for when you go home, too."

A well-dented five-franc coin fell into her palm. She stared at it.

"What's this for?"

"For good luck."

Rochat turned and shuffled outside. He stopped and looked back.

"Be not afraid, because Otto the Brave Knight is bringing the cavalry to save the cathedral and the bells and the fire and the . . . the you."

"What?"

"That's what the funny words mean that you said in your dream. I have to go do my duties now."

He shuffled away and she sat listening to his steps along the balcony. She stared at the dented coin, she stared at the storybook, not knowing what to do. She picked up Monsieur Booty from the bed and raised the beast to her face.

"For God's sake, tell me I didn't break his heart."

A shadow crossed the open door.

"Alas, the heart you break is mine."

Katherine froze, helpless for breath.

She raised her eyes to the tall elegant man in perfect black. Long silver hair pulled to the back of his head, dark round glasses over his eyes. Stepping through the doorway and moving slowly toward her.

# forty

Harper shoved the lantern in the spire atop the belfry and kicked the door closed. That's when he heard the scream. He ran to the northeast turret and down the corkscrew steps. He slammed into a shadow transmigrating into the form of a half-breed. Killing knife in his hand, dead black rushing through his eyes.

"I bring you forever death."

"Of course you do."

The half-breed came down with his knife. Harper dodged, kicked the back of the half-breed's knees, and knocked him down. He grabbed the half-breed's head and smashed it against the stone steps. Blood splattered against the close-in walls. Harper ripped the killing knife from the half-breed's hand. Another shadow appeared from above, took form, and flew at Harper. Harper swung the killing knife, caught the half-breed's throat. The thing squealed and fell to the steps. Harper rammed the knife deeper. The half-breed thrashed a few seconds, then stilled.

"Die forever, goons."

He raised the head of the still-breathing half-breed under his knees and set the blade at the side of its neck. He slashed open its throat.

"And give my regards to the big nowhere."

He stood, pressed his back to the wall, moved quietly down the turret.

Komarovsky dragged Katherine onto the south balcony.

"Let me go, bastard!"

"A few nights ago you called me your forever and ever love."

"Funny what a girl will say when she's drugged stupid."

He kissed her as if he was drawing the life from her body. She pulled back and spat in his face. Komarovsky touched the wet and tasted it.

"How bittersweet the wrath of the righteous whore. And may I say, I love what you have done with your hair. It goes so well with the pretty scar on your face."

"Where's Marc, what have you done with him?"

"Why, what any spurned lover does to the rival."

Komarovsky dragged her through an archway and tossed her onto the east balcony. He stepped to the side, his sweeping hand like a magician revealing a turn.

"Behold the crippled fool of Lausanne Cathedral."

Rochat was on the balcony flagstones. The tall skinny one had his boot crushing down on Rochat's chest. His face was bruised, his right eye nearly swollen closed.

"Marc, Jesus, Marc."

Rochat saw Katherine; he struggled under the tall one's heel. "*Non*, don't you hurt her. She needs to go home."

"Does she now? Then let's send her airmail."

"I don't know what that means."

"Then I'll show you, fool."

The tall one tore the floppy hat from Rochat's head and tossed it from the belfry. Rochat reached for it.

"My hat! That wasn't very nice! You go away, you bad shadow, you don't belong here."

The tall one's fist smashed down on Rochat's face.

"Where is the fire?"

"We hid it, you big stupid, and you'll never find it."

The tall one pulled a killing knife from his belt and held it by the quillon, the tip of the blade dangling over Rochat's chest. "Then I get to carve out your beating heart and crush it in my hands."

Katherine jumped for the knife. "Leave him alone!"

Komarovsky caught her by the arm, snapped her back. "Your affection for the crippled fool is most amusing. Did you caress his misshapen body in your whoring arms? Did you let him touch your secret places with his dirty little hands?"

"Fuck you. Marc's right, you don't belong here, you belong in hell."

Komarovsky smiled from behind his dark glasses. She felt herself being lifted from the flagstones and drawn toward Komarovsky by unseen hands.

"But have you not heard the poet's truth, my dear? Hell is empty, and all the devils are here."

He passed his hand before her face; she stiffened like a pillar of salt. He turned her around, and Katherine stared off the balconies in disbelief.

"Jesus . . . what?"

All light disappearing as dark matter descended through an almost liquid sky. Enveloping the cathedral, separating it from Lausanne and the lake, the mountains, and all the world beyond. Then shreds of black mist, tens of thousands, born from the dark matter, swirling around the belfry and growling with hunger.

"What is this?"

"The shadows of the devourers, my love. Remember how they suckled at your flesh and carried you like a goddess in breathless waves of pleasure? How you opened to them, loved them as you love yourself? How they prepared your body to receive our sacred seed?"

She looked at Komarovsky, saw her terrified reflection in his dark glasses.

"This isn't real, none of this is real."

He touched her trembling lips. "Be still, my dearest, and feel shadows made flesh within your womb."

Katherine turned toward Rochat. "Marc . . . am I imagining?"

Rochat squirmed under the tall one's weight. "Stop it, she's not like me. You're hurting her."

The tall one let the killing knife fall from his fingers. Rochat closed his eyes, heard Katherine cry, "No!" He felt something prick his skin. He opened his eyes and saw the tip of the blade scratching his flesh. The tall one leaned close to Rochat and sneered. "Fooled the fool, don't you know."

A lone seraphic breath blew through the carpentry.

The tall one, sensing the presence of another, looked toward the northeast turret. He saw Harper standing in the archway, fresh blood dripping from the killing knife in his hand. The tall one turned his eyes to Komarovsky.

"He's here."

Komarovsky held Katherine close to him. "Then our stage is set for the final act. Do join us, good and noble warrior."

Harper stepped from the archway. "Sorry I'm late. Had to slaughter a few of your half-breed goons along the way."

"Not at all." Komarovsky nodded off the balcony to the dark swirling mass in the sky. "Plenty more where they came from."

"Good. Nothing like job security in today's uncertain economy." Harper's eyes shifted to Katherine. He saw the madness in her eyes, the kind that comes from seeing unknowable things. "Hello, Miss Taylor."

"How . . . how can this be happening?"

Harper focused the light in his eyes straight into hers. "You remember, Miss Taylor, all those things you'd never understand in a billion years."

A fragile smile crossed her eyes. "Yeah, I remember."

"This is just one more."

Harper looked at Rochat, the tall one's blade still

pressing at his heart. "Hello, mate. I see you met Dick-face. Seen his pal anywhere, little squirt with a goatee?"

"He came and murdered my snowman, then this big dumb shadow threw away my hat and now he wants to cut out my heart."

"Well, they are the bad shadows, aren't they?"

*"Oui, monsieur!"*

Harper looked in the carpentry. Bits of crushed ice scattered on the wood floor under Marie-Madeleine, door to the shed open.

"What were they doing in the timbers, besides killing your snowman?"

"They broke into the shed and took some buckets and bottles of cleaning things. Then they sneaked to the upper bells."

Harper looked up, saw black gel oozing through the wooden planks high above. Dripping down the carpentry and seeping into the gnarls and cracks of the timbers. He stepped closer and touched the gel. He rolled it in his fingertips, smelled it.

"What is it, monsieur?"

"Fire potions mixed with solvents, bit of murdered snowman tossed in for laughs."

"Is it a bad thing, monsieur, because I imagined it's a bad thing."

"Self-perpetuating potions with an ignition blast that'll shatter windows in Geneva. Yeah, I'd say that's a pretty bad thing."

"But you can stop it, can't you, monsieur, because we're the good guys, and—"

The tall one slapped his hand over Rochat's mouth, pressed the killing knife deeper. "Quiet, you blathering fool."

"Mmmmm! Mmmn!"

Katherine pulled at Komarovsky's grip. "Jesus, Harper, don't let them kill Marc!"

Komarovsky laughed. "Yes, let's play another round of Who Dies First? Perhaps, this time, the warrior will not make such a mess of it."

Harper stared into Komarovsky's dark glasses. "I'm guessing you're the one men call Azazel, but whoever the fuck you are, I want you to listen to me. You kill her, you kill the lad, you'll have no one to hide behind. I'll slaughter the lot of you in your forms before their bodies hit the ground."

Komarovsky made a mocking nod of the head. "Such a heroic performance. But you only need look to the sky to know your performance is, shall we say, lacking."

Harper's eyes shot to the sky. He saw the shadows of the devourers beating against a liquid sky. *What the fuck is he up to?*

Harper shrugged. "I see a time wake, I see you trapped inside with your pals. And I see the time wake fading, with the cavalry just beyond waiting to charge in and capture your sorry arse. I mean, you do realize you've walked into a fucking trap, right?"

"How satisfying to know the free will of men has given you a sense of humor."

Harper wiped the bloody blade on the sleeve of his sweater. "I wouldn't count on it, slick."

Komarovsky was silent a moment. Then he began to squeeze Katherine's neck with a clawlike grip. "Surrender the lantern or this cathedral and all Lausanne will disappear in a flash of fire."

Harper looked to the sky again. The shadows slamming harder against the liquid sky, ripples and eddies forming into cracks. *Christ, they smell mass death.* Harper looked at Komarovsky.

"Have you completely fried your brains on dead black? We're locked in a time wake. A blast like that won't just destroy the cathedral and Lausanne, it'll set off a chain reaction that'll ignite every molecule of oxygen in the atmosphere. You'll kill seven billion people in the blink of an eye. You're talking lights out for the whole bloody world."

"Then we shall weep in the void and feed on the uncomforted souls of men till another world comes along."

Harper felt an ice-cold chill run through his being. "You're on a suicide mission."

"More like the denouement of our little play, with a dramatic flourish."

"No way the rest of your kind know you're doing this."

"No?"

The pieces fell into place in Harper's brain. "You've gone bloody rogue. That's why you staged that slaughterhouse on the Internet knowing we'd cracked your comms. You wanted our side to track the rest of the Two Hundred Club, you wanted us to know the identities of the half-breeds hiding in the world of men. This is a fucking coup and we're helping you pull it off."

"I will have the fire from the well and rule paradise as the creator, or the creation will be no more."

Harper chuckled. "I take it back. It's fucking brilliant, all of it. But somehow I don't think you and your half-breed goons ruling the world is what the real creator had in mind."

"I have crossed aeons of time searching for the fire of creation and, now, I claim it as the creator of the new paradise."

"You call this fucking mess of a world you created paradise? You even looked at a newspaper lately? This isn't the way it was supposed to be."

"The creator is dead, long live the creator."

Harper flipped the killing knife and caught it by the handle. "Yeah, maybe you're right. Maybe there's nothing left of the creator but the intersecting lines of causality moving through time. Doesn't matter. All I know is those lines were never meant to be bent by the cruddy likes of you."

Harper backed up toward the turret.

"So, if you'll excuse me, I'll head to the upper bells. See what I can do to fuck up the denouement of your little play with my own dramatic flourish."

Komarovsky squeezed harder at Katherine's neck. "Then you would choose to save the many, at the cost of these two innocent souls?"

Harper looked at Miss Taylor, then the lad. He shrugged. "My job is to save what's left of paradise. Besides, orders. No interference with the time and manner of their deaths."

The tall one tore his knife through Rochat's overcoat, ripping it open. He set the blade at his throat.

"Then time to slaughter the fool."

"Hey, Dickface."

The tall one looked at Harper.

"Something you want to say, killer, before I slice open the fool's throat?"

"I'd be careful. He watches a lot of Cartoon Network, Tom and Jerry."

"Who?"

"Tom's a big stupid cat, Jerry's a clever little mouse who always gets away. Right, mate?"

*"Oui, monsieur!"*

Rochat bit hard into the tall one's hand and ripped away a chunk of flesh. The tall one dropped the killing knife and Rochat rolled free. Harper ran up the turret; Rochat dived into the carpentry. The tall one caught Rochat's ankle, pulled, and dropped him on the balcony stones, trying to stomp him underfoot. Rochat rolled left and right, dodging the kicks.

"What's the matter, you big dumb shadow, can't catch a little mouse? Ha, ha on you."

He scrambled into the carpentry again, jumping around timbers and crawling over the scattered ice under Marie-Madeleine's bronze skirt. The tall one flew between the timbers, landed on top of Rochat, and pounded him down to the wooden plank floor. He grabbed Rochat by his shredded overcoat, lifted him overhead.

"Know what happens to the little mouse when it's caught by the big bad shadow? It gets squashed."

He slammed Rochat into the great bronze bell.

The bell rang with a dull sickening sound. Rochat's eyes rolled back in his head; he tumbled to the wooden plank floor like a wounded animal.

Katherine pulled at the hands at her throat and screamed: "No! Marc!"

The tall one kicked Rochat in the guts and sent him skidding, his black mop of a head hanging out between the timbers. Katherine saw Rochat touch the timbers with his fingers, press his head against a crossbeam. The tall one smashed his boot into Rochat's face. A gush of blood spilled onto the flagstones of the balcony.

"Uhhh . . ."

"Jesus, Marc!"

Harper leaned around a pillar and recced the upper belfry.

Two half-breeds in the carpentry above the bells pouring fire potions down the timbers. Under the bells, the small goateed half-breed dumping the sticky liquid over the wooden platform running through the center of the belfry. Harper squeezed the grip of his killing knife, crept to the stone arch at the end of the walkway.

"Hello, squirt."

The small one dropped the bucket, jumped to the south balcony, snapped an iron bar from the railing as if it were a twig. He slipped away through the arches. The half-breeds in the carpentry pulled out their knives and flew down for Harper. He ducked under a low-hanging bell as they hit the walkway. He saw dead black pumping through their eyes as they closed in.

"I know, you bring me forever death."

Flashes of steel came at him.

Harper threw up his arms; the blades caught his forearms.

"Fuck!"

Harper kicked the closest half-breed in the stomach, pivoted, and smashed the butt of his knife into the half-breed's face. The half-breed flew back, smashed its head on an iron bolt jutting from a timber, and fell dazed to the walkway. Harper charged at the other half-breed, dropped low, and sliced the tendons at the back of its knees. The half-breed squealed and fell, still slashing at Harper's chest. Harper swung at the half-breed's face and sliced open its mouth. The half-breed squealed again and rammed its knife into Harper's thigh.

"Argh!"

The half-breed rolled, raised its blade above Harper's neck. Harper jerked right as the blade ripped by his head and bored into the wooden planks. He kicked up with his knees and shifted the half-breed's weight. He rammed his own knife into the half-breed's chest and twisted hard. A death cry tore through the tower, but the half-breed lunged still, digging its thumbs into Harper's throat. "To the darkness!"

Harper flipped his knife, the tip of the blade touching the soft flesh under the half-breed's chin. "After you."

Harper rammed the blade deep and sliced it to the side. Harper heard the crack as steel severed spine from brain. The half-breed froze stiff. Harper shoved the dead thing to the side. He scanned the belfry. The squirt with the goatee was nowhere in sight, maybe down by the lower bells. Harper got to his feet and limped toward the dazed half-breed. He swung back his killing knife to slice open the goon's throat.

"You next."

Something coming fast at his back. Harper spun around and saw the small one charging with the iron rod like a spear. Harper ducked right, but the jagged point caught his left shoulder.

"Shit!"

The squirt rammed harder, the iron rod digging deep. He heaved and lifted Harper off his feet. A paralyzing shot of pain screamed through Harper's body.

"Christ!"

The small goon heaved and lifted and skewered Harper on the rod till the ragged point shot out of Harper's back. He charged ahead and rammed the bloodied tip of the rod into a cross timber.

Harper was pinned like a half-dead butterfly.

"No!"

He tried to touch the tips of his shoes to the walkway to relieve the ripping fire in his shoulder.

"Bloody Christ!"

He saw the small one move to the dazed half-breed, point to the high timbers, telling him to hurry. Then coming to stand before him. Pulling at his goatee and tipping his head from side to side, as if admiring his killing work. Then spitting in Harper's face, mocking him.

Harper couldn't hear the words. He heard nothing but the screaming pain in his brain.

K omarovsky dragged Katherine to Rochat.
      "Make him tell you where they hid the lantern or I'll slash open his throat and you will drink his blood."

"No, don't, please."

Komarovsky opened his coat, showed the long-bladed knife in his belt. "I will not ask you twice."

He tossed her to Rochat. She crawled near him, brushed the hair from his bloodied face.

"Marc, I don't understand what's happening, what is it they want?"

"A secret fire, in my lantern, we found it under the well. They can't take it, they can't take you."

"Marc, forget about me."

Rochat raised his eyes to see her, his head still against the crossbeam. "I know who you are."

"Marc . . ."

"You have a soul and that makes you as precious as the bells. That's what the detectiveman said."

"Please, I'm not worth it." She saw his eyes lose focus; she grabbed his arm. "Marc! Marc!"

"I imagined you can hear them, like in beforetimes."

"What?"

The tall one jumped on the edge of the carpentry and shoved Katherine to the balcony railing.

"Time's up, my turn."

"No, don't hurt him!" She watched the tall one brace

his hands on Marie-Madeleine and kick hard into Rochat's sides. "Stop it!"

Rochat dragged himself slowly under the bell, drawing the tall one around, never taking his eyes off the tall one's hands as they inched along the edge of Marie-Madeleine's bronze skirt. Closer, closer. Rochat held steady, absorbing the kicks, keeping the tall one in place. He pressed his head to a timber, looked at Katherine. She saw a fragile light flash in his eyes and she heard a great creaking groan.

"Yes, Marc, I hear them! I can hear the timbers!"

Rochat rolled on his back and looked up at Marie-Madeleine.

*"Merci, madame."*

The giant iron hammer outside the great bell crushed down on the tall one's hand. His earsplitting squeal was swallowed in Marie-Madeleine's thunderous voice.

*GONG! GONG! GONG!*

The great bell pulsed through the carpentry. Harper felt the timbers vibrate; the iron rod running through his form shivered with pain.

*GONG!*

He grabbed the rod, tried to pull it free.

*GONG!*

"Oh, fuck!"

*GONG!*

The thunderous sound and vibrations faded away. Harper shook his head to clear his eyes.

The small one pouring the last of the fire potions on the wooden planks under the bells. The other half-breed spreading the liquid over the giant wooden yokes and leather harnesses above.

"No, you can't do this."

The small one looked at Harper and smiled. He kicked over the bucket, jumped up to look into Harper's face.

"Watch me."

He grabbed hold of the iron rod, gave it a powerful shove. Another slash of pain screamed through Harper's brain.

"JesusfuckingChrist!"

"That's it, killer, howl with all your might, because this time, no one rises from the dead."

"He's going to destroy the creation, all of it."

"What of it? Bring on the darkness, I say."

The small one jumped down from the bucket, signaled to the half-breed in the timbers to finish, and hurried to the turret steps. Harper shouted after him: "No, not like this!"

Harper felt numbness seep through his form, the phantom of a dead man named Jay Michael Harper struggling to stay alive for the second time in his life . . . *No, please, not like this* . . . But the weary weight of eternity crushed down hard.

Tired.

Two and a half million years of tired. His voice whispering to a forgotten will: "Not like this, please."

Then other voices, singing voices, racing through the belfry. Harper lifted his eyes.

The bells, the seven bells of Lausanne.

Rocking from side to side, clappers banging against bronze skirts. Seven brilliant voices swelling into a deafening drone.

Then powerful vibrations rushing through the timbers, straight into Harper's back. His weight began to push down on the iron rod.

"Yes! Come on, ladies! Do it!"

Flesh sliding on iron.

"Bloody hell!"

He slid free and collapsed on the walkway.

"Aw, Christ!"

The bells roared louder, the iron rod loosened from its hold and clanged next to him. Harper grabbed it with his good arm, jammed it into the planks, pulled himself to his feet. He wavered in the dizzying sound of the bells.

"Move, boyo, keep moving."

He focused on the north balcony, stumbled ahead. Dodging the faster-than-light iron clapper of the low-hanging bell. Something heavy smashed into his back, threw him down to the walkway. He rolled over, saw the half-breed dodging the swinging clapper, killing knife in his hand coming down like a pendulum swinging to the rhythm of the bells, closer and closer to Harper's throat.

"Here comes the chopper, to chop off your head!"

"And you forgot to duck, fucker."

Harper rammed his knee into the half-breed's groin. The evil thing winced and jumped as the iron clapper of the bell swung down like a sledgehammer and smashed open its skull. Harper rolled over, grabbed the iron rod, tried to pull himself to his feet. He fell, tried again. All life slipping from his form, all light fading from his eyes.

*Christ, not like this . . .*

S he felt powerful hands haul her to her knees, then a jagged blade across her throat. She looked up into the blackest eyes over a goatee.

"You, no! Harper!"

"Don't bother calling, the killer's busy being dead."

Komarovsky swooped down on Rochat. "Do you hear? The warrior angel is no more. You are alone in the cathedral. He has abandoned you, as your mother abandoned you."

"*Non*, there was an accident when I was born. Maman died and sent me to live with Papa and Grand-maman where I could be safe from the bad shadows."

Komarovsky gently stroked Rochat's black mop of hair, as if calming a suffering child.

"For too long you have been forced to bear an unjust cross for the sake of man. Come unto me and I will lift this burden from your crooked legs. I will make you whole and wise. Honored by men, adored by women, loved by all. Imagine such wonderful things as these."

Komarovsky opened his hand before Rochat's eyes. And Rochat, enchanted by the imagined and wonderful things, watched the hand move till its fingers pointed to Katherine in the grip of the small one, a deadly blade set at her throat. Rochat felt a rush of frantic emotion. Hearing his heart pounding with the bells, seeing the woman who once pressed a kiss against a window.

"She's like the bells."

"And you love her as you love these singing bells. I will give her to you and she will bring you pleasure all your days. Together, you will rule Lausanne in my name, as king and queen. All this I will give to you, if you give me the lantern."

Rochat saw tears well in Katherine's eyes. Watched her lips move, read her words through the roar of the bells: "Please, Marc, let them kill me." He looked at Komarovsky, saw himself in the lenses of the dark glasses. The crooked and battered shape of Marc Rochat, *le guet de la Cathédrale de Lausanne* . . .

"*Non!* You hurt her in beforetimes because you're a bad shadow, that's what you are. And you want to hurt the cathedral and the bells and steal my lantern because we found a secret fire. I won't let you, I won't let you!"

Komarovsky grabbed Rochat by the arms, yanked him from the ground. "You are alone, fool, you are abandoned."

"*Non.* There's Otto the Brave Knight and the skeletons and the lost angels and the teasing shadows. They're alive in the cathedral because I can imagine them! And I can imagine the detectiveman, too, you bad shadow. Because you didn't kill him and he can kill you because that's what detectivemen do!"

"What?"

"Look behind you, you big stupid!"

Komarovsky turned, saw Harper stumbling from the turret, spearlike rod in his hands, letting out a scream . . .

"Rhhhaaahhh!"

. . . and ramming it into the back of the small one's neck. The goon dropped his knife, let go of Katherine. His quivering hands clawing at the tip of the bloody rod poking from his throat. His silent squeal twisting his face into a grotesque grin. He fell to the flagstones, forever dead.

Harper reached for the small one's killing knife, but a butchering pain brought him crashing down. Katherine crawled next to him, pressed her hands over the holes in his chest and back. Red blood seeped through her fingers.

"Harper, Jesus!"

Komarovsky kicked Rochat aside and flew across the balcony and pushed Katherine away. He loomed over Harper.

"Once more unto the breach, dear brother?"

Harper raised his head, smiled through bloodied teeth. "Sure, brother. Too bad you've run out of goons."

"Oh, ye of little faith."

Komarovsky stomped on Harper's shoulders, drove Harper's head to the flagstones. He couldn't move. He watched Komarovsky wave his hand and draw the tall one from the flagstones like a half-dead thing. A stringy mass of mangled tissue hung from the half-breed's right wrist. Komarovsky pointed to Katherine and Rochat.

"Set them alight! Let their burning flesh be the flame of destruction!"

The tall one stumbled to the carpentry, wiped his mangled hand against the timbers to absorb the fire potion.

He stood over Marc and Katherine, squeezed the sticky goo over their heads and faces. He pulled a cigarette lighter from his pocket and opened the flame. He hoisted them to their feet and back to the balcony railing.

Komarovsky hauled Harper to his knees, forced his eyes to the sky. "Look out there, good and noble warrior. Look what awaits all the souls of the world if you do not give me the lantern. You are finished. Will it be your last act to condemn the world to perpetual darkness?"

Harper tried to focus.

The swirling mass of dark matter and shadows, ready to infect the world with mass death. Then a small shaft of light cutting through the liquid sky . . . *time wake shifting . . . a flash of light from across Pont Bessières . . . line of sight to the belfry . . . he felt something under his ankles, a killing knife . . . bloody hell, hold on . . .*

Harper looked at Komarovsky. "No, don't do it, please."

"Surrender the lantern."

"All right, all right." He nodded to Rochat and Katherine. "You'll kill them, I know it. But I want their souls to have safe passage to the next life. I give them comfort before. Do that and you can have your bloody kingdom on earth."

"And you will kneel at my feet and worship me as the new creator of paradise?"

"Anything. Just let their souls go in peace, I beg you."

Komarovsky smiled. "Thy will be done."

Rochat was watching them, reading their lips. He yelled through the roar of the bells. *"Non, monsieur!"*

Harper shook his head. "It's over, mate!"

"He'll hurt the cathedral, he will!"

"I can't fight anymore. Too weak. Save the two of you, all I can do. Hold Miss Taylor. Listen . . . my voice. My eyes . . . look."

Rochat watched Harper's eyes point to the killing knife poking from his ankles.

"I understand, monsieur."

"Hold her. Don't let go of her."

Rochat put his arms around Katherine. She quivered with fear.

"Harper?"

Harper drew a ragged breath.

"It's going to be all right, Miss Taylor, just look in my eyes, listen to my voice."

Komarovsky yanked back Harper's head.

"The lantern first. Where is it?"

Harper nodded to the turret. "On the belfry roof . . . in the spire. Behind a small door on the south side."

Komarovsky looked to the tall one. "Kill them and throw their souls to the devourers."

Harper screamed, "No, you said I could give them comfort!"

"Evil is as evil does, brother."

Harper smiled . . .

"That it fucking is, brother."

. . . and shoved his weight back into Komarovsky, kicked the killing knife to Rochat.

"Get her down, mate!"

Rochat grabbed Katherine and pulled her to the flagstones. He grabbed the knife and stabbed the tall one's foot. The tall one barely shrieked before his head exploded in a spray of blood and brains, the burning lighter tumbling from his dead hand. Rochat sprang and whacked it with the killing knife and knocked it from the belfry.

"Goawaybadthinggoaway!"

Komarovsky ducked into an archway. He looked out through the cracking-open sky. Across the bridge, open window of a top-floor flat above Rue Caroline. A sniper with a high-powered rifle braced across the sill. Cop in a cashmere coat next to him, binoculars at his face. Harper chuckled through the blood gathering in his throat.

"Go ahead, brother, take a fucking bow. Your kingdom awaits."

"And it shall be the kingdom of darkness! Watch as I put an end to this cursed paradise, once and for all!"

He kicked Harper hard in the head, sent him skidding across the balcony to Katherine. She grabbed Harper's hand; he didn't move.

"Harper! Harper!"

Komarovsky turned toward Rochat and screamed through the bells.

"And you, you crippled fool! The world will never again hear the song of the bells!"

Rochat saw Komarovsky transmigrating into shadow, drifting away.

"*Non*, I won't let you!"

He rushed after Komarovsky with the killing knife, jumped at him, and drove the blade into his back. Komarovsky shrieked; the dark glasses flew from his face. He spun around, his form becoming whole again. Rochat looked into Komarovsky's silver eyes.

"I know you. You're the bad shadow from my nightmares. I imagined you killed Maman, I couldn't stop you."

Komarovsky flew across the balcony, slammed Rochat into the timbers.

"Hear the truth before you die, fool. Once upon a time, a shadow crawled in your mother's womb as she slept. It was me who poisoned her with agony potions, trapping the eternity of her being in a dying form. And it was me who wrapped the umbilical cord around your neck and pulled. I made you the crippled fool you are, to be abandoned by your mother."

"*Non!* You're lying! Maman died!"

"It was an empty box they put in the ground. She tried to hide to protect you, but I found her. And after the longest night of pain—oh, how she cried your name—I dined on her whoring flesh."

"*Non*, Maman was an angel, the detectiveman told me! And he said I'm the same as him, too! That means if he can kill you, I can kill you!"

"You want to kill?" Komarovsky pulled his knife from his belt and rammed the blade deep into Rochat's stomach. "This is how you kill."

Rochat shuddered as the steel twisted through his guts. He turned his head, his eyes watching Marie-Madeleine swing from side to side, feeling her voice vibrate through the timbers and into his body.

"Don't cry, madame, it's my duty."

Komarovsky ripped the knife from Rochat's guts.

"Uhhh!" Rochat collapsed to the flagstones. Komarovsky slowly raised the knife over Rochat's neck for the death cut.

"I bring you forever death!"

In the longest second of betweentimes, Rochat saw Katherine and the dying detectiveman next to her. Her arms reaching for him, her voice crying, "Marc!"

"Be not afraid."

He pushed down on his crooked legs and burst up from the floor and smashed his fists into Komarovsky's throat. Forcing those silver and unbelieving eyes over the railing and into the sky.

And when he pushed the bad shadow away, he opened his arms like perfect wings. For a moment, he was flying. Higher than the lake, higher than the mountains on the far shore, higher than all the world. And when he began to fall, he saw the belfry of the cathedral against a clearing sky. He saw the woman he imagined to be a lost angel reaching for him still, and he heard the seven bells calling out over Lausanne.

"All is well, Rochat, all is . . ."


M arc, no! Marc!"

Harper opened his bloodied eyes. He watched Katherine sink to the flagstones as the bells slowed and quieted, the final chord hovering in the sky like something crying. He looked to the sky. The shadows of the devourers were gone. The time wake shifted again and evening stars were coming to light over the lake. He pulled himself up, sat against a pillar, and looked down through the balcony railing.

Komarovsky was splayed on a long spire beneath the belfry tower as if run through by a brave knight's lance, his entrails like bloody strings snapping in the wind. And out on the esplanade Harper saw the lad. On his back, arms to his sides, fingers of his right hand almost touching a floppy black hat nearby. Harper saw the lad looking up to the tower still. He saw a flicker of light in the lad's eyes.

"Miss . . . Tay . . . Miss Taylor."

Katherine raised her face, her eyes flooded with disbelieving tears.

"Tell me he isn't dead, Harper, tell me he's coming back, please."

"Have to hurry . . ."

"Tell me he's coming back."

"Listen . . . before sound fades."

"What?"

"My eyes . . . too weak. Lantern . . . in loge . . . under bed."

"Lantern, Marc's lantern?"

"Get it."

"But you said it's on the roof."

Smiling, blood dripping from his lips. "We lied . . . Second lantern in case they got away . . . Lad's idea."

She heard gurgling sounds in Harper's throat. "Jesus, I'm going to get help."

"Lad . . . needs to see fire . . . my eyes, too weak."

Katherine wiped blood from his lips. "Harper, you need a fucking doctor."

He grabbed her hand, squeezed with a failing grip. "Needs to see the fire . . . find his way."

"Find his way? Where?"

"Where he belongs."

"The cathedral? To the cathedral?"

"Can't explain . . . a billion years . . . one of those things."

"Okay, Harper. Hang on, please hang on."

Katherine ran to the loge and rushed to the bed. She pulled open the cabinet doors underneath and found the lantern. The most beautiful and delicate flame fluttering on a half-melted candle. She carefully removed the lantern, hurried back to Harper.

"Okay, I got it. What do I do?"

Harper drew a shallow breath. "Needs to see light, hear words."

"I don't understand."

"Words . . . the lad's words. *C'est le guet* . . . You know the rest."

"Yes, I know the words but . . ."

Harper shook with spasms, coughed up blood and water. Katherine wiped his face with her sweater.

"Jesus, Harper, you're dying."

"Doesn't matter, the lad needs you . . . Call his name, say words . . . Needs to see light . . . before it's too late."

Katherine rushed to the south balcony, saw Rochat down on the esplanade. She fell to her knees and held the lantern out through the balcony railing.

"Marc, Marc Rochat! *C'est le guet, Marc! Il a sonné l'heure!* Can you hear me? *C'est le guet! Il a sonné l'heure, il a sonné l'heure!*"

The flame in the lantern began to swell, growing brighter and brighter, burning Katherine's eyes.

"Do you see it, Marc, can you see me? It's Katherine, I'm with you . . . *C'est le guet! Il a sonné l'heure!*"

Streams of brilliant light shot from the lantern and into the sky and burst into thousands of diamondlike sparks, burning bright and fluttering down toward the crooked form in the long black overcoat far below. The sparks touched him, then disappeared. The diamondlike light in the lantern faded into a delicate flame.

"No, not yet. Oh, make it come back. Please, God, make it come back. *C'est le guet! C'est le guet,* please!" She began to sink under the weight of tears, still holding the lantern through the railing. "Please, don't go! *C'est le guet, Marc!*"

Something took hold of her.

She surrendered to gentle hands, watched them take the lantern from her, heard a kind voice.

"It's all right, Miss Taylor, he'll be all right now."

She turned to a large man in a cashmere coat, saw more men running from the tower steps onto the balcony, rushing to Harper.

"No, please, I have to help him, please. Marc has to find his way to the cathedral."

"It's all right, Miss Taylor, you comforted him before he died. He saw the fire, he heard the words, he knew it was you."

She looked into the man's face. She saw the softest light in his green eyes. "He did?"

"Yes, he's where he belongs now."

A young blond woman knelt down, rolled up Katherine's sleeve, tied off her arm with rubber tubing.

"This is Officer Jannsen, Miss Taylor. She's going to give you a sleeping potion."

The blond woman pushed a needle into Katherine's vein. Katherine felt something kind and warm as light; she heard the man in the cashmere coat whisper, *"Dulcis et alta quies placidaeque similima morti."* And as Katherine slipped deeper into the kindness, she saw the men around Harper stuffing bandages in his wounds and needles in his arms, connecting him to bags of fluids. The man in the cashmere coat holding the lantern over Harper's eyes, his voice calling softly.

"Look into my eyes, Mr. Harper, listen to my voice. *C'est le guet. Il a sonné l'heure, il a sonné l'heure.*"

Katherine tried to reach for him.

"Harper's dying . . . they're all dying."

She felt something soft brush against her hands.

She looked down, saw Monsieur Booty curling into a ball on her lap. The frightened beast looking up to her with sad-hearted eyes. She brought him close to her breasts.

"It's okay, Monsieur Booty. Marc's safe now, he found his way. He's in the cathedral with all the lost angels."

*Mew.*

# of a saturday evening
# three months later

It hurt like hell, but he did it anyway. Bracing his legs against the low stone wall, pulling his coat over the sling on his left arm, and leaning down to the stream of clear water pouring from the iron spout. He drank deep, straightened up, wiped dribble from his lips.

A dark blue Merc coming up Rue Curtat and onto the esplanade as five bells rang from the belfry. Harper watched it circle beneath the façade of the cathedral and stop where he stood at the fountain under the trees. Sergeant Gauer emerged from the driver's seat, circled the rear of the car, and opened the passenger door. The cop in the cashmere coat stepped out.

"Good evening, Mr. Harper. Thank you for being prompt."

Harper looked down at his arm in the sling, saw the beat-up watch on his wrist ticking its way to five minutes before the hour, on the nose.

"Inspector."

He leaned down for another drink.

"I would've thought you'd had your fill of that water in the hospital. You had poor Sergeant Gauer here running back and forth from the hospital like a pizza delivery man."

"Needed my ten glasses a day, Inspector."

"Yes, and very healthy it is. But you shouldn't shy away from the canton's wines. Our vineyards draw from the same underground source, you know. Mixes with the light in the grapes, very good for what ails you. Care for a stroll to the embankment, if it's not too taxing?"

Harper recced the fifteen steps to the view of Lac Léman, Lausanne, the snow-covered mountains above Évian.

"Sure."

The inspector walked slowly, Harper hobbled along with a cane in his right hand.

"Good to see you up and about, Mr. Harper. How are you feeling?"

Harper raised his sling. "Like I've had my wings clipped."

"Very amusing. You did give us quite the scare, thought we'd lost you forever that time."

They reached the embankment wall. The inspector pulled out his cigarette case, offered Harper one of his gold-tipped smokes.

"Care for one?"

"No thanks."

"Are you quite sure?"

"I'm well awake, Inspector."

"Happy to hear it. Though one should remember a

dose of radiance now and then does help ease the weight of eternity."

"So the medics in Vevey keep telling me."

The inspector lit up, took in the view. "Nice weather. A few more days like this and the chestnut trees will flower."

Harper looked at the branches of the trees, the tiny green pods on the smallest twigs. Then his eyes focused through the trees to the belfry of Lausanne Cathedral high overhead. He took a deep breath; it hurt. He dropped his eyes to the Swiss copper guarding the inspector's Merc.

"I suppose I should thank Sergeant Gauer for that cracking head shot."

"Not at all. He was quite keen to test our new long-range rifle. He's very pleased with the results. Says he had another hundred yards to spare. I must say, Mr. Harper, you did leave quite the mess behind in the cathedral."

Harper gave the place a quick once-over. Looked like the same tumbledown pile of limestone rocks it always was, with new scaffolding on the walls.

"Doesn't appear the worse for wear."

"No, but it was a scramble. We managed to stabilize the time warp long enough to fix things up before the locals became too suspicious. The doors are battered and don't quite fit properly, but I think it adds to the charm of the place. Other than that, new leaded glass in the windows, rose window back together again, new chairs in the nave, skeletons tucked in their graves. Everything in its proper place."

"Everything?"

"Yes, everything. You do realize you took a grave gamble with the first light of creation."

"Seemed like a good idea at the time. Especially as you didn't tell me what the hell was going on."

"You're not alone, Mr. Harper."

"You're joking."

"Contrary to what you may think, Mr. Harper, I don't know everything there is to know. Should have spotted it, though. Yuriev coming to Lausanne, trying to contact the doctor at the IOC."

"The Olympic flame; the fire of the gods."

"Quite the clever clue when you think about it."

"Not like you to miss a clue, Inspector."

"Indeed."

"What else?"

"I beg your pardon."

"What else do you know about it?"

"Like you, nothing more than the legends of men. That one day the light will be revealed to them again, and that the light will pass them on to the next stage of their evolution. And on that day, this place will be paradise once more."

"And our job is finished."

"Yes."

"Any idea when that might be? I mean, we've already been here for two and a half million years."

The inspector took a long pull of smoke. "The knowledge of the whens and hows of this place is well beyond your pay grade. Mine, too, for that matter. But there is a plan, I'm sure."

"Speaking of plans, how could you be sure I'd find the key, or figure out what the hell it was for?"

The inspector smiled. "I was wondering when you'd get around to asking that. We'd been tracking Komarovsky's communications, knew he'd gone rogue. We knew his plans to drug you and return you to the cathedral to kill the boy. All we needed to do was evacuate the cathedral of partisans and resting souls and leave you alone with the boy and Miss Taylor. There was every confidence you'd take the boy under your wing, as they say, and that he'd lead you to the key, and together you'd sort the rest. Which brings me to something I'd like to ask you."

"Go ahead."

"I read your debriefing report. Beyond your description of events, you didn't offer details about the boy."

"And?"

"One would think you had come to know him a good deal."

Harper slid back in time, saw himself trying to strangle the lad, then the faintest light flashing deep within his eyes.

"You mean that he was a half-breed, bred by our own side?"

"I think 'child' would be the better word in his case."

Harper looked away, his eyes watching ripples on the lake. "I've been fighting a war longer than . . . longer than time. And for what? Come back after a hundred years and find we're doing the same damn thing as the enemy. The very thing that started this bloody war."

"Mr. Harper, you know how it is. This is all the paradise there is for these creatures of free will. It was choking on the greed and fear. Our forces were decimated, things were desperate. It was an experiment."

"The Two Hundred bred a race among men and we called them traitors; we do it and it's called an experiment?" Harper tapped his cane on the cobblestones. "How many more half . . . children are there stashed away in that school of yours? Mon Repos is one of your operations, isn't it?"

The inspector gave it a few seconds.

"How do you know about the school, Mr. Harper?"

"The lad told Miss Taylor, she told me."

"I see."

"How many?"

"The number is classified. And with that, I suggest you drop it."

Harper looked up at the belfry. "Newspapers said he died in an accident, slipped over a patch of ice on the upper balcony and fell."

"It was the most plausible cover story."

Harper looked the inspector in the eyes. "Accident at birth, accident at death. He was bred for a job and died doing it. No part of that lad's sad life was an accident."

"Part of him was human, so yes, he had a life of some sadness. They all do. But he also had a life of dreams and wonder as only they can have. And I would've thought the manner of his death speaks to the best of him."

"He was listed, remember? What sort of choice did he have about the manner of his death?"

"The boy wasn't listed, Mr. Harper. We told you that to keep the emotions of your form in play."

"I don't get it."

"You're a warrior, Mr. Harper. You exist to hunt down and slaughter the enemy. Your social skills are—how should I put it—somewhat lacking."

"True. But I still don't get it."

"We'd been aware for some time the boy was awakening to the duality of his being despite having suffered a brain injury at birth. Our medical team had him on a regimen of potions to keep his imaginations in check, but his imaginations became increasingly profound. It must have been terribly confusing for him. We had arranged for him to be married to the daughter of a partisan, someone to care for him and give him a sense of normality in his life. We were planning to take him from the cathedral to a small cottage in the country. For his own good."

"He would have never left. To him, that place was alive. It's as if . . ."

"As if what, Mr. Harper?"

"He knew before any of us the reason the cathedral is sacred beyond belief."

"Yes, that does seem to have been the case, doesn't it? And in the end, he killed one of their chiefs and sent the enemy into a tailspin. Intelligence tells us they're locked in internecine slaughter. A rather good result for our side."

"And what about the locals? Lucy Clarke and Stephan . . . I never knew his family name."

The inspector took another pull of smoke. "Gomaz,

his family name was Gomaz. And for the record, the loss of their souls was unforeseen and regrettable, but it happens. You know it does."

Harper wanted to tell the inspector to fuck off. Then again, he thought, what's the bloody use?

"You really play hardball, Inspector, don't you?"

"And so do you, that's why we're here."

Harper looked at the lake, saw windtrails on the surface. "Mind if we walk back? I need another drink."

"Of course."

They walked over the cobblestones to the fountain. Harper handed the inspector the cane.

"Mind holding this?"

"Not at all."

Harper leaned over the well and grabbed the spout. He bent down, let the cool water run through his mouth. He straightened up, looked at the inspector. "Really does taste better from the spout."

"Glad to hear it."

"So that's what this chat's about, is it? Make sure I keep my mouth shut about the lad and your school?"

The inspector handed Harper his cane. "Oh, I'm sure once given the order to keep your mouth shut, you would. No, it's something else. Miss Taylor is leaving for America today."

"America, why?"

"Because I say so. She's going deep underground. We've given her a new identity, a complete backstory."

"Where?"

"I'm afraid you're not cleared to know the details. But

I will tell you she'll be in a very quiet and remote place where she'll open a candle shop."

"Candles?"

"Yes. She took up candle-making as part of her recovery. Seems to have helped her immensely."

Harper remembered the night in the nave. Her holding a candle, talking about calling all angels in the darkest hour before the dawn.

"That's good."

"Officer Jannsen will be heading Miss Taylor's close-protection unit. They'll be traveling together."

"Does she know?"

"Does who know what?"

"Miss Taylor. Does she know she's pregnant? And if you give me that classified excuse, I'll drop you where you stand."

"My, my. We are feeling like our old selves, aren't we? Happy as I am to see it, I wouldn't push your luck. You're well within kill range of Sergeant Gauer—you know how serious those Swiss Guard types can be. Simple tone of voice can set them off."

Harper saw the Swiss copper next to the Merc. Jacket open, SIG sidearm and a killing knife in his belt.

"Point taken. Does she know?"

The inspector crushed his smoke on the fountain wall and tossed it in the nearby bin. "There was a genuine concern it would drive her insane. For the time being, we've masked it from her consciousness. Once she's in America, we'll help her through it. Given the trauma she's experienced, I think you'd agree it's the best thing."

"Maybe."

"Maybe?"

"Or maybe you're cooking up another one of your whiz-bang experiments. Raise one of their half-breeds as our own, see if you can flip him to our side."

"Mr. Harper, I understand you have . . . feelings. But I promise you it's not like that. Something's happened to her through all of this. Her light readings are off the chart. It could be her exposure to the fire, it could be the dream revealed to her in the nave. We just don't know."

"Have you debriefed Gabriel?"

"I'm afraid I'm forbidden to question him regarding his revelations to the locals. Always been that way. From the time of the unremembered beginning. Damn inconvenient, but that's the fact of it. However, we're picking up some interesting enemy chatter."

"They know Miss Taylor's pregnant and they want the child."

The inspector reacted with a steel-eyed stare. *No fucking comment.*

"Just tell me you're not using her as bait."

"Quite the opposite, Mr. Harper. We have a duty to protect her and the child, have we not? You do remember the First Law of Existence, I trust?"

"The souls of men are born of the first light; we are forbidden to snuff it out."

"Correct."

Harper heard the bells from Place de la Palud ring the quarter-hour.

"So, seeing as you didn't drag me out of bed to tell me

to keep my mouth shut or remind me there're things you can't tell me, why am I here?"

"I've received new orders regarding you."

"Orders? Rather quick, isn't it?"

"I'm afraid so."

"If that's the case, maybe I will have one of your flash smokes, Inspector."

"Of course."

The inspector offered his cigarette case and a light. Harper pulled a smoke and lit up, drew in the smoke, waited for clarity to seep into his blood.

"Right, I'm listening."

"HQ's expressed concern about the intense level of emotions you experienced on this mission, especially after the results of your last medical exam. It seems they aren't dissipating. In fact, they've become embedded to your eternal being. And now that you're out of danger of dying in your form, HQ wants you returned to stasis and separated from Captain Jay Harper, without delay."

Harper took a deeper drag. *Without delay.* Meaning right the fuck now.

"Understood. Where do I report?"

The inspector pointed to the cathedral. "In ten minutes, the bells will ring the six o'clock. Stand before the doors of the cathedral and place your right hand on the iron handle and wait for *la grande sonnerie* of the bells. When they finish, and before the sound fades, enter the nave. Monsieur Gabriel will meet you at the crossing square. I believe you remember the rest of the drill."

"From what I remember, it's a hell of a lot easier than awakening."

"Yes, it is. You're in for a very long rest."

"Long enough to sleep?"

"Perchance to dream, Mr. Harper."

Harper rubbed the back of his neck, feeling the weariness of eternity bearing down. "Now that would be interesting."

The inspector cleared his throat. "However, I've convinced HQ to come up with alternative orders, in the event you wish to stick around."

"You did what?"

"I do have considerable influence and managed to float the idea that the very emotions they're concerned about could prove helpful to our cause. Give us an edge in predicting what the enemy may throw at us next."

"Don't tell me you're offering me a choice, Inspector?"

"As a matter of fact, yes. Care to hear it?"

"Not really, but feel free to give it a go."

"You can return to stasis, or you can make your way down Escaliers du Marché to Café du Grütli. Have a *saucisse de veau* with a good bottle of Villette from our vineyards in Lavaux. Tell Monsieur Dufaux to put it on my tab."

"Then what?"

"You relax, Mr. Harper. Think about getting fit for the next battle. That will surely come sooner rather than later."

"That's your idea of a choice?"

"Unlike you, my experience is limited in that regard.

Let's call it the best I can do. Of course, there will be certain protocols to your staying on."

"What sort of protocols?"

"For one, that you have no further contact with Miss Taylor."

"Further? I haven't seen or talked to her since—"

"I mean from now, Mr. Harper."

The sound of tires on cobblestones coming up Rue Curtat again. Another dark blue Merc driving up the hill to the esplanade. The windows tinted and raised.

"Her?"

"She wanted to see the cathedral before she left. And to talk to you, of course. I must warn you—she'll have no memory of Jay Harper after today."

"Sorry?"

"The potions being administered to her to mask the trauma. We've adjusted them to remove you from the picture, as it were."

Harper felt something inside him sink, wanting to hold on to it, whatever it was . . . but knowing there was no choice but to let it go.

"Fair enough."

The inspector turned and walked away to meet the car.

"Inspector?" Harper nodded toward the belfry. "Up there, with the bells."

"Yes, there's someone new. A young girl from Iceland with a fine voice to call the hour."

"A girl?"

"I realize you've been busy and may not have noticed,

but the world has changed a bit since you were last here, Mr. Harper."

"I guess so."

"Plays classical guitar as well, likes to sit on the balcony near Marie-Madeleine on warmer nights to play. She imagines the old thing is sad these days and needs a bit of comfort. Monsieur Buhlmann's bringing her along. Seems the first thing she did upon coming into the loge was pick up the young boy's binoculars to have a look over Lausanne. Monsieur Buhlmann thinks she'll work out very well. If you choose to stay, you might come around of an evening and have a listen. Keep an eye on her, what?"

The Merc made a slow circle in front of the cathedral and came to a stop. Mutt stepped from the jump seat and scanned the perimeter. Harper saw Jeff at the wheel, Brügger & Thomet submachine gun on his lap, well-notched killing knife in his belt. The inspector had quiet words with Mutt and then turned to Harper.

"Only a few minutes, Mr. Harper, we need to get her to the airport. And the six-o'clock bells will be ringing soon."

The inspector pulled open the rear door.

Officer Jannsen slid out, turned back, reached in the car.

Harper saw her take a woman's hand and, for a second, he didn't want to see her. He dropped his eyes to the cobblestones. To where a pair of black penny loafers and nice ankles hit the ground. Then he couldn't keep his eyes from looking up. Black jeans, black sweater, a slender form draped in a long black cloak. Her hair and eyebrows gone blond, grown out some. She held a fat gray cat in her arms.

Officer Jannsen helped the woman from the seat.

The woman stood still a moment before walking toward him. Harper crushed out his fag, tossed it in the bin. He pressed down on his cane, stood to meet her. She stopped in front of him; she was quiet. He gave her a moment.

"Hello, Miss Taylor."

"Hi."

"Looks like the lad's cat's off to America."

"Yeah, we've sort of gotten attached at the hip. I can't seem to let go of him." She scratched the beast's head.

*Mew.*

"Maybe he doesn't want to let go of you."

"Yeah, maybe."

"The scar's gone."

She tried to smile. "Vitamin E, four times a day."

"You look fine, Miss Taylor. You're going to be fine."

"They won't tell me where I'm going, Harper."

"It's for your own protection, Miss Taylor."

"I know. It's just . . ."

Harper waited for her to finish. She couldn't.

"The inspector tells me you're opening a candle shop."

"I like making candles. I've gotten really good at it."

"That's swell, Miss Taylor."

She took a quick breath. "Anne's coming with me. She's going to live with me till I feel better."

"Anne?"

"Officer Jannsen."

"Right. Then you'll be very fine."

Katherine turned, looked at the cathedral, her eyes rising to the tower. "I didn't think I'd ever want to come here again, but I guess I needed to see the cathedral before I left. I asked Inspector Gobet if you could be here. Hope that's okay with you."

"I'm glad you did."

They faced the lake and the setting sun, listening to the wind circle the belfry and drift through the trees. He listened to her sigh.

"Sometimes, I hear him shuffling up behind me."

"Me too."

"But it's never him."

"No, it's never him."

She kicked back her head, trying to keep the tears away. Harper edged closer to her.

"It wasn't your fault, Miss Taylor."

"That's what the doctors keep telling me, but it's all so confusing. I can't remember things and I have the strangest dreams."

"Give yourself some time. It'll pass."

"They had me meeting with a counselor. He told me to imagine life never really ends, that people always come back. They just don't know it, and we can't see them the way they were."

"I've heard that, too."

"Really?"

"Yes."

"Then that means Marc could be somewhere in the world right now, and that makes me feel better. Even if I run into him and he doesn't know me and I don't know him, it makes me feel better thinking he's still in the same world. I really want to believe it."

"Then believe it, Miss Taylor."

The inspector called from the esplanade: "Mr. Harper, we must leave in three minutes."

Katherine rolled her eyes. "God, he's such a stickler for time. Keeps telling me I must be punctual in all things. I asked him if I could see you because I want to ask you something before I leave Lausanne."

"Sure."

"Before . . . before Marc died, I remember talking to him in the loge. I had a feeling he knew I was just a hooker hiding out in his tower. I was wondering if you said anything to him."

"Like what?"

"Like I wasn't an angel."

"No, he figured it out by himself."

"Honestly?"

"Yes."

She wiped a tear from her cheek. "What did he say?"

"Why are you asking?"

"I keep seeing him in the loge, looking at me and knowing I wasn't the angel he wanted me to be. And I keep thinking I broke his heart. Like I took something from his life that made him happy and I broke it, then he died."

"You didn't break his heart."

"Really?"

Harper looked up at the belfry again. "We were up there, on the roof, waiting for the killers. And out of nowhere he asked me about things girls like. Flowers, perfume. What kind of movies did they like, did they like to eat pizza on Thursday nights, Tom and Jerry cartoons? And he asked me if I thought you were beautiful. I teased him at first, said I didn't think so. But he kept saying you were the most beautiful girl he had ever seen till I agreed. Then he asked if I thought you might like to come to his flat sometime for tuna-noodle casserole. Seems he had a secret recipe from his mother back in Canada."

"Oh, God. What'd you tell him?"

"I told him I was very sure you'd accept his invitation with genuine pleasure."

"Please tell me it's the truth. You know what a sucker I am for fairy tales. I'm afraid I hurt him so terribly, I can't let go of it. I don't know what to do. Please, tell me something."

Harper stepped close to her.

"One thing I know, that love with chance
And use and time and necessity
Will grow, and louder the heart's dance
At parting than at meeting be."

Katherine looked at him. "That's lovely, Harper. What is it?"

"A poem by a soldier killed in the First World War. His name was Edward Thomas."

"Where would someone like you ever get something like that?"

"Just something I heard somewhere. You're going to be all right, Miss Taylor. Someone will be watching over you."

"I think someone already is, I just can't see him."

The engines of the Mercs turned over. The inspector stepped to Katherine's side.

"I apologize, but we must be going."

"Okay." Katherine scratched the head of the fat cat in her arms. "Say good-bye, Monsieur Booty."

*Mew.*

The inspector took Katherine's arm and they turned to leave. Katherine turned back to Harper.

"Oh, I almost forgot. This is for you."

Something in her fingers. He held out his hand and watched a five-franc coin, well-dented at the edge, fall into his palm.

"Where . . . How did you get this?"

"Marc gave it to me that night, before he died. He gave it to me for good luck. I thought you'd like to have it."

Harper stared at the remembered thing. "I'm grateful for this, Miss Taylor, I truly am."

She stood on her toes, kissed him on the cheek. "Good-bye, Harper."

He watched her walk away and settle in the backseat of the Merc, fat cat still in her arms. Officer Jannsen climbed in behind her and closed the door. The rear window slid down. Katherine leaned across Officer Jannsen and through the window.

"Hey, Harper, I didn't even ask you how you are."

"Ask me now."

"How are you?"

He put his weight on the cane and pulled himself up from the fountain wall and made himself steady.

"I'm good. Taking a bit of vacation."

"Send me a postcard?"

He waved. "Sure."

Car doors slammed and the convoy rolled quietly over the cobblestones of the esplanade, down the hill, and out of sight. Harper hobbled to the base of the belfry tower. He saw the cars speeding over Pont Bessières, flashing blue lights chasing evening shadows from the road. The cars rounded the corner at Rue Caroline and were gone.

Six deep-throated gongs rang from above.

Harper looked out over the lake, all that was left of paradise.

He turned and hobbled to the cathedral façade, standing at the massive wooden doors. He waited till all the bells began to sound. He placed his right hand on the iron handle. He stood perfectly still, waiting for the bells to finish, waiting to pull open the doors and enter the nave before the last bell faded.

He saw the coin tucked in the palm of his hand.

He curled the tips of his fingers and felt the dent at the side.

He looked at his watch. Five fifty-five. Still running five minutes slow.

"Bloody hell, what's the rush?"

He pulled his hand from the door and turned away. He dropped the coin in his coat and hobbled across the esplanade. He tucked the walking cane under his sling, grabbed the side rail, and slowly counted his way down the wooden steps of Escaliers du Marché.

## Acknowledgments

My deepest gratitude to Renato Häusler, who at the time this story was written was serving as *le guet de la Cathédrale de Lausanne*. His devotion to the cathedral was the inspiration for this story.

To Julian Magnolly of *24 Heures* and Omid Safi of Colgate University.

To Paul Reed, military historian and author.

To Georgina Capel, Doug Young, and David Rosenthal for their never-ending belief.

And to the bells of Lausanne Cathedral for allowing me the honor of their very fine company over the months I spent in the belfry loge writing the first draft.

Read on for a preview of the next thrilling book
in the Angelus Trilogy by Jon Steele,

## *ANGEL CITY*

Coming in hardcover from
Blue Rider Press in June 2013.

*Château Montségur, Occitania, March 15, 1244 . . .*

When the knight reached the stone steps to the ramparts, he realized was walking in circles. He stopped, looked around the courtyard. Till then there had only been the sensation of a staggering forward motion; now came an awareness of the world around him. It was the tower he recognized at first, rising like some singular presence against the late-afternoon sky. It was badly damaged during the bombardment, as were the battlements. In the early days, when French catapults were still halfway down the mountain at Roc de la Tour, the stone missiles did no more than bounce off the outer walls of the fortress. The knights made sport of collecting the stones, calling them "the Pope's turds" and bringing them into the courtyard, where the fighters of Montségur built their own catapult. After writing curses on the stones, the fighters returned the mountain from where they came. But in February the French broke through the lower defenses and scaled the cliffs, securing a foothold on the summit. Their catapults found their range and the final assault began. They leveled the terraced village on the north cliff in three days, forcing the folk who lived there to seek refuge within the fortress. Still, the fighters of Montségur would not surrender. The French adjusted their targeting and launched stones, a hundredweight each, into the courtyard.

Just now, seeing the crumpled shelters in the courtyard and the pools of blood on the ground, terrible images came to the knight's eyes. There was no defense from the bombardment, not even in the lower chambers of the tower. Fighters and folk were crushed to death. The French then attacked with infantry and captured the barbican a mere thirty chains from the fortress gates. It was Montségur's last line of defense. All was lost unless the Crusaders could be repelled.

The knight felt a cold wind at his back.

He turned to the smashed open gates, and for a moment, he was confused. He couldn't remember what had happened next. But as he felt the wind on his face, more images came to his eyes. He saw the fighters of Montségur mustering in the courtyard at evening, preparing for the last battle. Two young boys stood nearby, holding torches so the fighters could see as they dressed in chain mail, coifs and helmets. There was but a handful left now: nineteen knights with swords and shields, five crossbowmen and archers, twenty sergeants and infantrymen with lances and war hammers, a few Basque mercenaries with axes and cudgels. The knight remembered the fighters speaking quietly among themselves.

"What is the day?" one said.

"Why should you care?" another answered.

"Because I should like to know the day of my death, if this is to be the day of my death."

"Then it is a Tuesday, I think."

Such fateful words were a soldier's words, the knight thought. And he, too, tried to recall the day just in case this would be the day of his own death. It was a Tuesday, the first day of March. The day was named after the Norse god of war, *Tiw*. . . . The month was named after the Roman god of war.

"Not a bad day to die, then," the knight laughed to himself.

He fitted his helmet to his head, secured the chin strap and looked about the courtyard. The three hundred folk seeking refuge within the fortress had gathered to watch the preparations for battle. Farmers and shepherds from the surrounding valleys, craftsmen and merchants from nearby towns, dispossessed nobles from Languedoc. Many of them credents to the Cathar faith, all of them sympathetic to the cause of the Cathars. The leaders of the faith watched, too—the ones who called themselves *the good men*. They stood at the entrance of the tower, somber and silent in their black robes. The knight could see their lips forming words of silent prayer as was their manner.

The knight bowed to them; the good men continued to pray.

The knight turned to the fighters; the fighters fell quiet.

"Brothers in battle, I salute you this fine evening. For ten months, we have held an army of ten thousand soldiers at bay. Not just any soldiers, but soldiers of France. At our greatest strength, we were two hundred fifty fighters. I ask you to think on it. Outnumbered more than sixty to one, yet we have not been shaken from this rock. We are told tonight there is a full company of infantry at the barbican awaiting our surrender. We are told two more companies are making their way up the mountain and will be here by the dawn. They say Louis IX . . ."

Some of the fighters cursed, the rest of them spit.

"They say that Capetean donkey, then . . ."

The fighters laughed.

"They say he commands us to kneel and swear an oath of fealty to France. But I say as we live and breathe, this rock beneath our feet is all that is left of Occitania. It is our land, and I say free men do not kneel on their own land. And His Holiness the Pope . . ."

More curses and spit.

"I meant, that evil son of Satan . . ."

Laughter.

"He has blessed the French soldiers, calling them Crusaders, warriors of the Christ. He has decreed these Crusaders to be doing God's work in slaying the Cathars."

The knight pointed to the folk.

"His Holiness therefore orders us to surrender these men and women to the Inquisition, that they may be investigated for the crime of heresy. But I say these folk have fed us, tended our wounds, washed our braies and leggings, kept our worn shoes bound together with scraps of cloth torn from their own tunics. I say these folk have done all in the defense of Occitania but wield a weapon."

He nodded to the good men at the tower.

"More, we are ordered to surrender the leaders of the faith to be burned at the stake unless they repent. But I say these good men have prayed for us, offered our dying brothers the sacrament of *consolamentum*. I say we are bound to these good men and them to us. I say we will not surrender one pure soul to the tyranny of a corrupt and sinful church."

The fighters agreed with grunts and snorts.

"Brothers in battle, mark my words well: This alliance of Pope and King howling at the gates craves more than our lands to make them France. Pope and King crave our absolute destruction so that all memory of this place, all memory of us, will be wiped from the face of the Earth."

The knight pulled his sword from its sheath. He could see the chinks and nicks of battle on the blade. He admired the markings by torchlight.

"So, with apologies to the good men for my foul tongue, I say we tell Pope and King to go fuck themselves in the arse."

There was no laughter this time, only the sound of weapons being drawn and raised. The folk in the courtyard parted to let the fighters pass. The boys, bearing torches high, led the way to the north gate. As the fighters had arranged themselves in formation, the knight nodded to the boys.

"Douse the fires. Get you both to the tower."

The boys lowered the torches to the soggy ground. The fires sizzled out; the boys dashed away. The knight stood quietly, watching the sky, waiting for his eyes to open to the stars. There was the Great Plow of the heavens; there was Polaris. There were Draco and Cassiopeia. A voice whispered to him from behind:

"So, O noble knight, have you a prayer to offer the stars this fine evening?"

It was Jean de Combel, crossbowman from Laurac. Always good with a mocking word before battle to cheer the men. The knight turned back to him, touched the flat of his sword to the crossbowman's shoulder.

"I pray, 'Whatever you do, let me live one day longer than that ugly bastard de Combel.'"

The crossbowman laughed. "Then you shall live forever, knight, for I will never die."

The knight nodded. "Done. Now open the gate, de Combel, and let's put the bargain to the test."

Jean de Combel stepped forward with his archers. They lifted the cross brace, set it aside. The doors moaned and creaked open on iron hinges. The knight stared ahead, imagining. . . .

If they could retake the barbican and dislodge the forward company of French Crusaders, drive them over the cliffs, the fighters could capture the catapults. The machines could be turned around, used against the enemy soldiers scaling the mountain, and those encamped at Roc de la Tour. Two more catapults stood there. And in capturing those, the fighters would have enough firepower to break the siege. The folk could descend along hidden trails and disappear into the shelter of the Pyrenees, then over the peaks into Catalonia. But the French were dug in too well, and when the King's crossbows opened at the flanks, the fighters of Montségur were caught in the cross fire.

The knight winced, remembering a long bolt howling through the battle. He remembered hearing the killing thing before it hit him. Knowing the moment he heard its voice, it was meant for him. The bolt hit with the force of a war hammer, the tiny blades cutting through his chain mail, digging into the chest. He saw himself dropping his sword and shield, falling to the ground. He lay amid the battle, tasting his own blood in his mouth, knowing the blade had missed his heart but pierced his lung. The attack withered; the fighters fell back. Jean de Combel picked up the knight's sword, pulled the knight's arm around his own neck, lifted the knight to his feet. They hurried to the fortress. The knight pulled away from de Combel, fell against the stone arch of the gate.

"My sword! Give my sword!"

Jean de Combel handed it to him.

*"Va be, esta be!"* the knight cried. "This it! Stand at the forecourt! The bastards must not enter the fortress or the folk will be slaughtered!"

The fighters formed a line at the gate, drawing the French soldiers onto the narrow strip of land between the fortress and the sheer cliffs. There was little room to maneuver, and when the French pressed at the gate, the fighters forced them back with lances. The knight heard the screams of King's men at the rear falling to their death. He raised his sword and cried again, *"Va be, esta be!"*

Then he collapsed again to his knees and could not rise. Folk appeared in the courtyard to drag away wounded. Two folk grabbed the knight.

"No, I will stay!"

Jean de Combel turned quickly. . . . "You are finished here. We will hold. Take him!"

The folk carried the knight to infirmary in below the tower cellar, a dank and hellish place stinking of blood and puss. Torches formed a pool of light around two wood tables. One table was empty, dripping with blood; a fighter was strapped to the second table, screaming through the leather strap clenched between his teeth. The screams becoming shrieks as a surgeon, a barber from Carcassonne, sawed off the fighter's leg. A boy working with the barber removed an iron rod from white coals and cauterized the bloody stump. The boy had done it many times and he was good at it.

The barber saw the knight, nodded to the folk.

"On the table. Remove his chain mail and gambe-son," the barber said.

The folk did it quickly. The barber wiped his filthy hands on his tunic, hurried to the table. He tore open the knight's linen shirt, probed the wound.

"It's a three-sided blade," the barber said. "I'll try to dig it out, but you will not live, I think. Do you wish to receive *consolamentum*?"

The knight looked around the infirmary. More

wounded coming in. "Tell the good men to see to my brothers first."

"As you wish."

The barber turned to collect his knives.

The knight felt dizzy. The flame and smoke of the torches seemed to slow and take strange shapes. He eyes began to lose focus and close. . . . He felt an arm slip under his neck, raise his head. The knight opened his eyes, saw a fighter in chain mail and coif emerge. The fighter held a clay cup to the knight's mouth.

"Quickly, drink of this."

The knight looked at the fighter's armor. It bore no coat of arms and the chain mail was stained with blackish blood.

"Who . . . who are you? Bring your face into the light that I may see you."

The fighter leaned forward. The knight saw a battle-hardened face oddly painted with streaks of mud.

"I do not know you. Have reinforcements broken through? Are we saved?"

"There are no reinforcements, and there will be none."

"Then . . . who are you?"

"Someone who's been at your side these ten months, fighting the evil that surrounds this sacred ground."

"What evil do you speak of?"

"The enemies of light, the devourers of souls. They know I'm here. They're hunting for me."

"Your words are strange."

"Drink of this cup and sleep. When you wake, you'll understand."

The knight felt his consciousness slipping, then a flash of fear. . . . He tried to raise himself.

"No, this is a trick. You are a poisoner."

The fighter held him down. "You are mortally wounded and already falling into death; but you must live for one hundred more days. Look into my eyes. Listen to my voice. It cannot end here. It must not end here."

And when the fighter offered the cup again, the knight did not resist. There was a bitter taste, warmth, falling into light.

And now . . .

. . . the knight was healed, standing in the courtyard of the battered fortress. He looked down at himself, saw he was wearing a plain wool tunic and coarsely woven leggings. He thought he looked very much like one of the folk, then wondered which of the dead folk's clothes he was wearing. He pulled the tunic away from his neck, saw the bloodied scraps of linen bandages tied around his chest.

A voice called: "So it's true. You're alive."

The knight looked up to the battlements, saw a shadowed form at the ramparts.

"Who's there?" the knight said.

"Jean de Combel, best crossbowman in the fortress, that's who. Come up. The air is fresh up here."

For a moment the knight was taken aback by the crossbowman's familiarity. Then he remembered that was the way within the fortress. Nobles and peasants, knights and infantrymen, men and women even—all were equal before the Pure God of the Cathars.

"What about the others?" said the knight.

"What others?"

The knight had difficulty remembering who *the others* were; he tried to see them in his mind. Soldiers of France, arse lickers of the Pope; yes, that's them. He nodded to the walls.

"The ones beyond the walls, the French."

"Oh, them, the Crusaders. They're far too busy roasting a boar to care about fighting. Besides, there's been a truce for two weeks."

"A truce?"

"From the day you were wounded."

"It's been two weeks?"

"It has. We fought them back to the barbican, as you commanded. But we couldn't drive them off the mountain. It went back and forth all night. At dawn, we'd had it and called for a truce. The Crusaders could have stormed the courtyard and slaughtered us all; but they were in a hurry for their *petit déjeuner* and accepted the truce instead."

The knight looked around the courtyard again. The fortress appeared to be abandoned. "Where is everyone?"

"In the tower, watching the remaining folk and fighters receive *consolamentum*. The ones that stayed anyway. I was asked to keep an eye on the Crusaders, make sure they keep to the truce."

"Did many leave us?"

"More than half."

"Half?"

The crossbowman shrugged. "Can't blame them. The

King offered safe passage to all who promise to become good little Frenchman."

"Fighters, too?"

"Fighters, too, including you and the rest of the Avignonet assassins, if you choose."

"Avignonet?"

"You remember: you and your merry band slaughtering those seven Inquisitors in their beds last year. The very deed that brought us to this happy day."

The knight tried to remember it. He looked at his hands. Yes, he thought, the hands of an assassin.

"What are you thinking?" Jean de Combel said.

The knight looked up.

"Has there been any word from those who left? Have the Crusaders kept their word?"

"Some of the folk were paraded around the fortress this morning. The Inquisitor ordered them to sew a yellow cross to their tunics, to show the world they are heretics returned to the teats of the Whoring Mother Church. There was a priest with them, one of the Inquisitors, I'm sure. A fat slob of a Dominican, he was. He called to me. Promised the wearing of the yellow cross would be the extent of my punishment if I would surrender to him."

"And will you?"

"I showed him the crack of my backside and shouted, '*Vai t'escoundre!*'"

The knight laughed. Jean de Combel certainly would shout *Go fuck yourself* to a priest. And he would shout it in Occitan, refusing to even curse in the tongue of the French King.

"How many of us are left then?" the knight said.

"Fighters?"

"Yes."

"Twenty-six. Many with wounds."

"And folk?"

"One hundred ninety-two Cathars."

The knight stood still a moment. "So, it is true. We are defeated in this place."

"Yes, we are defeated. Come up and take the air. Enjoy the truce while you can."

"Yes, I will," the knight said. "I'd like to see what a truce looks like. I don't recall ever seeing one."

He climbed the stone steps, used his left arm to balance himself against the wall. There was some pain still, but he felt almost disconnected from it. As if it was happening to someone else, not him. Closer to the ramparts, he had a better view of Jean de Combel. The crossbowman was wearing a bloodied gambeson over a linen shirt. His leggings and shoes were bloodied as well. The crossbowman reached down, gave the knight assistance up the last steps.

"I was told you had died three times," Jean de Combel said.

"I'm not as fast on my feet as I used to be, if that make you any happier."

The knight stepped onto the ramparts and he felt the warm sun on his face. He looked beyond the battlements to see the lands of Occitania. Mountains like citadels, thick forest of pine and oak, meadows of poppy. Farther were sunlit rivers winding through maqui scrublands; and above it all, great winged vultures soared in loping circles. He closed his eyes and breathed. He smelled wild flowers, sage from the maquis, snow and ice from Mont Canigou. And Jean de Combel was right: There was the scent of roasting meat. The knight saw fifty or so French soldiers at the end of the summit. They wore swords at their belts but appeared relaxed.

"So, this is what a truce looks like," the knight said.

"It is."

The knight sniffed at the scent of meat. "Smells good, doesn't it?" he said.

"What are you saying? Only the French could waste perfectly good boar over a spit. I've half a mind to march down there and make those bastards a proper *sanglier* stew. We still have a few onions and garlic in stores. Some carrots, too. And the French have the boar. And the fat Dominican is with them. See him? Probably has a boy under his robes pulling at his fat dick. I promise you, *that* papist will have a skin of wine for the sauce."

The knight looked at Jean de Combel. "They might toss you a foot if you beg."

"Perhaps. But as the pure God would have it, it's too late."

"Why too late?"

The crossbowmen laughed. "Because I've received *consolamentum*."

"When?"

"With you, two days ago."

"Me?"

"Yes, well, you were delirious with fever. Not surprised you don't remember it. Your fellow assassin, de

Lahille was there, too. Took us some fakery to get you through the ceremony. We held you up and poked you in the back when you needed to reply. None too coherently, but you grunted well enough and the good men took pity on you."

"You tease me, de Combel."

"Not at all. I speak only truth now. I have to. Comes with receiving the one and only sacrament of the Cathars. And a serious business, it is. It means that for the rest of our lives, there is no meat. Has there ever been a troubadour with a more woeful tale? Locked up with these pacifist, vegetarians for ten months, not once a scrap of meat to eat for the fighters. Do you know how hard it is to do battle without meat in your stomach? What am I saying? Of course you do. Anyway, look out there. Crusaders cooking boar so close we can smell it. And, yes, they probably would toss us a foot. A hairy back foot, if we begged. But alas, it's forbidden to us both now."

The knight tried to imagine the sight of receiving *consolamentum* in a delirious state. He remember it; he had lost touch with the real world after someone held a cup to his lips.

"Something amuses you?"

"Twice so."

"Tell me."

"I'm amused that I've become one of the good men through the fakery of my brothers in battle."

"And good at fakery we were."

"I'm sure of it."

"And your other amusement?"

The knight smiled. "I'm amused a killer like me can now be considered one of the good men."

"And good at killing you were."

The knight looked at the French soldiers on the plateau, then beyond to where the shadows of hills began to creep over the land.

"Do you believe in the faith of the good men, de Combel?"

The crossbowman sighed.

"I believe that these good men believe it, and I believe it is a comfort to these gentle folk."

"So what is to happen to them?"

"You don't know?"

"You're the first person I've seen since I woke up, or the first I can remember seeing. I'm not even sure how I made it to the courtyard."

The crossbowman chuckled.

"You'd best come with me, see for yourself. Make your own choice about going or staying now that you're on your feet. It's still not too late to leave the fortress and become a good little Frenchman."

The knight followed the crossbowman along the ramparts, careful not to trip over rubble and spent missiles in his path. At the southwest wall, Jean de Combel leaned through the battlements and pointed down.

"That is what happens tomorrow."

Five hundred meters down, in a clearing at the edge of the forest, hundreds of French soldiers appeared small as ants. They were busy as ants, too, carrying tinder and buckets of pitch to a large square palisade. There were wood ladders at the walls and the soldiers took turns climbing the steps to empty their burden. Soldiers inside the walls spread the stuff over a thick flooring of straw.

"They will burn us as heretics," the knight said.

"They will."

"When?"

"Tomorrow, at dawn. And that will be the end of Montségur and the good men, I think. And a foul end it is. I'd hoped we could do more for them. But, alas, there is no choice but to watch them force marched to their death."

The knight looked at Jean de Combel, having never before heard such a sadness in the crossbowman's voice.

"How do you mean, de Combel?"

The crossbowman's eyes betrayed a secret knowledge, one he tried to conceal with a mocking smile.

"Why, I . . . why, I only mean these Cathars are a gentle folk. They deserve better than extinction."

The knight stared at the crossbowman. "You fought bravely as anyone to defend them, de Combel. You will burn with them at the dawn, will you not? What more could you do as a fighter?"

The crossbowman turned his eyes from the knight, looked down on the palisade. The French soldiers were done with their work and drinking wine from skins. After a long silence, the crossbowman looked at the knight.

"You said it yourself before the last battle. Pope and King wish to wipe all memory of this place from the face of the earth. I feared your words as you spoke them. I fear them now more than any words I've heard from a man. Shall I tell you why?"

"Yes."

"Because more than battle, more than what will come at the dawn, I fear a world without the Cathars."

The knight nodded, looked up to the sky. There was Saturn. There was Mercury. There was Mars hanging at the edge of the falling dark.

"Fear not, de Combel. It cannot end here. It must not end here."